I0523933

Mrs. Alexander

Her Dearest Foe

A Novel

Mrs. Alexander

Her Dearest Foe
A Novel

ISBN/EAN: 9783337042790

Printed in Europe, USA, Canada, Australia, Japan

Cover: Foto ©Andreas Hilbeck / pixelio.de

More available books at **www.hansebooks.com**

HER DEAREST FOE

A NOVEL

BY

MRS. ALEXANDER

AUTHOR OF "THE WOOING O'T," "WHICH SHALL IT BE?" ETC.

NEW YORK

HENRY HOLT AND COMPANY

1876

HER DEAREST FOE.

CHAPTER I.

" YOU have been good ! very good to me ! "
The sounds were slowly, brokenly uttered, as though
the mechanism that had produced them had well-nigh run down
for ever.

The speaker lay helplessly back upon his pillow, his gray hair
disordered, ashy pale, with the shadow of the great King already
on his brow—a somewhat rugged, but not ignoble face—the
lines about the mouth, so hard in life, relaxed—the keen, stern
eyes dim and dreamy.

The bed on which he lay, the luxuriously-furnished room, the
many appliances to relieve pain and assist weakness—all bespoke wealth. At some distance, in a large easy chair, sat a
stout elderly woman, evidently the professional nurse ; and beside the bed, holding the sufferer's hand tenderly in both her
own, stood a lady, tall, slight, wrapped in a dressing-gown of
soft gray, her eyes fixed intently on him, as if gathering up his
words, and unconscious of the tears that had welled over and
slowly coursed down her cheeks.

" I have loved you very much ! I wish I had been less stern,
less exacting," he went on with difficulty ; "but remember
always, I loved "—the voice dropped to a whisper with the last
word, and he closed his eyes.

" You have always been most kind and generous," returned
his hearer, softly ; "you have nothing to reproach yourself
with ! " and she bent down to kiss his brow.

" I have ! I have ! " Another long pause, during which he
seemed to sleep. Again the poor dim eyes opened. "Kate !
Are you there, Kate ? "

" Yes, dear. Here always."

" You will think I have been unjust, that I have done too
much for—"

I

A few moments after he added, "I am sorry, but it is too late—"

"For what?" asked his wife, gently. The question was never answered.

For nearly an hour he lay silent. The nurse after a while rose and advanced a chair so that the lady might rest without relinquishing the thin, bony, helpless hand that lay in hers; then the door opened to admit the doctor, who, with a whispered word or two to the nurse, and a silent bow to the mistress of the house, took his station at the foot of the bed. Once more the deep-set eyes opened wide with something of their old light, and the dying man breathed out low, but distinctly, the word "Remember!" A few long-drawn sighs, and the watchers listened in vain for the breath that had ceased for ever.

The doctor bent over the bed, then uttered, slowly and gently, the words, "It is all over!"

Still the lady did not stir; still she held the cold hand for a few moments longer, then laid it softly down, and stood, her own clasped together, the picture of profound, sad abstraction.

"Call Mrs. Mills," whispered the doctor.

The nurse nodded and left the room, returning almost immediately with a tall, angular-looking, elderly woman, whose air and attire bespoke the housekeeper or confidential maid. She, too, paused and gazed reverentially on the prostrate form that had been her master; then, passing on to the lady, who still stood motionless, said, in a low but harsh whisper, "Come away, my lamb! come away! You have done all that woman could for him, and you may rest now. Come with me!"

At the evidently familiar sound of the voice the lady turned, and leaning her head against Mills's shoulder, wept bitterly, though quietly, trembling all over.

Mills drew her arm through her own, and with a slight nod to the doctor, repeating, "Come away!" led the wearied mourner out of the room.

After a few directions to the nurse, the doctor too left the chamber of death, and passed out into a large square landing, well warmed and lighted, upon which various doors opened. He descended the stairs and went into the dining-room.

A well-dressed man, probably a gentleman, was slowly pacing to and fro, and stood suddenly still, face to face with the doctor. He was slightly above middle height, with sloping shoulders. Tolerably regular features, glittering, anxious eyes, and abundant, well-trained hair and whiskers, made up what their owner considered a decidedly good-looking whole. "Well," he said, with a sort of effort and a nervous twitching of the lip; "Well?"

"Our poor friend is at rest," replied the other; "passed away very tranquilly—nature quite exhausted." He stepped to the fireplace as he spoke, and rang the bell.

"And she is?" resumed the first speaker, in a curious broken voice, catching his words abruptly. He stopped an instant, then continued more quietly: "Mrs. Travers? Is she—" He paused again.

"Tolerably calm! sensible woman. Still I must write a little prescription for her. Nerves are not made of iron. She has really had great fatigue, and . . . Oh, Edwards!" to a staid, elderly man-servant who answered the bell, "I want some writing materials; and, Edwards, I think I must ask you to give Mr. Ford and myself a glass of wine."

"Yes, sir, certainly," replied Edwards. He proceeded to set forth the desired refreshment with alacrity, and then went in search of the writing materials.

"Not for me," said Mr. Ford, rejecting the glass offered him, with upturned hand; "it would choke me."

"Nonsense!" said the doctor, a cheery, chirruppy little man; "it will keep out the cold and the fog. I am glad you are here, Mr. Ford; you will perhaps be so good as to see Mr. Wall this evening, give him my compliments, and say I will see to the registry, as I was present at our poor friend's death. You and he, of course, know whom to write to; but it seems to me that the widow is terribly alone. Some female relative now, to stay with her; but I am perhaps going out of my proper sphere to offer any suggestion. Ah! thank you, thank you, that will do nicely"—this to the servant, and the little man began to scrawl hastily over the paper placed before him.

"You are right, sir," said Mr. Ford, drawing a chair to the table, and smoothing back his hair slowly and reflectively. "She, I mean Mrs. Travers, stands singularly, sadly alone. I may say that, although but a humble individual, I am her oldest, almost her only friend."

"Dear me! Indeed, indeed," returned the doctor, absently, as he read over his prescription and again rang the bell. "Here, Edwards, will you send this round to the surgery at once—*at once*, Edwards?"

"Yes, sir," and the man retired.

"You were saying?" observed the doctor, interrogatively, as he placed himself on the hearth-rug.

"We were speaking of Mrs. Travers," resumed Ford. "She has been kept singularly apart from her former friends; and there is no one now, save myself, who knew her in her early days. I knew her dear mother also, and all the circumstances —that is— Perhaps, under the circumstances, she might like to see me before I return to town?"

" What ! this evening ! now ? " asked the doctor, in evident
surprise. " Well, you know best. You might inquire."
But the doctor's tone seemed to steady Mr. Ford's nerves and
recall him to himself.

" No, no," he returned ; " not now, of course ; in a few days,
no doubt, she will send for me ; in the meantime, my best
efforts will be directed to arrange everything so as to cause as
little trouble to the executors as possible."

" I fancy there is a large real and personal estate, eh ? "

" Tolerable—tolerable, sir," returned Mr. Ford, rubbing his
hands over each other, with an air of superior information.

" Well, you will lose no time in communicating with Mr.
Wall," said the doctor ; " and," glancing at the clock, "you
will just catch the 7.30 train if you start at once. Have a glass
of wine before you go ? Do."

" Not a drop ! " returned Mr. Ford, with stern resolution.

A few more words and he sallied forth, holding down his
umbrella against the driving rain of a December evening, to
make his way to the station, which was fortunately close at
hand.

Three days after, the following formed one of the entries in
that column which is supposed to possess so deep an interest for
the female readers of the *Times :*—

" On the 12th instant, at Hampton Court, aged sixty-three,
Richard Travers, Esq., of St. Hilda's Place, E. C., and Hereford
Square, Tyburnia."

This announcement caused some gossip at Lloyd's, the
Jerusalem, and even among Dick, Tom, and Harry at the lunch-
eon-bars in the neighborhood of St. Hilda's place.

" So Travers is dead," was observed among the underwriters.
" What will become of the business ? "

" Is there no one to take it up ? "

" Capital East Indian connection."

" Not a bad trade with the Cape."

" Left no son ? "

" No ; married late—a foolish marriage. Some country girl,
they say."

" Who is heir ? "

" Has none, believe."

" Ford, his manager, is a shrewd, steady fellow ; he might
keep the business together," etc., etc.

While over the luncheon-bar the dashing young clerks at
Travers's were condoled with on the possible " shutting up " of
the " concern," and questioned as to how much the " Governor "
was probably worth. " Travers & Co.," though a somewhat
old-fashioned house, not working any of your globe-girdling

speculative gigantic operations, was much respected, and looked upon as being safe as the Bank, and considerably safer than a joint-stock bank.

All persons belonging to "Travers & Co." had a well-to-do, not to say gentlemanlike air, and, generally speaking, were prosperous.

And now the inevitable vulgarities of every-day life must tread close after, in the very footprints of the mighty, irresistible King.

Whispers of inexorable business penetrated the quiet chamber where the lonely young widow sits and broods over the strange, sad, and yet not utterly unwelcome liberty that has come to her. She must not appear until clothed in the sable garments suited to her state. She has neither father, mother, brother, relative of any degree at hand to act for her; and so, when a card, bearing the inscription "Mr. W. Wall," is brought to her, late the second day after her husband's death, she observes to her maid, "I must see him, Mills, of course," and, rising wearily, moves to the door.

"Mr. Ford is below, and wants to know if you will see *him ?*"

"Indeed I cannot. I am very much obliged to him for all his kind thought and interest, but Mr. Wall will do all I want at present. Tell Mr. Ford I will see him in a few days; show Mr. Wall up to the drawing-room."

The lawyer, a tall, thin, close-lipped man, gray and angular with advancing years, was but slightly acquainted with his friend and client's wife.

He had long known and respected the deceased, whose marriage had sorely disappointed and chafed him. It was with a sort of resentful reluctance he presented himself to the designing syren who had entrapped and bamboozled poor Travers, and induced him to leave the whole of his handsome fortune away from his own relations and natural heir.

Yet even he was insensibly mollified by the half-stately, half-subdued air of the objectionable widow.

"Thank you for coming to me so soon, Mr. Wall," she said, holding out her hand frankly to him. "I wanted to see you so much, and yet I seemed too dull to know how to send."

"While I rather hesitated lest I should be intruding too soon," replied the lawyer. "But there is much to be done and thought of; and not knowing any friend or relative more intimate with you than myself—" He paused abruptly, feeling he was on delicate ground.

"Exactly," said Mrs. Travers. The low, clear voice, though very soft, had in it a certain finish, a musical completeness of intonation which generally secured attention, and Mr. Wall listened intently as she tranquilly piloted him out of his difficulty.

"I *am* singularly alone ; so, even if you do not like me very much "—a sweet smile, sad, not unamused, but perfectly frank, and free from the smallest tinge of deprecation—" act as if you did, for the present."

"My dear madam—"

"There! there! I am quite sure you will be a considerate and conscientious adviser, and help me to fulfill, even to the smallest minutiæ, the wishes of—of him whom we have lost." She hesitated, and her voice trembled as she alluded to her husband, and then she remained silent till she could recover herself.

"I shall be most happy to assist you to the utmost of my power," said Mr. Wall, more cordially than he had yet spoken. " I have a will executed by your late husband about four years ago ; are you aware that he has made any other? I find from Mr. Ford there is some idea abroad that he has ; if so, it is most strange that we knew nothing of it. He always consulted us in all matters—especially myself."

"I think he has ; I think he has," returned Mrs. Travers, thoughtfully. She had seated herself on a sofa, and, resting her elbow on the pillow, leaned her cheek upon her hand.

" You think he has ! " repeated the lawyer, much surprised.

"I can only so understand his last words to me," continued his client. " He said he hoped I would not think he had done too much for— Then he stopped, and never uttered the name. Now I immediately fancied that he meant his cousin Hugh, for I know when he made the will to which you allude, he was terribly irritated against him, and therefore far from being just. I have often made Mr. Travers angry by urging this upon him, and entreating him to make a fairer distribution of his property. But I always imagined he resented my interference too much to follow my suggestions, though he loved me well. Where shall I find such a friend as he was ! "

She covered her face to hide the tears that would come.

"Certainly his words point to another will," resumed Mr. Wall after a moment's respectful silence. " Yet I cannot but consider it most improbable. However, it is our duty to make every search."

" What reason did Mr. Ford give for supposing there was another will? " asked Mrs. Travers.

" I really did not ask him. He mentioned it only just now as we were waiting together in the dining-room. He seems an excellent man, full of zeal for his late employer, and rightly so ; a better master, a more honorable gentleman never existed."

The solemn panegyric, though stiffly, was not unkindly said. Mrs. Travers held out her hand silently and gratefully to him ; he bowed over it, and went on :

" Ford is a keen man of business, and thoroughly understands the management of the house. When you feel equal to see him, you will find him useful in many ways."

" I have no doubt I shall," replied Mrs. Travers, carelessly. " But, in the meantime, will you, my dear sir, see and ascertain from him what has been said or reported about the will. We may get some clue to guide our search, and there is no use in looking at the will you have until we feel sure there is no other."

After receiving Mrs. Travers's directions respecting the funeral and some minor matters, the lawyer returned to the dining-room, considerably mollified towards his late client's widow, though it would have puzzled him to give a reason for the subtle change. Probably the simple, straightforward sincerity of her tone, the evident effort to suppress rather than display a grief unmistakably real, these symptoms so widely different from the " drowned in woe " aspect he expected from the designing minx who had entrapped his friend, blunted his suspicions in spite of himself, though he was half ashamed to feel them slipping from him.

The dining-room was unoccupied when the lawyer entered, and, looking round, he passed into a smaller room which opened upon the garden, and had been used by the late master of the house as a morning-room or study. Here Mr. Wall found the man he sought, who, standing with his back to the door, was so occupied in examining a water-color sketch of Mrs. Travers, which, though unfinished, was remarkably like, that he did not hear the lawyer's approach, and started when he addressed him.

" I was afraid you had gone, Mr. Ford. I want particularly to speak to you."

" I am quite at your service—and," with a slight, almost imperceptible catch or hesitation, " I thought it possible Mrs. Travers might wish to see me. I have had the honor of being on such confidential terms with our late excellent friend, and having been fortunate in doing Mrs. Travers herself some little service—"

" Just so," interrupted the lawyer, blandly. " She has just now begged me to express her consciousness of your zeal and merit, and, a—, hopes to tell you the same herself when equal to receive any one."

Mr. Ford bowed in silence ; so that Mr. Wall did not notice his expression. He also passed his handkerchief across his brow, as if warm or oppressed, and then rubbed his hands over each other with a nervous pressure ; meantime, Mr. Wall proceeded :

" We are very desirous of ascertaining if Mr. Travers has made any disposition subsequent to the will executed in '54. May I ask what are the rumors you have heard on the subject?"

"Only this; that yesterday, one of our clerks, Poole, who used to come to and fro with papers and checks to our late worthy principal after his first attack last spring—Poole said, 'He did not make that will much too soon.' I naturally asked what will he alluded to, and he told me that some months ago Mr. Travers sent for him, and when he went into the private room, he found Gregory with Mr. Travers. Gregory was our cashier; you may remember he took a holiday last summer, the first for twenty years—went to the seaside and caught fever, which carried him off; we had a move in consequence, and you recommended young Pierson for—"

"I remember it well! Pray go on."

"Well, Poole and Gregory witnessed Mr. Travers's signature to what Poole understood to be his will—of the purport he was, of course, ignorant."

"Ha!" ejaculated Mr. Wall, and stood a moment or two in deep thought. "This is very decisive indeed. Yet it seems almost incredible to me that he should have kept such a matter from Mrs. Travers and myself! However, all that now remains is for us to make a careful examination of all papers, etc. Is it not strange this man Poole never gave any previous hints?"

"I think not," returned Ford. "The young men in Mr. Travers's employ were considerably afraid of him, and as Poole seemed to think there was no secret in the occurrence, he was the less likely to talk about it."

"True," said Mr. Wall, and paused, as if considering the subject; then repeated the word "True. I will see Mrs. Travers again. It is only four o'clock. Nothing can be done until we know who is to administer to the estate; the sooner we commence our search the better. I will just step up to Mrs. Travers, and return to you immediately." So saying, the methodical lawyer left Mr. Ford to his reflections, which seemed to be of a checkered hue. First, he returned to his contemplation of Mrs. Travers's picture; once or twice he pressed his hands together with a sort of nervous tension, holding his head now to this side and now to that, so as to catch the different lights thrown by the lamp which Edwards had brought.

"Yes, yes," he whispered to himself. with a smile—a not unkindly smile, yet with an undefinable tinge of malignity in it, a sort of anticipative triumph. "It is his turn to-day—mine will come."

"Mrs. Travers is quite willing we should commence our examination at once; but doubts that such a document is among the papers here. Are you aware that Mr. Travers kept any at his office? Indeed, I suppose he was scarcely there since the period this man Poole mentions."

"Oh yes, he was ! He attended to business with much regularity all last spring and part of the summer."

"Well, Mr. Ford, let us begin. Here are the keys of this *escritoire.*"

For more than two hours did the two men of business seek carefully and systematically amid the papers and documents contained in a tin box or two, in an old brass-bound writing-desk, in all imaginable places—but in vain. And after partaking of refreshment, they departed, baffled, and silent.

While Mrs. Travers sits wrapped in thought over the fire in her dressing-room, unable either to form any defined plan, or even speculate on her own future, and a subdued note of solemn preparation vibrates through the household, let us put some of the memories which crowd the young widow's mind into a tangible form, and supply a key to the position.

CHAPTER II.

ABOUT sixteen or seventeen years before the dates of this chapter, a certain kindly, scholarly, elderly clergyman named Lee was perpetual curate of the pretty parish we shall call Cullingford.

Though not remote, it was retired and unknown save to experienced anglers, for the trout fishing in its neighborhood was excellent.

The Rev. William Lee was a small celebrity in his way. He had for many years eked out a very insufficient income by preparing young gentlemen for the army, navy, and the universities.

It was before competitive examinations had been invented ; still some preparation was necessary.

Mr. Lee's young gentlemen did not do badly, so his school prospered ; and the village, with the fields and woodlands round about, were the more cheerful for the sunny, healthy young life constantly overflowing the boundaries of the parsonage.

Mr. Lee had been early left a widower with one son—his idol —and a costly idol.

This special worship, and a general tendency not to turn away from those that would borrow of him, prevented the good curate's earnings from remaining in that concrete condition favorable to ease of circumstances. Still he had enough, and thought his lot a fair one, until his son, "his only son," was cut off by a few hours of cholera in India, leaving a little delicate orphan baby girl, first to plague and then to delight her desolate grandfather.

The nearest dwelling to the parsonage was a very humble cottage, originally not much beyond a gamekeeper's or gardener's lodge in size and style, but bearing the outward and visible signs of its inmates in the refined prettiness of its bit of pleasure ground, in the dainty drapery of its muslin curtains, and in the carefully trained roses and honeysuckle which made its porch in summer time all blossom and perfume. Holmewood Cottage had, about this time, been tenanted for nearly two years by a lady with one little girl—the widow, so it was understood in the village, of young Reginald Lee's dearest friend, who had stood by his death-bed, and sent the sad tidings to his bereaved father. At any rate, the curate was for long the widow's only friend, nearly her only acquaintance. She was a fair, soft, sad-looking woman, with weak health and shattered nerves ; her one tie to life a bright-eyed, brown-haired, active, restless, joyous little girl of five or six, with a sweet smile and a laugh full of glee, that soon wound herself round both the curate and his stern housekeeper, and was the spoiled pet of even the most cynical girl-hater among the curate's young gentlemen.

It is a strong temptation to pause and hold up some pictures of those happy days of young life among the bowery lanes and shady woodlands, by the merry cricket ground, the fresh uplands, and especially by the glorious trout streams for which the neigh-borhood was famous ; to describe the peace, the dreaminess, the silent thought-progress, the gradual unfolding of ambition to know, to see, to leave the happy valley and try the eddies and currents of the great, dreadful, beautiful, beckoning world be-yond. But it must be resisted.

None save Mr. Lee knew how scanty were the widow's re-sources, and with benevolent alacrity he did his very best to as-sist the education of her daughter. But the time came when she must be sent to school. This separation seemed to rend the mother's life. Then came a series of partings—for the widow was sure to be seriously ill when Katie had been away a few months—and the child was sent for in haste. Her presence then wrought a cure, and the process was repeated.

Now this was a trial to Katie ; she was ambitious, and pas-sionately fond of study, but the tender, protecting love inspired by her gentle, timid mother, enabled her to bear this and many other small worries arising from the same cause with the quiet submission of strength. Mrs. Aylmer had been, and still was, a delicately pretty woman, refined to weakness, more by nature than by training, for she was the daughter of a respectable tradesman, who had left her and her brothers fairly well off. Her grace and beauty, unfortunately for herself, attracted the admira-tion and affection of a handsome, pleasant, well-born, but reck-less young officer, who seemed to her the embodiment of all her fancy had ever painted. Difficulties and opposition only served to add fire and resolution to the lover's originally slight admiration, and at length he persuaded her to run away with him. The marriage being equally objectionable to the relatives on both sides, the erring couple were solemnly and effectively renounced ; the young husband exchanged into a regiment under orders for India, and he and his plebeian bride vanished from the respectable and aristocratic circles to which they respectively belonged.

After a few years of checkered happiness, the lieutenant, having squandered more than all he possessed, fell a victim to climate and too much "brandy pawnee," leaving his widow alone in the world, with her baby, and a lieutenant's widow's pension to exist upon. To her, of course, he was a hero, towards whom fate and fortune were adverse ; but Katie, whose mind was inquisitive and exceedingly common-sensible, in spite of its streaks of poetry and an ardent love of the beautiful, used sometimes, even when she listened to her mother's loving reminiscences, stroking her hand the while tenderly, to reflect that, were she a man, with the smallest opening wherein to insert the point of the wedge, it would go hard but she would force some favor from fortune.

It was during Kate's absence at a school in Germany, to which her mother had with infinite grief permitted her to go for a few months, that Mrs. Alymer received an advantageous proposition from a cousin, the only member of her family who recognized her existence. Mr. Hicks, the aforesaid cousin, was the proprietor of a far-famed establishment for the sale of "fishing tackle" in all varieties, including flies for all seasons and quarters. He was largely patronized by the disciples of the rod who are to be found in the precincts of the city where his shop was situated, and was a prosperous, kindly soul, innocent of malice, and regardless of the letter "h."

This fishing-tackle cousin wrote to ask Mrs. Aylmer if she would be disposed to accommodate a "most desirable party" for a few weeks occasionally ; the said "party" being an elderly "gentleman" who had been recommended to try change and amusement for his health. The only change he could invent was fishing. He had been used to go down to the North, but not feeling equal to the distance, had called at Mr. Hicks's place, and asked him to recommend some quarters within an easy distance of town. Whereupon Cousin Hicks bethought him of the trout-fishing reputation of Cullingford, and of throwing a chance in the widow's way. Mrs. Aylmer took counsel with the curate and accepted the proposal.

The little woman was ravenous to make and save money, for that meant helping Kate, and keeping Kate at home. The respectable party paid well, and stayed longer than he at first intended.

The widow made him very comfortable, and was the more successful because the respectable party was undoubtedly a gentleman.

He was, in short, Mr. Travers, head of the well-known house of Travers and Co., St. Hilda's Place, E. C.

Cullingford agreed with him. He came there frequently, sometimes not in the fishing season. He, after the first year, rented his two rooms permanently, and his managing clerk was quite well known on the line between G—— and Cullingford, as he went to and fro with his black bag at such times ; for, with all its rural, quiet, remote style of beauty, Cullingford was but two hours from London.

This was the addition which Kate found on her return from Germany. She was inclined to resent such an intrusion. Home was not home, with a stranger installed in the best rooms, and demanding her mother's first attention. But she soon became reconciled.

Mr. Travers was the most unobtrusive of men, though not without a certain dignity in his carriage and manners ; and when Kate had occasion to see and speak with him, her mother being disabled by a nervous headache, she was considerably struck by the sort of grave chivalrous respect with which he treated her.

Gradually it grew to be a custom with him to pause a while on his way out and in, and hold some conversation with his landlady's daughter as she tied up the flowers or took off dead leaves. He did not say much, but that little proved him a gentleman of some cultivation, and then— he listened remarkably well.

Sometimes he brought Kate some new and charming books from town—not novels ; these he disapproved as much as Kate loved.

He never appeared to care for Mr. Lee's acquaintance, and indeed the curate was too much occupied in his pastoral and tutorial avocations to spare the time for its prosecution.

So two years slipped away peacefully. At the end of that time Kate paid a visit to the German school where she had spent eight or nine months, and where she had formed a close friendship with the daughters of the principal. She hoped to have made an arrangement by which her young friend Fanny Lee, now emerging from childhood, should enjoy the advantages of a complete plunge into a foreign language ; but all her plans and projects were nipped in the bud.

Scarcely a month after Kate's arrival at Schlanganstein, a bad type of low fever broke out in Cullingford, where sanatory science was at that time unknown, and one of the first sufferers was Mrs. Aylmer. Kate was at once recalled, and came right willingly, though not very seriously alarmed—"the dearest mother" generally got ill when she was away, and recovered when she returned, and so it would be now.

It was not so, however; the fever was conquered, but the tender, timid, childlike mother died of the prostration which ensued. And then Kate knew how she loved her, and what desolation meant.

The day after the funeral, as Kate sat in all the unspeakable dreariness of the time when one's occupation's o'er, and the possibility of a new one has not suggested itself—when the reaction after protracted hope and fear and strained watching has set in, and makes life colorless, aimless, tasteless—she was startled by the announcement that Mr. Travers was at the door, and would like much to see her. She had nearly forgotten his existence; nevertheless she felt comforted by the idea that he thought of her, so he came in—came in more hastily, with less rigid composure than she had ever seen before. He evidently felt for her. She put her cold hand into his silently.

"My dear young lady," said Mr. Travers—and his voice, which had always pleased her, sounded unusually soft—"I have but this moment heard of your bereavement. I came down as usual, little thinking of the change which has occurred. I shall not, of course, intrude upon you; but if you can see me to-morrow, I should like to know your plans, if possible to assist you."

Very little passed then. Travers carried away with him a keen impression of the bravery with which Kate struggled for composure, and suppressed rather than exaggerated her grief. He talked with kindly sensible interest to her the next day; and the third, in a friendly and frank manner, suggested a solution of all doubts and difficulties by a marriage with himself.

Kate was astounded; but she was heartwhole and no sentimentalist. Mr. Travers was well-preserved, well-bred, and did not look quite thirty years older than herself. The world was strange and desolate to her; gratitude warmed her feelings towards him, and she consented.

The marriage was solemnized with unbecoming speed, so the people of Cullingford said; but, as Mr. Travers urged, Kate had no home to leave, and the sooner she was in one of her own the better. To this her only friend, Mr. Lee, agreed. Something he distantly hinted, respecting settlements, was met with a haughty "Rest assured, sir, I shall not leave my wife unprovided for," which silenced the good man. Two days after Kate Aylmer was transformed into Mrs. Travers, and carried away

from the sweet, humble, happy home of her girlhood for ever.
Mr. Travers evidently wished to cut off all connection with her
former life, and correspondence with Fanny Lee, though not
forbidden, was discouraged.

Nearly three years after the marriage, old Mr. Lee died, and
poor Fanny was left unprovided for.

Kate's lot had its angles ; but, rough or smooth, it did not
last in this stage. At the close of her third year of marriage,
Mr. Travers caught a severe cold, an attack of bronchitis ensued, from which he partially recovered. He was ordered out
of town, and not wishing to be far from his business, in the pursuit of which he had been keener than ever of late, he took a
house at Hampton. Feeling better at first, he relaxed some
invalid precautions, caught a second and severer cold, to which
he succumbed ; and Kate was again alone, though scarce so
desolate as when her mother died.   .

The will, which had been deposited in Mr. Wall's hands
soon after the receipt of an ill-judged letter from the man who
had hoped to be his heir, written in reply to Mr. Travers's announcement of his marriage, was short, simple, and to most
widows would have been satisfactory,

After a legacy of five hundred pounds to his chief clerk, and
a few smaller bequests to an old pensioner or two and a super-
annuated servant, the testator's beloved wife was constituted
residuary legatee and executrix in conjunction with an old City
friend ; no directions or wishes as to the winding-up or continu-
ance of his business was expressed—everything was unreservedly left to the young childless widow.

It was this will that Mrs. Travers strongly believed had been
superseded by a later testament or codicil.

CHAPTER III.

BUT the search for the will was fruitless ; every probable and
improbable corner was ransacked in vain, to the grief of
Mrs. Travers, and the ill-concealed annoyance of her solicitor.

Mr. Wall was convinced that his late client must have destroyed his second will, as on inquiry, there appeared no doubt
that he had made one ; while Mrs. Travers was equally convinced he had not, and worked herself almost into a fever by
fretting and conjecturing on the subject.

The last melancholy ceremonies had been performed. The
windows were once more opened to the light, and the scarce interrupted current of every-day life flowed on as before, its crowd
of common things rapidly closing up the gap, so that even the

truest, deepest mourners wonder at the marvelous and often merciful operation of inevitable routine—the force that lies in the "strong necessity of living."

Kate Travers never attempted to persuade herself or others that she was broken-hearted, yet she thought much and sadly of her dead husband. He had loved her truly; but even to himself his love had been more a source of pain than pleasure. He had believed that a calm and fatherly tenderness would have tempered the warmth of conjugal affection, and have fitted him peculiarly to be the guide and guardian of the bright girl who accepted his proposal with such frank gratitude. He did not reckon on the spell which her individuality, and an undefined consciousness of the latent wealth of love he had not the power to draw forth, cast over him to torment and to fascinate. Before he was six months a husband he loved her with an exacting passion which was at once the misery and delight of his existence. He hated himself for the difference of their age; he would have sacrificed his all without hesitation for her sake; yet he resented the slightest liberty of action, lest it might be the result of indifference; and was so ravenous for proofs of her affection that, when they came, the sweet incense was all evaporated in the self-torturing tests on which his eagerness to prove its purity insisted. While she, discerning things more from sympathy than deliberate observation, was slow to understand him.

At first, while mourning the loss of a cherished mother, whose helplessness had only endeared her the more, she clung gratefully and tenderly to him, and he was satisfied; but her sunny nature reasserted itself, and her girlish pleasure in rich and becoming dress, the new enjoyment of driving in her own carriage —as she soon ceased to call it—and her openly expressed delight in wearing the handsome ornaments Mr. Travers bestowed upon her, opened up a hundred sources of offense. Her vivid enjoyment of books and music and painting converted these innocent objects of interest into hated rivals, and Kate never could get rid of the impression that she was in a golden cage; that, however the imprisoning wires might be jeweled and adorned, they were still there. Her good temper, grateful, easy nature, and ready tact, always prevented any open collision, save on the occasion when Mr. Travers opened a letter addressed to his wife, in which her old friend, Fanny Lee, warmly thanked her for a very opportune present of money when she had been left in sore poverty by her grandfather's death, nearly a year before our story opens; this acknowledgment, and an evident allusion to some expressions of regret from Mrs. Travers that she had lost sight of so valued a friend as old Mr. Lee, were

construed by the jealous husband into evidence of his wife's
preference of her past life, and a tendency to underhand dealing.
In vain she explained that, having abundance of pocket money,
she thought she might dispose of some of it without troubling
him on the subject.   He was for some time unappeasable.   A
severe attack of illness occurring soon after, Mrs. Travers was
glad to let the subject drop, and she gradually but very slowly
regained her ascendency.   At first, with fearlessness of a heart
secure in its own honesty and singleness of purpose, Mrs. Travers
tried to wean her husband from his morbid greed for her society
—for her every look, and word, and thought, and to brighten this
engrossing jealousy into pleasant, friendly, sympathetic intercourse.   But, finding herself misunderstood in every attempt at
a better and healthier tone, she lost heart, and gradually subsided into an adored captive.   She was young, and but partially
developed ; as yet she knew neither her own strength or weakness.   But four years of marriage and constant companionship
with a man of cultivated though somewhat narrow mind, had
greatly matured her intellect, and the last year being much
thrown on herself both in matters of action and judgment, she
began to feel that she might stand alone.

Now, even under her sincere sorrow, in which the principal
ingredient was regret that the departed, with all the materials of
happiness about him, had gone down to the grave under the same
dull shadow in which he had lived ; even under her tender grief
was a sweet consciousness that, however gloomily shrouded,
liberty had come to her at last.   Still it was very strange, that
sensation of being quite mistress of the roomy, comfortable
house in which she was domiciled ; of having the full command
of the stately and well-bred man out of livery who presided
over the plate and glass ; of being really at home in her house,
albeit but a ready-furnished one taken by the year, in order that
Mr. Travers might enjoy pure air within an easy distance of his
office.   It was too strange to be pleasant yet.   And then how
she shrank from the look of her own face in her widow's cap !
From no want of respect to the departed, she longed to throw
it off ; it was so unnatural, so oppressive !

She sat thinking dreamily of these things about a week after
the funeral, on one of the first days of the new year.   How rapidly and vividly the panorama of the past floated through her
mind, and how changed was everything !

" I wish I had a nice, kind, gentlemanlike uncle or cousin !—a
man is so useful.   How lonely I am !   I have lost my old
friends, and made no new ones.   Well, I shall never return to
that dreary house in Hereford Square.   I was wretched there !
I will let it, or sell it, *if* I have power !   How that 'if'

meets me everywhere! I wish the real will could be found. I can never feel settled until it is. I am so sure it was made after our last conversation about Hugh Galbraith, when Mr. Travers seemed so offended at my persisting that his first will was unjust! It was so like him to act upon my suggestion afterwards, and yet to conceal the act! Ah! with so much knowledge and real nobility of nature in many ways, how was it that he missed the true wisdom of frankness and trustfulness? I must find Fanny Lee; I might help her, and if she turns out anything like what I remember, she could live with me."

Thinking thus dreamily, Mrs. Travers lay back in a luxurious easy-chair imported from their town house, near a glowing, blazing fire. The drawing-room where she had once more established herself was a large and pleasant apartment, well filled with a mixture of old-fashioned and modern furniture. The mirrors, the chintz curtains, the larger tables, and the cabinets, were almost antique in style and pattern. Although mid-winter, the *jardinières* were not neglected; heaths, ferns, and chrysanthemums lent color enough to be agreeable. A grand piano filled up the farther end of the room; and a pretty, fanciful, but useful writing-table stood near enough to the fire for warmth and to the window for light. A look of comfort and good taste pervaded the whole.

After a few moments more of reverie, a brighter and more decided expression stole over Mrs. Travers's features. She rang, and, rising, walked slowly towards one of the windows; a pretty garden sloped to the river, now denuded of summer adornments, and while she gazed upon without seeing it, the grave "man out of livery" opened the door.

"You rang, if you please, ma'am."

"Oh, yes! I want the Directory, Edwards."

When it was brought, Mrs. Travers sat down to her writing-table, and looked earnestly through its pages, apparently in vain. But she was interrupted. Again the door opened. Edwards appeared, salver in hand, and presented a card to his mistress.

"Mr. Ford? Show him up." She left the writing-table, and stood ready to receive him.

Mr. Ford was a man made up of negatives; he was neither young nor old, plain nor handsome, tall nor short, gentleman-like nor caddish. He had fine large dark eyes, rather restless in expression, very thick black whiskers faintly powdered with gray, a large loose-looking mouth, and a smile not unkindly nor yet quite free from a tinge of malignity. He was accurately dressed in slight mourning.

"How do you do, Mr. Ford?" said Mrs. Travers, holding out

her hand with a smile—a very kind but pensive smile. "I am glad to see you."

Mr. Ford took the hand, and bowed over it in silence.

"I was so sorry Edwards did not let me know when you called last Tuesday," she continued, to give him time, seeing that from some cause he was agitated. "I should certainly have seen you."

"You are very kind," said Mr. Ford, at length, clearing his throat nervously, and looking up without absolutely meeting Mrs. Travers's eyes. "I ventured to hope that for various reasons you would have received *me.*"

"Come near the fire," was Mrs. Travers's reply ; "though so bright, it is very cold." She resumed her seat, and Ford placed himself near her.

"I almost feared to see you, dreading to find sad traces of your long watch," he continued ; "but I rejoice to find you looking better than I expected."

"I feel very strange, and sad, and puzzled, but not ill. Oh ! Mr. Ford, I have been quite longing to talk to you. You were so much in poor Mr. Travers's confidence ; you knew us all so well before I was married, that you can tell me more than any one else."

Mr. Ford colored slightly, and drew his chair a possible inch nearer to the widow.

"My dear Mrs. Travers, need I say how heartily I am at your service. I . . . a . . ." he hesitated, and stopped abruptly.

"Oh, I feel quite sure of your loyalty to me," she returned, with a frank, unhesitating, but slightly indifferent acceptance of his assurances not exactly flattering. "Now, tell me, what do you think about this will? I think it is simply mislaid. I feel sure Mr. Travers made one in accordance with my wishes, but I never can believe he destroyed it."

"It is impossible to say. The most excellent of men are liable to strange whims, sometimes much more unpleasant whims than leaving all their property to a charming lady like your good self."

A faint tendency to frown appeared in Mrs. Travers's distinct though delicate eyebrows ; but she only said, "Then you think he did destroy the will Poole witnessed?"

"I cannot come to any decision in my own mind on the subject. I only know that every possible depository for such a document has been most carefully examined, and not a trace of it is to be found. Even if it exists I do not now think it will be discovered, and indeed I incline to believe it cannot exist."

"It is most unfortunate," said Mrs. Travers, leaning her elbow on the arm of her chair, and resting her cheek on her hand, while her deep blue eyes grew larger and darker with earnest thought as she gazed at the fire—not more earnestly than Ford gazed at her, now her eyes were turned away. "Most unfortunate," she went on slowly, as if speaking to herself. "I do not know what to do or how to act. I feel certain Mr. Travers wished to provide properly for Sir Hugh Galbraith, and now, when I suggest a division of the property with him, Mr. Wall says, 'My dear madam, you must just wait.' When I suggest that your five hundred pounds should be paid to you, 'I must just wait;' and when I say I should like to go away somewhere to shake off the sort of oppression that hangs upon me, I am met with the same impressive 'I would not advise you to stir under the circumstances; you must just wait.'" She pushed back her chair slightly as if warmed by her own impatience.

"And very sound advice too," said Ford, with a smile at once admiring and superior. "There really is nothing for it but patience. If the will does not turn up within a week or two we may conclude it has been destroyed, and act upon the original one. Fortunately, there is nothing pressing; things can go on for a while as they are. Even should the missing document be found, we may well believe that the bulk of the property and all the authority may be with you—at least I suppose you have no reason to doubt this?"

The last words were uttered with a kind of insinuating curiosity, while the speaker, resting his arms on his knees, bent forward to look very keenly at his companion.

"No, I suppose not," she returned, carelessly; and then added, with much feeling, "I know *he* would have been guided in all things by a partiality beyond what I deserved, by a kindly consideration that never deviated—"

"What!" interrupted Mr. Ford, rising abruptly, and walking to the window; then, turning again, he repeated, "never deviated! Do I not well remember one evening in Hereford Square, not long before you came to this very house, the pain, the grief, the indignation with which I overheard words addressed to you as I waited in the front drawing-room, words which should never have been addressed to a creature so gentle, so devoted, so—"

"Hush! hush! Mr. Ford," cried Mrs. Travers, imperiously. "I always feared you had overheard those unhappy remarks, and, not knowing what led up to them, would exaggerate their meaning. It was an affair in which I now believe I was wrong. So good a husband had a right to my fullest confidence in everything."

"Even in so slight a matter as a small gift to a young girl friend, whose feelings you would have spared the—"

"You know more than I thought," interrupted Mrs. Travers, in her turn, and looking full and more sternly at him than her soft eyes seemed capable of looking a moment before. "But whatever opinion you may have formed, I beg you will forget the whole thing ; at any rate, never name it to *me.*"

Mr. Ford colored and bit his lip. "I see I have offended. You must excuse me if I sometimes lose my self-command. When I remember old times, your dear respected mother, who always extended so kind a welcome to me ; the sweet cottage, which seemed to me at one time an earthly paradise—" He again stopped and turned away, passing his handkerchief over his face. Mrs. Travers looked at him with a slightly wondering expression, and a vague, uncomfortable desire that he would take his departure arose in her mind.

"They were very happy, those old days," said she, soothingly, after a moment's pause ; "but I hope there are many bright and prosperous ones before you yet, Mr. Ford. I am sure, if I can in any way assist your fortunes, I should not only please myself, but best fulfill my husband's good intentions ; he had, I am sure, a sincere regard for you."

Mr. Ford made a gesture as if repudiating all worldly advantages which might accrue from the Travers connection.

"By the way," continued the young widow, "talking of poor dear Cullingford and old times reminds me I was looking for Mr. Reed's address when you came in. Perhaps you remember Tom Reed ; though I believe he had left Mr. Lee's before you knew us. He was a second or third cousin of the dear old man, and I thought he might know where Fanny is. I have quite lost sight of her since—" Mrs. Travers stopped, colored, and added quickly : "I once met Mr. Reed at dinner—oh, quite two years ago—and he told me then where he was to be found, but I quite forget ; some Inn (he was studying for the Bar or had just been called to the Bar). Perhaps you could find out, or shall I ask Mr. Wall ? "

"If you will permit me, I shall make it a point to ascertain."

"Thank you very much, Mr. Ford."

An awkward pause.

"I do not think," resumed the confidential clerk, "I need trespass any longer upon you. The power of attorney which I have will enable me to meet all present contingencies in the way of correspondence. Beyond this, Messrs. Wall and Wreford must advise. I see you have rather a pretty water-color sketch of the old parsonage, with the river. Very neatly executed ! But does it not strike you, now," putting up his glass, "that the clouds are a trifle woolly ? And the perspective between those elms rather runs up-hill."

"No, indeed, it does not," said Mrs. Travers with a sigh. "I only see a close resemblance to a scene I love. I had no idea you were such a critic, Mr. Ford."

"I do not claim so high a title" (with the proudest humility); "but I used to do a good deal in that line once, and I flatter myself I have a tolerably correct eye."

"Indeed! I did not think you were an artist in addition to your high business qualifications."

"Pray do not look on me as a mere machine," replied Ford, with his peculiar smile. "But I must not keep you standing. I wish you good day."

"Good morning; and, pray do not forget Mr. Reed's address."

As the door closed behind him, Mrs. Travers stood a moment or two in thought.

"There is a change somewhere; is it in him, or in myself! He seemed a shade presumptuous, or have I forgotten the equality that once existed between him, myself, and my mother? I think not; but I cannot go back to the old state—and though I will be kind and helpful, he must see in me *only* the widow of his late employer, only the present head of the house of Travers."

CHAPTER IV.

THE Euston Terminus was all alive, and a goodly army of porters ready to disentangle the passengers' luggage, with small regard to its well-being, one bright but sharp afternoon in early spring, as the 3.30 train from H—— rushed into the station, and the crowded carriages disgorged an eager, pushing, striving mob.

Through its eddies a gentleman who had been waiting about for a few minutes before the train came in, dexterously elbowed his way. Looking sharply into all the first-class carriages, he suddenly paused at one of the second-class, from which a fat female with a huge basket had just emerged, and raised his hat. "Miss Lee," he said; "if I am not much mistaken, Fanny Lee."

"Yes, yes," said a young lady, disentangling herself from a chaos of children, band-boxes, and brown paper parcels; and, putting her hand in his, she stepped out into the light. They stood looking at each other for a moment, as if trying to recall some half-vanished memory. The girl saw a gentlemanlike-looking man, moderately tall, very slight, with dark hair, a spare, expressive face, exceedingly keen dark eyes, and a half-kindly, half-mischievous smile on his clean-shaved lips. He was remarkably well dressed, and wore a sprig of lily of the valley in his button-hole. Indeed, he might have passed for a man of

fashion, were it not for the expression of alertness, of bright intelligence, that pervaded every line of his countenance and, I
had almost said, figure.

She was a little, delicate-looking creature, wrapped in a shapeless waterproof, above which, and shaded by a very indifferent
hat, appeared a pretty oval face, with soft brown eyes and a
quantity of pale brown hair, not very neatly or fashionably arranged.

The mutual survey scarce lasted a second when it was abruptly
terminated by a hasty shove from a heavily-laden porter, which
sent the young lady almost into her companion's arms; but,
quickly recovering herself, she exclaimed, "Is it possible you are
Tom Reed?"

"Quite possible," replied the gentleman, drawing her hand
through his arm. "Do you doubt it? Come, let us see about
your luggage. I suppose you have four or five trunks, three or
four packages, a couple of bonnet boxes, and—"

"Oh dear, no!" a little sadly, though with a smile. "I have
but two in the world."

"What a delightful girl to travel with! Have they any
special signs?"

"No, no—just my name. There!"—convulsively—"that
man is going away with one of them." As she spoke Mr. Reed
darted upon him, and rescued No. 1; the other was quickly
discovered.

"Now, then! I am afraid that we must take a four-wheeler.
Here, cab!"—as though he was monarch of every conveyance
that ever paid for a license; so his companion thought, as he
quickly but carefully handed her in, saw the luggage placed,
and finally jumped in after her.

"And so you are little Fanny," he said, as they got into the
comparative quiet of Gower Street, looking straight into her
eyes. "I should have known you anywhere. But somehow I
fancy you had rosier cheeks at the old parsonage. You are all
right, are you? No cold or nervous debility—that's the last
dodge, I believe?"

"I am very well," said the young lady; "but not quite so
bright as I used to be with poor grandpapa." She sighed and
smiled. "And I have had some hard work in Yorkshire. Hard
work never suited me, you know. But, there—I cannot hear
what you say, and I can't scream.' Shall we stop soon?"

"Presently. Let me put up the window. Have you no shawl
or wrap?—it's cold, though so bright."

And they rattled on; occasionally the newly-arrived would
utter a word as with a note of interrogation, "Regent Street?"

"No; Oxford Street."

"Opera House?"

"No; Covent Garden."

Twice Mr. Reed called to the driver to hasten, and at last they reached Waterloo.

"Train for Hampton Court?"

"Just gone, sir."

"Next?"

"Not till 5.30."

"By Jove! an hour and a half to wait. Come, Fanny, you look famished. There's soup or something to be had, and a glass of sherry."

"Thank you, I will take a bun or a biscuit. I have not had anything since seven o'clock this morning."

"No wonder I miss the roses; roses don't flourish under such an ethereal *régime.*" And the weary traveler was soon summoned to the refreshment room, where soup, sherry, a table in a quiet nook, a devoted waiter, seemed ready as by magic—the magic of Tom Reed's good-humored authority and contagious activity.

His young *protégée,* glancing at the very perfect minutiæ of his costume, drew off her own dingy and not neatly mended gloves with a laugh and a blush which became her greatly. "Well, Tom," she said, "you might have known me, but I am sure I should never have known you in such nice clothes."

"Clothes!" echoed Tom Reed, stretching out one arm, and regarding it with an expression of uneasiness. "Do you call these clothes?"

"What are they, then?"

"Dress," he replied, with much solemnity. "The porters here, and your friends in Yorkshire, probably clothe themselves. I dress." He waited till the pleasant laugh with which she heard him was past, and asked gravely, "And what incongruity do you observe between my garments and myself?"

"Oh! you look all right now," she returned; "but when we met last, you know, you had not an unbroken garment, as you call it, in the world. Though I was such a little thing, I remember poor Mrs. Green, the housekeeper, for ever lamenting that Master Tom never *was* fit to be seen. What a mischievous boy you were!"

"Do you remember all that! Why, it must be ten years ago. Well, little cousin," a very kindly, soft expression stealing over his face, "nothing has pleased me half so much for many a day as this plan of Mrs. Travers to have you with her. You will be quite comfortable."

"Do you think so?" a little anxiously, while she held a spoonful of soup mid-way to its destination. "It is *so* long since I saw her, and people change."

"She does not," emphatically. "She is a thorough-going brick—a splendid creature altogether."

"I was very fond of her as a child; but then she was always so much with her mother and grandpapa that we were never quite playfellows; and she is four or five years older than I am."

"Did you know the late lamented Travers?" asked Tom.

"I remember often seeing him, but I do not think I ever spoke to him. He was frightfully rich, wasn't he?"

"Delightfully, you mean. Yes, and I believe your old friend has it all now. Well, I suspect she earned it. He was a fine fellow, the type of the 'grand old English merchant,' but I fancy a trifle jealous and exacting; all Kate's old friends politely warned off the premises. I met her very unexpectedly, about two years ago, at a gorgeous banquet in Westbourne Terrace; she was delighted to have a talk over the old place and people, so I went to call, was presented to the proprietor, and asked to another gorgeous banquet, where I nearly died of starvation."

Fanny opened her pretty brown eyes in amazement.

"Moral and mental starvation, I mean. After that I saw no more of our friend. Next I saw the death of old Travers in the *Times*, and a fortnight or so after, I had a note from her, asking me to call; when I did, I found she wanted to know where you were, and how you were placed. I was ashamed, my dear girl, to be able to tell so little; but I had a clue, and so she found you out."

"And then I had to give a month's notice; and even after that, could scarce get away."

"All's well that ends well," said Reed, rising. "I am sure you will be as happy as—as a pet fairy! so make yourself comfortable. I imagine I might get the tickets now."

The young lady sat very quietly in deep, and, from her expression, not unpleasant thought—enjoying, as she well might, emancipation from a comfortless school-room, a troop of noisy, ill-mannered, and not particularly good-natured children, whose exacting mamma looked upon her as a bondmaid, for whom there existed no chance of manumission.

She had drawn on her shabby gloves again, and had just begun to expect Cousin Tom back, when he returned, and, taking his arm, they sallied forth to seek their train. As they passed the second-class refreshment room, a very seedy looking individual issued from it; a short, thin, red-faced man, with a dingy, battered white hat, a cutaway coat with baggy pockets, and palpably burst-out boots. Yet he had a hand thrust into one of the pockets and a short stick protruding therefrom, and wore his miserable hat with an indescribable slant, as though the 'tone of the turf would hang round him still." This unattractive figure placed himself exactly in their way.

"Tom Reed!" he exclaimed, in a hoarse, unsteady voice. "Mr. Reed—I don't think I am mistaken."

Tom Reed looked at him, as if puzzled, for a moment, and then said, "Why, it can't be Trapes?"

"The same, sir! All that's left of him. And how are you, Reed? World's been going pretty square with you?" continued his curious acquaintance, staring boldly at Fanny, and seemingly resolved on a talk.

"Oh, pretty well, thank you," returned Tom, civilly; "but we are barely in time for our train."

"Good five minutes to spare, if you are for Hampton Court. I say, old fellow, I want a talk with you. I have lost sight of you this age past. Where can I find you?"

"Oh, the old place—M. T. office."

"Still there! Well, I don't care to call," screwing up his left eye, knowingly. "I'll drop you a line."

"All right—good morning," cried Tom, hurrying his companion on, and into a first-class carriage.

"What a dreadful man! How could you know him?"

"Poor unfortunate devil!" returned Tom, thoughtfully. "A few years ago he was a sort of fine gentleman I half envied."

"Did he lose his money, poor man?" asked Fanny, compassionately. "Still he need not look quite so dreadful."

"No, certainly not;" and then Tom Reed turned the conversation and devoted himself to cheering up the pretty little cousin under his care.

But Fanny was nervous, and could not conceal it. Her sweet, slight nature had been too much tried by the sudden change from her grandfather's loving indulgence to the rugged discipline of her Yorkshire penitentiary. She was too unhinged to look forward brightly, now that hope had come—as fatigue sometimes banishes sleep.

Tom Reed felt her slight arm tremble, as he drew it through his own to conduct her the short distance that intervened between the station and the Travers mansion.

It was a clear frosty evening, a young moon showing coldly bright in the deep blue sky.

"What a pretty place!" said Fanny, looking round her, timidly. "Will Kate—I mean Mrs. Travers—always live here?"

"It is hard to say; but I fancy not," returned Mr. Reed. "There, you see those tall wrought-iron gates?—that is our destination."

A few moments more, and Fanny found herself upon the threshold in a flood of light, and in the tender embrace of her old friend, who seemed to her at once strange and familiar. The sudden warmth and glow of kindness was nearly too much

2

for poor Fanny, whose bright eyes, half sad, half mischievous, were dimmed, while her lip quivered.

"Dear child, you are quite tired out; come with me to your room," cried Mrs. Travers, observing her emotion. "Mr. Reed, you will find the *Times* and magazines in the drawing-room—if I may offer any literary attraction to one of the initiated ? *So* much obliged to you for bringing me this dear little waif. Come, Fanny ;" and the rescued bondmaid was swept upstairs to a charming room, next Mrs. Travers's, where a ruddy fire, fresh chintz hangings, a dressing-table all pink and white muslin, a dainty little white bed, looked welcome most pleasantly and impressively. "How cold and pale you look !" said Mrs. Travers, assisting to take off her cloak. ("And how shabby," she *thought*.) "Still, it is the same little Fanny, and will bloom out soon again with the roses of former years under my care, I hope." Here the respectable Mrs. Mills entered with a can of hot water. "Do you not remember Mills, Fanny ? "

"Of course 1 do ! And, Mills, do you not remember me ? " cried Fanny, seizing her hand and kissing her withered cheek ; a piece of spontaneous kindness that bound Mills to her from that moment.

"Dear, dear ! to think that this is little Miss Fanny !—grown quite a woman, I do declare."

"Yes, it is astonishing ; but we could not expect her to stand still," remarked Mrs. Travers. "Now, dinner will be ready in a few minutes, and I daresay Mr. Reed is quite ready for it. When he leaves, we shall have plenty of time to talk together ; and how much we have to tell each other ! "

"Indeed, we have ; but, dear Kate—I mean Mrs. Travers—you are quite different from what I remember you—older looking and better looking ; and yet the same."

"It is well you have qualified 'older looking,' little one, with 'better looking,' or I should prepare to be awful ! I will leave you to dress, or not, as you like ; and when you join us in the drawing-room, dinner will be ready . . . ."

"How did you recognize each other ? "asked Mrs. Travers, as she dispensed the filletted soles.

"Well, we jumped at each other," returned Reed, setting down his glass of sherry with an air of discriminating satisfaction. "As I glanced into the chaos of bundles, bandboxes, and babies in which she was engulfed, a vision of a silvery trout stream, a sensation of terror and wet feet, much exaltation, a trifle of conscience and a large proportion of gratitude, associated a slight young lady in a waterproof with a certain great deliverance, wrought by her opportune warning in days of yore, and memory whispered, ' That's she ! ' "

" Yes, yes! I remember it," cried Fanny, who had already revived marvelously under the benign influences around her; "and I think grandpapa was equally relieved. He had solemnly declared he would flog you if he caught you poaching; and I knew quite well he did not want to catch you, so I slipped away out by the Beech Wood, and gave you notice. It was quite as much for his sake as yours." A pretty little defiant nod closed her speech.

" Did Fanny know you? " asked Mrs. Travers.

" That is a doubtful point. According to her the general excellence of my attire militated against my identity."

" Well, Mr. Reed, I must say that my recollection of you in days of old does not hold you up as the glass of fashion or the mould of form."

" No indeed; you were a dreadful pickle; yet how fond poor dear grandpapa was of you," added Fanny.

" He was far kinder than I deserved," returned Tom Reed, with momentary gravity; and dinner proceeded without anything further than newspaper talk till dessert banished their attendant.

" I cannot tell you what pleasure it gives me to see you both," said Mrs. Travers, permitting Tom Reed to fill her bubble-like glass with claret. " Besides the pleasure of meeting old, and I think congenial friends, the relief from the sense of isolation that has oppressed me since—since my widowhood, is wonderfully delightful. I have never been very fond of Christmas since I grew up, but this one I spent quite alone. The people on either side here were very good in calling and leaving 'Kind inquiries;' but of course they are total strangers to me. So all I could do was to give the servants a good dinner, and let them invite their friends. They sent me up a piece of their pudding at my luncheon, and, by avoiding a late dinner, I managed to forget it was Christmas Day. I hope I shall not spend another like it."

" No, no! we must change all that," said Reed, cheerfully. " And may I ask how are all your affairs progressing? When I saw you last week, you were experiencing some difficulty with Wall and Wreford. They objected to your rather munificent suggestion of sharing your fortune with Sir Hugh Galbraith."

" Yes; Mr. Wall would not hear of it, which rather surprised me. I fancied he was annoyed at Mr. Travers leaving all his money away from Sir Hugh. Now I observe he is not so great a favorite. Still, Hugh had evidently been taught to look upon himself as poor Mr. Travers's heir, and I think he has been badly treated; nor have I a doubt that the missing will would have given him a share of the property, could we but find it."

"Still, to go halves with him voluntarily," said Reed, smiling, "was slightly Quixotic, if you will not quarrel with me for saying so."

"I do not think it was," returned the young widow, thoughtfully. "Fifteen hundred or two thousand a year, all my own, are great riches to me; but by no means such wealth to Sir Hugh, with a position to keep up, and I suppose the usual costly tastes and habits of his class. In fact, but for the fear of being thought idiotic, and outrunning Mr. Travers's real wishes, I would willingly have given Sir Hugh the lion's share."

"And what decision have you arrived at?"

"Oh, Mr. Wall would hear of nothing beyond a third of the whole being offered; and you must remember we do not yet know what the whole will be. Mr. Wall rather startled me by saying that too much munificence might suggest that the real will was more favorable to Sir Hugh than I liked, and therefore not lost, but suppressed! Do you think the general color of men's minds of so vile a tint, as to distort a simple wish to do right so basely?"

"What a horrible idea!" cried Fanny, who was listening with deep attention.

"I have by no means a bad opinion of my fellow-creatures. Still, they are inclined to attribute very base motives for acts they cannot understand or account for," replied Tom Reed. "I heartily wish the second will could be found; but I suspect something or other occurred to renew Mr. Travers's displeasure with his cousin, and, thinking it too favorable, he destroyed it."

"No, Tom, no!" cried Mrs. Travers, with animation. "You must forgive me," she said, interrupting herself, and smiling; "but when eager or in earnest the old name comes so readily to my lips."

"I shall *not* forgive you, my dear Mrs. Travers, if you go back to the newer and colder appellation. Pray let me be Tom, who is quite as anxious and proud to be your servant and ally now as in our old poaching days." There was a tinge of earnestness under this pleasant, airy manner, very acceptable to the fair but lonely widow.

"So be it," she said laughing. "I accept you as Tom, and my champion to boot. But to return. I do not think Mr. Travers ever destroyed his will. I should more readily believe he had not made a second, but that it seems so positively proved he did. I confess I have felt at times a strange uneasiness about it, but have now made up my mind that, even if found, it will make no material difference—Sir Hugh will probably have a handsome legacy, but the bulk of the fortune and all authority Mr. Travers has no doubt left to me."

"That is highly probable," observed Tom Reed. "Where is this Galbraith?"

"Somewhere in India. He was, I believe, on the point of coming to England when the mutiny broke out. Indeed, he was at Calcutta on his way, but he immediately returned to join the remnant of his regiment, the —th Light Dragoons, which was nearly cut to pieces at the beginning of the outbreak. I have seen his name mentioned once or twice as a very gallant officer; but I fancy he is a thorough aristocrat—brave enough, but proud and overbearing, and unjust. His letter to Mr. Travers on our marriage was almost unpardonable. Oh, the contempt with which he spoke of me!"

"And why, I should like to know!" exclaimed Fanny, indignantly. "I am sure you are as good as he is?"

"That depends on the exact meaning attached to goodness," said Mrs. Travers, smiling. "I can afford to forgive him, because he did not know what he was writing about. Indeed, I imagine these high-caste men *know* nothing thoroughly."

"Why, Mrs. Travers, you are quite democratic!" said Tom Reed.

"Dear me!" cried Fanny, with some awe, "I suppose Sir Hugh Galbraith is of a very old family indeed."

"So old as to be lost in the mists of antiquity. His ancestors did heaps of mischief on the border in bygone days, and no particular good, I daresay. Notwithstanding the difference in their ages, Sir Hugh and poor Mr. Travers were cousins. I think my husband acted as a sort of guardian to Sir Hugh. Yes, Fanny, he is a very great man indeed—a tiny acorn on the topmost twig of the family tree. Still, I should not like him to suffer from his cousin's partiality for me. Generosity may be an aristocratic virtue; I am content with more homely justice, and will try to practice it."

"And the upshot of all this is—" put in Tom, interrogatively.

"That Messrs. Wall and Wreford have written by my direction to inform Sir Hugh how matters stand; that it is my intention, as soon as they can be arranged, to make over to him a third of the fortune bequeathed to me. I cannot help imagining he will refuse to accept, estimating me as he does; but Mr. Wall says he is a poor man, every acre of the few left, mortgaged up to the gate of the family fortalice, for it can hardly be called castle."

"He has made a great ass of himself," said Reed, "and is in luck to find such a residuary legatee as yourself; you certainly give the best refutation to his insolence by your generous conduct."

After some more conversation about the happy old days at

Cullingford, Tom Reed, observing his cousin's pale cheek and drooping eyes, bid the ladies "Good evening."

"Do you know I like that cousin of yours so much, Fanny," cried Mrs. Travers, as the door shut upon her departing guest. "There is an undercurrent of good feeling with all his lightness and careless ease."

"I was so surprised to see him quite a fine gentleman."

"A fine gentleman! My dear Fanny, you must not use opprobrious terms in speaking of your cousin. I believe he is a good fellow, which is a different affair altogether. And now, dear child, you look quite worn out. You must go to bed. Tell me, do you feel as if you would be happy and at home with me? I want you to feel so. I am grieved to think I was obliged to lose sight of you for a while. Did you think I had forgotten you, Fanny?"

Fanny's frank bright eyes filled up suddenly. "Yes, Kate, I did; and oh! I cannot tell you how desolate and miserable I was. I felt that if you could forget me, there was no help anywhere."

Mrs. Travers was silent for an instant; then, throwing her arms round her young friend, exclaimed, "There! let us not talk about it any more. You know now I did not, that I could not help it; and for the future you may trust me."

"I am sure I can!" cried Fanny, returning her embrace, with much warmth. "And oh, Kate! what a lovely house you have; and what beautiful flowers and things! Are they all really yours? I feel half-frightened to hear you order about that polite gentleman who waited on us at dinner."

"Ah! the change in my exterior life is as nothing to the change within. But come, dear, to bed—to bed—to bed."

CHAPTER V.

THE two months which succeeded Fanny Lee's arrival at her friend's house were certainly the happiest either lady had known for a long time.

To Mrs. Travers the sense of freedom, at first suppressed partly by her tender and respectful regret for her deceased husband, and still more by her shrinking from her own natural feelings as unseemly, gained more strength each day.

While to Fanny the glorious consciousness of having nothing to do but disport herself in the sunshine Fortune had suddenly shed upon her, was enough delight for the present.

She played and sang prettily, and worked all sorts of fancy work neatly and tastefully; but it was wonderful to watch the

varied changes she performed in the course of the day—from
the piano to her work-table, from the work-table to the garden
(weather permitting), from the garden to a sudden and complete
re-arrangement of her own room or Mrs. Travers's, or an enthusiastic compilation of a cap for Mills. It quite fidgeted her to
see Mrs. Travers reading steadily for a couple of hours with
wrapt attention, answering her many questions with unswerving
good temper, though often at random. At first, the graver of
the two friends tried to preach fixity of purpose, but in vain, and
so wisely and quietly gave up the attempt ; finding that, although
the effort to inculcate first principles was hopeless, whatever she
gave Fanny to do as a task for *her*, was most faithfully performed.

Then, when a rare bright day came, how delightful it was to
order the carriage and enjoy a drive in the beautiful country
which surrounds Hampton Court ! Tom Reed was a great addition to the pleasure of their life. He was a frequent visitor,
and was always considered due on Sundays, when he generally
arrived armed with *Punch* and the latest numbers of the best
periodicals. Then Mrs. Travers enjoyed hearing the latest political rumors, and a little discussion of the various new opinions
perpetually cropping up. Tom Reed, as he was universally
called, was a very agreeable companion—bright, keen, accustomed to focus his thoughts, which, if not profound, were
shrewd, and sharpened by constant friction with other minds as
bright and often deeper than his own ; accustomed by his position on the staff of a high-class morning paper to observe the
conflicting currents radiating from the old centres of belief. For
Fanny he generally brought curious and valuable morsels of fash-
ionable intelligence, perhaps not so carefully authenticated as
they ought to have been, but not the less acceptable on that account. To Reed this easy admittance into the society of two
refined and accomplished women, the delightful, graceful home-
liness—if such a combination of terms may be used—of the
old-fashioned house at Hampton Court, was wonderfully·delight-
ful and wholesome. For Tom had had his evil times and trials,
and had run the not uncommon round of spending all his money in
finding out how to make more.

To Fanny he seemed a fearfully clever, brilliant, sceptical,
scornful man of fashion, whose wicked theories she constantly
set herself to contradict and subvert. Many were the stinging
little darts she contrived to launch against the pachydermatous
Tom, so that a sparring match between the cousins was generally one of the evening's amusements.

The next-door neighbors, too, were sympathetic. The woes
of a rich widow were naturally attractive to an impecunious

honorable, whose husband, though not defunct, was "nowhere" in the world of fashion and respectability. Many were the invitations pressed upon the friends by the Hon. Mrs. Danby and her daughters; but though Fanny Lee often availed herself of these opportunities to cultivate the great world, Mrs. Travers, rigidly intent on showing respect to her husband's memory, invariably refused. An amiable readiness to lend her carriage to the honorable mother and her graceful brood amply compensated for the lack of personal intercourse. Various were the scraps of intelligence collected by Fanny during her visits; sometimes it was a tit-bit of Palace gossip, for Mrs. Danby's ostensible attraction to Hampton Court was a "relative" located in that refuge of impoverished aristocracy. Oftener it was some scandal touching the High Church curate, and oftenest military reports.

"Do you know, Kate," she burst out one day after a drive to Kingston with Mrs. Danby and one of her daughters, "that the officer who is coming here instead of Major Cunliffe is a Captain or Colonel Upton; he is a brother officer of Sir Hugh Galbraith, and Mrs. Danby used to know Sir Hugh long ago, and says he was the most tiresome, overbearing man that ever lived, so—"

"I trust and hope, Fanny, that you did not speak unadvisedly with your lips, or launch out into abuse of my enemy!" cried Mrs. Travers, interrupting her. "I am most anxious that no syllable of depreciation should be traced to me or mine."

"I am sure I did not; or, at any rate, if I said anything, it was not much," returned Fanny, coloring guiltily.

"I am quite sure you did," said Mrs. Travers, smiling, though annoyed. "Confess, now, that no devil was ever painted blacker than you depicted poor Sir Hugh."

"No, no, indeed!" exclaimed Fanny, earnestly. "I think I did say that, from all I could learn, Sir Hugh Galbraith was an unforgiving, vindictive, insolent, greedy, disagreeable man."

"And that is not much," said Mrs. Travers resignedly. "Well, in future, my dear girl, will you kindly keep silence, even from *bad* words, if Sir Hugh's name is mentioned?"

"I will indeed, Kate, if you wish it. But I can tell you Mrs. Danby said three—oh! five times as much as I did, and"—lowering her voice—"she said, too, that Sir Hugh was on the point of running away with Lady Somebody, or the Countess of Something, a married woman, when her father, who was a rich solicitor, found it all out, and had him arrested for debt, and so he couldn't—that is Sir Hugh; but he was so violent that it took three or four of those dreadful people—bailiffs, I think—to capture him."

"Really, that was taking a very shabby advantage of poor Sir Hugh," said Mrs. Travers laughing. "But I do not believe that long story, Fanny; depend upon it, there is but a slender foundation for such a legend."

"Well, Mrs. Danby assured me it was true; she heard it from Lord—oh, I do not know who!—who was in the same club with Sir Hugh Galbraith, and—"

"It is really no great matter, Fanny; just promise me, like a good girl, never to talk of him again."

"Very well, Kate; but I must tell you that when Mrs. Danby heard poor dear Mr. Travers was a cousin of Sir Hugh's, she seemed to know all about him at once. She said, 'Dear me! I had no idea it was *that* Mr. Travers;' and went on about his high family, and his riches, and how much she felt for you, and what a distinguished looking woman you were, and what a pity it was for you to be lost to society, but that time would soon pass, and you could come out a little more. You cannot think what a nice feeling sort of way she spoke; and oh, Kate, she wants to know if you would kindly let her have the carriage to-morrow; she wants to go over to Kew to call on Lady de Courcy."

"I am very sorry, but she cannot have it," said Mrs. Travers, dryly. "I want to drive into town myself to-morrow. The Indian mail is in, and it is just possible Wall and Wreford may have a reply from Sir Hugh Galbraith. I do hope he will accept my offer, though I should not be surprised if he rejects it with scorn."

"What a stupid, strange man he must be!" observed Fanny.

Mrs. Travers, somewhat to her surprise, found her conjecture right. Messrs. Wall and Wreford had received a reply to the epistle they had written little more than two months before. They evinced such a decided disinclination to let her see it, that she insisted on perusing it herself. Feeling distrustful of her own self-control, she quietly pocketed it and departed, telling Mr. Wall she would see him after she had digested the contents.

On reaching home, Mrs. Travers felt much cheered on finding Tom Reed assisting Fanny in some energetic amateur gardening, which was her last and most lasting whim.

"You will stay to dinner, of course?" she said. "I want a committee of the whole house to discuss Sir Hugh Galbraith's letter. Mr. Wall has told me so much, that he rejects my offer, and, knowing this, I shall take time, and fortify myself with dinner before I read it. I am sure it is odiously insulting."

"Do you know that Mr. Ford is in the drawing-room?" said Fanny, with the slightest possible grimace.

"No, indeed. What does he want? I suppose only to pay a visit. Well, I cannot ask him to stay to dinner to-day, but I will for Sunday. I could not read out Sir Hugh's letter before—

2*

him.   Why, I cannot tell, for he has always been most friendly
and obliging to me.   So, Fanny, I will go in and see him."

Mr. Ford was deep in the *Times* when Mrs. Travers entered
and greeted him kindly, yet with a nameless something of caution in her usual frank cordiality, which he did not fail to notice
and interpret to the satisfaction of his immense, yet uneasy vanity.

"I trust, my dear Mrs. Travers, you will not consider me intrusive," he began.

"Certainly not, Mr. Ford.   I am very glad to see you ; but are
you quite well? you have been suffering from cold? which is
perhaps the reason you have kept so long away."

"You are very good to notice my absence when you have the
society of so new and agreeable a friend as Mr. Reed."   The
head a little bent to one side with a jerk, "I could scarcely
hope—"

"Oh, Mr. Reed is a very old friend, as well as a very pleasant
one," interrupted Mrs. Travers, carelessly, and by no means in
an apologetic tone.   "He is a relation, you know, of dear old
Mr. Lee, and was quite a playfellow of Fanny's and mine."

"Well," resumed Ford, "I have ventured to call, as I see the
Indian mail is in, to ask if there is any communication from Sir
Hugh Galbraith?"

"There is, indeed," replied Mrs. Travers, sitting down with a
sigh ; "and a very decided rejection of my offer.   I am quite
vexed ; perhaps when he thinks better of it he may change his
mind."

"Hum !   He is a great fool, that is, unless he has formed any
idea that a will more favorable to himself may turn up; and,
even if it does, he would probably be better off with your offer."

"I have no doubt he would," replied Mrs. Travers, slowly un-
tying her bonnet.   "I feel quite sure my husband would not have
left him as much as I wish to give."

"Suppose my late respected employer was subject to crotchets
like other men," answered Ford, rubbing his hands slowly together, and putting his head slightly to one side, interrogatively.
"What a cruel triumph it would be to Sir Hugh if the bulk of
the property had been left to him and a mere legacy to you?"

"Why imagine anything so improbable?" replied Mrs. Travers, calmly, yet with a perceptible tinge of contempt in her tone.
"Mr. Travers would never have been unjust to me."

"No, no, of course not ; but, after all, he must have been fallible like other men—very fallible, I should say, or he never would
have used such words as . . .   But I beg your pardon, you forbid me to allude to that unhappy occurrence."

"I did," said Mrs. Travers, shortly; "so you ought to avoid

everything that can possibly lead up to it," she added, good-humoredly. "And tell me now how is poor old Gregory's family getting on; you mentioned that he left a son and daughter not very well off?"

"His son is well to do in his way; he commands one of Duncan's ships; he sailed for China some time after his father's death; but the daughter is in bad health; she is a widow with several children, and very badly off. The brother does what he can for her, but he has a wife and children himself."

"Then, my dear Mr. Ford," cried Mrs. Travers, earnestly, "do pray see how she is, and provide what is necessary for her and the poor children. I would go and see her most willingly, but a total stranger—the widow of a man who must be to her in some degree a personage, having been her husband's employer—might be troublesome and oppressive. Pray assure her of my sympathy and readiness to help her. I know Mr. Travers would have done so. He valued poor old Mr. Gregory very much, and I feel quite sure he would approve what I propose."

"Certainly," said Mr. Ford, in a suppressed and rather choked tone. "Certainly," he repeated, clearing his throat; "Gregory was a very faithful servant—and—and—your amiable, generous readiness to relieve misfortune touches me to the heart."

"I imagine the power to relieve suffering, even in a slight degree, is too great a luxury not to require self-control as much as any other enjoyment," returned Mrs. Travers, carelessly, while she thought, "How like an old-fashioned novel he talks!"

"It is only one more token of that excellence long ago recognized by me," resumed Mr. Ford, throwing out his hand, which held a yellow silk pocket-handkerchief, as though about to throw down his gage to all comers in defense of the young widow's amiability and generosity.

"Well, well!" she exclaimed, good-humoredly, "I cannot allege the favorite excuse for keeping one's money in one's purse, for I have very few claims upon me. But, Mr. Ford, when sufficient time has elapsed to assure my authority under Mr. Travers's will, you, too "—she hesitated, blushed, and showed a charming gracious confusion—"you, too, shall find that I am not ungrateful for the friendship you have always shown us both."

"My dear madam—my dear Mrs. Travers, you are very good; but you must be aware that there are free-will services, which to pay—"

"Would be the cruelest insult," interrupted Mrs. Travers. "Certainly I should indeed be 'of the earth, earthy' if I knew it not. But, Mr. Ford, I am not without my ambitions. If the house of Travers really passes into my hands, I should like to keep it up, to increase its prestige, to renew its youth; to prove to the world—my husband's world—that I am no unworthy inheritor of his name and fortune." She rose as she spoke, and began almost unconsciously to move to and fro. "And in the pursuit of such an object might I not also do you justice, as well as prove my respect for you—my confidence in you, and improve your position? Not, I confess, that I should, unless I change considerably, like partners—even a junior partner. I should like to rule alone, but I might improve your position materially."

She paused. Mr. Ford listened eagerly as she spoke, and passed his handkerchief rapidly over his face.

"You are quite a mercantile Portia," he said, in a thick, husky tone, that cleared as he proceeded. "It is remarkable to observe the natural enthusiasm of youth directing itself into such a channel."

"Ah! you despise my youth," she cried, pausing, and leaning against the back of a chair, while a delicate color stole over her cheek, for it takes long experience to steel the soul against a sneer. "But, you must remember, I am older than my years; that I have studied to be old, and almost succeeded."

"Your ambition is, I am sure, worthy of all respect," returned Ford ; but he dragged out his words with a visible effort. A short silence ensued, and Ford resumed : "Then Sir Hugh Galbraith shows himself quite inimical to your just rights, as they at present appear ? "

"Yes—quite—nay, he threatens to contest the will ; indeed, Mr. Wall seems to think he has some idea that another exists. I have not yet seen the letter. Suppose," continued Mrs. Travers, with the odd sort of restless desire to get rid of him which generally came over her—"suppose you come and dine here on Sunday, and we will talk it all over. I am sure you will be interested ; and more, if necessary, you will help me to fight this man."

She smiled very sweetly upon Ford as she spoke. He made a slight sudden movement towards her, which he dexterously turned into typical hand-washing, and began to speak with eagerness.

"You know well ; " then checking himself, he recommenced— "You may, indeed, count on me ; and, insignificant as I seem, I may possess more power than you think. Be that as it may, I believe you know the deep interest, the—the—friendship, if you will accept the expression, that I entertain for you ; and whatever course you may decide upon, I shall be at your service, with or without reward. *That* is a matter on which I do not dare allow my thoughts to dwell."

"No, no! I am sure you do not," returned Mrs. Travers, with complimentary readiness, quite heedless of his dramatic

emphasis, her mind preoccupied by the letter she longed, yet
half feared, to read. "You are much above any personal con-
siderations ; but you shall not find me ungrateful, I assure you
so," holding out her hand. "Do not forget Sunday. We dine
at five on Sundays."

Ford's countenance darkened, and his smile, as he accepted his
dismissal, was very snaky.

"And, oh, Mr. Ford! be sure you see poor Mrs. Bell, old
Gregory's daughter. I wish you would send me her address."

"I will do so," he replied ; and, bowing stiffly, departed.

"There is something the matter with that man," thought the
young widow, as she walked towards her dressing-room. "He
is changed in some way ; but he is a very good fellow. He must
be—he always has been—and why should he change ! I wonder
why I am always so glad when he is gone ! "

Dinner passed less agreeably than usual, for the three friends
were oppressed by the anticipated unpleasantness of Sir Hugh's
letter. Tom Reed did considerably the largest share of the
talking. At last the more solid portion of the repast was cleared
away ; the grave and discreet Edwards gave the final touch to
the dessert dishes, which perfected their mathematical precision,
and departed.

"Now or never, Mrs. Travers—courage ! Take a glass of
sherry, and open the fatal scroll."

"Oh, I am quite equal to the occasion without such extrane-
ous aid," returned Mrs. Travers, smiling, as she drew forth
the letter and opened it slowly. "What a horrible hand ! but
cruelly firm. It has evidently been dashed off in hot haste. I
must glance through it before I read aloud." (Reed and Fanny
naturally looked at their hostess as her eyes eagerly scanned the
page. First, the quick color flushed up to her brow, then faded
away as rapidly, and left her almost pale. When she came to
the end she laid it down for an instant with a slight, bitter smile.)
"Listen to this ! " she exclaimed, taking it up again, and proceeded to read in a clear, quiet voice :—

"Gentlemen,—I am in receipt of yours of —, announcing
the death of my cousin, Mr. Richard Travers, and the liberal intentions of his widow towards me. Be so good as to inform
your client that I am not disposed, by accepting obligations from
her, to imply approbation of the deplorable weakness which dis-
graced the close of my unfortunate relative's life. I think it
right to add a report that another and a very different will is in
existence, has reached me. I am on the point of starting for
England, to ascertain, as far as possible, the truth, and, in any
case, to try if the law can uphold a will so infamously unjust,
and made evidently under the undue influence of a lady whose

antecedents could not have exactly fitted her to be Mr. Travers's adviser. I, therefore, prefer claiming my possible rights to sharing the spoil with her, and beg that I may receive no furthei propositions on the subject.

"I have the honor to be, gentlemen, etc., etc.,
"HUGH GALBRAITH."

When Mrs. Travers ceased reading, she looked up at her listeners and kept silence.

"What a bitter bad temper the man must have been in when he wrote that !" cried Tom Reed.

"I am sure he is a detestable, ungrateful thing !" added Fanny.

"You see Wall was not so far wrong when he said that too liberal an offer might suggest an idea of being bought off," continued Reed.

"To a mind of Sir Hugh's calibre, perhaps," said Mrs. Travers, slowly, with her eyes still fixed on the letter. "See," she went on, handing it over to Reed, "he had written ' woman ' before ' lady,' and put his pen through it, not liking, I suppose, to be conventionally rude."

"Yes, yes, I see," he replied, as he glanced over Sir Hugh's effusion. "A most unwarrantable letter—ungentlemanlike, even. You really deserve some credit for taking it so calmly."

"Do I ?" returned Mrs. Travers. "Do I take it calmly? If it ever happens that I can pay my debt to Sir Hugh, he will not fare the better for my calmness ! What have I ever done to deserve such treatment ? That he should be hurt and disappointed by my husband's will I am not surprised ; but does he think Mr. Travers had not a right to marry anyone he liked ? And why should I be so distasteful to Sir Hugh Galbraith ? Surely he does not fancy that we are still in the feudal ages, when humble birth was more disgraceful than misconduct ? Why should he disdain me without knowing me ? Pooh ! Why do *I* trouble myself with such conjectures ? What is he and his contempt to me ? I can well afford to despise both."

She had spoken with repressed vehemence, and stopped abruptly. Reed looked up earnestly, as if struck by her tone, and Fanny exclaimed :—

"And I daresay you are just as well born ! I always heard your father—"

"Nonsense, Fanny," interrupted Mrs. Travers. "I only know and acknowledge my mother's relations, who are of the people. The only help we ever had was from cousin Hicks, and poor cousin Hicks was not a model of good breeding ; but I do not think he would have attributed such an offer as mine to a desire to preserve the lion's share of the spoil."

"He certainly never would be such an idiot as to refuse a good offer and run his head against the *chevcaux-de-frise* of the law, as Sir Hugh threatens ; but it is a mere threat ! When he arrives in England he will find out how absurd any attempt to shake your position would be."

"I suppose he will, Tom," returned Mrs. Travers. "Still, this man will give me trouble and pain. He has been wronged, and I cannot make it right. Try and throw it back as I will, his scorn hurts me ; the material superiority of my position hurts me. You may laugh, Tom ; but I should like to give him his choice of weapons and beat him in a fair fight. My money is my weak point."

"Long may you continue to suffer from such weakness!" exclaimed Reed, fervently. "You really are the most chivalrous lady I have ever had the pleasure of meeting."

"Oh, I daresay you think me very silly—but I am what I am. He says he is coming to England. I feel that his arrival will be the beginning of troubles."

"I am sure I wish some one would give him a bear's hug and finish him," cried Fanny, indignantly. "Never mind, Kate ! He cannot take away everything from you, as he would like, I daresay. So you must try and forget him and be happy. Do not let him vex you."

"I shall try and follow your advice, dear," returned Mrs. Travers, smiling, and resuming her usual tone, as the indignant color which had mounted to her cheek faded away. "Come, let us go into the drawing-room ; and, to turn our thoughts, suppose we plan out that little tour I have projected for the summer ?"

Accordingly, the three friends adjourned into the pleasant, perfumed drawing-room, where "Bradshaw" and "Murray" helped them to much lively talk and delightful plans. Mrs. Travers was unusually bright, and Sir Hugh seemed forgotten.

But long after Tom Reed had bid good night, and Fanny Lee's bright eyes were closed in sleep, Mrs. Travers sat thinking, with her elbows on her dressing-table, and her chin resting on her hands, till her candle was burnt down in the socket; and then she started up, extinguished it, and, opening the shutter, brushed out her long chestnut brown hair in the cold moonlight.

CHAPTER VI.

THE next Sunday was one of those bright soft days that seem stolen from a riper season, just as a sample of the delights which more advanced spring has in store. Already the

almond and lilac trees showed attempts at budding, the crocuses
and violets made a respectable show in the garden, and Mrs.
Travers's rooms were sweet with hyacinths.

Thither, in Sunday garb of most irreproachable cut and hue,
with tightly-buttoned, handsomely-stitched gloves, and a silk
umbrella rolled into the dimensions of a walking-stick, came
Ford. He first loomed upon Fanny's active vision at church,
and she, with her usual impulsiveness, bestowed an energetic
nudge upon her friend, who was busied in finding the hymn
just given out ; but Mrs. Travers was not unaccustomed to
Fanny's nudges, and did not even lift her eyes from her book.

On coming out of church, the Hon. Mrs. Danby pounced
upon Mrs. Travers, for whom she had lain in wait ; for the
young widow generally kept back till the rest of the congregation had partially dispersed.

"How do you do, my dear Mrs. Travers ? I was glad to see
you in church, for Georgy and I fancied, from not seeing you
anywhere, that you were not so well—cold or something. It is
such uncertain, trying weather."

"Oh ! I am perfectly well, thank you," replied Mrs. Travers,
cheerfully.

"Suppose we walk on ? "

Here Mr. Ford drew near, looking slightly embarrassed, yet
determined.

"Certainly," replied Mrs. Travers ; then, holding out her hand,
"Good morning, Mr. Ford ; I did not expect to see you in
church. Fanny, here is Mr. Ford ! "—and Fanny felt he was
committed to her care.

Mrs. Danby and her daughter looked at him with an instant's
short, sharp curiosity, and then the party fell into a natural
marching order, the married ladies in front, the young ones,
escorted by the gallant Ford, in the rear. Now it is remarkable
that, although speaking very correct English, with a good accent,
although a well-informed and tolerably good-looking individual,
both Miss Danby and her mother decided in their own minds
that he was, according to their scornful generalization, some
"tinker or tailor, or candlestick maker " from the City. Meantime they walked on harmoniously together.

"I want you to waive ceremony and come in to us to-morrow
evening, my dear Mrs. Travers," said the honorable dame, per-
suasively. "There will only be my cousin Lady Georgina Ver-
ner, her nephew Lord Delamere, who is quartered here, and
Colonel Upton, who is an Indian hero just returned. You
might like to meet him, for he is a great chum of your connection, Sir Hugh Galbraith. It is quite a family gathering ; no
party, a little music and a rubber. There could not be the
slightest impropriety."

"Thank you very much," returned Mrs. Travers, gently but decidedly. "I could not think of leaving my own house for some months to come. Do not think me ungracious. In such matters, I suppose, individual feeling makes the law."

"I really think you are too scrupulous, dear Mrs. Travers. It is not wise, or even Christian, to indulge in morbid regrets, which only unfit us for the duties of that state of life to which we are called," observed Mrs. Danby, in a highly religious tone.

But Mrs. Travers was not to be moved; the prospect of meeting an old chum of Sir Hugh Galbraith was anything but attractive to her, and she politely though firmly repeated her refusal.

"Well, your charming young friend will perhaps join us?"

This Mrs. Travers left an open point, determined to ask Fanny to stay at home, as she did not at all like the idea of her "charming" but communicative young friend being brought in contact even with the enemy's most remote outpost.

The parties separated at their respective houses, and Mrs. Travers addressed herself pleasantly to Mr. Ford.

"Come in, Mr. Ford; I daresay we shall find Mr. Reed. He generally comes down on Sundays, but, I regret to say, does not appear at church."

"I must beg you to believe," returned Ford, following her into the house, "that, although compelled by railway exigencies to make my appearance at so unreasonable an hour, I do not intend to bore you all day; a walk across Bushy Park, after a week at the desk, will be a great refreshment."

"I am very happy to see you, Mr. Ford," said the young widow, simply. "Pray stroll about, or sit indoors and read, just as you like."

Contrary to Mrs. Travers's expectations, Tom Reed was not awaiting them, and luncheon proceeded much more formally in consequence. Mr. Ford was very elaborately agreeable. He conveyed all the latest news he could collect in the most polite phrases, but Fanny was rather inattentive, and disposed to watch the window opposite her, which commanded a view of the entrance; observing which, Mrs. Travers remarked, "We cannot expect Tom now, till quite late in the evening, and I do not think he will come at all."

"I daresay he will not," returned Fanny.

They shortly after adjourned to the drawing-room.

"I wish," said Mrs. Travers to her companion, "you would be good natured, and take a walk with Mr. Ford."

This was a whispered aside, while he was critically examining an illustrated work on church architecture, which the High Church curate had persuaded Mrs. Travers to buy.

"I will if you like," said Fanny, with her usual good humor. "Mr. Ford," she continued, "will you take me with you? or shall I be in your way?"

"My dear young lady, I am greatly gratified at the idea of such companionship; but shall we leave Mrs. Travers alone? would she not join us?"

"No, thank you, Mr. Ford, I never go out on Sundays; but a brisk walk would do Fanny a world of good."

Fanny made a pretty "mow" behind Mr. Ford's back, and ran away to put on her bonnet.

"I have heard, since I had the pleasure of seeing you," said Ford, drawing his chair near Mrs. Travers, "that Sir Hugh Galbraith was to have started, or had started, from Calcutta the first of this month; so that he will probably arrive in England in about a fortnight."

"Indeed!" she replied, and then remained silent and absorbed in thought, her large dark blue eyes distended, gazing fixedly on vacancy.

Ford looked at her intently, quite unperceived by her, until he suddenly rose from his chair, and executed his favorite flank movement upon the window. Then she said, with a smile: "Well, Mr. Ford, he may come or go. I must trouble myself no further about him. He has rejected my offer with more than scorn, and has evidently heard some rumor of the second will, for he threatens to dispute the first. Oh, what would I not give to find that second will, or to know certainly that it does not exist! I shall never feel really safe or settled until I am satisfied one way or the other."

"It *is* a painful position for you," said Ford, once more seating himself beside her; "but I think you may make up your mind that nothing more will ever be discovered, although I once knew a case somewhat in point where, after a year, the final will was found. But as to Sir Hugh's threats, they are not worth thinking of."

"So Mr. Reed tells me; and I will try not to think of them. Pray, Mr. Ford"—with an abrupt change of voice—"have you been able to see poor Mr. Gregory's daughter for me?"

"No, indeed, I regret to say," replied Ford, softly. "I have been much engaged since we met, but I have ascertained her address."

"Oh, thank you. Pray give it to me. Perhaps I had better call. I have much more time to spare than you, and I ought not to trouble you."

"Trouble!" repeated Ford, emphatically. "When did I ever think anything a trouble for you?"

There was a perceptible quiver in his voice. Mrs. Travers

looked up quickly with a startled expression, meeting his eyes steadily.

"Oh, you may be so good as not to consider me troublesome," she said, with a certain quiet, careless composure, very refrigerating to an ardent, vain, timid man. "But I am all the more bound not to give you trouble. So let me have the address, and I shall call upon this poor woman in a day or two."

There was a tinge of command in both voice and manner that suited her well; and Ford instantly obeyed.

"There," he said, taking a slip of paper from his pocket-book. "It is not a very attractive locality, you observe." Then, after a moment's pause, "I trust I have not unwittingly offended by involuntarily falling back to the tone warranted in former, and to me, happier days."

"No, no!" cried Mrs. Travers, her frank kindly nature dreading to seem unfriendly or haughty in her prosperity. "I always remember—"

The entrance of Fanny with her bonnet on saved the impulsive widow from too fascinating an *amende*, though perhaps the suggestiveness of her unfinished sentence permitted a wider range to Ford's far-reaching vanity than the most unguarded words.

"Well, Miss Lee!" cried that gentleman, with head erect, and sparkling eyes. "I am at your service. I daresay you can direct our steps to some pretty bits of scenery. Do you ever try any sketching? If so, and I could give you a hint or two, I should be most happy. In other days I had almost elected an artistic line, and, but for one circumstance, regret I did not."

"It would have been much nicer than doing sums all day, I am sure," returned Fanny. "Come along, Mr. Ford; it is past two."

Mrs. Travers felt unusally pleased when Ford disappeared, but was too much occupied with other thoughts to bestow any on him. The near approach of Sir Hugh Galbraith filled her with undefinable and unreasonable uneasiness; but she made a resolute and successful effort to banish him from her mind. "There is no use in going to meet trouble half way," she reflected; "he can do me no real harm." She looked at the address given her by Ford. '"Mrs. Bell, Duke's Square, Lambeth, near Vauxhall.' I will try and see her to-morrow; perhaps it is foolish and Quixotic to go myself, but it cannot be wrong; and I have so much time, and help must seem long in coming to her, poor soul." So the fair widow's thoughts flowed out in benevolent plans, in half-sad, half-sweet reminiscences. How long she sat in luxurious solitude she did not know, when she was roused by an opening door and the announcement of "Mr. Reed."

" My dear Tom, I am so glad to see you ! What became of you this morning ; and how have you managed to arrive at this unusual hour ? "

" Well, you see, one of 'our own correspondents' has just arrived from India. Has been with Outram at Delhi ; and we were late last night, or rather this morning. The ' Morning Thresher ' men gave him a supper ; so he offered to drive me down, as he was coming to see some fellow he knew in India who is quartered here."

" Well, I am very glad to see you. Will you have some luncheon ? "

" No, thank you ; I have just finished breakfast ; " and Tom Reed ensconced himself in a comfortable chair, yet seemed restless, while Mrs. Travers asked and received the news.

" What is the matter, Tom ? " she said, at length. " You seem on the look-out for something. Oh, I know ! I suspect you miss Fanny's attacks. She is out. She good-naturedly undertook to guide Mr. Ford to some picturesque points ; and I was not sorry to be left in peace."

" Oh, indeed ! they will be back to dinner, then ? "

" Yes, unless they elope ; and I am sure Mr. Ford is much too proper to suggest such a thing," returned Mrs. Travers, laughing.

" Then you do not think the difficulty would arise on Fanny's side ? " said Reed, a little querulously.

" Poor dear Fanny ! she would inevitably box his ears if the spirit moved him so far. Under enormous excitement, I could fancy Mr. Ford on one knee exclaiming, 'A carriage-and-four awaits us in the ravine ; fly with me !' or some such correct in- correctness ; but I cannot fancy Fan saying ' Yes.' Ah ! Tom, Tom, you must put up with me, only me, for the next half- hour."

" Only you ! " cried Reed. " And am I not the luckiest of dogs to have a *tête-à-tête* with you even for once ; to have the *entrée* of your pleasant home-like house. Seriously, you have done me a world of good. Do you know I am crystallizing into a degree of steadiness calculated to result in a millionaire condition, if I only had a trifle to begin with. As it is, I trust it may not impart a solidity to my pen which will unfit it for lighter literature."

" Do not fear. Volatility is so ingrained in you that any graver habits contracted here will be but the sponge-cake under- lying the whipped cream of your existence."

" Perhaps so," returned Tom, gravely. " All I can say is, that the cream of my existence has been very considerably whipped hitherto."

Mrs. Travers smiled. "Ah, Tom! you would not be so good a fellow if the rod of circumstance had been more sparingly applied."

"So be it ; but the process has had its unpleasantness."

"No doubt. Now tell me, what wonders did 'your own correspondent' tell of his adventures in India? I daresay I have read the best of them ; but a little private bit flatters one's vanity."

"Well, curiously enough, our talk all the way down here was about Sir Hugh Galbraith. Markham (that's our man) knew him well."

"You do not say so!" exclaimed Mrs. Travers, with much interest. "And what does he say of him?"

"He evidently likes him ; says he is not a bad fellow—a thorough soldier ; a keen sportsman ; rather silent and haughty, but as plucky as a—well, as a well-bred Englishman generally is."

"Or an ill-bred one either," put in Mrs. Travers.

"Well, as an Englishman, then. Perhaps, when he comes to England, he may be induced to hear reason, and do you justice."

"That I imagine he will never do," said Mrs. Travers. "How is it that he has not arrived as well as this correspondent of yours?"

"Oh! his passage was taken, I understand, but he was too ill to go on board. It seems he was rather severely wounded defending the entrance to a fort with a handful of men, to give the women and sick time to escape. I hear he is to have the Victoria Cross."

"Indeed," returned Mrs. Travers, coldly ; and, after a minute's silence, added, "then he can hardly be here before the end of March."

"I should think not ;" said Reed, rising, and walking towards the window. "It is very fine, Mrs. Travers ; do you not feel disposed to follow Fanny's example, and come out?"

"No, I do not, Tom," she replied smiling ; "but pray do not mind me. I see you are longing to be away—go ; and if you bend your steps towards Bushy Park, you will probably meet the truants."

"Ah! you want to get rid of me," cried Tom. "You have some delightful novel hidden away somewhere, which I interfere with ; so I am off." He waved his hand to his fair hostess, and ran down stairs with his usual alert rapidity.

Mrs. Travers looked after him with a kindly half-amused smile ; but though she rose and took a thick, tough-looking book from her writing-table, it lay open, unread, for a long time upon her knee. Partly she thought of Tom Reed's irrepressible uneasiness when he found Fanny was absent, but more of his careless sentence, "I hear he is to have the Victoria Cross." It was curious how it ruffled the repose of her mind to hear of any worth in Hugh Galbraith—any liking towards him in others. It always seemed to reflect reproach on her dead husband and herself—and how much she had offended in urging Mr. Travers to do him justice, no one save herself knew. It was such an effort to her to speak to Mr. Travers on any forbidden subject, and Galbraith was always tabooed. Now, all her efforts were worse than useless! Well, she had, at all events, striven to do right; and she could not help believing that her conduct would come to light some day, even if not . . . . She raised her book, and strove to read, but only succeeded brokenly; disagreeable thoughts would flit between her mind and the subject before it. It was quite a relief to hear Fanny's voice on the stairs, and to receive the three pedestrians.

"I was so surprised to see Tom!" cried Fanny, as she entered. "I could hardly believe my eyes when I saw him coming along. We have had such a nice walk; have we not, Mr. Ford?"

"I should be a very strange individual to deny it," returned that gentleman, with much urbanity. "I wish we could have persuaded you, Mrs. Travers, to have joined us; I think you would have enjoyed the delicious spring feeling, the charming views."

"No doubt, Mr. Ford; but I seldom go out on Sunday. Now, dinner will be ready in five minutes, so those who wish to adorn had better do so."

　　*　　　*　　　*　　　*　　　*　　　*　　　*

The day but one after this conversation, Mrs. Travers, yielding to a kindly impulse, determined to seek out the old clerk's daughter herself. A deep grateful sense of happiness had been developing within her, and gradually pervading her whole being during the three months of harmonious quiet which had succeeded her husband's death. It was in vain she reproached herself for this disloyalty to his memory; in vain she told herself that her mourning should be deeper and more prolonged for him to whom she owed everything. Nature was too strong to be held back from its irrepressible germination. She felt she was young and fair; she knew she was free, rich, full to the lips with life, and she looked round, longing to bestow some of her happiness on others. Subscriptions to useful charities were all very right; but she wanted to say to some sorrowful ones, "Here, take of my abundance; let me have the supreme pleasure of drying your tears." She longed to give relief, not merely by gifts, but by the balm of personal sympathy. So she started in the most generous mood—she went alone.

" Poor old Mr. Gregory's people must be superior," she thought. " His daughter will speak more freely to me, if I am by myself." She, therefore, took the train to Vauxhall, and a cab from thence to the address given her by Ford. It was a better locality than she expected. The square was a large grass plot, adorned by a few weeping willows, fenced by wooden rails painted white, and surrounded by old-fashioned, respectable-looking red brick houses. The one she sought had a brass plate on the door, which announced " Mrs. Bell's establishment for young ladies." As Mrs. Travers rang, the door opened, and a stout, square-looking man, in a brown overcoat and baggy trowsers, came out ; he had a tall fluffy hat that seemed to have been brushed the wrong way, and held a book with a brass clasp, out of which various papers protruded. He was followed by a small pale woman, with a strained, imploring expression in her eyes, and hair much whiter than it ought to have been at her years. She was dressed in rusty black, and had a small gray knitted shawl drawn tight round her shoulders ; yet was there no tinge of commonness in her aspect, nor in her accent, as she answered the man's imperative "On Monday, then, at farthest," with a low, sad-toned, "On Monday, if I possibly can ;" and then continued standing, the door in her hand, as he walked away—looking with surprise at Mrs. Travers.

" I wish, if convenient to her, to see Mrs. Bell," said she, advancing, and drawing a card from her case.

" I am Mrs. Bell," returned the little woman, with a sigh, as if the name was identified with trouble ; " walk in, if you please." She led the way into what was evidently a schoolroom, as the front and back parlors opened into each other, and were scantily supplied with desks and forms.

" Pray sit down," continued Mrs. Bell, drawing forward the only chair in the room, which had a relaxed cane seat.

" I presume you have called about my advertisement."

" No," said Kate Travers ; " I was not aware of any advertisement," and she placed her card in the little woman's thin, tremulous hand.

" Mrs. Travers !" she exclaimed in great surprise. " This is most unexpected !"—the tears stood in her eyes, and her lips quivered.

" I have taken the liberty of calling on you," said Mrs. Travers, coloring, and feeling keenly the awkwardness of venturing to intrude her knowledge of the difficulties with which this poor soul had to contend upon her notice—"because—because your late father was much respected by Mr. Travers ; and had not his own illness come on so soon after Mr. Gregory's death, he would, I have no doubt, made it his business to ascertain "—she paused, at a loss how to proceed.

"Yes," returned Mrs. Bell, breathlessly; her thin hands clutching nervously at her shawl.

"If he could have been of any use to you," resumed Kate Travers, clearing her difficulties at a bound ; "and I have come to act for him. Will you forget I am a stranger, and speak to me openly of your affairs ?"

The kind frank eyes, the sweet, modest, hesitating voice, that seemed to ask rather than to confer a favor, melted the struggling woman's heart. A sudden overpowering gleam of hope seemed to turn her giddy : she leaned her elbows on one of the desks, and, covering her face with her hands, she kept silence for one trembling moment.

"You are very, very good !" she exclaimed at length ; "and I heartily thank you ; but I fear, I greatly fear, it is almost too late for help."

"Do not say so," cried Mrs. Travers, feeling at ease now that the ice was broken. "I am sure, if you will confide in me, something can be done—some way of escape found." She spoke warmly and quickly, for, without a word of explanation, she perceived that her listener was in great trouble. After a few more sentences had been exchanged, Mrs. Bell's shy reserve gave way, and, while unheeded tears welled over and stole down her sunken cheek, she told her whole story.

While her father lived with her, she was comparatively prosperous ; he paid her rent, and further contributed to the cost of the little household. She had a fairly successful school, and had contrived to educate her daughter, now grown up, a son, who had evidently been a "ne'er do weel," whose illness and death not long before his grandfather's had helped to exhaust her scanty savings, and another boy, her youngest, who was not yet twelve years old. But with her father she lost her mainstay. Her school fluctuated ; she got behind with her rent. Her landlord had, perhaps unfortunately, been tolerably patient ; she had struggled on, not liking to throw away the connection she had formed, especially as "dear Gracey" had just come home "finished" from an excellent school, where she had gained nearly all the prizes, and worked with her whole soul in order to be a help to the "dear mother" at home, and Mrs. Bell could therefore offer fresh advantages to her pupils.

Do what she would, however, the net closed round the poor woman ; and, as the last chance of paying her debts and setting herself and daughter free, she had advertised her school for sale, hoping to make an existence by giving lessons, as she could no longer receive pupils. They had now nearly come to the end of all their resources—the widow's brother was at sea, had been unheard of for months—the landlord had just left, after informing her that, if not paid on Monday, he must seize her furniture. "And all will go," concluded Mrs. Bell, who had talked herself into composure ; "for, between rent and taxes, there are nearly twenty-five pounds due. Then I do not know where to turn! With this house will go my last chance of independence. And there is poor Georgie ; he has not been to school for three months —what is to become of him?"

"You must have courage still," said Kate, taking her hand, while sympathetic tears stood in her eyes. "The house shall not go, nor the furniture."

"But, dear madam, it would take such a large sum to set me straight."

"How much?" returned Mrs. Travers, quickly.

"Well, you see, I ought to be sure of six months' rent besides what is due, and just the little weekly bills, and a trifle of ready money for books and things. Oh, I am afraid I dare not stay on with less than seventy pounds, and that is a fortune!"

"Nevertheless you shall have it," cried Kate Travers, impulsively—"you shall indeed! I am certain, if my husband had known about you, he would have done as much or more."

"But, Mrs. Travers, pray think what a very large sum it is to promise! Your kind heart is moved by the story of my troubles. I should be so sorry to hurry you into anything you would regret."

"You shall have the half to-morrow," returned Kate, "and the rest in a week, so pray cheer up, and set to work to inform all your friends that your school is not to be given up ; and as to your boy,"—she stopped—a list of all the institutions of which Mr. Travers had been a governor, or a benefactor, rose before her mental vision—"we must provide for his education in some way."

But her hearer was faint, and overcome by this unexpected turn of fortune. Mrs. Travers, frightened to see her look so pale, hastily rang the bell, which was immediately answered by a graceful, pretty, dark-eyed girl, a youthful picture of the faded woman who was now sobbing hysterically as she sat upon one of the forms with her head against an ink-splashed desk. A few minutes of confusion and misunderstanding, and then the glorious news of their emancipation was made known to "Gracey," who, though preserving her composure, was evidently as much overjoyed as her mother.

"The good God has sent you to us!" she said, in a choking voice. "I have no fear of the future if we can but keep up the

3

school, and people always liked to send their children to mother. Then, if we can let a couple of rooms upstairs, we shall do well. Oh, you have indeed given us hope and strength ! "

Kate remained some time talking over the simple plans of mother and daughter, deeply thankful that she had come herself without loss of time, and utterly winning the hearts of both by the unaffected friendliness of her interest in their projects. She could collect from their conversation that theirs had been lives of unremitting industry and humble content ; no worthier recipients of her bounty could be found.

How little it cost to restore sunshine to their hearts—sunshine that reflected itself glowingly in her own !

After this visit, the pleasant monotony of Mrs. Travers's life was varied by an occasional visit to the quiet little schoolmistress and her daughter—not too many—Kate was delicately fearful of being oppressive—and in going through the forms necessary to procure admittance for her boy into one of the many institutions to which Mr. Travers had subscribed, to some of which she had also herself contributed.

Thus another month had almost slipped by, and the promise she had made to her *protégée* had been faithfully fulfilled. After consultation with Mr. Ford, Kate had determined to increase her gift by an additional twenty pounds, which would not make it much more than half a year's *post obit* salary on account of the long and efficient services of the old clerk.

Mr. Wall had now ceased to warn his fair client that she must "just" wait ; and she herself had begun to plan an early move to the continent, beginning with Naples, and intending to work her way northward as summer advanced.

A delicious scheme, over which her fancy reveled, yet in which Fanny somehow did not seem to take as vivid an interest as might have been expected.

ı

CHAPTER VII.

" I WONDER what solemnity Mr. Ford intends to perform to-day," said Mrs. Travers, looking up from a note she was reading as she sat at breakfast.

" Is he coming here?" asked Fanny, who was diligently spreading honey on her bread and butter.

" Yes. He says : 'A matter of deep importance induces me so to arrange my work here, as to enable me to present myself at noon, when I hope you will grant me a private interview.' "

" Oh, my goodness, Kate ! " cried Fanny, her eyes sparkling with fun. " Depend upon it, he is going to make you an offer, or a declaration, or whatever is the right word."

"Fanny!" said Mrs. Travers, indignantly. "How strange it is that a really nice girl as you are should be guilty of such glaring vulgarity, even in jest! Do you forget the position in which Mr. Ford stands to me? Never make such a speech again."

"Oh, mercy!" exclaimed Fanny, clasping her hands as if in terror. "Do not grind me quite to powder! But do you mean to say you do'nt know that nice, proper, polite personage is in love with you? because, if you do not, I shall begin to think I am more than your equal intellectually!"

"Absurd!" returned Mrs. Travers, angrily. "I have a sincere respect for Mr. Ford, and such remarks are insulting to him as well as to me; besides, I am vexed that you should be so regardless of all propriety—there, Fanny! I do not mean to be cross, but do not be so thoughtless again!"

"No, I will not, indeed, dearest. I know I am a wretch; but, Kate, I do not give up my opinion for all that."

"Think what nonsense you like, but do not utter it!" returned Mrs. Travers, looking to the second page of the note, in obedience to a "P. T. O." at the foot of the first. "Listen to this, Fan. 'I saw the junior partner of Booth Brothers this morning. He had reached London only last night, having traveled from Marseilles with Sir Hugh Galbraith, though not exactly in his company.' There," continued Mrs. Travers, "I feel as if I was before the enemy, and on the point of going into action!"

"Sir Hugh absolutely in London!" cried Fanny. "Is it not sooner than we expected? 'Ill birds fly fast!'"

"No, not sooner than is quite possible," said Mrs. Travers, thoughtfully, as she laid the note beside her plate. "Our life is so serene and happy, no wonder that we take no heed of time—is! I fear has been would be more correct! I feel quite a coward at the idea of the unrest that is before me; and an enemy is so horrible—an implacable enemy, who cannot be bought off!" she continued, smiling. "I am ashamed of my cowardice. If that man had not a sort of right to consider himself ill-used, I should be braver. However, he may annoy, but he cannot hurt me!"

"Take some more coffee, and I will cut you such a nice thin slice of ham," said Fanny, soothingly.

"No, thank you—nothing more."

"Why, Kate, you have scarce eaten any breakfast!"

"Never mind, I shall eat the more luncheon. And, Fanny dear, I wish you would write and ask Tom Reed to come down to dinner, if possible, to-day. I will put on my bonnet while you write, and go to the post myself—a walk will brighten my ideas and steady my nerves."

" Shall I go with you ? " asked Fanny.

" No. I want to think, and you would have to be silent, so you would be bored."

" Very well," returned Fanny, good-humoredly.

Although a dull gray morning, the air and motion revived the young widow. She strove gallantly to throw off the depression and fearful looking for evil which had fallen upon her spirit ; but though partially successful, she could not quite repress the sort of nervous watchfulness which constantly drew her eyes to the clock. It must be some matter of no ordinary importance that could induce Mr. Ford to leave the office in the morning, on a foreign post day, too !—then she remembered that Friday was the post day, and credited it with a reputation for unlimited ill-luck, at which morsel of superstition reason smiled and imagination shuddered.

The first ten minutes after midday had ticked slowly by, and Mrs. Travers, though fully prepared, could not help a nervous start when " Mr. Ford " was announced.

Even while exchanging the ordinary greetings, Mrs. Travers was struck by his altered appearance. His face was thinner than when she had seen him scarcely a fortnight before, and deadly pale ; his eager, glittering eyes had a haggard, strange expression, which impressed her painfully.

" I fear you have been ill, Mr. Ford ! " she exclaimed, almost involuntarily, as she pointed to a seat near the fire and opposite her own.

" Ill at ease I certainly have been since yesterday," he replied, laying a square, thin brown paper parcel, folded and tied with his accustomed accuracy, on the table, and moving his chair so as to sit with his back to the light.

" I trust you have no very bad news to tell me," said Mrs. Travers, while her heart beat loudly.

" Nothing good, I acknowledge," he returned, taking out his handkerchief, and passing it rapidly over his face.

Mrs. Travers made no answer, and, with a sort of choking sound in the throat, Ford resumed abruptly:—" The missing will, for which we have sought so diligently—I have found it."

" Indeed ! " cried Mrs. Travers, with a sensation of relief. " I am very glad."

" But, my dear lady," said Ford, lowering his voice and leaning a little forward towards her, " I—I—as an old and trusted friend, I ventured to peruse it, and—"

" Well, well, Mr. Ford," interrupted Mrs Travers, impatiently ; " I am sure you were actuated by the best motives. I do hope Sir Hugh is remembered."

" Sir Hugh ! " repeated Mr. Ford, in a peculiar tone. " You

shall see ; " and he began to untie the parcel. " I do not know,"
he continued, "what induced me to perhaps transgress the
limits of prudence but my deep anxiety and regard for your interests—in short, I read the document ! and I am most thankful I
did, for I at once decided that *yours* should be the first eyes to
fall upon it. You can then act as you think best."

" But, where," exclaimed Mrs. Travers, who had turned somewhat pale—" where did you find it ? "

" You remember the large, old-fashioned bureau that stood in
Mr. Travers's private room ?—but no, you were there but once."

" I have heard you and Mr. Wall speak of it," she replied.

" We had examined it carefully, for Mr. Travers used to keep
his private papers, bonds, securities—matters unconnected with
the business of the house—there. The day before yesterday I
had noticed, in a list of drawings published in the *Times*, some
numbers of Turkish coupons which I felt sure were held by our
excellent principal, and late in the afternoon, when I had breathing time, I determined to look for the numbers which I had
noted down. While so engaged, Poole came to me with one of
the large ledgers which I usually lock away in the safe myself,
as he had requested permission to leave early. I took it from
him ; but, as he closed the door, I remembered a commission I
wished him to execute next morning, and, turning abruptly to
catch him, the heavy ledger fell from my hand, striking the in-
laid border that surrounds the writing-table part of the bureau.
It is one of those enclosed by a semi-circular revolving cover,
which shuts all in. The corner of the cover must have come
with much force upon a spring, for I heard a slight click, and a
secret drawer on the right, outside the bureau, flew open, and in
it I found this,"—laying his hand upon a folded parchment
which he had taken from its brown paper cover while he spoke.

" And it is—" exclaimed Mrs. Travers, breathlessly.

"The missing will," added Ford. "And now, my dear
friend," he continued, with a tinge of unusual familiarity, " I
must beg you to nerve yourself, for you will find this document
to be singularly unjust. I may say, basely unjust ! " He
paused, nervously biting his under lip, and, as he met the young
widow's full, searching, almost stern gaze, he averted his eyes.
When he looked at her again, she was holding out her hand for
the parchment.

" I daresay you exaggerate its injustice, Mr. Ford," she said.
" Even if the bulk of the property is left to Sir Hugh, I shall
not complain. He is the natural heir. I have no right to more
than a fair dower."

" Read it," returned Ford, emphatically ; "read it, and "
—sinking his voice, and drawing his chair a little nearer to her

—" remember, whatever course you may adopt, whatever decision you may make, I am utterly at your service." He stopped abruptly.

Mrs. Travers looked at him as if puzzled, and then unfolded the crackling parchment, her eyes intently darting upon the stiff, legal writing with which it was covered. " Ah ! " she exclaimed, after a few moments, which were very long to Ford, " I seem lost in a maze of words, and cannot gather the sense."

" Allow me to read it to you," he said, moving to her side. " You can follow, and I will explain. You observe the date— March the 15th. Does that bring anything to your recollection ? "

" No, nothing," returned Mrs. Travers, quickly ; " pray read on."

Ford plunged into the wilderness of words, skimming the technicalities quickly, yet with a slight tremor and catch in his voice, and bringing out the important morsels, dotted like islets in an Ægean of verbiage, with slackened speech and clear emphasis. Mrs. Travers listened in steady, unbroken silence to the very end ; the hand with which she held one side of the wide sheet firm and still, while Ford's shook perceptibly. Cleared of circumlocution, the will, after some small bequests to old employés, all more or less different from similar dispositions in the first will, proceeded to express a wish that the house of Travers should not be broken up, but kept in working order, either by the inheritor or a firm of partners ; this was not distinctly directed, but left to the discretion of the executors. The testator then remarked, that, having provided for all just claims upon him by gifts and otherwise during his lifetime, he desired that all his property, real and personal, should go to his nearest of kin, Sir Hugh Galbraith. This bequest was untrammeled by any condition or reservation whatever.

When Ford ceased reading Mrs. Travers turned quickly to the signatures, and read them aloud in a wondering tone. Ford rose, and stood a little distance, silent, but watching her intently. Again Mrs. Travers turned to the beginning, as though she would read it once more ; then, letting it fall, she looked up full at Ford, and, pushing back her hair from her brow, exclaimed, " I cannot understand it ! I am never mentioned ! ' He has provided for all just claims during his lifetime.' What does it mean ? Oh, Mr. Ford, this must be a forgery ! You cannot believe it genuine ? "

" I would fain believe it false," he began, in an unsteady voice, which he brought more under command as he proceeded. " I dreaded its effect upon you when I found what it was, and at once decided that you, and you alone, should first peruse it before any living soul knew of its existence."

" Oh ! yes, yes," cried Mrs. Travers, impatiently ; " you are always very good ; but do you mean to say that you believe Mr. Travers—my husband—would execute a will in which I am not even named ; in which I am totally unprovided for—unthought of, unless the sentence about having provided for all claims by gifts during his lifetime glances at me ? "

"And I suppose he made no deed of gift or settlement upon you ? "

" No, certainly not. I remember being so vexed before we were married, by old Mr. Lee asking for some such thing. Mr. Travers was rather offended, and said I might trust him ; and I did completely—justly—for" (with suppressed vehemence) " I will never believe this thing is real. No, not if one rose from the dead to tell me so ! *Do* you believe in it, Mr. Ford ? "

Ford made an attempt to speak before he could command his voice.

" I fear, my dear Mrs. Travers, it will be difficult to disprove it. I am most reluctantly obliged to place the reality of the question before you. First, we have the fact that Poole, shortly before Mr. Travers's death, admitted voluntarily that he and old Gregory had, early in the previous spring, witnessed a will which Poole believes Gregory (who was one time a lawyer's clerk) had drawn up under Mr. Travers's own direction. Then we have your own belief that a will subsequent to that existed. Indeed, you thought your own strong wish that justice should be done to Sir Hugh, suggested a change in Mr. Travers's testamentary dispositions. We search for the will in vain, our idea being that, as for some reason Mr. Travers chose to keep his intentions a secret from Messrs. Wall and Wreford, the bureau in his private room was the most likely place to find his will. There, accordingly, I, by a curious accident, do find it. The witnesses are the same as previously mentioned ; the date also tallies with what we were led to expect ; and, should you unfortunately not be able to arrange a compromise with Sir Hugh Galbraith, and if my evidence was called for, as it no doubt would be, I should be compelled to admit that, shortly before the date of that will, there was a disagreement of a somewhat painful nature on the subject of money between you and your late husband." He looked very intently at Mrs Travers while he spoke.

" Of course you would have to speak the truth," she returned, sharply. " But you surely do not mean to say that the trifling altercation you unfortunately overheard could have influenced Mr. Travers in so serious a matter as his will."

" It is impossible to say," said Ford. " No one knows better than yourself that your late good husband was not altogether free from crotchets more or less unreasonable."

Mrs. Travers made no immediate answer, but seemed looking
through the document with some care.

"The names appear all written in a different hand from the
rest," she said at last. "It is strange! It is incomprehensible!"

"It is cruel and deplorable," added Ford; "and," dropping his
voice, "not the least painful result is, that Sir Hugh Galbraith,
that haughty, overbearing fellow, will find a triumph prepared
for him as soon as he arrives."

"Ah! then you believe this horrible, cruel, unjust will is genuine. You cannot, Mr. Ford, surely you cannot!"

"My dear lady—my dear Mrs. Travers, it cuts me to the heart
to be obliged to confess that you will find it hard, nay impossible,
to set it aside." She rose from her seat and walked towards the
window as he spoke; he paused a moment, looking anxiously
after her, and then resumed—"Still, I would beg you not to be
too much cast down. Sir Hugh cannot be devoid of all humanity; you observe Mr. Gervais, the executor to the first will, is joint
executor with Sir Hugh himself. He is, I imagine, friendly to
you; if he represents your case judiciously, I am sure the fortunate heir will not refuse you, his cousin and benefactor's
widow, the means of subsistence, especially as you had made
him a handsome offer of your own free will when you believed
he had no claim. I think we may hope that Sir Hugh will make
you some small—"

Mrs. Travers had turned and come slowly back from the
window while Ford spoke, and now broke in upon his speculations in a low, concentrated voice, while her eyes flashed.

"What are you speaking about, Mr. Ford? Do you think
the will of any man could lower me into a dependent upon Sir
Hugh's charity? Do you not see that he will immediately declare, and believe that I knew of this—this—vile forgery, and so
tried to buy him off and quiet my own conscience? Do you not
see what an abyss of mortification and misrepresentation has
opened at my feet?—and if—if this thing cannot be proved false,
I *must* plunge in; there is *no* way of escape!" She grasped
the back of a chair as she spoke, and Ford could see from the
tight clutch of the white hands how strongly her spirit was
moved.

"I do indeed see how horrible it is; how much more horrible it
will be!" returned Ford, the color rising in his cheek, and a
light beginning to sparkle in his eyes. "My heart bleeds for
you; and yet I must draw your attention to another point, of
which I feel sure Sir Hugh and others will make the most and
the worst."

"What more?" asked Mrs. Travers, as if her thoughts were
far away.

"There is another name omitted from this will that was honorably mentioned in the former one—my own. You did not perhaps remember that I was left five hundred pounds?"

"Yes, yes; I remember."

"Then," resumed Ford, "it is highly probable that the total silence of this document respecting us both, coupled, in the mind of a worldly and not very high-toned man, with my pure devotion to your service; our previous—"

"I cannot imagine how any person could see the least connection between them," said Mrs. Travers. "But, be that as it may, I feel the ground giving way beneath my feet. I know this wretched will is false, forged, untrue; and yet, where can I turn for proof? How can I save myself from the humiliation of yielding, rescue or no rescue, to my insolent enemy?"

The last word was uttered with intense *verve* from between her clenched teeth by the fair, soft-looking widow.

"Can we find no way of escape?" asked Ford, in a low tone, looking intently at Mrs. Travers. She did not reply, and he resumed: "You would do much, anything, to avoid submission to Sir Hugh."

"Yes, anything," she replied, slowly.

"Then, Mrs. Travers," exclaimed Ford, his breath coming short and quick, "as you believe this will not to be genuine, suppress it! Not a soul knows of it save you and myself; you think it forged; you will, therefore, do no moral wrong. Need I assure you how completely you may trust me; how I would guard you from discovery even more watchfully than you would guard yourself?"—he ceased abruptly with a gasp, as if for breath.

Mrs. Travers turned, and looked at him full and steadily for a moment. "No!" she said, "that would indeed be to humiliate myself in my own eyes, and put myself under my adversary's feet. No, no; your sympathy for me, your friendly indignation, blinds you for the moment; we will blot out the suggestion. I see you more than half believe this will is genuine, and you are the more indignant. I do not believe it. Nothing will ever make me believe it—cruel, base, my husband never could have been; meantime, I must show it to Mr. Wall, and get Poole to verify his signature. How unfortunate that poor Gregory is dead! He, no doubt, was acquainted with the contents."

Mr. Ford changed color as she spoke, and passed his handkerchief across his brow, pressing it for a moment against his eyes. "Your decision," he said at last, in an altered tone, "does more credit to your conscience than to your worldly wisdom. Yet, if the advice of one so *culpably* anxious for your welfare as I am may still be offered, I should say, Do not give this docu-

3*

ment too hastily into Mr. Wall's hands. Pause; think of all you resign—wealth, ease, freedom! think of the reverse, which you will unavoidably incur—poverty, obscurity, hard work, possibly a faint suspicion that your late husband had some good cause for so complete, so extraordinary a change in the disposition of his property."

"I see it all, Mr. Ford, painfully clear; yet I must not do this thing." She spoke sadly, but composedly.

"Then," exclaimed Ford, with some agitation, "I have placed myself in your power to no avail—my character is in your hands!"

"What can you think of me," cried Mrs. Travers, with much warmth, "if you do not believe that I would be as true to you as you to me? I am certain you would never do for yourself what in a moment of mistaken feeling you suggested to me. Let us forget it. To-morrow you will think differently; and, as to me, the proposition shall never cross my mind again." She looked kindly and frankly at him, but he did not meet her eye. "But," she resumed, "if I grieve at the prospect of losing my all, I do not forget that you lose the legacy you so well deserved. Nothing makes me doubt the authenticity of this," pointing to the parchment, "more than the omission of your name."

"The whims of testators are positively unaccountable," said Ford, sullenly.

"But then," urged Mrs. Travers, "there was no shadow of reason for showing disapprobation of you. Mr. Travers confided in you—liked you to the last. Yours was the last name he mentioned. Ah!"—suddenly she stopped, as, with a flash of memory's light, the dying man's words came back to her. "Still," she resumed, speaking to herself, "my faith is not shaken."

"Some expression of poor Mr. Travers no doubt recurs to you?" said Ford, anxiously, while he watched her keenly.

"Yes," she returned, with her accustomed candor. "Scarcely an hour before his death he said, 'You will think I have been unjust.' Then, after a while, he added, 'It is too late!' words which I always thought pointed to a second will, but not one like this."

"Perhaps not; still they would apply. As to myself, who can tell that some instinctive feeling on the part of Mr. Travers may not have biased him against me? He may have recognized the deep admiration I once—nay, ever have felt since those happy days when first I knew you! the ardent sympathy! the devotion—"

"Stop!" said Mrs. Travers, gravely, coldly, and raising her hand with an imperious gesture which arrested the movement he made towards her. "These are not words for me to hear; but I am willing to forget *them* also, provided they are never repeated. I say so with no disrespect to you."

They stood for a moment face to face, and Ford's eyes fell under Mrs. Travers's composed gaze: a nervous, sinister smile flickered on his lip. He controlled himself with a visible effort, and, bowing low—

"You teach me my place," he said,—"a lesson I shall not soon forget. Once there was little difference in our positions—there may be less once more! But I have accomplished my errand, and received my reward; so I wish you good morning."

"I do not wish you to leave me in anger," said the young widow, gravely. "Be just, be rational, and let us forget the whole of this morning's conversation."

"Forget—forget!" repeated Ford, bitterly. "It is easily said. I shall so far remember as not to intrude again. Good morning."

He turned away abruptly, and the next moment Mrs. Travers heard the front door open and shut violently. She looked after him with a sigh, and a troubled expression came into her face.

"There goes another enemy," she murmured; then, taking up the fatal parchment, she slowly and carefully folded it up, laid it in a drawer, which she locked, and, sitting down to her writing table, quickly penned the following:—

"Dear Sir,—I shall call to-morrow between eleven and twelve. Endeavor to meet me; I have something very important to communicate."

This was addressed to W. Wall, Esq., 107, B— Street, and she had it instantly dispatched by a special messenger.

"Where is Miss Lee?" asked Mrs. Travers, when the serious Edwards returned to say her orders had been obeyed.

"Miss Lee is gone out, ma'am. One of the young ladies next door called, and Miss Lee left word she was going for a walk, and did not like to disturb you, as you were engaged. Luncheon is quite ready, ma'am."

"Very well," returned his mistress, mechanically; "but, Edwards, I cannot eat luncheon! I shall ask for something by-and-by. Go—go to your own dinner."

The man left the room, and Mrs. Travers remained gazing out upon the garden, where a flush of green and many opening blossoms told that Spring's first breath had touched the earth. Vaguely she looked out, and listened to the dim whisperings of her formless thought. She saw Cullingford and her cottage home quite distinctly across that mignionette border. She felt again the fluttered pleasure which Mr. Travers's grave notice and conversation created. She saw Ford, always carefully dressed, open the garden gate, with his black bag in his hand, and stop to assist her in budding roses. She recalled the odd, mixed feelings with which she always regarded him. A sort of compassion—a dread of hurting him—a tinge of ridicule—a sensation of unsafety. And then her husband; so generous, so high-minded, yet so narrow and jealous! A hundred instances of his thoughtful affection returned to her memory. *He* leave her unprovided for, dependent on her enemy! Never could she believe it. Yet the effect would be the same as if that horrible will was authentic. -

A certainty of defeat—of a long, weary struggle pressed upon her. The pleasant visions of travel, of study, of the variety and repose which easy circumstances can realize, melted utterly away; and the only clear idea standing up out of this misty reverie was that, at least, she had none to provide for save herself.

It was rather a relief to receive a message from Fanny to the effect that Mrs. Danby had some children to tea, and she would be so glad if Miss Lee could stay to assist in amusing them.

When Fanny returned, Mrs. Travers had gone to bed with a slight headache.

CHAPTER VII.

KATE TRAVERS cut short all her lively friend's questions and conjectures when they met the next morning by exclaiming, " There, Fanny, dear ! ask me nothing, and say as little as possible. I am going up to town immediately. When I return I will tell you everything, and you shall ask fifty questions, if you like ! "

" I am sure something frightful has happened," cried Fanny, the tears springing to her bright brown eyes. " You look as pale as a ghost, and as stern as if you were going to the block. I wish you would tell me just the least little bit. But, no, I will not tease you. I will wait till you choose. And, Kate," after a few moment's silence, "will you order dinner before you go? for I fancy Tom Reed will be here to-day ; he neither came nor wrote yesterday."

" Oh, Fanny, I cannot. Besides, there is no time. You must be housekeeper for to-day. Order everything nice. And now I must go, or I shall be late for Mr. Wall."

" Mr. Wall ! " echoed Fanny. " It must be something terrible."

" Good-bye, dear Fan ! " cried Mrs. Travers ; " do not make

yourself miserable. I have a sort of faith in my own fortune.
I think I shall conquer in the end. Good-bye." And she ran
away to put on her bonnet and gloves, summoning Edwards to
walk after her to the station, as a tribute to the aristocratic prejudices of Hampton Court.

"How long shall I have a lacquey to follow me?" she
thought, as the well-bred Edwards handed her her waterproof
cloak and closed the carriage door, touching his hat. "And
how long shall I be able to pay first-class fares?" For, in spite
of her brave words to Fanny Lee, the young widow's heart sank
within her. It was impossible to doubt that this new will was a
very serious misfortune, even if, as she hoped, Mr. Wall's knowledge and experience enabled him to find some weak point into
which he might insert the wedge of resistance. A long course
of litigation! She shrank from the idea. Yet it was the best
result she dared to hope for ; and most resolutely she determined
to fight it out, were it to cost her fortune and embitter her life,
if—oh, potent monosyllable!—if there was a reasonable objection
on which to ground resistance. But Kate Travers was too
clear-headed to hope, save that Mr. Wall might perceive what
her ignorance overlooked.

* * * * * * *

"It is a bad business, Mrs. Travers ; a very bad business,
I'm afraid!" was the wise man's dictum after more than an
hour of anxious discussion and re-reading of Mr. Ford's unlucky
"trove." "I cannot understand it. Why my poor friend should
suddenly withdraw the confidence he had always reposed in this
firm, and in myself particularly, I cannot conceive, except—and
this is one of the worst features in the case for you—that he was
well aware I should never have assisted to draw up anything so
unjust towards you. I was vexed, I acknowledge, that he
should leave the man he once looked upon as his heir totally unprovided for ; and so, I *now* believe, were you. But Sir Hugh
Galbraith brought this upon himself. I could never have agreed
to such an unjust will—never!—Why, it lays you open to—to
—" The lawyer, who was unusually moved, pulled himself up
abruptly, and altered his phrase—"to refund all the moneys ex-
pended since the death of your late husband—all!" with
emphasis. He paused, and met his client's eyes fixed earnestly
upon him. A slight smile curved her lip.

"Lays me open to the most injurious suspicions, you were
going to say," she rejoined, quietly.

"I admit nothing of the kind. The realities of the case are
quite enough, without adding imaginary hardships."

"But, Mr. Wall, you do not seem to take in my idea that this
will is not genuine?"

" What are your reasons for that opinion ? " asked the lawyer, severely, leaning back in his chair and thrusting his hands into his trouser pockets.

" My reasons ! " repeated poor Kate, feeling how unreasonable they would appear to the legal mind. " Alas ! they are scarce worthy the name, though very convincing to me. First, nothing could persuade me that Mr. Travers would make a will and never name my name ; then his employing some stranger to draw it—his keeping it a secret—the different handwriting in parts—the change in all his former dispositions—his—"

" My dear lady," interrupted Mr. Wall, removing his hands from his pockets, and running his finger along the lines of the fatal parchment which lay open on his desk, " the law ignores innate convictions. I observe the various names are filled in in a different hand ; that is nothing, a very ordinary occurrence when there is a wish for secrecy. Now let me ask you, Whose interest would it be to forge this will ? No one's, save Sir Hugh Galbraith ; and I do not think, even in your present very naturally excited frame of mind, you could for a moment suspect a gentleman of unblemished honor, a soldier, to whom no amount of fortune could atone for the slightest taint—"

" I have not suspected him," returned Mrs. Travers, in a low, concentrated voice, " though *he* did not hesitate to write his suspicions that I had suppressed a will favorable to himself."

" That was quite a different matter," said Mr. Wall, disposed, as men usually are, to pooh-pooh a woman's claim to stand on the same platform as themselves in a question of honor. " It was very wrong, of course, but he was in a passion, and, you must remember, he knew nothing of you."

" Nor I anything to Sir Hugh's advantage. But I am not in a passion, nor do I suspect him. Mr. Ford—"

" My dear Mrs. Travers," interrupted the lawyer, " your doubts surely cannot wander in *that* direction ! The poor man loses his five hundred pounds, and probably will lose his employment into the bargain."

" You are too quick, Mr. Wall. I was not going to *say* "— with a slight emphasis—" that I doubted Mr. Ford."

" Well, excuse me. Now I must ask you one or two questions, which I entreat you to answer truthfully—I mean faithfully. More mischief is done and causes lost through the impossibility of getting litigants to tell the whole truth, and nothing but the truth, to their advisers than from anything else."

" I have always tried to be faithful and true," said Mrs. Travers, sadly, tears welling up in her large dark blue eyes, as she looked steadfastly into those of her companion. " Ask what you will—I have nothing to conceal.'

" I believe you—I believe you!" returned Wall, quickly and earnestly.

" Look back as clearly as you can, and, if possible, recall any quarrel, any little difference of opinion which may have arisen between you and your excellent husband :—every trifle you can remember may prove important—differences will arise even between the most attached ; and I am sorry to say the crotchets of testators are perfectly incredible, as well as the indolence which so often holds men back from undoing the wrongs into which temper, or jealousy, or heaven knows what has hurried them."

" Latterly, no doubt from failing health, Mr. Travers was rather difficult : but the only serious difference that ever arose between us was when, after the death of Miss Lee's grandfather, I sent her a small present of money. My allowance was very liberal, and I did not require Mr. Travers's help; so I sent it without letting him know. Her letter acknowledging the money fell into his hands, and I was astonished at the anger it caused. He said much that I have forgotten and he did not really mean, but he did not get over the irritation for some time."

" Did you do your best to soothe him and make the *amende ?*" interrupted the lawyer.

" I did my best. I told him I would never again repeat the offense, as it caused him annoyance; but I could not agree with him in thinking that I was wrong in doing what I had done ; and I am of the same opinion still."

" Just so," returned Mr. Wall, in a cynical tone. " You stuck to your own opinion, cost what it might—a very womanish proceeding, excuse me."

" Yes, I excuse you," replied Mrs. Travers, coloring slightly ; " only if you insist on women misrepresenting their opinions, do not quarrel with them for occasional departure from truth, which may not suit you quite so well."

" Anyhow," returned the lawyer turning aside from this thrust, "your steadfastness has probably cost you a fortune ! When did the altercation happen ? "

"Some time in February last year—about the end, I think."

" And this is dated the 15th of March ! I think that is strong presumptive evidence of the mischief you did yourself. No doubt Mr. Travers argued that, when a free woman, you would squander all his hard earnings on your own friends ; and men contract a wonderful affection for money they have scraped together ! Unjust as it is, I have known the disposition of large properties totally changed for a slighter cause. I fear you have yourself to blame for this," striking the parchment with his finger, and unconsciously finding a sort of relief in what he could not resist feeling was a certain palliation of his late client's cruel will.

"And can you believe this?" cried Mrs. Travers, passionately. She had kept herself well in hand hitherto, and now broke out only for an instant. "Can you be so unjust to your friend as to imagine that, in the full possession of his reason, he could have lived on, treating me with seeming confidence and affection, and yet be conscious of the treachery that would leave me penniless at his death! I knew him better, and nothing will ever make me believe this to be his genuine will!"

"It is not like him to have so acted," said the lawyer; "but," shrugging his shoulders with an air of superior wisdom, "if you knew as much of testamentary vagaries as I do, nothing would seem incredible. Nevertheless, I quite believe your late husband intended to change his will, and, as so many have done before him, put it off a little too long."

"He never signed this one," returned Mrs. Travers, sadly but emphatically; "and now what is to be done, Mr. Wall?"

"Ha—hum! It is really—" he began, hesitating, and looking again through the obnoxious document. "Gregory, one of the witnesses, is dead."

"Yes; he died last autumn. Mr. Ford says that Poole is under the impression the will was written out by poor old Gregory; but this is not his writing, so Mr. Ford says."

"Ah! that is nothing. I must see this man Poole, and try what I can make of him; but, my dear madam, I dare not flatter you with much hope. Everything tallies, you see, with the first report that another will was in existence. Poole mentioned the end of February or beginning of March as the period at which he was called upon to witness what he believed to be the will—"

"And then?" persisted Mrs. Travers.

"Well, then, if Poole is willing to swear to his own signature, we must inform Messrs. Payne and Layton, Sir Hugh's solicitors—a very respectable firm—and try to make the best terms we can for you. From all I have known of him, Sir Hugh Galbraith is not the man to—"

"What do you mean?" asked the widow, coloring very deeply, and opening her large eyes full upon him.

"That he must be induced to make you some allowance out of the estate; he ought—"

"Never mention such a thing!" cried Mrs. Travers, rising from her seat in her excitement. "I utterly forbid it! What! accept a compromise, and forego my right to dispute this base imposition—my chance of upsetting it! Never! I am young and healthy, and not uneducated; I will earn my bread somehow. But give up the possibilities of the future—never, never!"

The lawyer was a little startled by her suppressed vehemence.

" Very natural you should say so just now, my dear Mrs.
Travers; pray sit down again. We must reflect, above all
things—reflect carefully, before taking a single step. Nothing
need be done hurriedly ; but I would advise your quietly collect-
ing together everything poor Mr. Travers gave you in his lifetime ; remember you are entitled to *every* thing he has ever
given you—plate, pictures, furniture, jewels, books, etc.—and be
careful in your expenditure. For how long have you that house
at Hampton Court ? "

" Six months longer. Ah, Mr. Wall, I see there is no hope ! "

" I do not exactly say so—"

" I should like to see Poole myself," interrupted Mrs. Travers.

" Hereafter if you will. *I* must see him alone first."

" There is no more to be said now," returned the young widow,
drawing down her veil. " I will go. Thank you for the friendly
feeling you have shown. If there is the shadow of a chance
you will fight, will you not ? "

" Not for a shadow, my dear lady—not for a shadow. I
would rather secure a little substance for you."

" I will have none of the substance you mean."

" Well, well ! You must reflect calmly when you have cooled
down. Nothing is a bad alternative."

" Good-bye," said Mrs. Travers, turning quickly away.

The lawyer followed her to the door. " I will write the moment I have anything to communicate, depend upon that."

She bowed and was gone.

" An ugly business—a *very* ugly business," said the lawyer to
himself, as he went back to his desk, and penned a note to Mr.
Ford, requesting him to send up Poole immediately, and call
himself in the course of the afternoon. This he dispatched by
a special messenger.

*   *   *   *   *   *

Her present trial had in it elements of strength and bitterness
totally dissimilar from Kate Travers's former experiences.
There was nothing to touch her heart, for she exonerated her
husband fully, utterly, from the cruelty and treachery of which
Mr. Wall evidently suspected him. Impossible as it now seemed
that she could ever prove it, or even find a plausible theory to
account for her conviction, she was as certain that will was
forged as though she had witnessed the operation. A vague
idea that some one might have done it to obtain a hold upon Sir
Hugh floated through her brain, and was dismissed with a start,
as it suggested another suspicion which seemed so preposterous
that she strove to banish it immediately ; yet it would not go,
and haunted her for many a day and night, although she resolutely refrained from uttering it.

She was too natural and healthy a woman not to put a true value on the advantage of wealth—*i. e.* she was heartily sorry to lose it, but by no means overwhelmed with dismay at the prospect. The real sting lay in her adversary's victory—in the cause given to the malicious .and the idly gossiping to shake their heads and cry, " Fie upon her ! It is plain old Travers knew of something very disgraceful, as plain as if we saw it with our eyes." " After all "—she pondered, trying hard to keep fast hold of reason—" my possible errors and misfortunes will soon be forgotten ! But what shall I do, and where shall I go ? Not out of England—not too far from London. I will never lose the remotest chance of disproving that will."

The young widow had given up all hope for the present ; four days had elapsed since her interview with the lawyer, and she had heard from him in the interim. Poole, he wrote, had recognized his own signature, and was quite willing to swear to it. He was also convinced that Gregory's was genuine, so that there was nothing for it but to submit, and the sooner the new will was communicated to the opposite party, the better chance of making good terms.

In the meantime, Mrs. Travers had gone through some trying scenes with poor Fanny Lee and the faithful Mills. The latter was cruelly disappointed, and strongly inclined to quarrel with everyone, including her much enduring mistress. But Fanny's grief and terror at the idea that she might possibly be separated from her tender protectress, touched her to the heart. " You will not send me away, dear. I will do anything—be the servant, and sweep, and dust, and cook ! I can do a ch—chop nicely ! " sobbed Fanny. " I know I am a selfish thing, and very little use, but I'll break my heart and die if I leave you and go among strangers again ! "

" Dear child ! you shall not go if I can possibly help it," replied Mrs. Travers, soothingly.

Mrs. Mills, with much significant head-shakings and screwing up of the mouth, hinted her opinion " that, if *her* advice had been taken, things might have been different. It was true she hadn't much edication, but she could see how things was going clearer than most, etc., etc."

Tom Reed, too, the widow's prime counselor, had run down twice, and even he was overwhelmed. At first he could hardly credit the misfortune, but after he had seen Mr. Wall, and perused Mr. Ford's unfortunate " find," he, too, counseled compromise, and had gone away the evening before with *carte blanche* to agree to any suggestion of Mr. Wall's, except to ask for an allowance from the widow's triumphant foe.

Meditating on these unpleasant topics, Mrs. Travers strolled into the Palace gardens, at the hour when luncheon generally left them very much deserted. She wanted the freedom of loneliness. She wanted the fresh air, and to enjoy the beauty of the place, feeling that beauty might be a rare ingredient in her future every-day life.

She wanted, too, to re-read one or two advertisements in the *Times* which had caught her eye, and suggested plans ; so she took that famous broad sheet with her, and, seating herself on a bench that encircled a large yew tree, remained for some time in a sort of unconscious reverie—the nearest approach to stillness the waking brain can know. The delicate perfume of the early flowers, the first flush of tender green upon the trees, the joyous spring note of the birds, the delicious odor of the freshly-clipped grass, the high-bred beauty of the stately garden, filled her with a sad pleasure. To all this, and such as this, she must soon be a stranger, banished from the pleasant and lovely places of life by a caprice of circumstance ! She knew how well suited to her taste, her nature, nay, even her outward presence, was all that is noble and beautiful, and she never seemed to have fallen into her right place. She never grew to be at home with the richly-dressed and fairly well-bred wives and daughters of Mr. Travers's City friends, or rather acquaintances—there was a lack of subjects in common between them. They dimly looked down upon her as a person of no connections, and she, too careless in her innate strength to recognize the wherefore, felt there was an indefinable barrier between them—an invisible fence, harder to clear than a stone wall. "The upper ten have certainly never taken kindly to me, if my Hereford Square acquaintance can be so classed. I suppose Sir Hugh would scarcely look on them as equals."

While she thus conjectured idly, steps approached, and the scent of an excellent cigar reached her. Voices—men's voices —came nearer, and two gentlemen, one in undress uniform, sat down on the opposite side of the tree.

"It is a deucedly lucky turn for you, but hard lines for the other. I wonder what vexed old Travers, and induced him to cut her off?" said one of the voices ; and Kate could not resist listening eagerly for a few moments.

"Heaven knows," replied the other—a harsh, deep-toned voice, somewhat monotonous in its strength. "He must have been crazy altogether—first to forget all that was due to his age, his station, everything, and marry the low-bred daughter of a lodging-house keeper ; some bit of vulgar prettiness, whose highest ambition could not have soared beyond the owner of the general shop in her native village ! Faugh ! Give me a fresh cigar, Upton ! If in his old age poor Travers had such vagaries, could he not have been content to take her for a mistress? but to give her his name, and the fortune he once intended for me, and then to leave her penniless, dependent on my charity! It was insanity!"

"You had better not suggest the idea," said the other, dryly.

"It would be of no consequence," replied the second speaker. "It is no easy matter to upset a will. No lawyer would take up this female's case—but I shall not let the creature starve. By the way, she offered me a good slice of the property at the out-set; depend upon it, she knew there was another will some-where. Travers had found her out in some delinquency—con-science had made a coward of her."

"I don't know," began the other; but Mrs. Travers, coloring with shame both at what she had heard and for having stayed to hear it, sprang to her feet, and stole swiftly, softly away.

But for omnipotent appearances, she would have ran at full speed to hide herself in her own room, to try and silence the cruel words that rang over and over again in her ears. All her worst and bitterest anticipations were realized. The basest of her sex could not have been spoken of with deeper scorn. No spark of manly consideration tempered this *gentle*man's judgment of a defeated, and, for all he knew, friendless woman. And this was a man of the class and profession usually credited with chivalrous traditions; because he was reared in the purple of a higher caste he permitted himself to believe there was no honor, no principle, no heart, among the unfortunates in whose veins flowed the blood of those serfs over whom this proud man's forefathers had tyrannized, and who, in spite of every dis-advantage, had developed themselves into the strength and power of the nation. How she hated and scorned .him, and al-most prayed for a chance of putting her foot upon his neck. It would be no common revenge that would satisfy her. No more aristocracy or gentility for her. No! she would enroll herself in the ranks of the simple, undistinguished workers. Though far from being a crying, hysterical woman, Kate Travers, already a little strained by the resolute suppression of her feelings, could not control a violent fit of weeping, so helpless and humiliated did she feel under a sense of undeserved defeat. All around was so dark too! Not a gleam of hope in any quarter of the horizon! for more than the space of half an hour she felt beaten to the earth; and then her healthy, hopeful nature began to as-sert itself. She would rouse up and be doing something; and she had need to look round her quickly, for she was well-nigh penniless. And no stress of circumstances would induce her to accept Sir Hugh Galbraith's "charity."

At this point of her reflections there was a tap at the door, and Fanny's voice asked, "Are you there, Kate?"

" Yes."

" We have been looking all over the gardens for you. I did not know you had come in. Tom Reed is down-stairs and wants to see you."

" I will come directly."

But it took some time to bathe her eyes effectually, and she was vexed to see they were still red and swollen, when she felt ashamed to keep her visitor waiting any longer.

CHAPTER IX.

" DEAR MADAM,—I have had a long interview with Sir Hugh Galbraith's solicitor. He informs me, he is authorized to offer you an allowance during your lifetime from the estate of your late husband of three hundred (£300) per annum, on condition that you agree to accept the will to which Sir Hugh administers as the true and final expression of the testator's intentions, and sign a declaration to that effect.

" I urged that the allowance was considerably disproportioned to the estate ; and he very naturally replied that Sir Hugh was in no way bound to consider this, or to make any allowance whatever.

" Now, my dear madam, let me urge upon you the necessity of giving this offer due consideration. Both as your legal adviser and, if you will permit it, as your friend, I strongly advise you to accept. I see not the most remote prospect of being able to dispute this very unjust will, and you are, I am sure, too sensible a woman not to recognize the wisdom of the old proverb, ' Half a loaf, etc.' Messrs. Payne, Sir Hugh's solicitors, are willing to renounce all claim for moneys disbursed since the death of Mr. Travers, as I have represented that you simply kept up the establishment as your late husband left it ; and I must here warn you that rent, wages, etc., now due, should be paid by the executors out of the estate.

" Any further information you may require you can obtain from Mr. Reed, who is good enough to take charge of this letter, and with whom I would suggest your taking counsel ; he seems truly interested in you, and is also a man of business.

" Hoping to see you in a few days,

" I am, dear Madam,

" Yours truly,

" F. WALL.

" Mrs. Travers, Hampton Court."

This letter was handed to the widow by Reed as soon as their first greetings had been exchanged. And she read it through steadily, without moving a muscle of her countenance, while Reed watched, with the keenest sympathy, the traces of tears and mental conflict upon her fair face.

" Well, Tom," she said, with a brave attempt to smile as she finished reading, " it is all over. There is nothing now to be done but to go forth into the wilderness."

" It is by far the most infer—" began Reed.

" Hush, dear old friend," interrupted Mrs. Travers ; " do not rouse up the passion and bitterness I have scarcely succeeded in crushing down for the present."

" No, I will not," he returned, persistently. " But Wall commissioned me to mention one or two matters which he omitted to write "—and Reed paused abruptly.

" Disagreeable things, I suppose, Tom," said Mrs. Travers, with a sigh. " But you need not fear to ' put a name ' to anything. I fancy my thoughts have been before you. The strongest feeling I have is an ardent desire to leave this place, where I have now no right to be."

" Exactly," cried Reed. " That was the first point I was to speak about. The sooner you move the better. And Galbraith's solicitors, I was to tell you, are authorized to pay a quarter's allowance, annuity, or whatever it is,"—he stumbled a little over this part of his speech—" in advance, provided you can vacate at once."

An indignant look flashed from the widow's eyes. " Do they think I must be bribed to give up what Sir Hugh Galbraith looks upon as his property. I am quite ready to go ; but you must understand me, Tom. I take no money from my foe."

" A very natural reluctance," began Tom, soothingly, and launched into a sensible and persuasive speech—for this was the point specially confided to his tact and eloquence by Mr. Wall.

Mrs. Travers listened quietly, without the smallest interruption ; and when Tom Reed, having exhausted his subject, paused for a reply, she said, in a low, firm voice, " Do not waste any more words, Tom. On this matter my mind is unalterably made up. Had I children, I would decide differently. As I am, *no* necessity shall compel me to touch Sir Hugh's money."

" Poor Fanny ! " escaped almost involuntarily from Reed's lips. " She will be homeless again."

" She shall not," returned Mrs. Travers, glancing with a kindly smile at her companion, while tears stood in her eyes. " I could not bear to part with that dear, faithful, thoughtless child—for she is a child in many ways. But, Tom, I have a dim sort of project of which I shall speak to you presently.

And I am not quite without resources. I have some jewels, diamonds, and other things which Mr. Travers bought for me, and which are distinctly mine."

" What are they worth? A mere trifle; nothing to reckon upon," replied Reed, in a disparaging tone.

" They cost seven or eight hundred pounds, if not more."

" And they would not bring half that money when sold," he rejoined. "Even if they did, what is the interest of seven hundred pounds?—not enough to buy you scented soap."

And again Tom urged the acceptance of Sir Hugh's bounty, and almost lost his temper at the widow's senseless obstinacy, as he termed it. Then she shed a few tears, which disarmed Tom; so they parted, Mrs. Travers's resolution still unmoved, and Reed refusing to consider her decision final.

" Tell Mr. Wall," were her parting words, "that the day after to-morrow he can hand over this house to Sir Hugh Galbraith, or the owner. I shall leave it before noon."

" But, my dear soul ! you will never be able to pack up your traps, and decamp by the day after to-morrow ? "

" I shall. Poor Mills ! Fanny and myself have been preparing ever since I saw Mr. Wall. I only require to find a lodging somewhere in town. I can do that to-morrow ; and then, Tom, you will still be my counselor and familiar friend, though I am unfortunate, and stupid, and blind to my own interests, and everything else that is wrong ? "

" Look here, Mrs. Travers," cried Tom, grasping her hand, energetically ; " right or wrong, I'll stick to you through thick and thin ! "

" I believe you," she returned, trying bravely not to cry. "You shall have a ·line from me with the new address some time to-morrow ; and you must come and see us very soon."

" Won't I ? And now—excuse the question—have you any cash ? "

" Yes ; enough for the present. Go, and bid Fanny good-bye. I have too much to do to ask you to stay."

  * * * * * * *

A couple of days later, Reed found Mrs. Travers and his cousin comparatively settled in a small street in that part of Camden Town which considers itself entitled to write Regent's Park on its addresses.

The change from the airy, stately, old-fashioned house to the narrow front-parlor struck him with a keen sense of pain ; but he could not refrain from observing that Mrs. Travers looked brighter and Fanny less tearful than when he had seen them last.

It was evening when he reached their abode, and the little

room was somewhat gloomy with the fading light ; but Mrs. Travers lit the gas at once, and then he beheld a table laid for tea, with the addition of cold meat and watercresses. There were even tufts of primroses and violets on the mantel-shelf, and a general look of order and occupation inseparable from the presence of cultivated, thoughtful women.

"Oh, Tom, I am so glad to see you," cried Fanny, springing to meet him.

"And so am I," said Mrs. Travers, heartily ; while Mills, who had been seated at table, rose, with a rueful. countenance, curtsied, and made as though to leave the room.

"Do not stir, Mills. Tom, you will be pleased to have Mills at tea. We are all companions in misfortune," said Mrs. Travers.

"To be sure," cried Tom, cheerfully. "Sit down, Mrs. Mills. You look pretty comfortable. Tea ! I am dying for a cup. Come, Fanny ; I will let you sit next me, if you promise to cut my bread and butter."

And the friends gathered round the table with wonderfully cheerful exteriors, at all events ; and for a while the talk flowed as if nothing had happened.

"There is no use in moping," cried Tom, at last. "What do you say to a box at the Haymarket to-morrow night ? There is a capital piece on there, and I think I can get you a box."

"Take Fanny, by all means," replied Mrs. Travers ; "as for me, I do not pretend I should not enjoy it, but it would be most unseemly."

"If you think so, I can say no more ; but you will come, Fanny ! and I tell you what, we will take Mrs. Mills. I daresay her ' young man ' has not treated her to the theatre all the time she was vegetating at Hampton Court."

"Ah ! go 'long with you, Mr. Tom !" returned Mrs. Mills, slightly relaxing as Reed, raising his voice, addressed her. He was an immense favorite with the afflicted Mills, who remembered him in his school-boy days of tatterdemalionism.

"Yes, yes, Mills, you must come !" cried Fanny. "It will do you all the good in the world."

"Well now, Miss Fanny, I did think you would be the last to leave my poor dear lady all alone in her trouble, to fret and break her heart ; but you go and amuse yourself ; I'll stay and keep her company."

"But, Mills, you are so miserable yourself you won't do her one bit of good," returned Fanny, at the top of her voice. Then suddenly lowering it, and in deep penitence, "There ! what a stupid I am ! I have done it," watching Mills, whose face assumed an awful expression.

"You needn't tell me so, Miss Fanny, 1 know well enough 1 am no good now ; but you needn't tell me so."

"1 do declare, Mills, 1 never meant anything of the kind."

"No, no," said Tom, cutting a tempting thin slice of bread and butter ; "Miss Fanny only meant to say you and Mrs. Travers would do each other no good if you were left together. A little more bread and butter, Mrs. Mills?"

"1 am much obliged to you, I have had enough. No good, indeed!" and Mills, refusing everything, comfort included, made her exit, stating she had plenty to do.

"And now, Tom," said Mrs. Travers, when the table was cleared, "let us have a committee of ways and means ; bring over my writing-book and the ink, Fanny, while I get all my worldly goods for Tom's inspection."

"Oh, Tom!" cried Fanny, as Mrs. Travers left the room ; "do not let her send me away! 1 cannot tell you how miserable I am sometimes when the possibility of such a thing comes across me. I shiver and turn cold, and I know I look blue. I suppose I am very selfish and good-for-nothing to feel so ; I ought to be brave and go away and earn my own bread, but I can't, dear Tom, I can't indeed. It was so horrible before; 1 could do anything with her—but alone—"

She broke down abruptly. Poor Reed's heart was at his lips, he caught her hand in both his own, his keen black eyes softening with the tenderest sympathy. "Dearest, sweetest cousin!" he exclaimed, in such an unusual tone that Fanny looked up startled, "you must not fret yourself. I think Mrs. Travers will manage to keep you with her still ; and if she cannot—why, you had better come and manage my housekeeping." And he kissed the hand he held lovingly.

"Oh! Tom," returned Fanny, with a vivid blush as a consciousness of his possible meaning flashed across her, "that is nonsense."

"1 am afraid it is, just at present," said Tom, with a sigh and a smile, as he slowly relinquished her hand. "But if ever, Fanny!" interrupting himself, "1 must never indulge myself in such talk till it ceases to be nonsense. Eh, Fanny darling?"

"Nothing short of the profoundest sense should ever be addressed to such a sage as 1 am," returned Fanny, arranging the writing materials a little nervously; "so no more nonsense an you love me, Tom."

"As I love you, no!" said Reed, with unwonted seriousness.

Mrs. Travers re-entered at that moment, perhaps fortunately for Tom Reed's self-control. "I have restored Mills's equanimity," she said, smiling, "which kept me a little. Here,

here is all I possess!" and she placed sundry morocco-covered cases on the table.

"Ah! now for an examination," cried Tom; and the three friends drew in their chairs. "What have we here?" he continued, assuming a solemn and magisterial air. "Three diamond stars! By Jove! They are sparklers!"

"How lovely, Kate. Why did you never show them to me before? Is it not cruel to have to sell them?" said Fanny.

"Here are the earrings to match," said Mrs. Travers. "Poor Mr. Travers bought them after the first great dinner party we went to together, when he observed I was the only lady present without jewels; the stars cost a hundred and fifty guineas, and the earrings one hundred."

"Put that down, Fanny; mind you make nice figures. What next, madam?"

"These bracelets, opal and diamond, and emeralds. Mr. Travers gave seventy pounds for one, but I do not know how much for the other."

"The stones look very fine; but I am no judge," said Reed. And so they went through the whole array—bracelets, rings and lockets, jeweled hair-pins and earrings; the prices of but few were known to Mrs. Travers, and Reed tried to guess at their probable cost, always telling Fanny to put down considerably less. Yet on examining the list, he found a sum total of six hundred and thirty-five pounds.

"A decent little capital, if you could but realize it," cried Tom. "We must not hope for that, I fear. You may get something near the value of the stones, if we can find an honest jeweler. The diamonds ought to sell well, if we could find a private purchaser. My own experience in such matters is extremely limited—limited, in short, to small transactions in days bygone, with a relative whose natural and acquired sharpness, quite unsoftened by any kinsmanly consideration, was more than a match for my inexperience." Mrs. Travers laughed, and Fanny opened her eyes. "We must do the best we can," resumed Tom. "I shall take advice. Perhaps," insinuatingly, "when you find how little these pretty things will produce, you will give more favorable consideration to the offer—"

"If they only bring me twenty-five pounds, or nothing, my determination will be still the same; do not mention that man or his offer," said Mrs. Travers in a low voice.

"Do you know I have seen him!" exclaimed Fanny, with mingled horror and triumph.

"You! impossible!" cried Mrs. Travers and Tom together.

"Yes, I did. It was that day, just before we left, when I went to look for you, Kate, in the Palace gardens, I saw Colonel

Upton walking with a great, tall, ugly, red-looking man. I felt in some extraordinary way that it was—him," continued Fanny, suppressing the name. "And in the afternoon, when I was paying the bills, you know, Kate, I met that horrid Mrs. Danby, and she cried out, ' Has Sir Hugh Galbraith been to see you? for he is down here to-day with Colonel Upton.'"

"How has the charming Mrs. Danby become horrid?" asked Reed, looking up from his figures, to change the conversation.

"Oh! she was so prying and unfeeling, and—"

"But," resumed the prime counselor, turning to Mrs. Travers, who kept silence, "suppose you succeed in getting, say, half the value, or rather the cost of these pretty things. What is your scheme? for I see you have one."

"Read that," replied Mrs. Travers, opening her pocket-book and taking out a slip of newspaper; "read it aloud."

Tom took it and read as follows:

"To be disposed of, on moderate terms, in consequence of the owner's death, the goodwill and stock-in-hand of a first-class fancy-work and stationery business in a thriving town on the sea coast, not far from London, much frequented by summer visitors, and surrounded by resident gentry. The lease of the house (old-fashioned and commodious), seven years unexpired, to be included in the purchase. Address C. P., Messrs. Hook and Crook, Size Lane, City."

"Why, what in Heaven's name has this to do with it?" cried Tom, when he finished, looking up with a bewildered air.

"Everything," returned Mrs. Travers, quietly. "If, on inquiry, it turns out a promising speculation, and I can get money enough, I shall buy it and turn tradeswoman—you know I am partly ' to the manner born,' Tom."

"Keep a shop! you!" exclaimed Fanny in open-mouthed amazement, and then became silent, too stunned to talk.

"Well, this is quite in keeping with your refusal to accept the tolerable means of existence to which you have an undoubted right. I never heard anything so preposterous," said Tom, with some heat.

"What would poor old Travers say, if he could look out of his grave, to see his name over the door of a miserable shop!—and you always say you respect his wishes."

"His name was long enough on a door-post; but it shall not be over any shop. Have patience, Tom, hear all my scheme," said Mrs. Travers, with much sweetness, and then went on rapidly, "I have thought of everything! I must work to live—the question is how? There are only two lines open to women, teaching or business in a small way. I leave the miserable indefiniteness of ' companionship' out of the question. If I

adopt teaching I become at once a homeless waif, and Fanny
the same ;. while Mills will have to be provided for somehow.
True, I might attempt a school, where they would be of use to
me ; but I cannot find that I have courage for such a hopeless
struggle as working up a school. Now this ' business ' will give
me a home and evenings to myself. I have already written for
particulars. If they are satisfactory I will risk it, Tom ; but one
thing I promise you, unless I can pay the whole purchase-money
at once, I will give it up ; I will not begin with a burden of debt on
my back. Fanny shall be my assistant, Mills our housekeeper ;
so the whole home shall not be broken up ; and trust me I will
put heart and soul, energy and pluck into my new career."

"Career!" echoed Tom, "I never heard such insanity! you
will lose your money, and your position into the bargain.
Fancy *you* behind a counter, and Fanny matching wools ; I can
never consent to such degradation."

"Is that a suitable word from the sub-editor of a ' high class
Liberal paper '? For shame, Tom ! do not be false to your
principles. My career shall not be degrading ; but listen to me
I do not want any one save yourself to know where I am. I
want to lie in wait for some evidence about this will. I shall
never rest until I know the truth ; there is some unaccountable
mystery about it."

"Not much, I am afraid," said Tom, shaking his head.

"I always think that horrid Mr. Ford made it up to worry us
all," exclaimed Fanny, at the last speaking with her tongue.

"I see I shall have to secure berths for both of you at Han-
well," said Tom, resignedly. " Mrs. Travers wanting to keep a
shop, and you, Fanny, accusing that poor fellow, Ford—who has
lost his legacy, and will no doubt lose his situation, who has
always been Mrs. Travers's most devoted servant—of forging
a will directly opposed to his own interests !—really, you are a
pair of very charming madwomen ! "

" Do not be so ridiculous, Tom ; I never could bear Mr. Ford."

"Ah ! then I daresay he has committed a couple of murders
and forged no end of things," said Tom, with an air of assumed conviction.

" Do not talk such nonsense, Fanny dear," added Mrs. Travers, absently.

" Now, do not let us talk about this wild project any more,"
said Tom, rising. " You will think differently when you have
reflected a little more. It is getting late. I will make all the inquiries I can to-morrow as to the best course to be pursued with
the jewels ; and perhaps have something to suggest when I come
for Fanny to go to the Haymarket ; for we must not lose our expedition because we quarrel—eh ! mesdames ? "

" No, certainly not," replied Kate. " One word, Tom, before
you go. Your word of honor, that you keep this project of mine
a secret from every one, especially Mr. Wall and Mr. Ford."

" Trust me ! I would not mention your temporary insanity to
any one ! By the way, Ford was with me to-day—and deucedly
cut-up he looks—to ask your address. I said I did not know if
I was at liberty to give it ; but that I would forward any note.
He told me he heard old Mr. Gervais had refused to act as executor."

" Then everything is absolutely in Sir Hugh's hands," exclaimed Mrs. Travers. " Time, and time only, can unravel this
web ! Good night, Tom ; bear with me, yet."

" Good-night, Fanny," squeezing her hand ; on which the
mischievous little witch cried, " Oh ! you hurt me ; see the mark
my ring has made ! " whereat Mrs. Travers laughed good-humoredly, and Tom, also laughing, disappeared.

" Tell me, Fanny," said Mrs. Travers, thoughtfully, when they
were left alone, " would it break your heart to keep a shop with
me ? "

" Oh ! to tell the real truth, I do not like the idea of a shop at
all. I always fancy the Honorable Mrs. Danby turning up to
buy twopence halfpenny worth of wool, and her polite well-bred
surprise at finding you and me there. But Kate, dear ! rather
than be parted from you, I would help you to keep a rag and
bone shop ! " cried Fanny, heartily, falling on her neck and kissing her. " Only you must mind what Tom says. He knows
everything ! and, Kate—I did not like to mention it before him—
but there is that beautiful pearl locket and the turquoise bracelet
you gave me ! you do not suppose I am going to keep them.
There ! " taking two cases from her pocket, " I got them out
when I heard you say you were going to look over your things ;
and," continued Fanny, blushing, " I have five pounds left of
what you are pleased to call my quarter's salary—there it is ! I
am ashamed to have so little, and I would not even have that,
only it is so soon after quarter-day."

" I think, dear Fan, we may spare my little gifts ! at least, at
present. But I will gratefully accept the money. Keep a sovereign, just to keep you from being penniless ! "

" Oh ! I am nothing of the kind. I have five shillings left !
More, Kate—dearest Kate,—than I had when you took me in ! "
Another hug.

" Well, go to bed, dear ! " returned the young widow. " We
can do no more at present. I believe, Fanny, there is a happy
future before you—and for myself ! Somehow, I cannot fear, so
long as I can work in my own way."

Fanny disappeared ; but Kate Travers sat long alone, and in
profound meditation.

CHAPTER X.

TIME seemed very long to our dispossessed heroine and her dependents. While Tom Reed sought, with all the energy and shrewdness for which he was remarkable, to do the best for his friend. Of the three, Fanny seemed to bear the lingering days best. Mrs. Travers noticed that since her visit to the theatre under her cousin's escort, there had been a remarkable look of quiet happiness in her eyes, a little less of flightiness in her conversation, from which she drew her own conclusions, though she asked no injudicious questions.

Meantime the reply to her inquiries respecting the fancy-work business duly arrived, and seemed satisfactory and straightforward. The last possessor had maintained an invalid husband and a daughter besides herself upon 'the proceeds. The daughter was married and in easy circumstances, so was not disposed to carry on the undertaking. She therefore wished to sell it as soon as possible, and sink the money and some small savings in a life annuity for her father. The sum asked (four hundred pounds), though not large, was the difficulty, as Mrs. Travers found the prices offered for her jewels were far below what she had anticipated.

If she had any other scheme within the bounds of reason on foot, Reed said, she might take counsel with, and obtain assistance from, Mr. Wall, though he was deeply incensed by her refusal of Sir Hugh Galbraith's offer.

But one of Mrs. Travers's objects, indeed, her chief object, seemed a desire to vanish from the scene into obscurity, at least for the present. "And," she thought, for she was pondering these things as usual, while dressing one morning, a few days after the interview last described, " I must not forget Mrs. Bell, poor old Gregory's daughter. I daresay she knows nothing of the changes that have taken place. I must let her know that it is out of my power to fulfill my promise of a further gift. What a disappointment it will be to her ! I will call upon her to-day ; and I will also see Mr. Wall, and ask him to intercede with Sir Hugh, and induce him to make her some small allowance or present. I dread seeing that severe lawyer, but I must, and this is a topic that will nerve me."

Mrs. Travers's expectations of a chilling reception were amply fulfilled. Mr. Wall was expressively silent on the subject which was uppermost in the thoughts of each, though he slightly relaxed the terrors of his countenance, as the young widow, her violet blue eyes suffused with tears, thanked him, in her low, clear tones, for the friendly interest he had shown in her.

" I could have done much more for you had you acted with

the same common sense you have hitherto shown," he replied, gloomily. And Mrs. Travers remarked, with an inward smile, the subtle change in his tone. It was far from being careless or disrespectful; but it was perceptibly more familiar than in the days so short a time ago—yet so infinitely far back—when she was surrounded by the halo of that divinity which doth hedge the owner of real and personal property.

"And have you formed any plans?—though perhaps you do not care to divulge them to a person whose advice was so unacceptable."

"I cannot fix anything until some jewels I have are disposed of. I have thought of going on the Continent. I know German and Germany tolerably; and it has been suggested that I should try and establish a school for English girls in one of the Rhine towns," returned Mrs. Travers, hesitatingly.

"Ha! not a bad idea. And the jewels—may I ask their probable value?"

"Seven or eight hundred pounds. At least, they cost that sum. Do you think you could assist me to dispose of them?"

"I do not think I could. I *don't* think I could; but you might let me see them," added the worthy lawyer, melting more and more.

"I will. And now, Mr. Wall, I have a great favor to ask," began Mrs. Travers, and proceeded to unfold her benevolent plan of representing poor Mrs. Bell's case to Sir Hugh Galbraith.

But this proposition had a most unfortunate effect in rousing Mr. Wall's indignation at the idea of asking that consideration for another, which she rejected for herself; and he absolutely refused. "The application, if it be made, should come through Mr. Ford," concluded the lawyer, in a chilling voice.

"But may he not be dismissed by this time?" asked Mrs. Travers.

"I should say certainly not. Ford is too essential to the winding up of the business, if it is to be wound up. I should not be surprised if Sir Hugh Galbraith bestows upon him the five hundred originally bequeathed. If he is wise, he will; and I daresay *he* will not reject it."

"Then I shall ask Mr. Ford's assistance," replied Mrs. Travers, with some spirit, and rising as she spoke. "I need not trespass any longer on your time. If we should not meet again, pray remember I shall always be grateful for your friendliness; and I consider your displeasure proves a high degree of friendliness," concluded the young widow, holding out her hand, with a smile half sad, half playful.

The old lawyer, slightly thawing once more, began, "I shall

always be happy to be of use to you." Then, checking himself, added, "But excuse me, no one can be of use to a willful woman."

"Good-bye," returned Mrs. Travers, declining the combat; and she hastily left the room.

It surprised her to feel such a choking sensation in her throat when she found herself once more alone and in the street. Was her courage going to fail? That must not be. Yet it was rather appalling to look round and see everyone against her— Tom, Mr. Wall, Fanny, and, last, far from least, Mills. Could she alone be right and all these wrong? How hard it is to have faith in one's own convictions, especially for those frank minds who can believe heartily, and are yet free from obstinacy. "Nevertheless, I will persevere. If I can muster money enough for this purchase, I will make it. What a grand triumph it would be to make a business pay! to prove myself the best judge of my own affairs, even if my other 'dim religious' hope be unfulfilled. Yet I risk and resign much."

So thinking, she persevered in a hot, dusty walk, and a still hotter, dustier "ride" in an omnibus, in order to reach Mrs. Bell's abode.

It was past four o'clock, and she was delighted to see quite a stream of little girls, bag or satchel in hand, issuing from the door. The whole aspect of the house was changed, as was also that of Mrs. Bell and her daughter.

"I am sorry to be the bearer of what is bad news for us both, Mrs. Bell," she began, and at once plunged into the narrative of her changed fortunes; her listener's countenance fell as she proceeded.

"Dear me," she observed, when Mrs. Travers stopped, "I can hardly believe it! It *is* a shame, and you can do nothing? Surely the law can stop such a will as that?"

"I fear not, Mrs. Bell. Pray have you ever heard your father speak of having written out a will at Mr. Travers's dictation?"

"I have heard something about it, but I forget what. What was it now?" striving painfully to remember, while she mechanically pleated up the edge of a large black stuff apron which covered her dress. "It was something I heard my father say one evening, not long before my brother sailed last time, nearly a year ago, about working after hours for Mr. Travers, and that / he thought he ought to have a rise when Mr. Travers trusted him to do private business he did not give even to Mr. Ford. I think those were his words."

"Do you think your brother would know anything more?" asked Mrs. Travers, eagerly.

"He might, and he might not. You see John has a great deal on his mind; but that is all *I* remember."

" When do you expect Captain Gregory back ? "

" I do not exactly know. He was to have been home next month, but my sister-in-law had a letter last week, and he is taken up to carry rice somewhere in India, and he does not seem to know when he will be home."

" You will let me know whenever he returns, will you not ? " said Mrs. Travers, impressively.

" You may depend upon me."

" Mrs. Travers then proceeded to tell her poor, downcast *protégée* of her intended application to Sir Hugh Galbraith, with what success she could not pretend to foresee, and after some kindly, friendly talk, left Mrs. Bell somewhat cheered, and leaving her own address to Reed's care.

It was late, and she felt greatly wearied when she reached her lodgings; and although Mrs. Mills met her with many half-testy, half-sympathetic expressions of regret that she should go and just wear herself out, she was wonderfully disappointed to find that Fanny had gone away with Mr. Reed for a walk in the park just before she had come in.

But she was not left long alone : by the time tea was prepared the cousins returned, and Mrs. Travers fancied there was the promise of something cheering in the expression of Tom Reed's countenance. He said nothing, however, till the tea-things were removed, and they were once more in committee.

" Well," he exclaimed, " I think I have found a chance for disposing of the diamonds at last, Mrs. Travers. A friend of our chief, a young fellow from Lancashire, who is up in town spending his money and seeing life, wants to present a lady with some diamonds—I suppose his *fiancée*. I overheard him ask Renington (that is our editor) what a regular turn out would be likely to cost ? He said, 'Oh, eight hundred or a thousand pounds.' This seemed to stagger our young rustic ; so I put in my oar. ' I could get you a first-rate set for four hundred, good as new, from one of the first houses in London '—yours were from H——, were they not ? He pricked up his ears at this, and, in short, I have agreed to show him the jewels, if you will trust them with me."

" What a good fellow you are, Tom," cried Mrs. Travers. " You never lose a chance."

" And be sure you make him pay four hundred guineas ! " exclaimed Fanny.

" Oh, you greedy creature ! No, Tom ; I shall be quite satisfied if I can get what they cost."

" Diamonds is 'riz' since those were bought," returned Reed, solemnly. " The young man shall have them at a trifle below the

4*

present value—if he will buy them. You will please to remember there is an "if" in the case."

"I am quite aware of it," said Mrs. Travers. "There, Fanny, is the key of my dressing-box: bring down the three red morocco cases." Then, as she left the room, she added, "How well Fan looks, and what a comfort she is to me! I do hope, Tom, you will not, as her next of kin, raise any serious objection to her joining me in business. I would not feel justified in deliberately opposing you."

"I do not think she would mind me if I did," returned Reed, smiling and shrugging his shoulders. "But I have no right to interfere—at present. Remember, this admission is without prejudice to any future interference I may feel entitled to."

"I understand," replied Mrs. Travers, smiling kindly upon him.

"For the present we must only think of you, and how best to help you," he resumed; "and though your scheme at first seemed the maddest idea, I begin to think it might be managed if you had the least knowledge of business; but I am afraid you will come to grief."

"I think I shall manage it," said Kate Travers, thoughtfully, "if I can only get a margin, after the purchase, to live upon for the first year, and make the business feed itself."

"And what margin would you require?"

"Well, the rent is low, and we have plenty of clothes: I daresay a hundred and thirty or forty pounds."

"A hundred and thirty pounds!" echoed Tom. "You will never do it."

Here Fanny returned with the diamonds. They were again examined and admired. The high preservation of the cases was pointed out as a most favorable circumstance. Then Tom Reed put them in his breast-pocket, buttoned up his coat, and swore melo-dramatically that whoever attempted to take them would first have to rifle his mangled corpse.

"Talking of mangling, Tom," said Fanny, "I saw that dreadful-looking man you spoke to at Waterloo Station the day I came from Yorkshire, in the park to-day, sitting under the trees near the canal; but I would not tell you for fear you would speak."

"You saw him, then? So did I; but said nothing, lest you should do anything to attract his attention. Poor devil! he looks worse than ever. I wonder who he has got hold of—a well-dressed, respectable-looking fellow."

"Yes, he was," replied Fanny, "and I have an idea I know his face!"

"Nonsense, Fan!" cried Mrs. Travers. "You are always fancying you remember people."

"I have a wonderful memory for faces," said that young person, shaking her head gravely.

"And now farewell, and peace be with you," said Tom, rising.
"One moment," exclaimed Mrs. Travers. "I had almost forgotten. Have you given Mr. Ford my address?"

"No, I never thought of it."

"I will write to him myself, then. I must see him about
that poor woman, Mrs. Bell, though I would much rather not.
Remember, Tom, should you meet him, not a word of my
plans."

"Sovereign! to hear is to obey."

Writing to ask a favor of Mr. Ford was an especially distasteful task to Kate. She felt it must lead to the unpleasantness
of an interview, there was so much to be discussed between
them. Moreover, she was anxious not to show anything like
resentment for the troubles he was the innocent means of
bringing upon her; and, with the effort to compose a suitable
note, came a curious train of thought. Old feelings of distrust
and undefinable, unreasonable aversion came back upon her;
suspicions she could not drive away, and was ashamed to express, thronged her mind, thick, shapeless, like volumes of
bodiless vapor, too vague to be combated, too pervading to be
resisted.

Yet, if she did not speak her thoughts, how was she ever to
make an onward step in her progress towards unraveling the
mystery of the will! "Ah, there is no use in thinking about it
now. I must wait—I must wait," said Mrs. Travers, with a
sigh, resuming her pen and hastily finishing her note, not at all
to her satisfaction; but she could do no better, so she let it go.

It was speedily answered. Mr. Ford stated, in the best possible English, that he had been somewhat seriously indisposed,
or he should have made an attempt to see Mrs. Travers before;
and, as it was impossible to discuss the matter mentioned in her
note except in a personal interview, he would do himself the
honor of calling on Mrs. Travers on the following Thursday
evening.

Mrs. Travers laid down the note with a sigh, and opened one
from Reed, which informed her that "the Lancashire lad" was
favorably disposed towards the diamonds, but wished to look
about him before purchasing them.

"So there is still an 'if' in the case," wrote Reed, "but it is
no longer in italics."

*   *   *   *   *   *   *

Mrs. Travers was positively startled at the change in Mr.
Ford's appearance when he presented himself on the appointed
evening. He looked years older, grayer, thinner, less erect, and
ghastly pale.

"You must have been ill indeed, Mr. Ford," said the young
widow kindly, as she gave him her hand.

" I have been somewhat seriously unwell, which was very inconvenient, as my services were much wanted. But, Mrs. Travers, to see you here—here, in this mean abode. It is more almost than I can bear!" His voice failed, and he sat down hastily, as if unable to stand.

"Dear me! Have a glass of wine, or a little brandy and water," cried Fanny, quite melted from her hardness of heart by the evident feeling of the obnoxious Mr. Ford.

"Nothing, I thank you—nothing. And Mrs. Travers, it is astonishing to see how well you bear yourself under such a reverse ! And how well you look !"

" I am quite well, and far from hopeless."

" May I ask if you intend to remain here, or—"

" I have made no plan as yet," returned Mrs. Travers, quickly. " In fact, I cannot until Mr. Reed has made some arrangements which he has kindly undertaken for me ; but we think of going on the Continent."

" On the Continent ! " he repeated, and then went on with the sort of deprecatory smile and slight catch in his voice which Mrs. Travers always thought an indication that he was forcing himself to say something he knew to be disagreeable. " It has been some slight consolation to me to reflect that at least you possessed jewels of considerable value. I well remember filling up the checks to pay for them. And it has struck me that my services might be useful in disposing of them."

Mrs. Travers colored vividly. This determination still to interfere in her affairs roused a degree of indignation quite disproportioned to the cause ; but she carefully restrained herself.

" You are very good, Mr. Ford ; but Mr. Reed has undertaken that matter ; so I need not trespass on you. You must be fully occupied, and I fear not equal to much exertion."

Ford looked down and wiped his brow. " I felt obliged to crawl back to the office the day before yesterday," he said, "and there I saw Sir Hugh Galbraith. I cannot say he made a favorable impression upon me. He is a cold, haughty, overbearing man, who, though passably civil, evidently looks upon all the employés of the house as infinitely beneath him. Even if the firm is still kept on, nothing would tempt me to continue in his employment."

" And is the old firm to be broken up ? " asked Mrs. Travers, with deep interest, remembering sadly her own dreams on this subject.

" I do not know certainly ; but I think so. The refusal of Mr. Gervais to act under the will has, I believe, greatly annoyed Sir Hugh. He is, I understand, anxious to realize, and cut all connection with the City. I had an opportunity of speaking to

Sir Hugh Galbraith to-day. When, though much against my inclination, in obedience to your wish, Mrs. Travers, I mentioned Mrs. Bell's case to him, he listened not unfavorably, and said he would consult his solicitors on the subject, and added some remarks very favorable to myself, which yet," added Mr. Ford, fervently, " did little to reconcile me to the terrible change of rulers. Sir Hugh Galbraith, in your place, my dear lady, is an hourly living torture. I—I—cannot stand "—and Mr. Ford again pressed his handkerchief to his brow.

" I trust this man will have some respect for your interests," replied Mrs. Travers, feeling a little puzzled how to reply.

" My interests," he returned, waving his hand, " are of small importance if I only could "—he paused abruptly.

" They are of importance to yourself, at any rate," observed Mrs. Travers, to break the awkward pause which followed.

" Will you excuse me ? " said Ford, with a sort of desperate effort to Fanny ; " but I have a few words to say to Mrs. Travers, which are for her ear alone."

" Certainly," replied Fanny, rising.

" But, Mr. Ford, I have no secrets from Miss Lee," exclaimed Mrs. Travers.

" Nevertheless, I trust you will grant me a few moments," said that gentleman, his brows slightly contracting, as he marked the young widow's substitution of " Miss Lee " for " Fanny," when she spoke of her friend to him.

" Oh, as you will," returned Mrs. Travers, and Fanny left the room. Then a painful silence ensued. At last Mr. Ford began in a tremulous voice, and evidently contending with some strong emotion. " My dear Mrs. Travers, my head is in such painful confusion I scarce know how to express the thoughts that throng upon me. I have known no rest since the discovery of that hateful will. Over and over again I have regretted not de-stroying it—not leaving matters as they were ! But to have in-jured you — to have benefited that haughty, contemptuous fellow ! Can you forgive me ? " He clasped his hands together in an attitude of entreaty, quite carried away beyond his ordi-nary conventionality and studied phraseology by the force of his feelings.

" Pray do not speak in this way, Mr. Ford ! I have nothing to forgive. You have simply done your duty—your unavoidable duty," said Mrs. Travers. Then, fixing her earnest eyes full upon him, she added in a lower, graver tone, " And I pity you—pity you deeply."

Ford, with a rapid, involuntary motion, pressed one hand over his eyes, as if to shut out hers ; but recovering himself immedi-ately, asked quickly, " Pity me ? Why ? I know I am wretched, but why do you compassionate me ? "

" Because you have been the means of causing mortification and loss to one whom you profess to like and respect."

" You are very cruel," cried Ford, his pale face flushing.

" I do not mean to be so," returned Mrs. Travers quietly, and still looking at him.

" Perhaps not ; but hear me. One purpose of my visit to-night is to inform you Sir Hugh Galbraith has expressed his desire that the legacy of five hundred pounds originally left me by Mr. Travers should be paid over at once. He is pleased to say that I have amply deserved it, and he cannot understand why it was struck out. Now, Mrs. Travers, I consider this ought to be yours. It is yours. I will never touch it. By all that I hold sacred, I will never touch it. You will take it, will you not ? " he urged feverishly, rising from his seat and clasping her hand in a burning, trembling grasp.

Mrs. Travers was much moved, but instantly withdrew from his touch.

" It is a very kind, generous impulse that prompts you, Mr. Ford. I shall always remember your offer with gratitude ; but when you are stronger and better able to reflect calmly, you will yourself see the impossibility of my acceptance." .

" I do not see it. The money is of no value to me. I have lived sparingly. I have saved. I have money enough—more than people think ; and I am alone—alone ! "

" Yes, at present," said Mrs. Travers kindly, but firmly, with the indefinable tone of superiority which always subdued, yet maddened, Ford. " But you are quite young enough to form the closest ties—to create a house for yourself ; and hereafter, when you may want to push the fortunes of your children, you will be glad of the money you would now give away."

" Never," he cried, walking up and down the room. " Nothing is of value to me, except so far as it is of use to you. I have injured you. I mean, I have involuntarily been the means of injuring you. Let me atone. All that belongs to me is yours—my whole life, if it can be of the slightest use."

" Mr. Ford, these are expressions I cannot listen to. You are unnerved ; you are not yourself. You must understand that it is impossible I could entertain such a proposition for a moment. I cannot listen to such wild words."

" But I will speak out for once," cried Ford, greatly agitated.

" Why should you despise and turn from me ? What is the difference between us ? When first I knew you, mine was the best position of the two. I always loved you. I strove and saved to make you my wife ; but my master "—with great bitterness—" stepped in and robbed me. And do you think I did not watch how he spoiled your life, and felt nearly mad between a sort of joy to think he was leaving your heart for me, and the bitterest sorrow for you? And then to find you—you that I had always dreamed of as in a measure dependent on me—assume the mastery, and treat me as a favored servant. Oh, Mrs. Travers! Oh, Kate! God pardon you for the suffering you have inflicted on me. Now it is all over. You are poor and alone. I am wealthy compared to you. Take it all! take my whole existence—be my wife. There, I have broken through the strange spell you have always laid upon me. That is my hope—my heart's dearest wish; nothing short of it will satisfy me."

He paused out of breath, his heart heaving, yet not brave enough to diminish by a step the distance between them.

Mrs. Travers was greatly moved; half frightened, half revolted.

"You give me infinite pain," she exclaimed, after a moment's pause.

"Do you not see how distressing, how shocking it must be to a woman so lately widowed to hear such words from any man? They are almost an insult."

"Then," cried Ford, interrupting her, "when may I speak? Some months hence? Oh! I will wait if—"

"*Never* dare to address me in the same strain," said Mrs. Travers, her curious antipathy to the unfortunate Ford flaming up into a sudden activity that quite overcame her self-control. "I do not mean any disrespect to you. I know that your position was as good as my own; but I now represent my late husband, and your words are an unseemly anomaly. More. However worthy of regard, it is not always given to men to meet with reciprocity. Position out of the question, you should have seen there was no chance for you with me. We can never meet again. I—I do not want to be harsh or unfeeling, but you have brought this on yourself How *dared* you think of me with such feelings during your master's life! We must never meet again."

"Enough," cried Ford; "you have finished your work and restored me some strength. Good evening, Mrs. Travers. In all probability your wish will be fulfilled. We may never meet again; but you may regret it."

With a ghastly pale face and gleaming eyes, full of rage and hatred, Mr. Ford snatched up his hat and departed.

Mrs. Travers sat down to collect and recover herself before meeting Fanny Lee. She was considerably puzzled by her own emotions. Here she was, a democrat by conviction, recognizing the right of men to work their way up from the lowest rung of the social ladder. Why should she be so indignant with her

husband's managing clerk for raising his eyes to her? Had it
been Tom Reed, or another Mr. Travers, or even that starched
Mr. Wall—her acquaintance with gentlemen was very limited—
she would no doubt have refused them all, and thought they
were rather premature ; but she would have done so with tenderness and sympathy, and certainly without indignation. Why,
then, did she feel so angry and degraded in her own eyes? Is
it because Nature has her own nobles, amid which Mr. Ford
certainly held no place ? But then, did Tom, or Mr. Wall, or
even Mr. Travers? Yes ; these men had reached manhood.
They were straightforward, and gifted with the average pluck
of every day. Mr. Ford was not unkindly or uncultivated ; he
was very nearly a gentleman. It was the sort of nameless moral
slinking—a constant soreness at the nonrecognition of claims he
dared not uphold—a serpent-like mingling of the crawl and the
sting, from which Mrs. Travers shrank, revolted and antagonis-
tic.

"And perhaps this is all owing to some defect in the circula-
tion, or the nerves, or some of the marvelous mechanism by
which the inner self works," she thought. "Why, then, do I
feel disgust instead of compassion? Is this instinct in me
wrong or false, and ought I to control it with reason ? Heigho !
I shall find no time for such puzzles when I am matching wools
and tracing patterns at Pierstoffe. I wish I was there now."

CHAPTER XI.

THE next morning brought a welcome distraction to Mrs.
Travers's thoughts in the shape of an answer from the agent
to whom she had written for further information respecting the
fancy business. He stated that the price asked included furniture and fittings, which were certainly worth two hundred
pounds, and suggested a personal interview, as there were other
parties making inquiries, and she had better not lose time.

This communication sent her in haste to try and catch Tom
Reed before he left his chambers for the day ; but she missed
him, and she was obliged to wait with what patience she could
till evening brought him in reply to an urgent note.

"Four hundred pounds," said their kindly mentor ; "four of
my teeth sooner ! Look here, Mrs. Travers, I have been making all sorts of inquiries, and I imagine the sea-side party will
jump at three hundred ; if not, an additional ten or fifteen will
clinch the matter,—that is to say, unless you take my advice and
give it up. And I have seen my Lancashire friend. He has
been making inquiries, too, and is willing to give three hundred

for the diamonds ; that is not so bad, and I think you had better
take it. You would not get so much from any jeweler."

" Oh ! what a mean, stingy creature your Lancashire friend
must be. Did you tell him what they cost ? " cried Fanny.

" Indeed I did not, or he would not have offered so much."

" Tom ! " exclaimed Mrs. Travers. " I have a sudden in-
spiration. I will 'not sell any more. The diamonds are your
friend's at his price. Get the money as soon as you can, but all
the rest I will take to those people you call ' Relatives.' "

" I Lombardi ? " asked Tom ; " pawnbrokers—not to be un-
intelligible ? "

" Exactly. They may give me more than the jewelers, thinking that I will release them."

" Relatives of that class are not given to flights of imagination,"
remarked Tom.

" At any rate I shall have the chance of redeeming them ;
and if I disprove that will, I shall," said Mrs. Travers.

Tom shook his head ; while Fanny observed, parenthetically,
" And you will ! as sure as I see Tom shaking his head and
making himself ridiculous." Mrs. Travers went on, not heeding the interruption.

" At the worst, they can but go. Then I need not part with
all at once, you know. Will you help me in this too, Tom ? "

" It is not such a bad idea," said her chivalrous counselor ;
" and in your cause I'll beard every ' uncle' in London in his own
particular den."

" You are a darling," said Fanny.

" You're another," retorted her cousin. " And remember,
Mrs. Travers," he continued, " you are on no account to go near
those Size Lane people without me. It would be the spider and
the fly over again."

The progress of a transaction such as Kate Travers, with
Reed's help, was now trying to bring to a conclusion, though
deeply interesting to the parties concerned, is not exciting to
read about. Suffice it to say, the bargain was accomplished
with the proviso that Mrs. Travers was to inspect the shop and
house herself, and personally test the business by residing on
the premises for a fortnight, before paying over the price, which
was to be, as Tom suggested, three hundred pounds for all.

" Pierstoffe, Maltshire," read Tom Reed from a " Guide Book,"
the evening after matters had so far been arranged. " Population, 4372½."

" You have added the half yourself, surely, Tom."

" Silence, Fanny, do not interrupt the lecture. A picturesque
and rising town, in much request as a bathing-place. It commands a fine prospect of cliff and sea, and several blocks of

commodious houses have lately been erected. Hotels : ' The
Marine Hotel,' ' The Queen's,' and ' The Robinson Crusoe.' Objects of interest in the neighborhood : Colnebrooke Castle, the
seat of Sir Hervey Brooke, Bart., D. L. ; Acol Court, the residence
of Colonel Craycroft, J. P. ; Weston, formerly a moated grange ;
and the ruins of St. Olave's Priory, all within an easy drive.
Distance from London, four hours and fifteen minutes. Express,
three hours and a half."

" I shall always travel express when I come to see you," said
Tom, shutting up his book.   " But I am afraid a population of
4372 will not supply custom to the extent of twenty pounds a
week, as that man asserted were the trade returns of the ' Berlin
Bazaar.' "

" No, I do not expect so much as that," observed Mrs. Travers.
" But remember — he said in the season.   By the way, I am
glad our future abode has a title already.   I would rather not
have an assumed name over the shop."

" Yes ; by the way, I observed Hook addressed you as Mrs.
Temple. "

" I do not intend to resume that of Travers until I regain the
property that ought to go with it," said Mrs. Travers, closing
her mouth tightly.   " So begin to practice at once, Fanny."

" I am sure I shall never remember."

" Is it wise to change your name ? " asked Reed.

" Yes, dear Tom ; I want to be altogether lost for a while.   I
shall be happier for feeling I have left no traces."

" And who would trace you ? "

" Oh, I do not know—Mr. Ford, perhaps.   And then that
horrid man is tormenting me to accept his miserable offer of an
allowance.   I had another note from Mr. Wall to-day : I am
sure Sir Hugh feels insecure, or he would not press the matter."
Tom shook his head incredulously.

" I should not be surprised if he induced Mr. Ford to perse-
cute me about it," Mrs. Travers went on.   " And now, Tom
and Fanny, for my latest scheme.   I am to go down to Pierstoffe
on Wednesday—this is Saturday—Monday our week in these
lodgings expires.   Fanny and Mills must live somewhere while
I am studying trade under the excellent young lady whom Mr.
Hook describes as left in charge.   I propose that we all go over
to Boulogne ; I know it a little ; I was at school there for a few
months before I went to Germany ; apartments are cheap ; I
shall leave Fanny there with Mills until I am ready to receive
them, and return on Wednesday to go down to Pierstoffe.   You
see " (drawing a paper from her pocket) " a steamer sails for
Boulogne from London Bridge on Monday evening at six.   I
will thus give every one the slip, and will be able, when writing

to Mr. Wall, to say with truth that I leave London for the Continent on Monday. You will keep our heavy boxes, Tom, and guard my address religiously."

To this, after some discussion and remonstrances from Fanny, who strongly objected to be left alone with Mills, all agreed.

Monday was a close, damp day, with an occasional drizzle of rain, most depressing to the spirits, and poor Fanny's were at the lowest ebb. Mrs. Mills was calm and resigned. Her beloved mistress had talked long and confidentially with her, and succeeded in piercing the rough and bristly exterior husk of the old woman's nature, and touching the sound, good heart that lay within ; so for a while Mills was lifted above her crotchets and ill tempers, and graciously promised to take care of Fanny. Mrs. Travers was the unflagging leader of the expedition, for Tom Reed, in his ardent sympathy and efforts to console his cousin, was less efficient than usual.

" I'll come and see you, Fanny, in a week or ten days—I will, indeed. I will run over next Saturday till Monday, and by that time you and Mrs. Mills will be qualified to lionize me all over ' our French watering-place,' as Dickens calls it."

" But it will cost you such a heap of money," said the tearful Fanny.

They were now somewhat tightly packed in a cab, and somewhat painfully crawling through the city.

" Who is that man ? " cried Tom, sharply, to Mrs. Travers.

" What man ? "

" The man that just passed now, and crossed under the horse's nose—you bowed to him."

" Oh, that was one of poor Mr. Travers's clerks—Poole—the witness to the will."

" Yes, I remember him now."

" Why, that was the man we saw the other day in the park," said Fanny, " was it not, Tom ? "

" I think you must be mistaken."

At last they reached the steamer, Tom Reed exerting himself to the last to secure what comfort he could for them in that abode of misery, the ladies' cabin. He bid Fanny a private adieu at the foot of the companion ladder, and then followed Mrs. Travers, who had gone on deck. " Good-by ! God bless you ! You are the best of good fellows, Tom," she said, holding his hand in both her own.

" And you—I can only say you are no end of a brick. Good-by ; you will be off in another moment," and Tom hurried on shore.

*   *   *   *   *

Pierstoffe was not unfaithfully described in the advertisement which had fascinated Kate Travers as a thriving town. Originally a fishing, smuggling village, the latter line of business had created a certain degree of wealth, and the style of houses which the successful owners of the various schooners and luggers plying between Pierstoffe and the coasts of France and Holland built for themselves in later years were of a very superior description from the lowly cottages which used to cluster round the "point," as it was emphatically called. The point being the southern promontory in which a bold range of cliffs ended, and which sheltered the wide open bay from the prevalent winds. But the cottages, the original nucleus from which Pierstoffe had sprung, had been pulled down more than ten years before, and an enterprising builder had erected in their place, and on the very verge of the shore, a huge, square, hideous marine hotel, with a sea wall and a terrace, a ladies' bathing place at one side, and, screened from observation, a gentlemen's on the other. Having accomplished this patriotic work, he smashed up, and other men entered into his labors.

Pierstoffe began to look up, and a row of lodging houses were built close down on the sea by the sons and grandsons of the old smugglers, now citizens of credit and renown, and in front of a little, narrow, tortuous street of shabby shops which crept along the base of the overhanging cliffs, to where they sunk somewhat suddenly into a valley which widened as it ran inland, and where the sweep of the bay compelled the new houses to cease, and permit some of the better and later edifices of old Pierstoffe still to face the sea, where, on a wide slip, the pleasure-skiffs lay drawn up for hire, and where the fishing-boats came in, and the weather-beaten fishermen disentangled their silvery, scaly treasures from the dark-brown nets.

Here the old coach-road turned inwards, and a few furlongs further bifurcated, one line ascending by steep zigzags to the opposite heights, the other leading away down the valley to where the open country, rich in corn-fields and pastures, with patches of woodland sheltered by the high cliffs from easterly gales, afforded first-rate sport to a fox-hunting gentry. Further on, past the slip, were the most genteel, the most costly, and the newest houses in Pierstoffe, called the North Parade, behind which the cliffs again rose to a great height. Many improvements were being carried on. A branch line from the " East Mercian, Stoneborough, and Barmouth Junction " had been brought by a tunnel almost to the door of the Marine Hotel, and a small pier was being built also near that favored spot, where summer sailors might more conveniently land from their pretty vessels. There was a library and reading-room also, where a visitor's book was kept, and there was talk of a yacht club ; but they

had got no further than erecting a flag-staff before the library
on the esplanade, whence the flag of the club was to float when
ever the one and the other had been called into existence.

Such were the principal points of the residence Mrs. Travers
had chosen. She was very weary, and consequently dispirited
when she reached her destination by the last train. It was dusk,
but not quite dark, and she could trace the outlines of the cliffs
and bay as she stood on the open space before the hotel, while
a porter called a cab—or, as it is usually called out of London,
"a fly" (will some Max Müller of the future account for this
variation in the growth of language?) The soft salt breeze (it was
a lovely April night), came to her cheek like a caress. The
breath of the sea seemed to call back her scattered forces, and she
had roused herself from the weariness of spirit which had hung
upon her since she had parted with Fanny and Mills, by the
time a very stuffy conveyance had rattled her over some rough
pavement, and through a street so narrow that she wondered
the jolting did not overturn her vehicle into a shop window on
the right hand or on the left. Then she felt once more in the
open, and heard the gentle dash of the waves as the driver
drew up at a corner house.

"This is it ma'am—' Berlin Bazaar.'"

"Will you please stop at the private door round the corner?"
said a shrill, treble voice, and a dim figure, tall and narrow, appeared at the shop door.

A small boy was putting up the shutters (the early "closing
movement" had always been moving at Pierstoffe), who hastily
desisted and ran round to carry up the luggage. The next moment Mrs. Temple (as we must call her in future) stood in a
short, wide, low, panneled passage, where a thin, angular female,
with flat bands of hair secured by a couple of rows of narrow
black velvet and a high back-comb, held a tall thin candle in a
brass candlestick. She was evidently an elderly young lady,
with a sweet simper, which displayed very large teeth—in fact,
her bony system was largly developed. She produced on Mrs.
Temple a general impression of being brown. Her dress was
brown merino, so tightly and accurately fitting, that it conveyed
the idea that she had been melted down and poured into a
brown mould. Her neat collar was fastened with a brown bow
of ribbon, her hands were covered with brown leather mittens,
and her complexion was not many shades lighter.

"Mrs. Temple, I am sure I am very glad you have arrived,"
she said, with a gracious bend, which made the composite grease
of her candle drip over. "I expected you somewhat earlier."

"Miss Potter, I suppose?" returned the young widow
pleasantly. "I hoped to have been here earlier, but I have had
a long journey."

"Dear, dear ! I daresay you are quite overcome with fatigue Here, Sarah, take up Mrs. Temple's box. Perhaps you will step into our little sitting-room at once." And Miss Potter, with the most scrupulous politeness, and holding the candle above her head, opened a side door and ushered her guest into a long, low room, also panneled, with a narrow door at the opposite angle from where they entered, and beside it, stretching towards the fireplace, was a long window, not more than one pane in height, but many in width, across which hung a muslin curtain.

A small fire burned in an old-fashioned grate, with wide hobs and extensive "cheeks," to limit its dimensions, and before it stood a three-legged iron stand, or " footman," with a carefully covered dish upon it. A table set with tea-things stood very near the window, and a small copper kettle hummed upon the fire.

"I am very thankful to be here," said Mrs. Temple, looking round her, not displeased by the aspect of things, as she untied her bonnet and laid it aside. "I hope my late arrival has caused you no inconvenience."

"Oh, none in the least, I assure you, ma'am," said Miss Potter, bustling about actively to get the tea. "And I think you will like the place and the business. Poor Mrs. Browne, the late owner, as nice a woman as ever lived, did not make it what it might be, as I have told her times and times ; but it is steady, and regular, and particularly genteel." Miss Potter, when not excited, talked in a loud impressive whisper. "It is like keeping a stall at a fancy fair, in a manner of speaking. Indeed, I tell my brother—my brother is in Australia in a very large way of business, and I am going out to him. I should have done so long since, but that I could not leave Mrs. Browne ; for as she said to me over and over again, 'If you leave me, Maria' (my name is Maria), 'my whole dependence is gone ; for Mrs. Penny' (that is her daughter) 'is not exactly the sort of'—but there, censoriousness is not my line. Poor dear soul, I was her whole stay." By this time Miss Potter had wandered through so many parentheses, that she had forgotten what she had told her brother, so wisely dropped the subject, and allowed Kate to take her tea in comparative quiet.

Although her acquaintance with Miss Potter soon came to an end, and she dropped out of her life altogether, Kate Travers never forgot the relief which the even flow of her unoffending though very small talk proved on that trying night. It gave a welcome tinge of the ludicrous to the awful strangeness of her position ; it held back the rising tide of sorrowful, half-indignant recollections that threatened to engulf her courage and composure, as gently sloping sandy beaches hold back the ocean. Then

the bird's eye view of the "business" which her ready intelligence gathered from this chatter, roused her interest in what
had now become her career, and so the first evening, in what
was to be her new home, passed over less painfully than she expected.

She woke early the next morning, and soon was up and
dressed. A fresh breeze from the southeast was crisping the
bay into short tossing foam-crested waves, and dashing them
with a sound full of lust and vigor upon the slip before described, and which her window overlooked. The bright clear
sunshine, the wide stretch of open sea, the tall cliffs which sheltered the little town to the north, and of which she caught a
glimpse on her left, all seemed to her very good. Her spirit roused
itself in response to the tumultuous activity of the nature she
gazed upon, and seemed to promise her success. To succeed in
a "Berlin Bazaar," is not an "o'er-vaulting ambition," scarcely
in accord with the idea of "deep calling unto deep," which certainly suggested itself to the young widow, as she stood gazing
at the wild play of the waters, and conscious of the sympathy
between her inner self and the speechless world without ; the
"voice" of which is yet to articulate. But *not* to succeed in this
humble enterprise, implied so terrible a defeat, such an incapacity
on her part to judge for herself, and to stand alone, that success
was thrown up into colossal proportions by the depth of shadow
behind it. Shaking off her thought fit, Mrs. Temple, as she
schooled herself to think she was, descended to the parlor where
she had partaken of tea the night before, and found a small girl
in a long sort of linen bib that reached from her throat to her
instep, setting the breakfast things ; she stopped short and
dropped a sort of staccato courtesy, when she perceived the
strange lady, continuing to gaze at her with a scared expression
and without moving.

"I suppose you are the housemaid ?" said Mrs. Temple,
good-naturedly seeking to break the spell by the charm of
speech.

" Yes 'm,—and I does the cooking, too 'm ; only mother comes
in twice a week to help clean up. Leastways, she used—but I
does all for Miss Potter, now," said the small statue, restored to
consciousness.

"Is Miss Potter up, yet ?" asked Mrs. Temple, measuring the
child in her mind, and conjecturing whether she might do for an
assistant to Mills—for Mills could not manage everything quite
alone.

"Oh, yes 'm ! Miss Potter is dusting of the shop. I was to
tell her when you comed down,—I'll just get the kettle."

Though April was drawing to a close, a fire was not unacceptable in the chill freshness of a sea-side morning, and Mrs. Temple had placed one foot upon the fender, when Miss Potter came in through the narrow door which led into the shop.

"Dear, dear! I did not know you were down. I hope you have not been waiting long." Miss Potter held a feather-broom and a duster, and another cleaner duster was tied over her head. She was attired in a print morning-wrapper, washed out to a dim ochre tint. "I told that girl to let me know directly you were down ; but she is so stupid."

Mrs. Temple exonerated the girl, and Miss Potter went on—

"I am glad you are an early riser—I always was—and it's a great thing *here*. You see, ours is that sort of genteel business, that there is no need to open much before ten. Indeed, for that matter, before eleven, only for the appearance ! and one can get a deal done between an eight o'clock breakfast and ten—as you will find. I think you said you were never in business before ? "

"Never," said Kate.

Miss Potter shook her head gloomily as she made the tea. "Business is uphill work for them that haven't been brought up to it."

"Yet, it cannot be so mysterious that a woman of my age cannot learn it," replied Kate ; and added, smiling, "with your good help."

"Oh, I am sure I am willing to do the best I can ; but I can't help thinking that a little outlay would fetch up the business wonderfully. I always told poor dear Mrs. Browne that she starved it ! Indeed, at one time, when I thought of taking it myself, I used to be rather annoyed. Then, poor Mrs. Browne had heavy expenses. Now, you see, you have no husband," as if this was an enormous advantage in an economic point of view. "At least—you'll excuse me—I understood you were a widow ? "

"I am," said Mrs. Temple, smiling ; while her eyes filled with tears, at the recollection of the husband who had so carefully guarded her from all of pain, save what his own jealous love inflicted.

"Poor Mrs. Browne suffered a deal with hers. I am sure I little thought she would go before him ! " in a slightly injured tone, as if Providence had made a decided mistake. "But, though I do not mean. the least disrespect to you, I can't say I have any right to like widows ! "

"I am sorry to hear it ! May I ask why ? "

"Well," with a deep sigh, "if it wasn't for one, I would be in a very different position to what I am." Whereupon Miss Potter plunged into a very lengthy parenthetical history of certain love passages which had passed between herself and one of the assistants at Mr. Turner's. This was *the* shop *par excellence* of Pierstoffe—a most elegant young man from London—quite a "millingtary" looking young man; but a designing widow, nothing at all to look at, the widow of a small farmer in the neighborhood, had won him from her, and they were now married and established in quite a large business in Stoneborough. "She had a little money," concluded Miss Potter, with a deep sigh, "and I believe he has never regretted it but once, and that was always."

"Probably it was the widow's money, not the widow, which attracted him," began Mrs. Temple in a consolatory tone; but she was interrupted by a sharp click and the convulsive tinkle of a little bell, whereupon Miss Potter started to her feet, exclaiming, "Dear, dear! I had no idea the time was running on so," and darted into the shop. Mrs. Temple, wondering at the revelations she had just heard, almost as much as if one of the wooden dolls of a past generation had opened its vermilion lips to speak of a heart within, could not resist looking with some curiosity through the wide, low window from which the blind was partially withdrawn. A small child in hobnailed shoes, whose snubby nose was scarce on a level with the counter, was holding up a penny in a paw as brown as the coin, and Miss Potter was drawing forth two skeins of black wool from a carefully papered parcel.

"My first customer," thought Kate, "and a specimen of the gentility of my business! I shall do away with that bell; it reminds me of poor old Sally Martin's sweety shop at Cullingford, where Tom used to spend so many pennies." Here Miss Potter returned, and proposed to show her over the house before any one else came.

It was a better sort of abode than Mrs. Temple had hoped for. Only two stories high, it was larger than it looked; for, being built on a corner piece of ground, its depth was greater than its frontage. The centre was divided into good square rooms, leaving snippets of space to form curious little crooked chambers, and three-cornered cupboards with odd, unexpected steps leading to them. The furniture was scanty but clean, the best things being placed in a sitting-room upstairs, which possessed a large window over the front door, commanding the Stoneborough Road and the new North Parade houses. Next to this was the bedroom which had been prepared for Mrs. Temple. Behind these, somewhat shut in by the high ground at the back, were three other bedrooms. Below the shop and parlor before described, at the other side of the hall, a pleasant, retired sitting-room with one large window opening on a neglected garden, which lay between the house and the lower cliff, which there sloped steeply down to the roadway. The kitchen

5

came next, with various convenient off-shoots in the shape of sculleries and wash-houses. "If the business will only answer. I have not made a bad bargain," thought Mrs. Temple.

Once or twice in the course of their inspection, Miss Potter had been called away by a shrill yell of "Shop!" from the diminutive girl, and had each time returned breathless, exclaiming at the unusual number of early customers.

"Poor dear Mrs. Browne was rather fortunate latterly in letting the upstairs rooms. Dr. Slade was a very good friend to her in that way, though he is rather peculiar; but he used to recommend invalid gentlemen—two guineas a week for the season, everything included."

"Oh! she let lodgings?" asked Mrs. Temple, smiling to herself at the turn of Fortune's wheel which had brought her back to the point from whence she had started.

"I think I shall do the same; it will lighten the rent."

"Oh, considerably, I assure you! but we had better go into the shop now."

CHAPTER XII.

THIS first day was both wearisome and depressing. Mrs. Temple felt bewildered by the effort to understand the mystery of marks and all the technicalities which the accomplished Miss Potter so glibly poured forth, and cast down by the trifling nature of the sales. A few girls, with broad, country accents, and exceedingly unpolished manners, came in for pennyworths of this and sixpence worth of the other. One young lady, the clergyman's daughter Miss Potter said, asked for some traced muslin-work, which cost the large sum of two shillings and sixpence. And a huge, good-humored looking farmer, with yellow leggings, a low-crowned hat, a whip, spurs, and a fiery-red face, who called Mrs. Temple "mum," brought a considerably-rubbed Berlin wool pattern, and asked that all the requisite wools might be supplied, and he would call for the parcel on his way home in a couple of hours, which he did, and paid for it standing in the doorway, his face redder than ever, the reins of his nag over one arm, his whip under the other, while he exclaimed at the cost of "such-like darned fiddle-faddles, and hoped his lass would be satisfied now."

"This has not been a fair average day," said Miss Potter, as she counted up the day's gain, and found it amounted to eight shillings and fivepence-halfpenny. "In short, I have never known it so low."

"That is curious," said Mrs. Temple, dryly and discouragingly.

"It is," returned Miss Potter, candidly; "but I wouldn't mind if I were you. There are many things to account for a temporary depression. It is just after the Easter holidays; and the young ladies at Miss Monitor's have scarcely settled to their work and their studies. And a great archery *fête* at Colnebrook Castle was to come off yesterday, you see ; so none of the county ladies would have time to think of fancywork the very day after. You must just wait a bit."

And the young widow resolved to be patient, more especially as she liked the look of the place, and felt still more disposed towards it after an evening stroll past the North Parade houses, to where the roadway widened into a graveled sweep, from which she discovered a narrow path leading along the base of the cliffs, now descending almost to the beach, now climbing steeply up over some projecting crag, which was lashed or caressed by the waves at high water. Following this, in some places, rather giddy footway, Mrs. Temple reached a spot where a sudden inward curve of the cliffs formed a tiny bay. The path she had followed zigzagged upwards to a coast-guard station, but another branched off here, and led gently down a few paces to a little rough wooden jetty, bleached almost ghastly white by the constant wash of the sea ; while some outlying standing timbers, set up to break the force of the waves, were covered with black-green seaweed, which, as the tide was now half high, and coming in, floated mournfully on the waters, like the long locks of some drowning creature. The shelter afforded here had permitted a growth of grass and brambles mixed with the gorse, now in full yellow bloom, and loading the air with its honeyed sweetness, to tone down the rugged grandeur of the cliff, and in the deeper hollow where the slope was least steep, and more of soil would lie, a small group of stunted oak trees nestled, throwing out thick gnarled branches with the ungainly strength of misshapen dwarfs.

The utter silence, the unspeakable repose enchanted Kate. She descended to the little pier, and strolled leisurely along it, resting for awhile on a low bench at the end, and drinking in the loveliness of sea and sky. By and by, a gray-bearded coast-guard's man, in a little boat, pulled round one of the points which sheltered the bay, and fastened his skiff to the pier, ascending by a straight sort of ladder made between the timbers, with a goodly basket of fish on his arm, and a loose heap of brown net on his shoulder. He gave Mrs. Temple a friendly "good even," and they exchanged a little talk. Then she watched him lazily as he walked up the path, after having spread out his net to dry, and looked into a sort of cave half natural half artificial where a large six-oared boat was safely stowed.

"What a relief it will be sometimes to come here after the toils of the day," said Mrs. Temple, as she rose, wonderfully refreshed, to return. "If I can at all make an existence, I will stay here." And, as she mused, the memory of the last time she had sat in the open air came back to her, with Sir Hugh Galbraith's cruel words, which had so often sounded in her ear since. She had never breathed them to any one; she never would, but not the less clearly were they remembered. Generally, the thought roused indignation, and a fierce desire to show that, at any rate, she had held the same place in her husband's estimation from first to last, by proving that the will which had robbed her, to enrich, him, was false; but to-night the loneliness, the beauty of her surroundings inclined her to a kind of melancholy regret that she should be so misjudged, so cruelly wronged! It was sad, too, after a glimpse of all that life might have given to her, young, rich in a sense of enjoyment, and rich enough in material wealth, to be suddenly cast out into the outer world of poverty and hard work. "I must not be false to my own principles," she thought, rallying her forces as she hurried on, slightly alarmed by the increasing darkness. "Work is a good in itself. All I hope is that Fanny will not find life insupportably dull here. I shall not keep her long, that I can see. It will be terrible to be without her."

Miss Potter's astonishment was loud when she found where Mrs. Temple had directed her evening walk. "Dear, dear! It is such a lonely, dismal place! I don't think even the visitors go there unless indeed in a party, to gather seaweed at the cove when the tide is out."

The succeeding day was considerably more animated. Some young ladies on horseback rode in from one of the neighboring places, and made quite a clatter outside, while one of the attendant grooms came in for a variety of articles, and Miss Potter herself had to go out and receive directions.

Later in the day, a very tall, thin, elderly gentleman, with glittering black eyes and rather hectic color, thin iron gray hair, brushed back from a bony brow, a huge shirt frill, and a long single-breasted green coat, came in with some importance.

"Good morning! good morning!"—knocking the top of his hunting-whip against the brim of his hat. "All blooming, I see. And this is our new proprietress—eh—eh?"—a keen stare at Mrs. Temple, with slightly knitted brow.

"Yes, Dr. Slade," simpered Miss Potter; "this is Mrs. Temple."

The Doctor knocked his whip against his hat again, and Mrs. Temple bent her head with a sudden strange feeling of being out of her place—the introduction was so unlike anything she had ever experienced before.

"Well, ma'am," said the doctor, "shall you let lodgings, like your predecessor, or have you a tribe of children to overflow into the nooks and crannies of this old Noah's Ark?"

Mrs. Temple had time to school herself while he spoke, and was ready to answer with a smile when he ceased.

"I daresay I shall let lodgings, Dr. Slade; but I scarcely yet know what I shall do."

"Well, you had better let me know when you make up your mind. I am the dispenser of fortune, as well as physic, in this direction. I fancy I'll have a couple of invalids on my hands this season; but you must give better cooking than the last sufferer had. Chops frightened by frizzling till they were black in the face, by jingo! That's not nutritious diet."

"But *my* chops, if I ever have the honor of serving any to your patients, shall 'blush celestial rosy red' at their own perfection," said Mrs. Temple, laughing good-humoredly.

The doctor stared for a moment, and then cried, "Shall they? By Jupiter! those are the sort of chops, and you are the sort of woman that will do." Then, turning to Miss Potter, he asked, "Have you, among the rubbish of your nonsensical bazaar, a piece of court plaster? I know I have none; and a —— bramble caught my hand here" (holding it out) "as I was cutting across a corner of the dingle, after being kept nearly an hour listening to that old blockhead, Farmer Owen, maundering about his inside. So I thought I would give you a chance before going on to the chemist."

"Dear, dear! what a bad place," said Miss Potter, sympathizingly; "and I am really afraid we don't keep such a thing as court plaster."

"I ought to have known better than to have looked for anything useful here," retorted the doctor, with an awful scowl.

And then an instinctive "trade" impulse stirred our young widow to exclaim, "If it is not in the shop, Dr. Slade, I have some in my dressing-case. I will bring it, and put it on for you, if you will promise never to go elsewhere for your court plaster in future."

"Done!" cried the doctor, slapping his hand against his leg; "but mind and don't let yourself be out of it. By George!" he continued, as Mrs. Temple left the shop, "that's a clever baggage! Why, she would buy and sell you and poor Mrs. Browne, before you would know where you were."

"She is very pleasant, I am sure; but rather inexperienced—new to business—and depends a great deal upon *me*," returned Miss Potter, with her sweetest smile.

"Depends upon you!" repeated the doctor, with anything but flattering emphasis. "Who is she? where did you pick her up?"

"Oh! I know nothing of Mrs. Temple, except that she answered the advertisement about the business, and that she comes from London."

"London is a wide place," said the doctor.

Here Mrs. Temple returned with the required plaster, and proceeded coolly and dexterously to cut and affix it undisturbed by the doctor's announcement that he was in a desperate hurry; that he had left his horse outside with the reins over a post, and he dared say he would chuck them off and run away, to the damage of all juvenile Pierstoffe.

"Do you want to test my nerve?" said Mrs. Temple, suddenly lifting her soft, dark eyes to his with a smile, which produced a very different effect from poor Miss Potter's.

"I fancy you are equal to it, if I do," said the doctor, with a sort of grim gallantry. "You are a deuced wide-awake young woman, my dear."

"Thank you," returned Mrs. Temple gravely. "There; I think that will keep your hand comfortable. Remember, in future you are to come here for your court plaster."

"That's a bargain," cried Dr. Slade; "and, moreover, I shall make my wife buy all her stuff to knit my socks with here—that is to say, if what you sell isn't rotten."

"Thank you, again," said Mrs. Temple.

"Mrs. Slade always did patronize us," simpered Miss Potter.

"Did she? I know she used to send for balls of worsted yarn—what do you call it?—to Stoneborough—ay, to London. Don't you believe all she told *you*. Good morning to you." Another knock of the whip against his hat, and the doctor strode away.

"Your doctor seems something of a character," said Mrs. Temple, looking after him.

"Oh! indeed, he is a most extraordinary man. He was looked upon as quite the king of Pierstoffe; but I think things are a little different now. There is a new doctor here—a quiet, grave, exceedingly genteel young man—who is making his way wonderfully even with the best families in the town. But Dr. Slade still keeps in with the county people. You see he hunts with the gentry, and they are used to him; but it is said that young Mr.—I mean Dr.—Bryant made one or two extraordinary cures of people that had gone on years and years with Dr. Slade. Any way, Dr. Slade hates the other like poison, and abuses and swears at him quite awful; but Dr. Bryant, I am told, never mentions Dr. Slade but with the greatest respect. The young doctor is not married, and that made matters worse when Miss Monitor called him in; every one said that an elderly—not to say old married man, was the proper person for a young ladies' school (though there are very curious stories told of Dr. Slade some years back). But Miss Monitor declared that a great London doctor said if Miss Goldfrass (that's a great heiress, who is at school) was ill, and she generally is, no one was to be called in but Dr. Bryant. Then he is so regular at church ; and poor Dr. Slade never darkens the door of church or chapel."

" Not a very pleasant account," said the young widow, thoughtfully. " Still I seem fated to accept this rather rampant Hakeem for my partisan."

" What did you say ? " asked Miss Potter, puzzled.

" Oh, that Dr. Slade seemed inclined to be friendly. What is his wife like ? "

" A very nice lady indeed, but that timid and nervous it makes one uncomfortable. I believe she was a great beauty once, but there is very little of it left now."

Ten days flew away with wonderful rapidity, and Kate Travers was astonished to find how quickly things, so new and strange, were growing familiar. The hardest nut of all was to take kindly and easily to the peculiar style of civility with which women, often her inferiors, never her superiors, addressed her, as some one quite out of their sphere. But she was too sensible not to school herself to look on this as a mere accident of business, not touching her real position.

" I hope when Fanny comes she will not be thoughtless and offend people, our fellow-citizens in trade," mused Kate ; " for it will not do to hold aloof, and make ourselves unpopular. After all, they have the same natures, the same objects in life, the same affections ; the difference only lies in our exterior coats of varnish. What an amount of vulgar ignorance exists among nominally educated ladies, who speak correctly, and are sufficiently well-bred not to rub you the wrong way unless it suits them ! Women are generally tolerable, but men, without the ' outward and visible' signs of gentlemen, must be dreadful, and yet real gentlemen must be exceedingly rare in every class. Still there is knowledge to be gained from every fresh page in the book of life, and ere long I shall turn another page.".

Then, as usual, her thoughts flew away to the standing obstacle of her life. She counted largely on what old Gregory's son would have to tell of his father's communications, touching the will he had witnessed, and was supposed to have written. But when would he return ! She had carefully kept up a correspondence with his sister, Mrs. Bell, who had told her that she had received a handsome present from Sir Hugh Galbraith, that had quite re-established her school, and hoped to do well ; but there was still no news of her brother.

As the fortnight progressed Mrs. Temple saw, or imagined

she saw, her way to a fair amount of success in the new life she had adopted. Many things were asked for which were not in stock, and she thus gathered ideas as to the further development of the business already existing at the Berlin Bazaar. Moreover, a judicious selection of magazines and periodicals, sent by the indefatigable Tom, took Pierstoffe by surprise, and acted favorably on other branches of her trade.

She, therefore, made up her mind to close with the agent, and with infinite pleasure wrote for Fanny and Mills to join her. With what delight she looked forward to seeing them once more, after being plunged in such a flood of strangeness! All this time she had had frequent letters from Fanny, written in better spirits than the faithful little soul really felt; on one point they were unanimous, Mills was perfectly angelic. "If she had not a tolerably fair appetite, I should think she was going to die," concluded Fanny in one of her epistles. Tom had paid his promised visit, and was more delightful and audacious than ever. So the young widow's mind had been kept tranquil in the direction of Boulogne.

It was the day after she had dispatched her letter of recall, and market day besides, so they had been quite busy all the morning. Now dinner time was past, and the little shop had been empty for a few minutes—Miss Potter was absent—when the door was suddenly darkened by the entrance of an exceedingly large lady, tall as well as stout, richly dressed in a thick violet silk, a black velvet mantle trimmed with costly lace, a green velvet and satin bonnet with crimson roses, and Brussels lace veil, a chain round her neck, and bracelets slipping down on the fat, pudgy hands, which were tightly crammed into violet gloves; one of them held a violet and lace parasol, the other a ribbon, the other end of which was fastened to a painfully corpulent pug, at whose collar a little ball-like bell tinkled perpetually. All this finery, it must be confessed, looked like every-day gear, not Sunday clothes, on the stout lady, who waddled into the middle of the shop, and then, gazing full at Mrs. Temple with little, sharp, green-gray eyes, exclaimed in a fat voice, but with a good accent and pleasant manner, "I do not think I ever saw you before! Where is Miss Potter?"

"She has only just left the shop, and will be here directly."

"And, in the meantime, have you any materials for this sort of lace work?" resumed the lady, taking a small parcel from her pocket, and opening it.

Mrs. Temple examined it with much interest. "I am very sorry to say we have not, nor have I seen anything like it in England."

"Then, have you been lately on the Continent?" asked her customer, quickly.

" I came from France ten days ago."

" Oh, indeed! Well, and what am I to do about the work? There is a young lady staying with me—a charming girl, but very delicate—and quite crazy about this work. I promised to bring her back patterns, and everything."

" I am exceedingly sorry not to have it. Could the young lady wait three days, and she shall have several patterns to choose from?" said Mrs. Temple, thinking of Fanny's arrival.

" I daresay she would. It would take as long to send to town. Oh, Miss Potter, how do you do?" as that individual returned. " What is going to be done now? Has the Berlin Bazaar been sold—are you going to desert us?"

" Well, my lady, I suppose I shall be going out to my brother soon. Can I get you anything this morning?"

" Yes; there is a list of cottons and tapes my maid gave me. And tell me—how is poor old Mr. Browne? has he gone to live with his daughter?"

" He is pretty well—at least was—when I heard last. He is not living with Mrs. Penny."

" Well, he ought. Where has she sent him?"

" Oh, he is quite comfortable, I assure you, my lady. He is boarded with a very respectable party quite near Mrs. Penny's farm."

" Ah! the respectable party will take the money and starve him, probably."

" I hope not," replied Miss Potter, meekly. She had permitted Mrs. Temple to take the list and select the articles named in it, in order to attend to her ladyship's cross-examination.

" And who is this person?" continued the stout lady, in an audible aside.

" Oh! Mrs. Temple; she is going to purchase the business and settle here."

" Doesn't look the least like business herself." Then to Mrs. Temple. "So you are to be our old friend Mrs. Browne's successor? I hope the Bazaar will be equally successful with you."

" Thank you," said Mrs. Temple, bowing slightly.

" But latterly there has been a decided falling off. Miss Potter is always ' just out ' of whatever one wants."

" I shall, of course, renew the stock, and hope to add some useful branches to the business. I have already some of the newest publications."

" Ah! yes, I see," interrupted her ladyship, wheeling her chair round with a sudden, violent effort, and beginning to overhaul them. " ' Household Words,' ' The Family Herald,' ' The

5*

Cheerful Visitor,'—newspapers, too ! that's a good idea. And, pray, had you a shop in France, Mrs. Temple ?"

"No," said the young widow, gently. She could not bring herself to add "my lady," which slipped so readily from Miss Potter's tongue.

"Ah ! perhaps your husband managed the business ? "

"He did."

"Ah ! you will be quite a tyro, then. Pray, have you many children ? "

"I have none."

"So much the better ; so much the better. Children and business do not agree, I imagine. And are you going to live here all alone ? Have you any friends in Pierstoffe ? "

"I know no one here ; but I shall be joined by a young lady— I mean person," correcting herself, with a smile, "who will be my assistant when I lose Miss Potter, who cannot, I fear, stay with me as long as I should wish."

"Hum ! that may do ; but you must be very circumspect. You must indeed—a handsome young woman like you. Are you going to send out circulars ? "

"I shall act on your suggestion," said Mrs. Temple, gravely, "as soon as I have finally arranged the purchase."

"Do ; and be sure to send me one. And I tell you what— you ought to give credit. There is so much inconvenience and vulgarity about ready money. I would certainly give three months' credit to residents, and the county, if I were you ; but don't trust the visitors ; they are a doubtful set."

"I shall consider it," returned Mrs. Temple.

"Well, are these my cottons and things ? "

"Yes, my lady."

"How much does it all come to ? "

"Three and fourpence-halfpenny."

"What a quantity of money ! There, I have only three and three-pence, and I do not care to change a sovereign. I will pay the three-halfpence another time. You see "—to Mrs. Temple—"there is a case in point. I feel the cost of those wretched reels of cotton because I see three shillings go out of my hand into yours ; but if your account for five pounds, or more, came in at the end of three months, I would write a check for it as cheerfully as possible. It is wonderful what a melancholy effect it has seeing the actual coin go away from you. Now I must leave you ; I have to pay a visit at No. 6, North Parade. Do you know anything of the people ? " To Miss Potter, " Have they been in here ? "

Miss Potter professed complete ignorance.

"*I* know nothing about them," continued the stout lady ;

" but a cousin of mine in town begged me to call; there is a sick child or some such reason for coming here so early. Good morning. Mind you get the lace patterns, Mrs. Temple. I shall look in soon again, and see how you are getting on." Another unmitigated stare—" I can't help thinking I have seen you somewhere before. Good morning ! " and she walked out of the shop with surprising briskness for so heavy a figure.

" And, pray, who is that remarkably curious personage ?" cried Mrs. Temple, when she was fairly out of hearing.

" That is one of our great ladies, and best customers," returned Miss Potter. " That is Lady Styles, of Weston. She has a beautiful place about four or five miles away, on the road to Stoneborough. She is a wealthy lady, and quite her own mistress, for Sir Marmaduke Styles is very sickly, and is often away in London for his health ; but she is the greatest gossip in the whole country. She will come and buy things here if it was only to cross-question you, till she finds out everything. She is not ill-natured, I believe, but so dreadfully curious. There is no keeping anything from her."

" I shall try, however," thought Mrs. Temple to herself. " I wonder if she has ever really met me ! I think not ; I think I should remember her." And Mrs. Temple ran quickly upstairs to write for the post, enjoining Fanny on no account to quit Boulogne without a supply of patterns and materials such as had caught their attention during the only ramble for which they had had time in the Rue de l'Ecu.

CHAPTER XIII.

KATE TRAVERS, or rather Mrs. Temple, had not felt so light of heart since the day on which Ford disclosed his unlucky discovery, as she did when welcoming Fanny and Mills to their new home. First, there was the great joy of having them once more with her—the consciousness of her own courage in having opposed the opinion of those she most regarded, justified as she felt by the strong hope of success in her brave undertaking, and then a certain satisfaction in the pleasantness of the locality where her lot had fallen. She had had tea laid in the best sitting-room, and as she had permitted herself the extravagance of a man to put the garden in order, and prune its wild luxuriance, things looked their best.

" What a pretty place, Kate ! Quite a lady-like-room," exclaimed Fanny, who was enjoying her tea with a traveler's appetite. " Do you know, I quite long to be in the shop, coaxing people to buy all sorts of things they do not want. What is the next article, madam ? Is not that the style ? "

" Bless me ! Miss Fanny, how you do run on ! " said Mills.

" I trust you may like it," returned Mrs. Travers. " But you will find standing all day very fatiguing. I did at first, but I have become used to it."

" Must you *never* sit down ? "

" Oh yes ! you can, sometimes, when there is nothing to do. But we hope to have very little of that sort of rest."

" Dear, dear ! "—a deep sigh from Mills.

" And have any of your neighbors called upon you ? " continued Fanny, helping herself to more brown bread and butter. " *Do* shopkeepers call on each other ? "

" I really cannot tell," said Mrs. Temple, smiling. " I am not thoroughly initiated yet. I imagine they have no time for these ceremonies ; at any rate, no one has called upon me except the doctor, and, although he generally buys a pennyworth of this or sixpence worth of the other, I always look upon his visits as personal ; he gets so much talk for his money."

" Indeed ! " cried Fanny. " And has he a wife ? Is he old or young, or nice or nasty, or—"

" Rein up your curiosity a little, Fanny. He has a wife—he is rather old—and I cannot exactly say he is nice."

" My curiosity is at an end, then. Do you know, Mills and I grew rather fond of Boulogne. We would have been quite fond of it had you been there."

" *Me* fond of it ! no, indeed ! It's a queer, unnatural place," quoth Mills. " Why, if you even go to thread a needle, the more you twist the thread the more it comes untwisted. And then the soup and the messes ! Why, you get up near as hungry as when you sat down."

" All the better for digestion ; but come, Kate, let us see your new abode," said Fanny, rising.

And then a pleasant excursion through the various nooks and corners, the more dignified apartments and domestic offices of the house, ensued. Fanny expressed the most ardent admiration, and sketched the outline of a romantic tale, as she inspected the principal rooms, which Mrs. Temple intended to let. A melancholy and mysterious invalid, of refined habits and blighted affections, was to occupy them. Mrs. Temple was to soothe his last moments ; he was to prove a millionaire, and leave all his wealth " to you," concluded Fanny, " or to me—and then we should go shares ! "

" No more wills, if you love me, Fan ; " said Mrs. Temple, laughing. " Why should he not recover, find balm for his wounded heart, and marry *you ?* "

"Oh! but I couldn't, you know," cried Fanny, and stopped, blushing brightly. ·

"I *know* nothing," returned her friend, "but I guess a good deal."

Mrs. Mills did not commit herself. She found no fault, neither did she bestow much approval. The "wash'us" was, she admitted, handy, and the cupboards convenient; but this was balanced by considerable doubts touching "no end of work" to keep such a heap of odd corners clean. Then the "girl" underwent a grim examination, from which she evidently drew unfavorable auguries of her own future, and asked if she might go home "to see mother." Then, as the evening was lovely, and Miss Potter quite willing to take entire charge of the shop for the short time that remained before closing, the young widow proposed a stroll on the beach, as Fanny did not seem very tired.

"Tired! I am as fresh as a lark; ready for anything!" was the reply.

"Here, Miss Fanny," said Mills, coming downstairs at that moment; "here's the parcel you said Mrs. Travers was—"

"Hush!" cried that lady. "Do be careful, Mills. I am Mrs. Temple now. You really must not forget. Give me the parcel!"

"But, Kate," said Fanny, as they left the house together; "it is very hard to remember; and I spoiled ever so many envelopes when I wrote to you. I was sure to have 'Travers' down before I could think. I wish you had not changed it. Was it necessary?"

"Yes; I thought so. I did not like to associate poor Mr. Travers's name with a shop, for I know my being here is not his fault. Besides, I have an odd, obstinate, perhaps stupid dislike to the idea of resuming it again until I have won my rights."

"Heigho!" said Fanny.

"Which means," returned Mrs. Temple, a little sharply, "that Tom has persuaded you that my hopes and convictions are insane crotchets. You think Tom an oracle; but he is not infallible."

"No, indeed, I do not; but he knows a great deal about law and things, more even than you do; though you are very, very clever, Kate dear. I wouldn't make so sure of . . . of anything, if I were you."

"Patience, patience! time will show," returned her friend, a little wearily; then, after a few moments' thought, she exclaimed, passionately, "you cannot know how deeply this blow has sunk into my soul! I shall never be quite the same again till I have rolled back that man's triumph on himself, and proved that I possessed—even if I did not deserve it—my husband's love and confidence to the last! After all," she went on, speaking slowly, dreamily, "my lot has been a little hard. I have never known real love—love I could heartily return—now I am compelled by fortune to turn aside out of the way of it. And I do believe that not only is love the whole fulfilling of the law, but of life, too, to a woman. But," in a cheerier tone, "there are many pleasant things left—among them success and revenge; not desperate, cruel revenge, you know, but a little pinching of one's enemy, just to give salt to the success. Tell me about yourself, Fan?"

A long confidential talk ensued, for Fanny was unusually sensible and satisfying, yet she avoided her own affairs somewhat; so Mrs. Temple concluded that her engagement to Tom, if it existed, was a tacit one. It was dusk when they reached the house.

"And, Kate! how long is that horrid, skinny Miss Potter to stay?"

"Another month," said Mrs. Temple, laughing. "It will take all that time to train you! She is very useful, and a good creature."

"I hate good creatures," said Fanny, with a pout.

"Which shows you are not one yourself," returned Mrs. Temple, putting the latch-key in the lock. "How thankful I am that everything has turned out favorably so far, though we must not expect it to be always sunshine! What a comfort that Mills seems tolerably pleased and in good spirits!—where is she, by the way?" Mrs. Temple opened the kitchen-door as she spoke, and beheld Mills seated by the fast-dying fire, her feet stretched out resting on each other, her hands clasped together, her apron thrown over her face, a picture of hopeless affliction.

*   *   *   *   *

Time flew by with amazing rapidity in the busy monotony of the new life upon which Kate and Fanny had entered. To the former it was far from uninteresting. Her self-esteem was deeply pledged to its success, and she soon began, under the pressure of such a motive, to understand her work. Misunderstanding is at the root of so many dislikes; to be thoroughly known is often, to the least attractive, to possess sympathy and liking. Then it was very delightful to perceive that, as the town filled, so did her trade increase. The possession of a little ready money, too, was a great advantage at the outset, as it enabled her to renew her stock on good terms, and without any difficulty respecting references, which would have been puzzling to find. As soon as she began to ascertain the kind of goods most in demand, she felt emboldened to add sundry fancy articles to her stock of jet ornaments and trinkets—she even ventured to run up to town from Friday morning to the following evening and visit the great emporiums in Cannon Street, where, if "fancy" was not originally "bred," she has developed to an extraordinary degree. All Pierstoffe was attracted by the dazzling array which resulted from this visit, and Mrs. Temple could not refrain from laughing at the sort of pride she detected in her own heart on finding that for some time both Fanny and herself were decidedly overworked, while the average of receipts was a trifle under fourteen pounds a week.

"What do you think of that, Tom ?" wrote the widow to her faithful ally ; " I have put away half the money to replace what has been sold, and the rest I shall keep in the bank, as I shall want nothing for our house or other expenditure for six months at least."

Meantime Fanny had caught the taste for business, or pretended she did, though Kate shrewdly suspected she viewed the whole undertaking as playing at shop-keeping, and could not believe that in sober earnest they were always to work.

Small troubles, of course, arose. Mrs. Mills started with a fixed and unalterable hatred to the unhappy "girl" who had been kept on by Mrs. Temple. Mills knew too well what was due to herself to hear any reason on the subject ; and her mistress, though sorely tempted to give way, was determined not to yield to an unjust prejudice, consequently "Sarah Jane's " was not a life of unbroken sunshine ; some respite, however, was afforded to all parties by her returning each evening to "*do*" for her grandmother, and her remaining under the maternal roof till nine the following morning.

Lady Styles was another thorn in their side, though by no means an unmixed evil. Being rich and idle, she was an excellent customer, and not only bought herself, but brought many to buy ; for her house was always full. Her extreme curiosity was distressing, and so alarming to poor Fanny, who had been solemnly warned by her friend against gratifying it, that her ladyship's first visits generally cost the pretty little assistant a fit of crying. Lady Styles took the deepest interest in the Berlin Bazaar and its owner, who had taken her advice respecting the credit system, to which fact her ladyship attributed the entire success, so far, of the young widow's speculation. Perhaps the true source of Lady Styles's interest lay in her unslaked curiosity. Mrs. Temple and Fanny grew quite skilled in fencing off her queries, and tacitly permitting her to form one theory after another as to their previous history. Her con-

jectures, always stated with the most insolent candor, were
often curiously ingenious ; but the fact of Mrs. Temple having
come direct from France baffled her a good deal. That there
was a mystery about the fair, sedate, attentive widow, she felt
quite sure, and she also felt herself bound to unravel it, if only
to keep up her character. In this Dr. Slade was somewhat
a hindrance. The doctor and she were old acquaintances—
often partners at whist, at the various dinners to which the former, in his double character of sportsman and doctor, was
frequently invited—but always more or less rivals in pursuit
of the latest, the most correct, and the most startling intelligence ; Dr. Slade generally mentioning Lady Styles (in safe
quarters) as that " blundering old gossip, who always has the
wrong end of a story ; " while Lady Styles usually spoke of him
as " poor dear Dr. Slade ! you never can *exactly* depend on
anything from *him*." Therefore, whatever theory started by
her ladyship was either openly negatived by the doctor, or he
shook his head with a calmly contemptuous smile, as if he knew
ever so much better, only he could not speak, which, as Lady
Styles remarked, would be " perfectly ridiculous if it was not
maddening."

The doctor continued very friendly, and masked his batteries
more skillfully than Lady Styles. He fulfilled his promise by
introducing an invalid gentleman and his valet as tenants to Mrs.
Temple, whose three months' occupancy of her rooms very
nearly paid a whole year's rent ; but this piece of good fortune
was not altogether without its unpleasantness also. The
"valet," a thick-set, " down "-looking individual, unaccom-
plished in any of the suave graces which usually distinguish a
"gentleman's gentleman," gave a good deal of trouble about
his own and his master's food, and attracted so much of Mrs.
Mill's wrath and indignation upon himself that she had none to
spare for " Sarah Jane," and grew quite friendly towards that
victim during the period of counter-irritation. The tenant himself—a red-faced, gray-whiskered, short, slight man of mild
aspect, well dressed in an old-fashioned style, and always wearing shoes and gaiters—developed a curious tendency to slide
down the bannisters when he thought no one was looking, and to
sit in his open window when all Pierstoffe was out in its best
attire, with his nightcap over his hat. Whatever doubts these
peculiarities might have suggested were quickly resolved into
certainty by Lady Styles on the first opportunity.

" I have just been talking to Dr. Slade, Mrs. Temple " she
said, " and I told him it was a great shame to quarter a madman and his keeper on you. Yes, a madman ! but immensely
rich—made a fortune in one day on the Stock Exchange, and

lost his senses in consequence. They *say* he is not dangerous; but you can never be sure. He may get up any night and murder you and this nice little creature in your sleep. ' His valet sleeps in his room, you say? Oh! the cunning of madness is so extraordinary! he would escape the keeper.''

A suggestion which gave Mrs. Temple no small amount of trouble, as Fanny could neither control nor conceal her fears, and every night went through nearly an hour's searching in cupboards, behind curtains, and under beds before she finally locked herself into her room.

On the whole, this slightly capricious young person was of more real use than Mrs. Temple had ventured to hope, and for the first two or three months things went smoothly in the main. By that time, however, their fellow-townspeople began to evince a desire to make their acquaintance, and Mrs. Temple determined not to hold aloof from the proffered intercourse.

Among the higher class of tradespeople, none stood higher than Mr. Turner, of " Turner and Sons," the grand, and indeed only drapery emporium of Pierstoffe. He was a very honest, respectable man, understanding his own work thoroughly, but little else; for education in the " good old days " of his boyhood was held to be an unholy thing for any one below the rank of an esquire; and gentlemen thought they best served " God and the king " by heaping up barriers of difference between them, and the brethren like unto themselves, whom Providence, for some wise purpose, had placed upon this earth to do their bidding. Education or no education, Mr. Turner managed to amass a good deal of money, and the more he advanced in wealth and consideration—which are indeed synonymous terms —the more he felt the want of what he himself would have termed " learning." Not that he said so, even to the wife of his bosom—he said very little on any subject—but he resolved that his son—his only son, Joseph—should have all the advantages he had never known.

Now Joseph, though an only son, was not an only child; three elder sisters alternately cuddled and cuffed him through an early boyhood of much spoiling, while two younger ones afforded ample scope for the tyranny over weaker vessels so natural to incipient man. But no only child could have been an object of fonder hopes. He was carefully instructed at the Stoneborough Grammar School; he was sent from thence to a commercial academy in the neighborhood of London, and finally placed in a West-end establishment, to learn the higher and more elegant mysteries of business.

He was far from a dull boy. He learned something of all this, and a good deal more besides.

Mr. Turner and his family attended the little old parish church, which modern Pierstoffe had far outgrown. He was equally opposed to attending the Baptist Chapel, Salem Chapel, Little Bethel, or St. Monica's Church, a brand new edifice erected by subscription to accomodate increasing numbers both of inhabitants and visitors (as a man of business, Mr. Turner had subscribed to it ; as a man of Protestant religion, he refused to attend it), and supported by an offertory which an excellent, hardworking, lantern-jawed, long-coated Anglican priest toiled to fill with energy and ingenuity that would have been invaluable in the purveyor to a music hall—in all respect, be it written—for the Rev. Claudius St. John cared little for this world's goods, but he loved to see his church beautiful, and he heartily cared for the poor. To recommence : Mr. Turner attended the old parish church, and insisted on his family attending it also. Although he looked on his son as a superior, or rather a fancy article, his will was on some points law to the young man, and this was one of them ; so it fell out that Mr. Joseph Turner saw Mrs. Temple and Fanny. They had also elected to sit under the rector, a mild, well-bred, indolent old gentleman, who, as the poor people used to say admiringly, " never harmed no one." In the animated discussions which ensued respecting the new people at the Berlin Bazaar, Mr. Joseph was unusually silent ; and although he frequently took occasion to saunter by the Berlin establishment of an evening in an admirable, London-made, sea-side suit, and a cigarette (refinement was his forte !) in his mouth, he never met the new proprietress and her assistant save once, when they were very simply attired, and moving briskly towards the Barmouth Road, evidently bent on a refreshing country walk. A few days after, a movement among the more enterprising townsfolk to water *the* street and roadway of the Esplanade, culminated in a meeting and a resolution to that effect, which was neatly drawn out on a sheet of foolscap, and ordered to be taken round by some one of the committee to all the principal houses to collect subscriptions. Mr. Turner, senior, as a churchwarden and a representative man, felt that he ought to be first in such an excellent work ; but he by no means fancied the undertaking. He was, therefore, doubly gratified when his son volunteered his services —first, because such a mark of interest in mundane affairs was rather rare in the sullen young gentleman ; secondly, because it was a personal relief. Thus it came about that just after the early dinner hour, when things were quiet one blazing afternoon in early June, Fanny peeped between the half-worked cushions and slippers, the traced screens and ornamental baskets that adorned the window, and exclaimed, " Here comes that elegant young man who stares so at us in church !—and, Kate, I protest he is coming in ! "

The next moment Mr. Joseph, in unquestionable attire, was raising his hat with metropolitan grace, as he stood in the centre of the shop, Macassar in his locks, a moss-rose in his button-hole, and a handkerchief redolent of *millefleurs* in his hand.

"A thousand pardons!" he said, in a mild and rather squeaky voice. "I have taken the liberty of calling in the character of a petitioner. Fact is, a number of respectable buffers belonging to this town, my governor among them, have decided on levy-ing—a—contributions for the desirable object of laying the dust, and I have therefore to request you will come down with your dust—if you will excuse that form of address."

This speech, though carefully conned, and delivered with a certain fluency, cost the speaker no small effort. He was in a violent perspiration before it ended, and, as usual, the effort to conceal his real bashfulness, of which he was heartily ashamed, made him assume an unnecessarily brazen front. As he paused, he drew forth from a breast-pocket and presented to Mrs. Tem-ple the foolscap aforesaid. She received it with a gracious bow and smile, proceeding to peruse it before committing herself to speech. While she did so, Mr. Joseph addressed some remarks on the weather to Fanny, in much less an audacious tone than that in which he began. That volatile little lady, infinitely amused by the young man's air of fashion and elaborate ele-gance, replied with much suavity, quite running over with smiles.

"A very necessary undertaking," said Mrs. Temple, interrupt-ing their conversation, as she finished perusing the "resolution." "I shall be most happy to contribute;" and, drawing forth her purse, she returned the paper with a smile and a half-sovereign.

"Very handsome indeed," observed her visitor, "for a new-comer."

"But I hope to be long reckoned among the townsfolk," re-turned Mrs. Temple.

"If I may be considered in any way representing Pierstoffe," replied Mr. Joseph, gallantly, but not without a tinge of self-im-portance, "I should say the town is honored by the addition of two such ladies to its residents. Perhaps," he went on, half-jest, half-earnest, "I may one of these days be its Parliamentary representative—who knows!—the age of progress, you know; a—impossible to say what it may lead to. As strangers, you may not be aware that my father's Mr. Turner, of the Empo-rium, ma'am—is the oldest-established firm in the place, except Prodgers, the grocer; but then the difference of position is enormous! My governor is desperately fond of the concern though there is really no necessity for his working it. Were the choice left to me—" A graceful flourish of his perfumed hand-kerchief, and the rest was left to imagination.

"Does Pierstoff return a member of Parliament?" asked Mrs. Temple, a little puzzled how to reply, and seizing the only point of general interest in his speech.

"Not as yet," said the future M. P., lifting and re-arranging his hat on his Macassar curls. "The narrow-minded agriculturists, who absorb Parliamentary powers, have as yet ignored the growing—I may say, the fast-growing claims of this rising town. Nevertheless, the hour is coming—perhaps the man will not be wanting."

Mrs. Temple generally hoped all possible success to that mysterious individual.

Still Mr. Turner lingered. He talked of "Town" with an air of exhaustive knowledge, and strove, though not very persistently, to ascertain if they were Londoners. Fanny's knowledge of what had been going on at the theatres six months before fixed her *locale;* but Mrs. Temple was impervious, and to a point-blank inquiry, replied, as was her habit now—

"I have lived in London, but I came last from France."

This reply, coupled with an admission that her husband dealt in Eastern produce, gave rise to a generally-received theory that the late Mr. Temple had been in the grocery line, in a large way ; had failed ; had fled to France to escape his creditors and get brandy cheap, as he took to drink, and, after inflicting much suffering on his wife, died and left her in the direst poverty. Her friends and Miss Lee's had bought the " Berlin Bazaar " and set them up—the money was chiefly Miss Lee's. She came of a high family in some mysterious way—the natural daughter of an earl—of a marchioness—of a general officer. It was easy to see *she* was unaccustomed to business, and the most independent of the two, etc., etc.

Meantime, Mr. J. Turner, jun., as was printed on his cards, which had led to his being familiarly styled J. T. J., posed and talked till, to Mrs. Temple's relief, the entrance of some customers obliged him to retire ; not, however, before he expressed a hope on the part of the ladies of his family, which they had not authorized him to do, that on some suitable occasion they might become acquainted with Mrs. Temple and her friend.

So gradually the widow found herself drawn into social relations with her fellows. She accepted their advances with a frankness that proved her best safeguard against intrusion, as what seems within the grasp is never too eagerly sought. But the only intimacy she found was with the chemist's wife—a gentlewoman by nature, but " sair handen doon " by a large and ever-increasing family. To her Mrs. Temple and her friend were real " God-sends ; " so much help, refreshment and courage did she glean from her kindly and congenial neighbors.

Thus the first months of their life at Pierstoffe rolled over for Kate Travers and her friend.

CHAPTER XIV.

" I N spite of prudence and all the other reasonable bugbears you array against me, I will run down on Saturday and see how you are getting on," wrote Tom Reed to Mrs. Temple a week or two after the visit of Mr. Turner, described in the last chapter; for Mrs. Temple had requested that for a while he would abstain from visiting them until they had established themselves, fearing that Tom's hopelessly gentlemanlike air might afford food for scandal and conjecture. "You will be quite satisfied with my appearance. I have invested in a traveling suit of the most 'gent '-like aspect. I shall put rings on my fingers, and would put bells on the other fingers (as the French have it), if they would facilitate matters. In short, I hope to look the character of your London agent perfectly, and expect to be welcomed literally and metaphorically with open arms."

"How delightful it will be to see him!" cried Kate, after reading this aloud. "But it is almost too soon for him to come. Don't you think so, Fanny?"

"No, indeed, I do not," returned that young lady candidly, and sparkling all over with smiles. "I have rather wondered why he kept away so long—I mean after Miss Potter went;" for "Mrs. Browne's right-hand woman" had departed a considerable time before, much gratified by a small present over and above the sum agreed upon for her services, and eloquent in her good wishes for the young widow's success.

"You know I have always warned him not to come."

"But for all that," pouted Fanny, "he has been marvelously patient."

"You are an unreasonable little goose," said her friend. "However, I shall be delighted to see him. He cannot be here till late. We must have something very nice for supper, and an extra good dinner on Sunday. I will go and speak to Mills." And Mrs. Temple rose from the breakfast-table, where this conversation took place.

"I do not think Tom cares much for eating," said Fanny, with a slight sigh and a tinge of sentiment in the outlook of her bright brown eyes.

"Nonsense," returned Mrs. Temple. "There is a strong dash of the Epicurean in the dear old fellow. Depend upon it he loves sugar and spice, and all that's nice, in his heart of hearts, though I believe he is man enough to do without anything cheerfully, if necessary." And Mrs. Temple went off quickly to consult Mills, whose countenance relaxed even towards the ex-stockbroker's gentleman when she heard she was to "kill the fatted calf" for Master Tom.

Business was quite over, and the "shutters up"—phrase suggestive of repose—when Tom arrived. The best sitting-room had been prepared; the lamp was burning soft, but bright; the window, open upon the garden, let in the delicious perfume of mignonette mingled with new-mown grass, for the little plat had been carefully shaven in the afternoon, that things might look their best; the old furniture judiciously arranged, with some telling additions of ornamental needle-work.

"I am sure it all looks lovely," said Fanny, putting the finishing touches with trembling fingers. Both friends were in a state of joyous excitement at the prospect of Reed's visit. To Fanny it was all joy; but Kate was surprised and vexed to feel how keen and painful were the memories revived by the prospect of seeing him. Bravely as she worked and faced her destiny, she still quivered under the sense of defeat and injustice; she still burned with the desire to right herself and revenge the insults that had been heaped upon her, which were none the less bitter for being unconsciously offered.

"Listen! a carriage, or something has stopped at the door," she exclaimed, turning gladly from her own stinging thoughts; and the next moment all their past life seemed to rush back upon them as Tom entered, in a bright purple-tinted 'heather suit,' with broad stripes down his trousers, and an indescribable felt hat on his head, which he speedily removed. "My dear Tom! how delighted I am to see you!" cried Mrs. Temple, holding out both hands.

"And I am not sorry,"added Fanny, trying with shy coquetry not to look too happy.

"What's your delight to mine!" exclaimed Tom, clasping the widow's hands warmly, then letting them go to grasp Fanny's, and further proceeding to a hasty, ecstatic hug. "I have been the most desolate and disconsolate of bachelors since you left. Nothing but the hope of getting leave to run down to see you has kept me from going utterly to the bad. And what a jolly place you have!" sniffing the sweet air. "The perfume of the garden is heavenly; and how well you are both looking! By Jove! I fancy this is the ornamental side of shopkeeping."

"It has its uglier aspects," returned Mrs. Temple; "but we are not worn to skeletons yet."

"No?" said Tom, interrogatively; then holding out his arms again to Fanny, "I should like to test the truth of that assertion."

" Ah," said Fanny, retreating, " this ' London assurance ' will not do, Tom."

" Come, you must be famished," remarked the fair hostess, moving to the table.

" Nearly," said her guest ; " but before proceeding to business I will secure quarters for the night. Where shall I go ? I want to avoid the haunts of a bloated aristocracy, lest the arrival of so distinguished an individual might be bruited abroad."

" Oh, I am sure I do not know any hotel except the 'Marine,' and that is—."

" Far too fine," interrupted Tom ; " but my cab is at the door ; I'll confide in the driver. I shall return in ten minutes, and devour everything before me."

" He may say what he likes about being desolate," cried Fanny, " I never saw him look better."

" I am sure I have," returned Mrs. Temple. " And what an absurd suit of clothes ! "

It was a very joyous supper that night. Tom was in the wildest spirits. A little piece he had written for the Anonymous Theatre had been accepted, and was to be read by the writer to the company on the following Tuesday. " You see I could *not* refrain from coming to tell the news in person," continued Tom, settling himself at table and unfolding his napkin, while Mrs. Temple supplied him with cold lamb, and Fanny, on the other side, became the ministering angel of cucumber, mint sauce, and admirably-mixed salad. " Of course the thing will succeed ; lots of ' go ' in it, sparkling dialogue (I had your repartees in my head, Fan, as I wrote), delicate sentiment (reminiscences of Mrs. Travers—I mean Temple), Attic salt, myself."

" And a little Durham mustard, I hope," added Fanny.

" You small barbarian ! "

" Now, Tom, what will you have in the way of liquids ? " asked his kind hostess.

" Oh, barley wine—known to the vulgar as bitter beer," returned Tom.

" Yes, there is some to be had here quite equal to Bass or Allsopp, though its bitterness is somewhat wasted on the obscurity of Pierstoffe. Fanny shall be your Hebe, and I will draw the cork."

So the two fair women petted and pampered their friend and champion, till, throwing himself back in his chair, he protested he could eat no more, finishing with the quotation, " And oh, if there be an Elysium on earth, it is this—it is this ! "

" Although behind a Berlin Bazaar," added Mrs. Temple, laughing. " And now you have appeased the pangs of hunger open your budget, and tell us the news."

"Which means tidings of the enemy. I have not much. The chief enemy, I hear, made a capital book on the Derby."

"His star is in the ascendant at present," murmured Kate.

"And the report is," continued Tom, "that old Scrymgeour, of some great banking concern—a Liberal of the stingy order—is going to retire from the representation of Ribbleston, and Sir Hugh Galbraith is going to contest it in the Conservative interest, as the descendant of some Galbraith in the good old times who used to harry the inhabitants."

"Indeed," said Mrs. Temple, thoughtfully. "And, Tom, there are no tidings at present of poor old Gregory's son. I trust and hope he has not gone down at sea!"

"By the way, I met Poole—one of the witnesses, you remember—at the Derby. I am sorry to say he was with that fellow Trapes, who seemed rather flourishing than otherwise; and, just to keep him in sight, I made a small bet with him. Strange to say, I won, which I do not often, and Poole begged I would allow him to call and settle it, as he was a little short of cash. I willingly agreed, took his note, and when he did call, had some chat, but could get nothing out of him—in short, he has nothing to tell, I imagine. I gave him a still longer time to pay up, warned him against the turf and turfites; he smiled; and then we parted. No, by-the-by, he first told me that Ford had cut St. Hilda's Place, had set up as a stockbroker, and was doing well."

"And Poole, then, has no suspicion about that will?"

"None, I should say. He seemed uncomfortable and shaky, but I think that is owing to his pursuits, poor devil!"

"I wish—" began Mrs. Temple; but her wish was cut short by a mysterious pounding overhead.

"What the deuce is that?" asked Tom.

"Oh, it is only our tenant," said Fanny, laughing, "going to bed; we always hear that sort of noise about this hour, whenever we sit in this room. I fancy he performs an Ojibbeway war-dance round his bedstead before turning in."

"Is he a madman?"

"Something very like it," said Mrs. Temple. "He will not be here much longer; and, alas! for the lowness of my motives, he pays well."

"That is consolatory, at all events," said Tom. "*A propos* of pay, let me have a look at the accounts you write about Mrs. —a—Temple. I am always afraid to believe they are as flourishing as you describe. Ladies are not always able to see their way through figures. Now I am a tolerable accountant."

"You *used* always to be in trouble over the multiplication table, Tom, I remember quite well," said Fanny.

" That is invented for the occasion," he returned.

" Yes, Tom," said Mrs. Temple, " I should be glad if you would look through my books. I do not think I have many bad debts ; " and she went to fetch them.

Tom's head was very near Fanny's when she re-entered, and the former, to cover any awkwardness, immediately exclaimed, " I have just been consulting Fan whether we might not get a trap of some kind to-morrow, and make an excursion into the ' picturesque vicinity,' as the Pierstoffe guide says."

" It would be perfectly delightful ! " cried Fanny.

" It would indeed," echoed Mrs. Temple. " I daresay you can get some sort of conveyance at your hotel. Where are you putting up, Tom ? "

" Oh, at the ' Shakespeare,' the favorite house, I imagine, from its general aspect, of those knights errant of modern life, commercial travelers, who issue forth armed *cap-à-pie* with *Punch* and *Bradshaw* to uphold the firms they represent against all comers. Alas ! what a change, Tomkins and Co.'s genuine articles, instead of the peerless Isabelle or Sophinisba. Nevertheless, I daresay a trap and horse are to be found there. Now for the books."

The examination proved more satisfactory than the chief counselor anticipated. " Upon my soul, this is magnificent ! " he exclaimed. " I never thought you would turn out such a first-rate woman of business, Mrs. Travers. Your books are so beautifully clean, too ! where did you learn book-keeping ? "

" Some hints from Miss Potter put me in the way, and a keen sense of my own interest kept me there," she replied. " You know I always had a taste for business. Had matters not gone wrong, I should have liked to keep up and extend the old house of Travers. Heigho ! there is no use in thinking of that now."

" Not a bit," said Tom ; " let us return to the books. I really believe you will do a very good business here."

" Yes, just now ; but you must remember this is the very height of our season. The autumn and dreary winter are yet to come."

" True," returned Tom. " Could you not add something useful to your stock ? I confess it amazes me to see such a lot of money paid for things that every one could do perfectly well without."

" It *is* surprising," said the widow, quietly. " But your suggestion is good. I shall think about it, Tom."

" And Mr. Ford has left the house and turned stockbroker ? " said Mrs. Temple, as Tom Reed rose to say good-night. " Did he quarrel with Sir Hugh Galbraith ? "

6

"I do not know. Galbraith, it seems, has scarcely ever shown at St. Hilda's Place, and the concern is being wound up."

"Indeed! Do you ever see Mr. Ford?"

"Never. He is out of my way, and I never liked him. I do not know why, except that I always fancied him a bit of a sneak."

"I do not think that," said Mrs. Temple, thoughtfully. "I think his spirit was always willing, but his flesh was weak. There was a want of pluck—I can find no other word—in him, which I imagine always put him at odds with himself; for his impulses were very good."

"Perhaps so," returned Tom, carelessly. "By the way, I forwarded you a letter from Wall about a month ago, and was in hopes it might contain some good news; but as you said nothing, my hopes died away."

"I remember. It only contained a repetition of Sir Hugh Galbraith's offer; and enclosed a letter from the wife of our clergyman at Hereford Square. She was the only one of my neighbors there with whom I contracted any intimacy; and although I lost sight of her when we went to Hampton Court, she very kindly wrote, on hearing of the great wrong that had been done me, asking my plans—and if she could in any way serve me? It is the only offer of the kind I have received; few women have ever stood more alone than I do."

"You are a host in yourself," said Tom, cheerfully. "But in spite of the flourishing aspect of your affairs at present, I wish you had accepted the baronet's offer—certainty is certain—and this concern does not belong to the category."

"On this head silence, dear Tom! even from good words."

*   *   *   *   *   *   *

The next morning was an ideal summer's day, tempered by a delicious breeze. "I feel like a real tradeswoman going out for a Sunday jaunt," said Fanny, as Tom Reed was assisting her into a very presentable pony phaeton, which looked rather small for the steady Roman-nosed steed attached to it.

"I hope you are not a sham one!" retorted Mrs. Temple, laughing. "This is very enjoyable," she continued, as they bowled along at a better pace than the "Roman" seemed to promise. "I hope you have studied a map of the country, for Fan and I are quite unable to direct you; our expeditions have been limited to walking distance."

"Oh, yes. I have informed myself. In fact, after I left you last night, I improved my opportunities by cultivating one of the knights errant of whom we were speaking; and he was good enough to introduce me to the commercial room, for I assure you the men of the road are exceedingly exclusive. They gave me lots of information as to the surrounding country, and were exceedingly pleasant fellows—fanciful, perhaps, in the distribution of their 'h's,' but emphatically men of the world. I picked up some ideas from them, I can assure you. There was one curious specimen of an ambitious son of trade there, a Radical, a poet—an awful ass—and he was properly chaffed. I fancy he was a Pierstoffean."

"It must have been Turner, junior," said Fanny, aside to Kate.

"What! do you know any of the aborigines?" asked Tom, overhearing.

"Yes; we know several of our neighbors," replied Mrs. Temple. "It would never do to hold aloof, as if we were made of different stuff, which we are not. It is foolish, and yet so easy to make enemies. You remember the Italian proverb : 'Hast thou fifty friends, 'tis not enough ; hast thou one enemy, 'tis too much !' "

"Do you know, Mrs. Trav—Temple, I mean—I am lost in admiration of your common sense!" exclaimed Tom. "Though why we should call that common which is the rarest of gifts I do not know."

"Because it is chiefly exercised in every-day matters, perhaps," said she.

"You see mine is the *un*common sense," put in Fanny. "So I am a much higher sort of creature than either of you. Instead of stumbling along the ground over all sorts of reasonable impediments, I soar right away to conclusions, which, I am quite sure, time will prove to be correct."

"For instance?" asked Mrs. Temple.

"Mr. Ford," returned Fanny, promptly. "You and Tom blind and deafen yourselves to your own dislike of him, because he has always behaved well and been obliging, and it is unreasonable to doubt him. I don't care for reason. I do not like him ! I never did. I am certain he is a tiresome, conceited, spiteful creature ; and you will find him out to be a villain of the deepest dye !"

"Oh! Fanny, Fanny!" cried Mrs. Temple and Tom together, laughing.

"And there is Dr. Slade ; I don't like him. I can't tell why, but I am quite sure I am right—he is a tyrannical old humbug."

"Do not let us abuse people this delicious evening," said Mrs. Temple ; and then the conversation turned on Tom Reed's concerns, his hopes and prospects, while the three friends deeply enjoyed the fragrant fields and shady lanes through which their road led to the ruined Priory mentioned in the description of Pierstoffe which Tom had read aloud in the dingy London lodging.

Here a gaping boy was easily induced to watch the little carriage and the horse, while the trio rambled about the ruins, and drank in the still beauty of the place, the atmosphere, the sunset hues, with delighted eyes.

"Tell me," said Tom, as they neared the town on their way back, addressing Mrs. Temple in confidential tones, "are you really happy? You look well, but there is something in your eyes, your expression that used not to be there."

"You are a keen observer," she returned, smiling. "Yes, I am happy just now; but a feeling of weariness and dissatisfaction sometimes creeps over me. I *know* I cannot go on always living as I do now; I want a wider range. I often feel a wild delight to be in the thick of the world, not shunted into a corner as I am. But I can wait. I am young; I want to make some money, and I have an innate conviction, quite unreasoning enough to please Fanny, that there is a change coming."

"Why do you not write?" asked Tom. "There is more in that pretty, stately head of yours, I believe, than in half our women writers. Why don't you go in for a thrilling tale? I am sure you have *diablerie* enough to invent one."

"Thank you, no; I am afraid I have nothing to say the public would like to hear; so I shall reserve myself for the battle of Armageddon which is before me."

"I wish you would put that out of your head; a haunting, unhealthy dream like this will spoil your nature and your life."

"I cannot help it, Tom; I cannot," said Mrs. Temple, earnestly. "Life will be one long defeat if I cannot upset that will."

These words brought them to the door, and Tom checked his desire to press the subject farther.

"It is a lovely night!" he exclaimed, for the sun had gone down half an hour before. "As soon as I leave the trap at the stables, I will return, and perhaps you will take a stroll along the beach with me, Fanny?"

"Yes—if Kate will come too," said Fanny, with sudden shyness.

"Nonsense!" returned Mrs. Temple, laughing. "I think you may venture on a walk without my chaperonage."

When the cousins had departed on their stroll, and she had assisted Mills to prepare supper, Mrs. Temple sat down by her bedroom window to watch the glimmering moonlight growing more distinct as the last tints of the sunset died out, and listen to the soft, sleepy ripple of the advancing tide. The book she had taken up dropped upon her knee, and her thoughts flew away. Was she happy? No; not for many a long day; not since the old free days of poverty and light-heartedness at

Cullingford. Her husband—well, she thought of him tenderly, gratefully; but she would have been sorry to live the repressed life she had led with him, over again. Wealth had only been a hindrance to her; yet the loss of it, and all that it entailed, had been a bitter blow. She knew all the longing for a full, active, loving life that heaved and struggled unspoken in her heart; she knew the deep capacity for enjoyment, the thirst for knowledge, the desire to go out into the world and possess it through a full understanding of its varieties, that lay under the well-controlled surface of her life.

"I must break away from this routine sometime, but for the present I must be patient, and for the present I have done the best I could. Where, where shall I see the first glimmer of light to guide me out of the puzzling darkness of the present? Tom is right; this dream of mine, if unfulfilled, will spoil my life. Yet I cannot, will not give it up. But can those be Tom and Fanny coming back already?"

It was that happy couple; and no sooner had Mrs. Temple lit the lamp, and looked upon them, than she saw something was wrong.

"Had you a nice walk?" asked Kate.

"Oh, very!" replied Fanny, in a peculiar tone.

"Perhaps you thought so; I didn't!" said Tom, savagely.

"What has happened?" asked the widow.

"Why," exclaimed Tom, getting up and walking over to Mrs. Temple, "who do you think joined us? That unmitigated idiot who made such an ass of himself last night with those bagmen. He talked to Fanny as if he had known her all his life! And she encouraged him, and laughed and talked nonsense till he did not know whether he was on his head or his heels. I did my best to stop her—"

"You did," said Fanny; "you pinched my arm black and blue!"

"But it was no use! It is too bad that either of you should be obliged to hold any communication with such an insufferable snob! but that Fanny should encourage him to stay and spoil our walk was, to say the least, extremely bad taste!"

"How can you be so cross and disagreeable, Tom? I could not help it, Kate. It was so funny to hear him patronizing Tom, asking him if he knew this place, and that theatre, and Tom sternly denying all knowledge of everything, till Turner junior evidently thought he was a mere hard-working drone, utterly inexperienced in life! I know you would have been amused."

"Very well," said Tom, controlling himself, and sitting down to supper with a very bad grace, "I see you are fonder of fun than your friends, or your friend! I used to flatter myself that I was your friend *par excellence;* but if all is fish that comes to your net, provided they make you laugh, I do not care to be included in the haul!"

"Don't be so stupid and serious," cried Fanny, enjoying to the full the sense of power of which Tom's ill-temper gave her a glimpse. "I hav'n t you always, and I can't afford to quarrel with Mr. Turner, for he is constantly here ; so be a good boy and make friends."

But Tom was not to be pacified, though Fanny made some pretty little advances; still she held her ground gallantly. It was so delightful to be able to shake the airy composure she had so often admired in those days when her cousin appeared to her a mighty and irresistible swell.

So Tom's delightful visit ended less brightly than it began. Overnight he declared he would leave by an early train before Pierstoffe had opened its eyes ; but he, nevertheless, appeared at breakfast, and bid Mrs. Temple a tender adieu, contenting himself with shaking Fanny's hand coldly, and never once asked for a kiss !

CHAPTER XV.

TIME, inexorable time, sped on. The summer visitors had gradually departed, and the full torrent of "season" trade subsided to the ordinary yet not despicable rivulet of local demand. Autumn faded into winter; the short days brought with them long cozy evenings for reading and for work. And although Kate had occasionally to struggle with sharp fever fits of impatient longing for movement, for intelligence, for light of any kind to guide her to some outlet from the mystery of her present lot, she felt she was singularly fortunate in her career so far ; and that could she hold on and keep clear of debt, her humble undertaking might insure bread and independence.

Even through the depth of the winter a bright day generally brought customers from the neighboring country houses, for a visit to the Berlin Bazaar had become one of the regulation "objects" for a winter's drive, as the "Abbey" or the "Castle" were for summer picnics.

Fanny's misunderstanding with her lover gave Mrs. Temple a good deal of trouble. For a considerable time the offended parties kept up a transparent veil of indifference which on Fanny's side dissolved in tears, when she grew confidential alone with Kate, and exhaled again into a perceptible cloud of sauciness when she sent Tom messages, or wrote to him. But the matter was not finally settled till Kate went to town to make sundry additions to her stock, and had a good long ·talk with Tom, which resulted in a full, complete, and rapturous reconciliation, strengthened and confirmed by a happy visit of two days at Christmas, when the display of novelties and temptations at the Berlin Bazaar startled all Pierstoffe and the surrounding district.

So the days and weeks rolled by, scarcely heeded, save when one or other of the partners exclaimed at the rapid recurrence of Sunday. And now the daylight began to stay a little longer each evening, and blustering north-easters to show how fierce and rough the young year could be in its play.

It was the close of a bright cold day which had not brought many customers to the Berlin Bazaar, and Kate had looked at her watch, thinking that soon she might order the shutters to be put up, and retire to the coziness of the apartment usually termed the "shop-parlor." Fanny had yawned twice over a thrilling tale in the last *Family Herald*, when the door of the shop opened, the well-known tinkle of a dog's bell was heard, and to their surprise Lady Styles walked in.

"Good morning, Mrs. Temple,"—to Fanny—"give me a chair: I am quite tired and out of breath. Thank you ; thank you ! Oh dear ! "—sitting down, laying her muff on the counter, and turning round another chair to put her feet on the bar. " Well, I suppose you are surprised to see me here so late. I have been all the way to Acol Court. I have intended going there for an age ; and now I find the whole family away in town. What in the world takes them to town so early, and the father not even in the House ? My coachman declared he must rest and bait the horses before we attempted the long hill between this and Weston ; so I thought *I* would rest here, and they can take me up when Davis and the horses have refreshed sufficiently. And what has been going on ? Why, it is nearly ten days since I was here."

But Mrs. Temple had not even the ghost of a scandal wherewith to regale her ladyship, who felt a little impatient at this want of subject matter for conversation.

"I protest, my dear Mrs Temple, you are singularly unobservant for an intelligent young woman. Have you heard nothing of that new man, Bryant ? Old Slade declares there is something very odd, very odd indeed, in his being always called in to the rich West Indian girl at the school here. I fancied you must have heard something about it. You have, at all events ?" —turning sharply on Fanny, who was laughing quietly, as she thought, out of sight. "No ! then what are you laughing at ?

Well, I want a couple of pairs of gloves. Have you any black stitched with colors? They are very useful in winter. What a good idea of yours, to keep gloves!" and her ladyship doubled up a thick, pudgy hand for measurement, chattering all the time, while Fanny sought the required commodity and handed them to Kate.

"I suppose your rooms have been vacant all the winter? You did pretty well with them last season, did you not? It would be nice now for some of your London or French friends to come and pay you a visit?"

"It would," replied Kate, gravely, as she laid a black kid glove against the fist which lay on the counter.

"But visitors are expensive, hey?—pleasures of hospitality not to be had for nothing."

"No, indeed," echoed Kate.

"Of course, you can see your friends when you go up to town."

"Of course, Lady Styles."

"Don't you ever take a holiday?" suddenly twisting her chair round to face Fanny.

While the little assistant parried the attack, and the cross-examination continued, Mills was resting from her labors during the lawful interval "between lights."

The back of the house, where the kitchen was situated, was considerably darkened by the cliffs behind, and evening always seemed an hour older there than at the front. Mills's arms were folded in her apron; her cap looked erect and defiant, but the eyes beneath it were closed for that indefinite space of time known as "forty winks." The "gurl," respecting the repose of so august a superior, stepped cautiously to and fro, softly placing sundry articles in their right places and ultimately putting forth the tea-things on a small, round, deal table, which could stand comfortably near the fire and Mrs. Mills, whose feet were on the fender. In the attempt to shorten her work, the unlucky "gurl" took up too many cups and spoons in her hand, and one of the latter fell, ringing on the tiled floor.

"Eh! what mischief have you done now?" cried Mills, starting into full consciousness and wrath. "Of all the awkward— What is it?"

"Only a spoon, mum. I thought you would like your tea, so I was a setting it."

"Oh, ay! Well, I am just dying for a cup. Is the kettle boiling? Bring me the tea caddy."

Mrs. Mills proceeded solemnly to measure the required quantity, and held a spoonful over the mouth of a brown tea-pot, smoking from the operation of scalding just performed, when the front bell was sharply and loudly rung. This was unusual.

"Now, who *can* that be!" exclaimed Mills, pausing, the spoon still in her hand. "Who can it be at this hour? Anyhow, I'll wet the tea first."

The short delay seemed to exhaust the patience of the applicant for admission, and another peal startled Mills and her sub.

"I had better go, mum," cried the latter.

"Not while I have the strength to do it will I let a chit like you go to my missus's front door!" replied Mills, solemnly, and walking slowly out of the kitchen.

On opening the front door, a gentleman met her view—a slight man, with a plaid over his shoulder, and a black bag in his hand.

"Mr. Tom!" cried Mills, "is it yourself?"

"No other!" cried Tom Reed, who had turned at the sound of the opening door, and held out his hand to Mills with a radiant countenance as he crossed the threshold.

"Just walk in and sit down by the fire a minute, sir; I'll tell my missus and Miss Fanny."

"And how do you find yourself, Mrs. Mills?" said Tom, cheerfully, but not quite loud enough, as he placed his plaid and bag on a chair.

"Just the same as ever," returned Mills, shaking her head. "As flighty and troublesome. Yet if a body ails a bit, that kind and good that——"

"But yourself, Mrs, Mills?" interrupted Tom in a more audible tone. "How goes it with yourself?"

"Bless your heart, sir! I am that stiff with rheumatics and that heart-broken, I'm sure it is a wonder I am alive! Look there, sir!"—lifting a corner of the curtain hanging over the low side-window which commanded the shop, and pointing to the group still visible in the waning light. "*That* is enough to curl the blood in my veins! Oh, the ups and downs I have seen! Well, no matter! You'll have a chop to your tea, sir?"

"Oh, anything—anything! Do you think you could manage to call Miss Fanny?"

"I'll see, sir; but as I was saying—"

Here the narrow door leading into the shop was pushed open gently, and Fanny entered. Catching sight of Tom, she stopped short, and exclaimed, but in a suppressed tone, "Tom! is it possible? I am so glad to see you. What has brought you here? Some good news, I am sure."

"Are you really and truly glad to see me, you saucy, mischievous puss?" cried Tom, taking both her hands in his.

"I am sure you might have knocked me down with a feather when I opened the door and saw Mr. Tom!" ejaculated Mills.

"Do you know I am dying for tea or something?" said Tom very loud, his keen dark eyes flashing from Fanny to Mills with an impatient expression.

"Dear me ! to be sure you are," replied the latter, hurrying away. "You shall have it in a jiffey."

"Now, my darling !" began Tom—

"Hush—hush !" exclaimed Fanny. "If you speak so loud that terrible Lady Styles will hear you ; and I really believe she would walk in here *coûte que coûte* to find out who you are;"

She hastily rearranged the curtain Mills had displaced, and turning, found herself in her cousin's arms.

"There, Tom—that's enough. Not one more ! Only fancy if Lady Styles could peep in !" was Fanny's next exclamation.

"But she can't, dearest, sweetest Fan ! Who the deuce is this Lady Styles ?"

"The most tremendous gossip. Oh, you must have heard us speak of her."

"Very likely," returned Tom, placing himself on the sofa, and beckoning to Fanny to sit beside him. "And now tell me, how are you ? And how goes on the business ? I must say you look thriving !"

"Well, we really are. The winter has been much better than we ventured to hope. And oh ! it is quite wonderful the way Kate manages. Why, there is nothing on earth our customers don't ask for—and I do believe that if any one was to enquire for—for—oh, a Lord Chancellor's wig ! I believe Kate would say, with her air of grave attention, ' We do not generally keep them in stock—but I have no doubt I could procure one for you ! '"

Here Mrs. Mills entered with a tea-tray and proceeded to lay the cloth. "And now," continued Fanny, "do tell me what has brought you down here !"

"Ah ! that's a secret till I tell Kate !"

"Nonsense, she has no secrets from me ! Mills, that cloth is crooked !" jumping up to put it straight. "I wonder if Lady Styles ever intends to go," peeping under the curtain. "No ! there she is, talking away still. Mills, have you no shrimps ?—a Pierstoffe tea without shrimps is quite a contradiction."

"Yes, sure," returned Mills, testily ; "but I haven't two pair of arms, have I ? I cannot fetch everything at once, can I ?"

"No ! no ! of course not ! just go like a dear and do Mr. Tom's chop, and I will finish laying the cloth."

Mills had turned to the door when a sudden and violent ringing startled them all.

"That bell," said Mills, solemnly, "is gone mad."

"A runaway ring, probably," remarked Tom.

"There's never no such thing here," returned Mills as she left the room.

"Tom, dear ! would you not like a glass of ale with your chop ? It is really good—you liked it before."

" This is downright delicious," cried Tom, rising and rubbing his hands with an air of intense enjoyment.

" What is ? "

" Why, the little attentions ! the delightful homelike charm of—"

" Ah ! Tom," interrupted Fanny, " don't fancy you are writing a domestic tale for ' Household Words.' "

" You insulting—" but Mill's voice in the hall made both pause and listen.

" I don't hear a word you say ! You'd better step in and speak to Miss Fanny." She opened the door as she spoke and ushered in Dr. Slade.

Doctor Slade in top-boots, much splashed, in a green hunting coat, and a hunting whip in his hand.

" Where is Mrs. Temple ? " cried that gentleman in a hasty and imperious tone. " I must see her immediately—there has been a bad accident in the hunting field, and I have ordered the sufferer to be brought here."

" An accident ! Oh, what shall we do ? " cried Fanny.

" Fetch Mrs. Temple," repeated the doctor, slapping his boot impatiently.

" Kate, dear, *could* you come for a moment ? " said Fanny, going very softly and timidly through the shop door ; something in her face made Mrs. Temple come directly, after a hasty word of apology to Lady Styles.

" Doctor Slade ! Tom ! " she exclaimed—and then shut her lips in extreme annoyance that in her surprise the last name had escaped them.

" Bad business in the field to-day," cried the Doctor. " Accident just outside the town—man thrown—scarcely know what injuries yet—but I always try to do you a good turn, so I have ordered him to be brought here—your rooms are vacant, eh ? " then shouting in Mill's ear, " Get a bedroom ready immediately, sheets, blankets, baths, hot water ! Eh, what do you say ? "

" That I would really rather not have your patient," returned Mrs. Temple, " if you could take him elsewhere."

" Now don't be perverse ! this house is more than half a mile nearer than the hotel, and it is of the last importance that the unfortunate man should be attended to at once—besides, extreme quiet will be essential, and he will get that here—and I cannot unsay my directions ; they are carrying him here on a door, and may arrive any moment."

" It will not be very pleasant for Mrs. Temple if he dies," said Tom, gravely ; " pray who is the sufferer ? "

" I really can't tell—but evidently a man of position—anyhow, Mrs. Temple, you must not reject him ; I will be answerable for

everything—come—I must follow that capital old woman of
yours upstairs and see things put in order."

"Tom," cried Mrs. Temple, as the Doctor bustled away, "this
sudden appearance of yours half frightens me, yet how glad I
am to see you! You have news of some kind, but I must not
stop to hear it now. I shall come back as soon as possible.
Come, Fanny, we may be of some use upstairs ; it is useless to
resist Dr. Slade."

But Fanny had already vanished ; and Tom, being alone, proceeded to stir the fire, with due regard to a comfortable-looking
brown tea-pot standing before it, and then took up a position on
the hearth-rug meditatively. His reflections, however, were soon
agreeably interrupted by the reappearance of Fanny with a tray
in her hands on which were a dish with a bright tin cover, and
a pretty jug with some creamy-looking froth peeping over its
edges.

"There," said Fanny, arranging these articles on the table ;
"because a man is killed you need not be famished. I do hope
the chops are nice" (lifting the cover). "And there is some
beer, and tea, and shrimps and things ; and oh ! a brown loaf.
Do try and eat."

"Why, Fanny, it is a feast ! The chops are a picture ! If
there is one quality more angelic than another in a woman, it is
that tender regard for man's minor wants—that thoughtful pre-
vision which supplies the required provision just in the nick of
time. There is a wonderful charm in having a pretty woman
flitting about you at meals—pouring out the beer, handing you
the bread, adding fire to the pepper, and piquancy to the sauce
(query)."

"Ah, that's all very nice but I must not stop to listen," interrupted Fanny, with a smile and a nod. "Do make yourself comfortable," and she was gone.

Upstairs she found Mills and her mistress busy unfolding blankets, and hastily setting forth house linen, while Doctor Slade
stood writing some hasty lines on a scrap of paper upon the mantel-piece, which "the gurl," in bonnet and shawl, stood at the
door ready to receive and convey to the surgery.

The doctor's short, sharp, and decisive directions were rapidly carried out ; for having, partly from surprise, partly from compassion, permitted the doctor's arrangement to stand, Kate went
heartily into the preparations for her expected guest, while
Fanny sped up and down stairs with right good will to save
poor Mills some fatigue.

Soon the trampling of men and horses' feet outside made
Kate's heart beat with nervous anticipation.

"Stay here," said Dr. Slade to Mrs. Mills ; "I will go down
to direct."

Mrs. Temple stole softly to the head of the stairs, where Mills had placed a lamp, with a sort of shrinking curiosity, reflecting that the drawing-room offered a retreat close behind her. The open door below admitted a current of cold air, and it seemed as if a multitude of people, all hushed, yet eager, from the sort of suppressed murmur that arose, had thronged into the hall below ; then Dr. Slade's voice ordered, " Keep him as level as you can ; mind the turn ; steady ; straight on ; first door on the right."

As the slow, heavy steps of the bearers advanced, Kate retreated ; and at length, from the half open door of the " best sitting-room," saw several men supporting a long helpless form, in a red coat all covered with clay on the side next her—a ghastly, pale face, bruised and bloody, and a look of death upon the whole figure as it was borne past. A feeling of awe and compassion crept over her.

" Kate, dear Kate ! are you there ? " said Fanny in a frightened whisper out of a dark corner where she had hidden herself. " Have they quite gone ? "

" Yes, quite. I am rather faint, Fan."

" No wonder ! Why did you look ? You ought to have gone into a corner and shut your eyes, like me ! Now I will just go and see if I can bring Mills anything. Oh ! here is Mills. Well ! What are they doing, Mills ? "

" Just putting of him to bed, miss.. Eh ! but he is a tall gentleman, and knocked about terrible ! His own man is there, and seems very wise-like. I am going for hot water."

" I will fetch it, Mills," cried Fanny, running downstairs.

" Oh, Mills, do you think he will die ? " asked Kate.

" God knows, ma'am ; he looks like death."

In the meantime Tom had begun to discuss his chop with a grateful and satisfied heart—not to mention an excellent appetite —when his repast was interrupted.

The narrow door before mentioned, leading into the shop, slowly opened, and a stout richly-dressed lady, with nodding plumes, squeezed through. Tom, reluctant, rose.

" I beg your pardon ; but could I speak to Mrs. Temple for a moment—just one moment ? "

" Mrs. Temple has been called away to attend to a gentleman who has broken his back, or his leg, or both, out hunting," replied Tom.

" Dear, dear, how very dreadful ! As I know most of the gentlemen about here, I think I shall just stay and ascertain who it is. Pray do not let me disturb you. I beg you will go on with your tea or dinner."

" Well, if you permit me, I will, for I have had a long journey. Mrs.—a—"

" Styles—Lady Styles," supplied her ladyship, graciously, while she revolved the problem of Tom's presence in her mind with the keenest zest. " Very nice, respectable-looking young man," she thought. " What on earth brings him here? *Much* too young to be safe—quite right," she said aloud ; " a long journey is a hungry concern. Come from town, eh ? "

" From town," echoed Tom.

" Hum ! the man she buys her wools and things from," meditated Lady Styles. " What's this they call them ?—bagmen." ·

" Might I offer you some refreshment ? " said Tom, with a graceful wave of the hand towards the jug. " The beer I can answer for, and there's some tea there has been brewing the last half-hour."

" He means to be monstrous civil," thought her ladyship, smiling upon her companion. " He is really a very good-looking young man. I will sit down with him. People are always confiding and communicative when they are eating. Well, really," she said, as Tom lifted the tea-pot from the hob to the table, " I do not think I can resist ; tea is tempting, and this is the hour I generally have my afternoon cup." So saying, she sat down, drew off her gloves, and threw off her bonnet strings, while Tom returned to his chop. " I do not presume," he said, " to pour out ; that is a lady's privilege."

" Oh ! I can help myself, thank you. And do you often come down here, Mr.—a—? "

" Not quite often enough ; every three or four months."

" Ha ! in love with one or the other of them," said Lady Styles to herself. " I suppose there are fashions in everything," she continued aloud.

" Just so," returned Tom, who divined her conjectures.

" Bread, Lady Styles ! and if you are of an industrious turn, let me recommend the shrimps ; for securing the largest amount of occupation and the smallest possible return of enjoyment there is nothing like shrimps."

" Thank you ! I am rather fond of shrimps," adding to herself, "quite a chatty, pleasant young man ! so," she resumed aloud, " you do not require to come round often ? I presume there is not the same amount of change in your business as in other branches, drapery and millinery for instance ? "

" I don't know that," replied Tom, gravely. " There is a good deal of ' dressing up ' in my line."

" Indeed ! Costumes, as well as this style of thing, eh ? " nodding towards the shop.

" The British public, so the critics say, have ceased to care for a plain unvarnished tale."

"Oh, I see!" she cried, "periodicals and newspapers."

"Precisely," said Tom.

"I suppose you have only known Mrs. Temple since she began business?" resumed Lady Styles.

"Since she began business," echoed Tom.

"She is such a nice ladylike creature, I have always thought it extraordinary to see her behind a counter—very extraordinary!"

"Quite extraordinary!" ejaculated Tom.

"I suppose," said Lady Styles, pausing as she picked a shrimp, "I suppose there is the usual story of speculation and failure, and all that; but do you know that the gossips here (it is a monstrously gossiping place!) say that her husband is still alive, but undergoing penal servitude for forgery, and all sorts of crimes?"

"I assure you the late Mr. T. is as defunct as the shrimp which now occupies your ladyship's fingers!"

"Ah! then you knew her during her late husband's lifetime!" cried Lady Styles, sharply.

"Good Heavens!" exclaimed Tom, "what a cross-examining counsel you would have been! There was legal acumen in the way you pounced upon that inference."

"Life, my dear sir," returned Lady Styles, much flattered, "and experience, are first-rate wit sharpeners."

"Undoubtedly," said Tom, filling his tumbler, "when, as in your ladyship's case, there are wits to sharpen."

"And what was this husband? No great things, I fancy, or he would have left more money behind him," pursued her ladyship.

"Oh, he was in business too."

"What sort of business?"

"Why, he imported 'sugar and spice and all that's nice!'"

"I see—a grocer! Well, I am disappointed! I thought, from her air and style, there must be a romantic story attached to her. So the late Temple was a grocer!" pouring herself out another cup of tea.

"Don't you think they are a long time putting that man to bed?" said Tom, who was growing a little weary of her ladyship's company.

"What an odd way of expressing it! but these bagmen are great characters, I believe," thought Lady Styles. "Well, I daresay he requires a great deal of care and attention, and perhaps—"

Mrs. Temple, entering, cut short the sentence. "My dear Tom!" she cried, and then, seeing Lady Styles, stopped short. Lady S. made a mental note of the exclamation.

"You are surprised to see me, my dear Mrs. Temple, but I just waited to ascertain who is the hero of the accident. But, I assure you, your friend here has done the honors remarkably well—better tea, bread and butter, and shrimps I have never eaten!"

"You are very good to say so. I believe the gentleman, Dr. Slade's patient, is one of the party who occupy Hurst Lodge this season," added Kate, anxious to satisfy and get rid of her customer.

"You don't say so! Why, I am told they are a sad racketty set. I would get rid of him as soon as I could, or you will have the whole lot in and out, smoking, and Heaven knows what!"

"I rather think not," said Kate, quietly.

"It is certainly a long rough way to take him," continued Lady Styles, not heeding her, "and much more convenient to Dr. Slade to have him close by, than all that distance; but here *is* Dr. Slade. Well, Doctor, how is the poor man? and who is he?"

The doctor entered with a pompous air, followed by Fanny, who stole behind Kate.

"Well," replied the doctor, "he is still insensible, and not likely to recover consciousness for a few hours. His arm is broken, and I suspect concussion of the brain; but our good friend Mrs. Temple need not mind charging for trouble—he is a man of position and property—he is Sir Hugh Galbraith!"

CHAPTER XVI.

"SIR HUGH GALBRAITH."

This announcement sent a sort of electric shock through three of Dr. Slade's hearers. Mrs. Temple started, visibly—to Tom Reed—and her cheeks flushed, but she instantly recovered her composure. Fanny uttered a prolonged " Oh!" which Tom Reed covered by a fit of coughing, and Lady Styles exclaimed with great animation, "You do not say so, Doctor!" Then turning to Kate continued, "A most disagreeable man, my dear! refuses all invitations! would not dine with *me!* and we all know that if a man rejects respectable society it is because he prefers disreputable people. You must make him well as soon as you can, Doctor, and send him off."

"I certainly shall," returned the doctor; "but it may be a tedious affair; however, there are, I think, no internal injuries, and I have known men recover perfectly after lying insensible for forty-eight hours, or more." Looking very keenly at Tom Reed while he spoke.

"I trust it will not be a very bad case," said Tom, answering the look. "Mrs. Temple will find it tough work to attend to business and an invalid at the same time."

"This gentleman is Miss Lee's cousin, and acts as our London agent," Mrs. Temple hastened to explain, though she felt so be-

wildered that her own voice sounded to her as if some one else
was speaking.

"Oh," said Dr. Slade.

"Ah," said Lady Styles.

"Well," continued the doctor, "it seems I am all in the
wrong box. I thought I was doing Mrs. Temple a good turn
this dead season, by bringing her a tenant who is likely to be
tied by the leg for a month at any rate ; a rich man, who does
not care what he pays, and now you are all down upon me!"

"My dear Doctor!" cried Lady Styles, deprecatingly.

"I *am* obliged to you," said Mrs. Temple, quickly ; "I feel
sure you wished to serve me. We must all do our utmost to
make this—this gentleman well. I shall think nothing a trouble,
so as it is done quickly ; but," with great emphasis, "I trust in
heaven he will not die under my roof!"

"Die ! not a bit of it," exclaimed the doctor, cheerfully ; and
as to trouble, you need not take any. Sir Hugh's own servant,
who seems an intelligent handy fellow, can do nearly all that is
necessary ; if you want more help, why, get it, and put it in the
bill ; you need not be afraid to charge," and Dr. Slade took up
his hat in a sort of huffed manner.

"I am told Sir Hugh Galbraith has lately come into a large
fortune by somebody's will," said Lady Styles, as if inclined to
settle down to a fresh feast of gossip.

"There is some one in the shop, I think, Fanny," observed
Mrs. Temple, significantly.

Fanny left the room and returned almost immediately, while
Dr. Slade was remarking sternly, "I know nothing whatever
about the man except that he, Lord Herbert de Courcy, and a
Colonel Upton occupied Hurst Lodge for the hunting season.
I have heard, too, that this Galbraith was the rich man of the
party—so—"

"It is your servant, Lady Styles," interrupted Fanny. "Your
carriage has been waiting some time."

"Dear me ! I suppose so. It must be five o'clock !"

"Quarter to six," said Tom, looking at his watch.

"And I have nearly four miles to drive !" cried Lady Styles.
"I must really run away, Mrs. Temple ; but I shall send to-
morrow to inquire how Sir Hugh is going on. The day after
we are going into Yorkshire to stay with a niece of mine for a
month, but as soon as ever I return I shall call, and expect to
have a lot of news. Come, Doctor, I will set you down at your
house if you like."

"Oh, Doctor ! will you not come back this evening?" said
Mrs. Temple, anxiously.

"Certainly, certainly ! between nine and ten. And look here,

Mrs. Temple, give the groom a good supper, it will keep matters straight."

"Good morning, or rather evening, Mrs. Temple. Good evening, Mr.—a—Mr. Tom," said Lady Styles, graciously. "I shall always remember the shrimps whenever I hear of Sir Hugh Galbraith!" and she squeezed through the narrow door, followed by the doctor and Fanny to see her safe off the premises.

As Tom opened his lips, Mrs. Temple raised her hand to enjoin silence, and held it so, listening till the sound of the carriage driving off and the return of Fanny seemed to relax the tension of her nerves, and she sat down suddenly, as if no longer able to stand.

"This is the rummest go I ever knew!" cried Tom, taking up a position on the hearthrug.

"It has taken away my breath," said Fanny, heaving a deep sigh.

"Oh, Tom, Tom! how dreadful it will be if he dies!" said Mrs. Temple, clasping her hands.

"Awkward, exceedingly awkward!" returned Tom, thoughtfully. "However, as it cannot be helped, let us hope he will recover and clear out quickly. Don't you be tempted to put strychnine in his gruel or prussic acid in his beef tea."

"But, Tom, he looked like death!"

"Why did you look at him?" asked Fanny. "You should have kept back in the dark, as I did."

"Seriously, though," resumed Tom Reed, "this *contretemps* may prove very awkward. Suppose his solicitor comes down to see him, and recognizes you?"

"You forget! I never saw his solicitor in my life."

"That's all right; then there is nothing to fear. I fancied you had met Payne one day at Wall's. Keep out of Sir Hugh's way, and there need be no discovery."

"I do hope he will not die," repeated Mrs. Temple, recovering herself, "for every reason. Of course some one would inherit after him, and I should have to fight the battle all the same, but victory would lose almost all its charm were it won over any other antagonist."

"May we venture to sit down and talk *à propos* of this said battle?" asked Tom.

"Oh yes!" cried Mrs. Temple; "I am burning to hear your report. Fanny, will you see Mills and ask her to get some supper ready for Sir Hugh's servant? How extraordinary to give such directions! Is it a good omen, Tom—my enemy being brought in senseless and helpless just as the first dawn of light begins to break—that is to say, if you have brought me any information?"

"A little—a very little," returned Tom.

"Don't begin till I come back," cried Fanny. "And oh, Kate! I had better not tell Mills who it is to-night, and *you* must tell her. What a fury she will be in!"

Tom, disregarding Fanny's injunction, immediately began to detail an interview he had had with Captain Gregory, who had at last reappeared. He described him as a regular merchant seaman, rough, but kindly, evidently accustomed to keep his eyes open, and his wits ready for active service. He had heard nothing of the subject in question beyond the death of Mr. Travers, and the timely assistance afforded to Mrs. Bell by his widow. He was therefore greatly astonished to hear of the present state of things, and ready to give all the information in his power.

"He said he well remembered 'Father' mentioning the will, though not its contents. 'The old gentleman was a bit of a "grumbler,"' said Captain Gregory, 'and I remember now, nearly two years ago, his growling about Mr. Travers not being the man he was, or he would have raised his salary, for he used to see into everything himself, but now he left too much to Ford, and somehow Ford didn't use to be quite friendly to father; but for all that, says father, "Mr. Travers trusted me to draw his will, and I do not think Ford will like to have a woman over him by and by, as he will have." Whereby,' added the Captain, 'I thought Mrs. Travers was to have everything.'

"'Did your father say he wrote it himself, or employed some one else?'

"'He wrote it all—so I understand. Father wrote a splendid hand—two or three sorts of hands! and I remember his saying he thought he might have a rise in his salary, after being trusted so far, for Mr. Travers made a secret of the will; and, you see, my sister and her children were a terrible drain on father. And he said, too, that there was no mention of him in the will, for, says he, "I witnessed it, as well as drew it"—he, and a man he called Poole. But Mr. Travers said he would give Mrs. Travers some instructions respecting father, which,' added Tom's informant, 'I suppose he did, sir, from the great kindness she showed my sister.'"

This was the substance of all Tom Reed could extract from Captain Gregory.

Kate listened, without interrupting by word or motion the narrative, and kept silent for a moment after he had ceased.

"This strongly confirms my own belief," she said at last; "but what is it worth in the opinion of others?"

"Not a great deal, I fear," replied Tom, though the words were spoken more to himself than addressed to her. "You see Mr. Travers might have destroyed that will a week, a day, after

it was made, and executed another. To you this morsel of intelligence is confirmation strong; in a court of law it would be
valueless."

"What do you think yourself?" asked Fanny, who had crept
quietly back into the room.

"Well," said Reed, looking up with a smile at Mrs. Temple,
"I am exceedingly reluctant to encourage or suggest false hope,
but there are two points in Gregory's account that struck me as
supporting your view: first, the will drawn by his father must
have been executed, from what he says, about the same time as
the one under which you have been dispossessed; secondly, the
witnesses are the same. These facts certainly give color to
your impression, that a false document has been substituted for
the one drawn out by Gregory."

"What is the penalty for committing forgery?" asked Mrs.
Temple, abruptly.

"Penal servitude, for a term of years, according to the circumstances of the case. Why? Have you a vision of your unknown enemy in the dock?"

"I have," said Mrs. Temple; "and the horror of it makes me
hesitate, for it will yet be in my power to put him there."

Her voice faltered as she said this, and to the great surprise
of both Tom and Fanny, she burst into tears, and hurried from
the room.

"Poor dear Kate," cried the latter. "I do not know when I
saw her cry before. But she has been wonderfully upset by this
accident, and that wretched man being carried in! Is it not
unfortunate? I had better go to her."

"No, don't," said Tom. "I am certain she would be better
alone. Yes; it is most unlucky Galbraith being brought here;
yet after all they need not meet!"

"No, I suppose not. But, Tom, I would so much like to go
in and see what he is like—to speak to him, I mean—that is if he
recovers. In spite of poor Kate's tears, it is so funny, the idea
of having Sir Hugh,—the great bogie of our existence, absolutely living in the house, and Mills cooking for him. How *will*
Mills bear it when she knows?—and she must know! I really
think I will go and ask what he will have for dinner some day,
as if I was the housemaid."

"I beg you will do no such thing," said Tom, sharply. "You
are so thoughtless! You would never be out of a scrape if
you hadn't Mrs. Travers at your elbow."

"I am not quite such a stupid," pouted Fanny; "and I can
tell you I shall do as I like!"

"My dear child," returned Tom, "don't you think it is only
natural I should wish to prevent my pretty little cousin from ven-

turing into the den of an ungodly dragoon like Galbraith, and in the character of a housemaid, too! Heaven only knows what impertinence he might be guilty of!"

"Is he so very wicked?" asked Fanny, opening her eyes, but not appearing as much horrified as she ought to have been.

"I really know nothing about him," said Tom Reed, laughing. "He is like other men, I suppose, neither better nor worse. It is very natural for Mrs. Travers to dislike him; but, except for that foolish and insulting letter he wrote, he has done nothing exceptionally wrong or unjust. He certainly made a shabby offer—I mean the allowance—but I daresay he might have been induced to give more. Then you must remember he never had an opportunity of correcting his idea of Mrs. Travers by personal intercourse, and—"

"Tom!" interrupted Fanny, indignantly, "I am astonished at you! making excuses for Sir Hugh in that way! He is a brute! at any rate he behaved like one."

"I protest, Fanny, you are the most unreasonable, hopeless, faithful little partisan that any one was ever tormented with. I cannot afford to quarrel with you, because I must be in town on Monday morning and bid you good-by to-morrow."

The conversation accordingly took a more personal direction, and Mrs. Temple's absence did not appear so much prolonged as it really was.

"Perhaps, after all," said Fanny, who had gradually changed round to take a more rose-colored view of things in general, after a long, desultory but charming talk, "his coming here may lead to good; I mean Sir Hugh Galbraith."

"How do you make that out?"

"He may get to know Kate, and she him, and divide the property."

"Don't talk such preposterous nonsense, my darling! Don't you see, it would never do for him to know who Mrs. Temple is? It would be the most cruel mortification to her to be recognized by him in her present position. If you are all quiet and prudent, this *contretemps* will not signify; that is to say, if the man does not die. If he does, it will be most awkward."

Here Mrs. Temple returned. The sufferer, she said, still lay unconscious and insensible; but his servant, Mills reported, seemed not despondent. He had been in the wars, he said, with his master and had seen him worse hit and recover. "And, Fanny," continued the young widow, "I have broken the fatal intelligence to Mills. She was thunder-struck, indignant, speechless—but she is now calmer, and resigned to the necessity of the case. This is one difficulty off my mind," concluded Mrs. Temple, with a sigh.

Soon after Dr. Slade came in, and, having visited his patient, re-entered the parlor only to repeat that there was nothing to be done—nothing but patience ; that he hoped to-morrow would bring a favorable change.

He then proceeded to give an elaborate account of how the accident occurred, much of which was Hebrew and Greek to Mrs. Temple and Fanny, but interested Tom Reed considerably, so the doctor went on fluently. The rest of the Hurst Lodge party had left, he informed them, and Sir Hugh, who had remained for the finish of the season, was a stranger in the county when he came down, and had remained so. He was a silent, haughty, ungenial sort of man—though Dr. Slade himself had found him civil enough ! he did not seem to have many friends or relatives, for the only person, suggested by his servant, to be informed of the accident was Colonel Upton, —th Hussars, Dublin, and to him the doctor had accordingly written. The talk then flowed from hunting to politics, and the doctor, finding Tom Reed a companion of far different calibre from those to whom he was accustomed, prolonged the sitting till a late hour ; but at last he departed, and, greatly wearied by the events and emotions of the day, the two friends bade Tom good-night and gladly retired to rest.

Another day of great anxiety, though not of so much excitement, ensued. Several gentlemen connected with the hunt came and sent to make inquiries for the injured baronet. Lady Styles dispatched a man on horseback with a note to Dr. Slade, which drew forth some strong language from that gentleman, as he objected to the trouble of replying ; but, in spite of all these disturbances, Mrs. Temple contrived to enjoy some comfort in taking counsel with Tom. She reluctantly agreed with him in thinking there was no more to be done at present. Tom suggested that the substance of Captain Gregory's statement should be embodied in an affidavit in case the worthy seaman should be inaccessible when any further light came. Then they must fold their hands again and wait. This course was decided on, also —that it was unnecessary to open the subject again with Messrs. Wall and Wreford until they had more to communicate. " Do you know," said Tom, as he stood ready to depart, "I am almost sorry we have looked up this captain ? His information has not done you a bit of good. It only serves to irritate and chafe you, by confirming your suspicions of foul play."

" No, Tom," returned Kate. " In one sense it comforts me, by confirming my belief that my poor husband was worthy of my affection and respect ; that he was not base enough to leave me penniless, friendless, and scarred with the suspicions to which such a will leaves me open ! "

"You are unnecessarily sore on that head! The whims of testators never reflect upon those who suffer from them," returned Tom. "That would be too bad. Now I must be off; write to me every day, one or other of you, please. I shall settle that matter of the affidavit directly I get to town."

It was not till the evening of the day after his accident that Sir Hugh Galbraith began to show consciousness, after which beginning he recovered his senses rapidly.

The third day brought a solemn, carefully-dressed gentleman from London, who announced himself to be Mr. George Galbraith, and next of kin to Sir Hugh. He asked to see the mistress of the house, and Mrs. Temple sent Mills, who knew more of the patient's case than she did. Mills proved an excellent representative. She reported the new comer as a nice, civil-spoken gentleman. He had received intelligence of the accident from Colonel Upton, who had telegraphed to the doctor requesting further tidings, and stating that it was almost impossible that he could leave his regiment at present.

"Mr. G. St. John Galbraith" (such was the inscription on his card), had an interview with his cousin—not a very long one—and departed, "looking," said Fanny, who took a stolen peep at him through an inch-wide opening of the parlor door, "'a sadder and a wiser man' than when he arrived. Depend upon it, Kate, he is the next heir, and is quite disappointed."

"For shame, Fanny," returned her friend.

A few days more, and ten had elapsed since the accident. As Dr. Slade had assured Mrs. Temple, there was very little to be done, and very little additional trouble given to the quiet household. Mrs. Mills confessed that Sir Hugh's man was very different from "that other glum, dour fellow we had here. He doesn't talk much, but he has a civil word when he does open his mouth, and saves a body what trouble he can."

It seemed incredible that the arch enemy should be installed under Kate Travers's roof and make so little difference. A constant odor of beef tea in the kitchen, a little more compounding of light puddings, a larger roast for the one o'clock dinner, a larger consumption of the bitter beer which Tom Reed so highly approved—these were the outward and visible signs of the wonderful event that had so mightily disturbed the quiet current of the young widow's life.

Sir Hugh had now progressed into the sitting-room, and at times, when the shop was silent, Kate and Fanny could hear him slowly pacing to and fro. Every day the doctor paid him a long visit, after which he usually informed Mrs. Temple, rubbing his hands joyously while he spoke, that "Sir Hugh was going on very well—very well indeed—but could not move just yet; would do better if he was a little more patient."

Sir Hugh became a customer also. He had all the papers and publications Mrs. Temple could supply, besides books from Mudie's, Indian papers, literature in abundance of the lighter kind, and, as time wore on, the house became pervaded by the perfume of very good tobacco.

"Ah!" said Fanny, when she first perceived it, "that is delicious! it reminds me of Tom!"

One rainy afternoon, nearly a fortnight after Sir Hugh Galbraith had become her tenant, Mrs. Temple and Fanny were both in the shop—the latter at work on a piece of "grounding" she kept at hand for unemployed moments, the former sheltered behind a screen of pendent patterns, finishing a delightful, brilliant article in a "Westminster Review" left her by Tom Reed. It was a hopeless sort of day for business, scarcely any customers had crossed the threshold, and Mrs. Temple felt quite at liberty to obey a mysterious "nod and beck" from Mrs. Mills, delivered through the little parlor window. "Do you know, ma'am," said Mills, as soon as her mistress crossed the threshold, "Sir Hugh Galbraith wants you to go up and write a letter for him?"

"Write a letter," repeated Mrs. Temple, astounded.

"Yes," persisted Mills, frowning yet laughing. "I felt as if I could throw the jug I had in my hand at him. His man has gone over to the place he had; I believe it is to be given up to-morrow. So I went to answer the bell, and says he, 'Can you write?' 'Of course I can,' says I. 'Very well,' says he, quick; 'get the writing materials, and be so good as to write a letter for me.' 'That's quite different,' says I. 'I couldn't write well enough for you, sir.' 'Oh!' says he, 'you are not the woman of the house, are you?' 'No, sir,' says I. 'Well, I daresay she writes well enough; I wish you would ask her to come here,' says he, impatient like. So I just came to you, for I didn't know what to say."

Mrs. Temple stood silent, gazing fixedly at Mills without seeing her, for a minute or two in deep thought. Should she refuse? Should she send Fanny? No; Fanny was too young—too giddy. Moreover she had a strange sort of wish to stand face to face with her foe. While she hesitated, a sharp, angry peal of the drawing-room bell startled her into decision. "I will go, Mills," she said; "tell Miss Fanny." Without giving herself time to think or grow nervous Kate ran upstairs, and opening the door, which stood ajar, entered so quietly that Sir Hugh did not hear her. He was stretched upon the sofa, a cigar in his mouth and the *Times* in his left hand; his right arm tied up and in a sling. A tall, gaunt-looking figure, wrapped in a gray dressing-gown covered with Indian embroidery in the same color; a long, thin face, very pale though slightly weather-beaten; long red moustaches, hair a shade darker and somewhat scanty upon the temples, one of which was scarred, as if by a sword cut. As he made no movement, Mrs. Temple advanced to a table that stood in the middle of the room, and, leaning one hand lightly upon it, said, "You wished to see me."

At the sound of her soft, but remarkably distinct tones, Sir Hugh looked up in great surprise, and starting to his feet threw his cigar into the fire.

"I beg your pardon," he exclaimed, in a deep, harsh voice, though the accent was well-bred, and gazing at her intently with, she thought, the sternest and most sombre eyes she had ever met; "I beg your pardon; I wanted to speak to the woman of the house."

"*I* am the woman of the house," returned Mrs. Temple, quietly, meeting and returning his gaze unflinchingly, her large dark eyes lit up with an expression of which she was unconscious, but which Sir Hugh afterwards described to a confidential friend as "the sort of look you might expect from a man that stood foot to foot with you, his sword across yours. There was hatred and defiance both in her eyes."

For an instant they paused, gazing fascinated at each other, then Sir Hugh recovering himself said composedly enough, "Indeed! May I trouble you to write a few lines for me? I am anxious not to lose this day's post or I would not ask you."

"I will write for you if you require it," returned Mrs. Temple, simply. "Where are your writing things?"

"On the cabinet; but I will get them."

"Allow me," said Mrs. Temple; "you had better not exert yourself I imagine." She brought over a blotting-book and ink-bottle, and, setting them on the table, observed, "I see no pen, I will bring one," and went away quickly to her own desk. When she returned Sir Hugh was standing exactly in the same position in which she had left him. She immediately sat down, arranged the paper, and dipping her pen in the ink, looked up, saying, "I am quite ready." Again she met the same grave, surprised, inquiring gaze; again there was an unconscious pause of mutual contemplation.

"I am ready," repeated Mrs. Temple.

"My dear Upton," began Sir Hugh.

"If you begin in the first person," said Mrs. Temple, abruptly, for she could not feel him to be a stranger, "how will you sign your name? You cannot write! Had I not better begin: 'I am directed by Sir Hugh Galbraith?'"

7

"Then *you* must sign it, and that won't do," he returned. "I will try and sign with my left hand."

"Very well, go on then," said Mrs. Temple.

"My dear Upton. Thanks for yours. I believe I am nearly all right again, though still a little shaky. If your friend's horse is all you say, and you are a fair judge, I feel inclined to buy him."

"One moment," interrupted Mrs. Temple, looking up with a smile; "I am not writing shorthand."

"I beg your pardon," smiling in return, which greatly improved his countenance: "I never had the honor of having a private secretary before and scarcely know how to dictate."

"'To buy him,'" read Mrs. Temple, keeping her eyes on the paper; "go on." Sir Hugh did not go on for a moment; but Mrs. Temple did not move, holding her pen in readiness and her eyes cast down.

"If he is all you say," continued Galbraith.

"You said that before."

"Would you read it over to me?"

Mrs. Temple complied.

"Oh . . . ah . . yes; 'inclined to buy him.' Although now the season is over I really do not want a hunter. I shall therefore not give the price asked nor make any offer until I see the animal."

Mrs. Temple held up her hand, and Galbraith stopped abruptly, until her pen was arrested, and again without looking up, she read aloud, "the animal."

"Which," he resumed this time quite readily, "from what you say, I shall have an opportunity of doing, if I can only get up to town before Tattersall's next sale. What I want is a good weight carrier, that can stand the jar of big drops without giving way; for I think I shall hunt in ——shire, next season, and that is a very stiff country."

Again, a warning finger made him pause, nor was he prepared, when she read over the last word; so she was obliged to say "Well," and look up, before he continued. This time she met his eyes fixed upon her with the same grave wondering expression, but less stern than at first.

"'Country,'" repeated Sir Hugh. "Let me see. Oh . . . you know a horse must be deep in the girths and deuced strong in the forelegs to carry me well to the front in ——shire." Another pause.

"I must not trouble you too much," said Galbraith, slowly pulling out his moustaches, as if his inventive powers were exhausted. "Just say I am thinking of parting with my roan mare; she would make him a capital charger; that I am afraid my sword arm will never be the same again ; and that I hope to see him in London before long."

"Have you that down?" after a few minutes' silence.

"I have."

"Then just end it ; and I will try and sign my name."

"But what sort of ending shall I put?" asked Kate.

"Yours truly," returned Galbraith.

"Upton never had so legible an epistle from me before," he added, as she handed him the letter to read ; placing the blotting-book, ink, and pen near him, while he was thus occupied. Then a difficulty arose ; besides that of using his left hand, Sir Hugh had no other wherewith to steady the paper, seeing which, Mrs. Temple, with the natural impulse of a kindly self-forgetful woman, stepped forward and held it for him ; so he contrived to scrawl his signature. "Thank you. You really have done me a great service," said he, quietly, but very sincerely. "Now, will you direct an envelope, and I will release you. What a capital hand," he continued, still holding the letter, while Mrs. Temple addressed the cover ; "so clear—and—well spelled," as if speaking to himself.

"Tradespeople generally receive a good plain education," said Mrs. Temple, demurely, while the suspicion of a smile played in the corners of her mouth ; she could not resist the temptation to play with the piquante peculiarities of her position. "Shall I put up your note, or do you want anything added?" holding out her hand.

"Nothing more, thank you," replied Galbraith, slowly returning it to her ; and she proceeded quickly and methodically to arrange the writing materials much more tidily than they had been, and put them in their place.

"Pray," said Sir Hugh, moving slowly across the room, and looking to Mrs. Temple considerably taller and more gaunt than when lying on the sofa. "Pray, may I venture to ask your services as secretary again? I may have to answer a letter or two, and I am really helpless."

"I am sure," she returned, a faint increase of color enriching her cheek, "Doctor Slade would be happy to be of any use to you, and would be a more suitable amanuensis."

"I don't think so. Doctors write such fearful hieroglyphics. I trust you will be good enough to assist me in an emergency."

"In an emergency, yes," said Kate, quickly. "I will have your letter posted at once," she added. "Good morning."

"Good morning, and thank you," said Galbraith, holding the door open for her to pass through, while he bowed as deferentially as though she had been a duchess.

Mrs. Temple breathed a little quickly as she went into the

kitchen to dispatch Sarah to the post, and then proceeded to stand the brunt of a severe cross-examination from Fanny. "What a long time you have been," she cried. "What is he like? What was the letter about?" All of which, Kate answered more or less to her companion's satisfaction. Indeed, both friends made very merry over the interview. "I am sure, Kate, your description of the renowned Sir Hugh, sounds like an ogre."

"No; he is not like an ogre, though he is far from good-looking; evidently a cold, haughty man, yet not quite like what I expected."

"Nobody ever is," said Fanny, philosophically.

When Mrs. Temple was safe in her own room that night, she lit a second candle, and placing one on each side of her glass looked long at her own image; then rising from her seat, murmured to herself: "No, it would be undignified, unprincipled, unfair; yet, from all I can read and observe, men do not take disappointments to heart and suffer from them like women." Again she looked in the glass: "A bit of vulgar prettiness," she repeated. "He might have been contented to take me for a mistress." Might he? Of course it was optional to so great a man, "so superior to my lowliness; and he must have found me out in some delinquency." She paused. "It is a great temptation!" So saying, she extinguished the lights, and went to bed.

CHAPTER XVII.

SIR HUGH GALBRAITH was the last of a long line of careless, improvident country gentlemen. His own father put the finishing stroke to the family fortunes, as a highly cultivated taste for racing, gambling, yachting, and all the linked charms that thereabouts do hang rapidly dispersed what remained to him.

As soon as Hugh had reached a legal age, after a boyhood of most heterogeneous and intermittent training, he gloomily yet willingly agreed to join his father in breaking the entail. Gloomily, because his was exactly the nature to cling closely to the family estate, and to part with the acres which had so long supported the Galbraiths of Kirby-Grange was a bitter cross. Willingly, because the disgrace of unpaid debts was intolerable to his proud spirit.

So the late baronet, freed from his most pressing difficulties, took himself and his three daughters to the Continent, where they passed, on the whole, a very bearable existence. Two of Sir Hugh's sisters picked up good matches—the prettiest, and

the one he liked best, ran away with a German artist and died,
at which her brother sternly rejoiced, as he considered such a
marriage almost as disgraceful as if she had run away without
any.

As a boy, Hugh Galbraith had been left much alone at the old
country seat. His mother died while he was still a sturdy, passionate, bony urchin, in frocks—the terror of his nurses—the torment of his sisters. His father was generally away, his sisters
at school, and his only education what small doses of learning
the curate could induce him to imbibe. In other branches of a
gentleman's acquirements he rapidly progressed. There was no
horse in the stables or out of them he could not "back." He
was a good shot, and a bold sailor, for the Grange was close to
a wild craggy coast, where many a fisher's family had to mourn
the loss of the bread-winner and his boat in the stormy winter
time. To the fishermen the young master was always welcome,
and to them he could talk, not copiously, for his words were always few, but with a freedom that would have astonished his
father and his polite, worldly, elder sisters. These ornamental
members of his family designated him "a sulky bear"—"a
hopeless barbarian"—and not unjustly.

When he was about twelve, the curate left, and his father sent
him to a second-rate school for "Young Gentlemen," where he
was at first spoiled and petted as the sole representative of the
master's aristocratic connection; and then, when payments
grew more and more irregular, and the Dominie became enlightened as to the true state of affairs, the heir of Galbraith was
considerably snubbed—a process of annealing not at all condu-
cive to a healthy frame of mind.

It was about this time that Mr. Travers, who was first cousin
to Sir Hugh's father, fell in with the lad. Being himself of a
taciturn disposition, and having had a boyhood of hard knocks
and puddings without plums, he took a fancy to the young kinsman, whom no one else found attractive, put him to a good military school, bought him a commission in the line, and made him
a small allowance.

When Sir Frederick Galbraith died, and matters were arranged, a paltry pittance was all that remained of the revenues
once forthcoming from his estates. Every acre, save a few that
surrounded the old mansion, was sold; and these, with the
house, were let to a prosperous farmer, who wanted a little more
land and a little better abode.

Small as was his inheritance, Sir Hugh declared it sufficient,
renounced Mr. Travers's allowance, and exchanged into a dragoon regiment, with the prospect of going to India.

His relations with Mr. Travers continued to be most friendly.

He was looked upon and considered himself to be Mr. Travers's heir. In this light he shone in his married sister's drawing-rooms, when he condescended to go there, which was not often. To Mr. Travers he was heartily grateful, especially because he had not forced him to adopt trade, for which, said Mr. Travers, "I don't think you've brains enough." More, he liked and respected his benefactor better than any one else in the world—except, perhaps, his chum, his schoolfellow, his comrade, Willie Upton! and for him probably liking considerably outweighed respect. Nevertheless, it seemed quite right and natural that Mr. Travers should have toiled all his life to amass a fortune for him (Hugh Galbraith) to buy back his estates with and live on them as became a gentleman of high degree. When, therefore, the elder cousin announced his marriage—briefly, and with an unconquerable degree of shamefacedness which communicated itself to the inanimate pen—Hugh Galbraith was furious. It seemed to him a scandalous breach of faith—a base withdrawal from an unspoken contract, which should have been all the more binding on a gentleman because it had been unexpressed! And for whom was he thus defrauded? Some rosy-cheeked plebeian! some showy girl, that, in his own mind, he ranked with the barmaids and chambermaids who would not disdain addresses from the sergeants of his own troop! If she had been a gentlewoman, ever so poor, the injury to himself would have been the same, but he would not have felt quite the same loathing and contempt that added fuel to the fire with which he read Mr. Travers's communication.

"'The daughter of the lady with whom I have stayed for some years in the fishing season,'" he repeated scornfully to his friend Upton. "The woman who let him his lodgings, he means! How any man at any age can make such a —— ass of himself is beyond my comprehension; but a fellow like Travers!"

"Perhaps she was very pretty and taking," returned his confidant, who had an amiable weakness for the sex.

But Sir Hugh was not to be pacified, as we have seen, and not only spake unadvisedly with his lips, but, what was much worse, wrote unadvisedly with his pen.

It was a cruel blow. Hugh Galbraith had never been disposed to indulge in bright dreams of the future, although he had more imagination than any one gave him credit for. The bitterness of poverty in high places had eaten into his heart and closed it rigidly against the greater number of his fellow-creatures. He was strong to endure, and slow to speak—generally considered a cold, hard man, but too just, too real, not to have a certain amount of popularity with his brother officers. He

was just to his equals, and would fain have been generous to
his inferiors, as you would throw bones to a dog; not all the
severity of his training could expel the mighty selfwill of the
man. He would be kind to whoever obeyed and served him
but he burned to crush whoever crossed him. He was also
capable of a good deal of self-control up to a certain point, and
then "chaos came again!"

For women he had profound contempt, though it would have
surprised him to be told so. They rather bored him, yet he
would, if required, put himself to inconvenience for a woman, or
expose himself to danger, and would think the man who could
treat one badly a brute or a poltroon. A wife and legitimate
children were unavoidable duties to be incurred for the sake of
one's position, and to be held in all honor; but as for finding
companionship with women, or friendship, or a profitable exchange of ideas, such notions were never rejected by Galbraith
simply because they never suggested themselves. He had a
dim consciousness that devotion and observance from a well-
born, well-bred, very quiet woman would be pleasant, and a
sort of thing he had a right to expect by and by, when he was
older; but he was a little hard to please, for though he saw
plenty of well-bred women, and handsome ones too, there was
almost always a touch of affectation or unreality about them
which his own uncompromising nature detected and despised.

All this applied to women of his own rank. Those of a
humbler class were much more endurable than the men, and by
no means to be badly treated. But then the treatment was
measured by a totally different standard, and wounds inflicted
on a lady for which blood only could atone, might for a woman
of low degree be salved by golden ointment.

This is a tolerably correct sketch of Hugh Galbraith's ideas
on matters and things in general, though it would have taken
him a long time to extricate them with equal clearness from the
tangle of contradictions, prejudices, and habits, the growth of
years, round the primeval trunks of natural or instilled opinion.

The interview with his landlady had startled and astonished
him. He could not get her out of his head, nor did he try; he
had been supremely bored before she appeared, and it was
rather amusing to have a totally fresh subject to think about.
He could still see her distinctly as she stood, when he looked up
at her voice, the graceful, rounded outlines of her figure showing through a severely simple black dress, without trimming of
any description, and buttoned from throat to instep. No relief
except a white muslin frill at neck and wrist; her clear, pale,
oval face, with its rich, red, curved lips, delicate yet full; the
low, broad, white brow, and chestnut brown hair, braided care-

lessly, loosely back into a thick coil. Then her eyes! they
haunted him; he could not tell if they were deepest blue or
darkest brown, but the expression he would never forget; the
resolute, unflinching, repellent gaze that met his own, nor the
change created by the shadow of a smile that once flitted across
their grave depths.

Her quiet manner of acceding to his request, had in it something remarkable also. Not a shade of hesitation or embarrassment, no assumption of equality, no confession of inferiority,
and yet no amount of dignity, of hauteur, of grace, could have
produced so deep a conviction that she was emphatically a
gentlewoman.

Her composed performance of the task he had given her
enabled him to note well the haughty carriage of her head, the
long, dark lashes that swept her cheek, the white, slender hand
that held the pen so firmly and guided it so deftly, and the
result of his reflections was summed up by a half uttered observation, "She is a gentlewoman, whatever has driven her behind
the counter, that's clear enough! But why, in heaven's name,
did she look at me as if I was the most hateful object in existence? Do I give too much trouble? Don't I pay rent enough?
What is it? What a handsome creature! By Jove, Upton
and Harcourt, and fellows like them, who are generally maundering about some woman or other, would say I had fallen on
my legs, but," smiling grimly to himself, "that is not my line;"
and so thinking Sir Hugh, somewhat wearied with the slight
excitement of the interview, fell asleep. It was true that he
professed not to care for beauty, and said truly enough he never
thought about it, but its absence vexed him unconsciously.
Ugliness and want of grace were terrible sins in a woman,—I
ought to have written, gentlewoman. With the vagaries of
men in love he had neither patience nor sympathy, considering
them—

> "Still beguiled
> By passions, worthy of a fool or child."

He might have had his own indiscretions in early youth, but
these do not concern the present story.

*   *   *   *   *

"Fanny," said Mrs. Temple, the morning after the interview
just described; "did you write to Tom yesterday?"

"No; I wrote the day before. It is your turn."

"Well, when you do write, pray do not mention that I acted
secretary to Sir Hugh Galbraith."

"No! Why?" asked Fanny with undisguised wonder.

"Oh! because it is not worth while; because I would prefer
telling him about it, it would be more fun."

" Very well ! only I counted on a description of that event to fill up my letter. Now, Kate, I suspect you think he would scold you for going to him ! "

" Nonsense," returned Mrs. Temple, a shade haughtily. "Tom knows I am capable of managing my own affairs."

" Very well," repeated Fanny, meekly ; and the next instant exclaimed, " Here is that Mr. Turner ! "

It was Turner, junior ; who said, as the shop was empty, he ventured to call with a message from his mother, requesting the pleasure of Mrs. Temple and Miss Lee's company on the following evening to supper. He added, with a sigh, that they were quite strangers, as it seemed impossible to get a peep at them.

" I certainly do stick close to business," replied Mrs. Temple, pleasantly. " And I have never gone out anywhere, except to Mrs. Owen's when her children were so ill, since I lost my husband; but that is no reason why I should shut up my young friend. I daresay she will be happy to accept Mrs. Turner's kind invitation."

Fanny, to use her own expression, made " big eyes " at her " worthy principal " during this speech, unseen by young Turner ; but being always ready for a change, and by no means averse to amuse herself with the young man's ill-concealed admiration, she graciously accepted.

" And pray do not trouble to send for Miss Lee," added Mr. Joseph, eagerly. " I daresay there is enough to do with an invalid in the house. I shall be happy to see her home."

" Nevertheless, I shall certainly send for Miss Lee," said Mrs. Temple, gravely.

" I suppose you have had a troublesome time of it," continued their visitor, lingering ; for of course Sir Hugh Galbraith's accident, Dr. Slade's fortunate presence in the field, the conveyance of the injured man to the Berlin Bazaar, all this, with many variations and additions, had been buzzed about the little town with amazing rapidity ; such an event in the dead season was quite a godsend.

" No, indeed," returned Mrs. Temple. " He scarcely gives any trouble. His own servant waits upon him, and both are very quiet."

" I am told he is a regular tip-topper," remarked Mr. Joseph ; " and that the Queen telegraphed to inquire for him."

" Perhaps so ; but the telegram did not come here," said Mrs. Temple, gravely, while Fanny burst into a fit of uncontrollable laughter. " I am afraid the Queen is not aware of Sir Hugh Galbraith's existence," she cried. " He is not quite such a personage."

" But Dr. Slade told father he was a V. C.," exclaimed Turner.

" ' V. C.,' what is that ? " asked Fanny, who did not take much interest in public matters.

" Victoria Cross," explained Mrs. Temple ; adding, " I suppose Dr. Slade is well informed, but I was not aware of it."

" Couldn't you find out ? couldn't you ask him ? perhaps he wears it on his coat," peradventured Mr. Turner, junior, with true provincial curiosity.

" Why ! " exclaimed Fanny, indignantly, " you don't suppose Mrs. Temple ever sees Sir Hugh ! You don't think she waits upon him every morning with a curtsey and a ' What will you please to have for dinner, sir ? ' "

" I am sure I do not know," he returned, bewildered.

" Do not mind her, Mr. Turner," said Mrs. Temple, laughing good-humoredly. " She is always full of some nonsense. I fortunately have an excellent old friend, who manages my housekeeping, or I could not let lodgings and keep a shop at the same time."

" Just so," he returned ; adding, to the indignation of Fanny, with an admiring glance, " But, I say, what a jolly girl you are ! "

" I had a great mind," said Fanny, when he had stepped away triumphantly, " to refuse their horrid supper on the spot; only I was afraid of you ! Now I am like the Romans in Mrs. Markham, between the barbarians and the sea. You would be vexed if I don't go, and Tom will be cross if I do ! "

" I will bear you harmless with Tom. We must not be too distant with our neighbors ; Tom will understand that. But, Fan, how is it you can condescend to accept Mr. Joseph's unspoken admiration, and yet be so indignant if he ventures to express it ? "

" The humble adoration of the meanest votary may be offered at the loftiest shrine, but the smallest attempt at familiarity must be crushed," replied Fanny, grandly. " Kate, you have not told me half enough about Sir Hugh ! "

" There is really nothing to tell. He is a tall, thin, plain, tolerably well-bred, and, I should say, commonplace man. You are a perfect nuisance with your questions ! I think I shall fine you half-a-crown whenever you mention his name again."

" I am sure, Kate," resumed Fanny, with an air of the most profound wisdom, after a few moments' silence, " I hope our interesting lodger will not tell Dr. Slade that you wrote that letter for him. It will fly like wildfire through the town, and there will be no end of scandal."

The young widow colored even to her brow. " I am proof against scandal," she exclaimed, with a scornful flash of her bright eyes ; " I don't care ! " Then, stopping short, " What nonsense one talks when angry ! I must care—but," laughing, " it would be rather too bad to be ' talked of ' with one's enemy."

A covey of Miss Monitor's young ladies entering prevented further conversation, and the counter was quickly strewn with all the colors of the rainbow in Berlin wool.

That evening as the two friends sat, the one making a dress, the other reading aloud to her, in the comfortable home-like "shop parlor" which was their winter sitting-room, a knock at the door announced Dr. Slade, who generally looked in after visiting his patient. "Come in," cried Fanny.

"Well, ladies," said he, entering, his shirt-frill in perfect condition, his eyes glittering, his large white teeth displayed by a gracious smile, as he glanced approvingly round the neat room, "you might sit for a picture of industry rewarded by comfort."

"Sit down, Doctor," said Mrs. Temple, placing a chair for him. "How is your patient this evening?"

"Not quite so well; and d——d sulky and silent, in consequence, I suppose. However, he made one query that afforded me satisfaction on your account, Mrs. Temple," taking out his snuff-box and tapping it, while he assumed a tone of patronage. "Sir Hugh Galbraith interrupted me rather abruptly in what I was saying just now by exclaiming, 'I find that old woman who answers my bell sometimes is not the landlady!' So I explained that the real proprietress was engaged in the wool trade, ha! ha! ha! therefore that he could not expect to see her. He nodded his head and puffed away for a while, and then burst out with, 'What do I pay for these rooms, Doctor?' so I explained that the subject of rent had really not been mentioned; that he had been carried into the nearest place of refuge, and no one had thought of the question of payment. Then he said it was time to mention it, and that he was willing to pay whatever I thought, or whatever you thought was right. So I said the last inmate paid two pounds a week; but I thought that, considering he necessarily caused some extra trouble—he interrupted in his impatient, overbearing way, 'Of course, of course! Will three pounds a week do?' I said I thought it would suffice; but said I would mention the matter to you. I assure you I am very pleased to have secured you so eligible a—eh! what amuses you, Miss Lee?"

This interjection was uttered in consequence of a sudden outburst of laughter from Fanny, all the more noisy from her efforts to suppress it.

"What is the matter?" exclaimed Mrs. Temple, smiling from sympathy.

"Oh! nothing; do forgive me!" exclaimed Fanny, struggling to compose herself. "I ran the needle into my finger, and it startled me. I am rather hysterical, you know."

"Hysterical! stuff!" growled the doctor. "You are the picture of health; but what do you say, Mrs. Temple?"

" That your patient is disposed to pay munificently; and it would be a pity to check his liberality, for I suppose he will not be with us long."

" A few weeks longer, if he is wise. He asked me this evening when I thought he might travel, and seemed disgusted that I could not undertake to say when. After such a shock as he has had, quiet is essential. It is curious he has had no other visitors except that starched high-mightiness of a cousin."

Mrs. Temple was not disposed to pursue the subject, so the talk flowed towards other topics, and the doctor mentioned having been called over to Weston to see the housekeeper, and that Lady Styles was still absent, and would be for some time longer, as Sir Marmaduke Styles had been attacked by rheumatism, and heaven knows what all, in Yorkshire. " I am sorry for him," added the doctor, " but if her ladyship had been at home all Pierstoffe could not have prevented her from forcing her way into Sir Hugh Galbraith's room, though if any one could have turned her out again it would have been the sufferer himself."

After a little more conversation, principally carried on by the doctor and Fanny, he bade the friends good evening, rather to their relief.

" What made you laugh in that extraordinary way, Fanny ? " asked Mrs. Temple, when they were alone.

" Oh ! dear Kate, I could not help it ! when I heard that ridiculous old doctor talking so big about the tenant he had secured for you, and the splendid offer of three pounds a week out of your own money—for it is, or ought to be, your own money."

Mrs. Temple laughed for a moment. " The position is altogether very droll," she said, " and very uncomfortable ; but as to the money, I am not so sure. I should think at the worst of *his* times Sir Hugh could pay three pounds a week on a pinch."

" Then he was quite rich for an old bachelor, and need not have quarreled and worried about poor Mr. Travers's money," exclaimed Fanny, indignantly. " But it is evident he never mentioned your having written a letter for him ; and, *à propos*, I will just write to Tom before I go to bed, and only say that our interesting invalid is going on as well as can be expected."

The afternoon of the next day was a busy one, and in the midst of it Mrs. Temple received a telegraphic summons from Mills through the little window.

" Well, what is it, Mills ? "

" He says he would be greatly obliged, ma'am, if you could spare a few minutes to write a letter for him."

" You mean Sir Hugh ? indeed I cannot ! Say I am exceedingly occupied, and if he can put off his letter till the evening, I am sure Dr. Slade would write for him."

So Mills departed and did not return.

"It would never do to come when he calls," thought the young widow, as she diligently sought through a pile of "London Journals" for a back number to suit a schoolboy customer; "nor am I going to be his amanuensis always."

It was an amusing task to attire Fanny and dispatch her to her tea and supper engagement. The mixture of readiness and reluctance with which she prepared herself was most characteristic, as was the undisguised pleasure with which she surveyed her dress and herself in the largest looking-glass their very moderate furnishing could boast, and her openly expressed regret that so much trouble and success should be so thrown away.

"If Tom was to be there, or even some of those pleasant, merry hussars I used to meet at Mrs. Danby's! Heigho! Kate, dear, I really would like to run in and show myself to Sir Hugh!"

"Fanny, Fanny! that looks like going over to the enemy."

"Nothing of the kind, dear; I am ready for war to the knife! even though I am not fit to be anything more than the knife-grinder."

"The knife-grinder, in such a warfare as ours will be (if it ever begins), is a very important personage," returned Mrs. Temple. "I suppose the lawyers will be the knife-grinders."

"Ah! there will be no more peace once that begins," said Fanny. Mrs. Temple made no reply, seeming lost in thought, and Fanny went on: "Do, like a dear! write a line to Tom this evening and explain everything, and ask him to write to me. After all, though he thinks rather much of himself, he is the dearest, best fellow in the world! Good-bye! Be sure you send for me at nine, or half past."

CHAPTER XVIII.

KATE settled herself to perform her task of writing to Tom as soon as she had finished a little domestic talk with Mills, who informed her that Doctor Slade had called early, while she was dressing Miss Fanny, for he was going out to dinner, so Sir Hugh's servant had told Mills, as he passed through the kitchen, to go on some errand for his master. Safe, therefore, from interruption, Mrs. Temple wrote rapidly and fully to her prime counselor. After explaining her reasons for making Fanny accept Mrs. Turner's invitation, and taking the whole blame of that transaction on herself, she went on to say that she wished very much he would endeavor to see Ford, apparently by accident, to ascertain if he kept up any intercourse with Poole;

"for," she wrote, "although I am reluctant to confess what must seem unreasonable suspicions to you, mine have for some time pointed to Ford. Why, I am reluctant to say. When I make up my mind to tell you, perhaps you will admit I am somewhat justified. At any rate, accept such guidance from me, as to direct your inquiries towards this man. Ascertain, if you can, whether he has sought out Gregory's son, or made him any offer. Is Poole still in the old house, or has Sir Hugh Galbraith—"

As she traced the name Mills entered. "He has been ringing again," said she,—Mills seemed to fulfill some self-imposed duty by religiously avoiding the name of her mistress's enemy, "and he wants to know if it would be perfectly convenient to you to write a bit for him now ; he is very sorry to trouble you."

"I will come in ten minutes," replied Mrs. Temple, without raising her eyes, or ceasing to write. "Tell him so, please."

Mills retreated, grumbling vaguely.

Sir Hugh Galbraith was pacing slowly to and fro when she entered. He turned and greeted her with grave politeness, placing a chair at the table, and moving the writing materials ; in doing so he upset some of them, which Mrs. Temple hastened to pick up, with the strange weft of compassion that, since she had seen him carried helpless and inanimate into her home, had shot across the warp of her dislike.

"I have to apologize very heartily," said Galbraith, "for trespassing so perseveringly on your time, but I ventured to think that you might be more at leisure in the evening, and I really want a letter dispatched."

"I am disengaged now," returned Mrs. Temple, seating herself at once, and getting pen and paper, "but I never am in the morning or afternoon."

"I shall remember," said Galbraith, as if he intended frequent employment of his fair hostess. Some such idea suggested itself to her, and strive as she would, she could not restrain a smile, all the softer and sweeter from the effort to be grave. She kept her eyes steadily on the paper, however, and her resolute composure quickly returned. Sir Hugh took his place on the sofa opposite to her. "Are you ready ? " he asked.

"I am."

"My dear Upton. I had yours of the 2nd, yesterday. It crossed one I sent you the same day. I now write to say it is exceedingly unlikely I can be in London for some weeks." He stopped, at a sign from his amanuensis. "I feel very shaky still," he resumed, "and must keep quiet, so tell your friend to put me out of his head as a possible purchaser of his horse."

Again a long pause. Mrs. Temple read aloud her last word, to show she had finished, and still no others came. Thinking that he was in the agonies of composition, she kept silence for a moment, and once more, as a reminder, read softly, "purchaser of his horse," looking up as she spoke. She met Galbraith's eyes fixed upon her, as if so absorbed in contemplation that everything else was forgotten, and yet there was no shade of boldness in his grave reflective gaze. Conjecture and admiration might be descried, especially the former, but nothing to offend; still Mrs. Temple could not keep down the quick bright blush that flushed her cheek, and then faded slowly away, leaving her paler than before.

"Forgive me," said Sir Hugh, bluntly, yet in less harsh tones than he had hitherto spoken; and leaning his sound arm on the table, he bent towards her. "I had forgotten what I was about, while wondering what freak of fortune drove you to keep a shop!" Again Mrs. Temple's lip curved with a passing smile, and before she could reply Galbraith went on hastily, "I am aware that such remarks are altogether presumptuous, unwarrantable, but I could not keep the words back."

"As you are suffering, and I imagine very dull, I suppose I must not quarrel with you for amusing yourself with speculations concerning my insignificant history! You will find it much more interesting in imagination than in reality, so I shall not enlighten you."

Mrs. Temple looked straight into his eyes as she spoke, something of the dislike and defiance that had struck him so forcibly at first returning to her expression. "You do not suppose I would venture to ask?" he returned, quickly.

"Suppose we finish your letter," said Mrs. Temple, quietly.

"Yes, yes, of course; where was I?"

"'As a possible purchaser of his horse,'" read Mrs. Temple, demurely.

"Ah!—h'm—" Galbraith's ideas evidently would not come. "I really have nothing more to say—you must just end it, if you please."

"But that is so abrupt! Can you not tell your friend how you are going on—when you-are likely to leave—but I must beg pardon in my turn. I am going out of my province."

"I am very thankful for any suggestion," replied Galbraith. "Say I am still confoundedly weak, and fear I cannot move for four or five weeks, but that I am in capital quarters." A pause.

"'Capital quarters,'" read Mrs. Temple, looking up with an unrestrained smile, so bright and frank that it seemed a gleam of real light. "Shall I add, 'and a secretary on the premises?'"

"If you like," replied Sir Hugh, also relaxing into a smile. "But that is self-evident. Will you add, that as soon as I am strong enough I shall join him in Dublin, if he thinks he can manage to get away to the west for some trout fishing?"

Mrs. Temple bent her head, and wrote on quickly and steadily; presently she pressed the page on the blotting-paper, and presented it for Galbraith's signature, holding it as before with a firm, still, white hand.

"You don't know how obliged to you I am," he said, pausing with the pen in his hand, and looking up in her face with his grave sombre eyes, which had a sort of yearning expression at times. "I should be badly off without your help. As to letting that doctor write for me, I should let everything go to smash for want of a line, first. He is an infernal gossip—I mean a confirmed gossip."

"Yes, that is better," said Mrs. Temple, softly and gravely. "I should think gossip too weak a diversion for the Inferno! a devil is nothing if he is not strong!"

Sir Hugh looked at her with increasing curiosity; there was such a contrast between her words and the gentle accent with which they were uttered.

"That is one's idea of a devil, certainly," he returned.

"Had you not better sign your letter, and let it be posted? My good old Mills is going to fetch my young friend and assistant, who is out this evening; she can post it for you."

"Thank you; and I am keeping you standing!"

Galbraith hastily scrawled a hieroglyphic at the end of his letter, and handed it back to his fair secretary, who proceeded deliberately to fold and address it.

"There is sealing-wax somewhere," said Sir Hugh, who was by no means anxious to shorten the operation; "I think it had better be sealed."

"Very well," she replied, searching among the writing things. "But I cannot see any. If you want some, Sir Hugh Galbraith," pronouncing his name rather slowly, and for the first time, "I *sell* the article, and will be happy to supply you—an excellent quality twopence per stick, first-rate threepence!"

She paused as she said this, resting one hand on the table, and looking quietly at him, but with a sort of suppressed sparkle under her long lashes.

"And I shall be delighted to become your customer," returned Galbraith, laughing. "Shall I ring for your housekeeper to—"

"Oh! I know where to find it, and will not keep you a moment," interrupted Mrs. Temple.

"But it gives you so much trouble!"

"Consider the unexpected sale of twopennyworth of sealing-wax—or, shall we say threepence?"

She left the room as she spoke, swiftly but without hurry, and Galbraith was still smiling and pulling his moustaches when she returned with two pieces of sealing-wax and a lighted taper. " Twopence," said she, holding up one piece ; then, raising the other, added " threepence."

" The first quality, of course," said Sir Hugh, laughing, and with a brighter expression than she had yet seen upon his countenance.

" Now for a seal ; I could not see any."

" I have my ring," interrupted Sir Hugh.

" Which you cannot get off," said Mrs. Temple, " so I brought you one, with the latest motto, ' Reply quickly,' will that do ? "

" Very well, indeed ; your forethought is admirable, Mrs. Temple. You would make a good general."

" I trust I may prove a successful one, when my battle begins," said the young widow with a sigh, looking down at the seal she was affixing ; she could neither account for, nor resist the impulse to bring her masked batteries into play. Never before had she felt the same vivid interest as in the daring game on which she had ventured ; and which, even while it half frightened her, she could not relinquish. If she could only get well through it, and accomplish Galbraith's chastisement before Tom could find out what was going on, or interfere, or even look disapprobation ; for she dearly loved her kindly, pleasant, honest counselor, and highly valued his good opinion. Still, the game was worth the candle ; she only intended to bring down her foe from his proud pre-eminence, not to hurt him seriously ; but while she thought, Galbraith was saying,

" Is there a fight before you, then ? "

" Yes ; a worse one than you were ever in—a legal battle."

" I am sorry to hear it ; a law-suit is a serious affair. I was very near launching into one myself, and I don't feel quite sure I am safe yet."

" Indeed ! " said Mrs. Temple, pausing, as she closed the ink-bottle, and looking up quickly and keenly in his face, forgetting everything save the desire to glean some straw of intelligence to show her how the current was setting. " Indeed ! but if you *do* drift into such a contest, you have wealth, and rank, and influence. I have nothing, and am nobody." A sweet arch smile. " Nevertheless, once the fight begins, believe me, I will stand to my guns as long as I have a round of ammunition, Sir Hugh Galbraith ; so good evening."

" One moment," he exclaimed, eagerly ; for he was marvelously roused and stirred. " I wished to speak to you about a— one or two things."

" And they are ? " asked Mrs. Temple, pausing in her retreat.

" Oh—ah !—I hope my fellow, Jackson, gives no unnecessary trouble to Mrs. What's-her-name ?—that he behaves properly.

These troopers are rough customers ; but Jackson and I have gone through a campaign together, and he suits me much better than a fine-gentleman valet." For once in his life, Galbraith was talking against time, though thinking himself an idiot all the while.

" He seems to get on very well with Mills," said Mrs. Temple, feeling anxious to retire. " I hear no complaint. I hope you have all you require, and are comfortable. I feel I ought to justify Dr. Slade's recommendation."

" I never was so well placed before," returned Sir Hugh ; "and if you will be so good as to write a letter for me occasionally, there is nothing else I can want ; but," seeing her about to speak, " I will *not* have Slade for a secretary."

" Well, we will try and manage your correspondence for you," said Mrs. Temple, good-humoredly ; and repeating her "good evening," moved decidedly to the door.

Galbraith's resources were exhausted, so he opened it for her, exclaiming, " I am sorry for the opposite party in your coming battle, Mrs. Temple. You are a dangerous antagonist."

" I will endeavor to be dangerous, depend upon it," said she ; and bending her head in return for his bow, she swept away without raising her eyes.

" That woman has a history," thought Sir Hugh, closing the door after her. " Yet how fresh, and fair, and young she looks. She is a gentlewoman ; she must be a gentlewoman ; there's not a tinge of anything bold in her fearless frankness. How much more pluck Upton has in some things than I have. Had he been in my place, now—by Jove ! he would have asked her to pull off his ring to seal that letter ; I daren't. After all, would he have dared ? I doubt it. I wonder what the late Temple was like ? A white-chokered elder of some Methodist chapel, probably. These tradesmen are all dissenting radical hounds ! How could such a woman as that marry one of these fellows ; she never learned that style, those manners, behind a counter. By George ! perhaps—" he stopped even from consecutive thought, as some conjecture possibly more repulsive than the Methodist husband, suggested itself ; and with a look of anger and disgust, addressed himself to the task of lighting a cigar with a twist of paper, which burned his fingers, and evoked some bad language before he succeeded.

Fanny returned in due course, escorted both by Mrs. Mills and Joseph, junior ; she was considerably less bright than when she started. " Oh ! they were very kind and hospitable," she said, in reply to some inquiries from her friend ; " but I was obliged to eat a great deal more than was good for me ; and then we had an adorable young man from Stoneborough, and another who sells fish, I think. The Stone man is evidently Miss Turner's property. The fishmonger, I flatter myself, fell to my spear. He wasn't nice—and Mr. Joseph lamented to me privately, as we walked home, that his parents had done him irreparable injury at his baptism, by bestowing such a ridiculous name upon him. I consoled him to the best of my power, and advised him to turn it into Beppo—the idea pleased him ; but he wanted to know who Beppo was. So I exclaimed, 'What ! an admirer of Byron not know one of his leading characters.' At which he was annihilated, and we arrived here in peace. I was so glad he said no more, because I began to be afraid Beppo wasn't in Byron at all. But he is, isn't he, Kate ? "

Mrs. Temple reassured her.

"Then he proposed driving me and his sister over to Stoneborough, which was alarming. And oh, they perfectly stupefied me with questions about Sir Hugh. Never send me there again, Kate."

"I think we had better let him know you are engaged."

"But I am not ; not regularly, you know ; only if—"

"Fanny ! do you consider yourself free to marry any one ? "

"Well—no, not exactly."

"That is quite enough. We had better say good night."

"And what have you been doing all the long evening ? " said Fanny, yawning.

"Nothing particular. I have read ; written one letter to Tom, and another for my enemy."

"Another for Sir Hugh ! Oh ! my goodness, Kate."

"Yes ; and he coolly declares we must manage his correspondence for him. He will not have Dr. Slade. So as he will be here but a short time, we must make the best of it ; only you must do your share."

"Me ! I should be afraid to go near him, after what Tom said."

"Nonsense, Fan ; he is a quiet, civil, grave personage, more like a parson than a soldier ; though, I fancy, full of pride and prejudice ; but come, let to-morrow take care of itself—to bed, to bed, to bed."

A few days passed unmarked by any event ; for Sir Hugh Galbraith's requirements and correspondence had become almost a daily occupation. Fanny had been sent once in Mrs. Temple's place, and had returned utterly discomfited. "I knew I should make a mess of it," she said. "I never saw such a cold, proud, stern, disagreeable man. I went in trembling, and he made me shake in my shoes ! the sort of bow he made and the stare he gave, was enough to turn one to stone. And oh, the muddle I got into with the letter—writing the same thing over two or three times, and leaving out other bits; even Sir Hugh laughed at last, and said, 'You are not quite so good an amanuensis as your sister.' Then 'I exclaimed, 'She is not my sister;' 'and, perhaps, I ought not to have said so. I will not write any more for him, Kate! that I can tell you."

Meantime Tom had not been idle; and in due time Kate received a report of his proceedings.

"Your suggestions are very good," wrote the London agent of the Berlin Bazaar; "and so far as I can I will carry them out; but it is not so easy to invent an accident that will bring me in contact with Ford. I am not in a position to require a stockbroker, and if I were, your views would not incline me to entrust much capital in his hands. However, I will be on the look out. I could not manage to see Gregory till last night; and, curious enough, your ideas are so far justified, that Ford has called upon him, but did not see him, as Captain Gregory was out. So far, the stars in their courses fight for you! I warned Gregory to say nothing of the will, beyond the bare fact of knowing that his father drew one for Mr. Travers, also to keep his communications with myself, and the affidavit, as dark as possible. This, I think, the worthy captain will do, as he has a prejudice against Ford, because of his supposed injustice to 'father.' I think, therefore, Gregory is armed at all points; at the same time, I must say that your suspicions of Ford seem to me, to say the least, unfounded. What object could he possibly have in bestowing so great a benefit on a man, who would unhesitatingly hand him over to the powers that punish if he found out the fraud; for even you do not imagine Sir Hugh would be a party to it. I cannot help thinking that your best plan would be, now you have such a curious opportunity, to make Galbraith's acquaintance, see what sort of a fellow he is, and then let me come down and negotiate between you. I am certain he would make a very much better settlement in this way than the lawyers proposed. And after all, you wished him to have a fair share of the property. The fact is, that although an advanced Liberal, I cannot reconcile myself to think of you and Fanny always behind a counter, and open to the addresses of any accomplished Turner of your society. It may do for a picturesque episode, but will never answer in the long run. Think over my proposition, and don't reject it with scorn right off. Thank Fan for her description of the supper, and say she *might* write a little more legibly, etc, etc."

"Make terms with Hugh Galbraith—never! unless I dictate them," was Kate's mental comment on this epistle. "For even if the discovery of another will released me from any compromise I might have made I should feel bound in honor not to look for one. It is deplorable that this wrong-headed man should have so mortally offended poor Mr. Travers! All would have gone right then. Why should he despise me so fiercely, at least the 'me' he thinks I am?" a half-pleased smile parted her lips as she thought. "But to submit to the will that placed me at his feet—at his mercy—never! As to the rest, I think he likes me: I have set the wheel in motion, but can I stop it?"

Kate pondered long and vaguely. Though she had been a wife, she knew nothing of love or lovers, save from books, which she was inclined to believe greatly exaggerated the subject. Matrimony had been a most prosaic and disenchanting condition to her, and though too natural and sympathetic a woman to be indifferent to admiration, her own heart was almost an unsolved mystery to her, and she scarcely believed in love. Freedom, knowledge, movement, color; pleasant friends, and the power of serving them; a bright home, and the power of embellishing it—these were her outlines of happiness. For the present it was infinitely amusing to play with Galbraith's evident curiosity and dawning admiration, which, by relaxing his mental fibres, would do a man of that description infinitely more good than harm; and, come what might, she felt no fear of consequences to herself, as she was quite resolved to act the prudent, quiet landlady to the last.

Absorbed in her own thoughts, she had not noticed the flight of time, and was startled by the entrance of Fanny.

"It is quite seven, isn't it?" said that young lady, looking at a watch which lay on a stand. "The boy may put up the shutters? I am quite tired of staying there by myself, in the dusk, and it would be sinful to light up for nothing."

"Oh, yes, dear," returned Kate, folding up her letter; "it is quite time to close." So saying, she stirred the fire and lit the lamp, for one of the charms of the "shop parlor" was, that it had no gas. It was, as has been said before, a low, wainscoted room, with a wide, tiled fireplace and carved oak mantel shelf, over which was a tall, narrow glass, with old-fashioned girandoles at each side. A few bits of good old china enlivened it, and a couple of gay prints under the girandoles finished it off pleasantly.

The objectionable horsehair chairs and sofas had been covered with bright chintz. A sort of sideboard of stained wood ran along the side of the room opposite the fire, with a cupboard at each end, and open shelves in the centre filled with books. This was adorned by a saucer or two full of moss and primroses prettily arranged, and a tiny pierced flower-vase of raised Dresden ware was stuck full of violets, scenting the room with their delicate fragrance.

The lamp stood on a solid, old-fashioned, octagon table, which had been rescued from a remote corner of the house, and its cover of rich red cloth gave just the amount of color to complete the picture of a pleasant, unpretending interior, which nevertheless had the indefinable expression in its general effect which bespoke the presence of gentlewomen.

When Mrs. Mills brought in the tea-kettle and equipage, she observed to her mistress, " I made a couple of rounds of buttered toast, ma'am, for you didn't eat much dinner ; and he "—a motion of the hand upwards—" wants his letters wrote as usual ; and he desired me to say that, if you like, he will come down here to save you the trouble of going up to him."

" I really think it would be better," said Mrs. Temple, looking at Fanny.

" Perhaps so ; but if you once let him in you will never get rid of him—that's my opinion," returned Fanny, sagely.

" My compliments, Mills ; say we are just going to tea, and afterwards we shall be happy to write for him, if he chooses to come down, unless he would like a cup of tea."

" Oh, Kate ! " cried Fanny ; " what would Tom say ? "

" That I am heaping coals of fire on my enemy's head ! It is so churlish to tell him to wait till we have done eating."

" Am I to say that ? " asked Mills, with unmistakable disapprobation.

" No, no ! " cried Kate, laughing. " It would be cruel to let him devour your toast, Mills. Say I will receive him after tea."

That meal had hardly been dispatched, and the things cleared away, when a knock at the door announced their visitor.

He paused a moment, as if struck by the simple, graceful comfort of the room. Mrs. Temple rose and advanced a step to receive him. " I am glad you are so much better," she said, " as to venture downstairs."

Fanny murmured, " Good evening," and dropped a slight curtsey.

" Thank you for permitting me to come ! I must trouble you with a very short letter this evening," returned Sir Hugh.

" Sit near the fire," said Kate, feeling it was a totally different matter, receiving him in her parlor, from visiting him in his.

" What a pleasant, cheerful room this is," he observed, taking the chair indicated ; " quite different from mine."

Fanny observed that he had discarded his dressing-gown, and, although only in a velveteen shooting-coat, was got up with some care. He was certainly tall and gaunt, and plain, but had, she thought, a soldierly, distinguished air.

Meantime she settled herself to her needle-work in demure silence, and Mrs. Temple, producing pen, ink, and paper, replied to Sir Hugh's remark, "You must not disparage my drawing-room, it is the pride of my house."

"Oh, it is very nice indeed! but it is somehow rather desolate."

"Shall I begin?" said Kate.

"Yes, if you please."

"Dear Sirs,—I feel somewhat surprised not to have heard again from you on the subject of yours of 2nd inst."

Kate, having written this, looked up.

"That's all," said Sir Hugh. "Will you direct it to Messrs. Payne and Layton, Gray's Inn?"

Mrs. Temple obeyed in silence, with an odd sense of danger. What if by chance it fell into Mr. Wall's hands? He knew her writing so well, what would he think? She could only hope it would not.

Fanny, in the meantime watching Galbraith sign his name, could not hold her tongue any longer. "How hard it must be to write with one's left hand," said she, timidly.

"The result is not very satisfactory," replied Sir Hugh. "At any rate, it could not be easily imitated."

A long pause ensued. Galbraith was evidently in no hurry to go away, and Mrs. Temple would not start any topic of conversation. At last Sir Hugh observed that he hoped, from what Slade had told him, to be able to write his own letters in another month.

"How nice that will be!" exclaimed Fanny.

"Because you will then be freed from the chance of having to write for me?" asked Galbraith, with a good-humored smile.

"Oh, no! I did not mean that!" she cried, blushing very prettily.

"Fanny was dreadfully distressed at having been so indifferent a secretary the other day," said Mrs. Temple.

"It was as much my fault as hers," replied Sir Hugh, turning his eyes full upon Kate as she spoke. "You teach me how to dictate as we go on. You seem to understand your work thoroughly."

"I used to write a good deal for poor Mr.—I mean my husband," returned Kate, pulling herself up just in time.

"Ah! I suppose he was also in business?"

"He was. All my people were."

"Except me," said Fanny, quickly; "that is the reason I am so little good now."

Galbraith then made some remark on the probable age of the house, which led to a discussion on the origin and rise of Pierstoffe; and Mrs. Temple promised to look out a quaint history of ——shire she had bought at a book stall, where some interesting particulars were to be found respecting their present locality. Then Fanny, with some dexterity, turned the conversation to India, and induced Sir Hugh to give some description of the country and its sports. The moments flew quickly, til' Mrs. Temple, glancing at her watch, said, smiling, "In the absence of Dr. Slade, I must remind you that invalids must keep early hours."

" I fear I have intruded too long," returned Sir Hugh, rising. " *I* am greatly obliged to you for the relief of a little society."

" Well, Kate," said Fanny, when he was quite gone, " if it was not my duty to hate Sir Hugh Galbraith, I should say he was rather awful, but very nice."

CHAPTER XIX.

A BRIGHT sun and a keen wind were playing havoc with the old and infirm, the weak-lunged and the rheumatic, in famous London town about a month after Sir Hugh Galbraith's accident, and Tom Reed was walking thoughtfully down the Strand, after witnessing the last rehearsal of his smart little piece previous to its production. His thoughts were agreeable. After a long, brave struggle with fortune she was beginning to yield coyly to his embrace. He was tolerably sure of the editorship of the " *Thresher*," should P—— not be able to resume that office, and altogether he felt it due to himself, to Fanny, to Mrs. Travers, that he should run down to Pierstoffe on Saturday and have a talk with them. " I have not heard from either for two or three days," thought Tom ; " I suppose Galbraith is gone by this time : what a curious eddy of circumstances that he should be carried into Mrs. Travers's house ! I wish she would hear reason about this will. It was an infamous affair, but she will never upset it—Oh, Mr. Ford ! "

This exclamation was elicited by a gentleman who stopped suddenly before him, so as to arrest his progress.

" Mr. Reed," he returned, " I was determined not to let you pass me as you did before."

" Did I ? " cried Tom, shaking hands with him ; " where? "

" At the Exhibition of Water-colors ; but you had some ladies with you, so I did not speak."

" Well, I am very much obliged to you for stopping me now ; I was lost in thought. How have you been this age? Why, it is just a year since I saw you."

" Yes ! just a year," echoed Ford. " Oh ! I am quite well— never was better." But he did not look so. He was thinner and more haggard than of old, and had a more restless, shifty expression than ever in his eyes. "Have you been always in town?" he continued. "I thought you must have been away, from never meeting you."

Tom's caution was aroused by the sort of suppressed eagerness underlying his efforts at easy cordiality.

"Yes, I may say I have, except for a night or two, and one short run to the Continent; but I have been desperately busy, and our lines are not likely to cross."

"Exactly so," said Ford. "I will turn with you as far as Hungerford Market. Pray, have you any news of our friends Mrs. Travers and Miss Lee?"

"Yes; I had a letter from Mrs. Travers a short time ago; they were quite well—flourishing, in short."

"At Weisbaden?"

"I am not at liberty to say where," said Tom Reed, smiling pleasantly.

"I should have imagined," returned Ford, with the old, nervous catch in his voice, "that considering the long-standing acquaintance I had with Mrs. Travers, and the devotion I ever showed to her interest, an exception might be made in my favor."

"I daresay she would herself; but you see I couldn't."

"Well, Mr. Reed, will you satisfy me on one point?—is she living in tolerable comfort? Is her plan of a school succeeding?"

"I assure you, Mr. Ford, she is very comfortable at present, and her plan is fairly successful."

"Fairly successful," repeated Ford, thoughtfully. "Well, I too have been fairly successful, and have some idea of taking a holiday this summer in order to enjoy a trip on the Continent. Should my presence annoy Mrs. Travers I would avoid any town she resided in—if you would tell me where she is!"

"Nonsense!" cried Tom; "I daresay she would be very pleased to see any 'auld acquaintance.'"

"But you forget, Mr. Reed," with a wavering, mechanical smile, "I was unfortunately the means of discovering that unlucky, that disgraceful will; I even placed it in her hands; and, innocent as I am, I fear she will never forgive me."

"I think you do Mrs. Travers injustice," said Tom; "she is not that sort of person."

"But ladies" (Ford would not have said "women" for the world) "ladies are not always very just in their conclusions; though, of course. *you* must see that I was quite an involuntary agent."

"Of course, of course," said Tom, yet a strange doubt seemed to come to him, even while Ford was protesting his innocence. "What are you doing now?" he continued, to change the subject.

"Oh, I am working up a tolerable business as a ship-broker and insurer—underwriting on a small scale ; but I should be very happy to see you, Mr. Reed, any evening you are inclined to look in at my place. I have changed my quarters ; stay, here is my card."

"Thank you. I fancy you had better look in on me, No. 6, —— Court, Temple ; I am more in your way coming out of the City—and tell me, what is 'Travers & Co.' doing."

"Winding up as fast as they can. Sir Hugh Galbraith had a bad fall out hunting I saw by the papers."

"Yes, I heard so. By the way, do you ever see anything of Poole, the fellow who was one of the witnesses to that unfortunate will ? "

"No ; do you know anything of him ? "

"Not much ; but I am afraid he is not in very good hands, and has a dangerous taste for the turf."

"A great mistake on his part."

"Well, I must leave you, for I have to meet a man at the House of Commons at two. By-the-by, I have a play coming out at the 'Lesbian' to-morrow night. I'll send you orders if you like." "Must keep him in sight," thought Tom to himself, "though there's not much to be got out of him."

"Thank you," returned Ford, "I should very much like to go. By the way, as I presume you have Mrs. Travers's address "— Tom nodded—"perhaps you would have no objection to forward a letter for me to her ? "

"None whatever," exclaimed Tom ; "send it under cover to me ; she shall have it, and will reply, I have no doubt, in due course."

"So I suppose," said Ford, stiffly ; "why should she not ? "

"Why, indeed," replied Tom, politely and indefinitely. "Good morning."

So they parted. Reed hurrying on to his appointment and thinking what a worthy, respectable, tiresome prig Ford was, in spite of a spasm of suspicion that once shot across him as they were speaking, but which had vanished as the conversation continued. "He is evidently full of thought and sympathy for his late employer's widow. I wonder why she is so inveterate against him ; it is not like her to be so unreasonable. To be sure, I have never heard her reasons."

Ford plodded moodily on to take a boat at Hungerford Stairs. He was evidently in deep thought ; he jostled in an unconscious way against several passers-by, and stood so lost in his own reflections upon the platform that he missed one boat, and would have missed a second, had not an amphibious creature, with a rope in his hand, called out in stentorian tones, "Now, then where are you for?" His face looked older, grayer, and more pained in expression, when he stepped ashore at London Bridge than when he parted with Tom Reed half an hour before. Perhaps all the grief and disappointment, the smouldering indignation, the bitter sense of being undervalued, and, worse than all, the unconfessed consciousness that he could not rely upon himself; all these vultures which gnawed and tortured him, more or less at times, had not in them such elements of tragedy as in two words which seemed to trace themselves on the atmosphere before him, and on the thought within him; they were—"in vain."

If Mr. Ford had been a tall, dignified patrician with a schedule of debts and a doubtful past, or an eager, fiery democrat, burning to right the wrongs of every one under the sun, but leaving his children to fight their own battles the best way they could, the task of dissecting such characters—demonstrating their defects, demanding admiration for their nobler aspects, asking sympathy for their trials, compassion for their weakness, and justice tempered by mercy for the total—would be deemed no unworthy task for a novelist's or biographer's pen. But when the subject "of the sketch" is a middle-aged man of middle height and sloping shoulders—of good business capacities, of undoubted integrity, of unimpeached morality, guiltless of any excess, his principal recreation a mild taste for art and a keen ambition to be attired as becomes a swell—which of our young lady readers would care to be informed how vanity and weakness combined to ruin and corrode much that was good, and how, in a man whose life of quiet, unvaried work knew little that was bright, an intense, unresisted passion, too strong for the character it dominated, mastered his reason and drove him into the wilderness where right and wrong were confounded in outer darkness.

Tom Reed had finished his letter to Mrs. Temple, describing his interview with Ford, the day following. He had written it at intervals as the interruptions of the M. T. office would permit, and perhaps less clearly than usual as he was somewhat excited by the event which was to come off that evening at the "Lesbian." "You may depend on my posting you a line with the result, good or bad, before I sleep to-night." He had just added this as a P. S., when a boy—an inky boy—in shirt-sleeves, entered with a crumpled card on which was inscribed "Mr. J. D. Trapes."

"What a —— nuisance!" growled Tom; "I can't see him. You did not say I was in, did you?"

"No, sir, I said I'd see."

"And so did I," cried a thick voice behind him; a loud laugh ensued, and Mr. J. D. Trapes presented himself.

"Excuse me! I really do want a few words with you, most particularly, or I shouldn't intrude. Reed, it's a shame for you to deny yourself to an old friend."

"Must do so in the office, you see; or we would get no work done," returned Tom, putting the best face he could on it, as he shook his visitor's hand. "And as time is precious, what can I do for you?"

"Oh, a great many things! Fork out a fiver; put your name to a little bill at thirty-one days; give me three to five against 'Leonidas' just to square my book. Lots of things, which I know you won't do! However, the thing I really want won't cost much. Who is the man you were speaking to in the Strand yesterday, just by the turn to Hungerford Market?"

"Why? What do you want to know about him?" asked Tom, with a sudden dim sense of a necessity for caution.

"I only want his name and address. I have a strong idea he is a fellow I have lost sight of for some time, that owes me a pot of money."

"Oh! then I am sure it cannot be my friend," said Tom, laughing. "Ford never owed any one sixpence, I am quite sure."

"Ford, did you say?" repeated the other, sharply. "No, that was not the name. Who is he?"

"He is a ship-broker, I believe; he was the head clerk in a large City house."

"So was my man," returned Trapes, carelessly. "What was the firm?" ·

"Travers & Co."

"Ay! I remember; you used to go down to Hampton Court to see old Travers's widow. Saw you with her once in Bushey Park! Sly dog! Something wrong with the will, eh?"

"How the deuce do you know?"

"Aha! I know lots of things that would surprise you, though I am a failure and you have shot ahead. Reed! we've changed places since we were first acquainted."

"I am sorry to hear you talk like that, Trapes," said Tom, kindly. "If you feel yourself going down, why don't you stop and turn round?"

"It's easy to talk," returned the other, with various expletives, which must not be reproduced here. "Did you ever know a man stop and turn round, once he was fairly set a-going down hill? If you catch him before he is over the brow, well and good, you may put on the drag; but not after—not after!" he repeated, gloomily. Then brightening up, if such an expression could be applied to a face like his, and before Tom could speak, he went on: "The fact is, I never could plod. I never

was like you. I wanted to go the pace from the beginning, and
I went it! too much quicksilver in my veins. Eh, my boy,
Never mind, I begin to see my way to a good thing, and if I
succeed I'll reform —— if I don't! Look here now. What does
respectability and morality and all the rest of it mean? A good
coat on your back, a good balance at your banker's. But look
at the difference: you are a jolly good fellow if you can pay for
your vices, or virtues—upon my soul I believe they are convert-
ible terms—but an infernal blackguard and a blockhead to
boot, if you can't. Look here, Reed; I daresay you think you
are a —— cleverer fellow than I am; but I can tell you, you are
not; you are steady and industrious, which being interpreted,
generally means a sneak and a grubber; nothing personally intended, you know! and look where you are."

"Well," said Tom good-humoredly, seeing his old acquaintance had had something stronger than tea for his breakfast.
"I am glad your free translation was not personally intended;
and I am very glad you have something good in prospect; in
the meantime—"

"In the meantime," interrupted Trapes, coarsely, "you'll lend
me five pounds, till times mend?"

"No, I shall not," said Tom, still good-humored, but decided.
"I will gladly try to put you in the way of earning something;
you used to turn out good work; for I am quite ready to admit
you are a cleverer fellow than myself. Why, you ought to do
something even in copying. You wrote, and probably still write,
a capital hand?"

"Not quite so steady as it used to be," replied the other, with
a leer. "But you are right; it's a capital hand, and it shall
make me a capitalist yet. By the way," with a sudden change
of tone, "if five is too much, could you manage a sov.?"—

"Perhaps I can," returned Tom, smiling, and thinking he
would, by a moderate outlay, purchase immunity from the in-
roads of Mr. J. D. Trapes. "But I can assure you, my success
has by no means reached that height at which five-pound notes
become plentiful. However, if a sovereign is of any use,"
drawing out his purse, "you are welcome to one."

"Thank you," said Trapes, pocketing it. "Will pay back
with interest—twenty per cent. 'pon honor, if I succeed in my
grand coup." He threw on his hat, which, as well as the rest
of his attire, was of the seediest, but still some degrees better
than the garments he wore when Tom and Fanny met him at
the Waterloo Station; and with a defiant air was turning to
leave Tom's dingy little den, when he suddenly stopped, and exclaimed with an oath, "I nearly forgot; where does this Ford
hang out? What's his place of business?"

"That I do not know," said Tom. "And you know City men don't consider it the correct thing to give their private address to any except personal friends."

"Oh, never mind," returned Trapes, with a wave of the hand, intended to express contempt; "I know a man who was in the same office with him, he will tell me."

"But, if Ford is not the man who owes you money, what do you want so particularly with him?"

"If it's not him he is uncommon like him! perhaps he is his twin brother, and can give me information," said Trapes, with a grin. "At all events, Master Tom, you may be clever enough to succeed, but you are not clever enough to suck my brains, or find out my little game, I can tell you; though, I daresay you are calling me a drunken vagabond in your own mind. I'd like to hear you say it, sir! I'd like to hear you say it!"

With a gloomy and threatening countenance, the wretched man abruptly turned his back upon Tom, and departed. With a mixture of disgust and regret, Tom resumed the work he had interrupted.

"I wonder if anything could have saved that fellow? The best and the worst of us have turning points; and it's an awful business if the pointsman is not at hand to keep the train on the right line! But what does he want with Ford? for it is evident Ford *is* the man he wants. Ford was never on the turf, even in the mildest form. I doubt if he ever went to the Derby." As no solution offered itself, Tom shook his head, and proceeded in his task of demolishing the arguments in a rival "leader" of that morning; but at intervals the unanswerable question would recur: "What can the fellow want with Ford?"

The night brought triumph! Tom's piece was received with genuine hearty laughter and applause. The smiling manager promised its repetition, every night till further announcements; and the author bowed his acknowledgments from a private box. But faithful to his word, though wearied by work, excitement, and the laughter of a jovial supper-party, Tom did not sleep that night till he had written and posted a few joyous, loving lines to Fanny, enclosing a letter, which he found on his table, from Ford; and adding a word of warning for Kate. "I would not reply too quickly were I you, nor mention the date on which I received the enclosed missive; dates might suggest the probable distance of your present locale from the twelve mile radius. Though why you choose to preserve such strict incognito, I don't pretend to judge."

Mr. Ford's letter gave Mrs. Temple some food for thought; it was as follows:—

" My dear Mrs. Travers,—I trust you will not deem me intrusive if I avail myself of your friend Mr. Reed's permission to address a few lines to one whose interest and welfare have ever, since the days of our early friendship, been most dear to me. I feel that, hurried on by an impetuosity which blinded me to the requirements of good taste and sound judgment, I wofully offended you at our last meeting ; also that the fact of my having been the innocent instrument of discovering the document which has so fatally injured your fortunes, has affected your opinion prejudicially against me, and I have long wished for an opportunity to remonstrate against your severity, and, if possible, win back the confidence you once reposed in me. I acknowledge with much penitence, that the expression of my feelings was premature ; that I did not show the delicacy due to your recent widowhood ; but, now that time and distance have intervened, is there no hope that a devotion so true, so lasting as mine, dating from those days of simple happiness, when I was a favored guest of your dear and respected mother, may not at last win some return—may not ultimately, meet success ! I would not venture to urge my suit upon you were it not that fortune has smiled upon me, however undeserving, more than she has upon your excellent self, and I venture to offer you the comforts of an unpretending, though not, I hope, unrefined home. As regards that most disgraceful will, need I remind you that I hastened to place it in your hands—and myself at your disposal. Your present position is not of *my* making ; and that position is an unceasing source of agony ; I repeat the word, agony, to me ! Young, beautiful, accustomed to a life of luxury and observance, how can you contend against the difficulties which surround you, and which are, or will be, aggravated by the cruel malice of an envious world. While on this topic, suffer me to point out that the fact of your residence being known only to a young and not over-steady man like Mr. Reed, whose estimate of himself is rather above than below par, is, to say the least, liable to misconstruction.

" I think it right to mention that in one of my interviews with Sir Hugh Galbraith, he questioned me as to your surroundings and associations with a brutal directness, which almost urged me, contrary to my habits, to personal violence. He then, with a sneer, observed that he was told your only confidant was a good-looking young vagabond connected with the press. I feel, therefore, justified in recommending that you should reveal your abode, either to myself as an old and trusted acquaintance of your late husband, or to Mr. Wall, a very respectable and trustworthy person.

" Would I dare hope for permission to visit you and urge my

cause! When I remember the happy evenings in which I was permitted to share your graceful task of tending your favorite flowers, I feel the bitterest regret at the unaccountable estrangement which has occurred. Then I flattered myself that a strong sympathy existed between us, and that you were not unconscious nor quite averse to my unspoken admiration ! How my hopes and your happiness were blighted by untoward circumstances, it is not for me to recapitulate. It is, though no doubt for different reason, engraven on both our hearts !

"Again, entreating your pardon and favorable consideration,
"I am, dear Mrs. Travers, as ever, devotedly yours,
"JAMES W. FORD.
"P. S.—Pray excuse all errors in this hurried scrawl."

It had cost him a night's rest to polish and elaborate !

The effect of this epistle on the young widow can only be described by a line in Fanny's reply to Tom Reed :

"Whatever was in Mr. Ford's letter, it has set Kate dancing mad !"

CHAPTER XX.

IT would not be easy to disentangle and define the mixed feelings which brought the bright color to Kate Travers's cheek, and made her heart beat indignantly as she perused the foregoing effusion. She scarcely herself knew why Mr. Ford's pretensions were so peculiarly offensive, nor did she take the trouble of inquiring, but had that devoted friend been within reach he would have received a crushing rejoinder. The passage about Sir Hugh Galbraith annoyed and yet amused her. She had now grown tolerably familiar with his modes of thought and expression, and she could well picture the quiet profound scorn with which he had spoken of herself "and the good-looking young vagabond connected with the press."

If there was one point upon which Kate Travers was more specially sensitive than another it was on the respect she thought she deserved. Naturally of a sunny disposition and easy temper, loving pleasure, and luxury, and beauty with a certain amount of graceful indolence, which in prosperous times entirely masked the strong will and untiring energy stored up against the day of need, she never dreamed any one would suspect her of the fleshly weaknesses to which others were liable ; she knew the childlike purity of her own life, and suspected that the long winter of such chilling circumstances as hers had been, might have had a hardening influence on her nature ; but she shrank from a disrespectful word as from a blow, and had her knowledge of men been equal to her knowledge of books, she would no doubt have resisted the temptation to play with the grave, surprised admiration evinced by Galbraith lest it might lead to unpleasant results.

Now she could not draw back without a display of stiffness and a change of tone which might lead to awkward explanations, and as her enemy progressed towards complete recovery, she told herself that it did not matter, he would soon be gone, and not remember much about the adventure until she reopened the will-case and defeated him. Then, indeed, their present acquaintance might lead to his accepting some portion of the property he had so long considered his inheritance, for after the friendly intercourse they had held, she never could contemplate robbing him of everything.

These thoughts flitted through her brain in and out of her daily routine of answering inquiries and matching colors, finding patterns and making out bills. It had been a busy and a profitable day, but although the lengthening evenings tempted many to keep their shops open later, the shutters of the Berlin Bazaar were always up at seven. The sweet repose of the after-hours was too precious to be curtailed even for the chance of a trifle more profit. On this particular evening—the one following her first perusal of Ford's letter—Mrs. Temple was considerably bored by a summons from Dr. Slade to speak to him in the best sitting-room, as tea was being laid in the shop parlor.

"Well, Mrs. Temple, I suspect you will soon lose your tenant, and I daresay you will not regret him," cried the doctor, who looked rather displeased as he stood by the window in the waning light, his head erect, his very shirt frill bristling with indignation. "A more quietly insolent personage I have never met. He has just told me I was a gossip!—me!—merely because I made a harmless jest. He is evidently an ill-tempered, crotchety fellow, and must be a great nuisance to his sisters—the Hon. Mrs. Harcourt and Lady Lorrimer—to whom I have written on his behalf. Nothing can be more charming than the letters I have from them, fully recognizing my care and attention, especially Mrs. Harcourt, who wanted to come and nurse him, only he forbade it in terms I should be sorry she heard. I have given him a great deal of time over and above professional attendance, and written, as I said, to his sisters and a cousin of his for him, and now he repays my well-meant attempts to amuse him by telling me I am a gossip!"

"Very rude, indeed, Doctor," said Mrs. Temple, sympathizingly.

"However," he resumed, "I only want to tell you that he has
8*

been asking me when he will be fit to go to London, and I really cannot advise his leaving for another week. He has still symptoms about the head which indicate that he requires perfect rest —freedom from excitement—and London would just be the worst place for him. No medical man likes to see a case he has treated successfully going out of his hands, but I suspect, if he chooses to go, nothing will stop him."

"I suppose not," said Mrs. Temple.

"I thought it right to warn you, as you might like to make some other arrangement, and I hope the letting of your rooms has been a help, a—"

"A decided help, and I am very much obliged to you," returned Mrs. Temple, pleasantly.

"That's all right. Now you must not keep me talking here when I have twenty places to go to. Do you know I met that young schemer Bryant walking with one of Miss Monitor's girls three miles off, on the Barmouth Road, near Jones's, the curate of Drystones. You know Jones? Well, near his house. I believe Jones's wife is Bryant's sister. It did not look well at all. I wouldn't trust Bryant farther than I could throw him. Good evening, Mrs. Temple; good evening."

Kate politely attended him to the door, and as she turned to join Fanny, was seized upon by Mrs. Mills, who carried her into the kitchen to speak to Sarah's mother. She was in great tribulation, being afflicted with a wild son, who turned up every now and then to work mischief. On the present occasion he had got hold of the poor woman's little hoard, had absconded, and left her penniless just as the week's rent was due. She had, therefore, made so bold as to come and ask if Mrs. Temple would be so kind as to advance a little of Sarah's money. This, in the mouth of Sarah's mother, was a very long tale. But Kate listened with the gentlest untiring sympathy, for hers was a very tender heart, and a full half-hour and more was occupied in giving help and comfort.

When at last she returned to the parlor she was not surprised to find the lamp lighted and Fanny seated behind the "cosy"-covered teapot; but she was surprised to find Sir Hugh Galbraith seated opposite to her, apparently quite at home, leaning easily across the table as he talked pleasantly with the pretty tea-maker. Kate could not help being struck by the altered expression of his face since she had first beheld it.

It was softer, brighter, younger-looking, but while she paused, still holding the handle of the door, Sir Hugh rose quickly and came a step towards her. "I have ventured to ask admittance, although I have no letters to write, or rather to have written for me, and Miss Lee, as commanding in your absence, has graciously assented," he said.

" Pray sit down," replied Mrs. Temple, moving to the place Fanny vacated for her. She was startled and disturbed at finding him there : but he was going away next week ; it was really of no moment, this unexpected visit. Still Ford's letter and her own previous reflections ruffled her composure. She colored and grew pale, and felt Galbraith's eyes fixed upon her, though she did not look up to see them.

" You are not well, or something," he exclaimed. " I had better go away."

" No, Sir Hugh. I am happy to see you," a little stiffly. " But the light affects me after the dusky kitchen, where I have been listening to a tale of woe. Fanny dear, will you bring the shade ? " Thus, effectually sheltered from observation, Kate quickly recovered herself and dispensed the tea, stretching out a hand white and delicate enough for a lady of high degree, as Galbraith observed, when she offered him a cup, which Fanny followed with a delightful slice of brown bread and butter.

" A tale of woe ! " exclaimed that young lady ; " and in the kitchen ? What took Dr. Slade there ? "

Mrs. Temple briefly explained.

" I could not think what kept you, and Sir Hugh said he was sure the doctor was gone."

" Old humbug," observed Galbraith. " I thought he would never go. I had to tell him some unpleasant truths before he would stir."

" Did you ? " asked Fanny, who, in consequence of Tom's note, was in towering spirits. " What did he say ? "

" I know," said Mrs. Temple, slyly. " He was making his complaint."

" Indeed ! " exclaimed Galbraith, looking under the shade to get a glimpse of her smile. " What did he say ? "

" That you are an ungrateful man ; that he has devoted himself to your service, and that your return is to tell him he is a gossip."

Galbraith smiled rather grimly. " Did he tell you what led up to it ? " he asked.

" No ; he did not give the context."

" He is not a bad sort of fellow," resumed Sir Hugh, " only spoiled by a country-town life and associating with women—I mean old women."

" And pray, why should women, young or old, spoil him ? " cried Fanny, aggressively. " I am sure we are much better than men in many ways."

" I think you are," returned Galbraith, gravely ; " still I don't think men or women the better for associating exclusively with each other. Military women, for instance, are not pleasant. Have you ever met any?" addressing Mrs. Temple.

"No," said she, answering the real drift of the question; "I have never, of course, been in that sort of society, and have never reckoned any military ladies among my customers."

Galbraith was silent until Mrs. Temple asked him if he would have any more tea. "If you please. I assure you no old woman likes tea better than I do. I have always found it the best drink when hard worked in India," he returned, with a smile. "Some fellows have a great craving for beer, and I confess it is very tempting in a warm climate."

"And are you strong enough to resist temptation?" asked Kate, carelessly, as she again held out her fair hand with his cup in her long, taper fingers.

"As far as eating and drinking go, yes; but I suppose all men have their assailable point."

"Pray, what is yours?" asked Fanny, who, in her present state of spirits, was irrepressible.

"I really cannot tell."

"And I am sure, if you could, you are not bound to answer a decidedly impertinent question," said Mrs. Temple. "Fanny, you are rather too audacious."

"I knew you would scold me!" exclaimed Fanny; "but I could not help it."

Galbraith laughed. "Suppose you set me the example of confession, Miss Lee. What is your weak point?"

"I could not possibly tell, like you; but for a different reason; all my points are weak; the puzzle is which is the weakest."

"Then I suspect your friend has enough to do to keep you in order; irregular troops are generally mutinous."

"I am the meekest creature in creation," cried Fanny. "The moment K——, Mrs. Temple, I mean, even looks as if she was going to find fault with me I am ready to confess my sins and go down."

"Only to rise up again the next instant not one bit the better for your penitence," said Mrs. Temple, walking over to the bell to ring for Mills.

"That is exactly like irregular cavalry. They disperse the moment you charge them, and immediately gather on your flanks and harass your march," remarked Galbraith.

"I cannot say Fanny has harassed my march," replied Mrs. Temple, smiling kindly at that delinquent as she placed the cups and saucers and plates neatly on the tray to save Mills trouble. "But I suppose it would be easier to keep a regiment of superior men—I mean educated men—in order, than the waifs and strays you pick up."

"I assure you soldiers are not on the whole bad fellows; but as to educated men, I can't say I should like to command a regiment of straw-splitting, psalm-singing troopers who would probably dispute every order they didn't fancy."

"But you, you are an educated gentleman, and don't you think," rejoined Mrs. Temple, "that if you had undertaken certain work and certain service you would be more obedient, more dutifully subordinate, than a poor, ignorant, half-blind creature who cannot see an inch beyond the narrow bounds of his own personal wants and pleasures, while *you* could grasp some idea of the general good?"

"There is, of course, some truth in your view," said Galbraith, somewhat surprised; "but a regiment of gentlemen, in the first place, is out of the question. There have been, I grant, body-guards of kings who were all gentlemen, but from what we know of them they were not exactly models of sound discipline or serious behavior."

And in the heat of argument Sir Hugh rose, drew his chair near his antagonist, and clear of the obstacle presented to his vision by the lamp-shade.

"There is your work," interrupted Fanny; "you know you promised that should be ready to-morrow:" "*that*" was a banner-screen of beads and silk, and each section of the pattern was to be begun, in order to save the fair purchaser from too severe exercise of brain.

"Thank you, Fan," and Mrs. Temple proceeded quickly and diligently to thread needles and sew on beads, glancing up every now and then with eyes that sparkled and deepened, and laughed and grew dim with a slight effusion if she was very earnest. Fanny placed a large work-basket before her as she took her seat opposite their guest, who felt wonderfully interested and at home.

"Oh! the people you mean would not be called gentlemen now; they were only polished barbarians, incapable of self-control; any tolerably educated shopboy would conduct himself better than the 'de's' and 'vons' of those days," said Kate.

"By Jove! men were better bred, more high bred, then. I never heard that doubted before," cried Galbraith.

"High bred! that is, they took off their hats and bowed more gracefully, and treated their inferiors with insolence none the less brutal, because it had a certain steely glitter, and were more ferocious about their honor; but they were mere dangerous, mischievous, unmanageable children compared to what men *ought* to be."

"You are a formidable opponent, Mrs. Temple. Still I will not renounce my ancestors; they were gallant fellows, if they had a dash of brutality here and there. And you will grant that without a regard for honor they would have been still more brutal."

" I do.   Nor do I by any means undervalue the good that was in them, only it seems so stupid either to want to go back to them, or to stand still."

" And what good does progress do?   It only makes the lower classes dissatisfied and restless, and wanting to be as well off as their betters.   There is nothing they don't aim at."

" Oh, Sir Hugh Galbraith ! you have concentrated the whole essence of liberalism in those words.   That is exactly what progress does; it makes people strive to do better.   I have no doubt the first of our British ancestors (if they were our ancestors) who suggested making garments instead of dyeing the human skin was looked upon by the orthodox Druids as a dangerous innovator."

" That has been said too often to be worthy of such an original thinker as you are," returned Galbraith, leaning forward and taking up some of the bright-colored silks which lay between them.

" It cannot be said too often," observed Mrs. Temple, stoutly, " for it contains the whole gist of the matter.   I will trouble you for that skein of blue silk.   Thank you."   Their hands touched for a moment, and Galbraith felt an unreasonable, but decided inclination to hold hers just to keep her eyes and attention from being too much taken up with that confounded stitchery.

" But," he resumed, " you cannot suppose men born to a certain position like to feel those of a lower sphere intruding upon them, and treading on their heels."

" Step out then !   Put a pace between you and them, and keep the wonderful start ahead that circumstance has given you," she returned, with great animation.

" You are too ferocious a democrat," said Galbraith, laughing, " and to look at you, who could believe you had ever been, even for a day, behind a counter?   There ! " he exclaimed, " I am the clumsiest fellow alive.   I have made a horribly rude speech."

" I quite absolve you," said Mrs. Temple, frankly, and looking at him with a sweet half smile.   " A counter has not hitherto been the best training school to form a gentlewoman ; but the days are rapidly passing when women could afford to be merely graceful ornaments.   We must in the future take our share of the burden and heat of the day.   God grant us still something of charm and grace !   It would be hard lines for us both if *you* could not love us."

" Not love you," repeated Galbraith, almost unconsciously ; he had hitherto been thinking the young widow rather too strong-minded—a description of character he utterly abhorred. "I imagine your ideal woman will seldom be realized, unless, indeed, in yourself."

"Oh, dear me!" exclaimed Fanny, "I have run the needle into my finger, and it is so painful."

Due commiseration being expressed, Fanny said she must put it in warm water and darted away.

"Do not imagine I am such a narrow idiot," said Galbraith, drawing his chair a trifle closer, "as not to respect a man who fights his way up to fortune from a humble origin, but then he ought always to remember the origin."

"Yes; you of the 'upper ten,'" said Mrs. Temple, smiling, while she hunted with her needle an erratic white bead round an inverted box cover, "are decently inclined to recognize the merits of such a man *when* he has achieved success in the end, but you do your best to knock him on the head at the beginning."

"How do you mean?"

"By creating difficulties of all sorts. Mountains of barriers for him to climb over; barriers of ignorance—it is unwise to educate the masses; barriers of caste—none but gentlemen must officer army or navy; barriers of opinion; social barriers—Oh, I talk too much! and I am sure so do you. Dr. Slade told me just now you were to be kept as quiet as possible and undisturbed; and here am I contradicting you most virulently. Do go away and read a sermon or something, or you will never be able to go to London next week."

"Next week! Does that confounded old humbug say I am to go away next week? I intend nothing of the kind."

"He said you wished to leave for town; so I warn you to give me due and proper notice, or I shall charge accordingly."

Mrs. Temple glanced up as she spoke to see the effect of her words; but no answering smile was on his lip. He looked grave and stern, and was pulling his moustaches, as if in deep thought. There was a moment's silence, and then Galbraith exclaimed, in his harshest tones, with an injured accent, "You never let one forget the shop."

"It was the lodgings this time," said Mrs. Temple, demurely. "I did not suppose you would mind."

"Do you want me to go away?" asked Sir Hugh. "I can go to-morrow if you do."

"I am very glad you feel so much better. Pray suit yourself. I could not be in a hurry to part with so good a tenant."

Galbraith muttered something indistinct and deep. There was a few moments' silence, and then Sir Hugh said gravely, "I am quite aware what a nuisance an invalid inmate must be;

and I hope you believe I am grateful for all the care you have
bestowed upon me."

" Indeed, I am not.   I have not bestowed any care upon you ;
Mills has, a little, and your servant a good deal."

"The fact is," returned Galbraith, with a tinge of bitterness,
" I have never had much care in my life, and I am, therefore,
especially grateful when I find any, or fancy I have any."

"Grateful people deserve to be cared for," said Kate, laying
her pattern on the table and gravely regarding it.

"And you have been very good to write my letters," continued
Galbraith.   " I never knew the luxury of a private secretary before, and as I believe ' the appetite grows with what it feeds
upon,' I shall miss your assistance greatly.   I never found my
correspondence so easy as since you were good enough to write
for me."

" A private secretary would not be a serious addition to your
suite," returned Mrs. Temple, without looking up.   " There are
many intelligent, well-educated young men would be glad of
such an appointment."

" Pooh ! " exclaimed Galbraith.   " I never thought of a man
secretary."

" Indeed," said Mrs. Temple.

"No ; men are so unsympathetic and slow to comprehend."

" I always thought so," replied Mrs. Temple, frankly ; " but I
didn't think a man would."

Sir Hugh's face cleared up as he looked at her, and laughed
" We are agreed, then," he said ; "and I don't think you put ?
much higher value on Slade than I do."

" I do not know what your value is ; I like him, because he
has always been a friend to me from the first."

"And that is how long ? " asked Galbraith, shrewdly.

" Oh ! if you want gossip you must apply to himself."

" I shall never put a question to him, you may be sure," said
Galbraith, gravely.   " But I confess I should like to know how it
happens that you are keeping a shop here ?   Nothing will ever
persuade me that you are 'to the manner born.' "

" You are mistaken, Sir Hugh Galbraith "—he always fancied there was an echo of defiance in the way she pronounced
his name—" my grandfather and great-gandfather, nay, so far as
I know, all my ancestors—if such a phrase may be permitted —
were knights of the counter.   The best I can hope " (with a
smile indescribably sweet and arch) " is that they never gave
short measure."

" It's incredible ! " said Galbraith, solemnly.

" Nevertheless true," she continued.   " Don't allow your imagination to create a romance for my pretty partner and myself,
though we are weird women, and keep a Berlin bazaar."

As she spoke Fanny entered. "It is all right now," she said. "Sir Hugh, if you ever run a needle into your finger, plunge it into hot water immediately, and you will find instantaneous relief."

"I shall make a note of it," replied Galbraith; "and in the meantime must say good-night."

"How fortunate you are," cried Fanny. "You are going to London next week and will go to the theatre, I suppose?"

"I scarcely ever go to the theatre," said Galbraith, "but I imagine most young ladies like it."

"I would give a great deal to see 'Reckoning with a Hostess,'" cried Fanny, unable to restrain herself.

"Suppose we all meet at Charing Cross, and go together," exclaimed Galbraith, who felt convalescent and lively.

"It would be perfectly delightful," said the volatile Fanny, while Kate, who felt keenly the absurdity of the proposition, hid her face in her hands while she laughed heartily.

"I must say good-night," repeated Sir Hugh, bowing formally.

"I trust you will not be the worse for our argument," said Mrs. Temple, rising courteously.

"I am not sure," he replied. "I shall tell you to-morrow."

"Well, Kate," cried Fanny, when he was gone, " has he proposed? I really thought he was on the verge of it when I ran the needle in my finger. It would be such fun."

"Fanny, you are absolutely maddening! What can put such nonsense into your head? To tell you the whole truth, and nothing but the truth, I have permitted Sir Hugh Galbraith the honor of our acquaintance simply because I wish him to feel however appearances may be against me, that his cousin married a gentlewoman; for he will yet know who I am."

"That sounds very grand and mysterious, Kate. I wish you could contrive to make him give you a proper allowance out of the estate— Well, there; I did not mean to make you look like a sibyl and a fury all in one!"

"I am both indignant and disgusted, Fanny, because there is so much levity and vulgarity in what you say," cried Mrs. Temple, warmly. "But we have something else to think of; read this"—and she drew forth Ford's letter, doubling it down at the passage adverting to herself, as having for sole confidant "a good-looking young vagabond connected with the press."

"I suppose," cried Fanny, "that stupid conceited old duffer means Tom."

"I suppose so; but pray remember it is Hugh Galbraith who is represented as speaking. Now you say Tom is coming down on Saturday; it is most important he should not meet our tenant. I imagine Sir Hugh knows his name."

" Oh yes, very likely ; but Sir Hugh has never intruded on us on a Saturday, and we must try to keep them apart. How delightful it will be to see Tom—and this is Thursday ! "

" Yes ; I shall be very glad to have a talk with him. Have you written to him ? "

" To be sure I have."

No more was said ; and Mrs. Temple pondered long and deeply before she was successful in composing herself to sleep. What was she doing ? was she acting fairly and honestly ? was she quite safe in trusting to the spirit, half-defiant, half-mischievous, which seemed to have taken possession of her ? Well, at any rate, it could do no harm. In a few days, Hugh Galbraith would be removed out of the sphere of her influence, and nothing would remain of their transient acquaintance save the lesson she was so ambitious of teaching him, viz., that whatever her circumstances were, she was a gentlewoman, and that some excuse existed for Mr. Travers's weakness in making her his wife.

CHAPTER XXI.

HUGH GALBRAITH was a very English Englishman. In opinion, as in battle, he was inclined, even when beaten by all the rules of combat, to resist to death. His prejudices would have been rigid to absurdity but for a thin, nevertheless distinct, vein of common sense which streaked the trap rock of his nature ; while here and there, carefully hidden, as he thought, from all observers, and scarcely acknowledged to himself, were sundry softer places—" faults," as with unconscious technicality he would have termed them—which sometimes troubled him with doubts and hesitations a consistently hard man would never have known. A vague, instinctive sense of justice—another national characteristic—saved him from being a very selfish man, but did not hinder him from an eager seeking of his own ends, so long as they did not visibly trench on the rights of others ; and at times, if the upper and harder strata of his character was, by some morally artesian process, pierced through, capable of giving out more of sympathy than his kinsfolk and acquaintance in general would believe. But he possessed very little of the adaptability, the quickness of feeling and perception, which gives the power of putting oneself in another's place ; and therefore, possessing no gauge by which to measure the force of other men's temptations, he had, by a process of unreasoning mental action, accumulated a rather contemptuous estimate of the world in general. Men were generally weak and untrue—not false, habit and opinion pre-

vented that—and women he scarcely considered at all; the few
specimens he had known intimately were not calculated to impress him favorably. His sisters, accustomed to the ameni-
ties of foreign life, never disguised their opinion that he was a
hopeless barbarian, until, indeed, their last few interviews, when
they showed a disposition to treat his *brusquerie* as the eccen-
tricity of a noble sincerity. The younger sister, who had always
clung to him, and whom he had loved with all the strength of his
slow-developing boyish heart, had chilled him with an unspeakable disgust by bestowing herself on an artist, a creature considered by Galbraith in those days, and, with some slight modi-
fication, still considered, as a sort of menial—as belonging to a
class of upper servants who fiddled and painted and danced
and sang for the amusement of an idle aristocracy. He would
have been more inclined to associate with the village blacksmith,
who, at any rate, did real man's work when he forged horse-
shoes and ploughshares by the strength of his right arm. In
short, he was a mediæval man, rather out of place in the nineteenth century.

In politics a Tory, yet not an ignoble one. He would have
severely punished the oppressor of the poor. Indeed, he
thought it the sacred duty of lords to protect their vassals, even
from themselves; but it must be altogether a paternal proceeding, given free gratis out of the plenitude of his nobility. Of
the grander generosity to our poorer brethren that says, "Take
your share of God's world, it is yours; we owe each other nothing, save mutual help and love," he knew nothing; he had
never learned even the alphabet of true liberality; and his was
a slow though strong intellect, very slow to assimilate a new
idea, and by no means ready to range those he already possessed
in the battle array of argument.

Nevertheless, he was very little moved by his charming landlady's opinions; they were a pretty woman's vagaries prettily
expressed; still, as he thought over every word and look of hers
that night, while smoking the pipe of peace and meditation
before he went to rest, he felt more and more desirous of solving the mystery of her surroundings. That she and her friend
were gentlewomen he never for a moment doubted, driven by
poverty to keep a shop, though it was an unusual resource
for decayed gentility. For poor gentry Galbraith had special
sympathy, and. had a dim idea that it would be well to tax
successful money-grubbers who would persist in lowering the
tone of society in general and regiments in particular by thrusting themselves and their luxurious snobbish sons into those
sacred ranks—he had, we say, a dim idea that such members of
the community ought to be taxed in order to support the help-

less descendants of those who had not the ability to keep their estates together. Still, how any woman with the instinct of a gentlewoman could bring herself to keep a shop, to measure out things to insolent customers, perhaps to old market-women, and stretch out that soft white hand to take their greasy pence, he could not conceive. She ought to have adopted some other line of work; yet if she had he would not have known her; and though he put aside the idea, he felt that he would rather have missed far more important things. She was different from all other women he had ever known; the quiet simplicity of her manners was so restful; the controlled animation that would sparkle up to the surface frequently, and gave so much beauty to her mobile face—her smile, sometimes arch, often scornful, occasionally tender; the proud turn of her snowy throat; the outlines of her rounded, pliant figure; the great, earnest, liquid eyes uplifted so frankly and calmly to meet his own—Galbraith summoned each and every charm of face and form and bearing that had so roused his wonder and admiration to pass in review order before his mind's eye, and " behold, they were very good." It was the recollection of their first interview, however, more than a month back, that puzzled him most. "She must have fancied she knew something of me," he thought, as he slowly paced his sitting-room, restless with the strange new interest and fresh vivid life that stirred his blood, and in some mysterious way, of which he was but half conscious, deepened and bright ened the coloring of every object, until Fanny declared, as she bid Kate good-night, that " Sir Hugh must have a bad conscience to keep tramping up and down like that,"—"and something to my discredit," he mused. "I shall not soon forget the first look I had from those eyes of hers ! It was equivalent to the 'Draw and defend yourself, villain !' of old novels. How could I have offended her, or any one belonging to her ? I'll ask her some day—some day ! By Jove, I can't stay here much longer ! Yet why should I not ? I have nothing to take me anywhere. This accident has knocked my visit to Allerton on the head. The Countess and Lady Elizabeth will be in town by the time I am fit to go anywhere. That pretty little girl, Miss Lee, is not unlike Lady Elizabeth, only she has more 'go' in her—but Mrs. Temple !" even in thought Galbraith had no words to express the measureless distance between his landlady and the Countess of G——'s graceful, well-trained daughter. The truth is, Galbraith had, after his accession of fortune, seriously contemplated matrimony, He had no idea of being succeeded by a nephew of a different name, or a cousin whom he disliked. Moreover, it behooved him to found the family anew— to impose a fresh entail—especially if he could buy back some of the old estates ; and Payne had written to him that it was probable a slice of the Kirby Grange estates might before long be in the market. If he married, he would go in for family ; he did not care so much for rank. Accident had sent him down to dinner at his sister's house with Lady Elizabeth, who seemed a pretty, inoffensive, well-bred girl ; and he even began, by deliberate trying, to take some interest in her, after meeting at several parties by day and by night, where he had, rather to Lady Lorrimer's surprise, consented to appear. Lady Elizabeth, although her father was not a wealthy peer, had a few thousands, which would not be unacceptable ; and, though Galbraith had bid her good-bye in Germany, where they had again encountered, with his ordinary cool, undemonstrative manner, he had made up his mind to accept the invitation then given him, if duly repeated, to go to Allerton, the family seat, for the close of the hunting season ; and should Lady Elizabeth stand the test of ten days or a fortnight in the same house, he would try his luck. A wish to enjoy his friend Upton's society to the last of his stay, induced Galbraith to postpone his visit for a week ; and then he met with the accident which made him Mrs. Temple's inmate ; and, lo ! all things had become new. Whatever his lot might be, it was impossible he could marry a pretty doll like Lady Elizabeth—a nice creature, without one idea different from every other girl, without a word of conversation beyond an echo of what was said to her. No ; he wanted something more companionable than that ; something soft and varied enough to draw out what tenderness was in him ; something brave, and frank, and thoughtful ; to be a pleasant comrade in the dull places of life. At this point in his reflections, Galbraith pulled himself up, with a sneer at the idea of his dreaming dreams, waking dreams, at that time of his life. "I'll just stay a week longer," he thought, "I really am not quite strong yet, and then I will go to town ; by that time I shall manage to penetrate that puzzling woman's mystery, or I shall give it up. I shall have Upton or Gertrude coming down here to see what keeps me in such quarters, and, by Jove! I would rather neither of them did. *She* would make mischief with or without grounds." So saying, almost aloud, Galbraith lit his candle, and turned down the lamp.

On Saturday morning, after due consultation with Fanny, Mrs. Temple wrote a little note to Sir Hugh, presenting her compliments, and begging to say they expected their agent from London that evening, and would be engaged on business, but if Sir Hugh Galbraith wished any letters written, Mrs. Temple or Miss Lee would be happy to do so between two and five.

"There," said Mrs. Temple, as she wrote these lines rapidly in pencil, "that ought to keep him out of the way."

"Yes, it ought, and will. Poor fellow! how moped he must be all Sunday, and, indeed, every day, by himself."

"Well, he need not stay if he does not like. I am sure he is quite strong enough to travel. He was out driving for three hours yesterday."

"Oh, it is the quiet Dr. Slade recommends. Oh, Kate! how I wish he would lend us his dog-cart to take a drive with Tom to-morrow! I am sure he would if I asked him—may I?—it really ought to be yours, you know."

"Oh, Fanny! you do not know what you are talking about, you are so delighted at the idea of Tom being here this evening."

"Of course I shall be glad to see him, but if you think I am out of my mind with joy you are quite mistaken. I feel as calm and collected as possible."

Which calmness was manifested by the most erratic conduct throughout the day—total forgetfulness on various matters, and frequent rushings to and fro between the shop and the kitchen, just to see that Mills did not forget this or that ingredient in her preparation of one or two niceties devised by Fanny herself, who had a delicate taste for the finer branches of cooking.

Saturday being market day, the morning was always a busy time at the Berlin Bazaar; but the rush of customers was generally over about three, as most of the Saturday visitors had a long way to go home; and, on Fanny's return from one of her excursions, she found only two old ladies of the better class of farmers, one requiring a pair of gloves for her daughter, the other some worsted yarn, wherewith to knit her husband's stockings—simple needs, which yet took an unconscionable time to satisfy.

At last they were gone. "I feel quite tired," said Mrs. Temple, sitting down. "I wish, Fanny, *you* would go up and write for Sir Hugh Galbraith; he sent word that he was sorry to trouble me, but if I could write a few lines for him before five o'clock he would be greatly obliged; you had better go, dear, for you are no particular use here."

"And I am sure I should make a fearful confusion of Sir Hugh's letter! Indeed I cannot go, Kate! I feel quite dazed to-day."

"Oh, I thought you were peculiarly cool and collected! No matter! mistakes in Sir Hugh's letters are not so fatal as mistakes in our business. If you will not go he must do without a secretary."

"Well," cried Fanny, with sudden resolution, "I will write for him this once. Do you know I am half sorry to be obliged to hate Sir Hugh Galbraith; but don't be afraid! I never allow myself to think well of him for a moment! I have not a doubt he is a deep designing villain, but he doesn't look like it, though there is something intolerably haughty in the sort of 'snuff the moon' air with which he looks over one's head."

"Don't talk such nonsense, Fanny, dear! I wish Sir Hugh would go; he is growing troublesome."

"Not to me," returned Fanny, gravely, shaking her head; "he takes no more notice of me than if I was a kitten when *you* are by; I will see how we get on without you to-day."

"Pray be prudent and steady," cried Kate, laughing, "though I am sure Sir Hugh is a pattern of propriety."

Fanny ran away upstairs, dashed hastily into her own room, pinned a blue bow on the side of the pale brown plaits into which her hair was braided, re-arranged her collar, and put on a fresh pair of snowy cuffs, then with a pleasant approving nod to her own image in the glass, walked away softly and tapped at the drawing-room.

"Come in," said Galbraith; and Fanny entered in some nervous dread, but nevertheless with a firm determination to tease and annoy the enemy so far as in her lay. He was standing near the window and looking towards the door with an eager, kindled look in his eyes, which altered visibly and unflatteringly.

"Mrs. Temple desired me to say," began Fanny, advancing with evident timidity, "she is sorry not to be able to come as she is very busy, and would you mind having me?"

A smile—a rather kindly smile—brightened Galbraith's face again. "You are very good to come," he said, "I ought to consider myself fortunate in having so charming a little secretary, but I must say your cousin is the better amanuensis of the two."

"He is very impertinent," thought Fanny; "he never would venture to talk like that to Kate. He wants to find out all about her! he shan't!—So I told Mrs. Temple," she said aloud, "and that I was more stupid than usual, but she said it was better to make mistakes in your letters than her business," concluded Fanny, looking up in his face with an innocent smile.

"The deuce she did," exclaimed Galbraith, looking grim for a moment; and then laughing, "I am much obliged to her; possibly she is right! Did she tell you to say this?"

"Oh, no! and pray, Sir Hugh, don't tell."

"I never was a tell-tale. Come, I will not keep you long." And he placed a chair for her at the table, where he had already

laid the writing materials in readiness. He was indeed bitterly
annoyed and disappointed. When Mrs. Temple's note had
reached him that morning he determined not to let all Saturday
and Sunday, and probably Monday, pass without having a letter
written by his interesting landlady—and not a word with her
either! No, it was the only shadow of amusement or occupation he had, and he was not going to resign it. Of course if he
hadn't been unhinged by that confounded accident he never
would have been driven so hard for one or the other, but it
is wonderful how soon a fellow gets used to things, and then
there was the oddity and curiosity. So he framed his verbal
reply, as he thought very cunningly, to secure one interview
before five o'clock, and now that provoking widow had sent her
silly, insignificant little assistant in her place, and cheated him
after all. Still he must not confess that he could do without
a letter being written very well, and when Fanny was seated, he
began rather rapidly. Standing opposite to the little half-
frightened, wholly daring scribe, and grasping the back of a
chair with his bony, sinewy hand—" My dear Upton,—Thanks
for yours of the 30th. I am nearly all right, only not quite able
to manage my own correspondence, as you see."

" Stop, stop, stop!" cried Fanny; "who in the world could
keep up with you? I am sure you do not run on like that
when Mrs. Temple writes for you. I have only got to 'all
right,' now; do forgive me, and go on again."

" I beg your pardon," returned Galbraith, smiling and recommenced.

" Are there two r's in correspondence?" was Fanny's next
query.

" It's not the least matter," he replied. " He will know what
you mean."

" What *I* mean," repeated Fanny, still writing. " What *you*
mean rather; but it would be better this Mr. Upton thought
you were with properly educated people than real shopkeepers."

Galbraith made a mental note of the expression, and grew
less anxious to dismiss his secretary.

" Upton must be delighted to have nice legible letters, I imagine—'s double e,' " spelled Fanny. " I have done that."

" I am much obliged for your offer of a visit, but I hope to
leave this in a few days ; it is a dull hole, with nothing in the
shape of sport or occupation and not a soul to speak to but a
gossiping old doctor; I would rather meet you in town.—At any
rate it would be an infernal bore to have him here!"

Galbraith had dictated the first of the sentences slowly, and
then unconsciously spoke out his reflection. ' Have you that
down?" he asked, after a pause.

"Just finished," said Fanny, with an air of great diligence, and spelling as she wrote "b o r e."

"Why you haven't written *that?*"

"Yes, of course I have! I thought it was a little uncivil. Oh, dear! I am so sorry! I knew I should be stupid! Pray don't be angry. I will make a nice clean copy if you will tell me the rest."

"Angry! what business have I to be angry? I am under great obligations to you and Mrs. Temple; besides it was my own fault. Just add, if you please, that I hope to be able to write in a few days myself at greater length, and that will do."

Fanny wrote diligently for a few minutes, and then with an air of profound attention read over the letter, crossing out here and there. "I really feel quite ashamed of myself," she said, taking a fresh sheet of paper. "But Mrs. Temple *would* send me."

To this Galbraith made no immediate reply—he even moved away to the window, not to draw his secretary's attention from her task—but as soon as it was accomplished, he said as he glanced over the result. "Then it bores Mrs. Temple to write for me?"

"No, no!" returned Fanny in a tone of palpably polite denial. "She is always very obliging, but to-day she was busy, and anxious to get everything out of the way before our London agent comes—his coming is always an event, you know."

"Indeed," said Galbraith, availing himself of her disposition to talk. "Perhaps he is a friend as well as an agent."

"Oh, yes," replied Fanny, dotting the "i's" and crossing the "t's" of the letter he returned to her to be folded and addressed, and just glancing up at intervals to see the effect of her words, "he is a dear old friend of Mrs. Temple's, she knew him before she was married, and he is so kind."

"Indeed," said Sir Hugh, pulling out his moustache and staring away into vacancy, "indeed! I suppose he is an old experienced man of business."

"Oh, very experienced! but as to age. Well, he is older than I am."

"Older than you are!" echoed Galbraith. "Why you are younger than your sister, or cousin, whichever it is?"

"You mean Mrs. Temple," said Fanny, avoiding a direct reply as to the relationship. "Yes, she is older than I am; but you know the great firms don't like elderly travelers."

"He is a traveler, then?"

Fanny nodded.

Galbraith hesitated, he felt it would not be honorable to cross-examine this little, good-humored chatterbox, still he longed to have some more talk upon the interesting topic of the "London agent," for he felt strangely savage at the idea of a confounded commercial traveler—a fellow redolent of bad cigars, audacious with the effrontery acquired by bar and billiard-rooms, vulgarly fine, and hideously ill-dressed, coming into close contact with his queenly landlady—indeed, the notion of any man, high or low, coming into that quiet, simple Eden where he had hitherto been the Adam, was infinitely disgusting and vexatious. Meantime, Miss Fanny watched with supreme satisfaction the dropping of his brows and general clouding over of his countenance; silence had lasted long enough she thought, so she said softly, "You will not mention what I repeated just now? I mean what Mrs. Temple said."

"You may trust me. Would the consequences be dreadful? Would she give you a wigging?"

"No; but it would vex her, and she has had enough to vex her."

"I feared so. Reverses, and that sort of thing?"

"Yes; oh, she has been robbed and plundered in the most shameful manner, and basely treated altogether."

"Did you know the late Temple?"

"No; but I have seen him."

"Well," said Galbraith, gallantly resisting his inclination to get the whole truth from Fanny, "I shall have a melancholy evening all alone here. You have been very good to let me come and have a talk with you sometimes; I imagine you have done more for me than old Slade. However, I must make up my mind to solitude for to-night."

"And to-morrow night," said Fanny, pressing the top of her pen against her lips, as she looked up mischievously.

"You need not warn me off the premises," said Galbraith, with a smile. "I did not intend to intrude to-morrow evening, nor until I am asked."

"Now, there! I never can do or say anything right!" cried Fanny, in pretty despair. "I only meant to say, that although to-morrow will be Sunday, we must talk of business, because he comes so seldom, and then you might not like Tom, and Tom might not like you!"

"'Tom,' might not like me, eh? So you call your agent Tom.'

"You would not have me call him Mr.—Jones," cried Fanny, picking herself up just in time, and then reflecting with horror, "that is a shocking story, I wish I hadn't said it."

"Tom Jones," repeated Sir Hugh, laughing, "a dangerous sort of name. No, you are quite right to prefer Tom to Mr Jones."

"I must go away," exclaimed Fanny, "I have quite finished

the letter. Oh! I forgot, Dr. Slade left word that he could not call this evening, because Lady Styles has returned, and he is going to dine with her."

"Lady Styles!" repeated Galbraith; "does she not live at a place called Weston? I believe she is an aunt, or cousin, or grandmother of Upton's."

"Of this gentleman's," said Fanny, holding up the letter. "Then I am sure you will not be at a loss for society any longer, she will come and see you every day and tell you everything, and make *you* tell everything. She is fond of K— Mrs. Temple," remembering the strict injunctions she had received not to breathe the name of Kate; "but she nearly drives her mad with questions."

"But what would induce her to trouble herself about me?"

"She was here the evening you were brought in like a dead creature (what a fright we had!), and you may be sure she has written to this Mr. Upton to know all about you."

"This will be a visitation! I am glad you have given me a hint," returned Galbraith, "and you must go? you couldn't leave Mrs. Temple and her agent to talk business and make my tea?"

"Indeed I could not," said Fanny, indignantly.

"Well, good-morning, Miss Lee," rejoined Galbraith, laughing; "remember I will not venture downstairs again unless I am asked."

"And then Mrs. Temple will know I have been committing some stupidity," cried Fanny, forgetting her dignity. "Do come down to tea on Monday, Sir Hugh!"

"What! even if 'Tom' is there?"

"Ah! there is no chance of that," said Fanny, shaking her head.

"If I have any letters to answer I will venture down then to ask for assistance," replied Galbraith, smiling, and opening the door for her to pass out. As he did so the sound of a man's voice, and some slight commotion rose up from below, while Fanny started, blushed, and brightened all over like some rippling stream when the sun suddenly shines out from behind a cloud, and with a hasty "good morning," went quickly away.

"I suspect 'Tom' is in clover when he comes down here," thought Galbraith, closing the door and resuming his arm-chair and a tough article in the "Quarterly." "He can't make love to both of them, and that nice little thing takes no common interest in his coming. Who the deuce can he be? What can they all be! They are more than tradespeople. I wish I could get at their history. Miss Fanny let out they were not real shopkeepers. Pooh! what is it to me, I have no business to pry into Mrs.

Temple's affairs, she would pull me up very short if I tried. I will go away next week if I feel strong. The doctor says I must take care of my head, and I shall never be so quiet anywhere as here: I wish that old woman may break her leg, or her neck, or anything to prevent her coming here to destroy one's comfort," for Galbraith felt it would never do to have his fair landlady's letter-writing and general intercourse with a man of his position known : over and over again he revolved the subject in his mind. The "Quarterly" was thrown to the other end of the room ; he could not bear the idea of leaving, and yet go he ought, he must. At last he started up, put on his hat, and walked away to the stables he had taken, to have a chat about the "bonnie beasts" with his servant, a Yorkshireman, and get rid of himself. He had not yet given up his invalid habits of early dinner and a "something" mild and strengthening before he went to bed. Both in going out and returning he heard the sound of merry voices and laughter, pleasant, refined laughter, as he passed the door of the best sitting-room ; evidently "Tom" was an acquisition ; it was no wonder they did not want him, Hugh Galbraith !

His servant noticed that he was more than usually silent, and very severe about some trifling neglect in the stable.

Even Mills did not get a civil look when she brought him some admirable scolloped oysters, but at last the uncomfortable evening was over, Galbraith's last waking thought being interrogative, "Who the deuce is Tom ?"

CHAPTER XXII.

THE three friends, oblivious of the moody, bored baronet upstairs, talked far into the night. Tom Reed had to give an accurate and detailed account of his play, or rather after-piece ;—they had just begun to be called "curtain lifters" by people who had been to French theatres, and custom was veering round to the habit of having, by some Hibernian process, the after-piece first.

Both Mrs. Temple and Fanny were burning to see the production of Tom's pen ; they had, of course, greedily read all the notices and criticisms which had come in their way, still that was but judging at second-hand, and to see it was the grand desideratum.

"We could in any case only go to town by detachments," said Mrs. Temple ; "we could not both be away together, and though I could go up alone very well, it would hardly do for Fanny, unless you have some friend who would take her in, Tom."

"We must manage it somehow!" cried Tom. "It will run a tolerably long time, at any rate, and I will settle some plan. Of course," turning to Kate, "you will have to come up soon to lay in your spring goods—isn't that the term?—and then you can easily pay the 'Lesbian' a visit. I really should like to know your opinion; you are a tolerable critic."

"There!" exclaimed Fanny, with affected indignation; "you don't care a straw what I think! But I can assure you my judgment would be much more original, because I don't stuff my head with other people's notions out of books, like Kate."

"Bravo!" said Tom; "your own opinion pure and simple. To tell you the truth, my darling, I am half afraid of those keen little eyes of yours, they spy out one's failings so unrelentingly!"

"Little eyes, indeed! Mr. Joseph Turner thinks them big enough."

"No doubt he does," said Mrs. Temple, laughing. "But I imagine Fanny has choked him off, for we have seen little or nothing of him for some time; not since Fan supped at the paternal residence."

"I am surprised to hear it," returned Tom, gravely. "She is such an arrant flirt that in the absence of higher game she would not mind keeping her hand or eyes in by practicing on the nearest haberdasher."

"Another word of that description," exclaimed Fanny, "and I will try my hand, as you say, on Sir Hugh Galbraith! He is sulking upstairs, poor fellow! all alone! and wanted me to stay and make his tea for him. It's not too late to give him his supper."

"You know," said Tom Reed, with a slight change of tone, "I warned you to steer clear of Galbraith when I was down here last. He only knows you as the assistant in a shop, and he will very likely presume upon your supposed inferiority of position. If he had met you at—say at Mrs. Travers's table formerly, would he have ventured to ask you to make his tea? confound his impudence!"

Fanny clapped her hands with delight at this ebullition, and laughed aloud.

"Do not be ridiculous, dear Tom," cried Mrs. Temple; "do you think either Fanny or I would go near Sir Hugh if he was inclined to give himself such airs? I assure you no one could behave in a more unobtrusive, unobjectionable manner than he does. The only trouble he gives is caused by his perpetual desire to write abrupt, and it seems to me, objectless letters—he certainly has not a talent for composition—and his scarcely concealed curiosity to know who we really are. He openly professes his disbelief in our seeming; but I hope and think he will go away next week; there is really nothing to keep him."

"And still he stays! That is odd," remarked Tom, looking at his mischievous *fiancée*.

"It is not me!" cried Fanny, too earnest to be correct; "so don't think it."

"Do you know it is getting very late?" said the fair hostess.

"Eleven! by Jupiter," exclaimed Tom, looking at his watch. "Mrs. Temple," he continued, "is your resolution to go to church to-morrow as fixed as fate?"

"Why?"

"Because I want a long *tête-à-tête* consultation with you about my own affairs. Suppose Fanny represents the firm at morning service, and then she shall direct my steps in the evening to some pleasant glade, where we can discuss the result of the cabinet council?"

"Very well; that will suit me exactly," returned Mrs. Temple. "I too want a *tête-à-tête* consultation with you; so Fanny shall be devotional for us all."

"That is very fine," said Fanny, who had blushed becomingly when Tom spoke of consulting Mrs. Temple about his own affairs. "I am to be banished whether I like it or not."

Good-nights were exchanged, and Tom persuaded his pretty cousin to see that the front door was safely fastened after his exit.

The succeeding Sunday was the first real spring day which had visited Pierstoffe that year. The sky was brightly blue, and the sea, stirred by light airs, soft and balmy as though it were June instead of April, "broke into dimples and laughed in the sun." The tide, which had been full at an early hour, was ebbing gently—Pierstoffe bay was too open to be afflicted by a long reach of bare black sea-weed and sludgy sand when the water was low, and the difference of ebb and flow was not great; a soft feathery fringe of wavelets lapped the beach as if they loved it. On the slip before the Berlin Bazaar the gaily painted pleasure-skiffs were not yet displayed, but the strong brown fishing-boats, battered though still sturdy, were drawn up for their legitimate Sunday rest, and dotted about among them sundry fishermen, in their dark-blue guernsey jackets, with hands deep in their trousers pockets and the indescribable lounging movements indicative of respite from toil, smoked pipes of peace and made short interjectionary remarks. The cliffs behind the North Parade lay bathed in the young sunshine, so distinct in its tender radiance from the fierce glare of summer. The gray crags, cushioned here and there with patches of soft green turf draped with long pendent tangles of bramble and tufted with heather, showed wondrously clear, beautified by the magic of light : and Sir Hugh Galbraith, who dearly loved to look upon the face of nature—as dearly as though he could have written reams of verse to express his admiration, perhaps the more deeply because he could say very little about it—finding himself too early even for the active Mrs. Mills, strolled out to taste the delicious breeze, and talk, in exactly the abrupt unstudied manner that suited them, to the lounging fishermen.

" I'll have a yacht," thought Galbraith, walking slowly away past the empty lodging-houses of the North Parade ; "a small one, need not cost a fortune. I wonder could I manage to put up in the old place for the summer ? I hate London, I don't care for the Continent—the regiment will not be home for another six months ; and perhaps, after all, I may leave it and go into Parliament. What the deuce is Payne about, that he has given me no more intelligence of the purchase he hoped to manage ? I'll write to him to-morrow ; that is, if Mrs. Temple can spare the time to write for me. By Jove !" moving the hand that lay in his sling, " I believe I could write myself; but it would be more prudent not to try just yet. This is a pretty spot ! but very dull. I suppose I was a good deal shaken by that spill, or I should never be satisfied to stay here so long." At this point his reflections grew less clear. He knew in his heart that he never would have endured a life so different from all he had been accustomed to, had he not found such a fascinating secretary. Nevertheless he could not stay much longer ; even the pleasure of his sojourn was largely intermingled with annoyance, aye, with pain. Interviews with his landlady were always difficult to contrive, and required an amount of scheming most abhorrent to his straightforward and somewhat domineering disposition. Still, to go away and never see her face again, or look into her eyes and try to understand their varying expression !—Galbraith felt, and for the first time acknowledged to himself, it was a sacrifice for which he hardly had strength. Still it must be done. He was no trifler, nor was she a woman to be trifled with. " I will ask Slade to-morrow if I may go up to town next week," thought Galbraith, turning sharp round to walk back, and frowning to himself at the mockery of asking the doctor's consent. " I shall be all right when I am away. I am past the idiotic period of boyish spooneyism ; " which was true, but he forgot that childish disorders are always more dangerous in maturity. Comforting himself with this incomplete generalization, he strolled on slowly, enjoying the delicious morning air, the contagious joyful spring aspect of everything. As he approached the open, where the main line bifurcated into the Stoneborough Road and North Parade, his attention was attracted by a gentleman who was approaching from the town.

"That's not a Pierstoffian," said Sir Hugh to himself. "Perhaps he is some yachtsman, who has got afloat early; at any rate, he has a London tailor, yet it's not a yachting rig."

The object of his remark stopped for a few moments at the slip to look about him, and then turned and walked straight and decidedly to Mrs. Temple's door, which was opened the moment he knocked; and, unless Galbraith's eyes, which were keen and far-sighted, deceived him, by the young widow herself.

"By Jove!" exclaimed the mortified baronet, "By Jove! it's Tom! and he is a gentleman—or looks like one."

Here was an additional shade of mystery to meditate upon during breakfast, to which Galbraith did not do so much justice as he ought after his early stroll, and which he permitted Mills to remove without the brief but emphatic commendation he usually bestowed. In truth, Mills was an irreconcilable, and all the more so because she chose to interpret the genuine satisfaction expressed by Sir Hugh as feeble efforts to conciliate her, which she saw through and despised. Whereas, Galbraith was in some odd way taken by her gruff civility and stiff uncommunicativeness, and, quite unconscious of her carefully-nursed dislike, ranked her in his own mind as a "first-rate old woman, with no humbug about her."

"Wasn't the fish right?" asked Mills, jealous of her reputation.

"Oh, yes; all right, thank you."

"They have the same downstairs, and Mr. Tom says it's as good as anything he ever had at—somewhere in Paris."

"Oh! he does," burning to ask "Tom's" name, but disdaining surreptitious information. "It is very good. You can take away the things; and—oh, nothing, I forgot what I was going to say."

"Mills is evidently an old family servant, has known her mistress in better times," pondered Galbraith, "and she too was familiar with Tom, who was no Berlin wool agent, not he!—that was only a blind!" which Galbraith did not like. Mrs. Temple and Miss Lee had every right to keep their affairs to themselves—but false appearances! that was another matter altogether.

Here Sir Hugh hailed with pleasure the entry of his servant with the ordinary demand for "orders," and so disposed of a quarter of an hour.

By that time the church bells began to ring out, and Galbraith, arming himself with the *Field*, took his place in the window and watched a few proprietors of the deserted lodging-houses going to church. Presently he heard the entrance door open and shut. He was instantly on the alert, but instead of the two figures he had seen so regularly sally forth on preceding

Sabbaths, there was only Fanny in her pretty Sunday half-mourning attire. She turned as she came to the corner of the house, and kissing her hand with an arch smile to some one, vanished round it.

"So Miss Fanny is sent to church, and Mrs. Temple stays to discuss business *tête-à-tête* with 'Tom,' a pleasant arrangement for the 'dear old friend,' as that little minx called him," thought Galbraith, gloomily, as he resorted to his favorite method of relief when perturbed, a species of quarter-deck walk far from soothing to the dwellers beneath him, while he strove to divert his mind by planning his future movements, with an odd, irritated, injured feeling; for he resolved stoutly to quit the rascally hole where he had been so long yet so willingly imprisoned, next week at the furthest. But somehow no suitable scheme presented itself. The people, the places, the amusements of which he thought were all unutterably distasteful, absolutely revolting. "At any rate," he said to himself as he seized the paper once more with a desperate determination to occupy his thoughts, "I will go to London in the first place. I will find out something to do with myself there."

In the meanwhile, Tom Reed and his fair client seated themselves for a long confidential talk as soon as they had seen Fanny off.

"Tell me your affairs first, Tom," said Kate. "I do not fancy they will take so much time as mine."

"Oh, mine is a plain, unvarnished tale; but I thought I should like to talk it over with you before I spoke to Fanny."

"I rather fancy I know 'the burden of your song,'" she returned, smiling. "Say on."

"Well, you see," began Reed, drawing his chair closer; "things are looking up with me at last. This little piece of mine has made a hit; I have another bespoke and on the stocks. I have had a private note from poor Pennington, telling me that he does not think he can resume his editorial duties; and I believe I am pretty sure to be his successor. This advance will bring me in a decent income; and so I begin to think I may venture on matrimony!"

"I thought so," said Mrs. Temple, quietly.

"Looking at it coolly and dispassionately," resumed Tom, with sparkling eyes, "I think I may; but, my dear Mrs. Travers, neither Fanny nor I would dream of taking any step, even in a right direction, without due regard to the interest and wishes of so good a friend as yourself. If Fanny leaves you—and she must some day—what will you do?"

"I do not know—I do not know," returned Kate, thought

9*

fully; then looking suddenly at Tom with suspiciously moist eyes, " I daresay it is selfish, but I cannot face the idea of living here without her; she makes home for me; but do not let us think of this. It will be much better and happier for Fanny to be your wife than my assistant; only, dear Tom, make sure that you can afford to marry before you rush into matrimony !"

" You may be sure I will; but listen to me: I want to settl· something with you before I open the subject with Fanny. If she leaves you, will you nail your colors to the mast and go on with the Berlin Bazaar? You know the undertaking wears its pleasantest aspect now; but picture to yourself being shut up with a younger, and, therefore, more objectionable Miss Potter —being worse off considerably than if you were utterly alone ! You couldn't stand it ! I know you could not ! You would murder the assistant, and throw yourself into the sea, or be driven to perform some sort of tragedy before three months were over, believe me !"

" It is a dreadful look-out, I acknowledge," said Kate, smiling at Tom's prophetic energy. " Still I should not like to abandon a tolerably successful undertaking merely to avoid a little personal discomfort—it would be cowardly."

" Not a bit of it," replied her prime counselor. " It is an undertaking in which you ought never to have embarked. I was always opposed to it. I can see clearly enough that one of its attractions was the home and occupation it offered to Fanny; you have stuck to her like a trump; now join her in her home— in ours. You will get back your money for this concern; it is worth considerable more than you gave for it. You can afford to live till you find some more congenial employment. I will find that for you. If you would only write as you talk, what a lot of pleasant magazine articles you could turn out in a year! Come; give the matter a little serious thought! London, you know, would be the best place to hunt up the tracks of the true will."

" Tom," crie! Kate, holding out her hand to him, "you are a good fellow; but such arrangements seldom answer. Settle your plans with Fanny; tell her it would be a satisfaction to me to see her your wife; but put me out of the question. I may come and live near you. I may adopt some other line of life; but I will not quit my business yet awhile."

·'And I know Fan won't listen to any suggestion of leaving you," said Tom, gloomily.

" She may—you do not know; open the subject, and I wil follow it up if you wish," replied Kate. " Now have you quite said your say?"

" Yes, quite; and I am all ears to hear yours."

" First, I want a *vivâ voce* description of your interview with Mr. Ford. Your letter was a little hurried, though it was very good of you to write at all in such a whirl."

Tom recapitulated all he could remember of the conversation, and answered many questions. Then, after sitting quite still and silent for a few minutes, Kate exclaimed, quickly,

" And what impression does all this make upon you ? "

" Well, no particular impression. He is just the same crotchety, touchy, worthy soul he ever was ! The last man in the world to tamper with any document. I know what you are thinking of ; but he would not have the pluck—believe me, he would not."

" Perhaps so," said she. "However, I will, in the strictest confidence, show you the letter you forwarded from him. Not a word of the contents to Fanny ; she could *not* refrain from laughing and talking about it, dear thing ! "

" Of course she could not," returned Tom, as Kate rose, and, unlocking her desk, she drew forth the letter and handed it to him.

Reed read through in silence, except for a few indistinct growls.

" The presumptuous blockhead ! " he exclaimed, when he finished. " He seems to have lost his senses ! Why, he insinuates that he was almost an accepted lover before old—I mean Mr. Travers, came into the field."

" Which, I am sure, it is unnecessary for me to deny ! " cried Kate. " You, too, then, think him audacious? I was not sure if it was a true instinct or an unwarranted assumption on my part. Remember, Tom, I was in a lowly state of life enough when I first knew Mr. Ford."

" Whatever you were, if he was not a conceited ass he would have felt he was not your equal. And then to raise his eyes to his employer's widow—a woman of your stamp ! it is the height of presumption ! "

" Now, Tom, perhaps you think I am justified in doubting him ? "

" Well, no ! It is scarcely logical. Why should he try to reduce the woman he loved to penury? Why should he enrich her enemy, and defraud himself ? Why—"

" It seems a far-fetched idea," interrupted Mrs. Temple, " and yet I cannot get rid of it. You know the day he brought me that false will—as I shall always consider it ; he offered to cancel or destroy it—I forget exactly what he said—but something to that effect. I scarcely noticed at the time, but I have often thought of it since."

" Did he ? " said Reed, who was looking through the letter

again. " That was queer. What do you suppose was his object ? "

" I can hardly say ; he thought probably my dislike and indignation against Sir Hugh Galbraith might have tempted me to consent ; and then what a hold he would have had upon me ! "

" By George ! I could never believe that proper old boy would be such a villain ! I think, my fair friend, you romance a little —all the better for a literary future."

" Do not laugh at me, Tom ; and pray do not lose sight of Ford. My whole soul is as fixed as ever on the hope of clearing myself and my husband's memory from the foul slander of that abominable will."

" I will help you with all my wits ! " cried Tom, remembering his creditable acquaintance Trapes and his inquiries. " But I dare not encourage you to hope. You say this Galbraith is going to leave ; I would advise you when he is just off make yourself known, and then I'll take long odds that he will make better offers of a settlement, and you might arrange things comfortably. It need not interfere with another will should it turn up."

" Never offer me such advice again ! " cried Mrs. Temple, indignantly. " It is a positive insult."

" I am dumb then," said Tom, submissively. After a few moments' thought, he asked, " Do you think Ford ever dabbled in any betting or turfy transactions ? "

" I should say not—certainly not. Why do you ask ? "

" Because a very queer character was making inquiries about him the other day." And Tom proceeded to describe his conversation with Trapes.

" It is curious," said Kate, reflectively, after listening with deep attention to his account ; " but I cannot see that this supposed debt of Ford's can affect me in any way, even if true ; and I presume your friend has some powers of invention, as you say he was once on the press."

" No doubt ; I believe very little he says ; but that he wanted to find Ford—or the man he resembled—is a fact, whatever the reason ; and, moreover, he knows something of Mr. Travers's people."

" True," returned Kate ; and then fell into a fit of thought, from which she roused herself by a sort of effort to ask, " Where is this man Trapes to be found ? "

" Oh ! I have not an idea ; indeed, I had no inclination to keep up the connection."

" I wish we knew."

" Better have nothing to say to him ; he would only persuade you to throw away your money."

Mrs. Temple made no reply, but again opening her desk, took out a memorandum-book in which she began to write. "What was the date of your interview?" she asked. Tom gave it, for as it was identical with the first appearance of his play he knew it well. A few more questions proved she was putting down the substance of Reed's communication.

"May I ask what that is for?" said he.

"This is my evidence-book," replied Kate, turning over the pages. "I put down here everything, great and small, that strikes me as bearing in any possible way upon my case."

"I protest you are a first-rate solicitor spoiled by your sex! What suggested such a business-like proceeding, positively unnatural in a woman?"

"I cannot tell; dwelling intensely on a topic is something like boring for a well, I imagine. If you only go on long enough and deep enough, you are sure to strike an idea or a spring! Then you know poor Mr. Travers was always making notes of ideas and suggestions, and all sorts of things that might by any possibility be useful."

"Believe me, Mrs. Travers—well, Temple! I must try and remember it—you have admirable qualities for a writer. The keeper of a diary, if intelligent, is the possessor of a mine."

"I trust this will prove one to me; but—oh! here is Fanny," as that young person entered, prayer-book in hand, and announced triumphantly that she had been escorted back from church by Mr. Turner, jun.

"Have you finished your consultation yet?" she continued, "or shall I go out again? I daresay Mr. Turner is lingering outside, and will not mind keeping me company a little while."

CHAPTER XXIII.

SUNDAY was not yet over. It had been a very long day to Sir Hugh Galbraith. Some of it he had disposed of indifferently, by trying how he could drive without the whip-hand, and, accompanied by his groom, had gone nearly over to Stoneborough, and now he had once more taken his post of observation in the window. The day had been beautiful throughout, and the sun had nearly accomplished his daily task, so far as Pierstoffe was concerned. The church bells had not yet rung out. All was quiet—the inhabitants were at tea—and Galbraith's reflections were interrupted by the appearance of Mrs. Mills bearing a tray with a huge cup, a tiny cream ewer, and a plate of thin brown bread and butter, such as Sir Hugh loved.

"It's a thought early," she said, setting down these good

things on a small table beside him. "But maybe you won't
mind, because it's the girls' Sunday out ; and as my missus
is having her tea, I thought I would get it all over before I
dressed."

Galbraith nodded a reluctant assent, and Mrs. Mills departed.
So everything must give way to Tom—even a good solvent
tenant like himself. Tom, he supposed, wanted an evening
walk, and he, Sir Hugh, must have his tea forced down his
throat an hour too soon. He wondered if Tom was to have
a *tête-à-tête* walk as well as a *tête-à-tête* conversation. He
would have a look as they went out. If that nice little Fanny
was excluded from the walk as well as the talk, he must conclude that Tom—confound him !—was the widow's lover, and
poor Fanny was an ill-used girl. For he had never seen startled
delight if he had not read it in Fanny's eyes when she heard
that fellow's voice the evening before. And a dim sort of feeling rippled over his heart or brain—or whatever thinks—like
the momentary crisping of water by a sudden breeze, that it
would be very delightful to see any face brighten thus for him—
brighten honestly, naturally, even a plain face ; but how gloriously would such eyes as Mrs. Temple's light up ! Strange,
that the grandest, the most striking expression he had ever read
in them was defiance, almost detestation, and it always suggested the idea of how they would speak a different and opposite passion. However, the tea was very refreshing after his
drive, and the bread and butter not unacceptable. By the time
both were finished Galbraith heard voices beneath, and looking
out, beheld the two friends, escorted by Tom, sally forth—Mrs.
Temple, as usual, in black, with a white shawl over her arm.

"The three of them, by Jove ! " murmured Galbraith to himself. "I never expected that." He watched them to the
division of the main street into the high road to Stoneborough
and that leading to the North Parade. Here they paused and
seemed to talk awhile ; then Fanny and Tom went to the left
along the high road, and Mrs. Temple took the more direct line
to the right, as if intending to stroll along the Parade.

So far as Galbraith knew her stroll would be limited. He
was not aware of any outlet beyond the gravel sweep whereon
the dowager barouches and invalid chairs which in the season
moved slowly to and fro along the sea front—turned, and came
back again. He watched assiduously for ten, fifteen, twenty
minutes, still no sign of the figure he looked for. A genial glow
began to replace the dull, irritated, injured sensation which
oppressed Galbraith all day. Perhaps she was sitting down
with a book ! At the thought he caught up his hat and was off,
with long, swift steps, to test the truth of his conjecture.

But the few seats on the Esplanade were all untenanted. No one, save a few of those inveterate loungers, the fishermen, was about. Where had that puzzling landlady of his vanished? Reaching the far end of the Esplanade, where a rough sort of breastwork, formed of pieces of rock, stones, clay, and supporting timbers, had been piled up against the sea, he looked round carefully, and perceived the pathway which Mrs. Temple had discovered about a year before.

She must have followed this track, unless indeed she had gone in to pay a visit to one of the shuttered, blank-looking, North Parade houses. This was highly improbable; so Galbraith pressed on rapidly, with eagerness and exhilaration—his pulses beating fast, somewhat to his own surprise.

Meantime Mrs. Temple—as she must be called in this portion of the story—strolled on leisurely, glad to be alone, that she might examine and reason away a certain feeling of depression and distress that had been fretting her spirit since her talk with Tom. She had shared in the cheerful pleasantry of their midday dinner. She had played her part of hostess as brightly, as cordially as ever; but under all there was the unrest—the fear of an unavoidable and painful change.

The silence and beauty around calmed her perturbed thoughts —calmed, but did not cheer. The deeper chords of her nature vibrated to the mute language of sea and sky and rock, and resolute endurance rather than cheerful resignation seemed the key-note to which she would tune her spirit.

She reached the little jetty before described, and, walking to the end, seated herself upon the bench. It was evident that she must not count on Fanny's companionship much longer, and how would it be then? Could she face the terrible isolation of the life she had adopted? Worse than isolation, the company without companionship of an assistant of the ordinary shop-woman type?

For the first time Kate regretted her choice of an occupation, and with all her liberal tendencies, felt the impassable nature of the gulf fixed between the habits, thoughts, and manners of the class she had quitted and that which she had adopted.

"It will be less and less as education and common sense spread up and down; but at present it is harder to bear than I expected. Is it quite fair of Tom, when he knew that I undertook this business as much on Fanny's account as my own, to take her from me so soon? Pooh! how self blinds one. Of course Fanny is his first consideration, and it is far better for her to be his wife than my assistant. Dear Fan! I trust in heaven he will be good to her; but matrimony is a fearful trial, and does not want a third in the house to increase its dangers.

No! come what may, I will not desert the course I have marked
for myself until I have either succeeded in upsetting the will or
given up all hope, or find the Berlin Bazaar will not pay; but
when Fanny leaves and I am much alone, I will try if I can
write as Tom suggested. I have plenty of time before me, and
I must not allow myself to be a coward; but the loneliness—
ah!" Gazing out over the sea she let her thoughts drift freely,
vaguely to the past, its tenderness, its high hopes, its bright
anticipations, the long, dutiful suppression of her married existence, her glimpse of life and liberty, her cruel reverse. The
soft, solemn loveliness of the evening disposed her to think
compassionately even of herself.

The sun had sunk behind the cliffs, but the slowly-fading
light was still reflected on the sky opposite. Towards the
horizon "the raven down of darkness" was gathering, but
above it lighter and lighter shades of gray prevailed up to a
pale ashen hue, flecked with rosy cloudlets, varying from ruby
to faint opal or mother-of-pearl tints of exquisite delicacy. The
sea was still and smooth; the breeze of the morning had died
away, and the giant slept,—only the soft lulling lap of tiny
ripples against the huge wet black stones which lay round
the timbers of the little jetty broke the silence. The very air
was full of speechless feeling—soft, quiet, and yet not without
the chillness of early spring—a certain cold which seemed an
expression of sadness. Kate opened her shawl, and wrapping
it round her, leaned her clasped hands on the rail which de-
fended her resting-place, while she looked forth with keenest
appreciation on sea and sky. "To bear is to conquer our fate,"
she thought; "rather a heroic quotation *à propos* of Berlin
wool shop. Ah! how different all things might have been had
Mr. Travers not been separated from his cousin. If Hugh
Galbraith—"

At this point in her reflections she was almost startled into a
scream by a voice beside her. "Good evening, Mrs. Temple."

"I thought this haunt was only known to myself, the coast-
guard, and the sea-gulls," she replied, turning to face the man
she had just thought of, and in her surprise speaking more
hurriedly than usual. "How did you find it out?"

"By accident," said Galbraith, shortly, but he smiled upon
her as he spoke—smiled. Yes; his sombre, stern, and usually
inexpressive eyes dwelt upon her smilingly, tenderly. She did
not know the effect her natural impulsive address, the quick,
flitting blush, the welcoming smile into which she had been
startled wrought upon the enemy; but she had never spoken
quite like this to him before, and Galbraith for a moment forgot
there was any world beyond the few feet of planking on which
they stood, and the stretch of sea and sky before them.

" What a lovely evening ! " he said, not finding any more original remark after a short pause, and sitting down beside her. " This is a pretty nook—do you often come here ? "

" Not often. I cannot, you know."

" Of course."

" In summer it is always my holiday excursion. In winter I can never manage it, and the path is not very safe in rough weather."

" The cliffs are rather fine along here," resumed Galbraith, " but they are nothing to the cliffs near Kirby Grange. My place, or rather my ruin—it's not much more," for Kate had looked up at him inquiringly. He went on. " Great black beetling cliffs with jagged reefs running out to sea, and lots of sea birds clanging about. I used to climb the crags to get the nests. I was a tolerable cragsman in those days. I don't think I should like to try it now."

" I do not like the terrific in nature," said Kate, drawing her shawl closer, the rounded, graceful outlines of her supple figure showing through the thin soft folds. " It makes me think of despair and defeat, and horrors of that kind."

" Yet I fancy you are very plucky for a woman, Mrs. Temple."

" I cannot tell. I have not been much tried, and certainly peace and rest seem to me the greatest good in life."

There was something weary, almost sad, in her voice, and Galbraith was conscious of a very strong desire to take the little hands which were holding her shawl in his and ask if there was anything in the world he could do for her, but he only said, " To a certain extent, but peace soon becomes stagnation."

A pause. Mrs. Temple was not displeased to see Galbraith. It amused her, and gave a lighter tone to her thoughts.

" Have you visited your native place since you have returned from India ? " she asked at last, the silence growing awkward, especially as Galbraith had a stupid fashion of staring.

" No, I want to go there, and yet I dread it."

" Indeed ! Why ? "

" Because—you will, perhaps, laugh at me—I have scarcely an acre of the old lands left, and I can't stand seeing another lording it over what ought to be mine."

" Laugh ! No, I should be the last to laugh. I would stake my existence on a struggle to get back my own."

And she looked full into Galbraith's eyes.

" And you would be no mean antagonist, I fancy," said he, returning her gaze with an earnestness from which she did not shrink. " I wonder, Mrs. Temple, if you and I ever met before in some different state of existence ? for I sometimes think you look upon me as an enemy. '

" Me ! What an extraordinary idea ! " exclaimed Kate, laughing, but coloring too—a glow that mounted quickly and then
fading, left her cheek to its ordinary rich paleness.

" Yes. There was something in your eyes when first they
met mine I shall never forget. Had you been a man I should
have snatched up some weapon to defend myself."

" Pooh ! nonsense ! " she returned, again laughing ; but there
was a curious sound of suppressed pleasure in the low, soft
laugh. " I had been vexed in my business. Some one had
tried to cheat me, perhaps ; or I doubted your solvency, and
imagined I had a bad bargain in my drawing-room apartments."

There was a subtle tone of mockery in the last words, a curl
of the ripe red lip suggestive of playful scorn.

" I do not pretend to guess the reason ; I only know the
effect," returned Galbraith, and there was a pause longer than
the last, for Kate's eyes had fixed themselves on the distant
horizon unconsciously, as she reflected on the strange eddy of
fortune which had made Sir Hugh Galbraith her companion in
this remote corner, while he availed himself of her averted gaze
to drink in greedily the charm of the frank, fair face before him,
its sweet, firm mouth and soft pale cheek, the large eyes so
still and deep when she was silent, so changeful and expressive
when she spoke or listened ; the broad but not high forehead ;
the delicate yet distinctly marked brow ; the look, as if no mean
thought, no low motive could lurk in a brain so nobly lodged.

Galbraith had hitherto considered himself, and had been considered, a cold, immovable kind of fellow, but he was conscious
that these characteristics were fast melting away ; there was
something in his companion's beauty and bearing which exercised a magic effect upon his half-developed nature, as certain
chemical ingredients, at the approach of that which attracts, or
contains the complement of their being, rush forth to blend
with what has called them to life. The deep calm, the solitude,
the tender beauty of sea and sky, the unusual tinge of familiarity
in Mrs. Temple's manner, lapped him into a kind of Elysium
such as he had never before known. As yet, he could enjoy the
first warm breath of the coming sirocco, before the fever and
thirst were upon him.

" What a relief it must be to you to come here from the shop,"
exclaimed Galbraith, abruptly, fearing that if the silence continued Mrs. Temple might get up and walk away.

" It is, indeed," she returned frankly.

" Then you don't like your work ? "

" I do not dislike it," said Kate, falling unconsciously into a
semiconfidential strain. " I would rather earn my bread as a
high-class artist, or writer, but as nature has not made me of

suitable stuff, I must do what I can.   I do not fancy the restraint of teaching, or keeping a school."

" Still, such a position must be very unpleasant to you, for I never will believe you were originally intended for it."

" Oh, as to that, you may conjecture what you like, Sir Hugh ; but I have told you there is no romance about me or my position," said she, turning her eyes, which laughed sunnily, upon him.

" I daresay you will think I am a presumptuous fellow," returned Galbraith, leaning towards her, resting the elbow of his sound arm on his knee, and his cheek on his hand ; " but I am always conjecturing about you.   You are a constant mystery to me, and I am determined to solve it ! "

The earnest uncomplimentary manner in which Galbraith uttered these words took from them all appearance of love-making.   Nevertheless, they sent a strange gust of triumph along Kate's nerves ; her contemptuous enemy was growing interested in her.   He acknowledged her superiority.

" The presumption consists in telling me so," she said, still meeting his eyes with an arch smile.   " I cannot help your thoughts, only they must sorely want legitimate employment when you waste them on—your landlady ; " there was a slight pause before she uttered the last words with provoking emphasis, which she could not restrain ; there is such a charm in feeling oneself charming.

Sir Hugh raised his head quickly, as if about to speak, and then stopped.

" But in a few days you will be away, among your natural occupations and associates, the mystery you have created for yourself will cease to interest or annoy," she continued.

" I hope it will," returned Galbraith, bluntly ; " I hope it will —but," again resting his cheek on his hand, and looking up into her eyes, " am I to take what you say as a notice to quit ? "

" A Sunday notice is not a legal warning—so I was informed when I inquired into the laws affecting landlord and tenant, previous to letting lodgings," said Kate, demurely.

" But do you wish me to leave ? "

" No, not before you are quite fit to move.   But of course it is absurd to suppose you will remain beyond a week or so !   Your kinsfolk and acquaintance would think you daft if you stayed on here without any adequate inducement, and justly."

Sir Hugh's brow lowered and he twisted his moustaches thoughtfully.   " I suppose," he said, " a fellow may please himself in spite of his kinsfolk and acquaintance—mine troubled me deuced little in former days !   Do *you* wish me to go ? "

"Wish to lose a good tenant! Certainly not," she replied with a smile—an irrepressible smile.

"But I ought to tell you that, after the middle of April, I wish to have my rooms ready for a tenant of last year, who made me promise to take him in if he wanted to come!"

"Oh!"— a very dissatisfied oh! "I must march, then!"

He was more mortified than he liked to acknowledge; this woman, the hem of whose garment he could have taken up and kissed, so much had he lost his common sense, deliberately told him that he was to her a mere every day tenant, and no more. But it was better·so; otherwise he, Galbraith, might make such an ass of himself that he could never get into the lion's skin again.

"But it will be dark if I stay any longer," said Mrs. Temple, rising, "and the path here is not too safe."

"Don't go!" cried Galbraith, almost vehemently, "there will be an hour of daylight yet, and when shall we have such an evening again? I mean, when shall I have such an evening, if I am to get the route next week? I beg your pardon!" seeing the look of wonder in his companion's eyes at the sort of despairing entreaty in his voice. "I fancy I must have grown whimsical and—and unlike myself, after my long imprisonment. I do not think I am much of a sentimentalist, but I was always fond of evening and the sea—and all that sort of thing, even when I was a boy." This was said with a kind of burst, as if it came in spite of himself, and he was rather ashamed.

"And do you despise yourself for loving such beauty as this?" returned Kate, with a slight gesture of her hand towards the sea. "How strange the effect of a man's life must be when all that *we* are taught to admire and take pleasure in is despised by them. No wonder there is so little true friendship between men and women!"

"I don't despise myself for loving beauty in any shape," said Galbraith, as he traced an imaginary pattern with his stick on the boards of the landing-place, "but I can't talk poetically about it. I should make an ass of myself if I tried!"

"If you have the feeling it will out! How do you know you are not a mute inglorious Milton? · How do you know that you have experienced the whole circle of feeling?"

A grim smile, not devoid of humor, lit up his face. "I think you have made a capital random shot!" he said.

"Then did you never read any poetry?"

"N—not much. I have heard some read."

"Do you read novels?"

"No."

"Do you ever read anything?"

"Yes, Mrs. Temple!" laughing good-humoredly. "I have read a good deal on professional subjects, and history, and politics. Come, does that redeem me a little from the general ruck of blockheads?"

"A little—yes," she said, thoughtfully. "But do you not care for the living spirit that animates these dry bones—the skeleton frame of facts? Do you not enjoy the genius which, out of the clay of everyday events, the mere matter of action, moulds exquisite forms, and breathes into them the breath of life? and more —that touches the sleeping God within us? or gives the dull sullen prisoner in the body's cage a glimpse of light and liberty?"

"Go on!" said Galbraith, in a low voice. "I am not sure that I take it all in, but I like to listen."

"I daresay you laugh at my outburst! and I am not going to talk for your amusement," replied Kate, smiling. "Now, Sir Hugh, do not curtail your enjoyment of this delicious evening, but *I* am going home!"

"And so am I," said he, rising, "for at present your home is mine."

His pertinacity and unusual sympathetic frankness amused and interested her, yet it would not do to meet all Pierstoffe as it returned from church, accompanied by a baronet; for the present she let him go on, however. He was assiduous in his attempts to draw her back to the enthusiastic strain, which gave so much animation to her eyes, and mobile lips, but in vain. The effort, nevertheless, made Galbraith talk unusually well, and before they had accomplished the distance between the coast-guard station and the town he had risen a degree or two in her opinion. Hitherto her estimate of his intellectual powers was by no means exalted; she had told Tom Reed that he gave her the idea of a stupid, obstinate man, whose education had been neglected.

That he was well bred, though no drawing-room gentleman, she could not deny, and on the present occasion there was more than politeness in the excessive care with which he watched every opportunity offered by the slight difficulties of the path, to assist or guard her. "Had he been in England when I married, and seen and known everything, he would have been more just to me, perhaps! and all this mischief might have been avoided," she thought. "But no, he is a man of such strong prejudices, that I daresay if I were to tell him who I am now, his friendliness would stiffen into stern contempt. To him I shall always be an adventuress. Well, his opinion is nothing to me." Such were the ideas floating through her mind as she listened, with soft attentive eyes, to her unsuspecting companion's exposition of his views as to the best method of managing

the natives of India, with which it is needless to say she en
tirely disagreed. But they were too near the town to permit the
argument. Mrs. Temple stopped short, and said, " Be so good,
Sir Hugh, as to walk on, and leave me to return alone. All
Pierstoffe would be horrified at the incongruity of a baronet escorting the proprietress of a fancy bazaar." She smiled brightly
sweetly, and Galbraith almost permitted the words, " D——
Pierstoffe," which rose naturally to his lips, to escape; but he
changed them to " What bosh ! "

" No, it is not bosh," said Mrs. Temple. " It is only consistent with your own conservative principles."

" I do not like to leave you alone in the dusk."

" Neverthe less you must," she returned, decidedly.

" I obey," said Galbraith, raising his hat; quickening his
steps, he was soon out of sight, while Kate, slowly following,
reached her house without any further adventure.

She had a long tearful talk with Fanny, after they had bid
Tom good-night and good-bye, as he had to start by the first
train for town next day. Fanny had utterly rejected the idea of
leaving her friend at present, or till she had renounced the Berlin wool trade. She confessed to a quarrel with Tom on this
subject, but also to a reconciliation, the very recollection of
which called up dimpling smiles and blushes. No ! she would not
quit Kate ; she never thought she would be so important a person, but she now saw quite well that Kate could not get on
without her.

Mrs. Temple urged that Tom Reed would have just cause to
complain if Fanny preferred her friend to her lover, and at last
it was decided that when Tom was actually appointed to the
chieftainship of the " M. T.," it would be time enough to talk
about separating. In the interest excited by Tom and Fanny's
affairs, Mrs. Temple forgot, or omitted to mention, her rencontre with Galbraith, and having done so, did not care to revert to
the subject, especially as her friend had asked her no questions.
But, in the solitude of her own room, a review of the conversa
tion called up a smile half-triumphant and wholly amused to the
young widow's lip, as she remembered that little more than a
year ago she had sat under the yew tree in Hampton Court gardens, and quivered with indignant feeling at the scorn heaped
upon her by the man, whose tones of entreaty for a few minutes
more of her society still rang in her ear !

CHAPTER XXIV.

A S the friends anticipated, Lady Styles lost no time on her
return to Weston, in investigating the state of affairs at

the Berlin Bazaar, and on the day following Tom's visit, she made her appearance at an unusually early hour after luncheon.

" Well, Mrs. Temple, how have you all been ? I feel as if I had been away a year instead of six weeks. Do you know I don't like any neighborhood as well as my own ; it's a great advantage to be within a drive of a Berlin Bazaar—especially when it is so well managed, ha ! ha ! ha ! I want three skeins of yellow shaded, and two of green, five of crimson, and—there ! your young person can take the paper and put all the things together, while I talk to you. You are looking uncommonly well ; and how are you getting on with your tenant—your patient— the man that broke his head ? Slade tells me he is here still ; not a bad business for you."

" No, Lady Styles. It has answered very well to have my rooms occupied ; but Sir Hugh Galbraith leaves this week."

" Oh ! indeed—yes, Dr. Slade gives an indifferent account of him, says he is so impatient and proud, and—all sorts of things. Have you found him so, eh ? "

" I only know that he pays regularly, and gives very little trouble," replied Mrs. Temple, smiling placidly, and perfectly understanding the drift of the question.

" Oh, indeed ; that is very nice, very nice indeed. You know, you would make such a charming nurse ; I thought he might have claimed his landlady's personal care," cried Lady Styles, with a jolly laugh.

" My good old servant has acted the part of landlady and nurse for me," returned Mrs. Temple.

" Oh, very prudent ; quite right, quite right," said her ladyship, looking round with an eagle eye, in search of some chink into which she might insert the point of her wedge-like inquiries. " I don't think you have quite so many pretty things as you used. I hope you are not neglecting your business."

" I hope not," said Mrs Temple, drily. " But I have not yet bought my spring goods ; in a week or two I hope to offer a choice selection of novelties."

" That will be charming. Well, Mrs. Temple, if Sir Hugh Galbraith is at home I think it right to call upon him. I will go in, if you please ! "

" I never know if he is in or out, Lady Styles. But if you will go round to the front door the servant will tell you."

" Oh, very well, very well. You see, he is a great friend of a cousin of mine, and I wish to show him a little attention—to explain why I have not been to see him before. I will look in again, Mrs. Temple, for my wools and canvas, and tell you what I think of him." So saying, her ladyship walked, or to be more accurate, waddled away round to the entrance, and there made a tolerable imitation of her footman's knock.

Mills, "simple, erect severe, austere," in due time—not too soon—opened the door in a snowy cap, apron, and net handkerchief, the very picture of an old family servant.

"Ah! I see," thought Lady Styles, with a delighted sense of her own rapid perception, "this is the nurse. I wonder where Slade found her."

"Good morning," she said to Mills, who had now reached a condition which defied the most startling combination of circumstances to surprise. "How is your patient? If he is pretty well and visible to-day, I will come in and see him."

"Is it Mrs. Temple you're wanting, ma'am?" asked Mills, to whom this address was dumb show.

"She is as deaf as a post," exclaimed Lady Styles. "No, no," in louder tones. "Sir Hugh Galbraith. I want to see Sir Hugh Galbraith."

"Yes, he is in, ma'am."

"Just tell him Lady Styles would be happy to come up and see him."

"Walk in, if you please," and Mills ushered her ladyship into the pretty sitting-room opening on the garden, where she immediately occupied herself in a close examination of all books, photographs, etc., etc., which lay upon the table. Meantime, Mills bent her rheumatic steps to Sir Hugh's apartment. "There is a lady wants to see you."

"A lady!" echoed Galbraith, looking up from some notes he was trying to make in pencil with his left hand. "What sort of a lady?"

"Oh, a stout lady, as is often in the shop. A lady somebody, Sir."

"Lady Styles, by Jove!" he exclaimed. "She has not lost much time. Well, show her up," he added, resignedly, while he hastily put his papers together and shut them in his blotting-book, before Mills opened the door and ushered in his visitor.

"Sir Hugh Galbraith," said Lady Styles, in her best manner, as she entered, "I really could not let you be here in a sort of savage land without coming to look after you. Colonel Upton mentioned you to me as his particular friend, and had I not been detained in Yorkshire by poor Sir Marmaduke's indisposition I should have had the pleasure of calling upon you before."

"You are very good," returned Galbraith, advancing a chair. "Pray sit down," which her ladyship, being rather out of breath from the ascent of the staircase, did very readily.

"I think," she resumed, "I have the pleasure of knowing your sister, Lady Lorrimer. I met her at dinner, where I was staying in Yorkshire. I cannot say I see much resemblance between you." Galbraith bowed. "And tell me, Sir Hugh, are you feeling better and stronger?"

" I am very nearly all right, thank you. Can't venture to use
my arm yet, the doctor tells me. I hope to get away the end
of this week or beginning of next."

" Then, my dear sir," cried Lady Styles, with much animation,
" you had much better come over and spend the remainder of
your convalescence at Weston. We will take great care of
you ; and I have one or two very pleasant people staying with
me."

" You are really very good, Lady Styles, but I am quite comfortable here. When I am fit to be seen I will do myself the
honor of calling upon you."

" Fit to be seen, my dear Sir Hugh!" echoed her ladyship.
" The less fit you are to be seen, the more ready all my young
lady friends will be to admire you."

" My dear Lady Styles, I do not like young ladies, and I am
quite unaccustomed to be admired."

" What a monster!" cried Lady Styles, laughing. " But they
make you tolerably comfortable here?"

" Very comfortable indeed."

" Do you ever see your landlady, eh?" sharply.

" I have seen her," returned Galbraith, with an immovable
face.

" She interests me very much," resumed Lady Styles, with
animation. " I am quite sure there is some romance attached
to her. She is so lady-like, and quiet; yet an excellent woman
of business. Then she reminds me of two or three people.
Has it ever struck you?"

" What? her likeness to two or three people? I cannot say
it has," replied Galbraith, so coldly and indifferently that Lady
Styles was checked for a moment.

" What a nice, respectable nurse you appear to have. I must
ask Slade for her address; it is well to know such a person.
Pray, have you found her satisfactory in every respect? sober,
vigilant, and all that, eh?"

" Who?" asked Galbraith, puzzled by this flank movement.

" The nurse—the old woman who let me in."

" You mean Mrs. Mills ! She is the servant and manager of
the house. I thought she was the landlady till the other day.
I have never been reduced to a nurse."

" Oh, indeed ! Now, there, Sir Hugh! there is another remarkable fact; the very servant is out of the common. Mark
my words, there is some mystery here."

Sir Hugh bent his head in silence. " I imagine all sorts of
things about that charming young widow. They *do* say her
husband is still alive, and imprisoned for some dreadful crime,
but I cannot help fancying that she has never been married, but

10

has been well connected, and obliged to part with her protector? eh, Sir Hugh? At my age one knows, unfortunately, too much of the wickedness of the world—and—has n't it struck you?"

"No, certainly not," returned Galbraith, starting up and stirring the fire violently, "my experience of the world suggests nothing of the kind."

"Dear me! does n't it," said Lady Styles, innocently; "but you have been a long time out of England, and of course you have n't seen Mrs. Temple as much as I have. Then you have formed no theory respecting your landlady?"

"Why should I?" exclaimed Galbraith, abruptly. "A quiet woman earning her bread honestly, ought to be spared theories and conjectures."

"Now, Sir Hugh, that is too severe. I suppose you mean I am a gossip, and I am nothing of the kind; but I am hugely sympathetic. I confess I take a deep, a sincere interest in the people I live amongst. There's the Doctor! *He* is a gossip if you will, and, between you and me, not the most good-natured of gossips; but he affects to be above all that sort of thing. Have n't you noticed it?"

"I am not observant," returned Sir Hugh, wearing his grimmest aspect. So Lady Styles wandered to another subject.

"I was very pleased to hear that old Mr. Travers came to his senses at last, and made a proper will. It would have been shocking if he had left everything to the widow."

"She would probably differ from you," said Galbraith, drily.

"Oh! I fancy it was a bitter disappointment to *her*. I believe she was a very grasping creature; a connection of mine, the Honorable Mrs. Danby, lived next door, at the time of poor Mr. Travers's death, and tried to show her a little attention; but she was rather ungracious; would not accept any invitation, and was very unneighborly and disobliging about her carriage: would rather let her horses eat their heads off in the stable than allow a mortal to use it but herself, and was always closeted with a clerk of Mr. Travers's—over accounts—or heaven knows what—quite a low fellow!"

"Well," returned Galbraith, who would have stood up for Beelzebub himself against Lady Styles; "it was only decent to keep quiet after her husband's death, and people don't generally keep carriages for their neighbors to use."

"I protest, Sir Hugh, you are severely just. However, it was rather hard of the husband to leave her penniless; depend upon it, he had reason to think her undeserving. Does it strike you?"

"We have no right to say anything of the sort."

"Pardon me, Sir Hugh, such a will gives us every right. Do you know what has become of her?"

" No," returned Galbraith.

" Dear me! I wonder you had not the—the curiosity to inquire. Mrs. Danby heard she had gone abroad; depend upon it, she had contrived to get a sum of money, or a settlement of some kind; she could not live on air. It would be awkward now if she were to dispute the will."

" That is not likely."

" Well, I don't know; these sort of women—greedy, uneducated women, I mean—are very fond of litigation. Suppose she got hold of some sharp, unscrupulous solicitor."

" I never suppose things," very sternly.

" Well, Sir Hugh, I think you are looking very tired, and I shall bid you good morning," said Lady Styles, giving him up as a hopeless subject. " I am truly glad your uncle—wasn't he your uncle? No?—whatever he was then—that he disposed of his property as he did; by the way, do you keep up the business still?"

" The house still exists."

" Then I really do wish you would give one of the rector's sons a berth in it. Most deserving people, but poor—wretchedly poor. What between dilapidations, and thirteen children —terrible, isn't it? Now, do think of them. Men like you have a great deal in their power, and you ought to consider yourself a steward for the benefit of others. By the way, Willie Upton talks of coming over for a week or two. He has business in London; so you really must come and meet him. Don't let me keep you standing. Oh, by the way, I just want to speak a word to Mrs. Temple before I go. May I ring the bell?"—ringing it.

This unexpected stroke paralyzed Galbraith for a moment. It seemed a sort of sacrilege to call up the gentle, dignified lady of the house to be cross-examined by this rampant old woman.

" I do not think Mrs. Temple usually leaves her shop," he said, hastily; " Mills is virtually mistress of the house."

" Oh, she will come for me," said Lady Styles, with a provoking triumphant nod. " I was her first patron, and I know she looks on me as her sheet anchor." To Mills, as she presented herself, " Pray, give my compliments to Mrs. Temple; I should like to speak to her for two minutes—just *two* minutes."

" What, here, ma'am?"

" Yes, here," smiling graciously. "I wish to tell her, before you, what I want," continued Lady Styles to Galbraith, with many nods and smiles, and resuming her seat, while he, in gloomy discomfort, stood upon the hearth-rug. Lady Styles talked on, but he scarce heard even the sound of her voice so anxiously was he watching the door. At last it opened, and Mrs. Temple came in, her ordinary and exceedingly simple attire could not conceal the grace of her figure, nor had the unexpected summons disturbed the composed, collected expression of her face. Galbraith made a step forward, and bowed. She returned the salutation in silence.

"Well, Mrs. Temple, I have been persuading Sir Hugh Galbraith to come over to Weston. We should take excellent care of him, and I daresay with your shop and all, you have quite enough to do without attending to an invalid."

"My servant, Mills, attends to the house. I have scarce anything to do with it," said Mrs. Temple, coldly. "But I have no doubt Sir Hugh Galbraith would have more comfort and amusement at your ladyship's residence."

"I cannot go, however," said Sir Hugh, resolutely, "though much obliged, and all that—"

"Well, Mrs. Temple, if Sir Hugh fancies fruit or vegetables, or flowers, or anything, pray send for them. By the way! have you ever been over to Weston, Mrs. Temple? It is a very pretty place; people often drive from Stoneborough to look at it. If you come over some afternoon, about five, you will be in time for the housekeeper's room tea, and they will be delighted to see you, though I doubt if you will get such good bread, butter, and shrimps as I had here, ha! ha! ha! Well, good morning, Sir Hugh. Good morning, Mrs. Temple," and her ladyship rolled with amazing rapidity out of the room, attended by Galbraith, who with ·difficulty restrained his lips from bad words. The moment the door was closed upon her he returned quickly, hoping to meet Mrs. Temple, but she had vanished.

Galbraith was greatly incensed by this visit, and all the gossip he had been compelled to listen to. It stung him to hear poor Travers's widow spoken of in such a tone, though he was quite sure she deserved it. Then it vexed him to have the possible claims and probable destitution of that adventuress brought before his notice. He had urged his solicitor repeatedly to seek her out and relieve her necessities, which he felt to be a blot upon his scutcheon. What evil fortune ever brought the creature across his path! There was one morsel of her ladyship's outpouring that dwelt on his mind pertinaciously. "They say her husband is in prison for some crime." He took this sentence, and looked at it by every light that Mrs. Temple's bearing, expression, or surroundings threw upon it, and he finally decided that it was utterly false. But his reflections revealed to him what a burning agony it would be to know that she had a living husband. In vain he strove to banish the idea with half-

uttered exclamations that it was nothing to him, that he was unhinged by illness, or he would not give the subject a second
thought; it would return with threatening distinctness.

"This folly grows serious," thought Galbraith; "I must
shake it off; but I have been warned off the premises, so I will
go—positively next week—next Saturday; twenty-four hours in
London will no doubt effect a radical cure."

But he was desperately restless all day, and walked and drove
as if urged to and fro by an evil spirit. He was haunted by the
suppressed, amused, arch smile that flickered round the young
widow's lips at Lady Styles's general invitation to the housekeeper's room. It was the natural expression of one too much
above the proposition to be offended.

Finally, after walking up and down his room till he heard the
church clock strike seven, he seized his hat, put the last *Quarterly* under his arm, and stalked downstairs as if to go out, but
he did not. He knocked at the shop parlor door, and, in reply
to Fanny's "Come in," passed the magic portal with an apology,
and so gave himself up to one more enchanted evening. Fanny
was in great spirits, and chaffed her friend merrily on being invited to the housekeeper's room. Mrs. Temple was rather
silent, bestowing much attention on her work. But Hugh Galbraith was content. Nevertheless, when he rose to depart, he
observed, "As it is not the Sabbath, Mrs. Temple, I suppose I
may give legal warning that I intend quitting my pleasant quarters on Saturday."   •

"Very well," said Mrs. Temple, with unmistakable and mor-
tifying alacrity. "I accept it, and will be so far indulgent that I
shall not insist on your vacating your apartments before twelve,
which is, I believe, the strict law."

"If it is any accommodation to you," returned Galbraith,
stiffly, "I can turn out on Friday."

"No, no!" she exclaimed, with a smile so frank and sweet
that Galbraith could have kissed her for it on the spot; "I do
not wish to hurry you in any way; you have been an excellent
tenant, but I must not be too selfish, so I am glad you are well
enough to leave."

This was said in a tone of the most conventional politeness—
a tone that could not be complained of, and yet that robbed the
kind words of half their kindness.

"Thank you; good-night," replied Galbraith, shortly, and departed, without taking any notice of Fanny.

"Well!" cried that young lady, looking up from a book in
which she was writing out a wonderful receipt for a crotchet
border that had been lent to her, "you do your best to retard
that unfortunate man's recovery! You play upon him fright-

fully, though he is not a very harmonious instrument. Pray, have you the face now to say he is not in love with you ? "

"You know how much I dislike such idle talk, Fanny. I do not think Sir Hugh Galbraith knows what love means. A cold, stiff, stern man like him fall in love ! Pooh ! He is a little piqued, and puzzled, and interested in me—I mean *us*—but a day or two of his old occupations—a race, a pigeon match, would put his nearly six weeks sojourn here out of his head. Besides, it would be unpardonable presumption in a man like him to associate me with such ideas," concluded Kate, raising her head haughtily.

"I know it's a weakness," said Fanny, reflectively; "but I cannot help it. Sir Hugh has, I can see, a great contempt for me. Yet I like him, though I try not. There is a sort of lazy lordliness about him—a carelessness of small things ! I know he behaved very badly to you—abominably !" in reply to Kate's surprised look; "of course I hate him for that; but I can tell you I know a great deal more of love than you do."

"You might, easily !" murmured Kate to herself.

"What do you say ?" continued Fanny. "Oh, you think nobody ever looked at me but Tom ! Well, you are mistaken ! There was a man in Yorkshire (that dreadful place you rescued me from, you dear !), and I am quite sure he was in love with me !"—a little triumphant nod—" though you may not believe it."

"Yes I do, Fan ! Go on ; tell me all about it."

"He was ever so much older than I am ; a great, tall, gaunt-looking man, not at all unlike poor Sir Hugh—the same sort of sunken, melancholy eyes, but fierce sometimes. I was rather afraid of him. To be sure he did not speak like Sir Hugh ; he had the dreadful Yorkshire accent. I was always inclined to laugh when he spoke. He was the uncle of my pupils."

"What made you think he was in love with you ? "

"I can hardly tell. He was always coming into the school-room, and I am sure it was too miserable a place to come to unless you wanted something very much. Then he was horribly cross and savage to me ; but he was down on any one else that was rude. I think he was ashamed of himself for caring about me ; and I rembember once when he found me crying--"

'Well, do go on ! " cried her attentive listener.

"Oh, nothing, only he was rather foolish."

"Did he propose for you ? "

"Not he ! " said Fanny, laughing ; "he was far too prudent , he might, though, had I remained."

"And should you have accepted him ? "

"To be sure I should," returned Fanny.

Her friend was rather scandalized. "What," she exclaimed, "this man whom you feared and laughed at ! "

" If he had got over things enough to make me his wife, I should have known I needn't fear a man who was so fond of me, and I should have thought him too good a fellow to laugh at. Oh! Kate, you don't know how wretched I was!"

"Did you feel inclined to love him at all?" asked Mrs. Temple, her thoughts reverting to the absent lover.

"Not a bit," said Fanny, cheerfully. "Thank goodness, he did not make up his mind in time, or I should have missed Tom, and Tom is a thousand, million times nicer and better! I wonder why Tom took such fancy to a stupid thing like me? What luck I have had! But I shan't tell him that. He requires a good deal of keeping down," and Fanny shook her head wisely.

Mrs. Temple did not reply; she was thinking of the wonderful difference between her friend's nature and her own. She knew she had more courage, and firmness, and reason, than Fanny, yet she should never dream of "keeping down" a man she loved, if she ever did love. If she ever gave her heart, it would be to some one she could look up to so entirely that all her care would be to deserve his esteem, not to rise above him, or keep him down—an intellectual ideal very unlikely to be realized, and exceedingly unpleasant if it was. Yet Fanny believed Tom the first man of the day, and infinitely her superior even when talking and thinking thus. "She will, probably, always have more influence than I," thought Kate. "Why is this?"

But Fanny was talking again. "Now, Sir Hugh always reminds me of poor Mr. West. He is growing fond of you and hates you at the same time, and despises himself all the while for caring about you."

"Despises himself," repeated her listener, with scornful, curling lips.

"Oh! if you would hang down your head, and sigh, and seem mysteriously broken-hearted, I daresay it would be all over with him; but to see you face him like the rock that wouldn't fly (what is it in that poem?), and look right into his eyes with those big, earnest ones of yours, makes him feel that you are more than his match. Why, even _I_ feel half-afraid of them now!"

"Fanny," exclaimed Mrs. Temple, "how did you learn all this?"

"Learn it! I don't know, I am sure; it seems to come into my head of its own accord. But I am certain I am right!"

"You are wonderful; you astonish me!"

"Do I? Well, then, I am astonished myself! After all, I may turn out one of those swells who can 'Lay bare the workings of the Human Heart,' with capital H's. I shall write at once to Tom, and tell him what a wonderful discovery I have made."

" Do, dear ; but first give me your word never to talk in this strain of Sir Hugh Galbraith again ! It is unbecoming and absurd ! In a few days he will be gone, and we shall never see his face again, nor will he even hear of me—unless, as I trust in Heaven I shall—I come before him as the successful opponent of the will which robbed me to enrich him."

" We never know what is before us," said Fanny, sagely. "But there, dear ! I will never say anything to vex you, if I can help it."

For the two succeeding days the friends saw nothing of Galbraith, who was suffering from a severe fit of the sulks, and was constantly out of doors, although the weather was showery and rough.

˛ He certainly intended to leave, for elaborate preparations were made for a move ; and his servant informed Mrs. Mills that if his master did want to stay at Pierstoffe for a day or two longer, he would go to the hotel—a proposition which excited Mills's wrath as a flagrant act of ingratitude, after "her slaving and waiting on him hand and foot ; but it was all of a piece ! "— meaning his conduct.

Fanny collected some magazines and reviews he had lent. carefully made out a copy of his bill, to have it in readiness, She made an excellent chancellor of the exchequer. Mrs. Temple attended assiduously to her shop. She was really glad the enemy was going to retreat, for she was half afraid something unpleasant might occur, since Fanny had opened her stores of wisdom.

Lady Styles had made another incursion, with a carriage-load of ladies who purchased largely, while their conductress abused Sir Hugh Galbraith to her heart's content. "The most tiresome, conceited, ill-bred man she had ever met !—but the Galbraiths always were the most overbearing, ill-tempered people, my dear. The late Sir Frederick—this man's father—was the best of them, and bad was the best ! " Mrs. Temple smiled.

" My dear Mrs. Temple, who is it that you remind me of so very strongly, especially when you smile ? I seem to have known you all my life. Look here, Elizabeth ! " to a grand lady who was buying views of Pierstoffe. " Does Mrs. Temple remind you of any one ? " The lady appealed to squeezed up her eyes, and calmly perused Kate's features. " I am not sure, but I fancy she has a look of Lady William Courtenay ? "

" Yes, to be sure, that is it !—a niece of mine. How stupid of me not to see it before ! Pray what was your name before your marriage ? "

"Smith," returned Mrs. Temple, shortly; "but, excuse me, I cannot see that my appearance or name has anything to do with my business, which is to sell you fancy-work of all descriptions!"

"Very fair! quite right! I protest I beg your pardon!" cried her ladyship. "And so that disagreeable man is going on Saturday—positively, Slade tells me. I am sure I congratulate you! I imagine he is a good deal set up by getting his uncle's fortune so unexpectedly. The uncle married a doubtful sort of woman, and they feared he would leave her everything; but he changed his mind in time. Dear me, Elizabeth! Laura! There is Sir Hugh himself, just passing the window." A rather undignified scuffle to see the object of Lady Styles's remarks gave Mrs. Temple time to recover herself. She was astonished to find her story, at any rate partially, known in that remote locality.

She did not know the freemasonry of caste—the electric telegraphy that sends all reports and tattle touching themselves flashing through the ranks of those linked together by the common . possession of that mysterious attribute termed "blue blood."

CHAPTER XXV.

THE morning before Galbraith's departure the postman had only two letters for the Berlin Bazaar; one directed to "Sir Hugh Galbraith, Bart.;" the other to Miss Lee, in Tom Reed's well-known writing. It was not a lengthy epistle, nevertheless it evidently gave both pleasure and amusement, for Fanny's face was dimpled with smiles as she read. Mrs. Temple glanced at her kindly and sympathizingly, as she poured out the tea.

"I think, Fan, you have dropped something out of your letter," she said.

"Have I?" starting, and picking up a small note that had been enclosed in Tom's missive. "To be sure! He says it is for you."

Mrs. Temple took and opened it. It ran thus: "The day of miracles is not quite over yet! Trapes called here this morning, and absolutely repaid me a sovereign I had lent him last week, and which I had fondly hoped would have kept him at a distance for months. Though stunned, I remembered your desire for his address, and recovered sufficiently to procure it: 'J. Trapes, Esq., care of W. Bates, The Red Boar, King Street, Islington.' One word more: by no means communicate with this fellow except through myself or somebody equally devoted to your interest."

"This is very curious! It is a good omen," exclaimed Kate.

"What?" said Fanny.

10*

Kate gave a short explanation, the shorter because she saw
Fanny glanced from time to time at her letter, which she evidently wished to re-peruse.

When breakfast was over, Kate went to their best sitting-room
to lock away Mr. Trapes's address with her evidence book, and
a few other papers of importance; and after turning the key,
stood a moment in thought. She did not know why she permitted the idea of this man to associate itself in her mind with
Ford. She could not help believing that his tale of Ford's resemblance to some one who owed him money was a blind, and
that Ford himself was the object of his search. What Ford's
acquaintance with such a character had to do with her own history she could not tell. She fancied, if she could only see this
Trapes, she might get some clue. Now his unexpected restora-
tion of the sovereign looked like having extracted money from
Ford! She must think it all over coolly and clearly. " I must
not let imagination fool me ; yet imagination is the pioneer of
discovery." Here the sound of Galbraith's deep, harsh voice
caught her ear. He was down in the hall at that early hour,
speaking to Mills—asking for herself. " I am here," she said,
coming to the open door of the drawing-room.

" I beg pardon for intruding on you at such an hour, Mrs.
Temple," said Galbraith, turning to her ; " but I have had a letter
which I am very anxious to answer by to-night's post. May I
once more trouble you to act as secretary ? Your labors in that
line are nearly over ! Any hour before nine will do."

" I shall not be free before seven, and, as it seems a letter of
importance, I had better not attempt it till I am safe from interruptions."

" Thank you, thank you ! " returned Galbraith, earnestly. " I
shall expect you, then, at seven."   He paused a moment, as if
on the point of saying more ; then bowed, and retreated upstairs.

Mrs. Temple was struck by the animation of his look and
manner. " His letter is not a disagreeable one, I am quite sure,"
she thought. " It is quite as well he is going ; this secretaryship
would not raise me in the estimation of my fellow-townspeople,
if it were known ! What would not Lady Styles say ? Fortunately, poor Mills is deaf and incorruptible ; and Sarah leaves so
early, she sees nothing. I wonder, shall Hugh Galbraith and I
ever meet again ? That our courses will cross or clash I feel
quite sure ! "

So thinking, she went slowly into the shop and threw her attention into her business. Still, sudden, sharp conjectures respecting J. Trapes, Esq., would dart through her brain, and also
respecting Hugh Galbraith's letter. It came so naturally to her
to call him Hugh ! In the various conversations in which she

had urged his claims upon her husband, they had always spoken of him as "Hugh;" and now, had she not always been on guard when speaking to him, the name would certainly have escaped her. "I shall really be glad when he is gone, and the odd excitement of his presence removed;" so honestly thinking, she attended to the many demands of her customers, the day went quickly over, and seven o'clock came round.

For the first time Mrs. Temple had to pause and reason away a slight tinge of embarrassment before she presented herself for the performance of her task. "This is the fruit of Fanny's foolish talk," she thought, as she stood before her glass; "but I am no stupid school-girl, to be affected by it! Life has been too real for me not to have steadied my nerves beyond what the implied admiration of an accidental acquaintance could disturb," and with a faint increase of color, a shade more of hauteur in her bearing, Mrs. Temple followed Mills, whom she had sent to inquire if Sir Hugh was ready.

He was, quite. The curtains were drawn, and the lamp lit; for, though daylight had not quite faded, there would not have been enough to finish a letter by.

Galbraith had put his writing materials in readiness on the table, and was leaning against the chimneypiece, holding an open letter, and evidently in a state of expectation. "You are really very good," he said, earnestly, coming forward to meet her, and placing a chair at the table.

His manner put Mrs. Temple at her ease. His business, whatever it was, appeared to occupy him, to the exclusion of any other idea; and Mrs. Temple mentally accused herself of conceit and stupidity for listening to Fanny's suggestions. She accordingly took the offered seat, and dipping her pen in the ink, looked up to Galbraith for the words.

He dictated slowly and thoughtfully, often looking at the letter in his hand: "Dear Sir,—I have yours of the —th. I regret to find you are out of town, and that you have been unwell. The price asked for the property I wish to buy back is much beyond its worth, quite a third more than my father sold it for. I am aware that it is of more value to me than to any other purchaser, but I am not at all inclined to pay a fancy price, and I know that in its present condition much of the land is scarcely worth two pounds an acre. You are quite right in trying to keep me out of sight, though I fear you are too well known as my solicitor. Could you not find some respectable, local man who might act for you in ignorance of your client's name? If the upland called Langley Knolls, which is very good land, be included in the sale, or you can manage to get hold of it, I will go as far as ten thousand for the whole—as much under as you

like ; but I have this sum at hand, as you know, and I will not
go beyond it."

At this point Mrs. Temple stopped short, and placing her elbow on the table, instinctively shaded her face from Galbraith
by placing her hand over her eyes, for the words she had just
written stirred her deeply. That ten thousand pounds—she
knew exactly where it came from, how it was placed, and why
it was available. Little more than a year ago it was hers, and
she had her own plans respecting it ; now she was writing directions for its disposal in a way that, whatever happened, would
put a large portion of it out of her reach. And more, she felt a
strange sensation of shame at the sort of treachery she was involuntarily practicing; for if she succeeded in making good her
claim to the whole of Mr. Travers's property under the original
will, Galbraith would be placed in a position which, from all she
could observe of him, would be unspeakably degrading and distressing to his unyielding nature. So far her acquaintance with
him had softened her towards her enemy that she could wish to
spare him unnecessary humiliation, if she had ever, even in her
angriest mood, wished it ; and now, to let him run blindly into
the snare—was it honorable or right ? " What can I do ? " she
thought.

But Galbraith had gone on dictating, and stopping to let her
pen overtake his words, observed, with a little surprise, that she
was not writing. His pause recalled her.

" Excuse me," she said, in a low voice, not venturing to look
up ; " but are you wise to allow an utter stranger to know so
much of your affairs ? If you leave us to-morrow, shall you not
soon see your solicitor, and talk over your business? How do
you know that I am not a friend of whoever wants an exorbitant
price for this land, and will let him know who the purchaser
really is ? If there are any more very personal topics to come,
had we not better stop here ? "

Galbraith looked at her in great surprise. " Do you know the
man who wants to sell ? " he asked, sharply.

" No, I do not ; but—"

" You are not the material traitors are made of," said he, after
an instant's pause and a searching gaze at the downcast face before him. " I have no secrets. I must write to Layton, for he is
away at Scarborough. He has been ill, and has gone for change
to his native place. You may write on with a safe conscience ;
I want to end it, for I am giving you a great deal of trouble."

Mrs. Temple was at the end of her resources, and silently,
nervously resumed her pen as Galbraith continued to dictate.

" I am very glad you have found some traces of poor Travers's
widow, and beg you will lose no time in following them up. I

feel infinitely annoyed to think she is wandering about unprovided for—perhaps subsisting by doubtful means!"

"Have you that down?" asked Galbraith, who began to think Mrs. Temple was not quite up to her mark this evening.

She bent her head, and, with a cheek that first glowed and then turned very pale, wrote on with a beating heart. Traces of herself! What traces? She could make him talk, and so find out.

"Just add," continued Galbraith, "that I beg his attention to this. I should write to the partner about it, only I wish to keep the inquiry as quiet as possible."

Mrs. Temple wrote on in silence, trying, and successfully, to recover her composure and presence of mind. In a few moments she handed him the letter to read, which he did carefully, and then managed to scrawl his signature with his left hand. He returned it to her with an envelope, showed her the address on Mr. Payne's letter, and rang the bell. "Tell my man to post this at once, and that I want nothing more to-night," said he, when Mills appeared; and he proceeded to pace once or twice to and fro between Mrs. Temple and the door.

"Stay a little," he said, as she made a movement to rise : "so far from having secrets, I feel inclined to tell you something of my history, such as it is; but first tell me, why did this letter disturb you?—for you *were* disturbed."

"Well—you see ten thousand pounds is such a quantity of money," said Mrs. Temple, settling herself again and shading her face with her hand; "at least it is to me ; you are accustomed to large sums no doubt."

"By Jove, I am not! I have been a poor devil all my life till the other day."

"I should have thought you only knew one half of life, and that the half in which, as the children say, 'We go up, up, up,'" replied Mrs. Temple, looking at him with an encouraging smile.

"I have had considerable experience in being hard up," said Galbraith, who, in his desire to prolong this last interview, was ready to tell anything and everything that could detain his companion. "You must know that for years I considered myself heir to a rich cousin, who, when I was away in India, thought fit to marry a girl young enough to be his daughter, and low enough to be his housemaid! Not content with this piece of folly, he left her all his money—cutting me off without even the traditional shilling. I came back awfully disgusted. When, to my own and every one's surprise, another will turned up, making me the heir and cutting her off without the shilling. I suppose the old man had some reason that has never come out. Still, I do not think it was right to leave the woman who bore his name

unprovided for. I wanted to make up the deficiency, but, by
Jove ! she would not accept a sou, declares number two will is
a forgery, that she will have all or nothing, and has disappeared.
Now the information I wanted from Payne is about her. He
thinks he is on her track, somewhere in Germany, he says,"
looking at the letter, " that there is a girl's school lately started
at Wiesbaden by an English woman, a Mrs. Talboys—heard of it
quite accidentally—and that she seems to answer the description of Mrs. Travers."

" Your story interests me," said Mrs. Temple, as he paused.
She had quite recovered her self-possession and raised her eyes
fully and calmly to his as he stood opposite to her, holding the
back of a chair with his left hand. " And I hope all will come
right," she added, with a meaning smile, which, looking as he
was into her eyes, he did not heed.

" You see," he resumed, " one must always admire pluck in
prince or plebeian ; besides, she offered me a tolerable income
out of the estate—but that might have been to keep me quiet."

" Was she pretty ? " asked Kate, looking down again.

" That I cannot say ; I never saw her. I believe she has red
hair ; so Ford told me."

" Did Ford say that ? " exclaimed Mrs. Temple, with irrepressible indignation. Then checking herself, " I mean, it is surprising your cousin should have fancied so plain a person."

" And his landlady's daughter, by George ! " said Galbraith,
who had walked to the fire just to get his eyes away from the
fascination of his companion's, and now laid hold of the chair-
back again. " Now, poor Travers was rather a fastidious man,
but I suppose she was determined to have him. It was a great
catch for her, no doubt, still it is always revolting to see a girl
sacrifice herself to age."

" I suppose it is," said Mrs. Temple, pushing back her chestnut brown hair, which was often loosened by its own weight,
with a natural, unconscious action, and then clasping her hands
leant them before him on the table, while she yielded to the
temptation to plead her own cause to the enemy whose somewhat rugged, generous honesty appealed strongly to her sympa-
thies, her fair face and soft, earnest eyes uplifted to his with a sincere purpose that banished every shadow of embarrassment. " I
suppose it is ; but did it ever strike you what a terribly hard lot
it is for a woman to be poor and alone ? perhaps suddenly bereft
of those who surrounded her youth with tenderness, if not with
luxuries ? I do not think any man can quite realize *how* terrible
it is ; but, if you could, you would understand what a temptation
an honorable home and the protection of a kind, good, even
though elderly, man offers—an irresistible temptation ! And if

a woman's heart is quite, quite free, believe me, warm, hearty gratitude is no bad substitute for love." She stopped a moment, a little ashamed of the emotion with which she had spoken, and added, in an altered tone, "So I imagine it is in my world. I do not pretend to understand the shibboleth of yours."

Galbraith's words did not come very readily, so absorbed was he by her look, her voice. "I understand *you*," he said, at last ; "and if you will not consider my interest impertinence, I should say your description is drawn from experience—your own marriage was something of this ? "

"Something," she returned, looking down and arranging the paper and envelopes before her, a little nervously.

"Well," returned Galbraith, closing his large, lean, sinewy, sunburnt hand tightly on the chair-back, "an elderly husband might be satisfied with gratitude and all that sort of thing, but, by heaven, I should not ! I should want throb for throb as tender, if not as passionate, as the love I gave, or I would be inclined to cut my throat ! "

Surprised at his tone, Mrs. Temple looked up and met his eyes all aglow with such passionate adoration that she grew paler, and her heart beat with undefined fear at the fire with which she had been playing. Here was something more than she had bargained for, or had ever before met. Moreover, whatever Hugh Galbraith's intellectual powers might be he was evidently a man whose pertinacity and resolution were not to be trifled with. Had she created trouble for herself, and brought upon herself possibilities of insult far worse than anything she had yet sustained ? could she at that moment have borrowed a conjurer's wand she would have instantly transported Galbraith to a London hotel safe out of her way ; but, as she could not, her best plan was to rally her forces and retreat in good order.

"It is growing late," she said, coldly, "I must wish you goodnight."

"One moment," returned Galbraith, eagerly, his invention quickened by his ardent desire to keep her a little longer ; "it is my last chance of having so good a secretary ; may I ask you to write a few lines to Upton ? "

"They will scarce be in time for the post."

"No matter; they will go to-morrow."

Mrs. Temple replied by taking some note-paper, and dipping her pen in the ink. Galbraith dictated a few incoherent ungrammatical lines, telling his friend of Lady Styles's visit and invitation, and adding his London address, requesting Upton to join him there.

"Is that all ? " asked Mrs. Temple, writing on rapidly, anxious to end the interview.

" Yes."

Her pen ran on ; suddenly she half uttered a quickly suppressed "Oh ! "

" What is the matter ? " asked Galbraith, who was again pacing the room.

" Nothing, only I have stupidly made a blunder." She stopped.

" Let me, see," he said, snatching up the paper before she
could prevent him.

" You have signed your own name ! Kate ! I have always
wanted to know your name.   Kate ! it's the best name of all—
there is something sweet and frank about it.. Kate," with a
quick, eager glance at her face, he pressed his lips greedily on
the writing, and then, crushing the paper in his clenched hand,
dashed down his arm to its length as if furious with himself.

Mrs. Temple changed color, but to deeper paleness, and rising quietly—swiftly, though without hurry—left the room.   Galbraith stood still for a minute or two, and then burst into half-
uttered curses on his own despicable want of self-control.   He
had betrayed himself, he had startled and offended the woman
he passionately admired, yet could not ask to be his wife.   He
had altogether behaved like a weak, purposeless blockhead.   He
was glad he was going away, yet he would not like to sneak off
like a poltroon without making things right.   What should he
do ?

The next morning before twelve the widow's tenant was ready
to decamp.

" He is just going, 'm," said Mills, putting her head into the
shop, " and he says he wants to speak to you."

" Go, Fanny," was Mrs. Temple's reply.

" Won't you ?   Well, I suppose I must."

The door of the dining-room was open, and as Fanny approached she could see Galbraith standing near the window.

" I wanted to shake hands with you before I left," said he, not
without a little embarrassment ; "you have all been very good
to me.   I was most fortunate in finding such care and help.   If
there is anything I can do for you at any time, Miss Lee, there's
my card—you will be sure to hear of me at my club, and—
where's Mrs. Temple, I want to bid her good-bye."

" She is busy ; but I will tell her," and Fanny left the room,
but soon returned, "She is very sorry, but she is particularly engaged ; she desires her best wishes."

Galbraith stood a moment gazing at Fanny in deep thought,
" I will not keep her an instant," he exclaimed ; "go and ask
her again.   Make her come, like a good girl."

Very much surprised by this appeal Fanny went, but on a
fruitless errand.

"She can't come, indeed."

" I am exceedingly sorry that I gave you such useless trouble," said Galbraith, sternly ; "Good-bye, Miss Lee ! Stay—I had almost forgotten," and he took up a small morocco case he had placed upon the table, " do me the favor to wear this sometimes in memory of your secretaryship. Good-bye," and he was gone.

" Well, I do declare, it is a bracelet—a beautiful, solid gold bracelet !" exclaimed Fanny, eagerly peeping into the case. "Now this was intended for Kate ; but she would not come. It's an ill wind that blows nobody good."

"Just see what you have lost !" she cried, running in to her friend, who had retreated to the parlor, leaving the shop to take care of itself for a few minutes, lest Galbraith, seeing her there, might persist in making his personal adieu. "Look, is n't that a lovely bracelet ? "

" Did Hugh Galbraith give it to you? " asked Mrs. Temple.

" Yes ! that is what he wanted to see you so much for ; he intended to give it to you."

" Impossible ! " she returned, coloring deeply. " I do not think he would have ventured to offer *me* a present. Let me look at it, Fanny." It was more massive than pretty, and had a raised ornament in the centre which opened for hair or a minia- ture, and holding it out to Fanny Mrs. Temple pointed to the in- itials " F. L." inside. "It was meant for you," she said, " I thought he felt *I* was not a person he could offer presents to."

" Well, I am," said Fanny, "so he showed his sense ! I tell you what, Kate, when you are really going in for your battle, we will sell this and pay some lawyer to plead against him ! That is what Tom would call poetical justice."

" You little traitor ; " cried Kate, " the rack would be too good for you."

CHAPTER XXVI.

IT was a few days before Easter, when Galbraith found him- self at L——s Hotel. The town was full and busy, yet he had never, even in the dreariest of outposts, felt so desolate as when he began "to take his walks abroad." Society he found, to a certain amount, at his club, but he was rather an uncom- municative man ; he had never given or received much sympa- thy until accident had placed him within the influence of the first woman who had ever made a real impression upon him. Now he missed the quiet, home-like comfort and care which had sur- rounded him for the last two months. His full strength had not

Of course, as soon as his return to the haunts of civilization became known, invitations poured in. His sisters were quite kind in their attentions, having found him much more endurable than he used to be.

"I really think Hugh has been more seriously injured than he believes," said Lady Lorrimer to her younger sister, as they sat together after a friendly little dinner of about a dozen dear friends, which Galbraith had been persuaded to join. "He is as silent and morose as if he had lost a fortune instead of coming into one. Now, he was not like that last summer, when he first came back. He was wonderfully bright, and amiable, for *him.* I really thought I had never seen any one so improved by good fortune before. Now he is worse than ever. He often does not seem to hear what you say."

"Deafness," said the Hon. Mrs. Harcourt, arranging the lace on her upper skirt, "often proceeds from concussion of the brain. Poor Hugh! some one really ought to induce him to make his will. The life of a hunting man is so precarious."

"Oh, he is exceedingly likely to follow us to the grave!" said Lady Lorrimer, sharply; "but I wish he would stand for Middleburgh. Lorrimer says there will be a vacancy before the session is over, and it will be well for him to represent what used to be a family borough. The more members of a family are in the House the better. In short, the tendencies of the present age are such, that, politically speaking, peers are nobodies."

"Of course he will stand!" cried Mrs. Harcourt, thinking of the possibilities of patronage and her own fledgelings. "Has Lorrimer spoken to him?"

"Yes, and can get no decided answer—in fact he thinks Hugh far from being himself. However, he has nearly arranged a rather extensive purchase of the property my father sold, and that is a step in the right direction."

Here a mutual dear friend, who thought a close confab between two sisters would not be the worse for an interruption, broke in with some queries touching their disposal of the Easter recess.

"We are going to Paris," returned Lady Lorrimer. "I rather wanted my brother to join us, but he is asked to join the Helmsford party, which is much better for him. Lady Elizabeth G——, and Miss Dashwood, and some very nice people will be there, and we are naturally anxious he should marry into a good set."

But Galbraith was not made of malleable materials, and quietly threw aside his sister's efforts to guide his career. She was by nature and adoption a manœuvrer—a politician, she would have called it. Having no children of her own, she bestowed her care and thoughts on her husband's party, and the unmarried members of her own family.

Lord Lorrimer was a Whig of the old school, and his wife, considerably his junior, and one of the most exclusive women in London, affected a more advanced Liberalism. She was always attempting to create a party, a *salon*, a *côterie*, and failed signally. It requires a woman of no ordinary calibre to construct such a fabric out of the unsuitable elements of English social life, and the tattle of his sister and her familiars, with their storms in tea-cups, and ministerial crises that never stirred the ministry, excited Galbraith's profoundest contempt. However, he was not deaf to the voice of the charmer, when the charm whispered of political position, and to the suggestions of Lord Lorrimer he did seriously incline.

It was the only line of thought in which he found relief from a constant gnawing sense of loss and disappointment of something gone out of his life, that he was perpetually feeling after and longing for. It was all the more idiotic on his part, he told himself, to allow such weakness to master him, as it was evident that Mrs. Temple, if she had any feeling towards him beyond profound indifference, had an unaccountable aversion. Why, he could not divine. Galbraith was by no means inclined to overrate his own attractions; he was too strong a man to be conceited, and honestly believed he was not the sort of fellow women cared about—a conviction which did not in the least disturb him. But he perhaps exaggerated to himself the advantages which fortune had tardily bestowed upon him, and was quite ready to think himself acceptable to most undowered women on the score of position. Not that he resented this; it was the ordinary course of things, and Hugh Galbraith was not the sort of man to set up an ideal standard, and fret himself because society fell below it. But in Mrs. Temple he had met something different from all his previous experience. She was so frank and firm, so well bred in her bold opposition or ready agreement; her very reserve was natural, unstudied, and flecked with gleams of feeling and tenderness, suggesting possibilities that made Galbraith's rather inexperienced heart beat fast. Then, in his eyes, she was the most beautiful woman he had ever met—beautiful, with a rich, queen-like beauty, that touched the senses as well as the intellect—and as he recalled every look and gesture of hers in their last conversation, every varying modulation of her low, clear voice, he understood how men—aye, even men of his mature age—have lost or renounced everything for some fair-faced bit of humanity. But he, Hugh Galbraith, would not make a fool of himself about a woman of whose antecedents he knew nothing, and had no right to inquire, unless, indeed, he committed himself beyond retraction ; and she was not a woman to be mocked by shows, without the reality of devotion ; besides —and in this probably lay the secret of his prudence—she did not care a rap about him : perhaps she was attached to some other fellow ! He could never forget the air of cold, self-possessed disapprobation with which she rose up and left the room when he kissed her name, showing none of the fluttered feeling, half fear, half pleasure with which the first approach of a lover is regarded. He had kept that note, with " Kate " hurriedly • written at the foot of the page. He had taken it out of his desk several times with the intention of destroying it, but invariably restored it to its hiding-place, not always without committing the boyish folly of bestowing kisses upon the name, which he would fain have pressed upon the lips of the writer !

However, Galbraith fought gallantly against the terrible madness which had seized him. He rushed to and fro to his solicitor, to his club, to dinners and receptions—he tried hard to find some suitable woman to drive the unsuitable one out of his head. But the plan would not succeed.

Lady Elizabeth G——, whom he had found very nice, quite the correct article, in short, last season, now appeared an inane doll. The animation of some women, the quiet of others, all seemed alike unreal, forced, distasteful. Politics, and the pre- liminaries of his purchase, alone brought him relief and distraction.

" Mr. Ford was here yesterday," said Mr. Payne to him one morning he was calling at the office when he had been about three weeks in town. " He wished to ascertain if you had any tidings of Mr. Travers's widow. I simply said you had not. If I remember right, we had a suspicion at the time the matter was fresh (suggested by the omission of Ford's name from Mr. Travers's last will, coupled with disinheriting his wife), that he might possibly have imagined there was some tie between his wife and his clerk which he did not approve. And though Ford tried to be very cool and business-like, I could see he was deeply interested in finding her whereabouts."

" Does he not know ? " said Galbraith, carelessly.

" No, I do not think he does."

" Well, I scarcely believe that. You are a shrewder man than I am, Mr. Payne, but I fancy I could make out if he was shamming. I should like to see this Ford. Have you his address ? "

" I have."

" Give it to me, then. I want to talk to him. I always fancied he was in communication with the widow. What is he doing ? "

" I think he has started a stockbroker."

" I never could understand why he declined to remain as manager with me. I think I should have kept up the house if he had."

" He acted unwisely, in my opinion. He is too quiet, too respectable a man for his present occupation. It requires a bolder, rougher, readier man. I do not mean to say there are no respectable men on the Stock Exchange, but they are not of Ford's type." The lawyer wrote down the address as he spoke, and handed it to Sir Hugh.

" Thank you. By the way, you have not heard anything more of the widow ? "

" Nothing."

" I do not quite believe that report about the school. How did it originate ? She can't be fit for such an undertaking."

" I beg your pardon ; I believe she is a well-educated woman. The report originated thus : a nephew of mine, who is articled to me, was over in Germany a week or two ago, to bring home a sister of his who was at school at Wiesbaden, and he says the lady with whom his sister was at school, complained to him of the competition which was increasing yearly ; that only last autumn a young English widow had opened a new school, and succeeded in drawing away two pupils who ought to have come to her. My nephew, a shrewd young fellow, pricked up his ears at this, and made some inquiries, which informed him that the widow's name was Talboys, that she was tall, with reddish hair, and generally answered the description of Mrs. Travers."

" But why is she Mrs. Talboys—married again ? "

" Possibly," returned the lawyer ; " but more likely changed her name, if she wished to cut off all connection with her past life, and she would, for obvious reasons, choose a name that would not change initials."

" I don't see her object in changing her name. Why should she evade me ? Concealment almost always means wrong-doing."

" Perhaps so. I do not like her vanishing in that way—looks like working a masked mine. But then she can do you no serious harm ; that will cannot be contested, and if she has married privately, why, then, it will be evident that Mr. Travers had some reasons, of which we know nothing, for disposing of his property as he did."

" Did your nephew see this woman ? "

" No ; and it would have done no good if he had. He never saw Mrs. Travers."

" Are there no photographs of her anywhere ? "

" I think not. All such things—her clothes, books, jewels, personalities of all kinds—she was entitled to remove, and did. It was from Mr. Wall (Mr. Travers's solicitor) that I first heard of her disappearance. He says she told him it was her intention to open a school in Germany, and I think he is rather offended by her concealing herself from him, for he seemed very friendly towards her. In fact, he resents your employing any firm but his own, having known you so long."

"That is absurd!" exclaimed Galbraith. "How could I put my affairs into the hands of my enemy's solicitor?"

"True, quite true; and a somewhat bitter enemy, from what I hear."

"Then Wall knows nothing of Mrs. Travers?"

"Nothing."

"Who does?"

"Oh, a young fellow connected with the press (I believe he writes for some wretched Radical twopenny paper), called Reed. Ford knows his whereabouts."

Galbraith twisted his moustaches in deep, silent thought.

"By the way, Sir Hugh, I think we have found a tenant for your house in Hereford Square, if you are still determined to let it. But you may want it yourself; a wife and proper establishment is almost a necessity for a man of your fortune and position!"

A fixed, haughty stare, a sternly spoken "I wish it to be let," was the only reply Galbraith vouchsafed to this piece of presumption.

"Very well, Sir Hugh," returned Mr. Payne, blandly, while he inwardly chafed at being put down in that way by the insolent soldier, whom twelve months ago he would not have trusted with a hundred pounds! After a little more talk, and a promise that the deed of sale should be ready, and the purchase completed by the following week, Sir Hugh Galbraith rose, wished his solicitor "good morning," and descended the stair. He paused on the door-step, and drawing forth the slip of paper on which Mr. Payne had written Ford's address, read it over, thought for an instant, and hailed a hansom. "To Size Lane," he exclaimed as he sprang in, and cabby, turning sharp round, directed his horse Citywards. Since Galbraith's return to England, and obtaining possession of the fortune he had so nearly lost, his feelings towards his cousin's objectionable wife had been considerably mollified, and Mrs. Temple's words had sunk deep into his heart. His original idea of a tawdry, handsome, pushing, unscrupulous, vulgar adventuress had, he knew not how, dissolved into the portrait of a quiet, simple, though not well-bred woman, only anxious to exist comfortably, but liable, from credulity or ignorance, to be the tool of some designing man. He regretted that he had been harsh. He suspected she had had hard times with old Travers, and if she had a weakness for some fellow of her own station, could he, Hugh, blame her? Not when he knew how hard a battle he had to fight with himself, though he had a force of all arms, in the shape of self-respect, reason, and resolution, which a poor half-educated timid woman could not be supposed to possess. "I wish I could find her, and know what she is doing. If she has fallen into the hands of a blackguard, it would never do to give him money through her."

"Here you are, sir, Size Lane," cried the cabby, peering down through the square hole at top. "What number, sir?"

"No matter! I will get down here."

Mr. Ford's office was small, but smart and bright with highly polished mahogany, brass, and plate glass. The smell of fresh varnish had not quite vanished. Sir Hugh was asked to sit down while a clerk took in his card to the private room.

Presently a busy-looking man, with a parcel of papers, came out quickly, and Sir Hugh was asked to walk in. Tall, gaunt, erect, with his ordinary cold, stern expression, Galbraith entered, and found himself face to face with Ford, whom, if he had ever noticed in those distant days, when he used occasionally to visit his cousin's place of business, he was inclined to dislike as a feline kind of man.

Ford was well and accurately dressed, and his room was duly furnished with all the appliances right and proper for the private room of a high-class business man, but he looked very pale, perhaps yellow would be more accurate, very dark and wrinkly about the eyes, while the eyes themselves were painfully glittering and restless.

"Good morning, Mr. Ford."

"Pray be seated, Sir Hugh," he returned, placing himself opposite, and arranging the blotting pad and paper before him with a nervous hurried movement.

"I have called upon you," said Galbraith, dashing into his subject unhesitatingly, "to ask if you can assist me in tracing Mrs. Travers? I understand you knew her and her family previous to her marriage, and were on terms of some intimacy even after she became your employer's wife."

Ford's pale cheek colored faintly, and he passed his hand over his mouth to hide the expression he felt come to it at this abrupt speech.

"It is probable," continued Galbraith, "that although you may not know where she is, you may be able to suggest a clue, from your knowledge of her character and habits."

Ford cleared his throat, and thought how he should answer. He was in a mood of bitterest resentment, a resentment half love, half hate, against the object of his devotion. Yet he

scarcely liked to lose his last chance with her, by aiding her
enemy in his search.. "Before I make any reply," said he, "allow me to ask your object in seeking her? Having been honored with her friendship and confidence for some years, I should
be extremely sorry to be the means of bringing any trouble or
annoyance upon her."

"You do not suppose that I have such intentions towards the
widow of my benefactor?" returned Galbraith. "My object is
to find out her present position, and furnish her with the means
of existing comfortably according to her original station. But I
must see the woman before I make up my mind what to offer."

"I cannot help you, Sir Hugh! For some reason she has
chosen to conceal her movement even from me."

"Who knows anything about her?"

"Mr. Reed, a rather self-sufficient young man, connected with
'The Morning Thresher.'"

"Have you any reason to think that she is married again?"

"No, certainly not," with a start that overturned a ruler, and
gave him occupation in picking it up.

"Do you believe she has gone abroad?"

"I do; I am sure of it."

"Why?"

"Because one of our—I mean your—clerks saw her in a cab
with luggage, going towards London Bridge, about a year ago,
with this very Reed, just at the time you were put in formal possession; and I have never seen anything of her since."

"Who is the clerk?"

"Poole."

"Poole! Why he was one of the witnesses to the will?"
Ford bowed.

"And you have heard nothing of her since?"

"I will not say that," returned Ford, beginning to think he
would like to get the management of this search into his own
hands. "I sent a letter of friendly inquiry to her more than a
month ago, through Mr. Reed, and not hearing in reply as soon
as I expected, I called to ask if it had been sent. Reed assured
me it had, and added that he felt certain Mrs. Travers would
reply, but that she was much occupied, and would not have
leisure just yet; finally she did write, during the Easter recess,
which confirms the idea of a school at Wiesbaden."

"It does," said Galbraith, thoughtfully. "Did she write fully?
What did she say?"

"Not much, but she did mention that the undertaking in
which she had embarked was so far prospering. Now, the only
undertaking she ever mentioned to me was a school."

"Then I am sure Payne's information is correct," exclaimed

Galbraith, and forthwith repeated that gentleman's communication. Ford's eyes sparkled.

"There seems a strong probability here," he said. "Were I still in the employment of Travers & Co., I should volunteer to run over to Wiesbaden, and put the matter beyond dispute. As it is—"

"I could scarcely expect you to leave your business for mine," put in Sir Hugh. "But, Mr. Ford, I shall endeavor to communicate with Mrs. Travers through this Reed, and should I be unsuccessful, could I not send Poole to ascertain if Mrs. Talboys and Mrs. Travers were identical?"

"As you please, Sir Hugh," returned Ford, stiffly, "but I need scarcely point out that Poole would be rather a rough ambassador for so delicate and difficult an errand."

"I do not see much difficulty or delicacy about it!" said Galbraith, bluntly. "But I will see Reed if possible. Where is he to be found?"

"'The Morning Thresher' office, Wellington Street."

"Thank you," returned Galbraith, rising. "I shall call on my way back. Good morning;" and with a haughty bow he took his departure.

"The Morning Thresher" office was, as he remarked, in his westward route, and there he accordingly called, entering for the first time in his life one of the smaller thunder factories, whence issue the electric currents that link city to city, and unite men in the great commonwealth of thought.

A dingier, dirtier place Galbraith had seldom entered; there was a long deal counter, where grubby boys in shirt sleeves were slapping up piles of papers together, and shoving them across to other grubby boys in jacket-sleeves. There was a generally ink-splashed aspect about every one and everything, and when Galbraith asked for Mr. Reed, every one asked every one else if Mr. Reed was in, and finally a thin, pale, seedy young man, with inky fingers, opened a narrow door, much rubbed and marked by hands and shoulders, and ran up a crooked dim ladder-like stair. Coming quickly, clatteringly back, full tilt against the counter, he uttered the single word "Out," adding, with a sharp glance, "any message?" "My card," said Hugh Galbraith, writing in pencil after his name; "wishes particularly to see Mr. Reed, if he will make an appointment."

The young man took the card, read it, nodded, and darted up stairs again.

Sir Hugh Galbraith, with a deeper feeling of disgust than ever against the offenders of the press, left the office, re-entered his cab, and drove away to the club.

It was now three o'clock, and the butterflies were beginning

11

to come out ; carriages were beginning to gather at the doors of Waterloo House, and Howell and James's. The steps of the National Gallery were sprinkled with gaily-attired visitors ascending and descending, for the R. A. Exhibition was open, and as Galbraith drove past, he saw a well-dressed, good-looking young man, with a bouquet in his button-hole, and a gray kid-gloved hand, resting on the door handle of an admirably appointed brougham, while he laughed and talked with evident familiarity to a handsome woman, who sat arrayed in all her glory within.

Sir Hugh leaned forward and gazed eagerly at him, then, throwing himself back with a sort of indignant astonishment, he exclaimed, aloud :

"By Jove ! it's Tom."

CHAPTER XXVII.

THE first two or three weeks succeeding Hugh Galbraith's departure were very dull and uninteresting, as Fanny openly declared ; but all her dexterity failed to draw any expression from her friend and partner, beyond an exclamation that she was very glad he was gone. Business was rather quiet too, and, in short, the friends had to pass through one of those dull periods—which will come now and then—when the wheels of life have slackened speed, or come to a standstill, till some unforeseen circumstance happens to screw them up to full working condition again.

Nevertheless, Kate Travers was conscious that she missed the exciting antagonism of Galbraith's presence, although sincerely thankful that he had departed without any attempt to express the admiration which he had been betrayed into displaying. In truth, she was vexed with herself for the part she had played, or rather into which she had drifted, with no specially defined purpose.

When first she found her enemy within her gates, the temptation to revenge herself for his expressions of contempt towards her by proving her attractions were not to be despised, was irresistible ; but she never contemplated anything serious arising out of her little game. To charm her guest, while holding him in check by her own well-bred indifference and self-possession, was the utmost she aimed at ; to make her mark, in short, so that, when the *dénouement* came, her husband's insolent kinsman should acknowledge that he had in every way met his match. She did not, however, calculate on the material with which she had to deal being different from what she expected.

There was an odd sort of power in the very simplicity of Galbraith's character. His wants were few, but he knew what he wanted. He was by no means intellectual, according to Kate's standard, but then his decisions were never swayed and unsteadied by seeing two or three sides to a question. He was evidently a soldier by nature—prompt to deal with what he could see and grasp, and utterly intolerant of all opposition that might weaken or retard his plan of life's campaign, which, to do him justice, was never conceived without a certain regard to the rights of others as *he* saw them. He was an aristocrat without being a fine gentleman, and the full recognition of herself as a gentlewoman, which every word, and look, and tone of his accorded, was very conciliating. There was something, too, that appealed to the chivalry of her nature in the boyish transparency of his admiration, mute though it was. She would have blushed to have hurried him, by word or glance, into any avowal he would have regretted ; but she was too thoughtful an observer not to see that he was strong enough to be master of himself; and that if he could not quite conceal the feelings she inspired, neither would he be betrayed into expressing them when they could not be addressed to her as to a woman he would seek to wed. She felt certain of his respect, but she had been greatly startled by his momentary loss of self-control. The passion betrayed by his eyes—by his gesture—was a revelation of something that might be beyond her management— something that might give him more pain than she would like to inflict, even on her enemy, especially as it was her mission to rob him of his newly-found fortune. Not altogether ! She would deal generously by Hugh Galbraith, and not let him know who dealt the blow till all was settled ! So strong was her anticipation of triumph that she almost shrunk from thinking of the bitter mortification she was destined to heap upon him. "How desperately he will hate me !" she thought. "That cannot be helped ; but I am very glad he is gone ! After all, I may have to pass my life selling wools and canvas, while he may soar away to political regions, and add one more timber to the heads that shore up the obstructions of Toryism. Hugh Galbraith would be a grand acquisition to a party. His sense of discipline would keep him steady to any chief who on the whole carried out his views. He would never split straws, and he would be as true as steel ! Won't he despise me, when he knows I have passed myself off to him under false colors ! Great, stupid, honest fellow ! What do I care—he will never cross me again ! "

From these vague reflections and dreams of possible triumph, Kate was rather unpleasantly roused by news from Tom.

" Gregory sails to-morrow," he wrote, " for the Cape and Natal. It is well we got his affidavit in time. It would have been better if we could have produced the man, should you ever be able to make out a case for counsel. I was rather startled by finding the enclosed card on my table a few days ago. I must not meet Galbraith ! for I have a strong suspicion he saw me when I was last at Pierstoffe, and of course he would immediately guess the identity of his fascinating landlady. I therefore wrote a polite note, stating that I was overwhelmed with work, but would be most happy to answer any written communication. High Presto ! I received a short, sharp, decisive array of questions : but I enclose you the production. My answer distinctly says, ' I am Mrs. Travers's trusted friend, and I will neither write or speak a syllable that can betray the incognito she chooses to preserve.' Ford called here since I wrote, but I did not see him. I feel greatly disgusted with everything to-day, especially myself. There is a report that Pennington is better, and may return to his duties here. Upon my soul I *cannot* rejoice, and yet he is such a good fellow ! "

There was also a long epistle to Fanny, over which she looked a little grave. At tea she confessed she had a bad headache, and thought she would put on her hat and take a stroll along the North Parade.

" Do," said Mrs. Temple ; " and as soon as I can leave I will come and join you."

It was Saturday evening, and it had been a busy day. Kate felt very tired, or rather weary ; she had worked without spirit, and was in that sort of mood when even so slight a check as the not unforeseen departure of an unimportant witness appeared a mountain of misfortune.

Kate felt unusually bitter and implacable towards Galbraith. She had seen a small paragraph in one of the London papers in which a report was noticed that Sir Hugh Galbraith of Kirby Grange would probably offer himself to the electors of Middle-burgh, in the neighborhood of which he had nearly completed the purchase of a large property formerly belonging to his family, etc., etc. So with her money he was building up a position of power and prominence, while she was spending her days in gathering up a bare means of existence from the obscure popu-lation of a little out of the way corner. Was it to be always like this ? Would the queen never have her own again ? Was it her fate to be walked over ? Where, where could she turn to find munitions of war, the evidence which she felt certain must exist, and which would furnish the basis of her operations ? Where could she turn ? Why was Tom so distrustful of that man Trapes ? Tom was lukewarm, because he was unbelieving.

She felt on fire with indignant impatience. Next week she would go up to town to make purchases for her shop, and then, Tom or no Tom, she would manage to see Trapes, and find out what connection existed between him and Ford.

But although she was feverish and depressed, Mrs. Temple's customers were not the worse or more impatiently served, and when at last she summoned the errand boy to put up the shutters, the fair widow had done a good day's business, and felt she had earned an evening stroll.

The soft summer darkness of a May evening was beginning to fold its wings over sea and sky as she sallied forth, and drank in with an unutterable feeling of relief and refreshment the delicious balmy, briny air. She paused upon the slip to enjoy it to the full, when to her surprise she saw Fanny hastening towards her.

" Returning already ? " exclaimed Mrs. Temple.

" I shall not, now you are here," said Fanny, who seemed ruffled ; " but it's too bad ; one cannot sit down in peace by the sad sea waves—"

" What has happened ? "

" Oh, that goose, Turner, junior, came and sat down by me and made a scene."

" A scene ? How ? "

" Oh, he said—great nonsense ; that I was the ocean to the river of his thoughts ; that I would yet regret my disregard of a blighted but devoted heart. That he knew he had rivals—a favored rival !—but that he would seek oblivion in the poisoned bowl of pleasure, and a lot more. He quite frightened me ; but I fancied I perceived an odor of brandy-and-water about him, so I plucked up courage to say I was very sorry to vex him, but that I couldn't help being engaged, and that I was quite sure he would meet somebody he would like much better by and by. Then he jumped up and desired me not to speak in that way unless I wished to see him a mangled corse at my feet. I just said I wished nothing of the kind, and ran right away. Did you ever know anything so stupid and provoking ? "

" It is, very," said Kate, sympathizingly. " But you know, Fanny, I always warned you not to trifle with that young man, and I think you have—a little."

" No, indeed, I have not. I never thought he was in earnest. I don't think he was now. I do not think he was sober. He will go away and forget all about it—only we will not tell Tom ! "

" Yes, you had better ; everything in the world comes out some time ; and let Tom hear the first of everything from yourself, I would advise you."

Fanny passed her arm through her friend's, and they strolled

on in silence. At last Fanny exclaimed, "I believe the world
would be happier and better without men; don't you think so,
Kate?"

"Certainly not, Fanny; and you would be the last to like
such a world. Imagine the world without Tom!"

"Oh, I should have excepted him; but see what mischief and
trouble Mr. Travers, and Sir Hugh Galbraith, and little Mr.
Turner make."

"True enough — and Captain Gregory. Tom says he is
obliged to go to sea again." Mrs. Temple recapitulated the
contents of Tom's letter, and the friends strolled to and fro discussing it, and the possibility of Tom encountering Galbraith.
"I trust they may not meet till the game is played out," said
Mrs. Temple, " but I confess, Fanny, I feel greatly cast down.
I do not catch a gleam of light on any side. Is it possible that
I must live on always under this cloud, and never be able to assert myself? I confess that to drag out all my life in social obscurity never entered into my plans. Fan, do you think you
could manage the shop for a week, if I find I want to stay so
long when I go up to town? for I am determined to utilize my
visit to London when I go."

"Of course I could manage it," cried Fanny, readily, "I am
not half such an ignoramus as I was; and I have got over my
dread of Lady Styles. Indeed, she does not bother me half so
much as she did at first. You may go, dear; and you shall see
what a heap of money I shall make in your absence. When
shall you go?"

"Oh, in about a fortnight; that will give me time to have everything arranged by the time the season here really sets in."

Their talk flowed on, sometimes broken by pauses of thought,
but always with a pleasant confidence and oneness of purpose.

"How beautiful the stars look," exclaimed Fanny, as they
turned at last to go in. "I wonder if they are really worlds,
and have people in them, and if they can look down and know
what the people here are doing? How they could astonish us
if they sent down electric information."

"I would ask what is the connection, if any, between Mr.
Ford and that man Trapes; and you would inquire about Tom,
I suppose?"

"No, I should not," cried Fanny, "it would be mean, and besides, I know he is all right. No; but I should like to know
what Sir Hugh is about; broiling at some grand dinner, I daresay, looking as cross as the cats, and as solemn as an owl.
Couldn't he look cross, Kate?"

"Stern and forbidding, not cross."

"I daresay he often wishes himself back at Pierstoffe, whatever he is doing."

Could Fanny's wish have been granted she would, no doubt, have been greatly surprised.

The purchase of the Galbraith property had been brought to a successful termination, and Sir Hugh determined to give himself a holiday from the crowd, the rush, the perpetual round of unimportant nothings which made up the sum of town life. He would away, and refresh himself by a breath of the free moorland breeze; a glimpse of the bold craggy cliffs with their border of ceaseless foam, and setting of wide, green-blue sea. So, desiring his servant to put up what was necessary for a few days, he started without beat of drum on this same Saturday for the Great Northern Station with the intention of catching a train that started about six, and got into Middleburgh—the nearest point to his destination he could reach by rail—about eleven.

On his arrival, however, he found the time-table had been altered, and the six o'clock train now started at 5.45. He was, therefore, just in time to be late.

"What a—blank, blank—nuisance! When is the next train?"

"Seven, sir."

"And I suppose that creeps along all night?"

"It's a fast train as far as Stoneborough, sir; after that it stops at a goodish few stations."

"It's fast to Stoneborough, is it?"

"Yes, sir."

Galbraith stood a moment in thought, and then began to walk up and down thinking, while the words " Fast to Stoneborough " seemed at once to embody all his wishes. It would be a far better, pleasanter place to spend Sunday in than London. There was a fine country round. He could get a trap and drive over to Weston and see Lady Styles. Pshaw! Why not to Pierstoffe and visit Mrs. Temple and pretty little Fanny? The idea presented itself with a flood of delight. To be once more in what had been the only homelike dwelling he had ever enjoyed! To hear Kate's low voice—to look into her eyes, and puzzle himself once more over the possible interpretation of their language, even though the solution was unflattering! To be near her once more; be the risk what it might, he would risk it. Besides, he had himself better in hand now; he would make it just a friendly visit, to show her he had not forgotten them—and— but could he trust his self-control? No matter whether he could or could not, *nothing* should keep him back from that hour of happiness, for which his soul thirsted!

If Mrs. Temple would only tell him her history, and that history contained no passage derogatory to character, nothing his wife would blush to own, why should he not marry her? Whatever her origin, she was a gentlewoman ; and so was Miss Lee. But this was absurd. He was only going to pay a friendly visit and get over Sunday.

With the help of a cigar, a glass of brandy and soda, and a good deal of walking up and down, Galbraith passed the time of waiting, and started for Stoneborough about an hour before Fanny Lee hazarded the conjectures respecting him recorded above.

Sunday was a calm, gray day, more like autumn than spring ; and after their early dinner Fanny undertook to give Mrs. Mills a nice long walk, for Mills's life was a little lonely. A walk with her mistress or "Miss Fanny" was one of her treats ; and the old lady was still strong and active. Mrs. Temple was glad to stay at home and alone. It was often a help to her to think things through—to reason herself out of her depressed moods —to seek counsel with her own heart ; and she was vexed with herself for the fretful unrest that had of late taken hold of her. Arming herself with a favorite volume of Carlyle's strange poetic weird eloquence, she sat down in a low chair by the open window and gazed out on the prettily-grouped flower-beds, sweet with mignonette and heliotrope and gay with verbenas. It was very still ; so still that the soft dash of the waves, hushed by distance, came sleepily to her ear, and made her thoughts dreamy instead of distinct and consecutive.

"What an eternal effort life is," she thought ; "a struggle for existence, and with existence ; with material circumstances outside, and rebellion and treachery within !"

> "All things have rest ; why should we toil alone,
> We only toil, who are the first of things,
> And make perpetual moan,
> Still from one sorrow to another thrown :
> Nor ever fold our wings,
> And cease from wanderings—"

The door opening suddenly startled her from her recollections of Tennyson. Sarah in a Sunday frock and smiling aspect appeared. "Here's the gentleman, ma'am," she said ; whereupon Galbraith, hat in hand, walked in.

"Hugh Galbraith !" exclaimed Mrs. Temple, thrown too much off her guard by extreme surprise even to notice her own speech, and holding out her hand before she had time to collect herself.

"Yes !" returned he, gathering it up into a tight, feverish grasp for an instant, and speaking quickly. "I am on my way to the north, stopping till to-morrow at Stoneborough ; so I just drove over to ask how you and Miss Lee are—and— How is Miss Lee?" Letting Mrs. Temple's hand go and taking a chair opposite to her, his usually sombre eyes all aglow, the lines of his somewhat harsh face softened and relaxed as he gazed once more upon the eyes, the lips, the brow, which he had never quite succeeded in banishing from his mental sight.

" She is quite well," said Mrs. Temple, smiling in spite of herself, though she was quite as much annoyed as she was amused by her enemy's unexpected reappearance.

" Is she at home?" asked Galbraith, who seemed deeply interested in Fanny's movements.

" No ; she has gone to walk with Mrs. Mills."

" Oh, indeed !" with a hearty inward thanksgiving, " And I hope Mills is all right ; she is a capital nurse !"

" Quite well, thank you." There was an awkward pause, which Mrs. Temple mercifully broke by asking politely :

" And yourself, Sir Hugh Galbraith, I hope you are now quite restored ? I see you have discarded your sling."

" Yes, thank you, I am quite recovered ; but I do not feel the same in London as here. It's such a rackety, unnatural sort of place. I don't seem able to breathe there ; so I am going down to Kirby Grange—an old place of mine, I think I mentioned to you. Haven't been there for years."

" I daresay the change will do you good," said Kate, blandly, but coldly. " I see there is some mention of your standing for Middleburgh."

" Yes, if I give up the army. I must do something; and—" Galbraith forgot what he was going to say, for Mrs. Temple had lifted up her eyes to his with an unusual amount of interest.

" And you will, of course, go into the House as an obstructive," said she with a smile, filling up his pause.

"Exactly," he returned. " I shall be very glad to act as a drag on the wheel, to keep the state machine from going too fast down hill."

" Or up hill," she added.

" I suppose Pierstoffe is going on just as usual?" resumed Galbraith, who found this effort to talk on indifferent topics desperately hard work.

" Just the same. We are anticipating a brilliant season, and Lady Styles informs me there is really a good set of people coming. Now a ' good set ' for me means people inclined to invest largely in Berlin wool and embroidery cotton, and I am afraid the possession of ready money somehow does not seem to exercise a refining influence."

Galbraith got up and walked to the window.

" How sweet and fresh your garden is. What a relief it is to

11*

be here again ! Do you know, I never felt so comfortable and at home as in your. house."

" I am pleased to hear it."

Another awkward pause, and he broke out with, " You remember that property you wrote about for me ? Well, I have bought it, and am now on my way to have a look at it." As he said this their eyes met, and at the same moment the recollection of the episode which concluded their last interview flashed upon them both ; the yearning passionate look came back to Galbraith's eyes, and in spite of her cool self-possession, Mrs. Temple's cheek grew crimson.

" I wanted to beg your pardon for that piece of presumption," exclaimed Galbraith, answering the blush, " and you would not see me ! I know it was wrong ; but I declare to Heaven, I could not help it ! "

" Pray say no more," said Mrs. Temple, in a low tone, and rising with a vague notion of making her escape. " It was a piece of folly better forgotten. I will not remember it—pray put it out of your head ! "

" I cannot ! " returned Galbraith, unconsciously placing himself between her and the door—" I cannot ! and your look of displeasure is always before me ! Of course you were angry ! but if you think I meant anything disrespectful, you are very much mistaken ; my feelings for you are more like worship than disrespect ! " and Galbraith pulled himself up with a short scornful laugh at his own imbecility in thus betraying himself to so indifferent a listener, and yet the surprise and embarrassment of the moment brought a varying color to Kate's cheek—a tremor to her voice—a something soft and deprecatory to her manner, that completed the spell. Galbraith did not exactly lose his head, but experienced the kind of intoxication which strong drink, rarely indulged in, exercises on a man of sound health and powerful frame, urging his brain to greater activity and his will to daring deeds, often resulting in success. such as he would never have attained in complete sobriety. He now stood still, his shoulder against the window-frame, all hesitation and reserve gone, his eyes fixed tenderly yet defiantly upon his companion.

" You astonish and distress me ! " said Mrs. Temple, hesitatingly. " I beg you will not talk in such a strain ! You must know "—gathering firmness as she proceeded—" you must know that such words from a man of your position to a woman in mine mean—well, certainly not respect ! I wish you would still let me think well of you, and go away ! "

" Why do you refuse to hear me ? What have I done to make you dislike me ? The first moment I ever saw you, you looked as if you could murder me! I wish to Heaven you would tell me your history! You might. I am certain there is nothing in it you need be ashamed of."

"This is, indeed, presuming too far! What right have you to ask such a question?" said Kate, turning very pale.

"The right that loving you as I never thought I could love, gives"—cried Galbraith, coming a step nearer—"give me the right! Will you be my wife, Mrs. Temple?"

This point-blank question seemed suddenly to restore Kate's self-command. "No, Sir Hugh Galbraith, I will not!" she replied, uncompromisingly, and there was a moment's silence, Galbraith looking fixedly at her.

"I suppose," he resumed, "I ought to be satisfied, and go away! I know I am not a lovable sort of fellow! I don't believe any one ever cared a straw for me; but I should like to know your special objections!"

"I have no special objections. You have always behaved well and kindly while in my house," returned Kate, a little touched by his unexpected humility; "but I am the last woman in the world you ought to think of! Believe me, this is a whim, for which, were I fool enough to accept you, you would soon think you had paid too high a price!"

"You are mistaken, Kate!"

"I am not, Sir Hugh! Your voice said as much just now, when you asked me what *might* have been a fatal question for you! Besides, we are unlike in habits, opinions, and antecedents. Let us forget all about this temporary insanity"—smiling pleasantly, and trying to give a lighter tone to the conversation—"do not fancy you are not lovable because I do not love you in the way you want. I hate having to speak so ungraciously," interrupting herself with a sweet frankness terribly trying to her hearer. "You will find plenty of women of your own grade who will love you—make you very happy, and let us forget all about this!"

"You said that hearty gratitude was no bad substitute for love," said Galbraith, gloomily, walking slowly towards the door and back again. "Not that you would have anything to be grateful to me for; but you once married for a home! Am I such a disagreeable fellow that a miserable shop is preferable to a comfortable home if I shared it?"

"And *you* said, if I remember right, that if your wife did not love you as warmly as you loved her, you would put an end to yourself!"

"Better half a loaf than no bread!" exclaimed Galbraith. "Give me your friendship—your confidence, to begin with, and let me try to win the rest!"

"Pray, pray say no more!" said Kate, greatly surprised and moved at his perseverance. "You grieve me beyond measure. It is quite impossible that you and I ever could be anything to each other, even friends! Do leave me. I am not ungrateful for the feelings you express. I am so sorry to cause you pain; but, indeed, it is utterly impossible for us to be even friends."

She held out her hand to him, and, to his decided gratification, he observed her eyes were full of tears. However, he drew himself up a little stiffly.

"Forgive me, Mrs. Temple. It would be unmanly to intrude any longer upon you; though we must not be friends, I trust we will never be enemies."

He took her hand as he spoke—at first gently, but with a tightening grasp, looking into her eyes, and then laying his other hand over the one he held.

"I hope not," she replied, flatteringly, "but what will be, will be."

"I shall never be *your* enemy, at all events," continued Galbraith, still holding her hand,—"so good bye, Kate! I will do my best to forget you. Though you are the only woman in the world to me *now*, I will not be such a poltroon as to let you spoil my life!"

"God forbid!" said she. "I trust there is plenty of work, and love, and happiness, before you! Life can give nothing better."

Galbraith made no reply. Pressing her hand hard, and releasing it so suddenly as to have almost the effect of throwing it from him, he turned and left the room. The next moment Kate heard the front door shut hastily.

The most extreme surprise—the most sincere regret—were Kate's only distinct sensations as she ran hastily to her own room to recover herself before Fanny's return.

She thought she could perceive that Galbraith had allowed himself to be hurried into one unguarded speech after another until he felt compelled to make all consistent by asking her to be his wife. She had certainly said or done nothing to lead him on, and he had seemed painfully in earnest. He would get over his fancy for her of course. Men are, fortunately for themselves, seldom constant; but there was a certain intensity about Galbraith's nature that was likely to render all struggles severe to him. And then the future—what mortification it would be her lot to heap upon this man, who, whatever he might be, had certainly offered himself and his whole life to her. She absolutely contemplated the idea of her own possible success with a shudder. She had wished that his life should have plenty of love and happiness. Where was it to come from if she was to re-

duce him to poverty and to debt? for how could he ever refund
the ten thousand pounds he had taken from her property.' She
was quite ready to deal generously by him; but how would he
like to be always in her debt? And yet she must go on; she
must disprove that will, be the consequence what it might.
"How I wish Hugh Galbraith had never come here. How I
wish he had been in England when I was married first. Had
he known me all through he would not have despised me so
much, and things might have come right;" but with this reflection came a sudden thought that made her heart beat for a moment—a consciousness that if she had known Hugh Galbraith
before her marriage, neither poverty or loneliness would have
driven her to be Mr. Travers's wife. Not, she thought, that she
felt any tendency to reciprocate his feelings, but the interview
she had just had seemed to have revealed what love was—what
it might be to herself—more than all the volumes of poetry and
romance she had ever read.

Well, that episode was over, and it was not likely that Hugh
Galbraith and herself should ever meet again. He would, no
doubt, keep out of her way. If so, then why need he ever
know that Kate Temple and Catharine Travers were identical?
Then he need never be mortified by knowing he was under obligations to the woman who had refused him. And she need
not be lowered in his estimation as having played the part of a
traitor, written his letters, and let him confide in her and love
her—she, his enemy.

"I dare say he will marry somebody soon, and then if it is
some commonplace fine lady, how will it be for Hugh when the
trouble comes? I really must ask Tom to give him some
notice that I don't intend to keep quiet always, just to rouse him
from his security— Alas! what chance have I really of the
success I dream about? According to Tom, none whatever.
It is all very puzzling!"

Fanny's wonder and exclamations and conjectures may be
imagined when she heard of Sir Hugh's visit. She bitterly regretted her own absence when she found that no satisfactory
information was to be extracted from Mrs. Temple. "Had I
been here I could have seen with half an eye what had brought
him back."

After this somewhat painful break in the routine of her life,
Mrs. Temple and Fanny settled once more into the ordinary
course of their existence, sold their goods, and balanced their
books, undisturbed even by Turner, junior, who disappeared at
intervals. Gossip said he had been seen at the Stansborough
races, and other scenes of wild dissipation. He was certainly

absent during the Derby week, and Mrs. Turner reported the "governor" as "that cross" there was no doing anything with him.

Miss Fanny, too, had her sip at the bowl of pleasure (poison omitted). Kate and Tom Reed had contrived three glorious days for her in London. A married sister of Tom's had come up from Devonshire with her husband to see the horse show, and she was very pleased to have their pretty little relative, who cost them nothing, for a guest. She only knew that she was employed in some capacity by a Mrs. Temple, and shrewdly suspected that she was to be Mrs. Tom Reed. But Tom, from having been the object of head-shakings and lugubrious prophecy, had progressed into "a fine young fellow that may be in Parliament one of these days," and with his choice no sister dared to interfere. So Fanny saw *the* play and the pictures, and had some charming *tête-à-tête* walks in the park, and so returned refreshed to her daily labor. Mrs. Temple had run up to town also, but only on business, and her visit was more wearisome than refreshing.

The Pierstoffe season had now set in, and the rooms erst occupied by Hugh Galbraith were tenanted by an elderly couple, recommended by Lady Styles, who were very fidgetty and exceedingly economical. Still Mrs. Temple preferred them to single gentlemen, whom from henceforth she renounced. And so a fine glowing July was drawing quickly—with the quickness of monotony—to its close, when one Wednesday evening, without notice of any kind, Tom Reed made his appearance.

His tidings shall be told in due order.

CHAPTER XXVIII.

ONE evening as Tom Reed was leaving the theatre, after escorting some country acquaintances to witness the performance, he was tapped on the shoulder. This operation had no terrors for Tom, so he turned calmly round and was greeted by a young man somewhat older than himself, attired in a sporting style, with his hat on one side and a red and yellow tie. The face was at once strange, yet familiar, and Tom had to think a moment before he exclaimed, " Poole ? "

" The same, sir."

" Well, Mr. Poole ? "

" Well, sir, I believe you are a lawyer, and I want a bit of advice. Might I be so bold as to call on you anywhere ? "

Tom felt inclined to d—n his impudence, but there was a

queer good-humored, good-natured expression about the man's face that attracted Tom's fancy—and then he was one of the witnesses to the will, and it would be as well to get hold of him.

"I am neither a solicitor nor a practicing barrister," said Reed, smiling; "still, if I can give you any help I will. Call at the *Morning Thresher* office, Wellington Street, any day between two and three, and I will try and see you, but I am a good deal engaged."

"Thank you! I will," returned the other; "and—I beg your pardon for keeping you, Mr. Reed—but I hope Mrs. Travers is well? She *was* a real lady!—always had a kind, civil word for a chap. She always brought me up to time, when I used to be in an awful funk going to old Travers. Lord, what a hard-mouthed old buffer he was!"

"Mrs. Travers was quite well when I last heard of her."

"I am told she is away on the Continent?"

"So I am told," returned Tom.

"Well, I'll look in the first day I can, Mr. Reed."

"All right."

They parted; and several days elapsed before Poole made his appearance. Tom had almost forgotten the interview, when one Saturday afternoon he had been detained longer than usual, and was on the point of leaving the office, when a crushed piece of paper with the words "William Poole" written in a fine clerkly hand upon it was brought to him.

"If you can give me a few minutes, Mr. Reed," began Poole, after they had exchanged greetings, "I'll be awfully obliged."

"I am at your service for the next half hour," said Tom Reed, with his usual cheerful good nature; "after that I have engagements."

"I intended calling here last week, but times are changed at Travers's. We used to be kept pretty well up to the collar in the old gentleman's day, but we are near driven to death since the new manager came."

"You have a new manager?"

"Yes; you know Ford would not stay on, though Sir Hugh Galbraith gave him the legacy that had been left him in the first will, after he had had the books and everything examined by a regular accountant. Ford was in high favor for a while, but I suppose he saw his way to a more independent position, for he gave up his situation, and I believe Sir Hugh took our present manager on his recommendation. I think he might have said a good word for me, but he didn't. He was always a conceited chap; didn't think small potatoes of himself, *I* can tell you. Lord! how he hated old Gregory; and the jealousy of him, if Mr. Travers spoke a civil word to any one— But I am taking up your time, Mr. Reed. Now what I wanted to ask you about was a man of the name of Trapes. He says he has known you for years; in short that you are an old pal of his."

"I certainly have known Mr. Trapes for a long time," returned Reed, "but I have seen very little of him since the first couple of years I was in London. He has gone to the bad terribly, poor fellow! I wouldn't have too much to say to him, if I were you."

"I have had quite enough, I can tell you!" said Poole, shaking his head. "Why, he owes me a pot of money! There is lots I will never get back; but I want you to tell me if this I. O. U.," dragging out a much-rubbed pocket-book, and extracting a piece of bluish paper from its depths, "is of any use? You see, it is nearly two years and a half after date."

"Why have you let it lie over so long?" said Reed, taking the paper. "Hum"—a quickly suppressed look of surprise and interest gleamed in his face as he perused it. Then, raising his eyebrows, he looked keenly and steadily at Poole. "I see it is dated the 15th of March, 18—? Under what circumstances did Trapes give this to you?"

"Well, we were together at the Reepham Steeplechase, and Trapes had won and lost a lot of money. I had been rather lucky; but when we came to start for town, he hadn't a rap, so he persuaded me to lend him five pound ten. He owed me six besides, so he said, in his dashing way, 'Come, I'll write you an I. O. for twelve, and that will pay a couple of weeks' interest.' But I have never seen any more of the money from that day to this."

"And where is Reepham?" asked Tom, still holding the paper.

"Oh, in S——shire, a couple of hours from town by rail, and another by 'bus."

"Did he give you this before you left?"

"He did. We were just having a 'go' of gin-and-water before starting, and the barmaid gave us pen, ink, and paper; he wrote it out, and I gave him the cash then and there. I was very green in those days."

"Then I suppose this is the date on which you lent the money?"

"Yes, of course."

"Why do you think of using it now?"

"Because that fellow Trapes seems quite flush of cash. You never saw such a swell as he is come out! but he is an impudent blackguard, and scarcely ever sober. He was d—d impertinent to my wife and me, Mr. Reed (I was married last autumn), at the London Bridge Railway Station, when we were going to

Greenwich last Saturday. You would think he was a lord. So I will have my money if it is possible. You see, Mr. Reed, now I have responsibilities I must turn over a new leaf, so I thought I would ask your advice, because you knew this man ; and besides, if I went to a stranger on a matter of business one would have to pay through the nose for advice," added Poole, candidly.

"And how did you manage to get away from the office for a whole day ?" asked Tom, who had been thinking deeply, and scarcely seemed to have heard Poole speak.

"Well, it was not an easy matter ; but you see, I was taken with a bad headache and faintness the day before," returned Poole, with a wink. "As Ford was away—gone to bury his father, or his mother, or both of 'em—I got off. Mr. Travers was not a hard chap when you got the right side of him."

"Oh, he was going to the office then ?"

"Yes, and for a couple of months after. It was shortly before he went down to Hampton Court."

"Then it was about the time you witnessed that unlucky will ?"

"Ay, so it must have been."

"Was it before or after you witnessed it ?"

"Well, I am not sure—after, I think. Why ?"

"Nothing ; only I cannot help thinking what a rascally will it is. If poor Mrs. Travers had continued the head of the house you would probably be in a better position."

"I don't know that," returned Poole. "It's the head clerk, not the head of the house, that gives you a lift. But, be that as it may, I was always sorry for Mrs. Travers."

"Look here, Poole," said Tom, suddenly rising, "I cannot let you stay any longer now ; but leave me this," holding up the paper. "I will take care of it, though it has no legal value. I will see Trapes, and try what is to be done with him. You shall hear from me in a few days."

"Thank you, Mr. Reed," returned Poole, rising with alacrity. "If you take it in hand, you will make something of it ; and I can tell you, twelve pounds is no joke to a married man."

"Or to an unmarried one either," said Tom, gaily, as he opened the door for him.

The moment he was gone, Tom turned to the table where the I. O. U. lay, and seizing it, exclaimed almost aloud, "By George ! she is right, after all ! There must have been some roguery at work ! If Poole was away all day at a steeplechase on the 15th of March, it is clear he could not have witnessed Mr. Travers's will. Yet he was ready to swear to his own signature ! I wonder he never noticed the date—but I daresay the steeplechase had gone out of his head by that time. It is the necessity for money that has made him think of this I. O. U. and recalled the circumstance to his mind. Not a word of this must get out till I have secured Trapes's corroborating evidence. After all, Mrs. Travers's conjecture that there is some link between Ford and this man may prove true."

So thinking, Tom carefully folded up the paper and placed it in a strong box for present safety, and then went on his way rejoicing.

Kate Travers had met her reverse with a gallant spirit, but he knew well the bitter mortification with which that reverse had been fraught. The loss of money was as nothing, compared to the humiliating effect produced by the sort of legal declaration of her husband through his will, that she deserved nothing—and that, too, from a man so remarkable for strict justice and profound sense of duty. True, she did not believe he had been guilty of doing her such a wrong, but the world did. And what an occasion was thus given to her contemptuous enemy to blaspheme !

Tom's honest heart glowed at the idea of her possible triumph; but, though far from a profound lawyer, he knew it was a difficult task to upset a will, and he resolved not to disturb Kate's present quiet until he could offer some more tangible groundwork of hope than the present faint spark of light.

Of course Trapes was away, or did not choose to respond, or was laid up with D. T. Whatever was the reason, he took no notice of Tom's note, requesting him to call, for fully ten days, and then he did not come at the right time ; so Mr. Reed was out, and Trapes afforded the grimy boys, attendant imps of the office, a good deal of amusement by swaggering considerably, and professing himself unable to understand what Mr. Reed meant by being out of the way when he had asked him (Mr. Trapes) to call.

On that very day Tom had business in the City, and turning the corner of Lombard Street he came upon Mr. Ford, who seemed eager to speak to him, and as soon as they had exchanged salutations, asked if there was any news of Mrs. Travers.

" Nothing new," replied Tom.

" She does not talk of coming to England ? " asked Ford.

" How do you know she is out of it ? "was Tom Reed's counter-question.

" Will you say positively that she is not ? "

" No ; I will commit myself to nothing."

" At any rate, her reply to me seems to have been three days on the road."

" I assure you I lost no time in forwarding it."

" Very likely."

" Well, I suppose she told you all about herself? "

" All about herself? " returned Ford, with a sneer. " I presume you know how much. I dare say the polite epistle was sent open for your inspection ! "

" It was nothing of the kind ! " cried Reed, with some warmth.

" Will you step into my office, Mr. Reed ? " said Ford, after a moment's pause, and regaining his self-possession. " I should much like a little conversation with you."

" Very well," replied Tom. " I have a few minutes to spare, and they are at your service."

Ford led the way in silence through the roar and rush of the great tideway. His office was close at hand ; and the well-appointed private room soon reached.

Here Ford began to unburden himself ; he was evidently in a curious, restless, excited, indignant mood. He began by stating that considering the true friendship he had ever testified towards Mrs. Travers he considered that he had met with decided ingratitude. " No one, Mr. Reed, ever made more sacrifices than I did, for if you knew the terms on which I was received, both by herself and that excellent lady, her late mother, you would understand how trying the change that ensued. When in former times I used to go down with letters and papers to Mr. Travers, I was permitted, nay, encouraged, to assist in pruning the fruit-trees and tying up the roses. My opinion was asked, and my advice taken. I will not pretend to you, Mr. Reed, that this constant intercourse with a charming young lady—not, after all, so very much my junior—was without its effect. Feelings began to arise in my heart which I flattered myself were neither unperceived nor unacceptable. When suddenly the intelligence of the mother's death, of the approaching marriage of Mr. Travers with the object of my own wishes, came upon me like an avalanche."

Mr. Ford paused and wiped his brow ; while Tom, his face composed to an expression of solemn sympathy, sat listening, and inwardly wondering at this strange confession ; marveling that the every-day good sense of a shrewd business-man, did not show him the great gulf at all times yawning between him and such a creature as Mrs. Travers—

"Oh wad some power the giftie gie us,
To see oursel's as others see us ! "

—Perhaps it is better that the powers are more merciful.

" It was my impulse to quit a post so calculated to embitter my existence, and embark in the line I have now adopted," resumed Ford, clearing his voice with a portentous " hem ! " " but an expression of Mrs. Travers's prevented me—an expression which, no doubt, she would tell you she could not recall to her mind. She said, when we first met after her ill-starred marriage, ' I am glad to see you, Mr. Ford. I trust you will be my right hand as well as Mr. Travers's, for we are old friends, you know.' From which I understood her to mean that she relied on my sympathy and assistance in the difficulties with which she already found her married life bristling. The words were enough for me ; I effaced myself and remained."

" I am sure she always had the greatest respect for you," said Tom Reed, seeing he paused for a reply.

Ford laughed bitterly. " Yes, I stayed on, to be made use of, to do what I could to shield her from the whims and ill-tempers of 'my employer,' as that conceited beast Sir Hugh Galbraith called him ; and she always spoke to me so softly and courteously I thought she recognized the spirit that actuated me. But from the hour of Travers's death, sir," he continued with increasing vehemence, "she changed in a thousand delicate, un-definable, unmistakable ways ; she made me feel that I was the employed and she the employer. The very tone in which she promised me advancement as a faithful servant was intolerable. I confess I did not deserve this—yet the pain of finding that will ; the agony of putting it into her hands was almost more than I could bear ; and from that hour she threw off the mask. She showed the dislike I inspired—dislike, no doubt, arising from the fact of my knowing the humble position from which Mr. Travers had raised her."

Ford paused out of breath from his own excitement.

" I cannot help thinking you do her injustice, Mr. Ford. In the matter of feeling, one is so apt to be mistaken. She may have appreciated you without actually reciprocating your feel-ings, and you must grant that, however sincere her regard and respect, and all the rest of it, it would not have been very seemly to change her manner towards you immediately after her hus-band's death."

So spake Tom, advisedly, watching his quarry all the time· most carefully. " As for resenting your instrumentality in find-ing the will, I am sure you are quite mistaken. She is far too reasonable a woman. I think, on the contrary, she sympa-thized with the distress you naturally felt at such an unlucky 'find.' I remember thinking so at the time."

" Would to God I had never touched it, or seen it, or had any-thing to do with it ! " exclaimed Ford, with an intense bitterness that startled Tom, and resting his elbow on the desk before him he covered his face with his hands for a moment, as if bowed down with mortification, or grief, or some unpleasant emotion.

"You cannot blame yourself with regard to that," cried Tom, not without sympathy; but with a sudden vivid recollection of Mrs. Travers's doubts — which must be mere surmise — but nevertheless were curious.

"Of course not—of course not!" returned Ford, recovering himself, and raising his head. "I merely performed a painful and unavoidable task, but I have allowed myself to say much more than I intended. My object in asking you here was to beg you would tell me how Mrs. Travers is really placed. The change she has experienced must be very trying; her means must be painfully limited, and in spite of all I have suffered through her, I do not like to think of her in poverty. Do be candid with me, Mr. Reed."

"I certainly will, so far as I may," replied Tom. "Mrs. Travers, I am glad to say, has no material wants, and reports herself well, and comparatively content. You know she is a woman singularly indifferent to the outsides of things; but that she ever will be quite at rest until she has upset this will I do not pretend to believe."

"Upset the will," said Ford, with a look of surprise. "I wish there was a chance of it! but a greater delusion never existed than to dream of such a thing. What a pity Mrs. Travers allows herself to entertain such an idea!"

"So I tell her; but she clings to it nevertheless; and will make some move respecting it, one of these days."

Ford was silent and in deep thought for fully a minute, his glittering, strained eyes fixed on vacancy, then rousing himself said, with a bitter smile, "Another question or two, Mr. Reed, and I will release you. Sir Hugh Galbraith, when he called here in the spring, was under the impression that Mrs. Travers had contracted a second marriage; is this the case?"

"I can answer that definitely and emphatically," said Tom, with some zest. "No, certainly not."

"Pray, then, is he right in his surmise, that if not actually married, she is engaged, and to yourself?"

"She is nothing of the kind! *I* am engaged, but not to Mrs. Travers; of that I give you my honor!"

"Well, Mr. Reed, I must say I cannot understand why she so resolutely conceals her place of abode from me. I am always, and have been always, her friend."

"I do not pretend to understand her motives. I only endeavor to carry out her wishes," said Tom, rising. "And now I must really bid you good morning. I have already outstaid my time."

"I will not detain you," returned Ford, with a bitter smile. "I am obliged to you for this visit, though I cannot say you have afforded me any special information."

" Well, you see, I could not! Good morning, Mr. Ford."

Very much impressed by the malignant expression of Ford's face, Tom departed ; more inclined than he ever was before to lend his ear to what he had hitherto considered Mrs. Travers's preposterous notions on the subject of the will.

The extraordinary vanity and unreasonableness of Ford moved his mirth, and yet he confessed the consistent absurdity of the romance he had weaved for himself, and of which the chief object had been utterly unconscious. The tenacity with which the man clung to his delusion was amazing. His great desire to know how Mrs. Travers was situated, no doubt arose from the hope that poverty and privation might a second time drive her into a marriage of expediency. " He little knows his woman," thought Tom, as he walked swiftly through St. Paul's churchyard and on towards Fleet Street. " Nothing would floor her now ; she stands alone, that's enough to strengthen a strong woman. It is the children or parents hanging on them that overweight women for the race of life. Mrs. Travers would float anywhere. I don't think she likes the bazaar business. I don't think she would ever have gone into it but for Fanny, dear little saucy Fan! Please God ! she shall soon have a home of her own. Now to catch that blackguard, Trapes ! "

This was not so easy to do, but Tom accomplished it. Of course Trapes was furious about the I. O. U., which he had quite forgotten. He stated his opinion that it was "a d—d dirty trick for one gentleman to play another." However, Tom pacified him, gave an affecting picture of Poole's necessities, and promised to compromise the matter. Moreover, he managed in the course of the conversation, without raising Trapes's suspicions, to draw out sufficient particulars of the transaction to corroborate in every way Poole's statement respecting its date.

" By the way," said Tom, as his visitor stood up to go, " did Ford turn out to be the man you wanted ? "

" What man—what do you mean ? " asked Trapes, with a stare.

" Don't you remember coming to me in the spring to ask who the man was you had seen me talking to—"

" Oh ! ay, to be sure ! " cried Trapes ; "thought he was a man that owed me money, but he wasn't my boy !" slapping Tom's shoulder with a wink and a shout of laughter. " He wasn't ; still I haven't done so badly since."

" And you see Ford sometimes ? Have you been dabbling in the stocks, eh ? "

"See Ford! Never! Never set eyes on him since I called that time to ascertain—to ascertain—oh! what was the color of the winning horse. He's out of my line altogether," cried Trapes, with an insolent air.

"I should think he was," returned Tom; and then, as his visitor went heavily and noisily down the narrow stair, he added to himself, "but that's an unmitigated lie nevertheless."

Such were the circumstances which Tom had to detail to the fair partners in the Berlin business when he made his unexpected but welcome appearance that Wednesday, to rouse them from the dull routine of their lives; and set all Kate's pulses throbbing, with the strangest mixture of exultation, hope, dread, yet resolution.

CHAPTER XXIX.

"AND what is to be done next?" asked Kate, who was greatly moved, her hands like ice, and visibly trembling, after she and Fanny had listened in nearly unbroken silence and deepest attention to Tom's communications.

"Well, I think your best plan is to lay the whole matter before Wall, and be guided by him. This evidence is certainly of the utmost importance, but whether it is sufficient to upset a will is another matter; the opposite party will of course try to prove there is a mistake in the date of the I. O. U. We can easily prove there had been a steeplechase at this place, Reepham, on that particular date; but then again, Trapes is a very disreputable witness, and it will be difficult at this distance of time to show that Poole had been absent from the office on that special day. Still, I am now convinced there is truth in your conviction of foul play; and I shall hunt up evidence with a will."

"Ah, Tom, you never believed me before."

"He is naturally an unbelieving Jew!" cried Fanny.

"At last, at last," murmured Mrs. Temple, not heeding her, "there is a pin's point of light. But adieu to peace for many a day; it is war to the knife now! But should I be defeated, how shall I bear it, Tom?"

"Don't think of that. We must make our position sure before we take any step; we must mask our batteries carefully till the last moment."

Mrs. Temple was sitting with her elbows on the table, and her face hidden in her hands.

"And Hugh Galbraith," she said. "Have you heard anything of him?"

"There was a report a couple of months ago that he was going to be married to Lord C——'s eldest daughter; but I have heard no more of it."

"And if he marries, how terrible it will be for him! But then for the sake of others he must accept a compromise; he must accept a share of the property, even to—"

"Why, Mrs. Travers, you surely do not intend to show the white feather now?" cried Tom, much surprised at her tone.

"Rest assured I shall not. Nothing shall turn me from the task of vindicating myself and my husband's memory from the disgrace of that infamous will. But it is hard to be cruel to others."

Her voice trembled; she stopped abruptly, and suddenly left the room. Tom looked inquiringly at Fanny.

"She has never been quite the same since Sir Hugh was here. I think she is sorry for him. I am sure it would be much better if she had just said who she was, and they settled it without fighting, or lawyers," said Fanny.

"Perhaps so," returned Tom. "But then Mrs. Travers naturally wants the matter cleared up publicly."

"After all, what is the public to her? they know nothing about her, and care less."

"Very true; but you must remember that she had been in possession of the property; and it was publicly taken from her. I think she is right in insisting on its being publicly restored."

Fanny was silent for a few moments in a pretty, thoughtful attitude, with her hands clasped upon her knee; and after looking at her admiringly and expectantly, Tom proceeded to unclasp them, and take possession of one. He had just opened his lips to speak of his own affairs when Fanny said, softly and solemnly:

"Tom!"

"Well, what is it, my darling?"

"Tom, you won't say anything to any one, will you?"

"Not if I was put on the rack, or torn to pieces by wild horses."

"You need not laugh; I am quite in earnest."

"So am I. Go on. There is something tremendous coming."

"Do you know"—still in a carefully lowered tone—"I think Sir Hugh Galbraith is quite in love with Kate."

"Oh, indeed! Well, that's possible, though I have always heard him spoken of as a cold, stiff sort of fellow, not at all a subject for the tender passion. But the wisest have their weak moments; witness myself."

"Well, but Tom," reiterated Fanny, too absorbed in her subject to administer a deserved rebuke, "I really believe he is."

"What are the symptoms? I daresay he was struck with her. But love is a thing of many degrees; come, your reasons?"

"I can hardly describe the symptoms. I know he used to look rather disgusted or perhaps disappointed whenever I went up to write his letters instead of Kate."

"Oh, you used to write his letters? Had he a large correspondence?"

"Yes, he was always wanting two or three lines written to somebody or other, about horses, and different people in his regiment; and then whenever he came down of an evening—"

"Then he used to spend the evening with you sometimes?"

"Oh, yes—that is—I don't think I ought to tell you, Tom, though Kate never told me I must not. Don't say a word about it, like a dear."

"Provided my silence is properly paid for, I have no objection to preserve it unbroken."

"Do be serious. When he used to knock at the door, and ask to come in, and Kate would allow him, his long solemn face used to brighten up in the most wonderful way. He was absolutely good-looking for a few minutes; and he always listened to every word she said as if he was drinking in her voice, though she contradicted him perpetually—they never seemed able to agree. Then he had a way of resting his elbow on the table, and shading his eyes with his hand. But *I* could see it was just to stare at Kate without being noticed. Why, the very tone of his voice was quite different when he spoke to her."

"Upon my soul, this *is* a revelation. I always thought Mrs. Travers rather reserved about her lodger; but she is not the sort of woman the most audacious scoundrel would venture to—"

"Sir Hugh was nothing of the kind," interrupted Fanny, with some warmth. "He was as quiet and mild as if he was an archbishop. I really could not help liking him. And he gave me such a lovely bracelet. But I suppose if he knew who we are, he would be ready to trample us under his feet—so Kate says."

"This is altogether a curious revelation," reiterated Tom. "I had no idea you had been on such intimate terms. I don't think Mrs. Travers showed her usual discretion."

"Nonsense!" cried Fanny, sharply. "She always knows what she is about."

"Perhaps so. But, Fan, did she reciprocate at all?"

"No, not a bit. She does not think much of him in any way, only she can't dislike him when he seems to admire her; one always has a sort of kindness for any man who admires one!"

"That's a pleasant lookout for me," said Tom.

"It *is* well for you," returned Fanny, with saucy emphasis. "But do not say a word to Kate about what I have told you."

12

" Trust me," said Tom, more seriously. " I fancy Galbraith's admiration (if you are right) must have been a great annoyance to her, if not an additional source of dislike and bitterness, in spite of your theories, my philosopher. But why the deuce didn't she bundle him out when he began to moon and spoon ? I am sure she is plucky enough."

" I don't think she saw as much as I did ; I am *sure* she did not. She used to talk away as calmly and as unconcerned as if he was her grandfather ; and he did not 'spoon,' as you call it. (I am sure I hope you do not put such vulgar words in your 'leaders.') He was quite natural and often disagreeable."

" Then, my dear girl, he wasn't in love, and you have wasted some precious moments over an imaginary difficulty. I can't picture a man making himself disagreeable to the woman he is in love with."

" That is all you know ! I begin to think myself a much better informed person than you are—I can tell you that men can make themselves horribly disagreeable to girls they perfectly adore ! "

" Your experience alarms me," said Tom, gravely. "I grant that, given a jolly row, each party can annoy the other pretty considerably ; but at the stage Galbraith had reached, it ought to have been all fair weather ; at any rate I always feel, always *have* felt, desperately amiable and sunshiny in the adored one's presence ! Eh, Fanny ? "

" My dear Tom, you have been occasionally odious ! I am happy to say ; otherwise I should have believed you to be a rank impostor, and expected you to beat me when we were married," cried Fanny, laughing, yet blushing brightly too, when she found how her sentence ended ; then the conversation became purely personal, and will not bear repeating.

Kate left them together to enjoy a long confidential talk, and when she joined them at the cozy supper she had assisted Mills to prepare, she was quite herself. In the interim she had made up her mind. She would press upon Mr. Wall the necessity of speedy action, so as to give Hugh Galbraith the earliest possible notice of the trial before him. Never inclined to doubt her own success, or look at the reverse of a pleasant picture, this new gleam of hope acquired the most positive color from the medium through which she viewed it, and her great desire was to give a character of fair and open warfare to the coming battle. Galbraith would then be prepared, and when the truth came out fully, she would, through her lawyer, in a quiet and business-like way, insist on settling the bulk of the fortune upon him, asking only in return an acknowledgment that after all his cousin had not made so unworthy a choice. " Then he need never know

that I had appeared to him in an assumed character. He will
be humiliated enough without *that!* poor fellow, and I do not
want him to think of me—*me*, my own self, as different from
what he now believes. Years hence, when perhaps he is
married, and the outlines of the present have faded from their
painful sharpness, we might meet and be friends. But he is the
last man in the world to care a straw for any woman he is not
in love with or married to! He is far too English to have female
friends!"

"And suppose, Tom," said Kate, as they discussed "possibilities" after the evening meal, "suppose we get more evidence,
or whatever is necessary, to induce Mr. Wall to take up the
case, what is to be done? How will he proceed?"
"Why, at the very outset, we have immense difficulties. You
see, it seems that either Poole's signature is forged, or the date
of the will has been altered, or that Poole knowingly signed a
false document as witness. Now I don't believe he did this; his
manner is perfectly innocent and unembarrassed. My own impression is that the whole thing is fabricated, signatures and all.
Wonderfully well done! Our first task will be to discover who
did it. Once we make that out, we must lay information before
a magistrate!"
"Against Hugh Galbraith?" interrupted Mrs. Temple,
quickly.
"No," returned Tom, with a smile, and a glance at Fanny—
"against whoever we find has forged the will; and then the
magistrate will, on the evidence, convict the miscreant to take
his trial at the sessions. Upon the commitment Galbraith must
be communicated with, and required to give up the property.
Then will come the 'tug of war.'"
"It will, indeed!" returned Mrs. Temple, thoughtfully.
"And of course, coming before a magistrate, the affair will be
sufficiently public."
"Public! I should think so! and coming on, as I suppose it
will, before Parliament meets, a romantic case like that will be a
godsend to the papers. I will give you stunning articles in the
'M. T.'"
"I hope you will do no such thing, Tom."
"I must look at that book of Chabot's on the writing of
Junius," continued Tom, not heeding her.
"Who is Chabot?" asked Fanny.
"Oh, the expert—a man learned in handwriting, who is sup-
posed to detect forgeries and interpolations."
"A sort of detective, I suppose? I hope, Tom, the opposite
party will not be sending any detective after us!"

"Nonsense, Fan! that would be no use," returned Mrs. Temple.

"The great difficulty will be," said Tom, addressing her, "who to fix the forgery on, if Poole is, as I suppose, innocent. I am reluctant to take him into our confidence, for he seems not overburdened with sense. In short, I am almost sorry I jumped so impulsively to the decision of coming down here now I see what an effect my intelligence has had. I am greatly inclined to share your convictions respecting the will, but how to prove them— I wish," interrupting himself, "you would give me some of Mr. Travers's writing—his signature if possible—I suppose you have plenty?"

"Yes, you shall have it."

"And I will get C. to look at the will, and compare the two signatures."

There was a pause, and then Mrs. Temple said, slowly and reluctantly, "I have also some of Ford's writing, Tom ; do not fail to examine that."

Tom looked at her earnestly.

"You do not mean to say your suspicions are so strong?"

"I do! It goes terribly against me to harm him in any way, but he or I must suffer, and I will not be under a wrong. I must attack Mr. Ford, Tom! I must!"

After much discussion it was decided that Reed should examine the will, and if he thought it prudent, take Poole to look at the signatures, in short, do his utmost to collect evidence by the time Mr. Wall returned from his usual autumn excursion, and Kate declared her intention of going up to town to be present when the subject was broached to the wary old lawyer. "I think, Tom, he feels for me, and I might have more influence by speaking instead of writing."

"No doubt," replied Tom, "he will not return for another month, and then your busiest season will be over ; I will let you know when he arrives. But I say, Mrs. Travers, it is rather unlucky that Gregory is away at sea! He would surely know his father's handwriting. Well, at any rate, I will lose no time in getting C. to look at the will ; but, first, I will write to Poole, and procure his signature in reply, so that I may have some data on which to ask C.'s opinion ; give me the specimens of Mr. Travers's and Ford's writing you promised, and I will go. I must catch the earliest train to-morrow, for nothing *ought* to have drawn me away from the desk to-day! But how can a poor devil resist when love and friendship pull together!"

The weeks which succeeded this horrid and disturbing visit were exceedingly trying to Kate. The monotony of her occupation—the iteration of days behind the counter were almost intolerable when her nerves were on the rack, and expectation strained to the utmost. Yet she struggled bravely to resist the tendency to be irritable and depressed, or to sit down and think, and create visions of triumph, or ghosts of defeat from the mists of the future. One view of the subject helped to keep heart and nerves in a perpetual state of painful vibration. Whether the future contained victory or defeat both would be bitter to her. To be compelled to crush Ford, a man she had known well and long, and for whom she had the degree of sympathy which arises from comprehension, this was the worst consequence of success; but second only to this cruel necessity was the result to Hugh Galbraith. After tasting the sweets of fortune equal to his social position, to be hurled back into that "slough of despond," genteel poverty! He, so proud and sensitive as she knew he was, under the cold, plain, immovable exterior he presented to common observers, and by her, to whom he had frankly offered himself and all he possessed. "Though," thought the young widow, with a smile at the recollection, "that was a momentary impulse, a freak from the consequences of which he is no doubt by this time thankful to have escaped. He is by no means a bad fellow—yet not at all the sort of man I would fall in love with even had we met under different circumstances. He is so prejudiced and uncultivated, and innately tyrannical with all his sense of justice." Nevertheless she felt it would be a terrible grief to wound him—still, to fail would be intolerable, irreparable—to be conquered by Galbraith was the one thing worse than conquering him. To be condemned for ever to her present life with its narrow influences and deadening sameness—this would be unendurable. "Yet," thought Kate, "had I adopted this life without any consciousness of having been defrauded of my rights I could have borne it better, but not in such a corner as Pierstoffe. Alas! I fear the day is far off when common sense will have sufficient force to prevent the social disfranchisement which an employment such as mine entails. Even when it comes, will it not be moving the barrier a few steps lower down, rather than destroying the barrier. Inequalities will always exist, but they may be softened and lessened till perhaps, as Fanny says, a few hundred years hence Liberals and Revolutionists may be reduced to advocate the rights or wrongs of those ill-used and degraded creatures the gorillas and ourangs!"

But, as it has been said, Kate struggled resolutely with her own weakness; she busied herself in every possible occupation, she took long rambles with and without Fanny after the closing hour; and though sometimes silent and sometimes uttering, half jest, half earnest, more biting remarks on her customers and the world in general than she usually indulged in, she never permitted her suppressed irritation to touch the helpless creatures dependent on her.   She was as gentle to Mills, as kindly to Fanny, as in their most tranquil days.

How beautiful and grand is the tenderness of a strong, loving heart, that instead of despising and overlooking natures slighter and poorer than its own, seeks to uphold and enrich them with the forbearing generosity we give to children, and like the sunshine of a glowing summer's day, lends or develops beauty even in the common things which come within the influence of its radiance and its warmth.

CHAPTER XXX.

"WHAT is Tom about, I wonder?" cried Fanny, one evening nearly a fortnight after his visit; "we have not heard from him for more than ten days."

"We must have patience," said Kate, with a little sigh. "I am sure he is doing his best; but delays will occur. He said that man, the expert he wanted to show the writing to, was very much engaged just now."

"Think of that!" returned Fanny, indignantly. "Who could imagine that in a country like this there would be such heaps of forgeries as to keep a man busy finding them out?"

Mrs. Temple did not reply. She was making up her books, for it was Saturday; and she preferred "stealing a few hours from the night" to pass them sleeplessly in bed. Fanny, "dull sleep and a drowsy bed scorning," insisted on keeping her company, but found it hard work to be wakeful and silent while her friend added up long lines of figures and compared results.

At last Kate put down her pen. "I feel unusually stupid, Fan. I do heartily wish we had some news—something to do; I feel, oh so weary of waiting!" She leaned her head on her hand as she spoke.

"Poor dear! I am sure I don't wonder," said Fanny, sympathetically. "I saw you were nearly worn out when you spoke so sharply to Lady Styles to-day; but she was enough to drive any one frantic. What did she say about Sir Hugh?"

"Oh, that he had started a yacht, a superb yacht, and was launching into all sorts of extravagance; and that Colonel Upton had deserted her to spend the whole of his time or leave of absence with Hugh, and that such folly would come to no good end; but I believe very little of all this. Listen to me, Fan. If Tom fails in procuring sufficient proof—that is, if I find it imprudent to proceed—what shall we do?"

"I am sure I do not know. What do you mean?"

"Oh, Fanny, I hardly know myself, but I cannot stay here. You, I suppose, will marry soon, so I have only poor Mills to think of. Were it not that I do not like to desert her—the last bit of home left to me—I would sell the shop and go out as a governess to Russia, or Tartary, or anywhere!"

"My dearest Kate, what puts that into your head?"

"Because I feel so thoroughly unsettled. If this gleam of hope proves illusory I shall never be able to settle here—never! And yet we are not doing so badly, Fanny." She pointed to the large book which lay open before her as she spoke.

Fanny rose and looked over her shoulder for a moment, then, glancing at some other smaller volumes of figures which were also open for consultation upon the table, heaved a deep sigh. "You are a wonderful woman, Kate! How you can find your way through all these awful books, and know whether you win or lose, puzzles me. I can sell tolerably, but as for arithmetic! You could manage an office, I do believe. It is a pity you are not a man!"

"It is indeed," echoed her friend, resting her cheek upon her hand, and gazing absently away to the open window through which the garden could be seen sleeping in the autumn moonlight. "As I am, I have none of the privileges of either man or woman. I have none of the help and care which falls to the lot of most women, and yet I cannot use what gifts I possess to push my fortune as I should like because I am not a man. But I must do the best I can. Look, Fanny," drawing over the purchase-book, and pointing to a column of entries, "we have all this stock, and it is paid for; there is quite thirty-six pounds due to us, and there is a balance of twenty-nine pounds eleven shillings and sixpence in the bank. To be sure we must now begin to pay our house expenses from our earnings, but then we want but very few goods till spring, except for Christmas novelties. I believe we might do very well here if I could stay, but I feel I cannot—I feel I cannot. There are elements in the life which I did not calculate upon, or underrated. The existence is purely material; I would much prefer being a chemist or a bookseller."

Fanny listened in some dismay. "Yes, dear, I daresay it is very disagreeable; but just think of the smell of a chemist's shop, and all the horrid things that would stain your hands. Now this shop is clean, and nice, and pretty; I would think twice before I gave it up."

"Of course I shall," said Mrs. Temple, rising and closing her books. "Moreover, Fan, I shall do nothing till you are married."

"Well, that is uncertain. Tom said very little about it when he was down here," said Fan, with a slight pout.

"You unreasonable little puss," cried Mrs. Temple, laughing. "Did you not say you would hear nothing on that head till my affairs were settled? Well, I feel as if something would happen soon. Yet this waiting seems long—very long." She locked away her books in their proper drawer, and, walking to the window, stood looking out for a minute in silence; while Fanny somewhat stealthily put out her writing materials to indicate a scolding to Tom.

"Give me the *Times*, Fanny," said Mrs. Temple, rousing herself, "I have not looked at it to-day."

She drew a chair near the table and lamp and read on for some time without speaking, turning over the sheets somewhat listlessly; at length she asked, in a low and somewhat unsteady tone, "Do you remember what was the name of the vessel Captain Gregory commanded?"

"The vessel Captain Gregory commanded," repeated Fanny, looking a little puzzled.

"Yes. You remember he sailed last April, and I am sure Tom mentioned the name of the ship—try and think."

"Oh, I recollect his going away; yes, I do remember something—oh dear, what was the name; can't you remember it?"

"I imagine I do; but I want to hear what you can recall."

"It was," exclaimed Fanny, biting the top of her pen, "it was 'The Fairy,' or Fairy something."

"I believe I do—listen to this." And Mrs. Temple read from the paper : "'On the 4th instant the brig "Mary Jane," of Leith, John Collins, master, homeward bound from Bordeaux, picked up a few miles off the Lizard two men and a boy, who were clinging to an overturned boat. They had been upwards of twenty-four hours in the water, and were greatly exhausted. It appears they are the captain, a seaman, and the cabin-boy of the ship "Fairy Rock," which was run down by a large steamer on the night of the third as she was on her return voyage from Pernambuco. The steamer kept on her course without the slightest attempt to succor the ill-fated ship, which was almost cut in two; and while the crew were attempting to take to the boats she sank. The captain received a blow on the head as the vessel went down from one of the spars, and was partially insensible for a few moments. When he came to himself he was in the water near a boat floating bottom up; upon this he clambered, and afterwards assisted the boy to the same position, where they were joined by the sailor. They had nearly lost heart when they were rescued. The captain proceeded yesterday to make a deposition before the Lord Mayor, but fainted before the conclusion of his narrative.'"

" Now can this be Captain Gregory ? " said Kate, laying down the paper and turning very pale.

" Oh, I am sure it is—it can be nobody else ! " cried Fanny, snatching it up. " Poor man, how unlucky he is ! Now he will be laid up ever so long, and not able to look at the writing or anything. What wretches they must be on board that steamer ! If poor Captain Gregory had not been run down he would have been safe and well in London by this."

But Mrs. Temple hardly listened. " I must write to Tom," she said, nervously ; " you are writing to him, are you not ? Well, let us cut out this piece of news and enclose it, and I will add a line imploring a speedy reply."

A sleepless night was the inevitable consequence of this intelligence. In vain Kate told herself that Gregory's evidence could not really be of much importance—still, in her strained condition of nerves, every additional source of disquiet, however slight, became magnified.

However, the next day's afternoon post brought Tom's long expected letter, which contained things good and bad.

He had taken C—— to compare the signatures of the will with the writing supplied by Mrs. Temple, and his sentence was that he considered Poole's genuine, Mr. Travers's doubtful, and thought there was a possible trace of Ford's hand in Gregory's.

Tom had also examined a file of *Bell's Life* and found a report of the Reepham Steeplechase on the same date as Trapes's I. O. U. It was very desirable, Tom added, to obtain some corroborative testimony as to Poole's presence at these races on the day in question, which Tom did not despair of finding ; finally, he informed Kate that Mr. Wall was expected back next week, and he strongly advised her to come up to town on the following Monday or Tuesday, to be on the spot when he arrived, so as to lose no time in laying her hopes and difficulties before the experienced lawyer. Moreover, he (Tom Reed) would secure her a quiet lodging in the Maida Hill district, which would be preferable to, and less costly than a hotel. Then came a hasty postscript,—

" Had just finished the above when I saw the narrow escape of poor Gregory in the *Evening Mail.* I hurried off to his owners, got his address, and have just seen the poor fellow ; he is terribly cut up, and looks as gaunt as can be expected. It will be a considerable time before he will be capable of attending to anything, so I did not touch on your affairs. He goes down to-morrow to his native place, where his family have been for some time ; I have the address. Give the enclosed to Fan, and keep up your heart ; we will frustrate their knavish tricks yet."

12*

"Thank heaven!" cried Mrs. Temple, with renewed animation in her eyes. "There is some movement at last; I have been thirsting to be on the scene of action. I shall see this expert myself, though I suppose his visits are costly—one must risk something. This is Thursday; on Tuesday I shall go up to town. Fanny, dear little Fan, you will be able to manage pretty well without me?"

"Oh yes, don't trouble about me; I shall be as wise as a serpent and as harmless as a dove. Mills and I will keep shop and house, neck-and-neck, as Mr. Turner would say; and I am equal to Lady Styles now, though I shall have a severe cross-examination respecting your movements."

"Never mind," returned Kate, smiling; "remember you have but one *theme* whatever may be the variations. I have gone to town on business and will be back in a day or two—a 'day or two' is delightfully vague; once I am away, you are not answerable for anything."

"Quite true," said Fanny.

Although there were sundry arrangements to be made in order to simplify Fanny's work as much as possible during her absence, the time seemed very long to Kate till the Tuesday came round; and then an unexpected tenderness and regret for the humble home she had wearied of surprised her.

She felt she was going forth to war, that she was making the first step in her onward march to painful victory or unendurable defeat.

The journey to town was as depressing as damp, chill, drizzling weather could make it; and it was with a sudden sense of comfort and support that Kate recognized Tom Reed's sharp, pleasant face through the early gloom of an October evening. It was not only delightful to have a hand to help her out of the carriage and to extricate her luggage, small as it was; but, knowing his engagements as she did, it was a proof of thoughtful kindness that he should have stolen half an hour from the busy afternoon to meet her.

"My dear Tom! How good of you to meet me. I have had a miserable journey—two fat farmers for my companions half the way, and a severe female, who gave me a tract, the rest."

"Such creatures should be arrested by the police!" returned Tom, sympathizingly. "But come along. Have you only one portmanteau? Sensible woman! We will have a hansom."

And they bowled along speedily to the lodging Tom had selected, in one of the small demi-semi genteel streets which properly belong to Paddington, but prefer the more refined definition of Maida Hill.

"I put you here," said Tom, as a stout, elderly woman, with

a broad, good-humored face, substantial merino "afternoon" dress, an elaborate cap, and stiffly-curled front, secured by three rows of narrow black velvet, ushered them into her front parlor, of tolerable dimensions, with a window opening upon a damp garden, where a few mangy shrubs suggested forcibly the idea of living death, while the tables, chairs, and sofas were shrouded in ample coverings of crochet and netting, which caught on the buttons and hooks of the unwary, carrying away plaster Shakespeares and misshapen delft bandits in their treacherous sweep. "I have put you here," repeated Tom, noticing the desponding glance with which Kate surveyed the apartment, "because," with a complimentary wave of the hand to the landlady, who stood at the door holding Kate's traveling bag, "I know Mrs. Small to be a person of high respectability; and, as you are by yourself, it will be a sort of protection to you to be in her house. Her son is one of the best men in our office."

Smiles and a curtsey from Mrs. Small. "Would the lady like tea, sir?"

"Thank you," returned Kate, "I should very much."

"I'll send it up directly, ma'am. You would like to see your room? It is just at the back, here. I wish there was a door through, it would be more private-like; and the landlord promised," etc., etc., etc.

"I am sorry to say I have only a few minutes to stay," began Tom.

"Then send up tea, I will see my room afterwards," said Kate. "Thank you very much, dear Tom, for all your thought and kindness," she continued, as Mrs. Small left the room. "I am so glad you know something of this person. Now, have you any more news?"

"No, nothing, except that Wall was expected to-day; and Wreford—the partner, you know—said I might be sure he would be at the office to-morrow. Suppose you meet me there at twelve-thirty? I would come for you, but I am so desperately busy, as I will explain to you, that I can scarcely find time to eat. You do not mind going alone?"

"Not in the very least! I put aside all ladylike incapability when I went into trade, and I should be so glad to set things going, and return again as fast as I can. I never dreaded anything so much as this visit to London and my interview with Mr. Wall!"

"That is not like your usual pluck, Mrs. Travers. By the by, in engaging these rooms, I hesitated which name I should give you, and decided on Temple, principally to dodge Ford, if by any chance he were to get on the scent! He might worry you, and I do not think you are up to more than is unavoidable."

"Thank you very much for this," said Mrs. Temple (as we must still call her). "I am most anxious not to be known by my right name till I *have* my rights."

"Strange as it seems—unaccountable as it is," returned Tom, thoughtfully, "I begin to think—to fear—that your suspicions of Ford are well founded! Yet it is almost incredible that a quiet, respectable 'citizen of famous London town' should commit such a felony, merely to spite you, without the slightest gain to himself!"

"I think he intended to get me into his power as well as to spite me, Tom. If we prove this against him, what will be the end of it?"

"Penal servitude," said Tom, shortly.

"I can hardly bring myself to inflict that—yet I must go on."

"Of course," he rejoined; "but I must leave you, I am sorry to say. I would much rather spend the evening here. I have lots to say about my own affairs, but I must not stay. Here is a very good novel; sit down and lose yourself in it. A good novel is a benefaction; and as for the Philistines who prate about fiction, there is often more truth in a good novel than in a biography, which is generally carefully cooked to spare the feelings of friends and relatives even to the third and fourth generation, till a most distorted image, a complete fancy sketch, is offered to the public. There, 'Madame,' weep over the trials of the heroine if you will, but don't give a thought to your own."

Kate followed his advice. Cheered by the consciousness of his steady friendship and support, she contrived to keep the demon of depression at bay; and, somewhat fatigued after her journey, was fortunate in obtaining a good night's rest.

The next day was still cheerless and drizzling. However, wrapped in her waterproof, her face shrouded by a thick veil, Kate managed to reach the well-known office through the greasy streets by many a devious turning, without any misadventure. In her present mood it was a relief to walk rather than sit silent, pent up among strangers in an omnibus.

She thought she was too early; but Tom met her at the corner of the street in which Mr. Wall's office was situated.

"You are in capital time, but we will go on at once." And they walked rather silently to the door.

"Mr. Wall has not returned, sir," was the reply to Tom's inquiries. "Does not return till Friday."

With a bitter sense of disappointment Kate turned away.

"That means I cannot see him till Monday," she said, as they went slowly down the street.

"True. Yet you must stay on in town. Write a line making

an appointment for Monday, and then you may be able to leave the following day, which will just finish the week for which I engaged your rooms."

"I will, Tom; but what a wretched time I shall have of it! You really must come and see me whenever you can."

"Unfortunately," began Tom, but stopped himself. "Come, my dear Mrs. Travers," he resumed; "I breakfasted early, let us go down to Verey's and have a little luncheon. I am ravenous; and I daresay your breakfast was a nominal one." So saying, he hailed a cab, and, before Kate could well reply, handed her in.

* * * * * * *

"Take another glass; that St. Julian is not bad," cried Reed, as the waiter put some Roquefort cheese and celery on the table after their dinner rather than luncheon. "For I have a tale to unfold which you will not like. Yesterday morning I had a telegram from Pau, announcing poor Pennington's death, and requesting me to go over at once, which I must do, both for the widow's sake and for other reasons; however, I postponed my journey till to-night, for I could not bear you to find me gone. As I saw you were rather in the dolefuls I would not tell you till we had seen Wall. Now there is no help for it. I must start by the mail this evening, and you must face the interview, and, what is worse, the business, as best you can; and you will do it well, or I am much mistaken. Yours is a spirit of the right sort, and will always answer the spur."

"But, oh! Tom; you are a terrible loss. How I wish I had not come up to town."

"We could not possibly foresee such a combination of disappointments. Still you must remember there is nothing in them to damp your hopes."

"When shall you be back?"

"Possibly in a week, and when I do return, it will be as editor; then Fanny *must* make up her mind. I sent her a few lines this morning. I am really and truly sorry for poor Pen.; but it is a stroke of fortune for me. Now I must say my say, and leave you. Do not be cast down by the way Wall will probably receive your news. We must get more evidence. I know that, but his advice and guidance will be a great help towards finding it. That fellow Trapes has disappeared again. I cannot help fancying that he has something to do with the mystery. His knowledge of Ford seems so strange. When I return I will unearth him wherever he is. So keep up your heart, my dear Mrs. Travers. All will go well yet."

Kate did feel disproportionally cast down, though she knew as well as her adviser that in the *contretemps* of his departure,

and Mr. Wall's prolonged absence, there was no real check to
her hopes; but the hopes were so commingled with fears, that
at best they were oppressive; now to face a week's lonely self-
communing absolutely appalled her.   But she was not going to
torment Tom, her true, devoted friend, or punish him with a
dose of discomfort for what he could not help; for besides the
native generosity which in her was nearly as strong an instinct
as that of self-preservation, she had the knowledge of men's common weaknesses which four or five years of matrimony may well
impart to duller women than Kate Travers, and well knew that
the one unpardonable sin in the eyes of creation's lord is to make
him uncomfortable, mentally or physically.

   "Of course you are a terrible loss," she said, checking her in- •
clination to cry, and even managing a tremulous sort of smile.
"But I shall just possess my soul in patience, and beard Mr.
Wall boldly, and you will write a line to me, Tom?"

   "Certainly—undoubtedly," replied Tom. "Moreover, I have
given directions that a parcel of books and mags. shall be sent
to you.   So now I must run away.   Shall I put you into a cab?"

   "No, thank you.   I think I shall try to walk back; it will occupy the time, and give me a better chance of sleeping.   By the
way, Tom, why should I not go and see poor Captain Gregory,
as you say he is at no great distance?"

   "Ay, do!   Here—here's his address," hastily opening his
pocket-book, and producing a piece of paper.   "Lillington; it's
on the Great Northern line, and I think you have to change at
H——.   I fancy a return fare will be six or seven shillings.
Here's C.'s address, too, in case Wall wants him.   And now
good bye, God bless you; don't be downhearted."   And they
turned on their various ways at the door.

   Kate walked steadily back to her lodgings, thus occupying a
full hour; and then, when she had removed her damp out-door
attire, it was sufficiently dusk to shut out the melancholy garden, and light the gas.   A long, long letter to Fanny—and the
novel, helped her over the evening, so she retired to rest more
cheerfully than she had hoped to do.   Having consulted Bradshaw as to the trains for Lillington, she requested the landlady
to give her a very early breakfast, if the morning was tolerably
fine, determining to devote the day to her intended visit.

CHAPTER XXXI.

L ILLINGTON was a pretty, well-situated village, about thirty-five miles from Town, twenty of which were on the busy
main-line, and the rest a special little byway, a sort of railway

lane, if such a term may be used, on which the pace seldom
reached fifteen miles an hour, and the train stopped about every
ten minutes at diminutive toy-like stations, where neatly kept gardens, rock-works, and curious devices in white stones attested
the ample leisure of the station-masters. Yet the line had an air
of sleepy prosperity. It led through a richly cultivated country,
tolerably open and flat, with here and there stretches of wood
and young plantations, and peeps at lordly dwellings, and in the
season it was busy with passengers in horse-boxes—and their
owners scarlet-coated and top-booted—or sportsmen laden with
the most approved fowling-pieces by well-known makers, and
all the modern paraphernalia required to enable an Englishman
to spend "a happy day." The neighborhood of Lillington was
famous for its sporting merits ; wealthy proprietors vied with each
other in their magnificent hospitalities and strictly-guarded preserves, where the pheasants fared sumptuously, and Lazarus, in
the shape of the laborer, lay at their gates, if not full of sores,
sorely in need of almost all that civilized man deems essential to
life. True, the charitable gifts distributed in due season were
liberal, but somehow, to that slowly-moving mechanism, the
English mind, generosity is a sorry substitute for justice.

Kate enjoyed the journey—the varied tints of the woods, the
rich brown of the plowed fields—the sense of freedom in the
passing view of wide-spreading, gently-sloping uplands—of
comfort and civilization in the peeps at stately mansions or snug
farm-houses—yet, the color of her mind was russet, like the
woods—though not untouched by gold. How she wished to
have Fanny, or Tom Reed, or both with her. Solitary enjoyment was only half a pleasure to her. "If I succeed," she
thought, "I can take enough for every want I can possibly have,
without robbing Hugh Galbraith ; for after having been taught
to look upon the inheritance as his, it *is* robbing him to take it
all. I wonder where he is, and what he is about?" and then
her thoughts grew less distinct as she fell into a reverie as to
what she would do if she were free—that is, sufficiently well-off
to do what she liked. She would travel a great deal and study,
and have a sort of resting-place with Tom and Fanny, and then
collect something of a literary and political society around her.
So, cheating the time, and shutting her eyes to her companions,
who were of a rather unpleasant and horsey order, for she traveled second-class, and the train was unusually full in consequence of the sale of a well-known stud within a couple of miles
of Lillington, the minutes flew fast, and she was at her destination.

But Lillington was a larger place than she expected, and as
the name of Gregory was probably not very well known, she

directed her steps to the post-office, where her inquiries were answered by a big, good-humored, red-haired girl, who looked like the incarnation of country fare, fresh eggs, fresh butter, cream, rosy-cheeked apples, and dairy-fed pork.

"Captain Gregory," she repeated, " I seem to know the name, and yet I cannot tell where he lives. Here," calling through a door which she opened an inch or two, behind her. " Mary Jane, do you know a Captain Gregory, anywhere's about ? "

A shrill scream, as if from an upper chamber, replied, " I dunno' about captain, but there are some people name of Gregory living with old Mr. Thorne, at the Dene."

" Yes, sure," exclaimed the other, returning to the counter, for the post-office was also the general shop. " I remember now old Mr. Thorne (he is the collector) has his daughter and her children from London staying with him."

" They are the people I want, no doubt," said Kate. " How shall I find the place ? "

" Oh, it is quite easy ; go straight through the village, and up the hill t'other side, and at the top there's a lane on the left ; a little way down you come to a brook and stepping-stones, and the Dene cottage will be right in front."

Kate thanked her, and walked briskly on.

It was a typical autumnal day. The mists and fog that had prevailed for nearly a week had disappeared, leaving a cloudless, pale blue sky, a bright sun, and a crisp, clear atmosphere, like the vigorous health of hale old age. The village, neither squalid, nor yet the pampered plaything of some wealthy patron, was sufficiently untidy to be natural, sufficiently in order to be cheerful. Kate soon cleared it, and ascended the hill beyond more slowly, enjoying the fresh pure air, the delicious odor of a newly-plowed field, and the occasional chirping notes of the birds in the tangled hedgerows, all dank and damp with the week's wet.

At the top the lane described was easily found, and Kate followed it through a beech-wood, where the thickly-fallen leaves gave a tinge of dull red to the ground, and the fences were moss-grown and picturesquely decayed ; the sun, now at its height, gleamed through the thinned foliage, touching the smooth trunks with living gold, and lighting up the wealth of many-colored vegetation with a glory artists might vainly covet. Out again into the open, where laborers were digging up the mangel-wurzel, and heaping it into a bank, to be covered with straw and clay for winter use, past other plowed fields, with a background of tall majestic elms, and then the lane descended steeply to a rivulet, now swollen with the late rains, until the stepping-stones were almost submerged. The road rose again at the opposite side, and yet the bank had been cut away to diminish the ascent, for to the left a steeper portion remained clothed with stunted oaks and brushwood, above which rose the gables of a tolerably large thatched cottage, evidently of a higher and more pretentious description than the ordinary habitations of the village. Kate hesitated, looking at the stepping-stones, and reluctant to attempt the passage, when a lumbering lad in a smock-frock came whistling out of some cattle sheds which were on the opposite side of the road. He stopped suddenly and gazed with some surprise at the unwonted apparition of a lady so distinguished looking as the young widow, in spite of the severe simplicity of her attire.

" Pray can you tell me if that," pointing to the cottage, " is the Dene ? " asked Kate, raising her voice.

" Yes, it be ! "

" Is Captain Gregory there now ? "

" Yes, he be."

" Would you be so good as to give me your hand across these stones ? " continued Kate, smiling.

The boy rubbed that member carefully on his frock, and advanced with a sort of wooden alacrity. Thus assisted, Kate contrived to pass over scathless, save for wetting one boot considerably. Her cavalier directed her to a little green gate, which opened between two luxuriant bushes of lauristinas, and led by some steps into a neat garden in front of the cottage.

Here a black-eyed, curly-headed boy, of four or five years old, was teasing a solemn old house-dog, and on Kate's addressing him he immediately fled through an open door, shouting " Mother, mother ! " with all the force of his lungs.

" He will not fail to bring some one here," thought Kate, as she looked at her watch. " Just three quarters of an hour since I left the station. I must time myself not to lose the three-o'clock train." Here a neatly-dressed woman, of lady-like aspect, with fine black eyes, but a sad, anxious expression, came to the door.

" Pray do I speak to Mrs. Gregory ? " asked Kate.

" You do," she replied, with some surprise.

" I have come to inquire for Captain Gregory, and, if possible, to see him."

" Pray walk in ; I am not sure that he can see any one, for he is still but poorly ; but perhaps I may be able to speak for him." She led the way into a small, accurately arranged sitting-room, which, being fireless and rather damp, struck a chill to her visitor. Perceiving this, Mrs. Gregory said : " If you do not mind coming into the kitchen, there is a nice fire, and no one there just now."

"Thank you, I should much prefer it."

The kitchen was a cozy, highly polished, picturesque apartment, quite a typical kitchen, and Kate gladly accepted a wooden chair near the fire.

"I ought to apologize for intruding upon you," began Kate, "but I believe that your husband may be able to assist me in a matter of great importance. You will probably understand me at once when I tell you I am Mrs. Travers."

"Dear, dear! are you Mrs. Travers? I *am* surprised! Come all this way! I thought you were in France. I'm sure if I thought you were coming I should have had the best sitting-room fire alight." And the little woman's color rose nervously; for Mrs. Travers, the widow of the head of what had been to the Gregory family the "mighty" house of "Travers & Co.," was a personage of high degree, far beyond any social standing Mrs. Gregory ever hoped to reach.

"No room could be pleasanter than this," said Kate, gently. "And now I will tell you the object of my visit, and you shall judge if it be prudent for your husband to see me or not."

She proceeded briefly to explain that doubts had arisen from circumstances too long to be detailed as to the authenticity of the will by which she had been deprived of her husband's property, and she was anxious to ascertain when Captain Gregory would be fit to undertake the journey to town in order to examine his father's signature.

"I am sure, Mrs. Travers, if he would see any one it would be you; but his nerves have had a terrible shake, and his strength too. The doctor says that nothing but extreme quiet, and being away from everything like the sea and ships, will restore him. That is the reason we brought him away here. I had been with father before (he is so lonely since mother died), and my three little ones; my eldest daughter is at school, she is training to be a governess. I lost several children between her and the next. So, as I was saying, we brought my husband down here, and he is certainly better. I suppose you heard all about the shipwreck? I can't bear to think of it, or hear of it; but I sometimes fear we are too quiet. He wants a little cheering up. I'll tell you what, ma'am, it's close on his dinner-time," —here she lifted the lid of a saucepan and peeped in,—" and I'll take it in to him and tell him you are here, and see how he feels; and maybe you will take a bit with us? I have some potato-pie for the little ones and myself, for father won't be in till evening, if you would not mind putting up with such a thing for once. You must be famished, after your journey from town," etc., etc.

And little Mrs. Gregory bustled about, quite excited by having so distinguished a guest, for whose wrongs, moreover, she felt the most indignant sympathy, especially as the unpretending grace of Kate's manner made her feel at home as well as honored. The little boy now sidled up to the visitor—a charming, plump, rosy-cheeked rogue. Attracted by the kindly, smiling eyes of the strange lady, he condescended to get on her knee, and, soothed by the tender touch of her caressing arms, leaned his curly pate against her shoulder and gazed wonderingly into her face.

"Well, I'm sure," said the mother, when she returned, "Georgie has made himself at home! Get down, sir, and don't tire the lady."

"Oh, let him stay!" exclaimed the young widow; "I always feel flattered when a child seems to like me."

"Well, Captain Gregory is quite roused up at the notion of seeing you," continued his wife. "But I told him you should have some dinner while he was taking his; and now I will go light the parlor fire and set the table, for I let the girl out for the day, as ill-luck would have it."

"Then pray let us dine here," cried Kate. "It is so nice and bright and comfortable."

So it was arranged. The young widow removed her bonnet, and soon Mrs. Gregory felt at ease; for Kate possessed that indescribable tact, the product of many ingredients, but the basis of which is thorough and sincere sympathy with others, which no difference of habits or manner can put at fault, provided always a certain rectitude exists. To her all humanity was sacred, and among her fellow-creatures she found nothing common or unclean—save for absolute moral error—towards which her feelings were more akin to compassion than contempt.

Captain Gregory, and the little back parlor he occupied, had evidently been smartened-up for Kate's visit, and though a square-built man of powerful frame, he looked greatly worn and reduced.

He rose to receive her respectfully, with more of the manner of her own class than his wife possessed, looking at her intently with his keen gray eyes as he did so.

"I congratulate you on your wonderful escape," said Kate, holding out her hand; "and I am truly glad you are so much better."

"Thank you," he replied, "I am sorry you have had such a journey to seek me out. I should have willingly replied to any letter you had sent me."

"I am sure you would," she returned, sitting down opposite him. "But, Captain Gregory, I have long wished to speak to you about this unfortunate will, and now I think your opinion respecting your father's signature may be a help, as I think of making an attempt to set aside the will."

"I rejoice to hear it, madam, for, from the bottom of my soul, I believe it to be false."

"You do? I like to hear you say so. It is, of course *my* belief, but hitherto I have found no one to agree with me. I wonder we did not think of asking you to look at the signatures before, but Mr. Reed did not really give any credence to my opinion, and it requires a hearty faith to bring forth works."

"True," returned Gregory; "I would give a good deal to see the old man's writing, or what is supposed to be his; but I don't think I could bear a railway journey for another fortnight or so. You see I was knocked down with sickness before, and hadn't rightly recovered when I went to sea again. I am not a man for speechifying, Mrs. Travers, but as long as I live I'll never forget your kindness and help to my poor sister just in the nick of time. Why, she'd have gone to smash, only for you; and me along with her, for I had nothing to spare, yet I could not let my sister and her children starve. So far as I can help you, Mrs. Travers, you may command me."

"I am indeed glad I was able to be of use to her, Captain Gregory, but my period of usefulness was very limited; since that time I have required all my exertions for myself."

"Why," exclaimed the honest sailor with a start, and gazing with deep interest into the sweet, earnest face before him, "you don't mean to say you were ever downright hard-up?"

"No, I have done very well; nor would I fight for money only, though I prefer being well off, but there is more at stake upon this will."

"And didn't that chap—he that came into the property—make no offer of a settlement? What a d——d screw! I beg your pardon."

"Oh yes, he did; but I would not—could not tie my hands by accepting it."

"It will be a desperate hard fight for you. This Sir—whatever his name is—has the sinews of war and of course will use them without stint."

"Don't you think," said Kate, thoughtfully, leaning back in her chair, "an honorable man, once convinced that he has no right to the property he enjoys, would be ready to give it up?"

"Bless your soul," exclaimed Gregory, with animation, "that is just the point! It is uncommon hard to convince the most honorable man on earth that he has not a better right to three or four thousand a year than any one else! And from all I have heard of your adversary, I fancy he is a stiff customer."

Kate did not reply immediately; imagination had conjured up the face and form of her adversary as she had last seen him, his eyes darkened and glowing with the depth of his feelngs; his

ordinary cold, rugged composure fused by his ardor for herself
into visible emotion; and yet, in all this disturbance, making for
his goal with a certain force and distinctness, though without an
unnecessary word. It hurt her to hear him spoken of slight-
ingly. "I have always believed Sir Hugh Galbraith to be an
honorable man," she said, softly. "At any rate, once I embark
in this warfare I must carry it out, cost what it may!" Then,
after a moment's pause, she went on. "If it is not too fatiguing, Captain Gregory, will you tell me what you remember your
father said about the will he was supposed to have drawn up?"

"Well," began Gregory, looking straight away to the opposite
side of the little room, "it was the end of February or beginning
of March two years ago—I think it must have been March, for
it was about a week before I sailed for Shanghai, and we cleared
out of dock on the 10th. You see father was to have dined with
me at K.'s, in America Square, because I was too busy to go to
him. He was to have been with me at six, and he did not come
till half-past; and he said he could not help it, because he had
been kept by Mr. Travers himself. Then afterwards, when he
had been warmed up a bit with a glass of grog, he says, nodding his head, how with all his conceit Ford hadn't as much of
Mr. Travers's confidence as he had, for Mr. Travers had trusted
him about his will, and that he (father I mean) had witnessed it
that afternoon; nay, I am pretty sure he said he had written it
out, only I could not swear to that, and that it was a dead secret. Then he says—I remember the very words,—'It's rather
hard that, though I'm trusted, I am not promoted,' says he;
'and if Mr. Travers dies I would be worse off, for Ford would
be all in all with the new principal; she, knowing nothing of
business, would look to him for everything. He would be the
real master, and he hates me!' Then I said something about
Mr. Travers having left everything to you, ma'am, but father
pulled me up directly, and said that ill or well treated he was
not going to betray his employer. I thought no more about it,
but the impression on my mind was that you would be mistress
after the old gentleman's death; and when I came back after
being so ill, I never was more astonished than to find everything
upset—you gone, nobody knew where, and a new man at the
head of the house. Then your friend, Mr. Reed, came to question me, and the whole conversation came back to my mind. I
did not care to answer him at first, one is so afraid of the law;
but I am glad I saw him before that fellow Ford came sneaking
down to my place, for I was on my guard. Father always
hated him like poison; so do I."

"Why, may I ask?"

"Well, I can't tell exactly; he is too d——d polite by half,

and yet he seems to make little of you all the time. What's
your idea about the will, Mrs. Travers? I suppose Sir Hugh
bribed Ford to forge it?"

"That is not at all my idea. Sir Hugh Galbraith would
never do such a thing! Nor have I any reason to suppose Mr.
Ford would lend himself to such iniquity. Are you aware that
Mr. Ford lost five hundred pounds by the discovery of this present will?"

" No, he did not lose it all. I understood Sir Hugh made him
a handsome present."

" Still, there was a strong probability of his losing it, and no
visible motive for him to risk so much."

" Had he any spite against you?"

" None. I have no right to suppose he had."

" Well, I cannot make it out."

" And your impression is distinctly that the property was bequeathed to me?"

" I always thought so. I think so still."

" And you say this interview with your father took place late
in February or early in March. Now the will is dated in March,
so it must be the same will."

" Hold a bit!" said Gregory. " What's the exact date of the
will?"

" March the fifteenth."

" By George! then I'll swear I had that talk with my father a
week before. I tell you, we sailed on the 10th."

"That is important," said Kate, looking earnestly at him;
"but might not another will have been made in the interim?"

" Almost impossible, I should say."

" At any rate," said Kate, looking at her watch, "your evidence
will be of great importance. Here is my solicitor's address.
Let me know when you are able to take the journey to town.
I am most anxious to have your opinion of your father's signature to the will. Meantime, have you any of his writing you
could spare me, to compare with it?"

" Not at hand; but I will look some out and send to you,"
returned Gregory.

" Then I must leave you," said Kate, "for I fear to lose the
three o'clock train. Will you pardon the selfishness that induced
me to come here and tease you with my troubles?"

She rose as she spoke, holding out an ungloved white hand,
and looking into his eyes with her own—darkly fringed, softly
earnest—sending the magnetic glance straight to the sailor's
honest heart.

" My dear lady,"—his pale cheek coloring with the sincerity
of interest—" I am but too glad to have had an opportunity of

talking matters over with you, and you have done me good into
the bargain. I feel moped to death lying here on my beam-
ends. In ten days or so, I hope to be in town again. Meanwhile, I will look out one of my poor father's letters, and send
it you."

They shook hands heartily and parted.

Mrs. Gregory attended her guest to the ford, and summoned
a man from the yard behind the house to assist her over the
stepping-stones. Little Georgie and his sister accompanied her
part of the way down the lane, and then she went on, enjoying
the unwonted pleasure of a woodland walk, and the delicious
perfume of some young larch plantations, thinking of her old
home which the scenery recalled, of those happy youthful days
which had so soon ended, and since which, despite her large
capacity for happiness, she had never known any joy. Kindly and
gratefully as she remembered her husband, she sighed to think
how " cribbed, cabined, and confined " had been her early youth ;
and now, should she go through life without ever tasting the joy
of loving and being loved ? She knew herself, and murmured.
" It is just possible, unless my circumstances change." Then,
by some strange drifting in the midst of indistinct thought, the
idea sprang almost to her lips, " How could any one imagine
for a moment that a man in Hugh's position would risk the danger of felony ? How impossible for the untrained and uneducated to judge probabilities fairly ! "

She was in time, but no more, for the three o'clock train, and
was pushed somewhat unceremoniously by a rustic porter into a
carriage rather more than half full of the same class of objectionable men with whom she had traveled down. One—an audacious, flashy-looking personage much better dressed than the
rest—sat unpleasantly close, almost squeezing her into the corner. However, she endured it all with her accustomed philosophy, changing her place when a man left the carriage at one of
the intermediate stations.

At H—— she determined to try and find a carriage with other
ladies in it before taking her place.

Crossing over the bridge which led to the " up " platform, she
found the London train was signaled.

" Will you be so good as to put me in a carriage with other
ladies ? " said she to an official of a higher class, whose cap was
inscribed " collector."

" You must speak to the guard 'm. Ticket, if you please."

Kate felt for her purse. She turned her pocket inside out,
but in vain. It was gone.

" My pocket has been picked ! What shall I do ? "

" Very awkward. You had better speak to the station-master; I daresay he will telegraph for you. You must stand back now till the up-train is gone."

" But "—urged Kate, bewildered for a moment.

"Can't let you pass without a ticket," interrupted the man, misunderstanding her, and stretching out his arm as a sort of barrier.

Kate shrank back instantly, and stood quite still, striving to collect herself and think what was best to be done.

CHAPTER XXXII.

WHEN Hugh Galbraith turned away from the dwelling where he had known the most of pleasure that had ever brightened his somewhat sombre life, nearly five months before this stage of our story, he felt strangely sore and stunned, yet not indignant. He had always accepted the position of "a fellow women did not care about" with great philosophy, returning their indifference with full measure, yet not the least resentment. But this practical proof of his own unattractiveness struck home. Worst of all, it lent the additional charm of being out of reach to the woman who had so fascinated him.

She was a lady in the fullest acceptation of the word; delicate refined. The attendant circumstances of keeping a shop must be repulsive to her, yet she preferred battling with the difficulties of such a life to accepting the position, the ease, the security she might enjoy as his wife. Nevertheless he loved'her the more for her unwavering honesty; and, as he walked miserably to and fro, seeking to while away the weary hours till it was time to go to bed (for there were no more trains that day), he cursed his own precipitancy in having thus suddenly cut himself off from all chance of any more play in the game on which he had staked so much. He had not diverged from his original route with any intention of proposing to Mrs. Temple; he only wished to satisfy his eyes with the sight of her, and gladden his heart with the sound of her voice; and then in a moment a wave of passion carried him over the border of polite seeming into the reality of confession! Yet, after all, he did not know what was beneath the cards. He could not for a moment believe that Kate Temple's past contained any page she need desire to obliterate or conceal, but there *was* something there she did not choose him to know. He was too candid to attribute his rejection to this reason. He recognized her actual indifference, while he recalled with a certain degree of painful gratitude the kindly emotion in her voice as she spoke her adieux. "I suppose it will come all right," thought Galbraith, with a dreary effort at manful, reasonable resignation. "I suppose the time will come when I shall think I have had a narrow escape from a piece of folly, for it is about the last sort of marriage I ever contemplated; but it's infernally bitter to give it up at present. Still, I suppose it is better for me in the end. Might I not have repented had she said 'Yes' instead of 'No?'" But even while he strove to argue himself into composure, the recollection of Kate's great lustrous eyes, dewy with unshed tears, her expressive mouth, the rich red lips tremulous with kindly sympathy in the pain she inflicted, came back to him so vividly that he longed with a passion more ardent, more intense than he had ever felt before, to hold her in his arms and press his lips to hers.

The Grange, as it was familiarly called—or Kirby Grange, to give the full appellation—the old house of the Galbraiths, was even more desolate than Sir Hugh expected to find it. His boyish reminiscences presented him with a lonely picture enough, but not equal to the reality.

Yet he soon grew to be at home there. Galbraith, though essentially an aristocrat, was not in the least a fine gentleman; the plainest food, the simplest accommodation sufficed for him. His soldier servant, a man in the stables, an old woman and her daughter to keep the house, formed an ample retinue. Some modern additions to such portions of the antiquated, mouldy furniture as could still be used made a few rooms habitable, and here Hugh Galbraith spent the summer, perhaps more agreeably than he would have done elsewhere. The land he had newly purchased gave him a good deal of employment. There were fresh leases to be granted on fresh terms; but some of his new acquisition he would keep in his own hands. Farming was exactly the employment that suited him. Moreover, Galbraith had been too long a poor gentleman, striving bravely and successfully to keep out of debt, not to have acquired a liking for money. To improve his property and add to it had become his day-dream. To this end he contented himself with a small personal expenditure, although when he first felt the unwonted excitement of comparative wealth he was tempted to many indulgences he scarcely cared for, the first taste of life as lord of the soil awakened in him a thirst to extend his domains.

In the long summer days his greatest resource was a small schooner, in which he passed many a thoughtful hour, and which formed the canvas or groundwork on which Lady Styles embroidered her fiction of a "splendid yacht."

In short, Galbraith went wisely and systematically to work to

13

effect his own cure; nay, he sometimes thought he had succeeded. Perhaps for a few extra busy days the haunting, ach-
ing regret would .be silenced or kept at bay; but when he most
fancied the ghost was laid, a breath of mignonette wafted from
the garden, a gleam of sunset over the sea, the coo of the wood
pigeon, or even a wild easterly gale dashing the storm-tossed
waters with giant wrath against the dark cliffs that stood up
with savage strength against them—anything, everything would
touch the electric chain of association and bring back those few
weeks of strange companionship vividly before him. Again he
would see Kate's eyes, the exact color of which he never quite
made out—dreamy, earnest, tender, resentful—he knew them in
every change; and the rounded outlines of the pliant figure he
had so often greedily watched sinking down into attitudes of
natural, graceful repose, or rising into unconscious stateliness—
the restful manner, the frank, unstudied talk—all would come
back to him with painful intensity.

But on the whole he gained ground. He thought, he hoped,
these fever fits were growing fewer and further between. To
complete his cure he seized gladly upon the opportunity offered
by his friend, being so far on his way northward, when he found
Upton was the guest of Lady Styles, and soon succeeded in persuading him to forsake the gaieties of Weston for the ruder hospitalities of Kirby Grange, much to her ladyship's indignation.

It was September and the weather was glorious. Galbraith
and his friend had had a long enjoyable day on the moors,
which were a few miles inland from the Grange. They had not
"made bags" worthy of notice in the local papers, but they had
had sufficient sport to give zest to their long tramp over the
springy heather.

The wide horizon of the "fells" imparts a sense of light and
liberty which no rock-bound valley, however beautiful, conveys.
You are in no way shut in. The beauty and freedom of nature
impress themselves upon you, and her awful power is out of
sight. The far-stretching purple distance spread out in undula-
tions, like billows arrested in their swell, gives the idea of a
moorland ocean, with even a greater consciousness of liberty,
for it needs no imprisoning ship; you may plunge yourself on
any side over a boundless space of bloom and fragrance
towards the distant blue :—

> "And now in front behold outspread,
> Those upper regions we must tread
> 'Mid hollows and clear heathy swells,
> The cheerful silence of the fells.
> Some two hours' march with serious air

> Through the deep noontide heats we fare;
> The red grouse springing at our sound,
> Skims now and then the shining ground;
> No life save his and ours intrudes
> Upon these breathless solitudes!"

Neither Galbraith nor Upton were able to quote Matthew Arnold, yet both felt the influence of the scene; the breezy, healthy, life-giving atmosphere sent them back satisfied with themselves, and pleased with each other.

Colonel Upton's was a much lighter and more complex nature than Galbraith's. "Enjoyment," it must be admitted, was "his end and way," and he had hitherto accomplished this end very successfully. A little more of selfishness might have made him odious; a trifle more lightheartedness would have made him uninteresting: but, for once, no ingredient preponderated, and a pleasanter, more popular fellow than Willie Upton never existed. No one would have thought of confiding any difficult or profound undertaking to his guidance, but of the pluck and dash that would carry him over any five-barred gate of obstacle at a bound he had plenty. When we add that he was Irish on his mother's side, the un-English facet of his nature is accounted for.

The friends descended from the dogcart which had conveyed them to and from the scene of their sport, ravenously hungry and sufficiently tired to enjoy easy-chairs after a hearty repast in a window of the dining-room, from whence a glimpse of the sea glittering in the moonlight could be caught. Here they smoked for a few minutes in silence; silence seldom lasted longer when Colonel Upton was present.

"I think," said he, slowly waving his cigar, and watching the curls of smoke—"I think a certain amount of roughness is necessary to perfect enjoyment."

"How?"

"Why, to-day has been almost, indeed altogether, perfect—and yet it was in the rough-and-ready style—pardon my scant civility. But if we had had an array of keepers, and gillies, and ponies, and an elaborate luncheon awaiting us at a certain point, and several crack shots, and heaven knows what besides, it would have been infinitely less enjoyable than our quiet day with that queer specimen of a gamekeeper. Our sandwiches and biscuit with a dash of Glenlivat in that deliciously cold spring water was a banquet for the gods! It is a great mistake to paint the lily."

"I am glad you were pleased," said Galbraith.

"Be the sport what it may, I don't care to have the game beaten to my foot," resumed Upton. "I like to do my own stalking. By the way, Galbraith, I never saw such a queer, cold fellow as you are. If I had come into a fortune as you have, after having been in a hard-up condition all the days of my life, there would have been no holding me. You used to be livelier last winter ; but you are as grave, ay, worse, now as in the old times. I don't think you are a shade jollier for having 'a house and estate and three thousand a year '—or is it four ? "

"I don't think I am," said Galbraith, quietly. "There is so much in idea. A man can but have what he wants, and my wants are almost as easily provided with four hundred a year as four thousand. I tell you though, what I do enjoy, Upton ; I like living in this old den ; I like walking over the lands I have bought back ; I like planning to buy more, and watching my opportunity to do so. But I sometimes think of Indian camp-life with regret."

"I dare say you do. You are one of those fellows who are jolliest under difficulties. However, this might be made a nice place ; four or five thousand in repairs, and two or three in furniture would make it very habitable. Then a well-bred wife with a pretty sister or two, to amuse your friends in the shooting-season —and there you are."

Galbraith smiled grimly. "If the future Lady Galbraith requires three or four thousand pounds' worth of furniture, she must supply them herself," said he.

"What an extraordinary effect money has ! " cried Upton. "I suppose if you had never come into your uncle's fortune, you would have been marrying some pretty nobody without a rap ? Now you want more."

"Well, life in our grade is very costly, once a wife is added to its encumbrances,—my first desire is to collect a little more of the old estate—that will take all my spare cash, and not bring much of a return for some time to come, so the furnishing may wait." After a pause, during which Upton hummed the "Sieur de Framboisie," Galbraith resumed, "I suppose I must marry some day ; but at my age a fellow may count on seven or eight years' liberty."

"You may if you like, but you'll be approaching the 'old boy' period. However, I daresay you will find a spouse without much difficulty at any period. You are so desperately modest ; you always affect to believe yourself unacceptable. Did you ever try to make yourself agreeable to any woman ? "

"Yes," returned Galbraith, unmoved, "and failed signally."

Upton laughed, but gave his friend a keen glance.

"Then I am disposed to quote a scrap of verse my sister's little girl used to sing to me—' Try, try, try again.' "

"In due time," said Galbraith, gravely ; "I imagine it would be rather a nuisance to have a wife very much in love with you; but I shall probably by-and-by find a woman of good family, with a sense of honor and some intelligence, who will have no objection to add her fortune to mine, and share both with me, and we shall jog along very comfortably."

"Good God! what an appalling picture!" cried Upton, throwing away the end of his cigar, and pouring out a glass of claret. "Have you no warm blood in your veins, Galbraith? There is nothing half so delightful as being in love, except being fallen in love with. I intend my wife to be tremendously in love with me; and will do my best to keep her in that frame of mind, thinking all my sayings marvels of wit or wisdom, and my doings heroic action—and—"

"I wish you success," interrupted Galbraith, dryly. "If I ventured to form any special wish on such a subject, I should wish for a companionable wife."

"Companionable," returned Upton, doubtfully; "I am afraid that's a little like wanting the moon. I have met heaps of charming, amusing, tormenting, delightful, good, bad, and indifferent women, but the companionable ones are few and far between; and when found are a long way at the far side of a certain age. Then, if a wife is companionable, she will find it hard to preserve the little illusions respecting her husband's genius and capabilities, which make it so pleasant for both. She will be too much as one of us, knowing the difference between good and evil. After all, those old Greeks were very sensible fellows —the simple, unenlightened, respectable wife for the home—the dashing, accomplished, pleasure seeking and giving Hetaira for holiday life."

"I should like a mixture of the two."

"You are unconscionable; they can't unite; the mistake we moderns make is the attempt to smother the inevitable compensations of existence behind transparent bogie-covered screens of propriety. The Hetairae would not be such bad creatures if they only had property. It makes an enormous difference in any morality whether you have to dip into another's pocket for your necessities and luxuries, or have the wherewithal to pay for them in your own."

"Whether the Hetairae had property of their own or not, I imagine they would do their best to clutch that of their admirers."

"Well, that is an open question. I am thinking of companionable women. To be companionable, a woman must have a certain amount of liberty both of thought and action, which, owing to our insular prejudices, we would rather not see our wives possess. There is something of the sort abroad, but I shall not vote for importing it ; but I ask you, Galbraith, is there any creature on earth so uncompanionable as a well-bred, well-educated *good* English woman, a creature you would trust your life to, who would quietly go through fire and water for any one she loved, or even believed she ought to love ; but she has no more conception of the world as *we* know it, than one of her own babies (I put young girls out of the category). The realities of life must not be mentioned before her ; the sources of some of a man's most trying difficulties, even if she really knows them, she must assume to be ignorant of. If one differs on religious points with the tutelar priest whose ministry she attends, she either tries to convince you by the funniest little sentimentalities, or tells you she will pray for you, or does it without telling, if she is very much in earnest. By the way, it's a capital means of keeping yourself in her mind's eye to be horribly irreligious if you want to make an impression. Then politics. What are her views ? A sort of rose-colored conservatism mixed with faith and good works, and a deep regret that you should be so hard-hearted as to vote for the reduction of expenditure when poor men want employment and salaries so much. There is a philosophic summary for you."

" I do not know about the philosophy," said Galbraith ; "but I know I hate blue women."

" So do I ; but then, my dear fellow, I want to convince you of your folly in expecting contradictory perfections in the same individual. Heaven preserve us from the logical well-instructed female who understands everything a deuced deal better than our noble selves. Nineteenth century English woman ! with all thy faults I love thee still ! But talking of politics—"

" You were talking of women," interrupted Galbraith, in a sort of growl.

" Well, I think I have exhausted the subject. So, to talk of politics. I heard you were going into Parliament ? "

" I thought of doing so, and an absurd paragraph got into the papers, thanks to my sister, Lady Lorrimer, I fancy—there's a female politician for you, Upton !—but when I came down here, and went about among the people, I saw I had no chance till these shrewd, cool-headed north-countrymen knew me better. I would not care to represent any other constituency. Besides, Upton, I am such an ignoramus in politics. I want to feel my way a little before I commit myself to be moved hither or thither by the minister I follow."

" Oh, if you wish to reduce your importance to a vanishing point go in for independence."

" Meantime, I am quite content as I am, if I am only left alone. Thank God, I have no near neighbors ; but since the people began to come down to the country I have had four or five invitations. I have refused them, but I shall be considered a sulky, ungracious fellow."

"Of course, and your chances of picking up that companionable woman you are on the lookout for considerably diminished."

Galbraith nodded with a kindly, smiling look in his eyes, as though his friend's chaff was acceptable because of the chaffer.

"I tell you what, Galbraith : you had better leave them all behind. I mean the hospitable families, and come with me. I am engaged to pay a visit in H——shire about the seventh. Capital house, first-rate pheasant-shooting; man of the house my granduncle. Besides, I want your opinion of a young lady I have partly promised to marry."

"Promised to marry! Promised who?"

"Well, not the young lady, but my sister ; you see the girl is granddaughter to my granduncle—do you see the relationship? —and but for the laws of entail she would be a great heiress ; as it is, I step in and—rob her, I believe she thinks. Now, my sister is of opinion that the best reparation I could make would be to marry her. I shall see about it. Won't you come, old fellow, and support me ? We'll not stay too long ; and as my leave is nearly over you might come on and have a peep at Ireland. It is the queerest country. We are down at Cahir, a most barbarous locale ; but the change will do you good, for in spite of the content you profess, I can't help fancying you are somehow down on your luck."

After some difficulties and demurs on Galbraith's part, this was agreed. Indeed Hugh felt loth to part with his pleasant, cheery comrade ; and sundry schemes of sport and yachting were planned to occupy the ten days that intervened before the date on which Colonel Upton was due in H——shire.

"I suppose," he said, as they were about to separate for the night, "I suppose your arm is all right, quite strong again?"

"Yes, I suppose it is. I don't remember it now."

"You were lucky in your secretary.. I used to laugh at the frequent, neatly written notes I used to receive. I take long odds the writer was not old?"

"No," in a candid tone, "she was not old."

"Nor ugly either? That good-natured, idle gossip, Lady Styles, told me a wonderful story about a lovely widow at the Berlin shop. Indeed, she took me there one day to see her, but of course she was not visible. Now, had I been in your place, I should have had 'a good time,' as the Americans say."

"I do not think you would," returned Galbraith, coldly. "My

landlady was a very respectable person. I imagine a decayed gentlewoman."

" That sounds elderly, at any rate. Are you sure she was not a companionable woman ? Ah, Galbraith, it is enough to shorten one's life even to associate with a fellow so desperately in earnest as you are. However, you must come with me. Now, I remember, there is an elderly young lady at Storrham, aunt, I think, to my fair one. She is very enlightened and strong-minded, wears spectacles and a crop. She is sure to be a ' companionable woman,' the exact article you require."

Thus it happened that Hugh Galbraith became the guest of Philip Upton of Storrham Hall, Master of the Foxhounds, and owner of a grand country seat, which he had always kept up in a corresponding style. Having been blessed with a son, whose tastes were as expensive as his own, and who died a few years previously, he had not been able to save much for his grand-daughter. Her younger child's portion, though unusually good, he considered a miserable provision.

He was therefore anxious that a marriage should be arranged between his grandchild and the heir apparent. Upton and his friend were consequently favored guests. It was a very pleasant house. The absence of a stately, elderly dame from the presidency made life less conventional, and the spectacled aunt proved to be a very lively personage, harmlessly and amusingly eccentric. Galbraith had not for long found time pass so agreeably. Upton's cousin was a graceful if not pretty girl, rather sentimental and romantic, with whom he did not appear to make such rapid progress as he perhaps anticipated ; but there were other ladies who came to and fro of better, or at any rate, more appreciative taste, and on the whole the fortnight at Storr-ham was a success.

However, time and the Horse Guards are inexorable. Upton had business in London, and Galbraith, though cordially invited to continue his visit, did not care to remain after his friend. The weather, too, had changed, and they had not been able to have quite so much shooting. Moreover, Galbraith felt ready for movement of any kind, and quite satisfied that a radical cure had been effected, and that he should no longer be tormented with the memories and longings he had at one time vainly striven to resist.

In good spirits and placid mood, therefore, he started with his friend for the H—— Junction, where they arrived in suffi-cient time to allow Upton's servant to see to their luggage be-fore the London train came in.

They were standing together watching its approach, when Galbraith's eye was caught by a figure in black that passed close to him. A tall lady, with a waterproof over her arm ; a round cape-like cloak of black merino and lace, showed the fall of very graceful shoulders ; a pretty, quiet bonnet of some thin black gauzy material, white roses and black leaves, a rather thick, black lace veil—commonplace details—but the turn of the neck, the carriage, the quiet, even gliding step, were familiar to him ; he felt, with a thrill of delight, that it could be no other than his ex-landlady. He watched—he caught a glimpse of her face—he was right ! He saw her hasty search in her pocket ; he saw the ticket-collector put her back, but he made no motion, no sign, until the train was alongside, and Upton fairly seated in the carriage. He then said, "I shall follow you by the next train, and join you some time this evening."

"Why, what has happened ? What the deuce is the matter?" cried Upton, in great surprise.

"Nothing has happened. I shall probably tell you my reasons when we meet," returned Galbraith, smiling, and stepping back as he heard the whistle. Upton rose, and looked searchingly up and down the platform ; but Mrs. Temple was partly behind a pillar, and several people, male and female, were standing about. The moment the carriage containing his chum had passed out of sight, Galbraith, his heart beating fast, walked up to where Kate stood, striving to think, and feeling unspeakably adrift. Raising his hat he said very quietly :

"You seem to be in some difficulty, Mrs. Temple. Can I be of any use to you ?"

CHAPTER XXXIII.

KATE thought she had indeed reached the acme of her misfortunes when Sir Hugh Galbraith's well-remembered voice met her ear. She had been dimly planning to return to Lillington to ask a trifling loan from Captain Gregory, if the stationmaster would have trusted her to the extent of the fare to that place ; this would have made her return to London either painfully late or impossible. In London, Tom Reed being away, there was no one to whom she could apply—except indeed Mr. Wreford, whom she scarcely knew—and now the situation was brought to a climax by the appearance of Galbraith, the one person in the world who must not know of her visit to Captain Gregory. She felt absurdly nervous, and an uncomfortable tremor made her voice less steady than usual, as she raised her eyes to his and replied, "Why, yes. I am in a ridiculous though awkward difficulty. I have lost my purse—or, rather, my pocket has been picked." The color mounted to her cheek as she

13*

spoke, and she was conscious of a curious contradictory sense of comfort, as well as confusion, in having her friendly enemy at hand in such an emergency.

"Lost your purse," repeated Galbraith, "very awkward indeed. Are you traveling alone, may I ask?"

"I am."

"Then I am glad I met you, for I can see you to your destination and save you any further trouble."

"You are very good, but," coloring more deeply than before, and speaking with dangerous discomposure unlike her usual manner, "I do not wish to give you any trouble or interfere with your journey—or—"

"But if you know no one here, what can you do?" interrupted Galbraith. "Come, Mrs. Temple, let bygones be bygones! Because I was a presumptuous blockhead once, are you going to forbid my being friendly, or of use to you . now you have brought me to my senses?" This spoken in his pleasantest tone and with a frank smile, was a marvelously clever stroke for a big schoolboy like Galbraith to make. It put Mrs. Temple at ease, it assured her delicately that he no longer pretended to be a lover ; and, more than all, it bound her to accept his friendliness, or risk appearing to recur coquettishly to his former character. She took him gladly at his word. If he was going to be simply a friend many difficulties would disappear. "Thank you very much," she replied, frankly, as he himself had spoken. "I shall be very glad of your help, for I am alone in London as well as here, obliged to stay for a few days on business."

"Indeed," said Galbraith, resisting his inclination to look into her eyes whenever they were raised to his, "Where is Mr.—Mr. —Tom?"

"Mr. Tom," replied Kate, smiling archly, "is ever so far away—quite unavailable at present."

"That is very unfortunate, and what are you going to do about your purse? I hope you had not much in it?"

"A great deal too much to lose : a five-pound note and eight or nine shillings."

"Have you the number of the note?"

"No, I am sorry to say ; I generally take the numbers of notes, but of *course* did not on this occasion."

"That is unlucky ; however, we must see what is to be done. Porter, here ! when is the next train to Town?"

"Four ten, sir ; and it's sometimes behind a bit."

"Half an hour to wait ! Come, Mrs. Temple, you had better sit down in the waiting-room while I speak to some of the people. Don't go into the ladies' waiting-room, it is a cheerless den, the fire has gone out." So saying, and relieving her of her waterproof with a sort of friendly authority that amused Kate,—so much had they seemed to have changed places now that she was adrift and he knew his ground—Galbraith led the way into the waiting-room, established his precious charge near the fire, and went in search of the station-master.

The time that intervened before the London train was due was amply occupied by interviews with the station-master, the inspector, and others. Kate gave a detailed description of her purse, its contents, and also of her neighbor on the journey from Lillington, and added that a reward would be given if the contents should be restored.

"Will you allow me to look after this affair for you," asked Galbraith, "you can hardly manage it yourself in the absence of Mr. Tom?"

"Oh, thank you. I suppose there is nothing for either of us to do, once the thing is put into the hands of the police, and I have given them my address. You are probably not going to stop in town?"

"Yes, I am; for some little time." He was silent, pulling his moustaches thoughtfully for a minute, and then walked away after the retreating officials.

When he returned he had the tickets for their journey in his hand. "They are not without hopes of finding the thief," he said, cheerfully. "The inspector telegraphed at once to the police at King's Cross; and I thought it better to give my address in addition to yours. I am afraid these fellows will be sharper if they think a man is on the track."

"I have a better opinion of them," she returned. "I am sure they would work as well for a woman. I am almost sorry you gave your address."

"What!" exclaimed Galbraith; "you are not going to put me in punishment again?" a remark that somewhat silenced Kate. "But the train is alongside; we had better take our places," and he offered her his arm.

In spite of her difficulties present and prospective—in spite of the sort of resentment it excited in her to find herself obliged to follow Galbraith's lead—Kate could hardly refrain from laughing at the absurdity of her position. Here was the man, to ruin whom she had undertaken that journey, assisting her with, at any rate, brotherly care; absolutely conducting her in the most conjugal fashion to the carriage! The care bestowed upon her, the sudden smoothing of difficulties reminded her of her rare journeys during her married life—and she confessed to herself that it was very pleasant.

The train was full, yet no fellow-passengers were intruded upon their solitude; and, as Galbraith did not talk much, Kate,

relieved in spite of her embarrassment, had ample time to think
and form some towering air castles.

Galbraith's friendliness, and freedom from everything like a
lover's tone gave her great pleasure. He had probably found
some charming girl infinitely more suited to be his wife than
herself, and then a little sigh swelled her heart as she thought
of her own nearly six-and-twenty years, and that the first freshness of youth—more from circumstances than from time—had
left her forever! If she could establish a frank friendship with
Hugh, there would be no difficulty in arranging matters amica-
bly and justly when the time came for her to assert her rights :
whereas, if they were hampered with the complications of a
false position, things might go wrong indeed. Then she thought
in a somewhat melancholy mood of the loss of her five pounds
—it would make her week in London very costly. What would
Fanny say to her day's adventure! How she wished she had
that dear, impulsive, bright little goose to welcome her back
when she reached her destination. Thus chewing the cud of
sweet and bitter reflection, she leaned back with something of
languor in her attitude, gazing dreamily through the window at
the landscape as it flew past them.

Meantime Galbraith experienced an extraordinary sense of
elation and delight. When he first recognized Mrs. Temple
he acted almost without thought, on a prompt instinctive impulse, to get rid of Upton anyhow. He proposed no plan, no
object to himself. At the sight of the woman whose domina-
tion he fancied he had thrown off, every idea, every consideration was merged in the imperative necessity of speaking to her,
and hearing her speak once more. In the same mood, taking
no heed for the morrow, and further blinded and fascinated by
her ready acceptance of his professed change of tone, he
plunged recklessly into the golden ocean of delight which their
unexpected meeting offered.

It was so delicious, too, to have her even for an hour or two
all to himself—in his hands, dependent on him. Whatever
came of it, he was fiercely determined to enjoy the present
moment.

At this point of his reflections he leaned forward with alarming tenderness in his eyes. "You are tired—you look tired,"
he said.

"Yes, a little," returned Kate, rousing herself ; "I have walked
a good deal. I went to see an invalid friend, and the house is
some distance from the station."

"And how is Miss Lee, and Mills, and Pierstoffe generally ?"

Kate replied, and they continued to speak of it, its scenery
and characteristics, till Kate, half fearing the associations it

might recall, mentioned Lady Styles and her report of the " splendid yacht," which made a useful diversion. Then their talk drifted to Kirby Grange and Galbraith's belongings in the North.

This was a subject of much interest to his companion, and she tried to draw him out, not unsuccessfully. It made her heart ache to see how deeply he was attached to the old place—how his imagination was occupied by the idea of re-creating the Galbraiths of Kirby Grange in their original status. So, conversing with intervals of (to Galbraith) delicious silence, they reached King's Cross. Here, with the same promptitude he had shown since their startling *rencontre*, Hugh secured a cab, handed Kate in, directed the driver to the address he had heard her give to the inspector, and took his place beside her, remarking, " You said you would allow me to see you to your destination."

The noise of the streets and of their conveyance did not permit much talk, and Kate thought the journey never would end. What was she to do with him when she reached her lodgings? He would surely have the tact and propriety to go away without obliging her to dismiss him? The friendly footing he had established was very nice and sensible, but the friendship was safer at a distance. Kate in her inner heart distrusted it ; that he should so far trouble himself on her account was natural, as she really needed his help : the intercourse, however, must stop here. "But I shall manage it," was her concluding and consolatory reflection. "I have a great deal more *savoir faire* than he has."

Adelaide Terrace was reached at last. Mrs. Temple could not be so ungracious as to turn upon the threshold and forbid Galbraith's entrance, so he followed her into the little front parlor, from which she had removed the crochet snares, and rendered more habitable-looking even by one day's sojourn. Mrs. Temple did not sit down, so Galbraith remained standing, looking altogether too tall and lordly for so small an apartment.

It was now dark ; the polite landlady lit the gas, and left the room. Galbraith made a sort of effort to speak, stopped short, looked down, and seemed suddenly to have lost the prompt self-possession he had hitherto displayed ; then, meeting Mrs. Temple's eyes which expressed extreme uneasiness, he laughed, and exclaimed, bluntly, " You must have some money till you hear from your friends."

" Oh, no—no thank you ! " cried Kate, stepping back in the energy of her refusal. " I could not, Sir Hugh ! I mean, you have assisted me quite enough ! If you will be so good as to let me know where to write, I will send what you have already—"

"I shall be highly offended if you do anything of the kind, he interrupted ; " besides, I must come and tell you if I get any tidings of your purse: in the meantime, you can't get on without money."

"And how do you know I move about with no larger capital than five pounds?" said Mrs. Temple, smiling.

"That's another thing," said Galbraith, looking keenly at her. "Have you any money?" he added, with his natural directness.

"No," she returned, laughing at his point-blank question ; "still I do not need any from you, I assure you. I have my check-book with me, and my solicitor will cash a check for me to-morrow."

"Oh, very well," said Sir Hugh, a little disappointed, and he let his purse, which he had half drawn out, fall back into his pocket. "But I am sorry to hear you have a solicitor. Steer clear of those gentry if you can."

"Unfortunately, I cannot recover what is due to me without them," replied Kate, somewhat evasively.

"Take care that your dues are not swallowed up in the cost of recovering them," said Galbraith. He paused a moment: "I am keeping you standing"—another pause ; but no invitation to sit down came—"so I will wish you good morning."

"Good-bye, and thank you very much," returned Mrs. Temple, holding out her hand. It was the first time he had touched it that day, and it was given with a sweet, frank smile of recognition for his services ; yet Galbraith did not hold it a second too long, nor too warmly.

"I hope you are not overtired," he said, "and that I shall soon bring you tidings of your lost property." He bowed, retired, and the next minute Kate heard the cab drive away.

She sat down at once upon the stiff little sofa, and heaved a sigh of relief; then, starting up, she hastily set out her writing materials, and wrote a hasty note to Fanny, enclosing a check, and requesting her to forward a post-office order by return. "Quarter to six," she exclaimed, looking at her watch. She rang, and asked her way to the nearest post-office, where an additional stamp insured the conveyance of her letter.

"That is the best plan," she thought as she walked back more leisurely. "I did not like the idea of going to Mr. Wreford ; besides it would have betrayed my whereabouts, though, I suppose, I must tell Mr. Wall when I see him."

Tea was ready when Kate returned, and, though puzzled and somewhat annoyed by this unexpected renewal of her acquaintance with Hugh Galbraith, she was infinitely less depressed than on the previous evening. Why, she would have been puzzled to explain ; but she felt as if things would not end badly could she and Hugh come to a friendly understanding, but before all things it was necessary that she should first prove her rights.

The next morning came a long letter from Fanny. There is a wonderful pleasure in reading a long letter full of minute details respecting one's home, or any locality familiar and endeared—more welcome a thousand times than the most wittily and originally expressed epistle upon abstract topics.

"What a misfortune that Tom should have been called away," was the opening sentence. "I have been thinking of you ever since I had his letter, for I believe I knew all about it before you did. He is quite vexed himself; and Mr. Wall not come back yet! It is really too bad! You must be so miserable all alone in that awful London! I would cry my eyes out if I was in your place; but you will not, you are so strong and brave.

"It has been horribly wet ever since you left, and I have only taken three pounds eleven and sevenpence halfpenny, but Mrs. Jennings called and paid her account at last.

"I have had tea with Mills since you left, and we sit by the kitchen fire, so we do not keep the parlor fire in. She has made great progress with the stockings she is knitting for you; but conversation is rather a difficulty. I don't think Mills values my opinions as she ought, so I proposed reading to her. She was very pleased; but I didn't think of her deafness, and now I don't like to go back; so, if I shout at you when you return, do not be surprised. We are going through the 'History of Pierstoffe.' You remember you bought it last spring. But I am surprised to find how sceptical she is: she has grave doubts that it ever was so poor a place as it is represented to have been. The gray cat is much better, and his coat looking quite handsome again. Shall I have the garden done up? Some of the trees want pruning.

"Such a funny thing happened to-day! I was in the shop after dinner, setting up some screens in the window, when a sporting-looking man, well dressed, though not a gentleman, I think, strolled past. He was a stranger, evidently, and yet his face was familiar to me. He stared very impudently, and, I am afraid, he *winked*, as he went by; but I had hardly got back behind the counter before he returned and walked in.

"'Have you any—any—' He stopped, looked round, as if trying to find something he could ask for. 'Oh, ah, gloves—that will do. I want a pair of dogskin driving-gloves.'

"'We only keep ladies' gloves,' said I, with dignity, I flatter myself.

"'Well, it's a mistake,' said he, sitting down and rapping his teeth with a queer little stick he carried. 'Gentlemen pay bet-

ter, and are easier served, especially by a charming young lady
like you.'

" I can't tell you how indignant and frightened I felt. You
never saw such a horrid man ! He had a white face and a red
nose, and was altogether dreadful. Before I could think of anything grand and cutting to reply, he went on : 'Now, I'd lay
long odds you never were behind a counter before ! Your pretty
fingers are not used to handle a yard wand ! A pair of white
reins from the bits of a couple of thoroughbreds are the ribbons
you ought to handle ! I have a notion I had the pleasure of
meeting you before. Haven't I the honor of speaking to Miss
de Burgh ? ' and he stood up and made me a wonderful bow,
raising his horrible white hat ever so high. I didn't know
what to do, and I just said, 'No, indeed I am not.' How
I wished for you. 'Then,' said he, 'if not, what may your
name be ? ' It flashed across me that he might be one of the
detectives Tom talked about so ; so I said very steadily—though,
believe me, I was shaking in my shoes (boots, I mean)—'I don't
see what my name can possibly be to a stranger like you, sir.
Can I show you anything ? ' 'That's a hint, by Jupiter ! ' he
cried, with a roar of laughter. ' Do I look like a fellow that
would work Berlin wool, or crochet ? No, nothing, thank you,
my dear Miss de Burgh, unless, indeed, you can tell me where a
young chap called Turner hangs out. He says his governor is a
big-wig here ! Do you know the name ? ' I told him the only
Turner I knew here was Turner & Co., the great drapery shop.
Then he gave a great roar of laughter, and, taking off his hat
again, he said ' Good morning, Miss de Burgh,' and walked
away. I really felt quite ill after, and I puzzled over his face all
day, but only this evening at tea it jumped into my head who he
was. I am certain he is the same man that spoke to Tom the
day I was at Waterloo Station on my way to you, dearest Kate,
years ago—that is, two ! And he is just the sort of creature to
be a detective, or an informer of some kind. I have been
miserable ever since. What could he want with that unfortunate young Turner? No good, I am certain ! Do make
haste and come back soon ; we are lost without you ! I am
longing for an account of your visit to Captain Gregory ! Lady
Styles has not been here since. Ever your loving friend,
                                        " FANNY LEE.

" P. S.—Have I not written you a splendid letter ? It would
do for a chapter in one of Tom's stories ! I hope ours will end
in proper story-fashion—with virtue, you, me, and Tom, rewarded ; and vice, Sir Hugh, Ford, etc., etc., punished, though
they are not very vicious, after all ! "

Kate read this curious story a second time, and set herself to think the matter over steadily. She had forgotten the encounter at the Waterloo Station, if she had ever heard of it; but the description, and allusion to Tom's knowledge of the mysterious stranger, induced her to conclude that he could be no other than the missing Trapes. She did not see what possible connection could exist between this man, Ford, and her own affairs. His acquaintance with Poole was accidental, and not difficult to account for, but his connection with Ford was utterly incongruous—a mystery she could not understand. The more she reflected upon the matter, the more she acknowledged that there was no evidence whatever of Ford's complicity in the scheme to defraud her. Nothing but her own unreasonable instinctive conviction; but to that, after arguing round a whole circle of probabilities, she returned as tenaciously as ever.

It was a bright, crisp morning—a morning that asked you to go out—but Kate felt bound to resist. She felt, while she smiled at her dilemma, that she could not venture to take "her walks abroad" with an empty pocket. No, she would stay indoors and wait patiently for Fanny's letter and remittance, which would be sure to reach her to-morrow.

Meantime a minute search in her traveling-bag resulted in a "treasure trove" of fivepence-halfpenny, and Kate felt positively at ease when she put this slight store in her pocket. "How dreadful it must be to be absolutely penniless," she thought,— "penniless, with little children crying to you for bread! Yet what power, what perseverance, what ingenuity the consciousness that you had them to provide for would bestow! The worst poverty is genteel poverty after all,—the loss of caste in the enforced abandonment of the gentlewoman's habits and appearance. The position of women is growing more and more false every day: we cannot find men to work for us, and if we push our own way, we are supposed to forfeit our ladyhood and womanliness! Can it be that these graces, which ought to be innate, really depend on the purse? Is it possible we are compelled to admit the materialist conviction, that there is a money reason at the bottom of everything? I cannot! the common sense of mankind will right this in the future, for though its manifestations are very intermittent, there is a great deal of common sense in the world or it would be a vast lunatic asylum."

But the idea of a money question sent her to her personal expenditure book, over which she severely took herself to task for various unnecessary though trifling outlays which she considered self-indulgent. To be prudent and economical was no easy task to Kate Travers. Naturally appreciating artistic elegance—ugliness and vulgarity in her surroundings was positively painful. A large liberality, never stopping to count the

cost of what she bestowed, was inherent in her; moreover, the
physical perfection of her frame disposed her to a certain luxurious indolence.   It is your nervous, unequally developed nature
that prompts to restless action and objectless self-denial—the
richer, fuller being is content to stand at ease and wait, confi-
dent in its own force when the moment for action comes.   Moreover it was an enormous advantage to her that her intellect had
been so much cultivated before passion had stirred from the
sleep of childhood.   As yet her idea of passion was an intellectual flame; she did not realize the strong human necessity of
contact, she did not perceive that even "through the laying on
of the Apostle's *hands*, the Holy Ghost was given."

But the great corrective to Kate's most deeply-rooted faults,
pride and an imperious will, was an inexhaustible sense of justice
to others, or rather a sympathizing equity, which is above the
dry rigidity of barren justice.   A tender equity, ever ready to
pay the fines it was compelled to inflict—this, and a sturdy independence, a shrinking from obligation—money obligation—
kept the current of her energy from stagnating, and gave to her
air and manner the indescribable restfulness of strength.

When Hugh Galbraith reached his hotel the previous evening
he was informed that Colonel Upton had engaged rooms, and
gone out, intending to dine at the club.   Thither Galbraith
followed, but did not find him; and, rather to his satisfaction,
dined alone.   The evening was long, though assisted in its course
by a game or two of billiards with a chance acquaintance who
happened to drop in, for in October the clubs present a deserted
aspect.

The chums, therefore, did not meet till breakfast next morning,
when Galbraith, having made up his mind on more points than
one, was impenetrable and imperturbable.

"What became of you last night?" he asked, boldly taking
the initiative.

"Well, that is cool!" exclaimed Upton, looking up from his
poached egg and broiled ham.   "Pray what became of you
when you deserted me in that extraordinary fashion yesterday?
You are not afraid of a tip on the shoulder?   Are you a spirit-
ualist, and had you a sudden communication?   I looked down
the platform pretty sharp I can tell you, and I could see no
moving cause for such extraordinary conduct—come explain,
explain!"

"That is just what I am not going to do," returned Galbraith,
calmly, "at least not at present."

"You said you would."

"I have changed my mind.   I could not tell you all, old fellow
so I will not open the subject."

"So be it," returned Upton, resignedly; then after an interval of eating, he resumed, "Pray, am I still to have the pleasure of your company to Ireland?"

"No," said Galbraith.

"Nice treatment ; but I expected as much. Is it indiscreet to ask what you are going to do with yourself this morning?"

"It is ; but I will answer you. I am going to Scotland Yard."

"Scotland Yard! Why, in the name of heaven?"

"To try and trace a thief."

"Then I believe I am on a wrong scent."

"That is very likely."

"One word, Galbraith. Was the cause of your sudden defalcation at H——, male or female?"

"I decline to answer," said Galbraith, smiling.

"It was a woman," cried Upton, triumphantly.

CHAPTER XXXIV.

THE long, bright morning hung heavily on Kate's hands. She wrote a description of the previous day's adventures to her friend and partner; but that did not fill up all the time, though it carried her on well towards her midday chop. She tried to read, but an odd nervous anticipation distracted her attention. That Hugh Galbraith would make his appearance, she was quite sure—the only question was, when? Kate was too wise and womanly a woman, however, to be without the resource of needlework, which, as many a weary sister could testify, has a calming, satisfying influence of its own. She had carried with her a large piece of cloth appliqué work, and the intricacy of the pattern served to divert her thoughts. She had, however, hardly thus disposed of an hour, when the sound of a rapidly approaching cab woke the echoes of the dull little street. The sound came near, ceased an instant, and then the conveyance seemed to drive away. An uncomfortable, uneasy beating of the heart made Kate's fingers unsteady.

"What folly and weakness!" she exclaimed to herself. "I must conquer both."

"A gentleman for you, ma'am," said the landlady, throwing open the door, and the next moment her hand was in Hugh Galbraith's.

"I had hoped to be here earlier, Mrs. Temple," he said, in the easiest tone possible; for all his native pertinacity was roused and concentrated on preserving the character of friendship which he had adopted, until it led him—where?—well he did not at present care to ask. "I had hoped to be earlier, but I was kept waiting for an immense time in Scotland Yard, and then sent to another office ; however, here I am at last." He laid aside his hat as he spoke, and sat down, uninvited, at the opposite side of the table.

" And I fear," said Mrs. Temple, taking courage as she noticed his manner, and the tranquil glance with which he met her eyes, " I fear you have had your trouble for nothing."

" Not absolutely. The police are not quite without hopes of recovering your money. They know that a certain swell-mobs-man was at a sale of somebody's stud, near Lillington, and they are on his tracks. If you knew the number of your note, I fancy it might be all right."

" It is very unfortunate ! I drew it out of the bank the after-noon before I started for London, last Monday, and as I was very busy, I omitted to enter the number—a disgraceful over-sight for a woman of business," she added, smiling.

" I fear you will have to pay a rather heavy forfeit in conse-quence. By the way, the bank people would know the number ! Why don't you telegraph to them ? I'll go to the nearest office and do it for you—they can telegraph back directly—and if you send me a line to-night, I can see the inspector to-morrow, the first thing." He stretched out his hand towards his hat as he spoke.

" Stop, stop ! " cried Kate, " let me think for a moment."

" There is really nothing to think about," said Galbraith, who could not understand her hesitation, while she confusedly thought of all the mischief that would possibly and probably arise from his becoming mixed up with her affairs. It would be better to telegraph herself, so she said, looking earnestly into Galbraith's grave eyes, and then she remembered her bankrupt condition.

" But the nearest office is a long way off," he urged—" some-where near Oxford Street, I suspect " (it was before the days of postal telegraphs)—" better leave it to me."

" But the bank people will not tell you any thing—they will only do so to me."

" I will telegraph in your name, and give your address."

" Then telegraph to Fanny ! " cried Mrs. Temple, eagerly. " She can go to the bank ; they know her, and will give her the information, and she will lose no time."

" What's the hour now ? " said Galbraith, looking at his watch " two thirty—barely time. I wish I had not sent off my cab. I will drive down to the office as quickly as I can, and return immediately."

" I am sure, Sir Hugh—" began Mrs. Temple, but he was gone and a vigorous slam of the front door announced his exit. " He 's really very good," thought Kate. " It is a great pity we ever became enemies, or that he made the ridiculous mistake of fancying himself in love with me. He has evidently got over it, and is anxious I should think so. I must not on any account seem to look on him as a lover, but accept his friendship frankly! I wonder why he is coming back—he has said his say, and we really have very few topics in common? Perhaps he will not return. He is wonderfully alert—quite another creature ! " ,

But he did return, and sooner than she thought possible.

" I have accomplished my errand," he said, cheerfully, reseating himself in the place he had occupied, and throwing open the front of his overcoat, as if he intended staying.

" But you must forgive me for exercising a little discretionary variation from your instructions. I sent the message straight to the bank—there was really no time to spare."

" I suppose it was best ; but I trust you used my name. The whole of Pierstoffe would be hysterical with curiosity if *you* telegraphed on my behalf ! "

" I am not quite blockhead enough to do so," replied Galbraith, a little indignantly. " I daresay," looking at his watch, " you'll have the answer before six."

" I hope and trust he is not going to sit there and wait for it," thought Kate. His next words reassured her :

" If you can post to me by six, I shall get the note to-night. There is my address," laying his card on the table, " and I know yours is the pen of a ready writer."

Mrs. Temple smiled, and tried to keep back a slight blush that would come in spite of her.

" It's so unfortunate that I—I mean my friend, Mr. Tom—is away, or I should not have given you all this trouble ; but indeed, Hugh—" the name slipped out quite unnoticed by her, so accustomed had she been for years to think and speak of him as " Hugh." He shot a quick, keen glance at her, saw her unconsciousness, and shaded his face with his hand for a moment while she finished her sentence,—" Indeed, you need do nothing further in the matter. To-morrow I shall be liberated, for I am certain to have money from Fanny, and I can follow up the quest myself, if you will be so good as to tell me the proper quarter to apply to."

" Ah," said Galbraith, looking at her, " then you did not go down to your solicitor as you said you would."

" No," she returned ; then, laughing at his suspicious air, added :

" I *have* one, nevertheless, I am sorry to say ; but on second thoughts I resolved to send home for what I required."

" I expect you had not the wherewithal to charter a cab," said he, laughing. " That came of being too proud to borrow a little filthy lucre from me."

"A cab, indeed!" cried Kate. "Do you suppose a hard-working tradeswoman like myself, up in town on troublesome business, would indulge in cabs? No; an omnibus is the extent of my luxury. At any rate, I shall be in funds to-morrow, and able to manage my own affairs, so pray take no further trouble. I do not see why I need write to you to-night. I can see the inspector and give him the number of the note myself."

"You must not think of doing so," replied Galbraith, very earnestly. "It is not pleasant for a delicate, refined woman to go about alone to these places. I cannot allow you to do so, unless, indeed, you will let me accompany you. Besides, as I began the affair, you had much better let me finish it. Two inquiries will only create confusion."

Kate thought a moment. "Has my name appeared at all?"

"No," said Galbraith; "there was no necessity to mention it. A lady had lost her purse, and I was the agent in the matter."

If, then, no one was to know of her being even temporarily mixed up with her enemy, she would not mind so much.

"Well, then, as you are so good," she said, slowly, and looking down, fairly beaten by his pertinacity and resolution.

"I suppose a day or two will see it ended one way or the other. If not, you must promise me to give it up. I can always get my solicitor to assist me, you know."

"Ay, and he will charge no end of six-and-eight pences! Believe me, you had better leave it to your unpaid *attaché*."

"Let me substitute unattached assistant," said Kate, laughing and coloring most becomingly, "and I agree."

"So be it," returned Sir Hugh, thoughtfully, "so be it;" after an instant's pause he added, "and you will write, then, this evening?"

"Yes, I will write."

"As soon as I have seen the police people in the morning, I will come here. In the meantime, what a frightfully dull day you will have of it."

"I do not mind being alone—at least I should not if I had not an interview with a solicitor before me," she replied, with a little sigh.

"How long do you remain in town," asked Galbraith, standing up and taking his hat, yet lingering still.

"That depends on my solicitor. I hope to leave on Tuesday. It is not very cheerful here."

"I should think not. I must say good morning, Mrs. Temple."

"Good morning, Sir Hugh. By the by, I shall be out to-morrow morning, so pray do not take the trouble of coming all this way—a note will tell me all that is necessary."

His face clouded over. "I believe you are frank enough to speak the real truth," he said. "Do you distinctly wish me to stay away?"

Kate hesitated; she half wished he would, but only half. Moreover, if she forbade his visits, would it not be confessing that she did not consider him emancipated from his character of a lover? No, she would secure his kindly, friendly feeling— that would be some provision against future difficulties. So, looking straight into his eyes, she said with a bright smile,—

"No, I do not. You know we can be friends for a few days while the shop is out of sight, and inequalities forgotten," and she held out her hand.

Galbraith took it quickly, pressing it for an instant almost painfully tight. "Friends, anyhow," said he, "shop or no shop!" Then, turning away with the words, "Till to-morrow, then," he left the house.

When he was gone, Kate sat down, leaning her elbows on the table and burying her face in her hands. "I wonder if I am doing right in letting him have so much of his own way? Will he think me a treacherous wretch by and by? What can I do? I cannot forego my rights to save his feelings. I am almost stupid enough to do so; but what would Tom and Fanny say? I could not be so weak; besides, I may never succeed, and if I fail I shall hate him again—there is such unreasoning prejudice in his contemptuous disregard and disbelief in any caste save his own. He chooses from some whim to credit me with an ancestry, because he knows nothing about it. I almost wish I had no drop of so-called gentle blood in my veins, were it only to contradict his theories. How out of place such a feudal individual is in the middle of the nineteenth century, and yet—" What extenuations her intellect or her heart might have urged on Hugh's behalf remained unsuggested, for the landlady put in her head.

"I was thinking, ma'am, as the gentleman is gone, you'll be wanting your tea."

"Thank you, Mrs. Small, I shall be glad of some."

Meantime Galbraith walked away south-eastwards, in deep self-communing.

There was no mistake about it. Mrs. Temple had called him "Hugh" familiarly, unconsciously; and never had the harsh name sounded sweetly to him before. It was impossible she could have made such a mistake (as she would have considered it) had she not thought of him tolerably often; not as Sir Hugh Galbraith, Bart., of Kirby Grange, but as one near enough, if not dear enough, to be enshrined in her memory as "Hugh" simply. What did it mean? When he so abruptly, and almost rudely, asked her to be his wife, her tone and manner indicated complete freedom from the least tendency to reciprocate his feelings. The most conceited blockhead that ever curled his whiskers and waxed his moustaches could not mistake it for concealed preference or any other sentimental indication. It was as downright a refusal as ever man received, though not unfeeling. Yet—she called him "Hugh!" Was she coming round to him? Galbraith's veins thrilled at the idea. Though by no means a self-conceited man, like most others of his stamp, it never occurred to his mind that any woman in the world was too good for him. Still Mrs. Temple had hitherto been an unattainable good; and now a gleam of hope, faint though it was, seemed to dazzle him. But how about those battles which he had fought with himself during his lonely rambles and cruisings in the north? He had then come to the conclusion that it was well after all he had been rejected, though he should never again have the chance of finding such a glorious helpmate as Kate would be; but that past of hers, which she was so unwilling to reveal, what did it contain? Nothing really bad—nothing. Of that his whole heart acquitted her; but something brought upon her by others, that was possible, and would he not brave that for her sake? Yes, if she had loved him; but was it not well that she did not? Hugh Galbraith was sensitively alive to the honor of the family name. True, his father had somewhat tarnished it, but not in the world's estimation, for he (Hugh) had helped him to pay his debts; but to marry a woman who was in any way touched by disgrace, no weakness would tempt him to such a step he once thought, and now accident, the drift of a woman's fancy, was perhaps his only safeguard. If, therefore, the unconscious use of his name was an indication that the tide was turning in his favor, would it not be wise to seek safety in flight, instead of courting danger by every means in his power? Common sense had no hesitation in answering, but passion, imagination, and self-will are a troublesome team; and if Galbraith could have brought himself even to will obedience to the dictates of prudence, I doubt if he could have followed them, though it is a moot point. "To will" anything is, I suppose, to do it; but this is not a metaphysical treatise. Willing or not, Galbraith determined to see the present act of the drama played out. "If I impress her with an idea of my friendly interest, she may open her heart and tell me her story. She is evidently very much isolated; and at any rate for the next three or four days I shall have her all to myself in this wilderness of brick and mortar."

So reflecting, Galbraith hailed a hansom and rattled away to his club.

The next morning, having been relieved from her embarrassing penniless condition by a post-office order from Fanny, enclosed in an effusive letter, full of dismay and sympathy, Kate sallied forth to leave a note she had written, requesting an interview the following morning at Mr. Wall's office, intending to assure herself that he had arrived the previous night.

Her note to Galbraith had cost her much thought. The "reply wire," as it is familiarly termed in busy offices, did not reach her till seven o'clock the evening before ; and she decided to enclose the telegram as it was, which she did, merely saying, "This moment received. Yours, with many thanks, K. T."

She felt a joyous feeling of relief at being able once more to walk boldly forth, and this buoyancy carried her lightly and rapidly to her destination.

She was recognized by the clerk, who sat in a sort of wooden cage near the door, where he noted down the entrances of the seekers of justice or injustice, and he paid her immediate and polite attention.

"Note for Mr. Wall, madam ? Certainly, it shall be given to him directly he arrives."

"I am told he was to return last night."

"Unfortunately he is detained at Dieppe by a severe cold, and fears he cannot travel till Monday."

"I am very, very sorry for every reason ;" and Kate felt almost choked with a lump that would rise in her throat.

"Will you step in, madam, and speak to Mr. Wreford ? "

"No, thank you ; it would be of no avail." She turned away, all her buoyancy gone—everything seemed against her. Five pounds lost, and another costly week in London probably before her, while her presence was so sorely needed at Pierstoffe. She felt too much cast down to face the long walk back, so she took refuge in an omnibus.

The next day was Sunday, a rather wearisome day, under any circumstances, but doubly so in a small temporary London lodging.

Kate was half amused, half angry with herself for the sort of disappointment she had felt at the non-appearance of Galbraith on the previous day. She was naturally anxious, though not very hopeful, about her five pounds ; but over and above this motive she would have been thankful for the seasonable break in the depressing monotony of the day, which his presence, and perhaps a little argument, would have afforded.

To-day he would not of course come. Men like him generally went away somewhere to avoid the sepulchral aspect of a London Sabbath. Moreover a Sunday visit implied a certain degree of intimacy. "To be sure," thought Kate, as she tied on her bonnet before going to church, " our acquaintance is

14

altogether exceptional—a sort of byway not amenable to the rules that govern the turnpike-roads of good society."

She walked some distance to hear a celebrated preacher, and then, as the weather though not wet, was dull and chill and misty, resigned herself to remain indoors, made up a bright fire, and drawing a low folding-chair—the only tolerably comfortable seat in the room—near the hearth, selected the toughest book of those provided by Tom Reed's kindly thought, and settled herself for a few hours' reading. But her attention was not quite so steady as she expected, she caught herself listening to the passing vehicles which were few and far between, although she had quite made up her mind that Galbraith would not come on Sunday.

Half an hour had hardly passed thus, when something drove up very rapidly and stopped suddenly. Then an impatient rap with the diminutive knocker, which sounded on the thin, unseasoned wood more like " the woodpecker tapping on the hollow beech tree " than the regulation "thunder claps" which " Jeames " used to discharge upon aristocratic entrances before bells had superseded knockers. The next moment Galbraith was bidding her, "Good morning."

" Could not manage to come up here yesterday till it was later than you might have liked," he began, drawing a chair opposite her, as she resumed her seat, making himself quite at home, to Kate's amusement; yet her amusement was tinged with shades of compassion and regret.

" I did not get your note till nearly twelve o'clock yesterday," continued Galbraith. " I stayed at the club till after the last delivery the night before, and began to think you had changed your mind, and were going to cast me adrift. However, your note explained all, short as it was. I have received very few letters from ladies in my life, and I have always understood that brevity is not their characteristic, but yours was literally but three words."

" Yet it told you all that was necessary," said Kate, smiling.

" Very true. Well, when I got down to the —— Street Station the inspector was gone away somewhere, and I had to wait some time. He was very glad to get the number of the note, and said he thought they might manage it now. That is literally all I have to tell you, Mrs. Temple."

" Thank you very much." Then, after a little pause, she added, " Of course I must give some reward; there will be something to pay ? "

" A mere trifle. The police are paid for their work by Government, and I daresay you contribute quite enough in the shape of taxes towards their maintenance."

There was a pause—neither knew exactly what to say next, though their hearts were full enough.

"And are you off on Tuesday?" asked Sir Hugh, at last.

"No. I am sorry to say I find the solicitor I wanted to see does not return till Monday, and" (with a sigh) "he may not return even then. So I have not a very lively prospect before me ; and I want so much to return."

"It is very annoying," said Galbraith, sympathizingly, though a subdued smile lit up his eyes. "However, I hope you will have as little as possible to do with lawyers and the law."

"I am on the brink of a lawsuit, I believe," replied Kate, urged by she knew not what impulse to approach the deep but narrow gulf between them, of which her companion was so unconscious.

"Well, pull up before you are absolutely over," said Galbraith, earnestly. "I was once very near going in for one myself."

"Why did you not?" she asked, gazing away into the fire.

"Because I got what I wanted without it."

"I will give up mine on the same terms," retorted Kate, with a thoughtful smile. "Perhaps my adversary may come to some accommodation as it is termed. Tell me, have you ever found any trace of the lady you were in search of?"

"What lady?" asked Galbraith, looking puzzled.

"Perhaps I am indiscreet in alluding to the subject ; but in a letter I once wrote for you, you made some inquiries about your uncle's or some relation's widow."

"Yes, yes, of course. I am not in the habit of thinking of her as a lady. You mean Mrs. Travers. No ; we can find no trace of her whatever. It is very curious," he continued, musingly, "the way she has vanished. I mean, I cannot account for her rejection of my offers ; it is not in keeping with what I imagine the character of her class."

"What was her class?"

"Tradespeople ; at least, I heard she was niece or relation to a man who used to supply old Travers with fishing-tackle. I think Travers took the lodgings where he met her through him. She was daughter to the woman of the house. Whether she acted as servant or not, I do not know ; at any rate she fascinated my deluded relative ; but if the right will had not turned up she should have had a tussle for the property."

"Do you imagine she will ever try to disturb your possession of it?" asked Kate, leaning forward to replace a piece of coal which had fallen from the fire.

"No ; that is quite out of the question.. The will could not be upset ; but I confess it is very hard lines for her to be sent adrift upon the world without a rap, after living in luxury for a few years."

"It seems cruelly unjust."

"It does," returned Galbraith, thoughtfully; "and I always fancy poor old Travers must have found out some wrong-doing of hers to induce him to make so great a change in his intentions. My own idea," he went on, as if speaking to himself, "is that there was something going on between her and that clerk."

"What clerk?" asked Kate, quietly.

"Ford, the manager. He knew her before her marriage—knew her well, from what he has admitted to me; and there was always something devilish queer, a sort of sentimental kind of restraint in his tone when speaking of her, that suggested the notion that all was not right. Then there was the five hundred pounds bequeathed to Ford in the first will, and never mentioned in the second. I think it is all very suspicious!"

"What do you suspect?" said Kate, rising and taking a paper screen from the chimney-piece to shade her face.

"Various delinquencies," returned Galbraith, with a grim smile. "Perhaps they agreed to marry, and share the money after the old fellow's death. If such a thing came to his knowledge—and a stray letter or a moment's incaution might betray them—such a will as Travers left would be the best sort of revenge."

"But have they married—this Ford and your friend's widow?" asked Kate.

"No—not that I know of; though they may. I can hardly believe Ford to be as ignorant of her whereabouts as he pretends. They may have married privately, but in any case I do not think either can disturb *me*. I hope you are as safe to win your cause, whatever it may be, as I am in my possession!"

"I should expect any wickedness from a woman base enough to plan marriage with another during her husband's lifetime."

"Well, it is only my supposition, Mrs. Temple, and you must remember her perception of right and wrong was no doubt much less delicate and acute than that of a woman of your class. It is absurd to attribute the feelings and motives of our grade to those in a lower strata."

"'My class,' 'our grade,'" repeated Kate, turning her eyes full upon him. "What difference is there between your cousin's wife and myself? I keep a small shop—I let lodgings—"

"With as fatal a result," put in Galbraith, an unusual sparkle of fun gleaming in his eyes. The remark was irresistible.

"Hush, hush," returned Kate, good-humoredly, pleased at the lightness of his tone. "We have agreed to forget all tem-

porary insanities; but why should not this lady—well, this
young woman—not possess as keen a sense of honor as you
credit me with?"

" Because it's not natural. She might be honest enough to
keep from any wrong-doing during her husband's lifetime, but
not have the delicacy to resist planning what would do him no actual material harm. It is the associations, the habits of life, the
tone of every one and everything around that makes a gentlewoman what she is, or ought to be."

"'Ought to be' is well put in, Sir Hugh. Does nature,
which is after all the groundwork for our embro'deries—forgive
a professional illustration—does nature count for nothing? The
true kindly instincts of the heart—and, remember, the highest
good breeding is but the outward and visible sign of this inward
grace—will often make the humblest woman act with both delicacy and tact. Have you never met with absolute vulgarity in
high places? And let me assure you, though you choose to
imagine me—I scarce know what—my people are and were
what I am, shopkeepers, not on a large scale."

" I do not care what they were. I only know you look like a
princess very slightly disguised." As Galbraith said this he
leaned his arms upon the table, looking straight at her, pleasantly, frankly, but not in the least like a lover.

" I claim to be more than a princess, whatever my faults may
be," returned Kate, speaking softly as if to herself. " I claim to
be a true-hearted woman."

A silence ensued, which both felt to be dangerous, yet Galbraith dared not speak. At length Kate's thoughts, having
shot along some curiously interwoven lines of association, suddenly stopped on the topic of Galbraith's antagonism.

" But why have you so strong an antipathy to this woman—
this widow?"

" I certainly had a very strong antipathy to her."

" Had?" repeated Kate. " Is it, then, passed by?"

" Well, yes; one generally feels more amiable to a defeated
enemy."

" True; still why did you hate her? Did she injure you?"

" She did. She extinguished the hopes of my whole life," returned Galbraith, earnestly. " Travers always led me to suppose
I was to be his heir, and I had perfect trust in his justice. He
was as cold and dry and hard as a piece of granite, and he was
a gentleman of the same blood as myself; if it did not sound
absurd to talk of sympathy (I have picked up the word from
you, Mrs. Temple), between two such men as Travers and myself, I should say there was a good deal. I really felt like a
son, or rather a younger brother, towards him. If he had come

to grief, I would have shared my last shilling with him ; not as a mere duty, for I owed him that much, but gladly ; and then to find him throwing me over for a mere bit of vulgar prettiness, a girl nearly young enough to be his granddaughter—not even a gentlewoman !—at his age ! I never felt so disgusted, by heaven ! I was as much cut up at having my respect for the old man destroyed, as at seeing my prospects go overboard. Nor do I believe Travers would ever have been so unjust, so unlike himself, if a strong pressure had not been brought to bear upon him. I think his ultimate action proves that he found he had made a mistake, and was anxious to atone. Still he must have had some strong reason for disinheriting the wife ; and they lived peacefully together to the last. That is the strangest part of the story," added Galbraith, thoughtfully.

"It is, indeed," said Kate, who had listened with avidity and a beating heart to this long speech—unusually long for Galbraith—and now only forced herself to speak, lest her silence should permit him to wander from the subject. "I cannot, indeed, wonder at your hating this obnoxious woman." She was unconscious of the earnest, appealing gaze she poured into his eyes as she spoke, but it riveted his attention, and swept the wicked widow and his wrongs out of his thoughts. "Still," urged Kate, speaking soft and low, "she may have been innocent of any intention to harm you. She might have been very poor and desolate, as I think I suggested to you once before, and poverty is more terrible than you can know — real poverty. When your kinsman asked her to be his wife, she knew nothing of you or your hopes ; she may never have influenced him against you. Are you sure that in your anger you did nothing to offend this Mr. Travers ? " How strange it was to speak thus of her dead husband to her foe.

"Why, yes. I certainly wrote a letter on the spur of the moment which could not be exactly pleasant to him or the female he had been pleased to bestow his name on. But I don't regret it ; I should do the same thing again. However he did not like it, for he never replied, and I only heard vague reports of him for the next two or three years. Then came the news of his death, and of that infamous first will. The widow wrote me an insolent letter through her solicitors, offering me a third of the property as a free gift ; but the idea of being under an obligation to her for what ought to have been my own, was more than I could stand," and Galbraith, warming with his subject, started up as if to pace the room ; but its narrow limits forbade that favorite exercise, so he resumed his seat, and listened attentively to his companion's words.

"It was not such an illiberal offer after all," she was saying thoughtfully.

"I grant that. It was more; it was rather an extraordinary offer, and meant to keep me quiet; for I fancy she knew the second will existed, or feared I might find a flaw in the first. Of course, had I agreed to accept her terms, I could have made no move against her under the first will; and no one could have foreseen that a curious accident should have led Ford to discover the second one. Fortunately he was an honest man, or, rather, rational enough not to risk a felony, so he handed it over to my solicitors or her solicitors, and it was all right."

"For you—yes! Then, the sum of your opinion is, that this Mrs. Travers strove to alienate your benefactor's affections from you; was found out in some disgraceful intrigue; was ready to bribe you to silence, and to destroy the will made by her husband under the influence of his just indignation against her."

"Yes; that is a tolerably accurate outline."

"Never say again that you are an unimaginative man, Sir Hugh Galbraith," said Mrs. Temple, slowly, in an altered voice. "You built up an ingenious theory on very small foundation."

"Perhaps so. I confess this woman's disappearance has puzzled me. Sometimes I think it shows that she is all right, with more in her than I gave her credit for. Sometimes I think her keeping out of my way a confession of guilt; still I don't like to think of her being in want or difficulty. And, by Jove, I will find her! But I must have bored you with my affairs, Mrs. Temple. One of the privileges of friendship, you know. I can't tell how it is, but I think I talk more to you than to any one else."

"I am interested in your story, Sir Hugh, that is the reason. But I tell you candidly I am disposed to take sides with the widow against you."

"That of course. You are always in opposition. Still I fancy I am right in the main. I have heard traits of Mrs. Travers—small indications of the current, that show she is grasping and selfish and mean. She cannot be so pretty either! Ford said she had reddish hair, and of course she was bad style."

"I suppose she was," said Kate, composedly; "but if she were to make any attempt to disturb you?"

"Oh, fight every inch of ground. If my whole fortune went in law, she should have none of it."

"Would you resist a just claim?"

"It could not be just, you see. Nothing could upset the last will."

Kate sighed.

"I have been trespassing on you unconscionably," said Galbraith. "The shades of evening are closing, and I had better go. If you admit me to-morrow, I will promise not to prose about myself."

" To-morrow," returned Kate, dreamily. " Are you coming
to-morrow ? "

" Yes, of course," cried Galbraith, boldly, though for half a
second he had hesitated whether he should say so, or ask permission to come. " I hope to bring you your money to-morrow.
When is this solicitor of yours to return ? "

" To-morrow, I hope," said Kate with a sigh.

" I suspect you will be in the down-belows until you see him."

" And perhaps after," she said, smiling. " Good bye, Sir
Hugh."

" The fight will be a bitter one," thought Kate, as she sat
alone after her tea. " But I am bound to carry it through. In
justice to myself I must show that my poor husband never for
a moment doubted me. I wonder if Hugh Galbraith's friendship,"—even in her thoughts she emphasized " friendship,"—
" will stand the test of discovering my identity with ' the female
to whom his cousin was pleased to give his name ! ' Will not
the surreptitious winning of his—well, regard, be my crowning iniquity ? Oh, Hugh ! I do not want to rob you of what ought,
indeed, to be your own."

But Monday brought no Mr. Wall, nor Tuesday, nor Wednesday ; nevertheless they brought Hugh Galbraith with almost un-
deviating regularity to the commonplace little cottage, which
was a corner of paradise, though an uneasy paradise to him.

Kate felt a little worried by his visits. She felt she ought not
to allow them ; but she was an exceedingly unconventional
woman, and a fearless one. Moreover, she was interested in
her visitor. She did not acknowledge it to herself, but she
would have missed him. There was a subtle pleasure to her in
the sense that she was charming to him ; that Kate Temple was
thus revenging the injuries of Catherine Travers. Yet she did
not intend any cruelty, any real revenge. " When he knows
who I am, he will find the knowledge sufficiently repulsive to
give me no more trouble," she thought ; "and if he is brought
to confess that he did Mrs. Travers injustice, he may agree to
reasonable arrangements with Mrs. Temple."

It was very strange to have him sitting there familiarly with
her by the fireside in the dusk of the October evenings, just as
he might have sat with her in her more stately home had he
come back from India on good terms with her husband. No,
not exactly. Hugh Galbraith would never have permitted his
eyes and voice to speak the language they often did, friendship
notwithstanding, had he known her as his cousin's wife ; and as
she thought so, her heart leaped up in a great throb of delight to
know that she was free.

It was very strange to be thus swept by the eddy of her life's current into this still pool for an instant's rest before she was hurried on again into the rapids. Strange, but also delightful—more delightful than she confessed even to herself. But then it was only an instant's lull. It must not, should not, last longer.

CHAPTER XXXV.

THE only result of Mrs. Temple's daily visits of enquiry to the office of Messrs. Wall & Wreford was the promised communication from Captain Gregory, enclosing a letter of his late father's with his signature, which she placed carefully with the documents Tom Reed had left her for Mr. Wall's information. Kate felt greatly tempted to proceed to Doctors' Commons and compare the writing with that upon the will, but she feared to take any step without either Reed's or Mr. Wall's knowledge. She therefore strove to possess her soul in patience till the moment for action came.

Tom wrote also. He had paid the last tribute of respect to the remains of his chief, and hoped to be in London within another week. So far there was a slight movement in her enforced stagnation. At last, on Thursday morning, when she had gone down to the office more mechanically than hopefully, she found good tidings. Mr. Wall had arrived the night before, had been at the office that morning for half an hour, had read his letters, and left word that he would be happy to see Mrs. Travers the next day at eleven. (She had left no address, not liking to acknowledge that she bore a feigned name at her lodgings.)

This sudden fulfillment of her long delayed hope sent her back to her temporary abode somewhat tremulous, with a curious confusion of thought seething and bubbling round one central idea. "To-morrow I am to lay the first charge in the mine that is to shatter Hugh's fortunes! Will he ever accept the fragments back from the hands that wrought the mischief?"

She felt that in her present mood she could not meet Galbraith, so purposely made a long *détour* in order to reach her lodgings after his usual hour for calling.

"The gentleman has been here, ma'am," said the landlady, as she opened the door. "He was very sorry to miss you, and asked to come in and write a note : it's on the table."

Kate walked in, and looked at it, and then stirred the fire, took off her bonnet and wraps, and even folded them up with mechanical neatness, before she opened the missive. How would this straightforward, rather rigid nature judge her?

14*

Would she not seem false and double-dealing in his eyes?
Would not his idea of his cousin's widow be on the whole confirmed by the line of conduct she had adopted? What did he
write about? Perhaps to say he was obliged to leave town and
should not see her again. She hoped so; it would be better and
wiser. She opened the note, and colored with pleasure to find
her conjecture wrong.

"So sorry not to find you," ran the epistle, in large, ugly, but
legible writing; "for I cannot call to-morrow. Obliged to run
down to see my sister at Richmond; but hope to call the day
after with some intelligence of your five pounds. I trust you
have caught the lawyer at last, and found all right.—Yours very
truly, HUGH GALBRAITH."

Something had been begun below, and had been carefully
obliterated. She had to-morrow, then, perfectly clear for her
interview, and for reflection afterwards; but the day after she
would see him for the last time as a friend, probably for the last
time in any character. Soon he would be a bitterer, probably a
more contemptuous foe than ever. And then the thought arose
—ought she to see him again? Would it not be wiser and
kinder to avoid any further interviews? She blushed to think
she had not hitherto avoided them as she ought—she might!
Well, now she would check the culpable. weakness; she would
be firm. If it were possible, after her interview with Mr. Wall
the next day, she would leave town on Saturday, and send a few
lines of polite acknowledgment to Galbraith. Of the lost five
pounds they had almost ceased to speak. She felt it was now
but an excuse for meeting. Not altogether blinded by his
tolerable assumption of friendliness, Kate had formed but a faint
idea of the depth and reality of Galbraith's passion for her. In
truth, though mature in some ways, especially in a genial mellow-
ness, resulting from richness of nature rather than the ripening
of time, Kate was only learning the A B C of love. As yet she did
not quite recognize the direction in which her own feelings were
drifting. The ice of an uncongenial marriage closing over the
warm currents of her heart kept it pure and free from all the
false mirage-like shadows of the real deity, but ready to receive
the fullest, deepest, most indelible impression of the true god
once he either smiled or frowned upon her.

As to her lover, whatever chance of recovery he might have
had before, the last week of quiet, delicious intercourse had
utterly swept away; and with all the force of his will he resolved
that nothing but her own resolute rejection of him should separate them. Her past might be doubtful. He felt certain she
could explain everything. That any shadow of dishonor should
ever dim those frank, fearless eyes, he would not for a moment

believe. Whatever was in the past or future, the spell of her presence had struck the imprisoned fountain of youth and joy that had so long lain congealed in the dark recesses of his soul, and all the world was changed to him.

Having fully determined to explain everything to Mr. Wall, and arrange, if possible, to leave town the next day without seeing Galbraith, Kate started to keep her appointment. It was nearly two years since she had gone into that well-remembered room, with a suppressed sensation of bitter wrath and defeat, to place the will that laid her fortunes low in the hands of the lawyer, and now she was taking the first step towards the recovery of her rights with feelings not a whit less painful.

"Well, Mrs. Travers," said Mr. Wall, a little stiffly, "this is a very unexpected visit indeed. I thought you had disappeared altogether."

"And you are not the least glad to see me?"

She took the lawyer's wrinkled hand as she spoke, smiling with pleasant reproachfulness.

"I confess I should have been better pleased had you treated me with more confidence, of which I flatter myself I am not undeserving," replied Mr. Wall, visibly relaxing.

"You deserve, and you have my best confidence, my dear sir. I know you are displeased at my concealing my abode from you."

"I am, and naturally. Nor was it judicious to have for your sole confidante a young man—a young man of attractive manners and appearance," he interrupted.

"Instead of one older, certainly, but similar in other respects."

"Ah, my dear lady, that will not do," returned Mr. Wall, smiling in spite of himself, so sweetly and brightly was this morsel of transparent flattery offered.

"Well, well, Mr. Wall, let us speak seriously. I am going to tell you everything—everything—under the seal of confession. Had you known my abode you would have persecuted me to accept Sir Hugh Galbraith's splendid offer of three hundred a year, would you not?"

"I certainly would have urged your acceptance of it," he returned, entrenching himself behind his professional manner once more.

"Well, you see I have escaped *that* by concealing my whereabouts," resumed his client. "Moreover, my chief reason for hiding it was to save you the shock you would have probably felt had you known that I had made up my mind to keep a shop, instead of adopting any genteeler method of earning my bread."

"A shop!" echoed Mr. Wall, infinitely surprised, not to say horrified. "My late respected friend and client's name over a shop!"

"Considering that you believe your respected client capable of leaving the wife he professed to love unprovided for, penniless, to battle alone with the world, you have no right to exclaim at any honest use I may put his name to," said Kate, very quietly. "But as I have a higher opinion of him than you have, and never will believe that he was guilty of the cruel will *you* accept, I preserved the respect due—you would say to his name, I say due to his natural prejudices—and did *not* put his name over my— shop,"—a little pause, an arch smile as she pronounced the obnoxious word. "Nay, more, Mr. Wall; I dropped the name altogether."

"Have you been living under a false name, then?" asked Mr. Wall, dryly, in a tone which implied the highest moral disapprobation, and not only expressed his real feeling, but was a *quid pro quo* for the tone of quiet rebuke she had adopted, and which nettled the orthodox lawyer, as showing too high a spirit of independence for a woman, and a poor woman to boot. Mr. Wall was a very good, honest man, but thoroughly imbued with the "respectability worship" which pervades so large and so valuable a section of English life. He flattered himself that he had the presumptuous young widow, who was after all only reduced to her original nothingness by her husband's eccentric will, at his foot, morally, by the admission she had just made. "You have been living under a false name, then?"

"Precisely," she replied, looking straight into his eyes, with an expression he did not quite like, and very different from the smile that played upon her softly-curved lips.

"And may I ask if you consider such a proceeding respectable?"

"I really never thought about it," she said, slightly raising her eyebrows. "I don't suppose *you* think so. Our habits of thought are no doubt widely different. At any rate, I adopted the name of Temple, and started in the Berlin-wool and fancywork line. You see my intercourse with poor Mr. Travers developed my commercial faculties," she went on, rapidly. "I established myself at the little seaside town of Pierstoffe; and I have succeeded fairly. I determined to wait there in humble independence until I could find some evidence on which to found an attempt to upset the will that robbed me. I have found it; and I am come to lay it before you."

As she spoke she drew forth a paper, in which she had written as shortly as possible an account of Tom Reed's interview with Poole; the expert's opinion; Captain Gregory's assertion that the will his father signed must have been executed before the 10th of March, and drawing the lawyer's attention to the great improbability that another totally different will had been made within ten days of that drawn out by Gregory. This she placed upon his desk.

" You are really a wonderful woman, Mrs. Travers," said Mr. Wall, with a sort of reluctant admiration. " Before I look at this, may I ask who supplied the capital for your undertaking ? "

" I did, myself. You know Sir Hugh Galbraith could not claim my jewels. I have been completely on my own resources ; and I owe no man, or woman either, anything."

Strange ! in that office she could speak of Galbraith with something of her old enmity.

The lawyer applied himself to the memoranda she had handed him, without another word : even in the eyes of respectability, a woman who can make money is free of this world's guild.

Kate sat very patiently while her adviser perused her statement slowly ; oh, how slowly. She even forced herself to take up a morning paper which lay on the office table, that Mr. Wall might feel at liberty to take his time. But she did not follow the arguments of the leader with much attention. She kept repeating to herself, " I must not be cast down by anything he says ; he will be sure to decry the value of this information." She kept very still, just speaking the exact words necessary to answer an occasional question.

At last, after what seemed a whole hour of suspense, Mr. Wall laid down the paper, stared for a moment or two across the room at vacancy, then, putting his hands in his pockets, he exclaimed, " This is very curious, very ! " Kate refrained from speaking, although he was looking to her for words. " I suppose it seems to you proof positive that the will under which Sir Hugh Galbraith takes—is a forgery ? "

" Presumptive, at any rate. What does it seem to you ? "

" Well—" long drawn out—" strongly presumptive, but not conclusive ; far from conclusive. Has Mr. Reed seen this man Poole ?—seen him, I mean, on this subject ? " tapping the paper.

" No. He rather fears opening it up to Poole, who is a silly sort of man, and still in the office. I suppose I must say Hugh Galbraith's office."

" I must see him. Though I do not wish to encourage any false hopes, Mrs. Travers, this matter must be looked into."

After some pertinent questioning and discussion, from which Kate gathered that the dry old lawyer was more favorable to her views than she had dared to hope, he observed : " It would be folly to open up the subject without securing ample proof, for it will be a costly battle. I need hardly remind you that justice is a costly commodity."

" It is ; but in this cause I am prepared to sacrifice all I possess."

"And suppose you are beaten ; how afterwards ? "

"With these, and this," holding out her hand, and then touching her brow, "I shall never starve." Then, after a moment's pause, "but we must not stir openly till we are certain of victory."

"When does your friend, Mr. Reed, return ? "

"On Tuesday or Wednesday next, I am almost sure."

"I think I shall wait for him before I take any step ; he is a shrewd fellow, as well as I remember, and *remarkably* interested in you."

"He is," returned Kate, smiling at the suspicion of her adviser's tone. "He has taken up my cause almost as warmly as if it was his own."

"No doubt, no doubt," said Mr. Wall, dryly. "I shall, then, have an able and willing assistant in him. Meantime, I shall look over these papers quietly this evening at home ; and I think I should like to see you to-morrow, when I have digested the pabulum you have brought me. Can you call about the same time ? "

"Certainly, Mr. Wall ; and if you are not likely to want me any more, I think I shall return to Pierstoffe to-morrow afternoon."

"Yes, to be sure. How do you manage about your shop when you are absent ? "—a little emphasis on " shop."

"I have a very capable assistant."

"Well, it was a curious idea to adopt that line of business."

Kate smiled.

"However," continued Mr. Wall, "there is no reason why you should not return to-morrow. I wish to see you only because I wish to give you a more careful opinion than I can offer after such a cursory glance at your case ; and I am most anxious to prevent your exciting yourself with unfounded hopes. These will cases are most difficult, most doubtful ; and you see your adversary is in possession. However," rising in token of dismissal, "I am sincerely interested in you, Mrs. Travers, though perhaps not so ardently as your friend, Mr. Reed, for I acknowl-. edge you have been hardly dealt by ; still, if I could have matters arranged as I should wish, I would not have Sir Hugh Galbraith disinherited either. I always looked upon him as Mr. Travers's adopted son—a fine, honorable, well-conducted young man ! and if you change places with him, the hardship will be shifted to his shoulders."

"I think with you," returned Kate, very earnestly. " Believe me, my motive is not to rob Hugh Galbraith, but to right myself. But when I succeed, my dear sir, I shall trust to your good offices to make a juster division between us than will then be legally possible. You know my theory—"

"There, there, there," interrupted the lawyer; "just as I thought; on this slender suggestion, rather than evidence, you think you have the property in your hand again! And pray what is your theory?"

"I am not quite so sanguine, I assure you," said she, smiling; "though I confess to believing that at the other side of a range of difficulties we shall find success. As to my theory, I believe my late husband did make a second will, and one far more just, probably providing well for me, but leaving the bulk of his property to Hugh Galbraith; and it is for this that the present will has been substituted."

"But by whom, my dear madam, by whom? There is not a soul interested in the matter save yourself and Sir Hugh."

"That is just what we must find out," replied Kate. She could not bring herself to reveal her true convictions to that dry old lawyer. She was always so ashamed of acknowledging Ford's feelings towards her, it seemed such a lowering of herself. "But I must not keep you," she added, hastily, and bidding Mr. Wall good morning, she walked slowly down B—— Street, settling her plans in her own mind. There was a train to Stoneborough at one twenty, which would enable her to catch a little, sleepy, local one to Pierstoffe at six, and so she would be ready for a quiet, peaceful Sunday at home, without any chance of a disturbing, interesting, irritating visit from Hugh Galbraith, whose sombre eyes had of late acquired such a variety of expression, and had begun to produce an effect upon herself she could neither account for nor resist. Small chance indeed of ever meeting him on any terms again. Soon he would be plunged into trouble enough to obliterate any fanciful notions about herself. And then when he knew all! She would not try to imagine his possible condition of mind.

Coming back to the present, Kate remembered she had put a list which Fanny had sent, of divers and sundry articles required for the "Bazaar," in her pocket, and she would now go on to the City and procure them, so that, after her interview with Mr. Wall the next day, she should have nothing to do but to drive to the train. She accordingly made her way to Holborn, and took "omnibus" to Cheapside.

It was past four o'clock, and already dusk, when Kate neared her abode. She felt weary and utterly cast down. True, Mr. Wall was on the whole less unfavorable than she ventured to hope; true, she would be to-morrow in her safe, quiet home; still her native buoyancy seemed to have deserted her. As she walked rather slowly along, she turned over in her mind the terms in which she would write to Hugh Galbraith. Her note must be friendly, neither too warm or too cold; slightly playful, she thought would be best.   Here a hansom dashed by; the occupant glanced through the window, stopped the driver, descended, and paid him hastily; turning in the opposite direction from whence he came, he was speedily face to face with Mrs. Temple, who had recognized the tall, straight figure directly he had sprung to the ground.

" This is a bit of good fortune for an unlucky fellow, as I generally am," said Galbraith, raising his hat and speaking with a degree of animation that formerly was very unusual to him. " If I had not been looking this side, I should have driven on to your lodgings and missed you again."

" I thought you were to be at Richmond to-day," said Kate, whose composure was severely tried by his unexpected appearance, the color coming up in her pale cheek, and then leaving it paler than before.

" My sister writes to me to go to-morrow instead, so I have run up to see you to-day," returned Galbraith, walking on beside her, his eyes riveted on her face for a few unguarded seconds.

" And I suppose there is no news of my purse?" said Kate, quickly.

" None, I am sorry to say; in fact, I have come to tell you there is nothing to tell."   Galbraith twisted his moustaches and smiled as he spoke.

" It is a long way to come for nothing," exclaimed Kate, incautiously, and wished immediately she had not spoken, though Hugh only remarked:

" For nothing—yes."

A few minutes silence, and they were at Mrs. Temple's lodging.   Galbraith, without waiting for any invitation, followed her in very deliberately.

" Dear, dear, your fire is near out, ma'am," cried the landlady, as she threw open the door of the little front parlor.   " I will bring a few sticks and make it burn up in a jiffey."

" Do, Mrs. Small," said Kate, a chill feeling striking through her with a visible shiver.   " I am cold and tired."

The landlady lit the gas, and bustled away.

" You look tired and pale," said Galbraith, advancing to the hearthrug and leaning his elbow on the mantel-piece while he gazed kindly and gravely upon her.   " I suppose I ought to leave you?"   He spoke with the curious familiarity which had grown up between them.

" You may stay a while if you like," she returned in the same tone, and urged to the words by a strange reluctance to part with him all at once, without a little more talk, perhaps a last argument. The return of Mrs. Small, and the lighting up of the fire, was a seasonable diversion ; and while the operation was in progress Kate loosened her cloak and took off her bonnet, with the easy, graceful naturalness that was one of her great charms in Galbraith's eyes, seating herself in her favorite low chair, her hands clasped upon her knee, without once looking in the glass to see if her hair was rough or smooth.

"And you," began Galbraith, drawing a chair opposite— "have you seen this absentee lawyer of yours yet ? "

" Yes ; I have had a long interview with him to-day."

" Hence these—not tears, but pale cheeks ? " said Galbraith.

" No, indeed ; my interview was less crushing than I feared."

" That is, you are encouraged to go to law ? "

" Almost."

" If it is 'almost' only, take my advice and don't."

" Your advice ! You are not much of a lawyer, Sir Hugh."

" Perhaps not." A pause followed.

" Do you know," resumed Galbraith, "it was only a week yesterday since I met you at H——"

" Only a week ! It seems a year ago," said Kate, dreamily.

" It does," he returned ; "and it seems two or three since I looked up and met your murderous glance the day you were first good enough to write a letter for me at Pierstoffe."

This was dangerous ground, and Kate determined to lead away from it as soon as possible.

" How can you persist in such absurdity ! It was a sickly fancy of yours that I looked murderously at you. Why should I ?—you, a stranger I had never seen in my life before ? "

" It was no fancy, Mrs. Temple ! I shall never forget your look, and I have seen something like it since in your eyes."

" There is no use in arguing with you, I know, on that subject. Pray, do you ever feel any inconvenience from your arm now, Sir Hugh ? "

" No ; it is all right when I do not think of it. But sometimes when I do, I hesitate about using it ; " and he stretched it out and bent it. " And when are you to be released from your solitude here, and restored to your pretty little partner and Mrs. Mills ? "

" I am not perfectly sure yet ; not till I see the lawyer to-morrow : but soon, I am sure. By the way, Sir Hugh, you had better give me the inspector's name and address, that I may send him mine at Pierstoffe, in case he should recover my money."

" I can do that for you. It is just possible he might not like to give you your own except through me."

" Will you do this for me then ? "

"I will."

"Are you going to make any stay in town," she asked next, to break the silence.

"My movements are very uncertain. I find my friend Upton is going into your neighborhood next week. He is going to stay with Lady Styles, who is some relation of his."

"Oh, indeed!" in a rather dissatisfied tone; "and are you to be of the party?"

"No, I am not invited. I suppose I shall drift away back to the very tumble-down home of my fathers, if no good reason arises for staying in the south."

"And have you given up all idea of going into Parliament?"

"Far from it, but I have postponed that project. Next year I shall think of adding myself to the 'obstructives,' as I think I heard you once say, Mrs. Temple."

"I hope you will not! I do hope not!" she exclaimed. "You really must look about you and read, and convince yourself that it is a terrible waste of time and strength to attach yourself to the Conservative faction. It is impossible to stand still."

"Is it not rare to meet so decided a democrat as you are, Mrs. Temple, among women?"

"I do not know; and I do not think I am what is generally considered a democrat—that is, I am more disposed to raise up than to pull down." She spoke carelessly, without the earnestness and animation she usually displayed when discussing any topic that interested her. Galbraith noticed this, and persisted with his subject, fearing that if any longer pause ensued he would be compelled to leave her.

"And how far down would you extend your raising system?"

"To any depth where human life exists."

"And then, when all are masters, how would the work of the world go on?"

"Ah, Sir Hugh, you ask that because you do not take the trouble to think! Obedience is not the virtue of the ignorant. Who, in all dangerous or difficult expeditions, bears hardship and privation best? Who is the most subordinate, submitting cheerfully, for the sake of discipline, even to regulations the wisdom of which he doubts? The cultivated gentleman."

"Yes, that is true enough; but in ordinary life cultivated gentlemen would not be satisfied with rough labor—plowing fields and making railways; and we *must* have hewers of wood and drawers of water."

"By the time all men are wrought up to such a pitch we shall have found some substitute for hard manual labor, which, by the way, has nothing in it degrading; and God knows we are at so great, so enormous a distance from even a decent platform of education and habit—I mean among our lower classes—that the most rigid Tory among you might safely give a helping hand without fearing that a day of disabling cultivation will arrive too soon. But it is always the same. I suppose when slavery began to die out in England the Galbraiths of that day (I suppose there were Galbraiths then) thought the country was going to the dogs, and that law, order, property were endangered."

Galbraith smiled. "Still, if men are raised to a higher state of intelligence and cultivation, they will demand political power, and we know what *that* is in the hands of the multitude."

"Not a cultivated multitude," she replied, "we have never seen that. I do not think you make sufficient allowance for the natural common sense of Englishmen. Besides, I have a sort of dim notion that political rights are an education in themselves; a sense of responsibility makes a man think—teaches him self-respect. If a child is forever in leading-strings he cannot learn to stand alone. The French were in leading-strings all the hundreds of years of their national life, till the supreme moment when, with mature passion but childish intellect, they burst their bonds, and gave Europe a picture awful and horrible enough, but not worse than might have been logically expected."

"You think, then, that we ought to have no political privileges beyond those of our laborers and artisans?"

"My ideas are crude," said Kate, thoughtfully; "but I do believe that the key to the real position of what is termed the ruling class was given to us more than eighteen hundred and fifty years ago in the sentence, 'Whoever will be chief among you, let him be your servant.'"

"You are quite original, Mrs. Temple!"

"I wish I could think so," she said, smiling; "but I don't suppose I ever had an original idea in my life. My highest attainment is to understand other people's ideas. However, I have not converted you—I can see that, nor do I expect it; but I should be pleased if I could persuade you to believe there are two sides to the conservative question. Your opinions are of some importance, mine have none, except to myself."

"I'm not quite so pig-headed a fellow as you imagine," returned Galbraith, laughing. "I shall not bind myself hand and foot to any leader; but, though I do not like to see the people oppressed, as long as I live I shall do my best to keep them in their place."

"What is their place?" asked Kate. "Would you go back to the caste system of Egypt?"

But Galbraith had gained his point. He had drawn her out to talk and smile with animation and interest; and odious as political women generally, indeed always, were, there was a simple sincerity about Mrs. Temple's opinions that made them not only bearable, but pleasant to listen to. He did not pursue the subject. "You have great facilities for studying politics. I remember you take in lots of newspapers at Pierstoffe. By the way, how does Miss Lee get on without you?"

"Very badly, I imagine, which makes me so impatient at being kept so long here; and I miss her much! We are great friends."

"Yes; you gave me that idea. Do you never quarrel?"

"No; do you and—who is your great friend?—Colonel Upton?"

Galbraith bent his head.

"Do you and Colonel Upton never quarrel?"

"No; but I don't know how it would be if we were shut up in a small room or shop together all day, like Miss Lee and yourself."

"Well, we are always good friends. To be sure, Fanny gives up to me in everything. I am afraid I am rather imperious."

"I am afraid you are," said Galbraith, gravely.

"You cannot possibly know!" she returned, in some surprise.

"At any rate," continued Galbraith, "two imperious people never could get on; but when I hear Upton say that no such thing as friendship exists between women (he is a shocking heathen, Mrs. Temple), I always think of you and Miss Lee. He is equally sceptical, I am sorry to say, about friendship between men and women," and Galbraith stole a glance at her as he spoke.

"One doesn't often see it, I am afraid," she said, frankly, looking straight into the fire; "and it is such a loss. Women will never be in a right position until hearty, honest friendships with men are of everyday occurrence."

"I am afraid, then, your right position is a long way off. It is all very well to discuss opinions and exchange ideas with an old woman, or an ugly one; but," continued Galbraith, with a mixture of fun and admiration, "when one is talking to a lovely creature, or even a pretty girl, one's thoughts are apt to be distracted by the beautiful eyes that meet your own, or the sweet lips that contradict you!"

"Ah, Sir Hugh," exclaimed Kate, "you make me understand how it is that plain women have called forth the deepest, truest, highest love! The feeling that is always being influenced by the accident of personal gifts is ignoble and unworthy."

"Perhaps so," returned Galbraith, "but it is uncommonly natural; though I will not allow you to set me down as a devotee of merely physical beauty! I could not care for a beautiful fool. Indeed, I do not believe a fool could be beautiful; but I confess that, with me, friendship for a lovely, companionable woman would very soon warm into love—unless, indeed, I had already given that love to another."

"Is he warning me that he is provided with a safeguard?" was the thought that flashed through her brain as he made a slight pause, and then resumed:

"But in that case I doubt if I should have even friendship to spare." And as he spoke Galbraith leaned his folded arms on the table, bending his head towards her with wistful eyes that set her heart beating, and turned her cheek pale with apprehension.

"It is a vexed question," she said, coldly. "Let us hope the happy solution may be found in the future perfection which some think our race will reach."

The severe composure of her tone checked Galbraith. He kept silence for a moment, telling himself he must not spoil his chance by precipitation; and she looked so sad and quiet, and unlike her own frank, fearless self, that a tender dread of disturbing her unnecessarily, held him back. He was learning and developing rapidly in Love's school. Then he would see her again, and again—and win his way at last!

Meantime Kate looked at her watch. "I am going to treat you unceremoniously, as an old acquaintance," she said, smiling away the abruptness of her words; "but I have letters to write, and—"

"And I have kept you too long from them," interrupted Galbraith, rising, but not in the least ruffled. "I shall see you to-morrow."

"You are going to Richmond, are you not?"

"True; well, on Sunday, then—and hear when you leave."

"It all depends upon the lawyer," she returned, in a low voice. "Good bye, Sir Hugh Galbraith."

He took the hand she held out, pressing it close, tighter than he knew, and kept it, still not daring to trust himself to speak. Kate strove to withdraw it, and grew so deadly white, while she compressed her lips with a look of pain, that a sudden sense of coming evil struck him. He relinquished her hand, and with a hasty "Good bye—God bless you!" turned quickly away.

CHAPTER XXXVI.

KATE was astir early next day, and having settled her land-lady's claims, started away to deposit her luggage at the station before calling on Mr. Wall. She also posted a little note for Galbraith,—very short, saying good bye kindly, decidedly. "But where is the use of my decision?" she reflected. "He is so obstinate, that unless he chooses to give me up of his own accord, he will come down to Pierstoffe again! I trust I have impressed him with the conviction that it is useless to think of me. I would not for any consideration do him an atom more mischief than I can help." As she thought, how clearly she saw him as he looked across the table at her the evening before, and felt again the thrill his eyes had sent through her, she was quite glad to reach Mr. Wall's office, that she might get rid of the haunting idea of Hugh Galbraith.

Mr. Wall had nothing different to say from the day before. He was much impressed by the bearing of the evidence he had been studying. Still, the want of some connecting link, the doubt as to whom he should first attack, made him hesitate. So the result of Kate's interview with the cautious lawyer was the same as before. Nothing was to be done till after consultation with Mr. Reed.

"By the way, Mrs. Travers," said Mr. Wall, as she was about to take leave of him, "I wish you would let me have your version of the quarrel or disagreement between yourself and Mr. Travers, of which Ford, as well as I remember, made a good deal at the time we were discussing this unfortunate will, and its possible cause?"

"Did Ford make a good deal of it?" she replied, looking at him earnestly. "It was a trifle, but an unpleasant one. At the time of my old friend and benefactor Mr. Lee's death, I knew that his granddaughter, my former playfellow, was left in sore need. I sent her a sum of money, which I could well spare from my ample allowance, but I did not think it necessary to inform my husband. Her letter acknowledging it fell into Mr. Travers's hands, and he was more annoyed than I could have expected. He was ill and querulous. I fear I was not as patient as I ought to have been. He spoke to me as he never spoke before or since, as I would rather not remember. Unfortunately Mr. Ford was waiting in the back drawing-room to see Mr. Travers, while this took place,—not with closed doors, I regret to say. He overheard, and presumed afterwards to remind me of it. That is the whole story, and pray remember, that for upwards of nine months after that occurrence I was Mr. Travers's constant, trusted companion. Believe me, Ford has his own object for dwelling on such a trifle." —

"Then do you imagine Ford had any hand in substituting this present will for the true one?"

"I do."

"Very extraordinary, very! A rather groundless suspicion, it seems to me. Why do you suspect him?"

" Because I think he wished to injure me."

" Injure you ! I never saw a man more indignant than he was at the injustice done you ! "

" Well, Mr. Wall, you must hear Tom Reed on that subject ; you will accept his opinion more readily than mine."

" I think I always respect your opinion. But you have not told me everything about the quarrel ? It is so hard sometimes to get hold of real facts."

" Do you imagine I pervert them ? " asked Kate, as she held out her hand to say good bye.

" No, no," returned the lawyer, taking it cordially. He was always won over to her by a personal interview, although in her absence the old indignation and wrath against her, for having fooled his friend and client, would assert itself. " I have your address, but I confess it goes against me to write to you under your false name—"

Home, if one's abiding place deserves that name, is very sweet. Warm and tender was the welcome which awaited Mrs. Temple (the name seemed quite natural to her when she reached Pierstoffe). It was closing-time when she arrived ; and as she had kept up the fiction even to herself, that Mr. Wall might have changed his mind and asked her to remain in town, she had not written to announce her return.

When, therefore, she opened the parlor door, Fanny gave a small shriek of joy and surprise, darting forward to hug her heartily ; then Mills came in, full of motherly thought for her probable needs of food and rest and warmth, as the weather was damp and raw, Kate felt all the power that springs from our social instincts—the strength and wisdom and self-control, and all goodness to which love and sympathy help us. She felt she could face her destiny whatever it might be with double, nay treble courage and constancy, here in her fortress of home, and hearts dependent on her, than she could in the solitude of London, where her one companion was becoming too necessary.

" Oh, Kate, dear ! How delightful to have you back again. I felt so wretched when there was no letter from you this morning. I fancied all sorts of things except your coming back. I am sure you have been worried to death. I declare you look quite pale and thin."

" I have been worried, Fan."

" Now here is some nice buttered toast ; you must be perfectly dying for a cup of tea ! When you have taken it, you must begin at the beginning and tell me everything. I never knew anything half so extraordinary and romantic as your meeting Hugh Galbraith. Have you had any news of the purse ?

No! I am afraid it is gone! And what did Mr. Wall say? I never liked him, he is such a stiff old thing. Oh, by the way, I had such a nice long letter from Tom; it came by the midday delivery. He hopes to be in London on Wednesday morning, but he will be so busy that he fears he cannot come down for a week to see me—I mean us. And do you know he comes back chief editor."

" I suppose so; and wants to install a commander-in-chief as soon as possible. Eh, Fanny?"

"Oh, he must not be in a hurry," saucily. "And, Kate, do you know I had a visit from that dreadful man to-day!"

" Is it possible!"

" Yes. I felt frightened to death; but I sha'n't mind now you are here. I was dusting the shelves about ten o'clock, when I heard the door bell ring violently, as if the door had been pushed open with great force, and when I turned round there was my gentleman, looking a shade more horrible than before!"

" How curious! What did he say?"

" Oh, he asked me how I was, and said I looked as lovely as the flowers in May. Then he laughed so impudently, and said, ' Is the missis at home?' And I said, very dignified, ' Do you mean Mrs. Temple?' 'Exactly, precisely; Mrs. Temple?' he said, in a sort of mocking tone. ' Well, she is away at present.' Then he asked when you would be back, and I said, ' I really could not tell.' He seemed very anxious about that, and said at last, ' Do you think she will be back next week?' And I said. ' I thought you would.' And then he took off his hat, and desired his compliments to Mrs. Temple. I fancied he put a sort of emphasis on your name."

" You think he did, Fan! Depend upon it, then, he knows me. Perhaps he wants me to give him money? I shall not do that. If any difficulty arises about my identity, I shall drop my disguise. Yet I want to win my cause first. I want to share with Hugh Galbraith before he knows he is under any obligation to his landlady."

" Poor Sir Hugh! Did you see him again—I mean after you met him at H——?"

" Oh, yes, he came several times about my purse."

Fanny put her head on one side, and looked a little mischievous; but she did not like to worry Kate just on her return home, especially as she looked depressed and weary. So, with praiseworthy self-control, she kept silence for a few moments, hoping that Kate might unfold some more of her London adventures. And after the revivifying effect of a cup of tea she did—that chapter at least which related to her interview with Mr. Wall. But Fanny listened in vain for any further scraps of information about Hugh Galbraith. Kate named him no more.

" What an unsatisfactory old wretch Mr. Wall is, to be sure,"
said Fanny, meditatively, when Kate had finished her recital.
" I dare say he will create all sorts of difficulties, just to make
out that he is very clever to get over them."

" My success or failure does not depend on Mr. Wall," said
Kate, pushing away her cup. " I see myself how imperfect my
case looks without some distinct evidence to fill up the hiatus.
I do hope that man Trapes will reappear. I can't help imagining that he has something to do with Ford, and can give me
the information we want."

Mrs. Temple settled herself quickly to her ordinary routine,
and was to all appearance more absorbed than ever in her business. For the various neighbors and customers who dropped
in to welcome her return, she had a pleasant word of greeting—
a bright, pointed answer. She bore the brunt of a heavy charge
from Lady Styles, in line as it were, that is, unprepared, and
foiled her ladyship with charming frankness and beautiful good
breeding.

" Well," said Lady Styles, towards the end of the encounter,
" I am very glad you are back. You always know exactly what
one wants; not that I have any complaint to make of this
young lady—you are all ladies now, you know. She is very attentive, and all that sort of thing ; but there is no one like Mrs.
Temple. Ha, ha, ha! I wonder if you will turn out a countess
in disguise, my dear ! "

" I am afraid not, even to oblige you, Lady Styles."

" What has become of that agreeable young man I had tea
with, ha, ha, ha, ha !—the evening Sir Hugh Galbraith's leg
was broken ? "

" He is in London as usual, I suppose."

" Suppose ! Ah, my dear, that won't do. *I* suppose one or
other of you hear from him every day ? Which is it ? "

" Both," returned Kate, smiling. " He manages all our
business, and that necessitates frequent correspondence."

" And has Sir Hugh never made his appearance since ? "

" I do not think he ever visits Pierstoffe."

" Well, so much the better," nodding her head knowingly.
" He was not at all a proper sort of inmate for a handsome
young woman like you. You are well rid of him. To be sure
he is not a scamp like his friend, my cousin Upton. He is such
a stiff, stand-off sort of creature. I suppose he wouldn't deign
to have the weaknesses of other men. But though Willie Upton
is a '*vaurien*,' he is such a pleasant fellow ; always good-humored, always full of fun, that I am inclined to give him plenary
absolution. I hope he will get longer leave, and come down to

15

me next week. He is such a help when the house is full. But he is up in town with his chum, Sir Hugh ; and I think he wants me to ask him, but I will *not*. I consider that man Galbraith behaved most rudely to me. He refused every invitation I sent him ; and when I took the trouble of going upstairs here, to ask how he was getting on, he was as glum and taciturn as—oh, as I don't know what."

" Very rude, indeed," echoed Mrs. Temple, sympathizingly.

" I want two skeins of floss-silk and half an ounce of wool to finish grounding that banner-screen I bought here last spring. There, my dear, match that yellow and green for me. Do you know Mrs. Temple, your prices are very high. Lady Eccleston was spending a few days with us (Lord Eccleston is that great Welsh mine-owner—doesn't know the end of his wealth, they say; his grandfather drove black bullocks—you know those long-horned, wild-looking creatures—to the market-town, and never was married, but they don't mind that in Wales) ; well, Lady Eccleston was telling me there is a shop somewhere in a street off Holborn where she can get a lovely pattern and the wools to work it, for five-and-ninepence or five-and-ninepence-halfpenny. Now, *you* would charge eight or nine shillings."

" I should like to see the pattern and the wools," said Mrs. Temple.

" Ha, ha, ha ! very fair," etc., etc., etc.

*   *   *   *   *   *

Doctor Slade, too, came to welcome the fair widow back.

" Seemed quite unnatural not to see your face in the shop as I passed by, though you have not lost much by being away; bad weather banished the visitors earlier than usual. There has been a tremendous blow-up at the Turners'. The old man has been very dissatisfied with the elegant Mr. Joseph. He has been away and unaccounted for on several occasions; but about ten days or a fortnight ago a very fishy-looking individual —a sort of betting-man—swaggered into the shop, half-drunk, wanting Turner, junior ; swore he owed him money, and struck the old man, when he attempted to put him out. There's been the devil-to-pay, I can tell you. Poor Mrs. Turner had a nervous attack through it, and young hopeful has never come back, but I believe they know where he is."

This and much more gossip did the Doctor communicate, and then observed that Mrs. Temple did not look the better for her trip to Town—offered to prescribe for her, and, on being smilingly refused, took his shirt-frill, his ruddy, black-eyed physiognomy, his formidable white teeth, and long, lank self away.

" Why, Fanny, dear, this unfortunate young Turner has

evidently been Trapes's attraction, and in some mysterious way he has recognized you!" exclaimed Mrs. Temple, as soon as they were alone. "This plot is thickening. I feel so anxious about that man, anxious to see him, and yet fearful."

But though Kate thus upheld herself with courage and composure, her heart behaved itself very differently. The strained feeling of expectation and unrest drove sleep from her pillow, and her ordinary appetite from her meals.

She felt the deepest anxiety to know what line of conduct Mr. Wall and Tom would decide upon after their consultation. A few lines from the latter had announced his return, but no more. Then she felt surprised, and although she did not admit it even to herself, disappointed that Galbraith had taken no notice of her sudden departure, of her little note. It was quite wise and proper of him not to write (unless indeed he had any tidings of her lost purse), but it was not exactly the style of wisdom she should have expected from him. It was not to be wondered at of course, considering the struggle pending between them, that Galbraith should be constantly in her thoughts, but it sometimes troubled her to find how her memory was haunted by his voice, which, though deep and harsh, was far from inexpressive ; by his eyes, which she wondered she had ever thought sombre and stern ; by his tall, gaunt, but not undignified figure. How much he had improved since he had been carried into her house, looking like death—and, above all, how fond he was of her. This crowning merit she was compelled to acknowledge, and yet she scarcely knew the power it gave him over herself. To be loved —heartily, honestly loved by a man in whose mind is no wavering or irresolution or calculation is, to a woman of Kate Travers's calibre, almost irresistible, provided the lover is personally presentable, and not beneath her in character. Grateful and loving by nature, she could not undervalue a gift because it was cast unreservedly at her feet, as other and lower-class women would, and do. At first she had been startled and offended at the abrupt, and she considered presumptuous, manner in which Galbraith had asked her to be his wife ; but the way he had borne her refusal had touched a sympathetic cord in her heart, and now their long, friendly conversations during her London loneliness had shown her there was more stuff in her enemy than she had given him credit for. He was not a cultivated nor an intellectual man, but he was prompt to see his way in whatever direction he wanted to go ; resolute in purpose, with a controlled fire under his cold exterior, that threatened not to be quite so easily managed as she once imagined. Then he was so straightforward ! It made her heart throb to think how he would receive the intelligence that she had to a certain extent played him false, and won his love while she was preparing to win his fortune too !

What would he think of her ? If he despised her, good bye to love from him ! And though she did not wish to win it, how should she like to lose his love ? Would she ever find anything like it again ?—so true, so regardless of circumstances—the most objectionable that could be imagined to a man brimful of class prejudices as Hugh Galbraith was—and how was she going to reward his affection ! Would he permit her to act Providence to him, and restore with one hand what she took with the other ? " He must—he shall ! " was generally the conclusion of her reverie.

But this constant struggle in her heart wore her spirits, and a secret belief that Galbraith would suddenly appear, kept her on the alert. Still a sort of gentle humility, not always natural to her—a sort of doubt as to the wisdom and rectitude of her own conduct—made her most patient and forbearing. Nevertheless, Fanny's true heart, unerring in its instincts, saw that she was very unlike herself; and when at last, about ten days after her return, Kate received Tom's long-expected report, Fanny was shocked to see how pale she turned, and how her hand shook as she opened the letter.

The information contained in it was to the following effect: Tom Reed had seen Mr. Wall immediately on his reaching London, and had arranged a meeting with him and Captain Gregory (who was sufficiently recovered to travel) ; they together visited Doctors' Commons, taking with them the two signatures for comparison, and accompanied by the expert. The result of a careful examination was that they considered Gregory's signature false, Mr. Travers's doubtful, but all agreed with C——(the expert) that Poole's was genuine. " This," continued Reed's epistle, " is not at all what either Mr. Wall or myself anticipated ; however, we have agreed to take an opinion on the case, and will be guided by it. I have fortunately found out a man who remembers seeing Trapes at the Reepham Steeplechase on the date we want to prove, and also remembers that he was with another, who answers to Poole's description. I must get this fellow (he is an occasional sporting correspondent) to go and see Poole on some pretext, although I cannot believe that Poole knowingly signed a forged will. Time will show, and we must collect all possible evidence ; for however morally sure these small indications may make *us*, they are far from being proof positive.

" I shall endeavor, if possible, to run down and see you next Saturday, by which time we may know what course counsel recommends."

"It will be a long uncertainty, I am afraid," said Kate with a sigh—a quivering, anxious sigh—to Fanny, who had read the letter over her shoulder. "I only desire that, for or against me, it may be soon decided."

"Oh, you must not think of 'against,'" said Fanny, kissing her brow affectionately. "It never can go against any one so kind and generous and gentle as you are. I really should feel ever so much happier, if you would be just a little cross and un-reasonable—just to relieve your heart, you know! It's inhuman to be so quiet and—and like an angel, when I know you feel miserable and broken-hearted." The tears stood in Fanny's eyes as she spoke. "I know you do," she repeated; "I have seen you angry and sad, but never quite like you are now."

"*Resurgam!*" cried Kate, laughing, and returning her kiss. "I will do my best to be disagreeable, if that is any comfort to you. I *am* rather down-hearted just now, but it will pass away, and I shall be myself again."

CHAPTER XXXVII.

THE day after she had received Tom's letter, Kate's nervous depression culminated in an intense, disabling headache. She bore up against it bravely all the morning ; but after their early dinner she could endure the shop no longer.

"I think the air might do me good," said she to Fanny. "I will ask Mills to give me a cup of strong tea, and then I will creep along the beach, and perhaps rest awhile under the broken cliff. It is as bright and almost as warm as summer."

"Do so, dear," replied Fanny. "It is the best thing for your head, and I feel quite independent of your help in the shop, quite self-reliant ; equal to setting up an opposition over the way."

It was a St. Martin's summer's day, one of those brief smiles which the departing season sometimes turns to throw back to us before she is quite gone. The morning had been thick, but towards noon the mist had rolled nearly away, leaving a silvery haze out to sea, under which the water lay blue and still, just stirred with a sleepy ripple, and thinly edged with white where it lapped the shore as the tide stole in. Little birds twittered among the brambles and bushes of the North Cliff, and the click of the capstan came with a mellow ring across the water from a coal brig, which looked fairy-like through the faint mist, where the crew were heaving the anchor. "This is reviving," thought Kate, thankfully inhaling the briny air as she passed the North Parade houses, and leaving the path to the coast-guard's landing-place on the left, kept along the beach to where a mass of fragments had fallen from the cliff above and scattered themselves over the sand. There was a slight indentation in the shore just here, so that many of the fallen rocks were never washed by the sea, even at high water, and were, therefore, more or less covered with a growth of weeds and briers, but the smaller pieces had rolled further seaward. Advancing to where the wavelets were stealing up with a soft, caressing murmur, Kate stood awhile to enjoy the peaceful beauty of sea and sky, then retreating a few paces, seated herself on a small piece of rock apparently broken from a larger neighbor close to where it lay. She drew forth a number of 'Household Words' she had caught up as she left the house, hoping by its help to avoid dwelling fruitlessly on the problem of her own affairs.

But her thoughts were wandering and rebellious; they would not occupy themselves with the page before her, but kept darting away with irrelevant topics, presenting dioramas of old scenes,—her home at Cullingford, the German school where she had passed some busy, happy, materially uncomfortable days; her husband's death-bed—this came back very vividly.

She had not sat long thus thinking or dreaming, when she fancied she heard something like a step, an unsteady step, stumbling among the shingle which here and there lay over the smooth sand. She did not heed it at first concluding it was some boy hunting for winkles, or one of the fishermen, most of whom were known to her. But the step approached. With a sudden feeling of apprehension she turned to look, and beheld a man of middle height, with a red nose, and small, fierce, red-rimmed eyes, a hat not worn out, but though new, visibly bent in at one side : a sort of green shooting-coat, and leggings buttoned to the knee, but buttoned awry ; a short stick in his hand, and a short pipe in his mouth, completed his very disreputable appearance. Moreover, to her dismay, Kate observed an unsteadiness about his knees, a look of severe wisdom in his once tolerable-looking face. " Good heavens," she said, in her heart. " It must be Trapes, and he is tipsy ! " The next moment he raised his battered hat with an attempt at high-bred style, and said, " I think I have the honor of speaking to Mrs. Travers ? " advancing disagreeably close.

" My name is Temple," she returned, coldly, but keeping a brave front.

" Oh, Temple, is it," with a burst of insolent laughter. Then suddenly changing to profound gravity, he took his pipe out of his mouth, and waving it in the air gracefully, repeated, " Temple,—quite right in one sense ! Temple is the correct thing— shrine—what-you-call-'em for a beautiful goddess, eh ? "

Another sudden peal of laughter, as suddenly turned into stern gravity. "Now, then, Mrs. Temple Travers, compliments being passed, let us proceed to business—I say business! Let's sit down;" and, suiting the action to the word, he took the seat Mrs. Temple had just quitted. "Sit down, won't you, and we can talk comfortably—lots of room," he continued, drawing so close to the edge of the piece of rock that he nearly toppled over.

Kate, dreadfully puzzled what to do or say, frightened at his condition, yet not liking to lose the chance of discovering what was the mysterious link, if any, between him and Ford, said, as civilly and composedly as she could, "Thank you, I have been sitting for some time, and prefer standing now."

"Oh, well, please yourself Mrs. Travers Temple. You see I do not like to contradict a lady, but the last time I saw you, you were Mrs. Travers. Yes, you were."

"Where have you seen me?" asked Kate, graciously.

"At Hampton Court, with a young fellow called Reed. Do you know Tom Reed?"

"I do," returned Kate at once, seeing that the man really recognized her.

"He is a blackguard—a great blackguard!" returned Trapes, with solemn disapprobation. "I was like a father to that young man, Mrs. Temple Travers, like a father, 'pon my life! When he was first up in town, and one of the biggest greenhorns you ever came across; and now—" Trapes shook his head in silence, and replacing the pipe in his mouth, essayed to smoke, but in vain. "My pipe's out," said he, again waving it before him. "A common expression, you'll observe, but there is a good deal of pathos in it for all that. My pipe's out! I've drawn too hard and quick, and the 'baccy is gone, and nothing is left but the scent of the weed, which hangs round it still; so with life— my life—but," with sudden energy, "this is wandering from the point. As I was saying, I was the making of that fellow Reed. He hasn't an idea he did not filch from me. 'Who steals my purse steals trash,' eh? Well, would he lend me a fipun note now, as between two gentlemen? No, not to save my life! And that brings me to my point again. Will you, madam, have the goodness to *give* me five pounds? for I wish to be perfectly correct in all my dealings, and it is not my intention to return it." He lifted his hat as he said this, and re-placed it, considerably on one side, with a defiant air. Kate looked earnestly at him, trying to find out how far she might venture to speak rationally. He was not so very drunk after all. She would see on what he founded his claim for five pounds.

"And why should I give you money?" she said, smiling, "though you say you know me, I certainly do not know you. Why should I give you five pounds?"

"For value to be received," he returned. "For, 'pon my soul, if you trust me to that extent," an attempt at refinement of tone sadly marred by a drunken wink, "you shall receive cent. per cent., or rather four or five hundred per cent. on the capital advanced."

"Of course I should be very pleased to secure such a splendid return for so small an outlay," said Kate, pleasantly. "Tell me a little more about it."

"Ah, ha! Mrs. Temple, or Travers, or whatever you choose to call yourself, you are deep—deuced deep—but it won't do! I'll not let you pump me, and leave me high and dry afterwards. No, no; you must have faith, madam! Look here, now. It's a d——d shame to see a woman like you behind a beggarly counter, cheated out of your own, and all by a dirty trick! Now suppose I—"

Kate listened with the utmost avidity, seeing which, Trapes, with drunken cunning, broke off suddenly, and burst into a rude boisterous laugh. "No, no," he repeated, "that would be telling."

"Well, you must remember that, right or wrong, I am a poor woman now, and five pounds is a large sum. I might not hesitate if I knew what I am to give it for."

"If you are poor, I am sorry for you. I feel for you from the bottom of this blighted heart." Trapes's eyes filled, and almost overflowed with emotion. "Then, hark in your ear! as the stage fellows say. I can set wrong right! on my honor as a gentleman."

"Then," replied Kate, her heart beating, burning to hear more, yet not liking to talk longer with him in his present condition, "come to my house this evening, and we can discuss matters. You will find me neither unjust or illiberal. You know where I live." She bent her head to him and moved away.

"Stop a bit," cried Trapes, starting up and placing himself so as to cut off her retreat. "My dear creature, I am exceedingly sorry to be so pressing, but I haven't a rap; not a rap, 'pon my soul; not even a screw of 'baccy! I must have a half-sov., a few shillings to keep me going till to-night, when I hope the supply is 'to be continued,' like Tom Reed's trash. I am growing deuced hungry, and they won't give me a crust without the rhino in that cursed hole of an inn. Come now, five bob won't break you!"

Kate, moved by a mixture of pity and disgust, put her hand in her pocket. To her regret and dismay—for Trapes's red-rimmed eyes were beginning to look vicious—there was no purse there. She must have left it in her morning-dress. "I am really very sorry, but I have not my purse. I would willingly give you a few shillings, indeed, if I had."

" Now," said Trapes, savagely, and throwing away his pipe, " that is as shabby a bit of humbug as ever I heard ; and what is more, I shall take the liberty of rummaging your pocket myself, and if the purse isn't there you shall pay forfeit in kisses, —— if you sha'n't."

" Sir," exclaimed Kate, horribly frightened, yet striving to seem composed, "this insolent folly will do you no good. If you will have patience—"

But he had already seized her wrists ; his dreadful satyr face was close to hers, when to her joy, her relief, Kate, who was looking towards the cliffs, saw a figure moving from behind one of the largest fragments of rock that lay near, a figure whose gait and bearing she knew well. She was safe now. " Hugh !" she screamed, "dear Hugh, come to me !"

He was upon Trapes in an instant. Seizing his collar, he wrenched him away with such force that the half-drunken wretch fell at once to the ground.

" What is it ?" asked Galbraith, placing himself between Kate and her assailant, " Robbery—what ?"

" I am no more a robber than you are," said Trapes, sullenly, as somewhat sobered he gathered himself up from the ground. Galbraith's hand was on his collar again directly. " Let me alone, I say," continued Trapes, trying in vain to shake it off, " I meant no harm, it was only a bit a of joke," and he struggled hard to free himself from Galbraith's grasp, but in vain.

" You will find it no joke, you dog ! I shall march you back to the police station."

" Oh, Hugh, don't hurt him ! He is weak, perhaps he is hungry. I do not think he knows what he is doing ! Don't hurt him !"

" Let me go," said Trapes, in an altered voice, touched by the genuine pity of Kate's tones. " The lady is right ! I am sorry and ashamed I frightened her."

" Let him go," whispered Kate, and Galbraith puzzled, but by no means reluctant to be rid of him and alone with her, released his hold.

" Take care what you do," he said, sternly, "if I find you prowling about here, I shall warn the police against you."

Trapes slowly and sullenly withdrew, muttering to himself.

" You are frightened," said Galbraith, taking Kate's hand and drawing it through his arm, where in the confusion of the moment she let it remain, " you are trembling all over. Tell me what did that brute want ?"

Kate could not quite command her voice. She felt utterly in Galbraith's hands for the moment ; and if she let the tears which

15*

were ready to come, and would have relieved her, burst forth, she feared the effect they might have on her companion.

"Sit down and recover yourself before you speak," said Galbraith, with infinite gentleness, and he led her to the place from which Trapes had disturbed her. Moving a little apart, he leaned against an angle of the rock close by, while Kate, trying to smile, with white, quivering lips looked up at him and said as steadily as she could, "He said he was very badly off and wanted a few shillings, and when I put my hand in my pocket I found I had not my purse ; so he would not believe me, and wanted to examine my pocket himself. He was not sober. He did not, I think, intend to rob me."

"It looked very like it ; yet he certainly did not seem a common tramp. I think it is my duty to make the police look after him."

"Perhaps so. I will probably lodge a complaint against him myself."

"You should do so without fail, Mrs. Temple ! Are you feeling all right again?"

"Nearly," she said, passing her hand over her brow. In truth, she was much more upset by Galbraith's sudden appearance than by her adventure with Trapes, besides a natural embarrassment at being alone with him under such circumstances ; his presence, just when she had found perhaps the missing link of evidence, was most inopportune. Nevertheless, come what might, she could not help feeling a strange, unreasonable thrill of pleasure at finding him there beside her—caring for her. "But tell me, how is it that you are here just at the right moment?" she continued.

"When I went down to my sister the day after I last saw you in London," returned Galbraith, "I found that she had had a quarrel with her husband ; that he was in a scrape, and gone off she did not know where. I was obliged to go in search of him, so I wrote an explanatory note to you, which of course you never received. I had a good deal of running about after Harcourt, and I did not go to my club until yesterday morning —there I found your very unsatisfactory epistle. It was rather shabby of you to give me the slip in that way, so I took the train to Stoneborough yesterday afternoon, and came on here this morning—called at the Bazaar, was graciously received by Miss Lee, who told me you had gone with a book and a headache to sit on the rocks under the broken cliff. I just came up in the nick of time. Drunk or sober, that fellow must be punished. You are trembling still." As he spoke, Galbraith sat down beside her, taking one of her hands in both of his, very gently, yet he held it close.

"You are always good to me, and I don't deserve it," said Kate, unable to hold the reins of her self-control with her usual steadiness, her voice faltering while she tried to draw away her hand, not very resolutely, "I don't indeed, Sir Hugh."

"Perhaps not," he said, gazing at her; "but you see it is not so much what you deserve as what I cannot help giving. I can no more help loving you than I help breathing! Well, there," releasing her hand, "I will not keep it if you don't like. You know that I cannot live without you—no, that's nonsense! I shall have to live without you, if such is your will. But are you *quite* sure it *is* your will? Come, Kate, you must hear all I have to say. You have made me so miserable and unlike myself, I think I have a right to be heard."

"It would be so much better not," she said, with trembling lips. She was frightened and bewildered, but the tame and somewhat gloomy tenor of her life had never known such a moment of delicious pain before.

"No, it is better we should understand each other."

He leaned forward, his arm on his knee supporting his head on his hand, that he might look into her eyes. "I have done my best to forget you, and you, for some reason or other, have done your best to choke me off; but it won't do. You will perhaps think me a conceited idiot, but I can't help fancying you like me better than you think. I cannot get the sound of your voice just now out of my ears when you called me 'Hugh! dear Hugh.' I would give some years of my life to hear you say so again in earnest. Couldn't you try?" and Galbraith smiled entreatingly as he spoke.

"It was the terror of the moment," said Kate, very low. "I did not know what I said."

"Ay, but you have called me 'Hugh' before when there was nothing to frighten or disturb you! Tell me, have I no chance with you? Why will you not be my wife? I am a rugged sort of a fellow, I know, but there should be no ruggedness in your life, dear—all the best I have should be yours," and he again took her hand.

"Oh, don't talk to me like that," cried Kate, snatching it away and covering her face, "I must not let you. It is quite impossible you could marry me. If you knew everything you would see that I am the last woman you would like to marry."

"My God!" exclaimed Galbraith, the color leaving his face. "Is it possible there is any real barrier between us? Is it possible there can be any spot in your past life that you would wish to hide?"

"Do you mean that I have done anything wrong?" returned Kate, her face still hidden, her voice faltering, and keeping back her tears only by a determined effort. "No, there is nothing in my past life I need blush for. It is not my fault that there is any barrier—I mean that there are things—circumstances you would not like—!" She stopped abruptly.

"Is your husband really dead?" asked Galbraith, sternly, Lady Styles's gossip recurring to his mind.

"He is, indeed!" said Kate, recovering herself in some degree. "I am not quite such an impostor as you imagine. But, Sir Hugh, you are putting yourself and me to unnecessary pain, for I am most deeply grieved to be compelled to pain you! I acknowledge there is a secret in my past ; and, besides, I do not—I never entertained the idea of loving you—I really do not think I do—at any rate—" She quite believed she was speaking the truth.

"I suppose I must submit to be again rejected!" he interrupted, very bitterly. "I daresay you deserve a better man than I am ; but, such as I am, I could be satisfied with nothing short of your whole heart. I have heard of fellows being content to wait and win a woman's affection inch by inch ; but I could not stand that. I love you so passionately that if you were my wife, and I had a doubt that you were not fully, freely, utterly my own, why, I should go mad with despair and jealousy!" He rose as he spoke, and walked away a pace or two ; then returning, looking grim and stern enough, he resumed his seat by Kate, who, deeply moved by his words, but nerved to desperate self-command by a sudden sense of the effect they produced upon herself, turned to him, her long lashes gemmed with tears, her eyes soft with the most tender sympathy. "Do not fear, you will be well loved yet by some one more fitted to be your wife than I am!"

"That is like giving me a stone when I ask for bread," said Galbraith. "Turn to me now, put your hand in mine, and if you can say it with truth, say, 'Hugh Galbraith, I love you;' say it with your eyes, that tell so much ! as well as your lips, and, by heaven ! I will forget and forgive your past, *whatever* is in it—there ! I never thought I should say as much to any woman."

He held out his hand, and there was a moment's silence.

"I must not, Hugh!" replied Kate, with a deep, quivering sigh. "Nor do I need to have my past either forgiven or forgotten!"

"Then why make a mystery of it ? Mysteries always imply something to be ashamed of."

"I will tell you everything one day!" exclaimed Kate, stung by his tone, and taking a sudden resolution, "if you still care to hear my story."

"Ay, but when?" cried Galbraith, with animation.

" Before five months from this time."

" That is a long way off!"

" I may be able to do so sooner," replied Kate, rising ; " and, meantime, do—do forgive me for causing you so much discomfort. God knows I am wretched myself! and try to put me out of your head. I fear—that is, I think—that when you do know everything you will not wish—in short, do not trouble yourself about me. Go away among your friends, and you will see far more charming women, and more suitable." She stopped, for words and voice failed her.

" I will," said Galbraith, shortly. " I don't like mysteries, and I think you might trust me now. Still, I will claim your promise. Can you not make it three months ? "

" No, I cannot! and now I must say good bye. I must not stay here any longer."

" I will not allow you to go alone. I must insist on your taking my arm—that scoundrel may be lurking about. I will go with you at any rate as far as the houses. You must let me take care of you so far, Kate. I will not intrude my feelings on you any more. You may trust me. You have said ' No ' often enough."

It was a trying and embarrassing progress, Kate's arm held closely within Galbraith's. He guided her steps with the most watchful care, but in almost unbroken silence, save for an occasional inquiry, " Am I going too fast ? " " Would you like to stop ? " Fortunately the distance to the first houses of the North Parade was but short. Here Kate resolutely withdrew her arm. " I feel quite steady now, and can go on alone." He made no attempt to dissuade her, but held out his hand. Kate placed hers in it frankly, impulsively, and raising her eyes, met his—a long look ; then Galbraith said, " It must be good bye, then ? "

" It must, Sir Hugh ; " spoken sadly.

" And you promise to reveal the mystery ? "

" Yes, if you ask."

" And then—"

" Leave the future to the ' Providence that shapes our ends.' "

" Am I forbidden to visit Pierstoffe ? "

" Yes,—at any rate the Berlin Bazaar—for four or five months ; then, if your interest and curiosity are not diverted into other channels, you may write and ask the fulfillment of my promise."

" Kate," said Galbraith, sinking his voice to its deepest tones, while he raised the hand that still lay in his to his lips, " it is not all over with me yet ! "

" Do not let yourself think so," she replied, earnestly ; and turning from him, walked quickly towards the town. Galbraith stood still, gazing after her in deep thought till she had got well ahead, and then slowly followed.

CHAPTER XXXVIII.

"DID you meet Sir Hugh?" was Fanny's first question, when, after her day's work was over, she went up to her friend's room to see if that horrible headache was any better.

Kate had availed herself of that excuse to keep out of sight and in semi-darkness till her nerves had somewhat quieted down after the painful, pleasurable, overwhelming excitement she had gone through.

"Yes, Fan, I met him ; and who else, do you think?"

"I can't think. Not Tom?"

"No, indeed ; but that dreadful creature Trapes!"

"Trapes!" with a little scream. "And what did he say?"

"Nothing I can depend upon. He was rather, indeed very tipsy ; and among other things he offered to restore me to my rights, but wanted me to give him five pounds."

"Well, then?"

"Oh, he would have been content with an installment of five shillings, but unfortunately I had not my purse about me. Then he grew insolent, and wanted to examine my pocket himself; then Hugh Galbraith came and knocked him down."

"You don't say so! Why, dear Kate, it is just like a play; and I *do* hope that you have promised to marry Sir Hugh! He came in about half an hour after you went out; looking —oh, I never saw him look so well or so bright!—quite handsome ; and so pleasant! If it was not for Tom, I should not mind marrying him myself."

Instead of replying, Fanny felt her friend's hand clasp hers with a tremulous pressure.

"Do not talk of Hugh Galbraith just now," she said, after a minute's silence. "I will by-and-by. At present I am greatly troubled about Trapes ; he has disappeared, and I have no idea where to find him. Even if I did, he is such a disreputable creature to inquire about."

She paused.

"Oh, we must find him!" cried Fanny. "What matter about his disreputableness? He would not be at such a grand hotel as the Marine ; but there is the Marquis of Cornwallis, and the Shakespeare Tavern. Had I not better catch Jimmy before he goes, and send him around to ask?"

Jimmy was the errand boy, and Fanny's most devoted slave.

"No, that will not do. I wish I knew if Hugh Galbraith has actually gone," said Kate, thoughtfully.

"Gone!" echoed Fanny, in dismay. "Then you have refused him, after all? I think you are very ill-natured. Why don't you make up your minds, and share the property? and we might shut up shop and all be married on the same day!"

"Dear Fanny, you do not know what you are talking about. There, you are putting the *eau de Cologne* in my eyes and making them smart." For Fanny was treating her friend for severe headache to the best of her skill. "My head is better, and I will not lie here any longer. I must write to Tom by to-night's post. He said he was coming on Saturday; I will beg him on no account to fail me. I cannot do anything without Tom. I seem quite dazed and stupid."

She had risen while she spoke, and was standing before the glass, impatiently shaking back her long chestnut-brown hair preparatory to rearranging it. Fanny, who was always a little frightened when, to use her own expression, Mrs. Temple got into "a state,"—it was so rare—held the candle obsequiously. "You look dreadfully ill, dear," she said, soothingly, "had you not better take off your things and go regularly to bed, instead of twisting up your hair and trying to do impossibilities? and I will bring you a nice cup of tea and a muffin—"

"I believe, Fanny, you consider tea and muffins a cure for every earthly ill," interrupted Mrs. Temple, continuing her hair-dressing rapidly and deftly. "The sight of a muffin would make me sick. I want to be up and doing. Don't mind me if I seem cross. I don't intend to be, but I feel chained here while I ought to be rushing hither and thither to secure Trapes, and urge on Mr. Wall; time is so precious, and it seems impossible to hurry things; just like those dreadful dreams where life depends on speed, and yet one's limbs are lead-weighted and rigid."

"I would not fret myself so dreadfully," said Fanny, in a tone of strong common sense. "If that horrid man is so very much in want of money as to try to rob you, depend upon it he will come here to ask for some."

"He will probably be ashamed to see me."

"Poor creature, I fancy he has forgotten all about shame."

"Come downstairs, then, Fanny. I am ready, and I shall be glad to be near the fire, I feel so shivery. How I wish Tom were here!"

"So do I," returned Fanny, with cordial acquiescence.

It was considerably past seven when the friends established themselves in their cozy parlor, Fanny stirring the fire into a brilliant condition, sweeping up the hearth, and making all things orderly.

Mrs. Temple at once sat down to write to Tom, her heart still throbbing at the recollection of Galbraith's words and tone

and looks. Her letter was very short: an exhortation to come
without fail on Saturday, an announcement of Trapes's momentary appearance, but no word of Hugh. "If I mention him, I
must tell everything, and that is quite impossible. It would
be bad enough to tell Fanny, but Tom is out of the question."

Fanny had just returned from delivering this epistle into the
hands of Sarah, to be posted on her way home, when a low,
cautious ring of the front-door bell was heard. Mrs. Temple and
Fanny both started. Rings at the front-door bell were rare at
that hour, and this was a stealthy, equivocal ring, suggestive of
the door-chain and careful reconnoitring.

"Who can it be?" exclaimed Fanny, stopping short in her
approach to the fire.

"Tell Mills to be sure and put on the chain," said Kate.

"I will go too," said Fanny, with heroic courage. She did
so, but considerably behind the valiant Mills, who, candle in
hand, advanced to face the enemy. A short colloquy ensued,
and Fanny darted into the sitting-room on tiptoe. "It is
Trapes!" she exclaimed in a whisper. "I told you he would
come. He will not give his name, and Mills will not let him in.
Shall you venture to see him?"

"Yes, I must, though I don't half like it. But Fan, we are
three to one. Do you think he is sober?"

"He seems very quiet."

"Oh, go and bring him in," cried Kate, impulsively.

"Mrs. Temple will see the gentleman," said Fanny, demurely,
advancing to the door. Mills muttered indistinct, yet unmistakable disapprobation, let down the chain, and Trapes entered.

He had endeavored to impart an air of respectability to his
attire. The dented hat had been restored to shape, though the
mark of its misfortunes could not be obliterated. A dark overcoat in good preservation made him look a trifle less raffish,
while both tie and collar were straight and in good order.

"Circumstances which I will explain to Mrs. Temple, compel
me to call at this unseasonable hour," said Trapes, in the
best manner he could recall from his better days, as he stepped
in and took off his hat.

"This way, if you please," returned Fanny, opening the parlor door. Trapes bowed and entered. Fanny hesitated to go
or stay, but, at a sign from her friend, followed him.

"You wish to speak to me," said Mrs. Temple, who had risen,
and was standing by the table.

"Excuse me," said Trapes, still in a state of elegance, "but
my communications are for you alone; may I request this
young lady to leave us?"

"I have no secrets from Miss Lee," returned Kate. "Even

if she goes away now, I shall tell her what you tell me an hour hence."

"Still," replied Trapes, "considering what sages (ill-bred old buffers, I grant), say of confiding a secret to one woman, it is not very prudent to reveal it to a brace."

"You will tell me no secret without her," said Kate, quietly and firmly, "for I will not speak to you alone, and if your secret is to do me any good, it must be very generally known."

"Ay, the part that concerns you! However, Mrs. Temple, I cannot blame you after my disgraceful conduct to-day," continued Trapes, with an air of penitence; "part of my errand here this evening was to crave your pardon. I am heartily ashamed. I can only say that I was under the influence of the demon drink, to which I have been driven by misfortunes not all deserved—the base ingratitude of—but," interrupting himself loftily, "I did not come here to complain about the inevitable! May I hope you will forgive me?"

Fanny crept close to Kate, in a state of fear, dashed with acute curiosity.

"I do forgive you," said the latter, gently. "But it is very sad to reduce yourself voluntarily to a condition in which all the instincts of a gentleman, which you seem to possess, are lost."

"It is—it is, by George!" cried Trapes, heartily and naturally. "However, it's never too late to mend," he went on, taking the chair indicated to him; "perhaps I may recover myself yet. Anyhow, madam—Mrs. Temple, as you wish to be called—I shall not forget the kindly manner in which you interceded for me with that strong-fisted ruffian who knocked me over—not but that I would have done just the same in his place! I was always disposed to befriend a lady. I am especially so disposed towards this particular lady"—a bow to Mrs. Temple; "but" —a long-drawn "but"—"it is my duty to see that my impulses square with my interests." Here Trapes drew forth with a flourish a large pocket-handkerchief, bordered by a pattern of foxes' heads, and used it audibly.

"You are very good," returned Kate, looking steadily at him, "Now perhaps you will tell me the object of your visit?"

"Certainly, madam," he returned, then paused, eyed Fanny with some irresolution, and returned his handkerchief to his pocket.

"My object, ahem, is simple. It is, in the first place, to obtain the—the advance of ten shillings you were good enough to desire me to call for, when you found yourself minus your purse this afternoon." All Trapes's natural and acquired impudence was restored by the sound of his own voice.

"I do not think I named any sum," said Kate, smiling, "and I think your conduct exonerates me from any promise."

"Very logical," said Trapes. "Nevertheless, a lady like you is not going to sell a poor devil with such a pleasant smile as that?"

"I shall give you a trifle," she returned; "but before doing so, I should like to have some idea in what way you can serve me. I do not want you to tell all you know, but prove to me that you do know something."

"Deucedly well put,‒Mrs. Travers—Temple, I mean. Well, then, I can prove that your late husband's will—I mean the one administered by Sir Hugh Galbraith—is a forgery! I can produce the man who drew it out, two or three months after Mr. Travers's death, and I can produce the man who employed him to do it." Trapes pulled up short, with a triumphant wink.

"You can do all this!" exclaimed Kate, her eyes fixed upon him. "Then why have you not enabled me to assert my rights before?"

"'Pon my soul, I did not know till last spring how shamefully you had been cheated. Then I did not know where you were, and I always like to deal with the principal."

"But you knew Tom Reed!" cried Fanny, indignantly; "*he* would have told you."

"No, he wouldn't," said Trapes, quickly. "At any rate, I think I asked him; but my head "—addressing Mrs. Temple —"is not quite so clear as it might be. Be that as it may, I have shown you my hand pretty frank. There's the outline of what I can do. What are you prepared to give for the details?"

"I am too much taken by surprise to answer you," returned Kate, changing color visibly, quivering all through with a strange mixture of feelings—exultation and fear, pain and pleasure. "If you are quite sure of what you state, how is it that you do not reveal all from a simple sense of right?"

"Because I am not a simpleton, my dear madam," said Trapes, with an indescribable wink. "I am poor—infernally poor. I have been driven and chivied, and sold right and left all my life, and I want a trifle to keep me going for the rest of my days. Now I have told you the sum total, I know; but, by all that's good, the rack shall not draw the particulars from me, unless I have some profit." Trapes closed his lips firmly as he ceased to speak.

Kate felt dreadfully puzzled. She must not seem too eager, she must not lose the information. She did a little mental calculation during the momentary silence which ensued. This man had evidently been hanging on Ford since the spring, when he had gone to Tom Reed to inquire about him. He had then either exhausted or quarreled with Ford—probably both; if so, Trapes's only chance of turning his secret to account was with herself. It would be too bad if Ford was ruined, and the baser of the two rewarded. Her strong inner conviction of Ford's guilt gave her a key to the position which her shrewd legal adviser did not possess.

"Well, Mr. Trapes," she said at length (it was the first time she had mentioned his name—he looked up sharply), "I am still at a loss to answer. I do not know how far I might injure myself legally by entering into any bargain with you. I really can say or do nothing without Mr. Reed's advice. I expect him on Saturday; come here and talk matters over with him. I am not indisposed to assist you, Mr. Trapes. I have heard Mr. Reed speak of you as a man of excellent abilities, but unfortunate."

"Oh, —— his patronage!" interrupted Trapes, impatiently; "he is rather a keen hand to deal with. But as you like, Mrs. Travers—beg pardon, Mrs. Temple. If you don't think my information worth a trifle, why I may as well bottle it up. I am not sure I can see Reed on Saturday. I'm due at Bluffton on Saturday. I came here in the best of good feeling towards you, though that tall chap has warned the police against me. I had gone into the waiting-room at the station to rest a bit, and I saw him; he was just opposite the window, talking to a constable and describing me, till he stepped into the train and started. I had to slink out pretty quick, or I would have had more questions to answer than was agreeable. Yet I stuck to my text, and came to give you what help I could. I cannot say you have shown much gratitude."

"I am far from ungrateful, Mr. Trapes," replied Kate, very quietly and firmly. "But, you must see yourself, that in such a case it would be absurd of me to make you any promise. I do not yet know how far your information may be available."

"I should only ask a conditional promise," he interrupted.

"I can only repeat, Mr. Trapes, that without Mr. Reed I can do nothing. You may be quite sure that I am eager to assert my rights, and I am not the sort of woman to be ungrateful; but, as to meeting Mr. Reed, you must do what you think best. It might be," she added, after an instant's pause, in which a sudden flash of thought suggested a stroke she would probably not have played had she reflected. "It might be more to your interest to make your confession to Mr. Ford." Her eyes were on Trapes as she spoke, and though he kept his countenance with tolerable success, there was a momentary look of blank astonishment, instantly covered by an insolent laugh.

"And who the deuce is Ford, when he is at home?"

"I need not describe him. You know probably more of him than I do."

"Not I," he returned, carelessly. "Well, then, I suppose what you say is not so unreasonable. If, on reflection, I think it advisable to meet Reed here on Saturday, I will do so."

"Meantime," said Mrs. Temple, willing to conciliate him, "whatever course you decide upon I shall be happy to lend, or let you have"—amending her phrase with a smile—"the half sovereign we were talking about."

And drawing one from her purse, she laid it within his reach.

"I must say that is acting like a trump," cried Trapes, clutching it eagerly. "You couldn't make it a whole sov., eh?"

"I cannot, indeed, you see I am far from rich."

"Well, well, come to terms with me, and you may ride on velvet the rest of your life."

"We will see about it. Good evening, Mr. Trapes."

She bowed him out politely but decidedly, and he retired, Fanny holding a candle, and locking, bolting, and chaining the door carefully after him.

"What a fearful, dreadful, dishonest creature," she cried, when she was safe in again, sitting down on the side of a chair. "The whole place smells of bad tobacco! Why would you not promise anything, Kate? I am afraid he will not tell a word that will do you any good unless you give him some money. Do you really think he knows all he says?"

"I do; but I must not have anything to do with him. I must leave him to Tom. Oh, Fanny, there is an awful time coming! I wish I was through it. Imagine having to prosecute Mr. Ford for forgery—he was so respectable and kind and obliging—and then Hugh Galbraith! I do not seem able to face it all."

"No, indeed. I am sure it is enough to turn your brain. But as to Hugh Galbraith," insinuatingly, "you said you would tell me all about him."

"And I will, Fan, I will! but not now. I could not now—indeed I could not—I want to think. Give me my writing-book." After arranging her writing materials as if about to begin a letter, Kate suddenly laid down her pen. "No, I shall not tell Mr. Wall until I have seen Tom. Fanny, do take your work and sit opposite to me; I cannot bear you to creep about putting things away in that distractingly quiet fashion. Ah, dear, dear Fan! how cross and unreasonable I am—and to you who have been such a help and a comfort to me during my eclipse."

"Have I really?—then I am worth something. Never mind, the eclipse is nearly over, and won't you blaze out gloriously by-and-by!"

"Heaven knows! I fear the future more than I can say. I feel it is just a toss-up, apart from success or failure, whether my lot is to be happy or miserable; but it might be—oh, so happy!"

"I know," said Fanny, significantly, and took up her needle-work with her usual cheerful submission.

Mrs. Temple closed her writing-book, and drawing her chair to the fire sat there in deep thought the rest of the evening, occasionally addressing a disjointed observation out of her meditations.

The night was nearly sleepless. At first the fatigue of the many emotions through which she had passed insured her an hour of forgetfulness, but she was disturbed by dreams. Again and again Hugh Galbraith stood before her with outstretched hand, asking her to place hers in it for ever, and she woke, her heart beating wildly, and sobbing out the words, "Yes, for ever, Hugh!"

Then her busy brain set to work revolving the events of the day, picturing their results—the most terrible was the impending ruin of Ford.

As regarded Galbraith, she was not quite without hope. But Ford—how could she spare him? A daring project suggested itself: she thought long, and turned it on every side; then, slipping gently out of bed, she lit her candle, wrapped herself in her dressing-gown, and stole softly, noiselessly downstairs to the shop parlor. Here she took out paper and pen, traced a few lines, enclosed them in an envelope, directed and stamped it, placed the letter carefully in her pocket, and crept back as noiselessly as she had descended.

The changefulness of the English climate asserted itself next morning—all trace of St. Martin's summer had disappeared. A stiff southeaster was lashing the bay into foam and fury, and driving stinging showers of fine rain that seemed trying to get down, with only occasional success, against the windows and into nooks with bitter vehemence.

"And you have been out this wretched morning," said Fanny, reproachfully, as Kate joined her at breakfast.

"I have, I could not help it, I wanted so much to go; and I think a brisk walk has done me good."

"More harm than good I suspect," returned Fanny, disapprovingly: but she stopped there, for Kate's heavy eyes and anxious expression disarmed her.

CHAPTER XXXIX.

WELCOME as he ever was, Tom Reed was perhaps never so anxiously looked for as on the present occasion. Kate felt that he could disentangle the raveled skein of her affairs;

that he only could deal with Trapes ; and his tact so manipulate the difficulties with which her relations to Galbraith bristled, as to effect a fair division of the property, she hoped to prove her own without letting Galbraith know her identity until it was accomplished.

Kate enjoyed the rare advantage of being in sympathy with her adviser. Generally an adviser is an enemy, whose opinions, ranged under a different banner from one's own, are to be in some way circumvented or twisted into accord with the advised : or, possessing sufficient weight to impose them upon the hearer, they are so often acted upon in an unwilling spirit as to neutralize their possible good effect.

But there was a real accord between Tom Reed and the young widow ; even when they differed, each knew that he or she was thoroughly understood by the other.

Fanny was of course in a state of unconcealable joy. She had stolen half an hour in the afternoon to compound a lobster currie for the late dinner or early supper at which Tom was expected. A low and mundane method of preparing for a lover's reception perhaps, in the reader's opinion, but—ask the lover's !

The trains between Stoneborough and Pierstoffe were by no means patterns of punctuality, and the friends agreed not to expect Tom till quite half an hour after he was due. That half an hour was nearly exhausted, when their attention was diverted by the entrance of Mills with a note, an untidy note without an envelope, and fastened by a wafer. It was directed to T. Reed, Esq., in a very intoxicated-looking hand.

" This has just been brought by a boy from the Shakespeare Inn, ma'am, and he wants to know if Mr. Tom is come."

" Say he has not, but we expect him every moment," replied Mrs. Temple, scanning the note critically. " This is from Trapes, no doubt."

" Don't you think we might open it ? " insinuated Fanny, laying a couple of covetous little fingers on it. " It is all about yourself of course. I really think you might read it, Kate."

" You impatient puss ! I think we might wait for Tom to read his own correspondence. He will be here in a quarter of an hour if he comes at all."

" Ah, Kate, that is a cruel 'if' ! "

" Never fear, Fan— There, there is some conveyance stopping at the door. Here he is, and I shall run away ! "

" Indeed, Kate, indeed you need not ! "

But Kate was gone. The next moment a hearty hug, a long, loving kiss, put everything and every one save the donor out of Fanny's head. " It seems a hundred years since I saw you, my darling," cried Tom, who, though looking a little thin and worn, was in high spirits and full of animation. "You little, ungrateful, saucy coquette! you are as blooming and bright as if I had been at your elbow all the time! Where is the pale cheek and tear-dimmed eyes that ought to show the sincerity with which you mourned my absence, and the severe mental arithmetic you exercised counting the days till I came?"

"Ah, Tom, I should have had a dash of uncertainty to reduce me to the proper condition of paleness and dimness. But I know you, and I am at rest," a small responsive hug, and some half-uttered ejaculations interrupted, as may be imagined.

"I see I do not go the right way to work to show what a valuable article I am!" cried Tom.

"If you worried, or gave me any trouble, I should not care a straw about you," said Fanny, with a pretty moan.

"Now let me call Kate, she is dying to see you."

"I think she might give us a few minutes more law."

"Oh, here, Tom, is a note for you!" cried Fanny, darting to the mantel-piece and taking it down. "I believe it is from that strange man, Mr. Trapes."

"Trapes!" echoed Tom, in much surprise. "How does he know that I am here?"

"Oh, because—but I will leave Kate to tell everything. Just do look at the note!"

"There! you may discount your rights, if you choose," said Tom, laughing, and handing the scrawled morsel of paper to her.

"What a hand! What is that word?"

"Seriously."

"Read it to me, dear Tom."

"My dear Reed,—I am seriously ill, and cannot go to see you as I promised Mrs. T——. I feel as if I was near the end of the race, and nowhere! Look in on me, like a brick, to-morrow.
                    "Yours,   G. TRAPES."

"If Trapes knocks up, he will not last long," said Tom, gravely; "but call Mrs. Travers. I long to hear all about everything!"

"Now tell me how you unearthed Trapes?" asked Tom.

They were sitting round the fire after dinner, Mrs. Temple having insisted on his refreshing himself before going into any discussion of business.

' He came to the surface of his own accord," she replied, and proceeded to describe her encounter with him clearly and shortly, till she came to the part performed by Galbraith, where she broke down for an instant, paused, collected herself, and continued her narrative by a decided abridgment. "When I was sufficiently recovered to walk home, Sir Hugh Galbraith was good enough to come part of the way, and I have not seen him since." She then passed rapidly on to Trapes's evening visit, and his remarkable boast : " I can produce the man who drew out the will, two or three months after Mr. Travers's death ; and I can produce the man that employed him to do it ! "

" This is very extraordinary," said Tom, when Kate ceased speaking. " If Trapes can make good his promise, of course your success is an accomplished fact. But I must warn you that my former acquaintance is given to the wildest romancing at times. Still, I believe he does know something of importance. One point, however, I must press upon you, Mrs. Temple : do not see this scamp any more—leave him to me."

" Most willingly and thankfully, dear Tom."

" Very well. Now, do you think he recognized Galbraith ? "

" No ; I do not think he did."

" Mind," continued Tom, " I don't think it matters a straw whether he tells his tale to Galbraith or to you, if he can support it ; for of course, a man of Galbraith's position and character would not for a moment hesitate about restoring your rights. All I want to make sure of before we stir in the matter is, to be prepared with irresistible proof. As things are at present, we should only be knocking our heads against the stone wall of a long lawsuit were you to move. However, you must leave Trapes to me." There was a pause, during which Tom appeared lost in thought—a condition which Kate and Fanny respected too much to disturb. At last he roused himself, and assumed the attitude peculiar to Britons when about to dictate or domineer—that is, he placed himself on the hearth-rug, with his back to the fire. " It was a remarkable, though fortunate accident that Sir Hugh Galbraith came to your assistance. Is it permitted to ask what brought him to Pierstoffe just in the nick of time ? " And Tom, with an air of comical solemnity, paused for a reply.

Kate crimsoned even over her little ears, but answered steadily, though in a low voice, " No, Tom, you must not ask. I cannot tell you any fibs, so I would rather say nothing."

" Ahem !—and in spite of this gallant rescue and unexpected appearance—I presume it was unexpected ? "

" Most unexpected ! " she returned.

" You are determined to carry the war into the enemy's country ? "

" Quite determined ! " said Kate, rising and coming to the fire, where she leaned against the chimney-piece, " if I can bring an overwhelming force to bear upon his position."

" Do you mean to say," exclaimed Tom, quickly, darting one

of his keenest glances at the fair, downcast face before him, "that you have any fresh cause for vengeance?"

"For vengeance? oh, no!" she returned, looking frankly into his eyes. "My opinion of Sir Hugh is changed for the better. It is for his sake as well as my own that I wish matters hurried on."

"You are incomprehensible!" he returned, less amiably than usual.

"Then do not try to comprehend me," she said, gently laying her hand on his arm, "but act as if the chapter of accidents had never brought Hugh Galbraith to lodge under my roof—continue to be my best friend as you have been."

"You generally make slaves of your friends," replied Tom, resignedly. "However, I have not opened my budget yet. I saw Wall this morning. He had just had S——'s opinion, and showed it to me. He considers that there are grounds for taking criminal proceedings against Poole."

"And will Mr. Wall arrest him, then?" asked Kate, anxiously.

"No. He would in the first instance summon Poole to answer the charge of having wilfully perjured himself by swearing that he was present when Mr. Travers executed the second will. But, as nothing could be done till Monday, I advised his waiting my return before he took any step, thinking there might be something in your idea that Trapes could give us information that would implicate Ford."

"And he can, depend upon it, Tom!" said Kate, thoughtfully. "I dropped a hint that perhaps his information might be more valuable to Mr. Ford than to me, and I saw his countenance change unmistakably."

"You should be exceedingly cautious what you let out to a man like Trapes," returned Tom. "There is no telling what mischief he might make of anything—or nothing."

"I do not think I did my cause any harm by my remark, but it certainly affected Mr. Trapes."

"Well, I shall probably find out to-morrow. I am not sorry the poor devil is obliged to keep his room. Men of his type are always easier to manage when they feel the grip of their proprietor upon them! Do you know, I have always been sorry for Trapes. He was a very pleasant, good-natured fellow once, seven or eight years ago. Never quite free from a dash of the blackguard, but would perhaps have kept right if he had fallen into better hands."

"Perhaps," said Kate, doubtingly. "Yet I imagine, if we could open such a man's head or heart, and look at the works as you do at your watch, we should find some weak or imperfect

16

mechanism—some faulty bits in which the tempter can insert the point of his wedge."

"Still, with different influences, he might have been a different man."

Kate, gazing at the fire, made no reply.

"The long and short of it is," said Fanny, with sly gravity, "he had not your adamantine firmness, Tom ! At any rate," with a pleasant, almost tender smile, "Kate and I are inclined to believe that the mainspring of your heart's machinery works true and steadily." To which Tom's appropriate reply was a good, honest kiss, despite Kate's presence.

She smiled, and naturally inquired, "What have you two dear friends decided upon ? "

"You mean as regards a joint establishment ?" asked Tom. "I cannot get a distinct reply from your undecided assistant. I wanted her long ago to give a month's warning, and take another situation. I am glad to have a chance of pleading my cause before you, Mrs. Temple. As matters stand at present there is no reason why Fanny should not take me for better for worse, say,—come ! I will be reasonable—this day fortnight ! Meantime you might advertise the Bazaar. You will easily dispose of it. Come, join us in London, be on the spot to enact the importunate widow, and make life a burden to old Wall ! Come, now, like a brace of angels, say, Done ! and we will arrange preliminaries before we sleep to-night."

"There is no particular reason why Fanny should not marry you," said Kate, thoughtfully ; "but I cannot leave Pierstoffe ! This is not the most agreeable life to me, nevertheless I will not break up the little home I have made till the question I am about to raise is settled, *then* I shall in any case make a change."

"There !—I told you so," said Fanny ; "and as long as Kate keeps in this stupid, odious, disagreeable shop, I will stay with her. You don't think I am of much use, I suppose," a little querulously ; for, though true to her friend, poor Fanny's heart had leaped with delight at the picture presented of going to live with Tom in London ; "but I know Kate could not live without me, at least not comfortably—could you, Kate ? "

"No, indeed !" heartily. "Tom, will you think me very selfish ? Leave Fanny with me just a little longer. I feel we shall soon know something more of this will,—and—I do not know why, but I am very sad and fearful." She held out her hand, and her rich, soft voice faltered.

"My dear Mrs. Travers, you are our first consideration. It is a bargain. This case is postponed till this day month, when a decree will be given."

"Thank you, dear Tom. And now Fanny will entertain you. I feel weary and headachy, so will go to bed."

The next morning, after breakfast, Tom Reed announced his intention of going to see Trapes at once.

"Yes, do, Tom," said Mrs. Temple; "we can do nothing until we know what he has to reveal."

"Well, I shall go to church," remarked Fanny.

"And I will escort you there," added Tom. "Will you come?" addressing Kate.

"No, it would be a mockery. I could not attend to what was going on. I am too much on the stretch to know about Trapes. I shall pray at home."

Tom and his *fiancée* set out accordingly, and Kate bore the lonely waiting as best she could. Seated near the fire—her eyes fixed on the red coals, her thoughts roaming far and near—trying to picture to herself the effect of her claim upon Hugh Galbraith's temper and character, to recall the various indications of his nature which she had noticed, and from them to decide how he would take the final revelation. "I have done nothing wrong—nothing he has any real right to be angry with; yet will he not think that I ought to have told him the truth when I first refused him! but then, I never thought we should meet again. I never dreamed that I could care about him. I have such an extraordinary longing to vindicate my real self— the self he so doubts and despises—before he knows the truth; and, if I do, how will he act? At present, he has some romance about me in his head, practical and imaginative as he is; how will it be when he knows who I really am? Will he shrink from the plebeian adventuress? He is very prejudiced; but he can love! Half-past twelve. Tom is having a long talk with that dreadful man. I earnestly hope I shall not have to prosecute any one."

In a few minutes more Fanny came back.

"Oh, how glad I am to see you. I am dreadfully in the blues."

"Then it would have been much better for you to have been at church with me. The dean of some place preached such a splendid sermon. Made me feel as if I should like to clap some parts. The church was so crowded; lots of the county people were there. I saw Lady Styles and some ladies in the rector's pew. They put a strange gentleman into ours—a very elegant personage, I assure you. He was most attentive to me, and was good enough to offer me part of my own hymn-book! I don't think he imagined I looked sufficiently dignified to be even part proprietor of a pew. I found him there, and I left him there, for I came out quickly, hoping to find Tom."

"He has not yet returned," said Kate, languidly, "and as to your elegant neighbor, you had better see if your purse is safe! Highclass pickpockets generally attend the preaching of eloquent divines—at least, in London."

"How disenchanting," cried Fanny, feeling rapidly in her pocket. "I thought he was an earl at least ; not even disguised." It was considerably past their usual dinner hour when Tom reappeared.

"I think you are right," said he to Kate. "He knows something of importance ; but he is in a curious mood. Though well disposed to you, his ramshackle conscience seems to suggest some scruple about disclosing what he knows. He is in a state of great debility and penniless ; though I can see by the condition of his wardrobe that it is not long since he was flush of cash. He had been drinking very hard ; and now he has an extraordinary craving to go back to town with me. I shall indulge him, and settle him under Mrs. Small's care for a few weeks, at any rate ; he will then be safe, otherwise we shall lose him."

"But, Tom, this will cost you a quantity of money ? "

"Not so very much ; and when you have floored Sir Hugh, you shall repay me."

"Then, shall you take this man with you to town to-morrow ? "

"Yes, by the eight o'clock train. Nothing later will suit me."

"And you have gathered nothing of what Trapes really knows ? "

"Nothing ; or next to nothing. However, be sure of this, that I shall never relax my hold of him, till I *do* know."

"Thank you, dear Tom. And you believe it is not all talk, his boasted knowledge ? "

"I do. The fellow *has* the secret, whatever it is."

CHAPTER XL.

THIS same Sunday evening settled down with the orthodox Sabbath gloom at Weston. Sir Marmaduke Styles's preserves were known to be well stocked, and his lively partner had a certain undercurrent of good-nature in her gossip that gave her popularity in the minds of her kinsfolk and acquaintance. The autumn parties at Weston were therefore not to be despised ; and when Galbraith so suddenly deserted his friend Upton, the latter, having lost the incentive Hugh's company would have lent to an excursion in the wild West of Ireland, applied for extension of leave, and availed himself of Lady Styles's renewed invitation.

The household being conducted on the country type, dinner was celebrated on Sundays at half-past six instead of half-past seven—why, it would be difficult to explain, as the alteration gave no help to the well-disposed servants who wished to attend evening service ; but as it inconvenienced all parties, the ar-

rangement probably fulfilled its end : at any rate, in keeping up
the custom, Lady Styles experienced the conscious approving
glow that ought to wait on self-sacrificing christianity.

The ladies had assembled in the drawing-room after dinner.
It was a small party ; three or four, besides the hostess, lounged
comfortably round a glowing fire of wood and coal.

" I have heard the Dean preach better than to-day," Lady
Styles was saying ; " he had not his usual fire and go."

" A country congregation is perhaps refrigerating," remarked
the Honorable Mrs. A——.

" Ha, ha, ha ! I assure you Pierstoffe considers itself peculiarly intelligent or intellectual."

" There is a great difference between the terms, dear Lady
Styles," said Miss Brandon, a handsome woman in the earliest
period of the "turn of the leaf," who knew and could do nearly
everything, save how to make a fortune, or pick one up, and
who had a sort of relative's right to be at Weston in the autumn.

" A distinction without a difference, I suspect, Cecilia ; at any
rate there was a very full attendance. I saw all the principal
tradespeople there except my '*rara avis*' of the Berlin Bazaar ;
but her friend and partner represented the house. By the way,
if I am not much mistaken, they put Colonel Upton into her
pew. I wish he could see the young widow. I should like to
know his opinion of her."

" You must know," said Miss Brandon, in reply to an interrogative elevation of Mrs. A——'s eyebrows, " Lady Styles has a
sort of '*rêve de quinze ans*' about two women who keep a fancy
bazaar here. They certainly appear very distinguished compared
with the Pierstoffe standard, but I think their elegance would
pale beside Madame Elise's or Howell and James's young ladies.
Their principal charm consists of a mystery which the joint efforts of Lady Styles and Doctor Slade have failed to elucidate."

" Doctor Slade ! " cried her ladyship ; " pray do not imagine
I am a gossip like him. His gossip is of the commonest type —
mere surface sweepings to amuse his lying-in women with."
When speaking warmly, Lady Styles was not always limited by
sensitive delicacy in her phraseology. " He always imagines the
most commonplace solution even to the most piquant mysteries.
He has no grasp of mind, no real experience of the world."

" Doctor Slade is the man in a shirt frill, who is dining here
to-day ? " put in Mrs. A ——.

" Yes, and what an enormous time they are sitting," continued the hostess. " Barnes," to the butler, who appeared
with tea, " have you taken coffee to the gentlemen ? "

" Yes, my lady."

"It is always the case; that man always keeps Sir Marmaduke. He has a lot of old stories which Sir Marmaduke is accustomed to laugh at, and likes to hear over and over again. But for all that he is clever as a medical man. I believe his treatment of Sir Hugh Galbraith was masterly—he had concussion of the brain, compound fracture of the arm, various contusions, and I do not know what besides, and in two months he was nearly well. By the by, he—Galbraith, I mean—lodged at my charming widow's, and I believe he never saw her but twice all the time he was there, she is such a prudent, dignified creature. Ah, here they are at last. Colonel Upton, did they not put you in the Berlin wool pew at church to-day?"

"I cannot say," he returned, coming over and sitting down at the opposite side of the ottoman on which Lady Styles, in the splendor of her dinner dress, was spread out. "I saw no Berlin wool there, only a very pretty, piquant little girl. Who is she? The rector's daughter?"

"Nothing of the kind. Do you not remember, when you were last here, coming with me to the Berlin Bazaar and buying a purse, and how disappointed you were because you could not see your friend Galbraith's landlady?"

"Yes, very well."

"Then the pretty girl is the assistant at the bazaar. I wonder why Mrs. Temple was not there. Perhaps she has gone away again."

"Has she been away lately?" asked Upton, carelessly, as he helped himself to sugar.

"She was in London about a fortnight ago."

"I am really sorry to miss seeing this object of your speculations," said Upton, meditatively, while he stirred his tea, "I suppose she often runs up to town?"

"No, scarcely ever. At the change of seasons—and—"

"This last expedition of hers," struck in Dr. Slade, "was rather disastrous—she had her pocket picked, and lost five pounds."

"You don't say so, Doctor; are you sure? She has never mentioned the matter to me."

"Oh, I am quite correct, I assure you. I met little Miss Fanny, with a face of woe, going to the post-office for an order to replace it."

"Really, I am quite sorry for her," said Lady Styles.

"A serious loss for a Berlin bazaar," returned Upton. "Pray, when did it occur?"

"About three weeks ago. Why? did you hear anything of it?"

"No— nothing," slowly and thoughtfully.

"I do protest, Willie," cried Lady Styles, with much animation, "I believe you know more than you say, perhaps you were the pickpocket yourself—just to get an introduction! Do make a clean breast of it?"

Upton laughed. "I have not your acute curiosity about this fair shopwoman," he said, and he relapsed into silence, though an amused smile lingered on his lip and in his eyes.

"Come, Doctor," said Sir Marmaduke, who was setting forth the chessboard, "you must give me my revenge to-night."

The Honorable Mrs. A—— and Miss Brandon, followed by two or three young men who completed the party, sauntered to the music-room, whence the sound of sacred songs soon issued.

"Pray, Lady Styles," said Upton, interrupting a rambling, highly-colored version of the quarrel between Galbraith's sister and her husband,—"pray what became of your nephew, John? I remember thinking him such a fine fellow when I used to meet him here years ago."

"My nephew, John," repeated Lady Styles, in a tone of high-pitched surprise. "What put him into your head? He has disappeared I do not know how long. He was a nice creature once. All you scamps are. But he went to the bad completely cost his mother a heap of money, and died abroad—D. T., I believe."

"Did he not marry?"

"Well, I am not sure. I think it was doubtful."

"I heard he did."

"There were all kinds of reports; but I am sure I have not heard his name, nor any mention of him, for twenty years."

A pause, which was broken by Upton.

"If you will give me a mount, I think I will ride over to Pierstoffe, and reconnoitre the Berliners."

"My dear boy, let me drive you over."

"No, my gracious cousin, I prefer doing the part of a single spy. You shall then have the benefit of my pure, unsophisticated impressions."

"Very well, you shall have my groom's horse; it is the best in the stable."

But the next day was wet—not pertinaciously wet—what our northern relatives call "an even down-pour," though sufficiently moist to check Colonel Upton's fancy for a solitary ride.

It was the Wednesday after Tom's visit he had sent a hasty line announcing his safe arrival with his precious charge, and Mrs. Temple had resigned herself to an interval of patient waiting. The shop was empty, and Fanny had retired into the shop parlor, in order to trim a new straw bonnet in the latest fashion. Fanny sang to herself in a subdued tone.

Her heart was very light. She was not without sympathy, sincere sympathy, with Kate's depression ; nevertheless, her own prospects were so sunny that for the moment she doubted the possibility of serious sorrow. All would come right for Kate also, and that delinquent Galbraith, whom she could not help liking. She could give him plenary absolution too.

" Miss Fanny," said Mills, coming in, with the well-known curl on her mouth, which indicated distrust of and contempt for the world in general. " There's a gentleman—leastways he has spurs and a whip—wants to see you."

" To see me ? Who is he, Mills ? "

" I duno', Miss ; a pickpocket for all I know. You had better not—" But Mills's wise counsels were cut short by the appearance of the individual in question, whom Fanny, had she been left to her unassisted conclusions, would have considered a distinguished-looking man. Prompted by Mills's doubts she fell into a state of fear and confusion. Was he an emissary of Ford sent to discover and annoy Kate ? Was he a detective dispatched by Galbraith's lawyer, with the uncanny prescience of his tribe, to find out what was going on ? She stood up, bonnet in hand, looking prettily bewildered.

" I beg your pardon," said Upton, for he was the intruder. "I understood you were at home, and that I might enter."

Fanny, still holding her bonnet, which was filled with blond lace, ribbon, and flowers, made a little nervous curtsey, while Mills officiously dusted the chiffonnier. There was an instant's pause, broken by Fanny's saying, in an accent of unmistakable surprise, " You wished to see me ? "

" I do,"—a glance at Mills, who, finding no further excuse for remaining, departed with a portentous frown to Fanny.

" I took the liberty," resumed Upton, when they were left alone, " to look into your prayer-book, when you left your seat last Sunday. A great liberty, I acknowledge ; yet you must allow the temptation to ascertain my charming neighbor's name was a powerful motive," concluded Upton, with an insinuating smile.

" Well," exclaimed Fanny.

" You left your prayer-book behind you," drawing it from his pocket. " I confess, then, to having opened it, and read this inscription." He pointed to the flyleaf as he spoke, whereon was written, " John Aylmer to his wife Catherine, Gangepore, August, 1836."

Fanny's eyes dilated as she gazed upon it with doubt and dread. " I am going to be cross-examined," she thought, " and I shall make a mess of it."

" I see," said she, looking blankly up in her interrogator's face, " And what then ? "

" Have I the pleasure of speaking to Miss Aylmer?" said Upton, blandly.

" No, no, my name is not Aylmer!" cried Fanny, breathless.

" My reason for asking," continued Upton, "is that a distant relative of mine of that name died in India, I imagine somewhere about that date," laying his finger upon it.

" His relative indeed!" was Fanny's mental commentary. " I am sure I know nothing about it," she said, aloud. " The book is not mine. It was quite by accident I used it. I know nothing about it. I—" stopping in confusion.

" What is your name, may I ask?"

" Oh, Jenkinson," cried Fanny, with a desperate determination not to tell the imagined detective a word of truth.

" Perhaps the lady who—who keeps the shop could tell me something about these names," persisted Upton.

" No, indeed she could not," said Fanny, resolving at all risks to shield Kate from the terrors she was undergoing. " And you had better not see her. She is very clever, and would see through you in a moment."

" That is quite possible," exclaimed Upton, a good deal surprised ; but while he spoke Fanny's blond lace fell to the ground, and the gallant Colonel hastening to restore it, contrived to entangle the delicate fabric in his spurs.

" Oh, dear," cried Fanny, crouching down to rescue her treasure. Upton stood tolerably still, but as Fanny bent round, he could not help half turning to watch the pretty, troubled face. " Pray stand steady," she exclaimed, " or you will tear it. I thought it was your work to get things out of tangles, instead of into them."

" My work!" echoed Upton, greatly puzzled. " What do you take me for, then?"

" Oh, I think I know very well! You fancy I am a simple country girl, but I can guess what you are—at least, I think I can!" with dignity and triumph.

" I suppose a long course of regimental drill leaves its stamp on a fellow?" said Upton, good-humoredly.

" Regimental, indeed!" cried Fanny, with indignation. " That will not do."

" I see I have offended in some way," returned Upton, insinuatingly. " And I assure you I have but two motives in my visit : first, a strong wish—irresistible, I confess—to make your acquaintance ; secondly, a sincere desire to know the history of this prayer-book."

" He has the impudence to pretend he is smitten with me," thought Fanny, wrathfully. " I consider it altogether unwarrantable," she said, aloud, " your coming here to try and find out

16*

things from me! I daresay you thought you had an easy case, but—" Fanny had warmed up, and was now reckless of consequences.

" Will you be so very good as to say for whom you take me ? " asked Upton, with grave politeness.

" A detective of some kind sent by—"

A burst of good-humored laughter from Upton arrested any imprudence into which Fanny might have hurried.

" I am infinitely flattered," he said, drawing out his card-case. " Allow me to introduce myself."

" Colonel Upton," cried Fanny, glancing at the morsel of pasteboard he held forth, while a quick blush spread over cheek and brow. " I am so surprised ! Are you Sir Hugh Galbraith's friend we used to write to for him ? "

" The same. And I must say such a premium on breaking an arm as your secretaryship, is a temptation to fracture one's bones I never foresaw."

" I am afraid I spoke very rudely," said Fanny, with evident contrition ; " but I felt so sure you were a detective—though now I see you are quite different."

" At any rate, you have taught me a lesson of humility I shall not soon forget," returned Upton, pleasantly. " Perhaps you will have no objection to give me some information about the prayer-book, now you know who I am ? "

" Indeed I must not—I mean I cannot ! " And Fanny stopped, fearful of having committed herself.

" Of course I have no right to press you," returned Upton, noting the change of phrase.

" But wait," cried Fanny, anxious to atone for her scant courtesy ; " I will call Kate—Mrs. Temple—and you can ask her. Pray, sit down."

So saying, she rushed into the shop. " Do come, Kate. There is Colonel Upton asking all sorts of questions about your old prayer-book. And I have been so rude ! I thought he was a detective. Was it not *dreadful?* Pray go to him, and I will stay here."

To Kate's hasty, astonished queries Fanny could only reply, " It *is* Colonel Upton—do go and speak to him."

Thus urged, Kate went into the parlor and stood face to face with the supposed detective.

There was a nameless something, a gentle, composed dignity in her bearing that Upton at once recognized, and his own manner changed insensibly. He rose and stood silent, while he gazed keenly at the fair, quiet face opposite him.

" I have to thank you for restoring my prayer-book," said Kate, taking the initiative.

"It is yours, then. May I ask if this 'John Aylmer,' whose name is written here, is any relation or connection of yours? Do you know anything of him, in short?"

Mrs. Temple did not reply instantly. She paused, gazing earnestly at her interrogator. "May I ask why you inquire?" she said, at length.

"Because I had a relative of that name in India at this date; indeed, to the best of my belief, he was in this very place"— pointing to the inscription. "He is dead, and I have heard nothing of him for years. Yet I should like to know if you can give me any traces of him or his family."

"And you were related to a John Aylmer?" said Mrs. Temple. "How? In what degree?"

"That I can hardly say," returned Upton, smiling, and looking in vain for an invitation to sit down, for he was greatly struck by Mrs. Temple's appearance and manner. "I never could thread my way through the maze of cousinly degrees. But the man I mean was a nephew of Lady Styles, and she is a second or third cousin of my father: so you see we are all cousins together. It has roused my memory or curiosity to find his name in the prayer-book Miss Jenkins left behind."

"A nephew of Lady Styles," repeated Mrs. Temple, in much surprise, not hearing the conclusion of his sentence.

"Then you know something of this defunct kinsman of mine!"

"Whatever I may know, Colonel Upton," she returned, decidedly, though not uncivilly, "I do not feel at liberty to tell you now at any rate, so you must ask me no more questions."

"Certainly not, if you put it in that way," said Upton, bowing and handing her the prayer-book. "However, I fancy you put a slight emphasis on 'now.' Pray, will you allow me to call again, when perhaps you will be at liberty to tell me a little more?"

"No," said Mrs. Temple, a sweet, arch smile softening the rugged monosyllable. "I shall not be able to tell you for some time. But if you really care to hear, leave me your address, and I will write to you."

"Yes, I care very much, and will be greatly obliged by your taking that trouble. Perhaps you would be so good as to write my direction?"

Kate opened her blotting-book unsuspiciously, and traced the words as he spoke them—"Colonel W. Upton, ——th Hussars, Cahir, Ireland"— under his eyes.

"Not the first time I have seen your writing," he said, pleasantly. "I am almost sorry my friend Galbraith is able to manage his own correspondence—reading his letters has again become a difficulty, whereas—" He stopped abruptly, too genuinely good-natured not to regret having in any way disturbed Kate's equanimity ; for, in spite of her strongest effort at self-control, a quick burning blush overspread her cheeks, and even the stately, rich white throat that rose over the Quaker-like frill which adorned the collar of her dress.

" I saw Galbraith in town the other day," went on Upton, hastily, " and he seemed all right. You must have taken capital care of him, Mrs. Temple ! I really think I shall hunt here this season again, if only for the chance, should I be spilled, of falling into your hands."

" We could do very little for Sir Hugh Galbraith," said Kate, in a low voice, but recovering herself ; " Nature and his own servant seemed to accomplish everything."

She stopped, and Upton felt he ought to go, but preferred to stay. " I was sorry to hear you had met with such a loss," he continued, for the sake of something to say ; " Have you found any trace of your purse yet ? "

Again Kate colored ; this time with an acute feeling of annoyance. Galbraith must have spoken somewhat freely of her to this chum of his ; and the care and delicacy with which he seemed to guard their intimacy, and which had always touched her, must have been in some degree a sham. " I have not," she returned, coldly, adding, with a sort of haughty humility, "although, as you are no doubt aware, Sir Hugh Galbraith did his utmost to assist me ! "

" Did he," exclaimed Upton, with such unmistakable surprise that Kate instantly felt she had made a false move.

" Ah, he is not a bad fellow, Galbraith," continued Upton, "though he seems rather a rough customer. Well, I am afraid I have trespassed too long on your time, Mrs. Temple. I must bid you good morning ; and you will, when it suits yourself, give me the history of the prayer-book ? "

" I will, Colonel Upton. Meantime will you grant me a favor ? "

" It is granted," said the Colonel, gallantly.

" Then, if you have not mentioned this matter of the prayer-book to Lady Styles, pray do not. She is one of my best friends here, but you can imagine the effect of such partially admitted knowledge as mine upon her. I should not be able to call myself or my shop or anything else my own till all was revealed."

" Gad, she would hunt up the scent like a bloodhound," cried Upton, laughing. " No, no, Mrs. Temple, that would be too bitter a revenge even for having been taken for a detective. Your charming young friend owes me some reparation. Pray tell her so, with my best respects. So good morning, Mrs. Temple, and *au revoir*—for I have a strong presentiment that we shall meet again ! "

With a low bow, Upton retired, leaving Kate still standing in deep thought. No, Galbraith had not made her a topic of idle talk. She had betrayed herself; but Upton, however he heard of her loss, knew nothing whatever of Galbraith's communications with her in London.

"Fanny," she said, slowly returning to the shop, "did you ever tell Lady Styles that I had my pocket picked?"

"No, indeed, I did not!"

"Then who did you tell?"

"Not a creature: that is, yes!—now I remember it. The morning I was going for the post-office order for you, before you had told me not to tell any one, I met old Dr. Slade, and I told him!"

"Ah!" said Mrs. Temple.

"Was it very shocking?" asked Fanny, in deep contrition.

"No, never mind. Do you know, Fan, I quite like that Colonel Upton. I believe he is a gentleman."

"To be sure he is; and to think of my taking him for a detective! I am sure I shall never look him in the face again."

"You will not be obliged, I imagine," said her friend.

Meantime, Upton strolled slowly towards the hotel where he had put up his horse, meditating more profoundly than was usual with him. "I believe I have a clue to the maze," he thought. "By George, I fancy Galbraith has caught it hot and strong!—that Mrs. Temple is just the kind of woman to inspire a great passion, and Hugh, in spite of his cold airs, the very man to feel one. What with his pride and hers—for she will stand no nonsense, I suspect—there will be the devil to pay. I am certain he forsook me that day at H—— to go after her. Ay, it was the next morning he was going down to Scotland Yard; it is as plain as that pretty little Miss Jenkins's *nez retroussé!* Galbraith has had a squeeze: he had better go abroad; change of air and scene is the best remedy; but to apply that nostrum in such a case, the plan would be to take a new love. I have a great mind to offer a remedy to the fair widow in the shape of myself! I should not dislike making love to her at all. There is a world of undeveloped feeling in her eyes. What a 'cheerful visitor' I might make myself to Lady Styles if I were to sit down and treat her to a dish of my surmises and discoveries! But how did that Mrs. Temple come to possess poor Jack Aylmer's prayer-book? I should like to ask Lady Styles more about him and his possible marriage—but no, I have promised silence, and will keep my word in the spirit as well as the letter."

CHAPTER XLI.

IF Kate and Fanny, especially the former, waited with almost sickening anxiety for news of Tom's proceedings, they had at least the comfort of full faith in him. No doubts of his ardent friendship or his earnest action, complicated their pangs of endurance, even when Wednesday and Thursday brought no tidings.

In the meantime, Tom, who was overwhelmed with work on his own account, contrived to see Trapes every day, but without extracting any tangible information from him. He (Trapes), though recovering, was feeble, and always spoke as if it was his intention to "make a clean breast of it as soon as he had settled a little business he had on hand," or "as soon as he was able to go into the City to see a fellow he wanted to speak to."

"Come, now," cried Tom, at last, "do you want to see Ford? for if it is that, I will call and tell him. I shall be passing his place this afternoon, and I suspect it will be some days before you are equal to the journey due-east."

To this, after some demurs, Trapes assented. "Don't you let on that I have seen Mrs. Travers," he urged.

"Of course not. Ford is not to know that she is in England."

"Ay, to be sure. Perhaps, after all, Reed, I had better wait and write him a line."

"No, no, have him out here, and say your say! Then make a clean breast of it, and you will be ever so much better."

Tom was growing very anxious for Trapes's revelations. He feared a relapse of low fever, or a sudden failure of intellect. He was evidently linked in some strange way with Ford; how, it was impossible to conjecture. Tom therefore made it a point to call at Ford's office, and, on mounting the stairs, was struck by the evident increase of the ex-clerk's business : various anxious looking men—some with pocket-books, some with papers in their hands—were coming up and down ; the office door was open, and several persons were speaking to the clerks or writing on slips of paper.

In the middle of the office stood a very respectable-looking, gentlemanlike man older than Ford himself, evidently the manager. He seemed deeply engaged with an irate personage, whom he was endeavoring to soothe, and who held out an open letter. "I see, sir, that letter is very conclusive," he was saying, "but you need be under no apprehension."

"The delay is most annoying!" returned the other, a young man got up in a "country-gentleman" style. "You see he promises to procure me eight hundred pounds' worth of Turkish Fives and Russians, at once. Now, there was a fall of an eighth on Friday in one, and a sixteenth on Monday in the other, and he missed both opportunities!"

"I really am not in a position to assert anything," returned the manager. "I know Mr. Ford transacted business on the Stock Exchange on Friday and on Monday, but, being suddenly called away, he had not time to leave me full instructions. If you will call to-morrow, I shall, no doubt, be able to arrange matters to your satisfaction, and make the purchases you require. I shall have heard from Mr. Ford by that time."

"I hope so," said the other. "It is altogether very extraordinary;" and, with a running growl, he turned to leave, very nearly knocking against Tom Reed, who now advanced.

"Is Mr. Ford away, then?" he asked.

"Yes," said the manager, looking sharply at his interrogator. 'Obliged to run over to Vichy for a few days' holiday, but I shall be happy to do anything for you in his absence."

"Thank you," said Tom. "I only wished to speak to him on a private matter."

"Private," repeated the manager, thoughtfully. "I think I remember your coming here with Mr. Ford one day last spring."

"I did do so."

"Then, perhaps, you would do me the favor to call to-morrow, either early or after five? You might—that is, I shall probably be able to tell you something of Mr. Ford's movements." He paused, and then added, "I should feel obliged by your calling."

"I will, then, but it must be nearer six than five," returned Tom, feeling that the request was unusual. So saying, and placing his card in the chief clerk's hand, he left the office.

"I wonder 'wot's up!'" he pondered, as he rolled westward in the first cab he could find. "There is something wrong with Ford! I wonder if he is gone mad? There was a very suspicious glitter in his eye the last time we met." So reflecting, he called to the driver to set him down in B—— Street, where he spent a few minutes in explaining matters to Mr. Wall.

"Very well, Mr. Reed—very well," said the lawyer, "but I really begin to have serious doubts that this man Trapes knows anything at all! However, as Mrs. Travers seems content to await your rather tardy operations, I have no right to find fault. But if I find you have nothing more tangible to communicate by Saturday, I really must summon Poole! That is our line, I am convinced."

"No doubt, Mr. Wall, you will be all right in that direction; meantime, I hope to bring you a lot of information by Saturday." And Tom hurried off with more of hope in his manner than in his heart. It was too provoking to feel the goal almost within his grasp, yet evading his touch!

The next day was excessively occupied ; and six o'clock had tolled from the great clock of St. Paul when Tom Reed ran hastily up the stairs to Ford's office—those on the ground and second floors were already closed—and when he reached the door he met the manager just issuing forth. " I had given you up," he said, quickly, and in a different tone from that in which he had spoken the day before. " Pray step in."

Reed followed him. An old clerk was in the act of turning off the gas : " One moment if you please," said Reed's conductor ; "I want to speak to this gentleman. But you need not wait ; I will give the key to the housekeeper as I go down."

The old clerk bowed and withdrew, and Tom could not resist a chill, creepy sensation, as if on the verge of a discovery—whether of a crime or a tragedy !—while his companion raked the fire together and threw on some more coals.

" May I ask if you have known Mr. Ford long ? " he asked, sitting down at one of the high desks.

" Not very long, Mr.—," returned Tom.

" Rogers," said the other, gravely supplying the word. " My name is Rogers."

" Well, then, Mr. Rogers, I have not known Mr. Ford more than a couple of years."

" But you knew him when he was at Travers's ? My reason for asking is, that I am exceedingly perplexed ; and not knowing any friend of Mr. Ford's to apply to (for he led a singularly isolated life), I was in hopes you might afford me some information. The fact is, I fear he has committed suicide !"

" Suicide ! " cried Tom, aghast.

" I am not sure. I will tell you the whole story ; it will soon be noised abroad. I had thought him looking very wild and haggard for a few days, and on last Saturday was rather pleased to hear him say he would go over to Vichy for a week, just to recruit. There was really nothing to prevent him—no business I could not do ; so he said he would leave me a power-of-attorney to sign checks and letters, etc. On Monday morning accordingly, he came in early and transacted a good deal of business, gave me the power-of-attorney to act for him, and started off with one of those portmanteau-bags to catch the boat-express from London Bridge, saying as he went, ' You shall hear from me fully on two or three points towards the end of the week ; ' and I thought no more of it. But on Tuesday evening I had occasion to go to the strong-box for some coupons, and to my great surprise I found all the Continental securities—Turkish and Egyptian bonds, and a few Americans—which I knew were safe there on Friday evening, had been removed—altogether between two and three thousand pounds' worth. I confess I

felt great uneasiness, not knowing Mr. Ford's address; but, remembering his last words, I hoped the morning's post would
bring me his promised letter. It did not; but in the afternoon,
shortly before you called, I received from his housekeeper, a respectable, elderly woman, this long letter."

"This is very strange! Has he bolted, then?" cried Tom.

"Not in the ordinary sense. I do not feel at liberty to show
you the letter," continued Mr. Rogers; "but it is to the effect
that I am to use the power-of-attorney to settle his affairs; that
he has left ample funds to meet all claims upon him; that I am
to act as his executor, for I shall never see him again in this life!
I went up to his place last night, and found from the housekeeper
that he had not taken any clothes with him, and that on Sunday
night he had sat up late writing. On quitting the house he had
said: 'If I do not return on Wednesday evening, send this
letter'—which he gave into her hands—'in the course of the
next day to Mr. Rogers,' which the housekeeper accordingly did."

"An extraordinary affair!" exclaimed Tom Reed, rising and
coming over to the desk at which the other was sitting. "Do
you think it was his intention to commit suicide?"

"I do."

"I do not," returned Reed, quickly. "His object is to escape."

"Escape what?" asked the other, rather indignantly. "A
more honorable, straightforward man, never existed! Do you
know any reason why he should fly the country?"

"No, Mr. Rogers, I do not. I only judge from what you tell
me. A man who is about to terminate his existence does not
want a capital of two or three thousand pounds in the world he
is going to!"

"Then you believe he removed all the foreign securities?"

"Yes; don't you?"

"I do not know what to think. I hoped you might have
known something of poor Ford's real circumstances. He lived
singularly alone. I have telegraphed to a brother of his in Lancashire, and have set the police on the track, so far as I know it."

"Tell me, Mr. Rogers, has a man called Trapes—a seedy,
flashy, turfy-looking fellow, been in the habit of coming here occasionally?"

"Not of that name," he answered, "but decidedly of that description. He called himself Jones. However, I daresay he
went by various names. Yes, a fellow like what you describe
has been in here now and then. Sometimes he would be here
two or three times running, and would then disappear for a considerable period. Why, do you connect him with Ford's disappearance?"

"I have a vague idea—mind, very vague—that he has something to do with it. Should I ascertain more I shall let you know."

After some further desultory talk and conjectures, Reed took his leave, very much astonished at the result of his inquiries, and resisting as illogical the tendency of his imagination to connect Ford's strange disappearance with Trapes, and Trapes's alleged knowledge of the will.

He was determined to lose no time in communicating his curious intelligence to Trapes, for he could not help feeling that it would affect his broken-down *protégé* strongly. But the editor of a morning paper is a slave to the thunder he wields, and it was past Trapes's late breakfast hour before Tom could make his way to him next day.

"He was very bad last night, sir," said the landlady, as she opened the door, smiling, as she ever did upon the favored Tom. "He had such severe spasms as it took near a pint of the best brandy before he came right, and then he begged and prayed, and cursed and swore, because I took away the bottle, so that, if my son had not been at home, I don't know what I should have done. But he is as mild as new milk this morning, and I have given him a cup of fine, strong tea, but, bless ye, he won't taste a bit!"

"Now, Mrs. Small," said Tom, sternly, "Mr. Trapes must have no brandy without medical advice. Provide it at your peril. I will not pay for it, remember that!"

He opened the door of the little sitting-room, and found Trapes—a pipe in his mouth, and *Bell's Life* in his hand—leaning back in one chair, his feet elevated on another.

"Well, so you never looked in last night," he began, in a querulous, growling voice.

"My good fellow, I have brought you news enough to atone for any shortcoming. Your friend Ford has disappeared—decamped—is not to be found, in short."

Trapes started up, dropped his paper and his pipe, which smashed on the fender. "Bolted! What then! How the deuce did he get scent of what was brewing?"

"I know nothing of the whys and wherefores," returned Tom. "I only know what his head clerk told me," and he proceeded to repeat what he had learned.

"And has he smashed for a large amount?"

"I don't believe he has smashed at all. I believe no one has any interest in hunting him up, except his attached relatives—unless it's yourself, Trapes—for I strongly suspect you could read the riddle."

"I am not so sure of that. But it's an extraordinary move

on the part of Ford. To be sure, he threatened; but," checking himself, "that is nothing to the point."

He suddenly lapsed into silence, picking up the fragments of his pipe in an absent, mechanical manner. "And that fellow, Rogers, thinks he has made away with himself?"

Tom nodded, watching Trapes, who seemed from the changes of his countenance to be undergoing some mental struggle.

"Well, whether he has or not," cried Trapes, at length, with an oath, turning his face to Tom, "it seems as if his game was up, and I will make a clean breast of it!"

Whereupon he launched into a long narrative, at the end of which, and some talk with his friend, Tom administered refreshment in the shape of cold beef and a judicious allowance of brandy-and-water. A cab was summoned, and Tom Reed carried off his prize in triumph to Mr. Wall.

It was not until the afternoon post on Saturday that Kate reaped the reward of her faith and patience. The letters were unusually late, and seeing a packet of considerable dimensions, Mrs. Temple had the self-control to put it in her pocket till "closing time" set her free to plunge into its contents. Indeed, she felt she dared not commence its perusal until she was safe from the eyes of her customers. Then, with closed doors, and her faithful little friend by her side, she read the following particulars, which are here set forth free from Tom's introductory and explanatory remarks.

About the end of February succeeding Mr. Travers's death, Trapes, who had been suffering from a run of ill-luck, happened to pitch his tent—*i. e.*, take lodgings—in a small street off Gray's-inn-lane, where a former acquaintance—a law writer in very low circumstances, named Nicholls—managed to drag on a wretched existence. The poor fellow, moreover, was in a rapid decline, and Trapes, with the queer, incongruous generosity which flecked his reckless, ignoble nature here and there, was kind to the sufferer and shared what trifling supplies he managed to pick up with him; in return, the consumptive scrivener was glad to divide any windfall that came to him. The partners were, however, reduced to great straits; when one day, as Trapes returned from an aimless, hopeless walk, the law writer told him he had written to a former employer for help, and the employer had replied, promising a visit.

"Now he cannot come and not leave a blessing behind," said Nicholls. "He is coming this evening, and as he is uncommon particular, and a bit of a prig, I think you had better keep out of sight;" to which Trapes acceded. When the visitor had departed, Nicholls informed his friend that he had made him a present of a sovereign, and promised him a job of writing.

"Now I really am not equal to this," said the poor scrivener; "but I saw that his mind was set on it, and that I should get very little out of him if I did not agree. So I thought we might do it between us, for you can write a legal fist; but I did not mention you, for it strikes me there's some mystification in the matter."

In due time the "job" was put in hand. It was to copy out and engross a will, simple and short, with blanks left for all names, sums of money, and dates.

Some slight delay occurred in procuring parchment, etc. However, the task was accomplished in the given time; but by Trapes, as Nicholls, in going to purchase the materials, caught cold, and was really incapable of holding a pen. The gentleman for whom the work was done seemed anxious for speed and secrecy. He came himself for the document, and was satisfied with the manner in which it had been executed. He seemed, Nicholls said, concerned to see him suffering so much. He paid liberally, and called twice again. On his second visit he found Nicholls on his death-bed, and Trapes saw him distinctly for the first time. Very few words passed between them. The employer expressed becoming sympathy with the employed, bestowed an alms, and departed a couple of hours before the sufferer breathed his last, leaving no clue by which Trapes (had he wished it) could identify him. Nicholls had always carefully abstained from mentioning his name.

But Trapes forgot all about him, and scrambled on through another jagged, ragged year, when accident threw him once more into Poole's society, from whom he heard much gossip respecting his former acquaintance, Tom Reed; of his intimacy with Mrs. Travers (of which Trapes was already aware, forming his own conclusions thereon); also of the general upset in "The House" by the finding of a new will, and the disappearance of Mrs. Travers. This talk of wills did not recall any associated ideas to his muddy brains; he only chuckled with dull, gratified spite to think that Tom Reed was not to have his fortunes crowned by marriage with a rich, beautiful widow after all.

It was not till the previous spring that his curiosity and self-interest were roused by coming suddenly upon Tom Reed in evidently close and familiar conversation with the benevolent individual who had befriended Nicholls.

His visit to Reed followed. Directly he became aware that Ford, formerly manager at "Travers's," and the defunct scrivener's employer were one and the same, a light broke in upon him; ease, indulgence, fortune, were in his grasp! "That fellow Ford" had of course been employed by the baronet, and the thieving rascals should pay for their villainy by enabling an honest well-disposed party (himself) to enjoy a little peace and comfort! With a glow of conscious virtue he proceeded to expend a shilling of the sovereign requisitioned from Tom for permission to peruse the "last will and testament" of Richard Travers, Esq., late of St. Hilda's Place, E. C., etc., etc. A glance at the document confirmed all his suspicions. It was his own work, written nearly three months after the death of the supposed testator!

A visit to Ford, and an immediate improvement in the appearance of the fortunes—but, alas! not in the habits—of the lucky Trapes ensued. It was evident, even on his own showing, that he had extracted quantities of money from Ford, besides making life a burden to him.

At last Ford rebelled, and declared that, rather than drag on such an existence, he would give up the game, make a clean breast of it, and defy Trapes.

This suggestion by no means suited that ingenious individual. He therefore strove to collect all moneys due to him by hook or by crook, in order to give Ford time to cool and repent his rash intentions. With a view to turn what he would probably term "an honest penny," he attended the Stoneborough races, and there victimized young Turner, who, not being able to pay up in full, in an unwary moment gave his address at Pierstoffe. Thither Trapes hunted him, and thus stumbled upon Fanny. He knew of her relationship to Tom, of her connection with Mrs. Travers, and once more he felt on the road to high fortunes!

- Such were the principal facts contained in Tom's letter. It must be added that a tardy sense of compassion for Ford seemed to have induced Trapes to refrain from speaking out until he could give him some warning of the crash that was impending.

CHAPTER XLII.

WITH white lips, and in a low, parched voice, Kate read these astonishing details to Fanny, who at the same time perused the letter over her shoulder. When it was ended, the friends looked at each other, and Kate, resting her elbows on the table, covered her face with her hands.

"The murder is out at last," exclaimed Fanny; "and," with a hearty kiss, "the queen shall have her own again."

"Thank heaven!" cried Kate. "Mr. Ford is gone. I shall not have to prosecute him. How could he have permitted himself to act so basely, so treacherously, so fatally for himself. I am very glad he has escaped."

"Well, so am I; but he deserved to be punished. I wonder

what will be done next. I wonder if Sir Hugh will dispute your claim. But he cannot. I wonder—''

"You see," interrupted Kate, "Tom says, 'We are rather stunned at present. But Mr. Wall will write to you as soon as he has consulted counsel, and made up his mind.' We must just wait—wait still. All I hope is, that there will be no bitter, costly lawsuit. But how will Hugh Galbraith take it? I wonder where he is?''

"Then he did not leave his address when you parted," said Fanny, demurely. "You really must forgive him, and make friends, now you have beaten him."

"You must remember my victory is not an accomplished fact yet. But as to Hugh Galbraith, I have forgiven him long ago. Still, he has not ceased to trouble me, I fear."

"And, dear Kate, what shall you do? Shall you live in the grand Hereford Square house, or—''

"Dearest Fan, how far ahead of present probabilities you go. There are quantities of things to be done yet."

"If I were you I should advertise the Berlin Bazaar for sale at once; that would be doing something."

"Yes. Whatever happens, I shall not, of course, stay here when you are married. But, Fan," beginning to re-read the letter, "what an extraordinary history this is! With what skill and cunning Mr. Ford appears to have laid his plans! He must have thought that the secret of his iniquity was buried with the poor scrivener; and in his turn *he* thought that in concealing Ford's name he had kept full faith with his employer."

They talked far into the night, and then retired to dream, and conjecture even in sleep.

It was long, however, before tired nature's restorer visited Kate's eyes. Over and over again she pictured Galbraith receiving the news that Fortune's brief smile was withdrawn, and replaced by her heaviest frown. The stern impartiality with which he would set himself to sift the evidence, and, seeing it incontrovertible, the silent endurance with which he would submit to his fate. And all the time no sympathizing friend near to take his hand and say, "It is hard to bear."

Her heart throbbed, and the tears welled over on her eyelashes with the intensity of the longing she had to be with him, to assure him that all should be well, if he would only be reasonable; to tell him that she understood him and felt for him, and would be faithful to him. One more crisis was to come, and she knew it would be the greatest of her life. He must be told, sooner or later, who she really was; and everything depended on how he took that information.

The succeeding fortnight went by with the strangest mixture

of flight and dragging. Every day that was unmarked by a
letter from Tom seemed an age of inaction, and yet at the end
of the week it seemed but an hour since the first great news of
the solving of mysteries had arrived. Still no tidings of how
Hugh Galbraith had borne the bursting of the storm, or if he
had even heard of it.

It was from Lady Styles the first rumor reached Mrs. Temple,
more than a fortnight after Upton's visit.

Her ladyship, contrary to her usual custom, had driven into
Pierstoffe before luncheon, in order to take some departing visitor to the train.

"Did not expect to see me at this hour," she said, waddling
in with her usual vivacity. "Do you know, I think it is very
foolish to come out as late as we all do in winter; but it can't
be helped. My coachman would give me notice if I took him
out every day at eleven, and James would rebel. Yet in November it is almost dark before one can order the carriage
round. And how are you, Mrs. Temple? I cannot say you
are looking very bright. Any news of your purse?"

"None, I am sorry to say, Lady Styles."

"Sorry to hear it. I don't think I have seen you since Colonel
Upton paid you a visit. By the way, it's a mistake your not
keeping gentlemen's gloves. Lots of the men staying at Weston and other places would make quite a lounge here, and buy
heaps—"

"That is exactly what I should not like the Berlin Bazaar to
become, Lady Styles," returned its mistress. "It is a lady's
shop *par excellence.*"

"I am sure you are the most prudent young woman in the
world; still I am certain a mixed multitude pays. Do you know,
I do not think I should make a bad woman of business myself."

"Far from it, Lady Styles."

"Well, I want two pairs of black gloves stitched with red.
Have you any at two-and-ninepence? No? really, Mrs. Temple, your prices are extravagant; a Bond Street standard for
Pierstoffe won't do, I assure you. Well, have you any dark
violet at three-and-sixpence?"

Mrs. Temple could accommodate her ladyship; and while
she was undoing the parcels and turning a whole boxful over to
select a thin, elastic kid, she chattered on.

"Well, is there no news stirring? Have you seen Slade
lately? No! I am surprised at a bright, intelligent woman
living shut up like a mummy in this old house, never hearing
anything or seeing any one. By the way, that reminds me. I
had a letter from Colonel Upton this morning: do you know he
was quite struck with you. I can't tell you all the pretty things

he said : and envied Sir Hugh Galbraith having been your inmate, and declared, with his usual impudence, that had he been
in Galbraith's place he would have seen a good deal more of
you."

" I do not think he would," said Mrs. Temple, demurely.

" So I told him. But in his letter this morning he says he
had just seen Galbraith, who has been called up to town in consequence of some move of the enemy, that is, Travers's widow.
She is making a stir about the will. I suppose it will end in
smoke ; but it is curious that the day I took the trouble of going
up to see Sir Hugh Galbraith, when he received me so coolly, I
suggested to him that he had not heard the last of her yet, Of
course he pooh-pooh'd my suggestion ; but it was curious, wasn't
it ? "

" I think this pair will suit you, Lady Styles," said Mrs. Temple, anxious to draw her away from this agitating topic.

" Well they look very nice ! May I try them on ? "

" It is against shop rules," returned Mrs. Temple, smiling.
" But you may."

This little concession charmed her ladyship, who was further
gratified by finding they fitted admirably, and, after a little more
talk, she rose to depart.

" And how is your agreeable friend, the traveler ? "

" Who ? " asked Kate, considerably puzzled.

" Oh, you know who I mean ! The young man I had tea
with. Ha, ha ha ! "

" Yes, yes, I remember. He is quite well, thank you ! "

" Do you know I met a man in town last spring so wonderfully like him. I was quite startled for a moment ! It was at
Lady Lorrimer's, one of Sir Hugh Galbraith's sisters. She is a
blue and a politician, and has artists and editors, and a perfect
olla podrida at her house. Just as I went into the refreshment-
room I saw a gentleman handing a cup of tea to a very pretty
woman, and he was so like your young man that I nearly cried
out, ' Shrimps ! ' "

" Very extraordinary," returned Kate, laughing, " but he is
Fanny's young man, not mine."

" Oh, indeed ! " cried Lady Styles, with a twinkle of delight in
her good-humored black, beady eyes. " I always guessed he was
after one or other of you. And so he is her young man," reseating herself. " Now tell me all about it."

Kate, bitterly repenting her unguarded admission, had hard
work to ward off her ladyship's very leading questions, and after
a desperate encounter of wits, had at last the satisfaction of seeing her tormentor depart.

In the meantime Mr. Wall and Tom were working hard in

London. The revelations of Trapes rendered criminal proceedings against Poole unnecessary, although he was called upon to explain how his name came to be appended to a will executed when it was incontrovertibly proved that he was sixty or seventy miles away. He was greatly astonished at the circumstances revealed to him, but adhered steadily to his statement, that late in February or early in March, previous to Mr. Travers's death, he had been called in to the private office to witness, together with Gregory, what he understood to be Mr. Travers's will written out by the latter.

He acknowledged that, about a week or ten days after, he had had "sick leave," which he had employed in attending the Reepham Steeplechase in company with Trapes; but he felt quite sure the signature shown him was his own writing. After meditating on it for a moment or two, he suddenly struck his hand on the table and exclaimed, "I remember now!—between three and four months after Mr. Travers's death, I was very hard-up, and one day Ford noticed I was looking uncommon bad. As he spoke in an unusually kind, friendly way, I took heart, and asked him for a small loan. He said he could not oblige me then, but that if I would come over to his place and take a bit of dinner he would. So I went. We had a very good feed. Then he lent me two ten, and talked to me like a father, till he brought the tears into my eyes. Then he said he was making a little settlement on a sister of his, and asked me to be good enough to witness his signature. Of course I agreed, and he went over to another table and wrote something, and then he brought a parchment, all doubled up, and says he, 'Put your name there.' 'All right,' says I, 'only I did not really see you write yours.' 'Never mind,' said he, with a pleasant laugh, 'I am sure you heard it, for I never had such a scratchy pen.' I was ashamed to say any more, so I just wrote my name, though I did not exactly see where he had put his. I wonder if he really had any hand in this! But he was done out of money by it himself, wasn't he?"

Poole had been kept carefully in the dark as to the suspicions or rather certainties concerning Ford, and this fresh instance of the morbid cunning displayed by the late manager struck Mr. Wall and Tom, who were both present at the examination of the signatures by Poole, as confirmatory of the deep-laid and carefully worked-out scheme, by which he had endeavored to draw Kate into his power, and singularly illustrative of the keen foresight on all sides save the one where strong passion and unchecked desire had blinded his judgment and blunted his moral sense.

His whole plot rested its chance of success on the strength of

Kate's dislike to Sir Hugh Galbraith overcoming her sense of right. Had be been able to view these forces with sight undistorted by exaggerated vanity and enormous selfishness, he would not have embarked in so disastrous a crime. Once launched in it self-preservation compelled him to persevere.

"What an awful life that fellow must have led for more than two years!" exclaimed Tom to Mr. Wall, who was making a note of Poole's observations. "I imagine he has had his share of punishment."

"It is very much to be regretted he has escaped the hands of justice," returned Mr. Wall, sternly, "and I trust he may be caught yet. I have seldom heard of a greater villain. Just look at the confusion he has created! First, poor Mrs. Travers suffers, and then Sir Hugh Galbraith! Finally, Mr. Travers's intentions are frustrated, for there can be no question that at the end of February, 18—, he executed a will, which will this absconding forger has destroyed. So we are compelled to fall back upon the first will which Mrs. Travers originally proved. I must say that, although I am heartily glad Mrs. Travers is righted, I cannot help feeling for Sir Hugh Galbraith. He has laid out a good deal of money, too, in the purchase of property, I am told. Mrs. Travers can force him to repay all that, you know."

"Mrs. Travers will do nothing harsh or unjust," cried Tom; "but I agree with you it is much to be regretted the second will is lost. It is impossible even to guess at the true intentions of the testator. What course do you propose to take now?"

This was fully discussed, and with the advice of counsel it was decided to lay a statement of the whole matter, with Trapes's confession, duly embodied in an affidavit, and the circumstances detailed by Poole and Captain Gregory before Sir Hugh Galbraith's solicitor, who quickly summoned his client from the congenial retirement of the family den. Here Galbraith had lived not unhappily since his last interview and rejection by Mrs. Temple. Something he could not define in her voice—her look—her soft, hesitating manner, gave him hope. There might be some difficulties connected with her past, which she could not at once remove, but nothing that he would shrink from associating with the name of wife. He had her word for that, and it was enough. In another month or six weeks he would visit Pierstoffe again, or write and ask leave to do so. All hesitation and doubt had long since been exorcised by "the sweetness and light" of as honest a love as ever warmed man's heart.

Near Kate, life was a fresher, fairer thing than he ever thought it could be. To be understood—to be loved—to have the brighter, richer tints of his soul, which had so long been dulled by the mists and miasmas of every-day commonplace association with men who aspired not, nor knew, nor sought knowledge,—to feel them glowing forth once more, retouched by the penetrating nobility of a nature in many things weaker, but also in many loftier, than his own, all this was a vision of paradise. What a terrible awakening awaited him when he reached London. His dreams were even more substantial than the reality he had tasted.

At first he was very little moved ; but as one overwhelming proof after another was laid before him, he could no longer refuse acquiescence in his lawyer's conviction, that the will which had constituted him his cousin's heir, was a clever forgery.

Having admitted this, he demanded a day's reflection. It was spent in a brave, silent facing of his position on every side, and a careful, deliberate decision on his own future plans.

When Galbraith reappeared at Mr. Payne's office, he looked considerably older and sterner, but it was with perfect composure and apparent *sang froid* that he gave them directions to communicate to Mrs. Travers's solicitor his complete conviction of the justice of her claims, and the means by which he proposed to refund the money he had withdrawn from her estate.

While these events were occurring in London, Kate, finding herself too much over-wrought by the strain of constant anxiety and correspondence with Tom and Mr. Wall, to give due attention to her business,—Fanny, too, being quite distracted from her usual routine,—it suggested itself to her mind one morning, while lying wakefully watching for the dawn, that she would ask Mr. Turner for the "loan" of one of his young ladies to attend to the shop. It was more than she could bear at such a time to be hunting for subtile shades of Berlin wool, when her heart was beating with a variety of emotions, hopes, and fears, inextricably mixed together, so that every hope was largely streaked with fear, and every fear with hope.

Fanny, who was in a most restless, nervous mood, highly approving this project, Mrs. Temple started immediately after their early dinner to call on the proprietor of the chief shop, glad to be out in the air and doing anything.

She was most politely received by Turner, senior, who heard her proposition favorably and affably. In fact, in the dead season, he was not sorry to get rid of an extra shopwoman.

He rubbed his hands over each other, in the "Do-you-require-any-other-article, madam" style, and said blandly that he was always "happy to oblige a neighbor ; that there was Miss Newman or Miss Finch, both very clever, industrious young ladies, with a good idea of business, and she could arrange with either herself."

Mrs. Temple thanked him, and was about to request an interview with one or other, when, with a portentous hem! Mr.
Turner proceeded to inquire if she had any idea of giving up
business, or if it was only temporary pressure that made her seek
extra assistance. Mrs. Temple answered candidly that circumstances would probably render business no longer necessary to
her, and that the Berlin Bazaar would soon be in the market.

" Then, ma'am," said Turner, solemnly, " as a neighbor that
has always been on the best of terms, may I be so bold as to
ask for the first refusal ? "

" Certainly, Mr. Turner," she replied, smiling; " you are at
liberty to make me an offer whenever you like."

He, still solemnly, replied he would take a few days to consider, and then proceeded to summon Miss Finch, with whom
Kate soon agreed, arranging, to her great satisfaction, that the
young lady was to sleep at her old quarters, but to come to
breakfast at the Berlin Bazaar each morning.

" I think, Fan, I shall get rid of the business without the
trouble and delay of advertising," said Kate, after narrating her
interview with Mr. Turner ; " and this poor girl seems very good-
humored and inoffensive—you must go in and assist her sometimes."

" Of course I will, dear. But, oh ! I do feel in such an extraordinary state ! Every ring of the bell makes me expect Sir
Hugh, or news that Ford's body has been found ! or that Sir
Hugh has shot Tom, or Trapes has committed suicide ! It will
be such a relief when everything is really settled, and we have
left Pierstoffe."

" It will," said Mrs. Temple, slowly, while she took off her bonnet ; " but, Fanny, I shall always have a regard for Pierstoffe.
It was here I found I could ' learn and labor ' to get my own
living, and altogether I am not sure I shall quit Pierstoffe with
dry eyes."

" Ah," said Fanny, with a supremely knowing look, " I can
understand your having more tender reminiscences of Pierstoffe
than I have, but I will say no more. Goodness gracious ! " interrupting herself. " What a violent ring ! Mills !—don't you
hear, Mills ? " and Fanny started up with her hand on her heart.

" Law, Miss Fanny, it's only the post ; you need not be in such
a taking. There ! two for the mistress, and one for you."

" One is a circular," said Kate, taking hers. " But who is
this from ? "

" Just open it and see," cried Fanny, who had pounced upon
her own letter, which bore Tom's well-known superscription.
" There is nothing particular in it," she continued, glancing at
its contents. " No further news from Messrs. Payne. Sir Hugh

is in town—he supposes in consultation with them, and Mr.
Wall will let you know anything fresh.   Now, who is your correspondent?"

"Colonel Upton!" cried Kate, turning to the signature at the
end of her letter.

"How extraordinary!   What does he say?"

"Dear Madam," read Kate, "since I had the p'easure of seeing you, some circumstances connected with my relative, the
late John Aylmer, have come to my knowledge, which make
me especially anxious for any information that you can give me
respecting the prayer-book which so stirred my curiosity.   I
trust I am not indiscreet in troubling you.   Should you be inclined to gratify me, I shall be entirely guided by your wishes in
making your solution of the mystery public or not—"

"I wonder what he can have heard," said Kate, thoughtfully.
"At any rate, Fan, there is no longer any need for concealment.
I shall just tell him the fact that his relative, John Aylmer, was my
father.   I wonder if Lady Styles will still continue to patronize
the Bazaar when the news penetrates to her ears?   Perhaps she
will be disgusted!"

"Not she," cried Fanny.   "She will be far too much delighted with such a nine days' wonder.   Tell me, Kate, did you
know all along that she was your great-aunt?"

"No, Fanny; not until Colonel Upton's visit."

"And how could you hold your tongue about it?

The next day but one brought a long letter from Mr. Wall,
announcing that Sir Hugh Galbraith had resolved not to make
any attempt to uphold the will which had been proved in so extraordinary a manner to be false.   His solicitors, on his part, expressed extreme regret that he should, under an erroneous impression regarding his rights, have alienated so large a sum from
Mrs. Travers's property.   To refund this was quite out of Sir
Hugh Galbraith's power.   All he could propose was to give her
a mortgage, being a first charge upon property still remaining to him, and pay five per cent. interest.   He also proposed to
create a sort of sinking fund by quarterly payments into the
hands of trustees in order to liquidate the debt.

Various other details of business were dealt with, the letter
concluding thus: "No traces of the missing Ford have as yet
been discovered, nor do I think will be.   Being amply supplied
with funds of the least traceable description he is probably in
the New World by this.   I shall be glad to know what your
plans are.   If I might make a suggestion, I should say that
your presence in town would be desirable.

"Are you in want of cash? If so, pray let me know how much you require, and I will forward a check by return.

"I am yours, etc., etc."

"Ah!" said Kate with a sigh and a smile. "Have the old times come back; the quiet, stagnant old times, when I never had even the excitement of a want? But no, the game is not played out yet!"

She immediately replied to the lawyer's letter, entreating him to make Sir Hugh Galbraith understand that she particularly wished him to consider the ten thousand he had appropriated his share of the property, for she felt convinced that had the will for which the forged one was substituted been discovered, a larger portion would have been his. She pressed Mr. Wall to lose no time in making this proposition, and to let her know the result. She declined his offer of funds with thanks, assuring him that her *shop* had answered extremely well. Finally, she promised to come up to town as soon as she could arrange matters at Pierstoffe.

Now that she was free, she felt an extraordinary reluctance to move—why, she scarcely acknowledged to herself. But the real magnet which attracted her to her humble home was a vague but instinctive feeling that Galbraith would come to seek her there—that in the wilderness of London they might miss each other, and that now nothing was to be risked, for the happiness of both was balancing on a mere thread of possibility.

"Yet I must go soon—I cannot stay on ; and Fanny is visibly vibrating to the points of her toes in her eagerness to take flight!"

CHAPTER XLIII.

THE day after Kate had dispatched her reply to Mr. Wall's letter she was somewhat surprised by receiving an offer from the prosperous Turner for "the good-will, stock-in-trade, furniture, and fixtures" of the modest little establishment, she having only informed him of her intention to part with it a few days before. The sum he proposed was sufficient to reimburse her for any outlay she had made, and leave a small—a very small margin of profit.

It was enough, however, to satisfy the proprietress, who, sincerely glad to have the whole concern thus taken off her hands at once, only waited till the next morning to write, accepting Mr. Turner's offer, lest a more immediate reply should seem too hasty.

"Really," exclaimed Fanny, "nothing could happen more fortunately. We shall only have to pack up our clothes, and leave everything as it stands. When shall you go?—because if you will make up your mind, I had better write to Tom to take lodgings for us. Oh," with an ecstatic jump, and clapping her hands together, "how delightful it will be in London once more! —to go to the theatres!—and have Tom coming in to late dinner."

"I imagine you will soon have the privilege of choosing Tom's dinner for him; and I only hope you may be wisely directed in the choice, for I am convinced a great deal depends on how you feed a man," said Kate, oracularly. "And now run away, like a dear. I must look at my inventories, for of course Mr. Turner's offer is subject to a proviso that the furniture is in fairly good order; and I want to write to Tom besides."

"I am sure you could write in your sleep; the pen is never out of your hand. You are looking quite ill, more as if you had lost a fortune than gained one! Was there any bad news in Tom's letter this morning? I think you have seemed miserable since you read it."

"Yes, there was something in it that distressed me; but I cannot say anything more now, dear. I shall try and think what is best to be done; and do you go and help Miss Finch in the shop. It is a fine afternoon, and the people will be coming *out* and *into* the Berlin Bazaar, I hope."

When Fanny left her, Kate sat quite still in a low chair near the window, gazing out upon the sea without being aware of what she saw.

For greater quiet and seclusion she had settled herself and her writing materials in the upper sitting-room, which had been Gilbraith's. The table had been placed nearer the window that she might have the light as long as a November day would allow, but the sofa was still where it had been the day she had first spoken to him. She could still in fancy see him extended on it; still see the look of profound astonishment in his eyes, which, in spite of their light color, were so stern and sombre, when he turned at the sound of her voice. Was that day to prove fortunate or unfortunate to them both? Hugh Galbraith was specially in her thoughts, because of the concluding paragraph of Tom's letter.

"Johnston, formerly our correspondent in India, has just come in; he says he met Galbraith yesterday, who informed him he had nearly arranged an exchange into the ——th (a regiment which sailed for India last autumn) as his old corps the ——th Dragoons were on their way back; and he did not wish to remain in England. I do not know how far this may interest you, but I think it right you should be told."

She had not said anything of this to Fanny; but the words

had stamped themselves on her brain. Wherever she turned, the words, "Hugh Galbraith is going away out of my reach. I shall never see him again," seemed to blaze before her. How could she prevent it? How could she draw him to her? What right had she to address the man she had twice rejected, and yet she could not bring herself to resign? Perhaps all his trouble—the crushing reverse of his fortune—had driven her from his mind! to so many men, women are but the playthings of their hours of ease; and if she made any attempt to recall herself to him, might he not consider her importunate. Still she felt she ought—she must—make some effort to communicate with him. She might write and ask if he still wished to know the story of her previous life? Or she might send a formal request for a personal interview, as Mrs. Travers. How she wished some one would tell him her story for her.

"Thinking will do no good," she said to herself, rising and moving towards the fire, which burned bright, thanks to Fanny's parting attentions, and she knelt before it to warm her chill hands.

"I shall just write to Tom, and enclose a little note to Sir Hugh, asking if he is still curious to learn my history. Tom will find out where he is. Yes" (standing up and gazing in the glass, "I do look ill."

A pale, sad, sweet face was reflected, only the lips richly red, with a slight shade as of fatigue beneath the large yearning eyes; the slender pliant figure in its winter garb of thick, dark woolen stuff, looked a trifle less round than when she first stood before Galbraith. "However," she thought, "the anxiety and uncertainty cannot last. I will take courage and write."

She went quickly to the table, and set forth her writing materials, then, seating herself, traced quickly the words, "Dear Tom—" There she stopped, and the succeeding sentence was never written, for Mills came in, with an unusually benign expression on her face. In her hand she held a card; and as she gave it to her mistress, she said, "He wants to know if you will see him?"

Kate turned faint and dizzy as she saw the card bore the name of Sir Hugh Galbraith.

"Yes, yes, I will see him!" She went instinctively to stand by the fireplace, as furthest from the light, and strove to be composed, or to seem composed, though she trembled all over.

It seemed at once a long stretch of time, and yet but a second, before the door opened to admit Galbraith. He advanced and took the hand she held out, both remaining face to face and silent for a moment. Then she saw how gaunt and haggard and worn he looked; what deep gloom was in his eyes; what hard lines about his mouth.

"I hope you are not displeased at my coming here, Mrs. Temple," he said; and she fancied a touch of melancholy softened the harshness of his voice. "But you must forgive me; I could not leave England without seeing you."

"Leave England!" she echoed, sitting down on the sofa because she felt unable to stand.

"Yes," returned Galbraith, walking slowly to the window, and then back again to the fire, where he leaned against the mantelpiece opposite, looking intently at her, while she, in the great, the terrible strain of the moment, was unconscious how her own eyes were fully uplifted to his.

"Are you all right?" he continued, tenderly. "You look pale, disturbed, as if something had gone wrong."

"Oh, yes, I am well enough. But tell me why—why are you leaving England?"

"It is rather a long story," resumed Galbraith; "but considering how we parted last, and the sort of promise you made me, I thought it due to you to explain how matters are; besides" (a short quick sigh) "I wanted to look upon your face once more" (another pause, which Kate felt quite unable to break, and he moved restlessly away to the window and back). "Since I saw you last," he resumed, speaking quicker than usual, "I am sorry to say I have come to grief. You remember my telling you how I inherited a fortune from a relation who cut out his widow?"

"I do," in a very low voice.

"Well, the widow has come to the front, and proved the will to be a forgery."

"Has she really proved it?"

"Yes, there cannot be a doubt in any sane mind on the subject. There is nothing for it but to give up the fortune I had a short spell of. So I am going back to my profession as my only out-look now. There would be nothing in that alone I couldn't stand very well; but you see I took ten thousand pounds of this woman's money and used it; and I could as soon pay the national debt! It is this that hangs like a cursed millstone round my neck; and I shall be poorer than ever with a lifelong effort to pay it off."

"Surely she will not exact it," murmured Kate.

"I only know I am determined to pay," he returned. "But I did not come here to drivel about my troubles and distress you. I only want to show you my imperative reason for going on foreign service—to explain to you, that having no longer home or fortune or position to offer you, I must not press for the explanation you once promised me." He leaned against the mantelshelf, and covered his eyes with his hand for a moment. "What was once a bitter grief is something of a consolation now, for I

17*

should not like you to feel what I do; but I shall battle through, I suppose, Mrs. Temple," seeing her pressing her handkerchief to her eyes. " A new life and hard work will help to wear out both myself and my trouble. You will give me your hand "—taking it—"and bid me God speed, will you not?"

He sat down beside her as he spoke, trying to look into her face, which was half averted.

She did not reply. Her heart was beating to suffocation; she was trembling in every limb.

"Speak to me," repeated Galbraith, making a movement to relinquish her hand; but to his infinite surprise, her soft white fingers closed over his; it was drawn close to her; and, before he could find any word to express the mingling of pain and pleasure and wild emotion her movement excited, with a gesture full of grace and shy tenderness she laid her cheek upon it.

"God of Heaven!" exclaimed Galbraith, pressing close to her, "is it possible that my dim instinct did not deceive me?—that you care for me—love me?"

" Before you ask me any question, Hugh," said Kate, finding voice and courage, letting his hand go, and starting to her feet—"before you ask a single question, hear my story, then—"

" Ay, I will listen to what you like; but first, one moment of Paradise before I go out into the dark," cried Galbraith, rising also.

He caught her hands in his, drawing her to him gently, yet with a force she could not resist. He raised them to his neck, and, clasping his arms around her, laid his lips on hers as if he were athirst for life and had found its well-spring.

" Now tell me everything," he said, his voice husky with passionate delight,—"here—in my arms. I will not—cannot let you go!"

" You must—you will," said Kate, half frightened at this outbreak. " Listen, then. My name is not Temple! I am Catherine Travers. I am your cousin's widow. I am the woman you despised so much, and you—you are my dearest foe!" The last words sounded like a caress.

"What!" said Galbraith, in great astonishment, and holding her from him to gather her meaning in her face as well as from her words. " You Travers's widow? How did you come here? Why did you not tell me at once? And—but I see it all. And Mr. Tom—your man of business—is that newspaper fellow, Reed?"

" He is. There, you must let me go, Sir Hugh. That is my story." She drew herself away from him and stood near the table with downcast eyes, and an air half proud yet shy, one hand upon her heart, which throbbed almost visibly. " Perhaps I ought to have told you at once, but we seemed to drift into a sort of acquaintance which made explanation so awkward. And then I never thought we should meet any more; and I enjoyed making you feel I was a gentlewoman. But when I found that you cared so much for me, I was afraid you would go back to your feelings of contempt again if you knew who I really was. And I was so anxious to prove that my poor husband loved and trusted me to the end, that I was resolved nothing should turn me from my purpose of proving that dreadful will a forgery. And now, you will *not* go away?—you will forgive my half-involuntary imposition? Ah, Hugh! it went to my heart to hurt you—to rob you! You will take back your own?"

"It is the most extraordinary story I have ever heard," said Galbraith, still bewildered; "yet now that I know it, I seem to have been a blockhead not to know who you were. Forgive you! I do not see that I have much to forgive, though I have had some hours of torture lately. But tell me, do you love me —really, earnestly? Are you willing to give me your life?"

And Kate, with grave eyes, but a tender smile on her trembling lips, said, "I am, Hugh."

The night had closed in, and still the lovers sat in earnest talk by the firelight. Their explanations were full, outspoken, unchecked by a shadow of reserve. There are moments of rapture—diapasons of delight—which from their nature cannot last, but leave a blessing behind them: this was one.

"And I suppose, then, you agree with me, that there is now no necessity for your going on foreign service," said Kate, with an arch smile, when they had fully discussed all points.

"Well, no. I suppose we can manage a fair division of the property. Though I warn you, you might find a far more brilliant marriage than with a poor baronet—your debtor too, by Jove!"

"But if I happen to fancy 'a penniless lad wi' a lang pedigree,'" said Kate, abandoning her hand to his caresses.

"How did that fellow Trapes manage to warn Ford?'

"Oh, he did not warn Ford."

"Then who did?"

"I myself. I do not know what you will think of it, Hugh, but the night that Trapes made a sort of half confession here, I was so convinced Mr. Ford was implicated in the plot, that I wrote him a little line, saying that Trapes was in communication with me respecting the will, and that no decided step could be taken for a week, adding that my writing to him was a profound secret; then I suppose he ran away."

"And so you let the villain off! Well, I think you might have asked Reed's advice. It is too bad he should escape."

"Still, I do not think having to punish him would have added to my happiness—our happiness. I am glad he is out of the way; and, I imagine, so are you."

"You are a sage as well as a witch! By Heaven, I can scarcely yet believe you are my *bête noir*, Travers's widow—the embodiment of all I most detested. And this is the reason why you looked at me so murderously the first time I saw you in this blessed room?"

"Yes, I was very angry against you; which you cannot wonder at. Consider that, not ten months before, I had heard you tell Colonel Upton Mr. Travers might have been satisfied to take me for a companion on cheaper terms. Do you remember?"

"How do you know this? Where did I say it?"

"In Hampton Court Palace Gardens. You were talking to Colonel Upton under a large yew tree. I was at the other side, and then and there devoted you to the powers that punish."

"Yes; but how in Heaven's name was I to imagine you the sort of woman you are—a *rara avis* in any station?"

"But remember, Hugh, I am no aristocrat. My father was, poor fellow, what is called an officer and a gentleman; my dear —my dearest mother, was the daughter of a shopkeeper."

"I don't care a rap, Kate, who you are, so long as—"

"I beg a thousand pardons," said Fanny, pushing the door open slowly and prudently, "but it is six o'clock. Miss Finch is gone, and if Sir Hugh and yourself have not quite cut each other's throats, why, tea is ready."

"Fanny! you dear little soul," cried Galbraith, starting up, joyously; "I have such wonderful news to tell that you must give me a kiss!"

"Wonderful news—no news to me, Sir Hugh. I know what it is; but there, I will give you a kiss of peace and congratulation. You and Kate have been made more than friends! I always knew you would."

A few lines from Tom to Fanny, received that evening, announced his intention of running down the next day to talk matters over and make certain arrangements which, in his opinion, had been delayed too long.

"Will you not stay and see our good friend and prime minister?" said Kate to Galbraith, "I want you to know and value him."

"I had no intention of returning to town till Monday," replied Galbraith. "A letter to the army agent will do as well as a visit, and I think the redoubted Tom will back me up as to the arrangements *I* want to make."

So it happened that the next day a very happy *parti carré*

sat down to high tea in Mrs. Travers's (the name of Temple was now discarded) pretty drawing-room ; four happier hearts could not be found ; " quips and cranks and wreathed smiles " flew from lip to lip, mellowed by a real loving-kindness for each other. Galbraith confessed in his heart that, although a news-paper fellow, and a bit of a radical, Tom Reed was a gentleman and an acquisition ; while Tom's delight at the solution of all difficulties, and the righting of all injustice, by the prospective union of Kate and her " foe," was sincere and heartfelt.

Kate had begun to dispense that crucial test of a tea-maker, the second cup, when a long, loud, irregular rapping at the front door caused her to pause in her operations.

" Who can it be ? " cried Mrs. Travers.

" Oh, I do not care," said Fanny. " We are no longer two ' lone lorn ' females ! With Tom and Sir Hugh here, I am as bold as a lion."

They were silent for a moment, and then Mills opened the door. " If you please, mum, here's my Lady Styles wants to speak to you, right or wrong."

" Oh, have her in ! " cried Galbraith. " The sooner everything is known the better ; and she is a first-rate circulating medium."

But her ladyship waited no permission. Galbraith's words were hardly uttered before she was upon them.

" My dear Mrs. Temple ! you really must excuse my coming in ; but I *must* see you about an extraordinary—" stopping short, as she crossed the threshold and recognized the group before her. " The young traveler, I protest ! and Sir Hugh Galbraith—I really am surprised. Perhaps I am in the way ; but, my dear creature, I have such an extraordinary letter from Upton ! I only found it when I came in from calling at the vic-arage to-day ; and late as it was, I ordered the carriage and came straight away to speak to you." To the general company : " Pray don't let me keep you standing. I daresay you know what I mean, my dear Mrs. Temple ; would you rather come and speak to me in another room, or the shop ? "

" No, Lady Styles," replied Kate, with a smile and a blush ; " we are all true friends here ; we have no secrets."

" Very nice indeed ! " cried her ladyship, with a stare of un-disguised astonishment at Galbraith. " Well, then, Upton tells me you are the daughter of my nephew, John Aylmer ; and— and—that pretty girl he ran away with—and married—I believe ? "

" I am," said Kate, quietly ; " and I possess the marriage cer-tificate of my parents."

" Well, I protest, it's the most extraordinary, romantic, un-heard-of affair I ever knew ! My dear, I always thought your face was familiar to me ; now I recognize the likeness to my poor brother, your grandfather! Berlin Bazaar, or no Berlin Bazaar, you are a nice creature, and you shall come and stay with me." And Lady Styles took Kate's hand and bestowed a kindly, audible kiss upon her cheek.

"Now," she resumed, sitting down at the table, "come, do tell me all about everything! I can't make out what brings Sir Hugh Galbraith here. I am really sorry to hear such bad tidings of you," she went on, addressing him. "But I told you I thought that widow would be a thorn in your side yet; now, didn't I?"

"You certainly did," said Galbraith, laughing a genial heartlaugh very unusual to him; "but instead of rushing into legal warfare, I have persuaded her to become bone of my bone."

"Excellent! very judicious! a common-sense line of action. But pray, Sir Hugh, is she aware of your visits here? I am not straitlaced, but—"

"She highly approves," interrupted Galbraith.

"Oh, Tom, Tom!" cried Mrs. Travers, laughing. "You are accustomed to manage the *dénouements* of thrilling tales; will you tell Lady Styles everything?"

Whereupon Tom detailed a simple narrative of the principal events set forth in the foregoing pages; during which Lady Styles was a study. She followed his words with her eyes and a motion of her lips, as though she were absolutely drinking the delicious revelations. Her fat jeweled hands (for she soon drew off her gloves, in the excitement of the moment) twitched and clutched at her dress as they lay on what were unmistakably her ladyship's knees; and when he reached the climax of Mrs. Travers's approaching marriage with Sir Hugh Galbraith, her joy, her exultation knew no bounds.

"My dear creature, I never in all my experience knew anything half so wonderful, and delightful, and romantic, and satisfactory; only I should like to have hung Ford! And you, my dear Mr. Tom, are going to be married to this charming young lady! I tell you what, you shall all come to me, and we will have what Willie Upton would call 'the double event' at Weston. Why, it will supply the country with talk for the next ten years to come! I am sure, Sir Hugh, I already look on you as my nephew; and I shall always thank Heaven that I happened to be on the spot when you were carried in here insensible. Only for me, there is no knowing where that obstinate fellow Slade might have taken you, and then nothing would have come about," said her ladyship, throwing back her bonnet-strings, and stirring the cup of tea Fanny placed before her, joyously, while her broad, good-humored face beamed upon them.

"But, my dear Lady Styles—"

"Dear aunt, if you please," interrupted her ladyship.

"My dear aunt, then," repeated Kate, "I was under the impression that Doctor Slade ordered Hugh to be brought here from the hunting-field, and—"

"Not at all, not at all, my dear! You," turning to Tom, "must remember my standing up from that nice tea and shrimps, and my words to Slade were, 'Don't exhaust him by going further, bring him in here and keep him quiet.'"

"I cannot recall the words," said Tom, demurely.

"Never mind, I can," said her ladyship, with an air of deep conviction. "And but for me, my niece here, Mrs. Travers, would never have had an opportunity—"

She paused, and Tom finished the sentence—

"Of heaping coals of fire on the head of 'Her dearest Foe.'"

THE END

www.ingramcontent.com/pod-product-compliance
Lightning Source LLC
Chambersburg PA
CBHW032002120726
47898CB00005BA/1455